United Brth. of Carpenters and Jointers

Carpenter

Volume 3

United Brth. of Carpenters and Jointers

Carpenter
Volume 3

ISBN/EAN: 9783337383435

Printed in Europe, USA, Canada, Australia, Japan

Cover: Foto ©Andreas Hilbeck / pixelio.de

More available books at **www.hansebooks.com**

A MONTHLY JOURNAL FOR CARPENTERS AND JOINERS.

VOLUME III. NEW YORK, JANUARY, 1883. NUMBER 1.

Premiums to Subscribers.

We want to increase the circulation of THE CARPENTER and as a New Year's inducement to our old subscribers to renew their subscriptions, and also to gain new subscribers we have a proposition to make.

By special arrangement with a large publishing house, we are enabled to offer a library of standard works *at less than five times lower* than through the business channels of the book trade. And this offer we make will be carried out to the letter. The books we offer are printed from good type, on clear white paper, and bound in stout manilla, perfectly durable and are excellent in every respect. This affords a splendid opportunity for workingmen to secure a library at low cost.

FOR FIFTY CENTS,

the regular subscription price of this paper, we will send THE CARPENTER for one year, post-paid, and your choice of any of the following works:

Macaulay's Essays: Milton, Dryden, Bunyan, History, Samuel Johnson (two essays), Athenian Orators, and Robert Montgomery's Poems. By T. B. Macaulay.

On Self-Culture: Intellectual, Physical and Moral. By Prof. John Stuart Blackie.

Joan of Arc: By Alphonse de Lamartine.

Ethics of the Dust: By John Ruskin.

The Imitation of Christ: By Thomas A. Kempis.

The Light of Asia: Life and Teachings of the Founder of Buddhism. By Edwin Arnold.

Frondes Agrestes: Or, Readings in Ruskin's Modern Painters.

The Nutritive Cure: Or, how to get well and how to keep wel[illegible] [illegible]bout medicine. By Robert Walter, M[illegible]

FOR [illegible] DOLLAR

we will send THE [illegible]ARPENTER for one year, and any two copies of the works above mentioned, and any one of the following works complete:

Letters to Workmen and Laborers: By John Ruskin. In two volumes complete. 4to. Manilla.

Carlyle's Essays: Goethe, Burns, Luther's Psalms, Schiller, Memoirs of Mirabeau, Death of Goethe. By Thomas Carlyle.

Memories of My Exile: By Louis Kossuth. Complete in two parts.

Idyls of the King: By Alfred Tennyson.

Orations of Demosthenes: Translated by Thomas Leland, D. D. In two parts.

Sartor Resartus: By Thomas Carlyle.

Letters From a Citizen of The World: By Oliver Goldsmith.

Alfred The Great: By Thomas Hughes, author of *Tom Brown of Rugby*.

FOR ONE DOLLAR

we will send THE CARPENTER for one year, and a copy of each of the following works:

Christmas Stories: A Christmas Carol, The Chimes, The Cricket on the Hearth, The Battle of Life, The Haunted Man. By Chas. Dickens. With 16 full page illustrations by Frederick Barnard. Complete in two volumes. 8vo. Manilla.

Lothair: By B. Disraeli (Earl of Beaconsfield). Complete in two parts. 8vo.

FOR THREE DOLLARS AND A HALF

we will send THE CARPENTER for one year, and all the works above mentioned, complete, post paid. Or, we will send the same as a premium to any one who will send us $20 *for a club of 40 subscribers to* THE CARPENTER for one year. This offer holds good only for a few months.

A Library of twenty-three standard volumes

for THREE DOLLARS AND A HALF,

besides a year's subscription to THE CARPENTER.

All persons may avail themselves of any of the above offers by sending their money and orders to

P. J. McGUIRE,

[illegible], New York.

[illegible] to demonstrate the possibility of a higher economic system." We have tried [illegible]

A BOSS CARPENTER FLATTENED OUT.

Some time ago we referred to J. J. Withrow, a boss carpenter in Toronto, Canada, who had a sneaking ambition to become Mayor of that city. He was the candidate of the most popular party. There was every prospect of his election, were it not that like Banquo's ghost his anti-union career "would not down." The workingmen of that city did not forget that in 1872, during the printers strike for nine hours, Mr. Withrow went outside of his own trade to give the boss printers a helping hand. In that instance the men were locked out before they had declared a strike. And it appears Withrow was active in procuring the arrest of 25 printers under the Conspiracy Act.

So persistent an enemy of trades unions is Mr. Withrow that were it not for him last April, the carpenters would never have had so much difficulty in securing decent wages. His tyrannical and overbearing spirit prevented an amicable settlement at a time when many bosses desired it. And after being forced to sign an agreement with the men, Withrow was one of the first to break it by giving less wages. It is said he hired men at union rates and then at the end of the week paid off at 25 cents a day less. Last April it was Mr. Withrow who asked the Master Carpenters' Association to hire no man prominent in that strike. And further he discharged union men who had been in his employ for years, and employed non-union men in their places. He was also instrumental in publishing the secret black list of carpenters to keep trades union men from procuring employment. This is the pedigree with which Mr. Withrow went before the people of Toronto for their votes.

On December 30th last the Toronto Trades Council called a large public meeting and summoned Withrow to be present and answer the charges against him. The chair was occupied by J. Lewis, President of the Seamen's Union. On the platform sat Mr. Withrow and his principal accusers. The Master Carpenters' Association and other employers, contractors, bosses, clerks and friends of Mr. Withrow, attended in large force and acted in a very disorderly manner. The charges were read and Mr. Armstrong, Mr. Moor and other witnesses stepped forward and made their statements to corroborate them. Mr. Withrow was granted three quarters of an hour to reply, and before he had concluded one hour and a quarter had elapsed. He said it was the first time he had ever been on trial, at least for years. And, no doubt, it galled him severely and humbled his pride to appear among workingmen to answer their charges. At last the supercilious Withrow was on trial before workingmen—before the very men he had formerly scoffed at, and to their credit they gave him a fair and a full hearing.

In opening his reply Withrow attempted to give his hearers the stereotyped: "that he had been born and bred a mechanic and his father was before him." To which the Chairman pithily replied: "There is no charge against you being a mechanic!" Mr. Withrow then proceeded to deny each charge, but it was evident as he proceeded that he was merely equivocating, and attempted to evade all responsibility on some charges by throwing the blame on his partner, Mr. Hillock.

Bro. S. R. Heakes of Union No. 27 made a brief reply to Withrow which perfectly dumbfounded him. He showed the price lists of the various carpenter shops and that they were paying from $1.81 to $2 per day, Withrow's average rate was $1.75 and the highest $1.78 per day. Withrow failed to deny this. After further argument the discussion was closed and a vote was taken whether the charges were substantiated. Up went a forest of hands declaring the charges sustained. On election day, Jan. 1, 1883, the result was that in a poll of over 8000 votes Mr. Withrow was defeated for Mayor by 13 majority, after a very bitter contest, where employers of both parties forgot their political differences to support Withrow. Let his defeat be a lesson to others!

[illegible] to her [illegible]

EMPLOYERS AS DELEGATES TO LABOR BODIES.

A very important question to the welfare of trades unions has been brought forward in St. Louis and in New York. The admission of George Blair to the Central Labor Union of New York, and the admission of Andrew P. Brown to the Trades Assembly of St. Louis, have occasioned no little surprise and excitement in the labor circles of these cities. Both of these men are employers and bosses, and as such have no right to sit as delegates in a body of wage-workers. Trades unions very properly have drawn the line so that employers cannot become members. And if they cannot become members of these unions, then why should they be permitted to sit in a trades union body? On this score the *Peoples Advocate* of St. Louis rightfully says:

"Was it the intention when the Knights of Labor were invited to send representatives to the Trades Assembly to give them a voice in all Trade Union matters? If so, would it not be well to require all representatives sent to the Trades Assembly to be members in good standing in some trade union, or at least, be eligible to membership. We doubt the propriety of having men in the Trades Assembly with authority to vote upon questions affecting the welfare of Trade Unions, who could not, and who would not be members of Trade Unions."

—Carpenters in Atlantic City, N. J., get $1.75 to $2 per day; and in Sanford, Florida, $2.50.

—Carpenters in Australia work only 8 hours per day and get $2.75 per day, and have a half-holiday on Saturdays.

—The New York Plasterers, on Dec. 30, gained their strike to maintain $4 per day. They were out three weeks and compelled all the bosses to accede. The cause of the strike was that some employers were hiring men for $3 and $3.50.

—Philadelphia Union No. 8 have elected the following officers for the current term; Pres., C. H. Hudson; Vice Pres., James Brown; Rec. Sec., W. F. Eberhardt; Fin. Sec., Con. Thorn; Cor. Sec., Geo. Mann; Treas., Geo. Grimes; Trustee, James McKimm.

—On Jan. 8, the Bricklayers National Union held its Convention in Providence, R. I. Two years ago this body numbered only 15 unions, last convention it increased to 38 unions, and now it numbers 68 local unions. Henry O. Cole was reelected President. Action was taken in favor of reduced hours of labor.

—Hard times are coming! Reduction of wages and stoppage of work are the rule now in many foundries, machine shops, boiler works, and in the iron mills, also in the cotton and woolen mills, cigar shops and glass factories. Had not carpenters better prepare for the worst and join their union, and not be left at the entire mercy [illegible] the bosses!

SPLINTERS.

—Don't forget to subscribe to the Daniel Hurley Fund. Send for lists to this office.

—The Wood Carvers' Unions of various cities met in Philadelphia, January 16th, and formed a National Union.

—The Furniture Worker's International Union will publish a semi-monthly trade journal, beginning February 1, next.

—A labor paper—*The Labor Enquirer*—has been established in Denver, Col. [illegible] is a handsome sheet, well edited and [illegible] gorous.

—At Detroit, Mich., the Fifth [illegible] Convention of the Lake Seamen's [illegible]tional Union was held on December [illegible] and it was well attended.

—The men who pay their dues [illegible] Buffalo Machinery Moulders have [illegible] to no longer work with men wh[illegible] been suspended for non-payment [illegible]

—Two thousand workmen in [illegible] Works in Troy, N.Y., are on strike [illegible] 15 per cent. reduction in wages. The[illegible] great excitement in labor circles.

—The Baltimore houses of glass fac[illegible] evidently overreached themselves w[illegible] they had their striking employes arre[illegible] for inducing the Belgian blowers to [illegible] the Union.

—The Chicago Trades Assembly [illegible] augurated an early closing mo[illegible] among the clerks in various leading [illegible] and it has resulted successfully in [illegible] instances.

—The Deputy Sheriff of Gl[illegible] County, N. J., called upon the [illegible] Guard of that State to be ready [illegible] moment to shoot down the strik[illegible] workers at Malaga.

—John Swinton has returned [illegible] rope greatly invigorated in health. [illegible] common with others, we rejoice tha[illegible] has returned safely, after undergoi[illegible] very difficult medical operation.

—The workingmen and trades u[illegible]ists of St. Louis have established [illegible] headquarters in center of city wi[illegible] library and reading room, and me[illegible] halls for the unions. The Labor Ly[illegible] for the discussion of labor questions [illegible] been re-instituted.

—In Montreal, Justice Loranger h[illegible] clared that labor unions for dem[illegible] higher wages are illegal, and has aw[illegible] an employer $20 damages against [illegible] named Bourden, a member of a [illegible] who induced a fellow-workman t[illegible] his employer's service.

—Lorillard & Co., the tobacco m[illegible]turers who were boycotted for [illegible] their workers to slavish contracts a[illegible] proper searching, presented such a[illegible] a Christmas present of a [illegible] It cost the firm $15,000 [illegible] wipe out the stain [illegible] the [illegible] lesson.

[illegible]

[illegible]E CARPENTER.

[illegible]red at the Post-Office in New York, as [illegible]-class matter.

[illegible]EW YORK, JANUARY, 1883.

WORKSHOP NOTES.

—Saw-tooth is the name of a western [illegible]erritorial town.

—One of the uses for which straw lum[illegible]ber has been found to be very valuable, [illegible]s for the backs of picture frames.

—Wood worms in woodwork can be de[illegible]stroyed with benzine. When used in pro[illegible]per quantities it kills off the insects as well as the larvae and eggs.

—Western furniture makers are said to [illegible]oking to the south as a source of fu[illegible] hardwood supply. It is reported that [illegible] company has sent an agent into wes[illegible]tern North Carolina, with instructions to [illegible]purchase 100,000 acres of timber lands, and [illegible]hat others will follow the example.

—The importation of American joinery [illegible]ork into England next year will be watch[illegible]ed with considerable interest, as several [illegible] lines will be tried, including dressed [illegible]ards and dimension stuff. The mills of [illegible]eden are said to have an eye on the [illegible]glish market, and a vigorous competi[illegible] may result.

—The best preparation for restoring [illegible]iture, especially that somewhat mar[illegible] and scratched, is a mixture of three [illegible] of linseed oil and one part spirits of [illegible]e. It not only covers the disfigur[illegible] but restores wood to its original [illegible] in [illegible] a lustre upon the surface. [illegible] as [illegible] a woolen cloth, and when dry, [illegible] a woolen.

[illegible]NEERS THAT BEND EASILY.

[illegible]ent chemical treatment of veneers [illegible] successful in London, it is said, [illegible]e veneer can be made supple as [illegible] of less than the usual thick[illegible], [illegible] the strength and beauty of the [illegible] unaffected. The veneer thus [illegible]ed can be used with the utmost ease [illegible]afety on the most elaborate workman[illegible] bending around the most acute angles [illegible] most intricate curves. They do not [illegible]d any pressing by mechanical methods [illegible]r conforming with hot irons, a simple [illegible]ying on with glue and hand pressure be[illegible] all that is required.

[illegible] FLORIDA FANCY WOODS.

[illegible]rida gentleman urges the value of the native woods of that state, [illegible] in places where walnut and ma[illegible] are now used. The irregular [illegible] of yellow pine, when the convolu[illegible] [illegible] a twisting in and out of the [illegible] claimed to be one of the most [illegible] woods. The color is [illegible]ow and charming from its origi[illegible] contrasts well with walnut and [illegible] woods.

[illegible]agnolia, from its inherent [illegible] fineness of grain, makes a fine [illegible] wood. It is also well adapted [illegible] in imitating ebony. It is said to [illegible] in almost inexhaustible quantities in [illegible] hammocks of Florida and therefore is [illegible] easily to produce.

[illegible] red or sweet bay wood is said to [illegible]itable for ornamental purposes, and [illegible] in great quantities in the state. It [illegible] substantially the same as mahogany, [illegible] can be used for the same purposes. [illegible] gentleman alluded to can see no good [illegible] why it should not be called Ameri[illegible] mahogany.

NEW WINDOW SASH.

[illegible] invention provides a window, [illegible] sash of which slides up and down in [illegible] way, with counterweights [illegible] pulleys. A portion of the length [illegible] window jambs is a pivoted swing[illegible], so that both sashes may be run [illegible]

A MEMORIAL TO THE TRADES CONGRESS.

(Continued.)

If this then be true, it should logically follow that the principle of unionism, good in its local application, should be extended to effect the national and international organization of each trade. And it equally follows that these trades and labor unions should be combined in a Federation of Trades and Labor Unions.

That such a form of organization is necessary is amply proven by the experience of many trades during the past twelve months. Isolated Labor in conflict with consolidated Capital in many cases has been driven to the wall, defeated for a time, but destined to emerge victorious only as it learns from its defeats, the lesson that our Trades Councils and our National and International Unions must be affiliated practically, so as to form one unbroken chain of union for each other's defense and welfare. To accomplish this task, your Congress has assembled. Workmen, everywhere look with expectation to your deliberations, that they may be marked with a higher degree of statesmanship than marks the acts of our State Legislature, or of the United States Congress. It is for you to settle questions that these politicians can never comprehend, nor do they care to understand them. But these questions will be forced onward in spite of their Penal Codes and Conspiracy Laws.

The first thing to understand is the dual character of labor organization—its public and its secret side. We desire to be organized publicly wherever possible, so that the existence of our unions may be known and that they may be legalized. But where by acts of the capitalists this has become impossible than we favor secret organization. Both forms are necessary and instead of being hostile, they should be harmonized so as to cooperate with each other. There is no need for one trying to swallow the other, nor is there need for any conflict. The open trade unions, local, national and international, can and ought to work side by side with the Knights of Labor, and this would be the case, were it not for men—either overzealous or ambitious who busy themselves in attempting the destruction of existing unions to serve their own whims and mad iconoclasm.

This should cease and each should understand its proper place and work in that sphere. And if they desire to come under one head or to affiliate their forces, then let all trade and labor societies—secret and public—be represented in the Federation of Trades and Labor Unions.

The benefit of this Federation is not only to render pecuniary and moral assistance in case of strikes, or lock outs, but its very existence can lessen strikes, by playing with the fears of employers who in many cases would then hesitate to provoke strikes, that they know would be well supported. In addition to this, new unions could be organized, local trade councils could be formed, and national and international unions could be established and a systematic plan of propaganda inaugurated that would strengthen and enliven our unions.

By proper support of the Federation, a weekly official journal might be published and a labor literature of tracts and pamphlets could be printed at small cost for public distribution.

We find the workmen of Europe, in Great Britain, France, Spain, Italy, Switzerland, Belgium, Holland, Austria and Denmark, have held largely attended Trades Congresses the past year. And just as these National Labor Congresses develop, they will tend to correspondence with each other and open up friendly relations between the workmen of all countries, that will lead undoubtedly to an "era of peace and good will among nations." And hence before many years we may expect an International Trades Union Congress, to determine among other questions the importation of labor from one country to another in case of strikes, and to discuss the evil immigration of labor to flood a country at the behests of cheap labor capitalists.

While we consider these subjects there are other matters we must deal with. We desire a reduction of the hours of labor, Hour law. And in the next session of Congress the Legislative Committee of the Federation should demand the enforcement of that law, and also the creation of a National Bureau of Labor Statistics and the Legalization of Trades Unions. Let the Congressional work of the Federation be centred *primarily* on these three points; and *secondary* on such others as in your wisdom you may determine.

In asking these measures from Congress let us by no means sink to the level of party politicians. Let us not sacrifice our unions for the sake of any political party. But as union men let us work in harmony for those issues we do comprehend and upon which we are fully agreed, and let us ignore all those questions likely to disrupt and divide us.

Yours Fraternally,
P. J. McGuire.

Philadelphia, Pa., Nov. 20, '82.

AMERICAN JOINER WORK IN GREAT BRITAIN.

The *Timber Trades Journal*, of London, indicates a new use which is to be made of yellow pine in Great Britain, which is likely to increase the demand for that useful timber from across the waters. The *Journal* says: "Further information has reached us respecting the intended importation of American yellow pine mouldings and joinery work. There can be no doubt but that a vigorous effort will be made next season to create a market here for plain scantlings and other forms of American manufactured wood. Some novel forms of manufacture will be introduced, and, from what we can gather, every effort will be made to introduce them to the favorable notice of the trade here. The best recommendation which American joinery has is the really splendid quality of the material of which it is usually made. Few home-made articles at all approach it in this respect."

A PROCLAMATION.

The following proclamation issued by Prince Krapotkine and which is addressed to the Kings of Europe and to the monied Lords, expresses sentiments which are growing throughout the world:

"Where you number ten we number ten millions.

"Where you produce one necessity of life we produce a million.

"Where you cultivate one rod of land we plow and reap from a thousand fields.

"We build the ships and you sail them.

"We build the railroads and you own them.

"We grow the bread and you deny it to us.

"While you have unused millions of money stored in your vaults, our wives and ourselves work wearily forever for bread and water.

"You have pictures and music and dancing; the theatre, the feast, the wassail, the lecture and books, and do nothing.

"We have misery and hunger and thirst and crime, the prison, the workhouse, the asylum, and the grave, and yet we do all.

"We are tired of this and will suffer it no more.

"Give us what we earn, and a government to protect it.

"For if you do not we shall take it by force.

"We, in the name of liberty, knock at the doors of royalty, and bid the King, the Prince, and the Capitalist to come out and work with us in the field.

"If they come not then they must die."

SOME SUGGESTIONS.

A large proportion of the men working in our carpenter shops seem to have ideas and plans connected with their ordinary daily work which, though not absolutely wrong, are so far removed from the correct method, and sometimes so much opposed to nature, as to cause a great deal of extra labor and annoyance. Amongst these mistaken notions might be mentioned the various plans adopted by them to bring wood, when warped or twisted, back to the proper, or rather the required, condition. It is very often found to be the off the high corners, and thus make it perfectly true by reducing the thickness. But if it be simply cast, one side being hollow and the other round, the defect may be easily got over. If the man, by working on some other portion of the material required for his job, can let the defective pieces stand for a day or two, then by placing the wood "hollow side" down on a plane surface, or by putting two such boards one on the top of the other, with the hollow sides facing each other, the wood will draw straight without any more trouble on the part of the man. It is always best, when possible, to work up the wood in its natural state, as even if the tendency to cast be overcome previous to working it, there is always the probability of its returning to its normal condition. Some men, when pressed for time, heat the round side on the stove. This does indeed make the wood straight, but there is a great risk of the wood opening and splitting under this roasting treatment, and this liability is very much increased if the wood be at all shaky. If required, the wood can at once be straightened without this risk, by damping the hollow side with water, when the expansion of the fibre on that side pulls it straight. It sometimes happens that a piece of wood of some considerable width, such as a carcase end or a wardrobe panel, has to be reduced from 1 inch to ½ inch thickness. If this superfluous wood be all taken off one side, that side will become hollow, whereas if it be taken off equally on both sides the wood remains as before.

In veneering panels, etc., it is always best to veneer on the outside that is, the side opposite the heart side, the reason for this being that veneer is apt to swell with glue being laid on, and must therefore contract after it is fixed. As the heart side has always a decided tendency to curl, the two forces counteract each other, and the wood remains the same. For this same reason, it is always best to inlay on the outside.

To some people, these may appear to be trivial matters, but it is by keeping these and other little points in mind that a job may be turned out with more comfort to the man and satisfaction to the employer, and these hints, if carefully attended to, will frequently save time and expense.—*Builder and Wood Worker.*

"A SUPERANNUATED NUISANCE."

That is what the New York *Sun* calls our foreign diplomatic service, and we are glad to be able to agree with that journal. If a costly and ridiculous sham exists anywhere, it is our diplomatic establishment. Sending furbished and costly dandies to foreign courts, is certainly not in accord with the genius of a republic. Ocean cables and fast steamers can carry all our correspondence, and by them we can transact all our business with foreign countries. The whole diplomatic establishment is a huge imposition on Labor. Besides, a real representative man has hardly any chance whatever of being sent as an embassy or consul to a foreign country. As a rule our ministers represent, not the people, but the shoddy aristocracy—the fools and fops of "high life," the most useless and destructive class of society.—*Irish World.*

Something For Scabs And Luke-Warm Members.

Cincinnati, Ohio.—Union No. 2 has lately had a large attendance in its meetings, and the union increases in members every week. But now work is slacking off and men are looking for jobs and of course non-union men will take anything they can get. Nevertheless union men are holding the best jobs in general, and that goes to show that the best men are union men. Our members propose to fight to the bitter end for their existence, and in unity will uphold each other in securing a decent livelihood. Bad members and scabs seem not to care for decent treatment; they expect union men to fight and struggle for them, and then like dirty hogs they swallow the benefits. They ought to realize what union men are doing for them and their families. We are working for them as well as ourselves; we are elevating the

ORGANIZATION OF EXCHANGE.

LETTER No. 12.

Dear Sir:—All science to become constituted or established, or to be considered as a science, must discover by means of observation, experiment and comparison, the laws which govern the phenomena which it studies. Astronomy for instance became a science only when Newton by these means had demonstrated the law of gravity as applied to celestial bodies. Social science must therefore demonstrate the law of social movement. This law is VALUE; which value is cost of production measured, 1st, by the amount of repugnance to be overcome; 2nd, by the amount of time spent in production, which, like gravitation, is developed under the influence of force. Supply and demand are the two forces which constitute that value. All men in order to live are compelled to exchange the products of their labor; value is therefore the foundation of the social movement, since there is no exchange possible without a previous valuation of the products exchanged.

This valuation is effected by supply and demand.

Every member of society is at the same time producer and consumer; but on account of the diversity of functions, each produces that which he does not consume, and consumes that which he does not produce.

As producer a man acts upon value by the offer of his products; as consumer he reacts upon value by his demand for the products of others; as a producer, prompted by personal selfish interest he tries to get as much as possible for his labor; as a consumer, to give the least possible for the products which he wants. From this fact arises the constitution of value under the power of two forces acting in opposition—the action of which is known as competition.

As to-day the worker sells his labor and his intelligence for a stipulated wage, the conditions of competion are not equal for all; the *demand* is made by *all*, the *supply* is in the hands of a *few* holders of products and capital; hence the action of the law of supply and demand is controlled by such men—it is not left to work freely and great suffering to the poor is the consequence.

A simple illustration will show this fact more clearly. If there are say 10,000 barrels of flour in New York, and there are 8,000 persons each wanting a barrel of flour, evidently there are 2,000 barrels of flour more than demanded, in other words the supply exceeds the demand; Now, if these 10,000 barrels of flour are monopolized, or cornered, by the dealers in that city and they hold 5,000 barrels for a rise, that is to say if they refuse to sell but half the quantity which they have, evidently they make it appear that there is less than the demand. In other words they maliciously interfere with the free action of supply and and demand, and create *a fictitious scarcity amid natural abundance.* Nature gives food to the people, the monopolists starve them.

Therefore the market is completely controlled by the capitalist, and the value of products is always greater than the value of wages.

In spite of all the obstacles opposed to the free action of exchange, the proportionality of value exists all the same; if a certain product augments or diminishes, all others soon have to submit to an analogous fluctuation; laws, degrees, statutes nothing can obviate this natural result; values *will* tend to adjust themselves; but in view of the inequity of conditions this equilibrium always turns to the profit of a privileged few who possess fortunes.

To demonstrate the law of social movement and prove that the inequity of conditions is the cause of this law working for the benefit of a few, and to the detriment of the many is not sufficient: it is also necessary to demonstrate the possibility of a better economic system [illegible] to fulfil this last part of the programme, so far as the limited time and space will permit.

For the production of wealth, it is urgent that education and the instruments of labor should be equally accessible to all. The liberty left to all to produce and consume according to their tastes and aptitudes; to competition the care of maintaining the equilibrium between production and consumption.

For the distribution of wealth, it is necessary to put the producer in *direct communication with the consumers, by the suppression of all useless intermediate parties, traders or middlemen.* Also that the sign of exchange, or currency, should be the direct representation of the produce and that it should follow the law of production, that is to say that it should depreciate in value equally with the product which it represents.

In order to realise which, it is necessary to arrive at the following;

1st, Make of the workman a social functionary having a right to the use only of the instruments of labor and being retributed only for his labor.

2d, Destroy individual speculation by making exchange a social function.

3d, Regulate the value of all labor and of all products by free and untrammeled emulative competition freely and integrally exercised by all.

4th, Make of the sign of exchange (currency) a simple guarantee of labor performed.

5th, Make the depreciation of value in the sign of exchange, money or currency, equal to the depreciation of the value of the products which it represents.

6th, And I may add make scientific and professional education accessible to all.

Thus equity of conditions, liberty and solidarity will unite our country in harmony with all the world.

DRURY.

Philadelphia Pickings.

PHILADELPHIA.—Your christmas chromo with "Out of work" poetry did not seem to strike the funny fancy of some of our I-dont-want-to-see-any-of-your-reality young men. But, if I don't mistake the meaning of the idea expressed in the closing sentences of each stanza, I should say many are passing through that punishment too often meted out to the undeserving.

Yet it is a sad fact, Philadelphia is a poor town for carpenters just now, from the number seeking work and finding it not. But the man who advertised the other day for men to meet him at his office got himself in rather a hot box. His office was on the curbstone and his business in his hat. So many answered that he was obliged to send for a squad of police to disperse the mob. He only did it for fun, to see if there were any out of work. Men never answer advertisements where there is no fixed place of business. Only scabs do.

Union men are doing fairly, but a good many are out of work; wages average from $2 to $2.75. It seems to be a kind of a go-as-you-please race. But some say "get a job any how, never mind the wages, they will adjust themselves." And you bet your life they will too. But we must consider that when the stomach speaks for its quota of backing, the iron will of principle will bend in conformity with the demand.

Empty cupboards and empty drawers as well as empty pockets with want and the landlords power will make slaves of us all. There is some little excuse for men in the above conditions, making the best bargain they can under the circumstances. But if they were all in union there would be no such conditions.

In the balmy days of last Summer when work and wages were good, many did not realize the fact that it may be prudent to lay away a few dollars for a cold day and to have a union to uphold wages. Now some of them are in quest of free lunches.

The birds don't sing so prettily now in the Park; the benches are very cheerless and uncomfortable. If things continue the city will have to put a roof over Fairmount Park to accomodate her out-of-work mechanics. It would be no more than she has done for the Russian Jews. But this "brotherly love" does not go out to her own people.

Carpenters, save some money if ever so little. It is handy to have in the house. You may be sick, you may get crippled,—and worse than all you might get out of work and out of money, with false friends sneering at you. That implies to a sensitive man—Hell on earth.

Local No. 8 is thinking of sick benefits, tool benefits and other important changes.

Since Drury of New York spoke here in Union No. 8 we haven't had a first fiddle man in the Union. The new Sunday paper *The People* offers a ton of coal to every subscriber as a prize. For a few more subscribers it would be a house and lot.

NUMSKULL.

AN EMPLOYER WHO APPRECIATES HIS WORKMEN.

Mr. Geo. Tuckett, a tobacco manufacturer in Hamilton, Canada, has taken a step which is worthy of example and adoption by other employers. At every Christmas it is his practice to call the employes together and distribute prizes among them for the best workmanship, and at the same time give a gift of money to each one apart from the prizes. On December 23d, last, he called the employes together, and before distributing the prizes and gifts, he addressed the work people as follows:

I have been asked the cause of our success as a firm. For the benefit of young manufacturers I may say that during the 25 years I have had to employ help I have never had to cut down wages. (Applause). Nearly every year I have been able to advance wages. And why? Not so much because of any business ability of mine or my partners, but because of the careful and diligent manner in which every one of my employes has done his or her work. We therefore now propose to distribute among you a share of our property to which you have contributed so much. You have done well. The Tuckett tobacco stands as high in the market as any in the world which speaks well for your work. We compete with the manufactories of the lower provinces though the work is done cheaper there than here because of your good and careful system of working. To those who have recently arrived here from the lower province I wish to say that if they have any disputes which the foreman cannot settle, or if they are sick, let them come to me. I will try to prove myself their friend. (Applause). We also propose to distribute a share of our success among you in this manner. In future, during nine months of the year we will commence work at 7.30 in the morning instead of 7 o'clock; paying the same wages, (Applause), and paying you off at 4 o'clock Saturday afternoon. During June, July and August we will go to work at 7 o'clock A. M. and pay off at 12 o'clock Saturday noon, so as to give the boys a holiday. (Great applause). I believe that with our improved machinery and with increased intelligence among workmen such as now exists, we can do as much work all around in 9 hours per day as was formerly done in 12 hours. This result has not been brought about by strikes, but by consulting each other's interests as you and I have done. I hope the time will come, when my son, my junior partner will say to his employes, "Eight hours per day is enough for you to work." (Applause.) I wish you all a merry Christmas and a happy New Year. (Great applause.)

SHORTENING THE HOURS OF LABOR.

SIR: In the consideration and discussion of shortening the hours of labor per week, are we acting honestly in the matter. The first question that suggests itself to me in connection with this subject, is: are we really desirous of shortening the hours of labor? Do we now make beneficial use of one day in seven, that we have given to us by law, both in the United States, I believe, and in Canada? By our actions do we not allow employers of labor, and the public generally to think that we are not anxious to shorten the hours of labor per week, but make it a side issue only; and at the same time allowing it to occupy the prominent place for the purpose of getting higher wages? Thus wages and not the shortening of the hours of labor are the real bone of contention. Where we have the privilege of leaving off at four o'clock, or at twelve o'clock on Saturdays, how many croakers are there who cannot afford to lose the time, but who would willingly work not only the sixty hours per week but the whole seventy, if thereby they could roll up a big week's pay? Of course, I cannot believe the Brotherhood have many such [illegible] brethren, if any, who are so anxious for a big week's pay as to work seventy hours per week.

While putting these questions it may be proper for me to return to these questions and go over them again as a means to reach a solution of them. My answer to the first question is that *I am anxious* to see our trade work less hours per week. And I think I am consistent in my position in *seeking* to shorten the hours of labor per week. I believe in one rest day in seven, which the law of the land gives me; but instead of abusing the privilege thus given to me I endeavor to keep that day intact from any unnecessary physical labor, and use it to my mental and moral advancement and social enjoyment, as well as for the preservation and recuperation of my physical energies. While I believe in it, and enjoy the benefits of such a rest day it is my endeavor to keep it intact from spoilation by the selfish, unscrupulous white slave drivers. It is these selfish unscrupulous white slave drivers honest toilers have to fear, and it requires all their wisdom to guard against the insidious methods they use to entrap them into the abuse, and the nullifying of privileges they enjoy by the law of the land.

Of course the Brotherhood in Canada cannot speak, as *yet*, from so extended an experience of these species of white slave drivers as the Brotherhood in the United States can. We have not yet, on this side, the publication of Sunday papers, and sundry other abuses of the privileges of enjoying one rest day in seven.

But there are here, nevertheless, white slave drivers and their hirelings, both in the press and out of it, who are trying all they can to rob us of this rest, and bring us into bondage of continuous labor [illegible] white slave labor without any cessation.

If we are acting honestly in this matter of shortening the hours of labor, let us in justice to all classes of labor use our influence for the suppression of any [illegible] of labor that entails more than the [illegible]ous working hours per week. [illegible] labor upon others for the purpose of [illegible]istering pleasure to us, is to [illegible] consistent with the position taken upon [illegible] reduction of the working hours in [illegible] of the week. I must be candid [illegible] matter in asking the Brotherhood [illegible] their influence, consistently with [illegible] desire for shorter hours, that they [illegible] patronize for their own pleasure, [illegible] others' pain, any of those agencies [illegible] entail any extra hours of labor [illegible] toiling masses during the seven days.

I am furthermore consistent in [illegible] desire to shorten the hours of labor [illegible] sixty hours to fifty-five, or less, per [illegible] I have worked for the last five years the fifty-five hours per week, unless [illegible] urgently necessitated an extra hour [illegible] two, or may be the remaining five hours. Am I any the poorer in pocket, or worse in temper, for these less hours of labor it may be asked? I will leave [illegible] question to be answered by those [illegible] know me best. This question of [illegible] hours is with me a principle of self[illegible]vation of the trades from demoralization. The loss of money by this loss [illegible] has had no consideration on my part. [illegible] is with me, will this shortening [illegible] hours of labor help the trade [illegible] demoralized condition? Can eleven [illegible] by working fifty-five hours per week instead of sixty save an idle hand from [illegible] undermining one of us by offering to [illegible] less than the regular wages? For we remember that machinery helps to many an idle hand. And thriftless hands are sometimes very demoralizing to the trade.

Machinery and those selfish [illegible] lous white slave drivers with the hands are playing the terrible part [illegible] demoralization of our trade and working masses generally. Of course liquor is an insidious element in the [illegible] the demoralization along. Machinery, selfish greed, liquor and the idle are the combined evils acting against righteous condition labor should [illegible]

The unscrupulous capitalist encourages and uses these agencies for his own [illegible] to the injury of honest, righteous [illegible]. Labor has created and perfected [illegible] ry to ease off the heavier burdens, but unscrupulous capital commonly uses it against labor.

Let us look these facts squarely in the face and act honestly in regard to [illegible] and see that we are consistent in our [illegible] tion in seeking for the reduction [illegible] hours of labor.

Yours,

[illegible]

THE CARPENTER.

PUBLISHED MONTHLY

BY THE

Brotherhood of Carpenters and Joiners,

OF AMERICA.

Office: 184 William St., New York.

TERMS.—Fifty cents a year, in advance, post-paid.

Send all moneys and correspondence for this Journal to

P. J. McGUIRE, Secretary,
184 William St., New York.

NEW YORK, JANUARY, 1883.

—We extend our most cordial thanks to the daily and weekly papers which so kindly gave such a widespread circulation [illegible] our "Appeal to Carpenters." It has re[illegible] in many letters of inquiry asking [illegible] information in regard to the Brotherhood.

—Our Brotherhood is no local institution; it is not for Philadelphia, Boston, Chicago, or any one city. It does not exist for any one city, nor does its life or death depend upon any one union. Its jurisdiction extends over many cities and its work embraces the good of all carpenters unions.

—Official stupidity has never been more generously displayed than by the Mayor of East Liverpool, Ohio. He has issued a proclamation against the striking potters [illegible] that city, and in it he forbids assem[illegible] on the streets and even in halls or [illegible]dings, and also proclaims *whistling* to [illegible] a crime.

—A correspondent from a certain city, [illegible] we will not now name, says in a [illegible] homely and trite way: "The carpen[illegible] [illegible] are a set of ignorant asses, and [illegible]robably three or four thousand [illegible] can not be got to stick and make a [illegible] union. There are some good men, [illegible] they are dragged down by the prepond[illegible] of ignorance and apathy." And [illegible] it is in many other cities. Still we [illegible] keep right on with a firm faith that [illegible] non-union men will see their own [illegible], and be led into union with their fel[illegible].

THE CHANNEL TUNNEL.

For many years no public event has cre[illegible] a more profound and lasting impres[illegible] in all quarters than the visit of the [illegible] trades union delegates to Paris. [illegible] the Parisian dailies, and even the [illegible] Times gave full reports of the pro[illegible]. From first to last the affair was [illegible] complete success and a perfect rebuke [illegible] Chauvinistic spirit which desired [illegible] the Channel Tunnel by appealing to [illegible] of the timid and conservative in [illegible] and France.

[illegible] workingmen are not to be kept apart [illegible] old grannies. The peoples of dif[illegible] nations are no longer to be held in [illegible] of each other to satisfy the old feuds [illegible] potentates and despotic rulers. [illegible] working class of all countries has [illegible] that they have nothing to gain by [illegible] against each other.

[illegible] have never been consulted about [illegible]; all they have to do is to foot the [illegible] and pay the costs in toil and blood.

This has taught the workingmen of [illegible] and France that they have no [illegible] to take part in the quarrels of their [illegible]. They believe in peace and prog[illegible]! And taking this as their watchword [illegible] Tunnel Conference in Paris [illegible] the way to an era of amity and [illegible] more weighty and potent than [illegible] peace congresses ever held.

[illegible] better by far than all this, it has [illegible] workingmen of these countries to [illegible] each other's methods of organ[illegible] and agitation. And the result with[illegible] will be that the French workmen [illegible] some of the English methods, [illegible]

OUR THIRD YEAR.

This number of THE CARPENTER begins our third year of publication. Two years have gone, and what years of work and toil they have been to maintain our journal! At best the life of a labor journal is perilous and trying. It has to combat the molded prejudices of ages, to inculcate new ideas of government, industry and social life. It has to wage war against the iniquities and abuses of a class that has all the money and resources to command a servile press. With but little capital and no power, only that which has come from cohesion and numbers, the journeymen carpenters at last have a journal of their own. It is the property of the carpenters themselves; no capitalist or politician can control its destiny. It has lived two years in spite of them and will live to arouse the men of our trade to organise and act for their own common good.

What THE CARPENTER has been the past two years, it will continue to be—the unflinching enemy of all social and political wrong, and the advocate of better and nobler conditions for the men of Labor. When its issue was first projected, there were doubts among some of its success, but now its existence is assured. We are grateful to our co-workers and friends for their support, and ask them to not relax their efforts. THE CARPENTER can be made even better than it is, if each one will only add to our list of subscribers. There is a wild field among non-union men for this work. Send in the subscriptions. Fifty cents a year is all our journal costs. And every carpenter can afford it.

COMMENTS ON OUR SUPPLEMENT.

With our last number we issued an illustrated supplement which has provoked some very interesting comments. From one quarter we have heard it said that the illustration presented only the darkest side of the question. For the benefit of such critics the next occasion we have to print such a supplement, we will dress the man out of work in a "plug hat" and broad cloth suit, and have him feasting upon turkey and champagne.

Then there are some who think there was a little too much HELL in the poem, and it ought to have been milder. After this we will be careful to use the word HADES, and to avoiding shocking them we will expunge half the dictionary if necessary.

With the exception of these comments the reports generally were encouraging and spoke in no small measure of praise. One was so emphatic as to say: "That picture ought to be in the home of every scab to shame him." The labor papers have in many instances published the poem, and one labor paper—*The Buffalo Banner* makes extended mention of it and says: "The illustration speaks more than a page of the strongest and best editorial, and is a powerful appeal to carpenters to be true in union to each other's interests." The daily *N. Y. Volkszeitung* also gives it a hearty notice, and so did many other papers. On the whole we are satisfied with the results.

TRADES UNIONS NOT SOLELY FOR STRIKES.

Our enemies and even some workmen spread the statement that trades unions are organised for strikes. No better evidence of the falsity of such an accusation can be given than to present a fact or two.

The Amalgamated Carpenters in their history from 1860 to 1881, spent only [illegible] on strikes—or less than $814,000 in 21 years, while over $1,975,000 were expended on sick, funeral, tool and other benefits—only 15 per cent. for strikes and 85 per cent. for benevolent purposes. In [illegible]

DANIEL HURLEY.

The labor movement has suffered a severe blow in the loss of one of its purest, noblest and most devoted men. On Dec. 9th last, Daniel Hurley, aged 37, died in Brooklyn, N. Y., from a compound fracture of the skull, received while at his work of dock-building. He lingered three days from the date of the injuries. His remains were escorted to the grave by the Knights of Labor, the New York Central Labor Union, the Dock Builders' Union, Post Mansfield No. 35, G. A. R. and other organizations of which he was a member.

His sad and untimely end deprives us of a cherished friend, and one whose whole life was wrapped up in the work of doing good for his fellow man. It leaves a gap that will not be easily filled. For years he served the cause of labor. Many a night after toiling hard all day at his trade of dock building, he would leave his home and travel miles to address or encourage some meeting of workingmen. Not only were his time and talents given to this work, but his means also. This is but a poor tribute to DANIEL HURLEY! Had he devoted his ability and eloquence to men opposed to our interests, he could have placed himself and family beyond the reach of want. But he was too honest and too honorable for that. He has left a widow and five small children unprovided for. The working people of America owe it to themselves and to Daniel Hurley, to place this widow and the five small children beyond danger of want. And for this purpose a *Daniel Hurley Fund Association* has been organized and subscriptions are requested from every man, who desires to show that Labor is not so ungrateful as to forget those who devoted their lives to our welfare. Stephen P. Ellsworth, 584 Grand St., Brooklyn, E. D., is Treasurer of this fund. We ask our readers to contribute to this fund, no matter how small the trifle. All monies will be receipted for in *The Irish World*. Lists can be had by applying there or to the office of THE CARPENTER.

Men Should Join The Union of Their Own Trade.

HAMILTON, Canada.—Trade dull, still we initiate members continually. If the bosses took a notion to cut wages, we would have a great many more to join us or if we talked 25 cents a day advance it would be the same. But those kind of members don't last long anyhow. Some non-union carpenters have joined the Knights of Labor, because it is cheap—ten cents a month dues. And they expect great benefits from it. They are told that in case of strike they will get their full wages, the same as if working. How they can do it on ten cents a month is "one of those things no fellow can find out!" They are also promised other benefits, all for ten cents a month. But it is all promise, no realization. What I want to know is this: If one-third the carpenters of Hamilton were in the K. of L. and wanted a raise of wages or shorter hours, and the other two-thirds were not agreeable, how could they get it? But if they all join Union No. 18, or the Amalgamated, there would be sense in it, because they would be sustained by the men of their own trade in other cities. Men should join the union of the trade they work at. And if the carpenters do that, we are strong enough without rushing into a society of mixed trades which seems to be more apt to run into politics, than to work on for legitimate trade purposes.

—Labor is like a perishable commodity, the smallest overstock is sure to lower the market in an undue proportion. Take away but the trifling surplus and a fair remuneration will be obtained. The emigration of the surplus labor of Europe will, in a few years, equalize the wages of both, by lowering American wages to the English standard.

BROTHERHOOD NOTES.

—Business in Toledo is dull and Union No. 25 growing.

—The carpenters of Atlantic City, N. J., are forming a union under our jurisdiction.

—The Hartford carpenters union now embraces nearly every member of the craft in that city.

—Kansas City Union No. 13 has a slow and steady growth and its members are true timber that will stand to the last.

—Indianapolis Union No. 16 had a supper and festival on Dec. 24, which netted a handsome sum and was also profitable in arousing interest in the union.

—Bro. Edward Owens of San Francisco has founded a carpenters union in Oakland, Cal. The new union has obtained a charter and is known as Union No. 36.

—Whenever any of our members do not get THE CARPENTER, they should at once send a postal to this office and complaint will be entered at the Post Office, and the matter can be remedied.

A death benefit of at most $100 would work to better advantage and with less hardship to our local unions. Many of the local unions now find that $250 is too high a premium to pay in the infancy of our Brotherhood.

—Toronto Carpenters Union No. 27 has suspended the following members until their dues and fines are paid: James Smith, W. E. Pearce, James Gorrie, W. Jeffries, James Dawson, J. Ferguson, Geo. Breffith, T. Reynolds, T. M. Spitzinger and Alver Symonds.

—President Allen has revoked the charter of Buffalo Union No. 9 and a new union has been founded in that city by Vice President Hickey, Bro. Dillon and other members, formerly of Union No. 9. The Buffalo Union will be known as Union No. 37.

FROM OUR GENERAL PRESIDENT.

To the Officers and Members of the Brotherhood!

[illegible]: I desire through our official organ to lay before you some few questions that have been running through my mind for some time.

No doubt many of you have been watching the signs of the times, and therefore can discern the near approach of another financial crisis. Has any one told you that under the present system there would be no more panics? If they have, they are not very weather-wise. For, as sure as you trace these lines, just so sure have the workingmen got to face another crash in this country. And that in less than three years. It may not last long—who can tell? But it will last too long for workingmen to escape being victimized, degraded and forced deeper in the slough of abject poverty where greedy capitalists and employers are ever ready to push you.

Think of it! What have you as workingmen done in the past three years to ward off another hard struggle for bread and clothes? What do thousands of idle men mean to do, walking the streets, asking for work anywhere and everywhere? To-day, in Philadelphia, there are at the least calculation 1500 carpenters out of employment. Bricklayers, Plasterers, Stone Masons, Stone Cutters, and in fact every trade is represented in like proportion. About one-half at work; the other half *idle*. What are you going to do about it? Idle men won't join unions when trade is falling, and men in unions, or at least the majority of them won't support their unions on a falling trade. Are you making any provision now that your unions may stand the stress and storm of another financial smash?

I say to you plainly, you cannot hope to build up unions on the sole principles of high wages and strike benefits when as many men are idle as are at work. You have got a burden to hold the wages up, let alone agitating higher pay.

You cannot depend on political issues to save you and your unions from the crash. The moment you take up political questions, political tricksters, bummers and demagogues crowd your union. You are given the bag to hold, and after election find the bag as you received it—empty. Why? Because the working men of this country are not educated enough yet in trade union principles. They don't see nor understand the principles and benefits of [illegible] to do their duty at the [illegible]. And this has been proven [illegible]

THE CARPENTE

PUBLISHED MONTHLY

NEW YORK, JANUARY, 18

THE CHANNEL TUNNEL

1883.

NEW YEAR'S SUPPLEMENT

—TO—

THE CARPENTER

OUT OF WORK!

(ORIGINAL.)

Out of work! Said a Carpenter brave,
My saw is the last thing I have to pawn;
There's little that stands between me and the grave.
Out of work! My last dollar and tools are gone!
They tell us of paradise,—well, ah well—
I know naught of that. But this is Hell!

I lost my neat cottage I lived in so long;
Took two rooms in this shanty. I thought it was cheap;
Since we live here I find I am not so strong,
And my wife in her grave now takes her last sleep.
She may be in Heaven. I cannot tell,
But for me and the young ones, I know this is Hell!

I thought I should clear the mortgage, when
I fell out of work and Shylock foreclosed;
My wife she was buxom and lovely then,
And the children's cheeks were ruddy and rosed.
What now may happen I cannot foretell.
Don't tell me of Heaven! I feel I'm in Hell.

The Press and the Pulpit, they tell us to hope,
They preach bread and water and tell us to pray.
As well might they tell us—Go swing by a rope,
As labor and live "on a dollar a day."
When in work 'tisn't Heaven, that's easy to tell,
Out of work! It is certain no better than Hell!

Out of work! Oh, what misery's told in those words!
While fiends flourish proudly in crime and in greed,
Why should Providence kindly look after the birds,
And leave men to suffer in hunger and need?
The reason is surely quite easy to tell
Nature made this Earth, heaven—men made it a Hell!

Out of work! Out of work! I sit here and pine,
And ask in vain to work for my food,
The bosses say I should not repine
That times are hard and "The Lord is good."
Fools—Have ye never learned to spell;
Dynamite—nor the fear of Hell!

Patience be Damned! as the public may be
According to, he of the Vanderbilt crew
Who, nursed in the lap of luxury,
Thinks this world was made for the wealthy few.
I may sit here and moan, but I feel the spell
Coming o'er me to make for such men a Hell.

Beware! Beware! Ye men of the hour!
Beware! Beware! We are crying for work!
The eternal Samson will shake your tower
And put you to sword like the cimeter'd Turk.
Beware! Beware! 'Tis the truth I tell,
You are making your Pile, but you're breeding a Hell!

Out of work! Out of work! Do you know what it means?
Stomach empty, limbs numbed and brain aglow?
With indignation the human heart teems,
And breaks and anguishes, who can know?
He alone who is out of work can tell
With a cupboard bare, the meaning of Hell!

Rich! Rich! look up and your duty learn;
Perceive what a Moral Dury implies;
Perform it well, or the future will spurn
Your memories and lives as a system of lies.
For the only heaven of which you can tell
Is to say I have lived and "My Life was well."

Druer.

Now I suggest to you to make your unions beneficial. Have a sick and funeral benefit and, if possible, insure tools. Raise your dues in proportion to enable you to keep up these benefits. This will have the effect of keeping your unions together; sufficient at least to hold your organizations together, until after the threatening storm has passed. You have then the nucleus of an organization, and the ground you formerly went over you will not have to retrace. You will not have to struggle two or three years after the return of good times, agitating to get men enough together to get decent pay. You will be prepared at the start to claim your rights. Think of this before you reject it.

We must and should make a move for short hours, either 9 or 8 hours per day. [redacted] I earnestly ask you for your sake, for the sake of your families, for the sake of suffering humanity, do something to shorten your excessive hours of toil. Bankers, brokers, lawyers, and many more such useless leeches in society work only 4 or 6 hours per day, defrauding the public and all they come in contact with. And they fare sumptuously every day and wear fine linen, while the labor element who produce all the wealth, struggle 10, 12 and 14 hours per day, and are compelled in many cases to go in rags and buy the cheapest cuts at the butchers, the commonest provisions at the market. And if they lose two days work, they feel the effects of it for weeks to come. Surely something is wrong, and it remains with you to remedy the evil.

[redacted], I want you to look at another matter. That is the postponement of our coming convention, and not to hold any until August, 1884. If every union will consider this matter, they will understand the importance of it. If they do not, then I am ready to give the full reasons. You can elect your officers for the B the coming year by general vote and make any changes necessary just in the same way. Of course, it requires a general vote to lay the matter over. Give these questions your serious thoughts, and better results may be achieved.

As we did a fair amount of good in 1882, let us be able to say in 1884 that we have achieved one of our main objects—the shortening of the hours of toil.

Fraternally,

J. D. ALLEN.

PHILADELPHIA, Jan'y 8, 1883.

The Results of Trades Unionism.

NEW YORK. In England, as most of your readers are probably aware, it has been the custom to speak of the ruling powers as the three estates; the King or Queen being the first, the Lords the second, and the Commons the third estate. Since the press has begun to wield such a power, it has been dignified by the title of the fourth estate. But now, through the cautious, patient and persisting action of the trades unions, a fifth estate is forcing recognition, in the organized workingmen of England, who now exercise an influence which is becoming more and more powerful on the legislation of that country, as exemplified in the many measures, the adoption of which they have compelled, for the bettering of the conditions of labor.

But not only that, they are also sufficiently powerful and intelligent to have them enforced, and any infraction of them heavily fined. The Factory Act, the Education Act, the Employers' Liability Act, the Public Health Act, Truck Act, an act for shortening the hours for female and juvenile labor, an act making it obligatory on both employers and employes to give notice to quit service and many others which do not occur to me at present, are all enforced.

The English newspapers daily bear witness to the enforcement of the beneficial measures proving the increasing intelligence and consequent power of the workers for the demonstration of which they are indebted to their thorough organization in trades unions.

Be it also remembered that it has not been without much hard labor and sacrifice that they have done so much.

And also that there is no organization which possibly can do the work of labor's emancipation so certainly, so well and so safely as the trades unions.

Working people cannot oppose them unless they do so without thinking.

Let us study this question with the attention it deserves.

Let us consider the difficulties which have been overcome from the time that the unions had no status, legal or other, [illegible] the right to hold property, so that even if their treasurer absconded with their funds, they had no redress.

France, also, can justly attribute the advancement slow but sure, of her working classes to the same agency, which is gradually placing them in a position to command respect, as proved by the recent action of the Municipal Council of Paris, *according* to associations of workingmen, the right to compete for the execution of public works, and establishing a Labor Exchange and Bureau of Labor Statistics.

And this action is a proof that just as soon as the workers know what they want, there will be plenty to assist them in the ways and means.

England and France are pioneers in this labor movement, industrial and economical, and notwithstanding the objections of interested or ignorant opponents, we cannot do better than to follow their example in the organization of labor, modifying our action, according to our conditions and necessities. P. H. MCNICHOLAS.

The Good of our Order.

INDIANAPOLIS, Ind.—There are a few things that should always be aimed at and secured by our members, for we will be approved or condemned by our words among mankind. A man, and especially a brother carpenter should adopt it as an inspiration of his life to work for the good of the order. This is kept before the eye and the heart of every member who is regular in attendance upon his union, because at every meeting in the business the question is proposed: "Has any brother anything to offer for the good of the Order?" And yet I dont know whether many of the members fully comprehend the importance of the question. It is so common a question that it is passed with little thought, yet it is a most important part of the programme of business at every meeting. For under it there is a wide range of remarks, and an opportunity for the expression of thoughts and the presentation of suggestions embracing all that is good in our Brotherhood. And the place that is given to it in the order of business is the proper place: it occurs as the last question not because it is of least consequence, but that everything passed over or neglected may be brought up in the end. There is sometimes a large amount of care, and anxiety and trouble in the union, and it is rather pleasant after it has occurred to hear the president ask: "Has any brother anything to offer for the good of the union?"

Now, is it not a good thing in our unions at this point for some good brother to present to the union some case of sickness in the neighborhood, or the necessity of some helpless widow or orphan of our craft who have no claim on our Brotherhood; but being accustomed to that kind of work in the household, he speaks of it that the Brotherhood may learn of the case, and if in their power, make a free will offering of time, attention or means? Sometimes there is some sojourning carpenter or a suspended member dropped for non-payment of dues and he is in distress, the case is brought up, and the members are let out in their feelings and are at once enlisted, and are led to develop the principles of our Order toward them.

Under this head a brother may have a word of cheer to offer the brother or some counsel or advice to give that will be a benefit to others exemplifying and setting forth the principles of the Order, and encouraging the brethren in their work. This is in place, and would always be appreciated. Then an interchange of views, and feeling and sentiments warms the heart and invigorates the spirit of the moral man, and each brother leaves the union room for his home in a happy frame of mind and anxious for the return of the hour for the next union meeting. And when the time comes, each brother goes with a light step and a glad heart, feeling sure that something good is in reserve. To the members of the Brotherhood for whom I write, I say: My brethren, if you desire peace and happiness, and the approval of your own conscience, go look up the poor, relieve the distressed, help the necessitous, develop fully the principles of our Brotherhood. And if you have an enemy anywhere, and it is in your power, do that enemy a kindness. If you do not feel quite right towards a brother, make advances of friendship and a disposition to reconciliation. Never neglect an occasion to speak and work for the good of the Order, and make our Brotherhood as heavy among men.

A. [illegible]

LECTURES ON LABOR.

III.

PROPERTY AND POSSESSION.

In our former observations we have dwelt upon the fact that the activity of society finds its expression through the operation of five elements or mediums:

The first of these elements, *Land*, we have dealt with somewhat too briefly.

It now remains to speak of the other four elements, viz: Labor, Capital, Exchange, and Insurance.

Before, however, taking up the question of Labor, we want to say something further upon the question of Land; and to claim a few moments attention to the difference which exists between *Property* and *Possession*.

The only ideas which have prevailed in the world up to the present time, in relation to the social and economic condition of the people, are those which have been promulgated and maintained by the political economists of various schools, and although it is not my intention to go through a lengthy discussion of their relative merits and demerits, I should greatly desire that we (as working-men who have to work out our emancipation), should know briefly what position the economists occupy on the question of land in relation to the labor problem, in order that we may the better understand the evils under which we suffer, and thus more efficiently labor to overcome them.

The ancients knew nothing of national or political economy—or as some of the moderns have falsely called it "The Science of Government."

A few moral sentiments and commonplace remarks is all that is to be found, scattered here and there, throughout their literature.

It is true that Aristotle in his writings had remarked the great advantages to be derived from the division of labor. He had noted the fact of the transition from barter to the use of money, and also the difference between value and utility. Plato, in his "Republic", gave a sketch of what he considered society should be. It may perhaps be possible that in these hints may be found the possible germs of social science, but they were never followed up, nor were the laws which underlie them ever investigated.

The prosperity of Genoa and Venice which excited such jealous rivalry in all other parts of Europe, and the commercial supremacy which had for four centuries gradually been acquired by the Hanseatic league, first led men to study the subject, and we find it occupying a place in the literature of Italy, Spain, France and England, from the sixteenth century onward.

Europe at that date had revolted against all schemes of universal monarchy. This was the period of national history. Independent sovereign kingdoms, with national languages and national literatures, divided the area of Europe among them. Thus the circumstances of the times gave shape to these studies, and the *mercantile* school of writers, as they are now called, set their wits to work in order to devise means whereby they could make their own nation rich, while at the same time they sought to discover means whereby all other nations could be impoverished.

This may be said to be the first school which worked toward the discovery of the laws of social science.

The second school was that of the economists or physiocrats, founded by Quesnay, under Louis XV. This school maintained that agricultural labor produced more than was consumed by the farmer and his household, and that this surplus was the origin of all wealth.

Benjamin Franklin became Minister to France at the time when the teachings of the physiocrats held sway, and became a pupil and disciple of Quesnay. This school held that it was better to be a [illegible]

The third school of economists was founded by Adam Smith, a Scotch professor, who was also a friend of Quesnay, the French writer. This school has been falsely called the industrial school. It would be more properly designated by the title of *commercial* school, which teaches selfishness, for he maintains as a truth that if every man is left to do what he likes with his own, no matter how he gets it, and to use it in whatever way will secure the largest possible returns to himself, society will reap the largest possible benefit.

Thus he fairly and squarely defends monopoly—the oppression of the poor by the rich, and all the train of evils which follow.

The great work of Adam Smith, "An Inquiry into the Nature and Causes of the Wealth of Nations", was published in 1776, and in 1778, R. T. Malthus, published his "Essay on Population," which furnishes a discussion of the other side of the question—viz. the poverty of nations. Malthus was a member of the Tory or Conservative,—*i. e.* aristocratic party; at that time of political disturbance, when the impoverished workers of Europe were calling Governments to account for the bad policy which led to so much misery. He was led to the study of the economic condition in which that misery originated in order to close the mouths of the so-called agitators by showing that Government—*i. e.* aristocracy—had nothing to do with it; that it arose from causes which were beyond the control of the [illegible] classes.

He found that the cause of [illegible] the excessive growth of population, led to the pressure of numbers upon means of subsistence, and could only controlled permanently by the self-restraint of the lower classes, and by the discontinuing to give birth to so many children. He demonstrated that population increased in a geometrical ratio while subsistence could only increase in arithmetical ratio. He says the human species would increase as the numbers 1, 2, 4, 8, 16, 32, 64, 128, 256, and subsistence would increase as the numbers 1, 2, 3, 4, 5, 6, 7, 8. In the view of Malthus the condition of the people was a change from ease to misery; as soon as they advance to welfare, they are thoughtless as to the future, and their increase in numbers will always keep them in poverty and will cause years of scarcity to follow quickly upon the footsteps of years of plenty.

Thus the aristocracy, who were monopolists of the land, threw [illegible] for the existence of distress upon [illegible] causes not within their control.

Somewhat later arose another economist, David Ricardo, who belonged to the Whig party, or as it was then named, the Liberal party. He carried the investigation a step further, and attempted to account for the inequality of conditions which distinguished different classes of society, and he declared that it did not arise from natural and unavoidable causes, but from the effects of an artificial monopoly—the tenure of land. He maintained that those who had been fortunate enough to obtain possession of the best soils in the settlement of a country form a privileged class that can live in idleness [illegible] the labor of others by means of [illegible] payment for the use of the natural [illegible] of those soils.

Thus, we see the aristocracy of [illegible] who monopolized the land, laid the [illegible] to natural causes, while the aristocracy of money—the *bourgeoisie*—who [illegible] the instruments of labor, laid [illegible] to the monopolizers of the [illegible]

We may, therefore, [illegible] school of polity three months' founded, with [illegible]

[illegible] Comstock,

must come forward, and give the subject the attention and study which will enable them to deduce the laws which govern the industrial relations of mankind. And this must be done from a close attention to all the phenomena which present themselves in the industrial domain of human activity. And perhaps one of the most fundamental things which we have to consider in meeting the arguments of the economists in relation to the tenure of land, from whence springs all other things, is the difference of which I spoke a few moments ago, between property and possession.

There are two different manners in which a thing may be owned, or, we may say that there are two different views which may be taken of ownership—viz., property and possession, and between the two there is a subtle difference, which calls for a definition; for the source of all the errors of those who sustain the right of property, as also of those who combat that right, arise from having confounded the one with the other.

The etymological sense of the word "property"—that which is proper to—indicates clearly that man is the proprietor of all that is proper to, or inseparable from his being; his senses, organ faculties, acquired knowledge, etc., but none of those things which are separable from his being, which are outside of himself. He can possess these latter, but he cannot make them proper to himself—cannot assimilate them with himself.

[illegible] our notions concerning property [illegible] to us from the old English com[illegible] law, which, in its turn, was derived [illegible] the old Roman law.

The Roman law gives the definition of [illegible]roperty *(Jus utendi, et abutendi re sua)*, which is the right to use and to abuse one's [illegible]ings, and maintains that the proprietor [illegible] *"Jus in re,"* which is the right *in* the [illegible]ing; while the definition which it gives [illegible] possession is: *"Jus utendi,"* which sig[illegible] the right to the *use* of the thing, [illegible] declares the attribute of possession to [illegible] *"Jus ad rem,"*—the right to the thing. [illegible] Roman code, therefore, clearly dis[illegible]guishes between property and posses[illegible]ion. To the proprietor it gives the abso[illegible]e right in the thing, to use and abuse, while to the possessor it gives the right to make use of the thing to render it produc[illegible]ve.

[illegible] the eye of the Roman law, property [illegible] a right, a legal faculty—a man is pro[illegible]etor by virtue of a legal convention which confers upon him the right to abuse [illegible] property.

A man is possessor from the fact that [illegible] has become the first to occupy and [illegible] the use of that which he possesses. [illegible]ession is therefore a natural right. [illegible]perty is a fictitious right.

This distinction between use and abuse, [illegible]ween property and possession, has not [illegible] maintained either in principle or in [illegible]ctice. We have been working under [illegible] which we have copied from barbar[illegible]), and while we have eliminated some [illegible] of the barbarism which those laws [illegible] admirably adapted to perpetuate; we [illegible]ve not modified the laws accordingly; [illegible] have not even taken cognizance of the [illegible]istinctive difference which those laws [illegible]ognized and maintained.

The proprietor disposes of that which [illegible] owns during his life, and after his death [illegible]cording to his caprice. He may own a [illegible]use, leave it unoccupied, and let it fall [illegible] decay. He may leave his fields un[illegible]tivated and non-productive, while those [illegible]und are without shelter and without [illegible]; he does not want to use so he has [illegible] to abuse. None can use his prop[illegible] [illegible] it productive without sub[illegible] [illegible] by far [illegible] which he chooses [illegible] workingmen of whom live as an idle [illegible] each other's [illegible] of those who [illegible] and agitation. And the [illegible] [illegible] will be that the [illegible] [illegible] more of the [illegible] [illegible] their English [illegible] will be [illegible]

he owns, and it ceases to belong to him when he ceases to render it productive.

In Japan, the tenure of land depends upon this recognized principle of the difference between use and abuse. Those who cultivate the soil are bound to conserve it in proper condition, under penalty of forfeiture of possession.

How different was the tenure of land in the Southern States of America, where, by the right of property, the planters were permitted to exhaust the fertility of the soil to the detriment of the nation.

The devastations of the forests in the West is another example of the abuses springing from proprietorship. The evils of this example will not be recognized until it is too late to avoid the consequences. If, however, it teaches the American bourgeoisie that *"Apres nous le deluge"* sentiment is as fatal to it, as it was to the French aristocracy, the lesson will not have been taught in vain.

It is eminently unjust that any man should monopolize that which he cannot use, and the right of property in land is doomed to disappear before the *fast* increasing knowledge of the producers, which is proven by the fact that every step which humanity takes on the road to progress manifests itself by an abbreviation of the privileges which this fictitious right confers on the proprietor.

When he emerged from the savage state, man, impelled by want, found the means of living only through labor, and the right of the first occupant was a necessity. Possession, that is to say, the use of that which he occupied, from being the *fact* became the *law*.

Each man may then be said to have become proprietor of the little bit of land which he could cultivate, and defend against the encroachments of ferocious animals, and of men still more ferocious.

At that period man knew no other law than that of brute force; the strong subjugated the weak, and property became established in its most complete form, that of slavery.

Throughout all antiquity, the prisoner of war, the insolvent *debtor*, were slaves according to law; the proprietor had absolute right in man as in the land; he had the right of life and death over his wife, over his children, over his slaves; for all these things were *his* things *(re sua)*, he could use them and abuse them at his pleasure.

The feudal system which destroyed slavery and instituted serfdom, destroyed the right of property in man. The serf was no longer a thing belonging to man, but he belonged to the land, with which he was bought and sold. It was a step in advance. The serf had a family; the slave was but cattle.

The feudal aristocracy was overthrown by the commercial aristocracy, who dealt a severe blow at the right of property by the abolition of the law of primogeniture; by the enactment of laws concerning inheritance; the right of expropriation for public utility; by the laws concerning mortgages, corporations, limited liabilities, etc., the tendency of which is to transform individual private property into collective public property; but above all, to transfer serfdom into wagedom, *i. e.* chattel slavery into wages slavery.

Those who work *for* wages are certainly not free; they are industrial slaves, since they cannot produce without having a master, commonly called a "Boss;" but they are no longer either the thing belonging to man, nor the thing belonging to the land; they have conquered their position of comparative dignity as men and citizens. These successive restrictions of the rights of property, these limitations of the right to abuse, will not be complete until the right of property shall have become restricted simply to the right of possession accessible to all, under well defined and absolute conditions. The [illegible]

ever-growing power and ever-increasing arrogance of corporations, is but the prelude to the association of labor, which will lead the producing masses toward equality of conditions with unerring fatality. It has been proved beyond the possibility of a doubt, that those who hold the land command the use of all the elements of life. Land, air, water, and light are linked together in such intimate connection, that exclusive property in any one of them extends to all, and no man has a natural right to claim as private property a larger portion of those united elements than he can employ or cultivate for his own use, and that of his own family. It is therefore held that land, air, light and water are common property, which ought to belong to the State alone, as a source of public revenue, and not as a source of rent for the exclusive benefit of private landlords and their families.—BRUTUS.

[illegible]

Der Carpenter.

New York, Januar 1883.

Der Schreinergesell.

(Bearbeitet für den „Carpenter".)

Mein Handwerk lernt' ich wohl, ja ja, ja ja,
Doch [illegible] mir's [illegible] besser an, ja, ja
[illegible]
[illegible]

[illegible]
[illegible]
[illegible]
[illegible]

[illegible]
Mein [illegible] Meister [illegible]
[illegible]
Ich [illegible] Meister [illegible]

—. [illegible]

Theile und herrsche!

Schlau sind die Mächtigen, das muß man denselben lassen. So oft gegenüber der großen Masse ihr Interesse in Frage kommt, stehen sie ohne Unterschied der Partei und der religiösen Anschauungen wie ein Leib und eine Seele zusammen. Sie sind in volkswirthschaftlichen Fragen eben nur Kapitalisten, die sich in erster Linie fragen: „Bringen wir Schaden oder Nutzen?" Kein Mittel wird als zu verwerflich befunden, um den Profit zu retten.

Anders die arbeitenden Klassen. Da dünkt sich der Meister besser als der Geselle, der Bauer besser als der Lohnarbeiter. Da sind selbst unter den einzelnen Handwerksbranchen Kastengeist und Dünkel vorhanden.

Das „Theile und herrsche!" wird von den Gegnern des Volkes und deren Vertretern so bethätigt, daß die Masse sozusagen nie zur Einsicht ihrer ursprünglichen Interessen kommt, daß sie im eigenen Fleische wühlt und so den Gegnern das Ausbeutungsgeschäft bedeutend erleichtert.

Arbeiter, Brüder! Die Großen haben allenthalben ein gemeinsames Interesse: die Arbeitskraft der arbeitenden Massen nach Kräften auszubeuten und wir haben hinwieder das übereinstimmende Interesse, diese Ausbeutung, die uns zu Noth und Elend verdammt, zu bekämpfen.

So lange wir dies nicht international, d. h. ohne Unterschied der Nationalität thun, besiegen wir den gemeinsamen internationalen Feind, den Kapitalismus nicht.

Mitbrüder! „Seid einig, einig, einig!" Der Schrei eurer Kinder nach Brod, der kummervolle Blick eures Weibes, der barsche Ton eures Lohnherrn wie die kahlen Wände eures Heims, sie alle mahnen euch zur Vereinigung. Ein menschenwürdiges Dasein zu erringen, die Existenz eurer Lieben zu sichern durch Bekämpfung des Kapitalismus ist des einigen Vorgehens gewiß werth! — —

Arbeitendes Volk, fühle dich der einigen Kapitalistenklasse gegenüber auch als Klasse, die der einigen reaktionären goldenen Internationalen gegenüber ihr gemeinsames Proletarier-Interesse wahrt. Dann wird eine bessere Zukunft für die Enterbten anbrechen. Dann werden die Gegner mit ihrem Wahlspruche „Theile und herrsche!" keine Geschäfte mehr machen. Getrennt sind wir nichts, vereinigt Alles!

(Arbeiter-Stimme.)

— Man hat zwar keine zuverlässige Statistik über die Sterblichkeit der Negersklaven; das aber steht fest, daß es auf den Plantagen mehr alte weißhaarige „Onkels" und „Tantes" unter den Negern gab, als unter den weißen Lohnsklaven unserer Tage in Tenementshäusern und [illegible]

Ueber Gewerkschaften.

Die Gewerkschaften sind das einzige Mittel, um die Profite der Arbeitgeber zu beschränken, und was davon abgebrochen wird, dem Arbeitnehmer zuzuwenden. Wir wollen diesen Satz streng beweisen. Vorher jedoch möchten wir es verstanden zu sehen wünschen, daß sie dies erst dann können, wenn sie alle oder fast alle Arbeiter desselben Faches umfassen und verständig geleitet werden.

Der Profit entsteht dadurch, daß der Arbeitgeber den Tauschwerth der Arbeitskraft zahlt, aber den Gebrauchswerth, welcher größer ist, möglichst ausnutzt. Mit anderen Worten, wenn und weil mehr Arbeiter als nöthig im Markte sind, unterbieten sie einander, um lohnende Arbeit zu erhalten, und der Arbeitgeber giebt ihnen blos so viel Lohn, wie die Mindestforderungen verlangen, d. h. so viel, als die nothdürftige Wiederherstellung verbrauchter Arbeitskraft und die Fortpflanzung der Arbeiter erheischen; nimmt aber aus ihnen so viel Arbeitskraft heraus, als er kriegen kann, indem er sie mehr arbeiten läßt, als der Lohn deckt. Er läßt sie mehr Arbeit verrichten, und was diese ihm einbringt, ist sein Profit. Es bleibt sich bei Betrachtung dieses Verhältnisses gleich, ob er seinen Profit mit einem müßigen Dritten theilen muß, der ihm Kapital in sein Geschäft vorgeschossen hat, oder ob er selbst Kapital genug hat, wie wir noch zeigen werden. Kurz, was das Kapital gewinnt, das verliert der Arbeiter, und was der Arbeiter gewinnen kann durch Lohnsteigerung, das verliert das Kapital.

Die Gegner wenden nun ein, daß in demselben Maße, wie der Lohn steige, auch die Lebensmittel sich vertheuern, so daß der Arbeiter schließlich um nichts gebessert sei; denn wenn die Produktion theuerer werde, müßten auch die Waaren theuerer werden. Dieser Satz ist aber nur dann wahr, wenn die Profite durchaus sich sollen gleichbleiben. Dafür aber, daß die Profite gekürzt, also die Löhne gesteigert werden, sorgt einerseits der Wettbewerb der Arbeitgeber unter einander um den Waarenmarkt, wenn nur andererseits dafür gesorgt wird, daß die Arbeiter sich nicht unnöthiger Weise unterbieten, wozu eben die Gewerkschaften das Mittel sind.

Sorgen also die Gewerkschaften dafür, daß die Arbeiter einander nicht unterbieten, wozu Verkürzung des Arbeitstages das wirksamste und nächste [illegible] abgibt, so müssen die Arbeitnehmer, um ihren Profit nicht geschmälert zu sehen, entweder Kapital zu billigeren Prozenten als bisher zu bekommen suchen, oder irgendwo einen Waarenmarkt zu monopolisiren suchen, so daß sie dort ihre Waarenpreise steigern können; aber sie müssen die Arbeit intensiver (angestrengter) machen, so daß dieselbe in weniger Arbeitszeit denselben Mehrwerth erträgt als vorher.

Alle diese Mittel, den Profit hoch zu erhalten, sind schon oft, gewöhnlich zugleich, probirt worden, in Verbindung mit anderen wie zum Beispiel Erpressung an Produktionsmitteln, Versuche, Gewerkvereine zu sprengen, nicht unirte Arbeiter anderswoher zu bekommen u. s. w.

Allein diese Gewerkvereine haben Waffen gegen alle diese Maßregeln. In der Vereinigung mit allen anderen ihres Gleichen sind die Arbeiter nicht mehr die „willenlose Waare Arbeitskraft", welche sich Alles bieten lassen darf, sondern ein geeinter, vernünftiger Wille mit vereinten Widerstandsmitteln. Sie können — wie die Erfahrung lehrt — Frauen- und Kinderarbeit beschränken oder verwehren, fremde Arbeiter fernhalten, ihr Vereinsrecht [illegible] vertheidigen, übermäßig erschöpfende Arbeit verweigern, die Arbeitsstunden verkürzen, je anstrengender jede einzelne wird, staatlichen Schutz für ihre Menschenrechte verlangen und diejenigen Arbeitgeber, welche wegen ungenügenden Profits ausverkaufen wollen, schließlich auskaufen, um das Geschäft als Produktiv-Association fortzusetzen.

Die Profite müssen sinken, wie durch die Gewerkschaften der Lohn gesteigert wird, ohne daß die Waarenpreise gesteigert zu werden brauchen.

Die Erfahrung lehrt, daß mehr moralischer Zusammenhalt unter den Arbeitern, wenn vernünftig organisirt, herrscht, als unter den Arbeitgebern, weil diese blos durch den Profit, jene durch die Vertheidigung ihrer Menschenrechte zusammen gehalten werden; die Erfahrung lehrt, daß alle Arbeitseinstellungen (strikes) und Ausschließungen (lock-outs) unmöglich werden, wenn eine gute Organisation besteht, welche nicht nur alle Fachgenossen einig macht, sondern auch den Waarenmarkt aufmerksam beobachtet und dafür sorgt, daß nicht eine Zeit lang zu viel producirt wird, damit nicht die Arbeitgeber, auf ihre großen Vorräthe pochend, ihre Werke still stehen lassen können, sobald sie selben durch „Strike" oder „Lock outs" die Löhne herabdrücken [illegible], wie es noch jüngst den Vereinigten [illegible] und Eisenarbeitern widerfuhr.

Nur schlecht geleitete Gewerkschaften können einen Strike verlieren oder einen Lock-out erleiden; — und [illegible]

[illegible]

Widerstreiter eine Strike erlaubt wird, aber den Arbeitgebern ein Lock-out vortheilhaft werden kann.

Die Erfahrung lehrt ferner, daß in Großbritannien seit dem Bestehen der Gewerkvereine und ihrer Organisationsverbesserung die Löhne stetig gestiegen, trotzdem die Waaren immer billiger geworden sind. — Die Erfahrung aller civilisirten Länder lehrt übereinstimmend, daß immer zuerst die nothwendigsten Lebensmittel im Preise steigen müssen, ehe die Löhne zu steigen anfangen — wir wissen Alle, warum? — und daß die Löhne nie in demselben Verhältniß, wie die nothwendigsten Lebensmittel steigen, sondern in geringerem, wenn die Arbeiterorganisationen nicht sehr mächtig sind. Auch gelingt es, wenn die nothwendigsten Lebensmittel sinken, gut geleiteten Organisationen (wie z. B. noch jüngst in Wien den Buchdruckern unter Beistand der Organisation) ihre Löhne aufrecht zu erhalten, oder deren Sinken zu mäßigen.

Alles dieses sind unwiderlegliche Beweise für unseren obigen Satz. Also auf, ihr Arbeiter, zur allgemeinen Organisation!

(„Hammer“.)

Der zweite nationale Gewerkschafts-Congreß

tagte vom 21. bis 21. November in Cleveland, Ohio. Wir beschränken uns auf einen kurzen Auszug der wichtigsten Verhandlungen:

Aus der Platform des vorjährigen Congresses wurde die Schutzzollplanke gestrichen, hingegen zwei neue Forderungen hinzugefügt: Für Haftpflicht der Arbeitgeber bei Unfällen, und gegen die Ausgabe von Regierungsarbeiten an Contractoren.

Präsident Arthur wurde aufgefordert, das nationale Achtstundengesetz unverzüglich durchzuführen.

Bücherei-Staatssecretär French wurde wegen Umgehung des Anti-Chinesengesetzes auf's Schärfste verurtheilt und das Legislativ-Comite angewiesen, Amendements vorzuschlagen, durch welche derartige Vorkommnisse in Zukunft verhindert werden sollen.

Dasselbe Comite erhielt den Auftrag, Gesetzentwürfe einzureichen: für Incorporirung der Gewerkschaften, für Haftpflicht der Arbeitgeber gegen Unfälle, die ihren Leuten ohne eigenes Verschulden auf den Arbeitsplätzen zustoßen, und für Regelung des Lehrlingswesens, und die Gesetzvorlagen zum Verbot der Tenement-house-Cigarrenarbeit und zum Schutze des Lebens der Seeleute zu unterstützen.

Nach den Erklärungen von Robert Howard aus Fall River, in welch' schändlicher Art und Weise die Arbeiter der Pacific Mills in Lawrence, Mass., und der Harmony Mills in Cohoes, N. Y., bezahlt und behandelt werden, beschloß der Congreß, diese beiden Fabriken zu boycotten; ferner wurde beschlossen, alle Arbeiter aufzufordern, nur Cigarren zu rauchen, die von Kisten mit dem Union Label versehen sind.

Die Womens' Labor League von Washington suchte um Aufnahme in die Föderation nach. Dieselbe wurde gewährt und alle Frauen ermuntert, sich gewerkschaftlich zu organisiren.

Eine Resolution, welche verlangt, den Privatbesitz an Land abzuschaffen, wurde zurückgelegt, da der Congreß vorläufig nothwendigere Sachen zu berathen habe und die Lohnfrage der Landfrage vorangehen müsse.

Der Jahresbeitrag der Vereine wurde auf 1 Cent per Mitglied herabgesetzt. Lokale Gewerkschaften, die mindestens 6 Monate bestehen, sollen gegen Zahlung einer Steuer von $10 jährlich zur Vertretung berechtigt sein. Die Knights of Labor wurden in die Föderation aufgenommen, und gelten für die Districts-Assemblies derselben die gleichen Bedingungen, wie für locale Trades-Councils.

Das Legislativ-Comite für das laufende Jahr besteht aus: W. H. Foster von Cincinnati, Generalsecretär; Sam. Gompers von New York, Robert Howard von Fall River, W. Comerford von Washington und Richard Powers von Chicago.

Die Zeit für Abhaltung des Congresses wurde auf den dritten Dienstag im Monat August abgeändert und beschlossen, daß die nächste Jahres-Convention in der Stadt New York stattfinden soll.

Da der Congreß beschloß, Platform und Verhandlungen auch in deutscher Sprache zu publiciren, ist allen unsern Lesern Gelegenheit geboten, dieselben noch eingehender kennen zu lernen.

— Trades Unions werden in England zuerst in einer von Edward VI. im Jahre 1548 erlassenen Acte erwähnt. Es heißt darin: „Bäcker, Handwerker und Arbeiter haben Bündnisse geschlossen und sich durch gegenseitige Eidschwüre verbunden, nicht allein, daß sie Einer dem Andern nicht in's Handwerk pfuschen, auch daß der Eine eine Arbeit nicht fertig machen [illegible], welche die Andern angefangen haben, [illegible], daß sie festsetzen und ausmachen, [illegible] Arbeit sie in einem Tage thun und [illegible] [illegible]

Harmonie zwischen Kapital und Arbeit.

Die Arbeit erzeugt bekanntlich alle Neuwerthe, ohne Arbeit können keine Werthgegenstände entstehen. Da nun innerhalb der heutigen Gesellschaft sich der Grund und Boden, die Arbeitswerkzeuge und die nöthigen zu verarbeitenden Rohstoffe im Besitz einzelner Personen befinden und diesen Besitzenden gegenüber besitzlose Lohnarbeiter stehen, welche über nichts anderes als ihre Arbeitskraft zu verfügen haben, so stellen die Inhaber der Kapitalien, nämlich die Besitzer der Arbeitsmittel, die Besitzlosen zur Arbeit an. Die Arbeiter erzeugen dann durch ihre Arbeit mit Hülfe der Kapitalien neue Werthe, neue Reichthümer; die Arbeiter dürfen aber die durch ihre Arbeit erzeugten Reichthümer nicht für sich behalten, sondern sie arbeiten nur im Interesse derer, welche bei Beginn der Arbeit die Kapitalien besitzen. Für ihre Arbeit erhalten die Arbeiter nur einen gewissen Lohn, damit sind sie dann für ihre Arbeit abgefunden und haben kein Recht, darnach zu fragen, wie groß eigentlich der Werth war, den sie durch ihre Arbeit erzeugten.

Die Kapitalbesitzer haben natürlich ein sehr begreifliches Interesse daran, daß die besitzlosen Arbeiter möglichst viele neue Werthe erzeugen; dieses Interesse würde schwinden, wenn die Arbeiter das Erzeugte ausschließlich für sich behielten, aber das ist ja nicht der Fall, sondern die erzeugten Neuwerthe gehören dem ursprünglichen Kapitalbesitzer und er zahlt den Arbeitern für ihre Anstrengungen nur einen gewissen Lohn.

Es leuchtet nun jedem vernünftigen Menschen ein, daß unter diesen Umständen der Kapitalbesitzer ein hohes Interesse daran hat, daß die Arbeiter erstens möglichst viele neue Werthe erzeugen und daß sie zweitens für ihre Mühewaltung nur möglichst wenig von dem, was sie erzeugt haben, für sich beanspruchen. Es bleibt sich ganz gleich, wie hoch wir den Werth einer gewissen Arbeit taxiren, ob wir in unserem Beispiel, mit dem wir den feindlichen Interessengegensatz zwischen Ausbeuter und Ausgebeuteten illustriren wollen, 100 Dollars oder 1000 Dollars als geschaffenen Neuwerth annehmen.

Der Interessenstreit über die Vertheilung des durch die Arbeit geschaffenen Neuwerthes bleibt immer derselbe. Hat ein oder haben mehrere Lohnarbeiter z. B. 1000 Dollars an Neuwerth, nach Abzug aller Unkosten außer dem Arbeitslohn, geschaffen, so ist klar, daß wenn der oder die Erzeuger dieses Neuwerthes davon für ihre Arbeit 750 Dollars in Form von Lohn verlangen, für den Kapitalinhaber nur 250 Dollars als Ausbeutungsertrag oder als unverdientes, weil arbeitsloses Einkommen übrig bleiben. Sind die Lohnarbeiter hingegen mit 500 Doll. oder gar noch mit weniger Lohn für ihre geleistete Arbeit zufrieden, so verbleiben dem Kapitalisten 500 Dollars oder genau so viel mehr als die Arbeiter weniger für ihre Arbeit erhalten.

Als einen noch klareren Beweis, wie es mit der Harmonie zwischen Kapital und Arbeit bestellt ist, führen wir die Fabrik-Statistik der Ver. Staaten vom Jahre 1880 an. Wenn man die im Jahre 1880 gezahlten Arbeitslöhne und den Werth der verarbeiteten Materialien zusammenzählt ($947,919,673 und $3,394,[illegible],[illegible]) und die Summe $[illegible],342,[illegible]59,704 von dem Werthe der Produkte abzieht, also von $5,369,667,706, so bleibt ein Rest von $1,0[illegible]7,[illegible]48,00[illegible]. Das ist der Kapitalgewinn. Es ist nicht der Reingewinn der Fabrikanten, denn er schließt noch den Kapitalzins ein. Aber gleichviel für unsern gegenwärtigen Zweck. Es erhält also ein Arbeiter einen Dollar erhält, bezog das Kapital einen Dollar und acht Cents Gewinn. Rechnet man vom Kapitalgewinn vorher noch den Kapitalzins ab zu 10 Prozent, welcher bei $2,790,[illegible]23,566 die Summe von $279,0[illegible]2,350 beträgt, also $[illegible],314,[illegible]01,155 übrig läßt, so bekommen die Fabrikanten diese letztere Summe, also ebenso oft 98 Cents, als der Arbeiter 100 bekam, und das war ihr Reingewinn, wozu sie in allen Fällen, wo sie alles nöthige Kapital selbst besaßen, auch noch 10 Cents Zinsen bezogen. Also das gar nicht arbeitende Kapital erhielt von jedem Dollar Lohn des Arbeiters 10 Cents und das die Arbeit leitende Kapital 98 Cents.

Kann da noch von einer Harmonie zwischen Kapital und Arbeit die Rede sein? Wir sagen: Nein! Oder glauben etwa die Harmoniedudeler, daß das Harmonie ist, wenn der Arbeiter 1 Dollar erhält und das Kapital 1 Dollar 8 Cents? Eine solche Harmonie wollen wir ihnen gerne gönnen.

Aus dem Obigen folgt, daß, so lange es überhaupt Privatkapitalisten resp. Ausbeuter und ihnen gegenüber ausgebeutete, weil besitzlose Menschen gibt, eine Harmonie zwischen Kapital und Arbeit, d. h. Ausbeutern und Ausgebeuteten, oder, besser ausgedrückt, zwischen Arbeitgebern und Arbeitnehmern nicht existiren kann. Die Interessengegensätze sind durchaus unversöhnlich. Was die eine Gruppe von den Erzeugnissen der Arbeit mehr erhält, geht nothwendig der anderen Gruppe verloren.

Eine Harmonie zwischen Privatkapital, das [illegible] [illegible] wird, und

[illegible] monie zwischen Kapital und Arbeit überhaupt ist sehr wohl möglich und auch wünschenswerth. Der Unterschied in der Auffassung ist nur dieser, daß in jenem Satz, wie ihn die Arbeiter lesen, nicht von der Lohnarbeit und nicht vom Privatkapital die Rede ist, indessen die Harmoniedudler, welche der Phrase der Vertheidiger des Ausbeutungssystems gedankenlos Glauben schenken, sich dem trügerischen Wahne hingeben, das ausbeutende Privatkapital mit der ausgebeuteten Lohnarbeit in ein harmonisches Verhältniß bringen zu können.

Wir wollen das leblose Ding Kapital der lebendigen menschlichen Arbeitskraft untergeordnet. Das todte Kapital, das Erzeugniß früherer menschlicher Arbeit, soll der ganzen Menschheit dienstbar gemacht werden. Das Kapital, die Sache, soll nicht den Menschen beherrschen, wie dies jetzt der Fall ist, sondern der Mensch soll die Sache beherrschen. Das Kapital soll Dienerin der Arbeit sein, weil es leblos ist, nicht aber soll der beseelte Mensch Diener des Kapitals sein. Man schaffe das Privatkapital ab und alle Kapitalien werden gesellschaftliches Eigenthum sein. Dann hat plötzlich alle Ausbeutung aufgehört. Dann gibt es auch kein herrschendes Kapital mehr, sondern nur todte Arbeitsmittel. Dann gibt es keinen Kampf zwischen Kapital und Arbeit mehr, weil das Kapital nicht mehr selbstständig ist; dann herrscht wirkliche Harmonie zwischen Kapital und Arbeit, weil dann die Arbeit ungeschmälert die Früchte ihrer Anstrengungen genießen kann.

Dies ist der Sinn, den wir dem Prinzip der wünschenswerthen Herstellung einer Harmonie zwischen Kapital und Arbeit beilegen.

(„Progreß“.)

Was nützt eine Lokale Union.

Was nützt eine lokale Union oder Verein, wo nur die Mitglieder als Eintagsfliegen betrachtet werden können, indem viele Mitglieder heute hier und morgen dort sind, und sich jedesmal in dem betreffenden Ort immer wieder einer anderen lokalen Organisation anschließen müssen. Dieses ist geradezu Geldverschwendung ohne zu welchem Zweck und Nutzen für die Gesammtheit. Mitarbeiter! wir rufen Euch die Worte zu: „Einigkeit ist Macht!“ und diejenigen, welche frei werden wollen, müssen selbst Hand an's Werk legen. Jeder Lokal-Union muß unserer Brüderschaft beitreten, und fest und treu für unsere gemeinsame Interessen kämpfen.

Strikes.

Richter Ruppert Kettle sagt in seinem Buch über „Strikes“, das er kürzlich herausgegeben hat: „Die Gewerkschaften haben bewirkt, daß die arbeitenden Klassen anfangen, frei zu denken und zu handeln; und mehr noch, sie haben sie gelehrt, die Gesetze zu achten und sich moralischer Mittel zur Erlangung dessen zu bedienen, zu dem sie sich berechtigt halten. Es giebt jetzt kein Blutvergießen mehr bei den bittersten und längsten Arbeiter-Ausständen.“ Dazu bemerkt der in Cleveland erscheinende „Journeyman Builder“: „Und trotz solcher Erfahrungen giebt es schlechte Menschen, welche das Bestehen von Gewerkschaften bedauern und den starken Arm des Gesetzes zu ihrer Unterdrückung anrufen oder durch Sophistereien, falsche Logik und höhnische Bemerkungen die Gewerkschaftler als „Communisten“, „Agitatoren“ u. s. w. anschwärzen, damit die Arbeiter glauben mögen, daß Trades Unions ungesetzlich und überflüssig seien. Gehet Euch in der Welt um und wo Ihr eine schwächliche, sorgfältige Arbeiterklasse findet, werdet Ihr eine schwächliche, verkommene Nation finden.“

Läcerlei.

— In Missouri wird eine Staats Trade & Labor-Association gegründet werden.

— Jetzt werden in England Frauen beim Schmieden von eisernen Bolzen verwandt.

— Das Schreien der Unterdrückten nach Gerechtigkeit erschallt auf der ganzen Erde.

— Die Arbeiter von Muskegon, Michigan, bauen sich jetzt eine Halle, die $7000 kosten wird.

— Die Carpenterbosse in San Francisco wollen den Versuch machen, die Löhne ihrer Arbeiter zu reduziren.

— Der englische Statistiker Mulhall veranschlagt den Reichthum der Verein. Staaten auf $50,000,000,000.

— In Lynn, Mass., haben die Arbeiter Einen der Ihrigen zum Candidaten für das dortige Mayorsamt aufgestellt.

— Es ist ausgerechnet worden, daß in den Ver. Staaten Kinder unter 14 Jahren 44 Prozent der arbeitenden Bevölkerung bilden und [illegible] [illegible] 64 Prozent aller Männer.

— [illegible]

einmal 9,000 Hausbesitzer. Die Uebrigen [illegible] sämmtlich den „Landlords“ tributpflichtig.

— Es geschehen Zeichen und Wunder. Sämmtliche Arbeiter und Arbeiterinnen [illegible] Lorillard'schen Tabaksfabriken haben als Weihnachtsgeschenk einen ganzen Wochenlohn erhalten. „Es „kostet“ das der Firma $18,000 — von den Millionen, die sie den Arbeitern „gesetzlich“ gestohlen hat.

— Ein aus Arbeitern und Kapitalisten zusammengesetztes Schiedsgericht hat soeben entschieden, daß die Löhne der Arbeiter in den Schuhfabriken von Cincinnati um 10 bis [illegible] Prozent zu erhöhen seien und die Preise während der nächsten 6 Monate nicht geändert werden sollen. Ein Theil der Kapitalisten beschwert sich über diese Entscheidung und behauptet, das Geschäft gehe zu schlecht, um eine Lohnerhöhung rechtfertigen zu können.

Man hat berechnet, daß Sir Lord Vanderbilt's Einkommen von seinen Bundespapieren dem Jahreslohn von 100,000 Arbeitern gleichkommt. Keiner der südlichen Barone hat jemals so viele Sklaven gehabt und das Schönste dabei ist, daß diese Vanderbilts und Konsorten, wenn sie ihre Arbeiter entlassen, ihnen nicht einmal eine Brodkruste mit auf den Weg zu geben brauchen. Auch bedürfen sie keines Gesetzes von Flüchtlings-Gesetzes; sie brauchen nur dafür zu sorgen, daß die Arbeiter ihr Leben lang Puckesel bleiben.

— Die Negersklaven hatten nervige Fäuste und waren der Zahl nach ihren Peinigern weit überlegen, aber dennoch krümmten sie denselben kein Haar — weil sie nicht wußten, daß sie ein Recht hatten, frei zu sein. Die weißen Lohnsklaven von heute sind „freie“ Bürger, „freien“ Staates und haben das Stimmrecht, vermittels dessen sie sich der Räuber und Schinder, welche die Früchte der Arbeit des Lohnsklaven verzehren, mit einem Schlage entledigen könnten. Sie thun es aber nicht, weil sie nicht wissen, daß die Früchte ihrer Arbeit ihnen, Niemand anders gehören.

— Die Neujahrsbeilage des „Carpenter“, Organ der Bauschreiner, ist ein Holzschnitt, passendem Gedicht, welcher einen Bauschreiner darstellt, dessen Frau aus Entbehrung gestorben ist, dessen Haus mit einer Hypothek belastet und der keine Arbeit finden kann, um sein überlebendes Kind zu ernähren. Das Ganze beträgt mehr als 1 Spalte des Leitartikels und sollte den Bauschreinern dringender Mahnruf dienen, für ihren Zweck solidarisch einzustehen.

(Das Buffalo Banner.)

— Der „Carpenter“, das Gewerkschafts-Organ der Zimmerleute, ist gestern für den laufenden Monat in New York mit einer illustrirten Beilage erschienen, welche einen Zimmermann darstellt, der beschäftigungslos geworden sein Weib verloren hat und, am Bette seiner schlafenden Kinder sitzend, die ihm übrig gebliebene einzige Säge in der Hand hält und über sein Schicksal grübelt, das ihn zwingt, auch diese Säge noch zu versetzen, um die Kinder vor Hunger zu schützen. Das Bild und das dazu gehörige Gedicht von Drury sind von ergreifender Wirkung.

(N. Y. Volkszeitung.)

THE VOICE.

At last New York workingmen hav[e] press of their own! And the paper th[ey] have started is worthy of more than l[ocal] circulation. *The Voice* is the title o[f a] weekly labor journal just publishe[d in] New York, at 25, 26 and 30 Frankfor[t St.] It is a handsome 8 page paper of el[egant] typographical appearance and of a [most] dignified tone. It's make up is eleg[ant;] its editorials show no weak hand; and [all] in all, it is a worthy representative of [the] labor cause. May its *voice* never falte[r.] Its subscription price is 50 cents for th[ree] months.

BOSSES STRIKING AGAINST GOOD WORK.

Since Nov. 20, the ship caulkers of Ne[w] York have been locked out by their boss[es.] The workmen resolved in 1881 to do "g[ood] work", and in this they were encoura[ged] by the ship captains and ship owners. [The] The boss caulkers object because [there is] "no money in it." The caulkers con[tend] the ship owners desire it. Hence the [lock-]out has resulted. On the one side [the] bosses say: "You must do what w[e say] and never mind about good work." [On] the other side the men say: "We [re-]fuse to yield certain trade privi[leges] [illegible] upon our right to do [illegible] [illegible] is [illegible] at the [illegible]

. Introduction. The object and chater of our social.—L. E. Schneider.
. Are socials beneficial to our organiza ?—J. P. McGinley.
. Song: Think of your head in the rning.—Mr. White.
. The world's heroes.—Bro. Dixon.
. Education and self-culture.—Prof. D. nbert.
. Recitation. The modern orator.— White.
. Solo: Die alte Sagamore. L. E. neider.
. Why I am a union man. J. Blair.
. Labor and co-operation. Bro. White.
0. Balloting for boquet to handsomest y present. The two prizes were: First, opy of Moore's poems; second, a large quet. There were 1725 votes cast. Miss yle received first prize, carried by anch 4; Miss Wicks got second prize, ried by Branch 6. The meeting made avorable impression on both members l outsiders.

Trade is dull on account of cold weather; ges $2.75 to $3 per day, but the nineer plan of the bosses has reduced them and 30 cents less per day. There are reat many non-union men out of work. use for carpenters to come here this son.

From The Bricklayers' National Union.

NEW YORK, Dec. 20th, 1882.—It is with lings of deep gratitude that I now acowledge the receipt of your most intering journal—THE CARPENTER. Although one of your trade, I nevertheless have d THE CARPENTER with intense inter. In its columns I have found many uable lessons and wise sayings; not y in regard to your particular trade, lessons that could be taken up and ed upon by all organized bodies of wage rkers.

The true aim of all organizatio[illegible] rkingmen is to try and am[illegible] ndition of the va[illegible] read the [illegible] [illegible] th trade [illegible] work[illegible] par-[illegible] of labor must adopt [illegible]itimate means to arrive at the e solution of the various questions that m time to time may arise. And they ould be ready at all times to take a deled stand in support of their principles. itation and education will win the day Labor, if Labor will only accept that ich is so freely offered their trades ions and labor press. In my humble inion I know of no better way of enlighting the minds of all wage workers than rough the columns of just such journals THE CARPENTER—papers that are ned and controlled by honest workingn, and which cannot be bought by capilists or politicians, no matter how tempty the offer. I write these few plain facts th the hope that every carpenter and od worker will see the necessity of subibing for THE CARPENTER, and by so ing help to spread the light through the gth and breadth of this land.

HENRY O. COLE,
Pres. Bricklayers' Nat. Union.

The Situation in 'Frisco.

SAN FRANCISCO, Cal. Union No. 22 is riving rapidly. A spirit of organization abroad. Since we obtained the four lock quit on Saturdays, men have awoke the advantage of united action and like Sexton "we gather them in." Trade 'Frisco is fair; of course there is no usual demand for men, but our memrs by looking out sharply for each ner's interests, manage to keep fairly ployed for this season of the year. Carnters should be very slow about moving m any Eastern city here, as yet Califor, as far as our trade is concerned, is a te with but one city. When business is dull here so in San Francisco, there is show, unless to buy a blanket and go tramp seeking work from some rancher. ould the unfortunate mechanic descend that, he has reached the level of a inaman, as they constitute the bulk of farm laborers of this State.

We have achieved one victory here, for believe we have killed the piece work stem. The Chapter of Architects of is city are in sympathy with us in that vement. At one of our meetings a short ago, it was reported that the floors [illegible] block had been sublet [illegible]

following day to the job and met that gentleman there; he admitted that the contractor had sublet some of the floors without his knowledge, but said that he did not think the fellows who had taken them would desire another such contract, as he compelled them to take up several squares and relay it, also that he warned the contractor, that in no case would he permit any piece work on that or any other job under his superintendence. He also called for the foreman, the contractor not being around then, introduced me as President of the Union, and repeated the same injunction against piece work to him in my presence, telling him that the Chapter of Architects had assured the Carpenters Union that they would not permit it, and that they were determined to oppose it in the future.—EDWARD OWENS.

Free Labor and Slave Labor.

BOSTON, Mass.—I noticed in the Dec. number of CARPENTER the following paragraph: "Free Labor is cheaper than Slave Labor,' was the cry of the North to the South before the rebellion. And now the capitalists North and South have made it a fact."

Now I wish, if possible, to give a little more force to the above truth by relating a narrative which happened between myself and a man I worked for a year ago: One day in conversation I said to him:

"Suppose it were legal for you to buy me, and I was willing to sell *myself* to you, what would you be willing to give for me?"

"Not five cents." was his reply.

"Why not?" I asked.

"Well," he said; "In the first place I do not think I could support you for m[illegible] less than you earn, not enough [illegible] way to take any risk, as [illegible] support you whe[illegible] or not; in [illegible] [illegible] [illegible] [illegible] foot in the [illegible] somebody else, no [illegible] becomes of you or your fa-[illegible]

This was a reasonable answer every one will admit, but it proves plainly that "free,' labor is cheaper than chattel slavery was. If an employer of labor wants to hire a man, he gets him without paying one cent, and he has to furnish his chattel slave with food, clothing and shelter from the first hour he has him in his possession.

Hear what William Cobbett says: "But some may say, slaves are *private property* and may *be bought and sold* out and out, like cattle. And, what is it to the slave, whether he be property of *one* or of *many*; or, what matters it to him, whether he passes from master to master by a sale for an indefinite term, or be let to hire by the year, month or week. It is in no case the flesh and blood that are sold, but the labor, and, if you actually sell the labor of man, is not that man a *slave*, though you sell it for only a short time at once? And as to the principle so ostentatiously displayed in the case of the *black* slave trade, that '*man* ought not to have a *property in* man'; it is even an advantage to the slave to be private property, because the owner has then a clear and powerful *interest* in the preservation of his life, health and strength, and will *therefore* furnish him amply with food and raiment necessary for those ends."

H. W. BROWN.

A CARPENTERS' STRIKE.

We are indebted to the *Progressive Age* for the following:

The members of Chicago Carpenters Union 21 who have been employed on the Farwell building, corner of Monroe and Market Streets, quit work Dec. 16, in consequence of an imposition sought to be perpetrated on their foreman, Mr. Keeh, by one of the head employes of the establishment. The difficulty involved a principle of unionism, which the members of Union 21 had the requisite backbone to sustain.

— Cincinnati Union No. 2 has had an election of officers with the following result; Pres., John Ellick; Vice Pres., John Valerius; Rec. Sec., Robert Hamond; Fin. Sec., Geo. Brethauer; Cor. Sec., Chs. Rumpler; Treas., Jos. A. Leininger; Conductor, Jos. Rouse; Warden, Ben. Meader; Trustees, Jos. C. Stein, T. W. Noertker, John Cossmann, Wm. Winkler, Alfred Gennell.

VOLUME III. NEW YORK, FEBRUARY, 1883. NUM[illegible]

THE LABOR INVESTIGATION IN WASHINGTON.

Some months ago the United States Senate passed a resolution instructing the Senate Committee on Education and Labor to inquire into the condition of the working classes, and as to the cause of strikes. On Tuesday, Feb. 6, the examination of witnesses on the labor side of the question was opened. Robert D. Layton, Pittsburgh, Pa.; F. K. Foster, Boston, Mass.; P. J. McGuire, Philadelphia, Pa.; Samuel Gompers, New York; and William Baird, Elkhardt Mines, Md., were summoned, and appeared as witnesses in behalf of the working classes. Layton and Foster were the only witnesses examined, and as their examination extended over several days, the Senate Committee for want of time was compelled to postone further investigation until after this session of Congress.

The testimony offered was very full and complete,, showing the actual condition of the working people, their wages, hours of labor, cost of living, etc. The remedies upon which all the witnesses agreed as the most urgent for Congress to pass are, the rigid enforcement of the eight-hour law, and abolition of private contracts on public works, the creation of a National Bureau of Labor Statistics, and the legalization of trades unions.

On February 7, a mass-meeting of workingmen was held at Shea's Hall; it was largely attended. Robert D. Layton, Grand Secretary of the Knights of Labor, said *the K. of L. did not conflict with trades unions, and that both forms of organization were necessary.* He advised the K. of L. men to work in harmony with the trades unions, instead of opposing them. F. K. Foster, S. Gompers, W. Baird, and P. J. McGuire spoke very emphatically in the same vein.

A FEW FIGURES—NOT TOO DRY TO READ.

The total number of manufacturing establishments in the United States is 253,-852, with a capital of $2,790,272,606. These industries employ 2,738,895 hands, two million of which are male adults, half a million female and 181,918 children and youths. The wages required to pay this large number of people is $947,953,795. The value of materials used is $3,396,823,-449, producing $5,369,579,191. This leaves a clear profit of $1,024,801,947, after wages and material are paid for. It is plain that this is 43 per cent profit on the capital invested, or over $4,000 clear for each concern; while the average yearly wages for each workman was $346, or less than *one dollar per day!*

While political economists claim that wages are fully one-half of the total product, we can see plainly in this instance that wages are barely twenty per cent of the total product.

—Branch No. 5 of Chicago Union No. 1 now meets on north east corner Centre avenue and Huron streets.

—Carpenters Union No. 86 has been organised in St. Catherines, Canada, and has applied to us for a charter.

—Among the new candidates for place the ranks of labor journalism are! The

TRADE NOTES.

—A building trades league has been formed in Pittsburg, Pa. Wages for carpenters in that city average $2.25 per day.

—Advices from Jamestown, Dakota, show trade is very fair and wages $2.50 to $3 per day. Trade it is said will be good there in a few weeks.

—From the last monthly report of the Amalgamated Carpenters we note a gain of 269 members,—a total of 20,659 members. They have 276 branches—36 of which are in London.

—*Truth* of San Francisco in speaking of our carpenters union in that city says: "The Union is progressive and well officered, composed of thinking men and should and will maintain always its present good standing."

—The carpenter bosses in Toronto, it seems, have combined to keep Thomas Moor from obtaining employment on account of his activity in the strike last Spring. Such a system of proscription and blacklisting will surely some day bring its retaliation.

LAW MAKERS GRANTING US CONCESSIONS.

The politicians in Congress and in several State Legislatures are making ready to throw a few sops to the workingmen. Not that they have any great respect for Labor—far from it—but simply because they fear the growing power of the workingmen. It is that alone which has produced their change of mind.

When pronounced enemies of trades unions like Bill Wallace of Pennsylvania —a man who has heretofore prosecuted workingmen for conspiracy—can stand up as he has done, and introduces bills in the name of Labor, then let us prepare for the millenium.

In the Pennsylvania Legislature Senator Wallace has introduced bills for the incorporation of trades unions, and for voluntary tribunals of arbitration to settle strikes. The bill for the incorporation of trades unions betrays the cloven foot when it requires trades unions to show their books and papers, and does not make the same demand on corporations of capitalists. Other labor measures are also pending.

New Jersey has passed a law prohibiting children under fourteen years, who have not been two years to school, and under twelve in any case, from working in factories.

The bill prohibiting the manufacture of cigars in tenement houses in New York City has passed both houses and now awaits the signature of the Governor.

In Missouri, Indiana, Colorado, Ohio, Massachusetts, Connecticut and other States, various labor measures are pending in the State Legislatures. In New York and Ohio the prospects are good for abolishing the contract system of prison labor. And all this is done simply because Labor is organising. If politicians will offer these concessions now in our present state of organization, how much more will they grant us when we are more perfectly organized?

—With encouraging results the Cincinnati trades unions are boycotting a Ger-

ACROSS THE SEA.

FRANCE. Over 2500 porcelain makers at Limoges are locked out on a general reduction of 20 per cent in wages. Everything is in favor of the men: English trades unions have sent 1000 francs assistance; relief is also provided by the French unions.

AUSTRIA.—The printers of Vienna lost their strike after being out twelve weeks. At first they struck against lower wages and then the struggle took shape in favor of reduced hours and the abolition of Sunday work. The men lacked organization beforehand, and were without funds.

SWITZERLAND.—In Zurich a mass-meeting of 350 carpenters was held and action taken to strengthen their union. The bosses warned their workmen to not attend under penalty of discharge; but this simply had the effect of stirring the workmen to attend in spite of the bosses.—In Berne carpenters wages are 1½ francs per day.— From statistics lately published we learn that over 70,000 mechanics in Switzerland are out of work, and in the main are dependent upon charity.

SPAIN.—The carpenters of Badalona are considering the question of joining the regional federation of trades as a step to aid the Spanish Federation of Trades.— At Gracia, Figueras, Cadiz and Puerto Reale the carpenters held public meetings to advocate federation of trades in those regions. All through Spain the carpenters are making rapid progress in organization and are preparing for a convention, to organise a National Union of Carpenters.— In Linares the carpenters have joined the Union of Building Trades which has been formed in that region.

ENGLAND.—Danl. Guile, for many years Secretary of the Iron Founders Union of Great Britain, and who was lately pensioned by that union and retired from office on account of old age, died on Dec. 14 last, aged 68 years. He was a faithful and steadfast trades unionist and his memory is universally honored.—A three days conference of delegates representing 257,000 coal miners was held in Leeds to restrict the output of coal in order to maintain wages.—Fifteen Annual Trade Union Congresses have been held in Great Britain; the first being held in Manchester in 1868, and the remainder in the following order: —Birmingham 1869, London 1871, Nottingham 1872, Leeds 1873, Sheffield 1874, Liverpool 1875, Glasgow 1875, Newcastle-on-Tyne 1876, Leicester 1877, Bristol 1878, Edinburgh 1879, Dublin 1880, London 1881, and Manchester 1882. The Congress of 1883 will be held during the month of September, in Nottingham.

OBITUARY.

FRANK SUNDERHAUS, late member of Cincinnati Union No. 2, died in the Cincinnati Hospital, Jan. 2, 1883, of small pox. He was admitted for treatment into the hospital, Dec. 26, 1882, and has been a member of Union No. 2 ever since March 7, 1881, and entitled to all benefits. Application in due form according to the constitution has been filed with us by the officers of Union No. 2, in behalf of the relatives of deceased, for payment of the Insurance Benefit of $250. This is our first death under the provisions of Endowment.

SPLINTERS.

—The workingmen of Massa[illegible] are demanding from their State [illegible] tion a law compelling weekly payment [illegible] wages.

—The census of 1880 shows the [illegible] average wages of workingmen [illegible] United States is a fraction over [illegible] per day.

—It is estimated that children [illegible] years of age constitute 44 per cent [illegible] working people of this country [illegible] does 24 per cent of the income.

—Prison labor in Colorado is [illegible] contractors for 50 cents a day. [illegible] victs in Sing Sing, N. Y., are [illegible] 40 cents a day to Perry & Co., [illegible] ers.

—John O'Brien, the man [illegible] bitter attacks on President [illegible] agement of the Amalgamated [illegible] decamped with $250 in money [illegible] his lodge.

—The N. Y. *Times* says [illegible] for co-operation to succeed [illegible] as Americans cannot be tied [illegible] one locality, or to the patronage [illegible] ticular establishment.

—Bills for the creation of bu[illegible] labor statistics are now pending [illegible] State Legislatures of Connecticut [illegible] York, Indiana, Colorado, Michigan, [illegible] consin, and California.

—At last the Trades Assembly [illegible] Louis has taken the proper position [illegible] employers shall not sit as delegates [illegible] their midst; they are of the opinion [illegible] wage workers can attend to their own business.

—A bill to repeal the conspiracy la[illegible] as to annul the common law and [illegible] workingmen the full right to combine [illegible] act in their own interests, has been i[illegible] duced in the N. J. Legislature and is [illegible] to pass.

—Commissioner Spannhorst of the [illegible] souri State Labor Bureau practically [illegible] commends the destruction of that Bu[illegible] What better could be expected from a [illegible] litician who had not even the most tri[illegible] ability for the work?

—A bill has been introduced in [illegible] Pennsylvania Legislature which make[illegible] a misdemeanor for an officer of any [illegible] *corporated* association to appropriate to [illegible] own use the funds of the society, wi[illegible] penalty attached of $500 fine and [illegible] years imprisonment. This bill should [illegible] passed. Then our labor societies and [illegible] unions can fix defaulting treasurers.

—Justice although tardy has com[illegible] last! The Supreme Court of New [illegible] has reversed Judge Haight's decision. [illegible] will be remembered that during the freight [illegible] handlers strike last summer, Judge Haight [illegible] sided with the railroads. Now the [illegible] preme Court decides that the State has [illegible] power to compel railroads to perform the[illegible] duties as public carriers. Had this [illegible] cision been rendered sooner, the [illegible] handlers would have won their strike [illegible]

CLEVELAND, O.—Trade is [illegible] wages $2.25 to $2.50 and good [illegible] Spring and Summer. Our [illegible] along faithfully and the [illegible] are of the true grit [illegible] fold. [illegible]

THE CARPENTER.

[illegible] Post-Office in New York, as [illegible]

[illegible], FEBRUARY, 1883.

[illegible]ARPENTER'S WOOING.

[illegible] my own to me!"
[illegible] addressing—
[illegible] years,
[illegible] glowing!"
[illegible] speak,"
[illegible] said with laughter—
[illegible] guileless girl,
[illegible] what you are rather;
[illegible] gave you but a bit,
[illegible] will you as me!
[illegible] be content with that,
[illegible] further lacks me!"
[illegible] saw, her words were square.
[illegible] me—
[illegible] I implore,
[illegible] brace me!"

The Sequel.

[illegible] to his arms;
[illegible] him only
[illegible] make a bolt for him
[illegible] could prepare,
[illegible] screw his courage up
[illegible] his level head
[illegible] matter then and there.
[illegible] unto her breast,
[illegible] square well for me,
[illegible] to hinge on this;
[illegible] plane to see,
[illegible] child wants a kiss."
[illegible] her lip, he kissed her cheek,
[illegible] her his adored—
[illegible] his saw-hammer next week,
[illegible] will share his board.

WORKSHOP NOTES.

[illegible] originated with the art of [illegible] and was in use among the [illegible] over 3500 years ago.

[illegible] floors are said to be in [illegible] which the highest grades of [illegible] are employed.

[illegible] dries much more readily [illegible] has been once or twice [illegible] ordinary glue, or that [illegible] bones, absorbs twelve [illegible] water in twenty-four [illegible] bones the glue absorbs [illegible] weight of water, while the [illegible] made from animal refuse, [illegible] three to five times its weight

[illegible] OF THE STEEL SQUARE.

For Miters.

[illegible]	and	12	Square	Miter.
[illegible]	"	4	Triangle	"
[illegible]	"	10	Pentagon	"
[illegible]	"	7	Hexagon	"
[illegible]	"	6	Heptagon	"
[illegible]	"	7½	Octagon	"
[illegible]	"	9	Nonagon	"
[illegible]	"	9	Decagon	"

Common Rafters.

[illegible] following figures on the Square will [illegible] plumb and horizontal cuts for the [illegible] enumerated below:

	Rise.		Run.
[illegible]	3		12
....	4		12
....	4	8-10	12
....	6		12
....	8		12
....	12		12
....	16		12
[illegible]	21		12

Hip Rafters.

[illegible] of hips may be got by taking [illegible] the run, instead of 12, using the [illegible] as for common rafter on same [illegible].

CHEAP HEAD-PLANE.

[illegible] you are caught out on a job without [illegible] and must have one for, per-[illegible] only a few minutes' work, just take [illegible] screw and screw it into a block [illegible] leaving the head project the [illegible] the head, and run this over [illegible] the slot in the screw-head [illegible] durably fair thread, and cuts a [illegible] may do for the occasion. A [illegible] off the corner completes [illegible] Journal.

[illegible] Labor League [illegible]

ORGANIZATION OF EXCHANGE.

Letter No. 13.

Dear Sir:—Man is a social being and capable of perfecting himself. In the time of the Egyptians and Greeks, and it is reasonable to suppose that in prehistoric times, the bees constructed their cells in the same way as at present; birds built their nests in the same manner and with the same materials; the greater part of the insect world is born after the death of the parent, and consequently never learn anything from them and yet perform the same acts as their parents. Therefore in the case of animals the history of the individual is the history of the entire species.

If animals know all that is necessary at birth, man is born in ignorance but with the faculty of acquiring all knowledge; he has aptitudes for self-progression, can appropriate to his wants and desires all science, and the progress of generations which have preceded him upon the earth; therefore, in order to study the history of man, we must study, not the history of an individual, but the entire species, and follow it in its successive stages of development from age to age.

The discoveries recently made in the geological formation of the globe prove clearly that man in the prehistoric ages lived in holes which he dug in the ground, or took advantage of those caves or holes in the rocks which nature had excavated. He must have been in existence for centuries, ere he conceived the idea of living above ground, or of constructing the very rudest hut by means of putting stones near to each other and filling up the interstices with mud, etc.,—a hole served him for a door through which he crawled on *all fours*, a stone rolled against the hole to protect himself from wild beasts during sleep. Centuries again elapsed before he conceived the convenience of having a hole in the top of his hut to let the smoke out, —other centuries passed, ere he conceived a window, and if we reflect for a moment at the passage of man from the hole in the ground to the 5th and 6th story of a well-built stone house, we shall catch a conception of the slow but continuous process of evolution which has raised man from a state of barbarism to a state of comparative civilization.

Hence as man is progressive, it is folly to suppose that although the same nest will serve for the bird the same cell for the bee, etc., etc., that the same system of money and the same methods of exchange will serve the purposes of mankind at the present day, any more than the old system of transportation of merchandise, letters and messages, by means of wagons, teams, and post-horses, would serve the people of to-day in the face of railroads and steam locomotion, the Post Office and the electric telegraph.

In the animals, under the influence of instinct, the faculties are the same for each individual of the same species and only differ in different species; in man who enjoys the liberty of action and of thought, the faculties differ in each individual, this diversity of tastes and aptitudes renders it necessary, in order to live and develop himself, that man should have the cooperation of his fellow-beings, that is sociability.

Man is not a machine subjected to the degrees of providence, he is the framer of his own destiny, since instead of instinct we find he possesses a free and progressive intelligence. Humanity then in its progress continually acts and reacts upon itself, without the intervention of any superior force whatever, but on account of the immutability of natural laws man cannot err without suffering, which fact makes society return in spite of itself into the path of justice and truth.

Neither is human nature merely body and soul, mind and matter; man was not made to suffer here and to permit himself to be crushed and maltreated by the more fortunate in this world, in order to receive a recompense somewhere else after he is dead; future felicity does not prevent the felicity of the present. Therefore we find that parsons, bishops etc., all pursue wealth and accumulate riches in order to enjoy felicity here on earth, which they would not do did they themselves believe that which they preach, that "Poverty is a Blessing." They believe what all men of clear intelligence know to be a *fact* that poverty is a crime.

Well! labor for the better time,
With our power of Press and Pen,
Believe me, 'tis a truth sublime
This world is worthy better men.
Darby.

ARE STRIKES A LOSS?

May people think that the iron strike of last summer was a failure, because the men returned to work at $5.50 a ton. This is not true beyond the loss of the half dollar for a few months. Their action last summer did away with a strike this winter against a reduction to $4.75 or $5 a ton. Such a demand would have been made, to take effect on January 1. There is no danger of it being made now. Employers know that they must be content with a smaller profit, pay the men the present wages, sell iron cheaper than last year, and still make a handsome dividend. That is what was gained by the strike, and it is worth all it cost the men.

There are people who contend that strikes do injury to a country generally, and to the men engaged in them in particular. This could be advanced by no one who has looked at strikes, their causes, and consequences, from any other standpoint than that of the employer. We, workingmen, know of no strike that did us injury. It has been said that no rebellion was ever totally unsuccessful. So with strikes. If one is unsuccessful, the employers learn the strength of the men, become familiar with the reason of their demands, and learn to respect their rights; while the men learn the condition of the trade, and under what circumstances they can be paid better wages.—*Sigma in Labor Herald.*

HOW TO SELECT A FILE.

Take the file to the light and hold it in a horizontal position, the point of it toward you. The teeth of the file will now be pointing toward you, enabling you to detect easily any and all imperfections that a bad file is heir to. If the conformation of the teeth is irregular or uneven, or if the color of the file is not uniform, let it severely alone. A spotted or mottled file denotes unevenness of temper. If, on the other hand, the file presents a clean, white color, it denotes that the temper of it is hard and even throughout; and if, besides this, it has regular and perfect teeth and bears the maker's name you may rest assured that it is an excellent file.—*The Wood Worker.*

SALT AND WOODWORK.

It is a curious fact that in the salt mines of Poland and Hungary the galleries are supported by wooden pillars, which are found to last unimpaired for ages, in consequence of being impregnated with the salt, while pillars of brick and stone, used for the same purpose, crumble away in a short time by the decay of their mortar. It is also found that wooden piles driven into the mud of salt flats and marshes last for an unlimited time, and are used for the foundation of brick and stone edifices; and the practice of docking timber after it has been seasoned, by immersing it for some time in sea-water, is generally admitted to be promotive of its durability.

LABOR JOURNALS.

No better evidence of the gradual growth of the Labor movement can be desired by the anxious, enthusiastic student than the multiplying of journals devoted to the interests of wage-workers, from the laborers own standpoint, throughout the entire country. Time was (and that not very long ago) when mechanics convened a public meeting it was the custom to solicit a lawyer, doctor, or prominent personage, or a business man to preside over their deliberations, not having the requisite confidence in the capacity or general fitness of an ordinary mechanic to discharge the duties of so important a position. In those days usually local celebrities of the "better class" were invited to expound the views and define the wishes and demands of the so-called "common herd"—the great unwashed. Nowadays, however, their meetings are managed differently, after their own fashion, in their own way, and they do not borrow the "thunder" of persons outside the ranks of labor. They now have trained men, in [illegible]

VICTOR HUGO TO THE RICH.

In his grand and masterly style, Victor Hugo has lately sent forth a thrilling appeal to the rich and to the poor. In vivid and characteristic language he depicts the powers and privileges of the rich and wealthy, and warns them that their vested rights are imperilled, and their day of judgment is at hand. In it he says:

"Abandoned, an orphan, alone in boundless creation, I made my entry into this gloom that you call society. The first thing I saw was law, under the form of a gibbet; the second was wealth. It is your wealth—under the form of women dead with cold and hunger; the third was luxury under the shape of a hundred men chained to prison walls; the fourth was your palaces beneath the shadow of which cowered the tramp.

The human race has been made by you slaves and convicts. You have made of this earth a dungeon. Light is wanting, air is wanting, virtue is wanting.

The workers of this world whose fruits you enjoy, live in death. There are little girls who begin at eight by prostitution, and who end at twenty by old age. Who among you have been to Newcastle-on-Tyne? There are men in the mines there who chew coal to fill the stomach and cheat hunger. Look you in Lancashire. Want of work everywhere. Are you aware that the Harlech fishermen eat grass when the fishery fails? Are you aware that at Button-Lasers there are still certain lepers driven into the woods, who are fired at if they come out of their dens? In Peckridge there are no beds in the hovels, and holes are dug in the ground for little children to sleep in, so that in place of beginning with the cradle, they begin with the tomb.

Mercy, have mercy for the poor! Oh, I conjure you, have pity!

But no, you will not. I know ye all. Devils bred in hell, and dogs with hearts of stone. Upward to your golden thrones for ages has gone the cry of Misery, the groan of Hunger and the sob of Despair, and ye heeded not. What mercy thou hast given shall be meted out to you in turn.

Bear in mind that the series of Kings armed with the sword was interrupted by Cromwell armed with the axe.

Tremble! The incorruptible dissolutions draw near; the clipped talons push out again; the torn out tongues take to flight, become tongues of fire scattered to the wind of darkness, and they howl to the infinite. They who are hungry show their idle teeth. Paradises built over hells totter. There is suffering, there is suffering, and that which is above leans over, and that which is below gapes open. The shadow asks to become light. The damned discuss the elect. It is the people who are on-coming. I tell you it is Man who ascends. It is the end that is beginning. It is the red dawning of Catastrophe.

Ah, this Society is false! One day, and soon, the true Society will come. Then there will be no more lords, there will be free, living men. There will be no more wealth, there will be abundance for the poor. There will be no more masters, but there will be brothers. They that toil shall have. This is the future. No more prostration, no more abasement, no more ignorance, no more wealth, no more beasts of burden, no more courtiers, no more kings—but LIGHT.

THE SPINNERS ORGANIZING NEW ENGLAND.

At a recent meeting of the National Mule Spinners' Association, Mr. Howard, of Fall River, Mass., was re-elected Secretary, and empowered to appoint two members from the Fall River branch of the National Association to organize the mill operatives in the States of Rhode Island, Vermont, Connecticut and New Hampshire, with a view of effecting a reduction in the hours of labor. They are to receive $12 per week for their services and their traveling expenses, and will be paid from the funds of the National Association. This is an excellent move, and it is hoped that it will result speedily in a uniform reduction of the number of working hours not only in New England, but throughout the United States.

A LETTER FROM ENGLAND.

MANCHESTER, England, Dec. 8, '82.

P. J. McGuire:

Dear Sir:

Your letter to hand, also copy of THE CARPENTER, which I receive regularly and always read with pleasure. I shall always esteem it a duty to maintain the friendly relations which exist between our organizations at the present time.

By this post I forward you a copy of our last month's report and also the official report of the late Trades Union Congress. Our yearly report will not be due until April next, but I will send you a copy when they are issued.

The Associated Carpenters and Joiners of Scotland have their office in Glasgow, and the General Union of Carpenters has its headquarters in Liverpool. These are national societies of carpenters.

Faithfully yours,
J. S. MURCHIE,
General Secretary.
Amalgamated Society of Carpenters and Joiners.

ENGLISH AND FRENCH TRADES UNION-MEN IN CONFERENCE.

[Special Correspondence to THE CARPENTER.]

PARIS, Dec. 30, '82.—The Workingmen's Channel Tunnel Conference has been the great event, not only of this year, but for many years no assemblage has attracted so much public interest; and more than a[illegible] it has cemented the ideas of fraternity [illegible]

[illegible]

[illegible] ring world [illegible] was undertaken and prosecuted with vigor, and no opposition was manifested until suddenly the military flunkies and old grannies of both countries conceived the idea that the Tunnel was dangerous and would be used for invasion in time of war. The trades unionists of England then stepped gallantly to the front and in the name of Industry announced to the world that the working classes of both England and France favored the Tunnel and feared no war with each other. To give expression to that feeling, a delegation of English trades unionists visited this country. On Saturday, Nov. 25, twelve delegates arrived here from London. Each one of them a representative man among his fellow workers in England and from different quarters of that country.

On the following day—the 26th—the conference took place. It was held in a large theatre near the Bastille, and although an admission fee was charged, over 3000 people thronged the theatre. The demonstration was very imposing. Jules Joffrin, a journeyman machinist, was chosen chairman. Joffrin is a member of the City Council in Paris and in London he was a member of the Amalgamated Engineers. A number of dispatches and letters were read from all quarters of France and England in sympathy with the conference. Then the speaking commenced. Each speaker spoke in his native tongue. Mr. A. Smith acted as interpreter.

The first French speaker, M. Chabert, said the fear of invasion was only a ruse to oppose the tunnel between France and England. The invasion the governing classes feared was not *one of armies, but one of ideas!* The two peoples have every interest to facilitate intercommunication. The English will inspire the French with their spirit of tenacity while the English themselves will imbibe the Gallican principles of social equality.

Mr. J. Fox then rose in the name of the West England laborers. He said the fears of invasion were puerile in the extreme. Attempts were made to frighten us by the prospect of a few thousand Frenchmen coming through the tunnel, but I say let them come, not in their thousands, but in their hundred thousands; come and bring us some of your ideas and your high principles; bring us your love of humanity and of liberty. Let those who opposed a scheme which is manifestly one of progress remember that the working classes are the very foundation of society, and that if they do not act prudently, the foundations may upheave and the entire social edifice crumble to the dust [illegible] French [illegible]

avoiding transshipment, [illegible] tunnel would reduce freights.

George Shipton and others followed in appropriate speeches in favor of the tunnel. The most intense enthusiasm prevailed in the conference.

And the result was the passage of a resolution unanimously in favor of the Tunnel.

On Monday eve, Nov. 27, the English delegates were entertained by the French Workmen's National Committee. Among the speeches of the evening, there was none of more interest than that of M. Gambon, a member of the French Parliament. He held that the presence of the English delegates would be the death-knell of the French law against trades unions. As the law now stood anyone attending that meeting might be condemned to from one to ten years imprisonment. But the moral influence of the presence of the English delegates would revoke that law. He thanked them for what they were doing to abolish hatred between nations and to lay the foundation of a Federation of the States of Europe. They had but one war to fight and that was against poverty, misery and militarism.

Benjamin Pickard of the Yorkshire Miners said that through the press of England he had been led to believe that the French workmen were hasty and lacked coolness to discuss, but that meeting convinced him it was untrue. When British workmen were told that they must not meet in the day, they met at night; when they were not allowed to gather together [illegible], they held secret meetings in [illegible] in caves. They had passed [illegible] and in spite of oppres[illegible] [illegible] of organization [illegible] the day. It [illegible], but [illegible] each man to [illegible] what [illegible] wo[illegible].

M. Camelina, in [illegible] name of the [illegible] workers and of other [illegible] societies, thanked the English Trades [illegible] for what they did to help the French workmen in 1867. By seeking out the company of English unionists during the years of exile, the French workmen had learnt that it was by perseverance and everyday work among their mates in the workshop that the strength of the union was made. In trade matters the union must be what the Commune was in politics. The Commune was independent in England. The Commune was an accomplished fact in England; but they had no Commune in Paris. The Federation of Communes brought political freedom; the Federation of Trades Unions would emancipate the working classes. Then might ensue an International Federation of Labor, and all based on the great Communal principle of local independence, of local self-government, or home rule, with federation to secure and preserve all general and collective interests.

The meeting concluded, as it commenced, by the reading of a great number of communications. The cabinet makers wished to renew the relations with the English trade, which were broken off by the massacre of 1871. The Compositors Society asked that the English Compositors Unions should act in fraternal relations with the French.

The next day the English delegates visited various workshops and conferred with the workmen, and in the evening they were received by Victor Hugo at his villa. The illustrious poet was surrounded by his grandchildren and family; the reception was magnificent. After welcoming each delegate by a cordial shake of the hand, M. Hugo delivered this brief address to the delegates:

"My dear fellow-countrymen—For most assuredly the French and English now form one people; indeed I can foresee the day when all differences of men will be effaced and all the frontier walls crumble to the ground. You have come for a most useful among many useful purposes. The submarine tunnel is a work that, in its results, will become the consecration of human unities, and achieve the fraternization of peoples. You may return to your country and tell the workmen of England that my voice belongs to you, that I approve your efforts and will second them with what little strength I have remaining. Human endeavors to benefit humanity go beyond geographical limitations; the union of men between men will not be checked by artificial barriers; and [illegible]

Mr. Geo. Shipton replied and at its conclusion said:

"We will return and invigorate our fellow-workmen by spreading the knowledge of all that you have done; by showing to them the example of your life, they will see that neither misfortune nor exile could damp the ardor of your devotion and the firmness of your heroic resistance against injustice and oppression. Our fellow-workmen will learn to revere in you the brightest example of the subordination of the person to the propaganda of a grand idea."

Those were the principal events of the English trades unionists' visit to France. And their visit has drawn the workers of both nations into closer bonds of sympathy and mutual effort, to the affright and horror of the bourgeoisie.

JEAN PROLETAIRE.

THE LAND QUESTION.

Of all the utterances on the land question there is none so pregnant with reason, and none so forcible in argument as that which Herbert Spencer published in his "Social Statics." It is worth repeated reading and suggests in itself a state of affairs not at all unlikely to occur if the present monopoly of the land is permitted to continue. Listen to the words:

"Given a race of beings having like claims to pursue the objects of their desires—a world in which such beings are similarly born, not made, and it unavoidably follows that they have equal rights to the use of this world. For if each of them has freedom to do all he wills, provided he infringes not the equal freedom of any other, then each of them is free to use the earth for the satisfaction of his wants, provided he allows all others the same liberty. And conversely it is manifest [illegible] not one or part of them may use the [illegible] such a way as to prevent the rest [illegible] using it, seeing that to do [illegible] greater freedom than the [illegible], permit prop[illegible] [illegible] of the [illegible] the [illegible] a [illegible] then [illegible] held; and, [illegible] surface may [illegible] now [illegible] to [illegible] Supposing the whole habitable [illegible] so inclosed, it follows that if landowners have a valid right to [illegible] all who are not landowners have no right to its surface, and *exist only by sufferance.* They are all trespassers. Save by permission of the lords of the soil they can have no room for the soles of their feet nay, should the others think fit to deny them a resting-place, these landless men might equitably expelled from the earth altogether."

SHALL TRADES UNIONS BE DESTROYED?

In the *Cigar Makers' Journal*, the delegate of the Cigar Makers' International Union reported:

"During the sessions of the Cleveland Trades Congress, the question to admit District Assemblies of the Knights of Labor at the future meetings of the Federation elicited a long and warm debate. Some of the delegates thought that it seemed to be the policy of that organization to increase its membership and influence, even if by so doing it had *to tear down Trades Unions*, and cited cases where that organization had opened its doors to dissatisfied and insubordinate elements; and were of the opinion that under such conditions no real harmony or affinity could exist under Trades Unions as such, and the Knights of Labor."

In regard to this we can cite cases in our own trade, of men who have been suspended from our Brotherhood for not paying their dues who are accepted into that order. And again we know that insubordinate elements that could get no foothold in our Brotherhood are joining the K. of L. This is not the policy that is best calculated to promote the Knights of Labor. Men who are no good for trades unions are not good for any other organization. And the sole object of these men is simply to join the K. of L. to make war on trades unions, hoping to destroy them. There is work for the K. of L. to do without antagonizing trades unions.

But some men in the K. of L. [illegible]

AN APPEAL TO NON-UNION MEN.

The journeymen carpenters of San Francisco are by no means backward in the cause of trades unionism. Organizer Edward Owens of that city has issued a stirring appeal, part of which we here publish, and for it we can say that it merits the widest circulation:

"The history of our Union has demonstrated that hundreds of the carpenters and joiners of this city have awakened to the importance of our principles as aids to progress and prosperity, and the great increase in our numbers proves that they have adopted them, and now believe that in union alone lies their surest chance of improving their condition.

We hold it as an axiom that in protecting our interests it is not necessary to injure the interest of our employers, or cause them to suffer any loss; on the contrary, we assert that by demonstrating our ability to take care of our trade and secure a fair remuneration for our labor, the more certain they are of obtaining a reasonable profit on their business.

It is well known that in all industrial and manufacturing pursuits the safest are those whose prices are regulated by intelligent organization among those who labor at them, and the most dangerous are those in which accidents or circumstances govern the conditions under which they operate. This is the belief of the founders of the Carpenters' and Joiners' Union. Therefore, we say [illegible] again to such of you, our fellow-craftsmen, as are yet doubting and hesitating: Be decided, be bold; apply for admission in our Union, take your place among us who are laboring to advance and uphold the common interest of all. Come and discuss with us those matters which concern you, or should concern you, more than any others; how to obtain fair remuneration for your labor, and guard yourselves and us against injustice and wrong.

In thus guarding yourself and protecting your interests you are serving humanity. He who has not the courage to demand his rights [illegible] his duty to his country, to his family and to himself [illegible] the willing, crouching spirit [illegible] directly menaces the freedom [illegible]. The portals of our Union are [illegible] all [illegible] worthy of admis[illegible] fraternal ties of [illegible] brother[illegible] which we belong [illegible] the [illegible] the Pacific, a[illegible] who will not b[illegible] a stranger and [illegible] his fel[illegible]

To all whom it may con[illegible] well [illegible] with the hand of friendship [illegible] we will welcome you among [illegible] round you with friends who are [illegible] to protect your interests as they pledge[illegible] their own.

Consider, then, if you can afford to ignore this greeting or despise this warning. Can you afford to fight your battle alone, unfriended and forgotten? If so, you are either a human prodigy or a hopeless imbecile, and for such we have neither greeting nor warning. But for the earnest, honest, thoughtful men of our trade we have all that the sacred name of brother implies. Fellow-craftsmen, you are called, will you answer?

E. OWENS.

THE TONE OF OUR PRESS.

Altogether, the progress of the labor press has been wonderful, and it demonstrates that the great masses are becoming interested in their own affairs, are breaking loose from the thraldom of parties and [illegible], are learning to think and seeking information. And it is a fact that papers owned, edited and supported by poor men [illegible] and wage-workers, discuss [illegible] social and political economy with a [illegible]ness, propriety, vigor and fund of general knowledge such as, forty years ago, was not looked for outside of a very limited circle of writers and thinkers. Articles appear every week, written by mechanics, which, at one time, would have made a national reputation for the authors, and for the magazines which secured them. There is every reason to hope that, before the crisis comes [illegible] before the centralization of wealth [illegible] reached the unendurable limit, the [illegible]

[illegible] the giving off of this superfluous energy. If conducted into a productive channel, will furnish more than necessary to repair the loss of that energy which is expended in producing. In other words, a man who labors sufficiently to keep himself in health, will produce more than he can consume; or we may say that his power of production is superior to his power of consump[illegible]

[illegible] succeed in [illegible] strike.

The main objects of our Carpenters' Union are: moral public support of the carpenters in all their demands; fixity of employment and proper counsel for all [illegible] fellow craftsmen from far and near. [illegible] propose to organize the entire trade [illegible] and [illegible]

[illegible] in einer Petition an den Reichstag gestellt [illegible] Die Conjunktur des Baufaches ist [illegible] nicht ganz ungünstig und hoffen wir [illegible] Streitfälle durchzukommen. [illegible] Grundbedingung unserer Bewegung: mora[illegible] öffentliche Unterstützung von allen Zim[illegible] (Carpenters) Deutschlands [illegible]

social forces, are compelled to take a much more comprehensive view of the word than our lexicographers ever dreamed of taking, and as it one of the natural forces without which society could not exist, we cannot, I should think, be accused of treating it with too much im[illegible]

[illegible] a union man, but in [illegible] no connection with us at all [illegible] every Winter they [illegible] expenditure [illegible] have been [illegible]

THE CARPENTER.

PUBLISHED MONTHLY

BY THE

Brotherhood of Carpenters and Joiners,

OF AMERICA.

Office: 184 William St., New York.

TERMS.—Fifty cents a year, in advance, post-paid.

Send all moneys and correspondence for this Journal to

P. J. McGUIRE, Secretary,
184 William St., New York

NEW YORK, FEBRUARY, 1883.

—THE CARPENTER is well worth 50 cents a year, and all we ask is for each of our members to increase our list of subscribers. We will give a premium of one copy of Henry George's "Progress and Poverty" to any one sending us a list of five subscribers.

—Another example of what we have to expect from the capitalists is the arrest and trial of the Glass Blowers in Baltimore for conspiracy. But in spite of all opposition the workmen have won their strike and influenced the imported Belgian workmen to join the union.

—Congressman Upton of Texas wants a stronger standing army to put down "labor strikes." Were the capitalists and millionaires to pay workmen decent wages, "labor strikes" would not occur. If any one needs shooting it is not the poor workmen, [illegible] the rascals who have defrauded and [illegible] the workers.

—Since 1878, the average wages of workmen have increased about seven per cent, while the necessaries of life have increased fully twenty-three per cent. And still we hear the raving that this is the [illegible] of prosperity. So it is for the vipers who coin wealth from the flesh and blood and virtue of human beings.

—Some journals speak very favorably of Gov. Crittenden's message to the Missouri Legislature, because he complains of the long hours of street car employes. [illegible] Gov. Crittenden [illegible] who called out the State [illegible] Militia in 1881 to shoot down the [illegible] car employes of St. Louis for [illegible] 12 hours should constitute a day's work.

—It is said "Hard times are not coming!" Well, if they are not, it does seem odd that the number of idle men are increasing, and that the bankruptcies are more numerous. The Mercantile Agency reports the failures in the United States the past year number 6,738, as against [illegible] in 1881. The liabilities in the United States are, for the last year, $101,000,000, as compared with $81,000,000 in 1881.

—"Strikes are no use; there is no good in trades unions; we must organize for political action!" This is the talk we lately heard from a workman. We turned [illegible] and asked him: "Have you a funeral fund, or a sick benefit, or any such features in your union?" And the answer was "No!" Then we calmly said: "Go [illegible] these benefits before you do anything [illegible], and then you will find some good in your union."

—In a very able article the *Popular Science Monthly* tersely says: "Two irregulated [illegible] overwhelming passions in this country [illegible] the growth of science—the intense [illegible] passion for wealth and the [illegible] infatuation for politics. Th[illegible] [illegible]

WHAT WE EARN, AND WHAT OUR BOSSES POCKET.

From the statistics of twenty principal cities, as furnished in the census of 1880, the wages of journeymen carpenters average three hundred and fourteen dollars per year, or the grand sum of *one dollar and two cents per day* for 308 work days, or less than *87 cents a day* to support a family the whole year. The cities selected are: Baltimore, Boston, Brooklyn, Buffalo, Chicago, Cincinnati, Cleveland, Detroit, Jersey City, Louisville, Milwaukee, Newark, New Orleans, New York, Philadelphia, Pittsburgh, Providence, St. Louis, Washington and San Francisco.

In these twenty cities there is a total of 37,809 persons employed at carpentry, and a total of $9,443,444 capital. The total wages paid, $11,762,930; cost of material, $23,430,649; value of work done $41,813,065, or a total profit of $7,600,290 for these twenty cities, which is equal to 77 per cent. profit on the capital invested. This ought to be overwhelming proof that boss carpenters are doing well enough to pay more wages than they do. According to these figures they can well afford to pay the workmen one-third more wages and yet these bosses would net 38 per cent. on their capital.

And bad as this condition of wages is in the cities named, it would be worse were we not organized in those cities; and it is far worse where we are not organized. Next month we shall present a tabulated statement taken from the census, showing the exact situation as regards carpentry in the twenty cities named.

Let the thieves give up their plunder,
Ere the storm has gathered head;
Before louder peals the thunder,
And the lightnings flash more dread;
For the storm, if once it breaketh,
No human hand can stay,
'Till the wrongs the people suffer
Have in blood been washed away.

C. C. POST.

IMPORTING FOREIGN LABOR.

In settling the Labor problem in America, there is one factor that has a powerful disturbing influence which we must well consider in all our actions.

The tide of emigration flows naturally [illegible] this country, and the thronging thousands that have poured in upon us each month the past few years, have come not only to swell our population, but also to overstock the labor market, and in many cases to reduce wages to pauper pay.

While under proper conditions this immigration would be a benefit to all, we find that it now inures chiefly to the interest of capitalists and monopolists whose only desire is to cheapen human labor.

But there are other facts to be considered. Most of these people come here under false inducements—the dupes of steamship agents and railroad sharks. In glowing and bright colors this country is pictured as a Paradise for workingmen, with cheap food and high wages! Our consuls abroad are mere puppets in the interest of the cheap labor capitalists of America. And thus the poorest peoples of Europe are thrown upon our shores penniless and forsaken. And this state of affairs is not confined to our own States; it extends also to Canada and the British Provinces. There the workmen also complain of this wholesale importation of foreign workmen.

Yes, it has come to this; that it is no longer a voluntary immigration of independent, manly workmen that comes to our shores, but it is an importation of hordes of slavish, badly fed workers unused to our standard of civilization and willing to work early and late for a bare pittance. From the poorer districts of Poland, Italy, Hungary, Russia and all parts of Europe and Asia they come in droves to [illegible] and to add to the [illegible] ses and rents, and privations, and to drag down wages.

Of course, after some years residence these elements rise to demand as much pay as others. But in the meantime we are left to suffer, and by the time these imported laborers have adjusted themselves to the wants of the country, the capitalists are ready to import more.

We do not wish to be understood as classifying all emigrants under this head. There are many good and noble workmen who come here and stand up for high wages far better than many of our native Americans. But these come mainly from districts of Europe where the force of labor organization has been felt.

This great eruption of imported labor has been brought here to counteract our unions. It was used against the workmen in the coal miners strikes of Maryland and Western Pennsylvania and it has crowded into every avenue of labor. The very capitalists who have howled in protest against the evil effects of competing with "the pauper labor of Europe"—as they term it—are mainly the ones who have brought cheap labor here. Hence we propose to no longer help the bosses to sustain *tariff on foreign goods* for their interests, while they give us *free trade in labor* to our injury.

Some Senators and Congressmen in Washington, in order to sustain tariff, now propose to place an embargo or duty on foreign labor. In doing this they do not strike at the real evil. The real evil is the scoundrels of capitalists, who have agents all over Europe to import slavish workers here. These modern slave traders are the ones the law should punish and not the immigrants.

—In this issue our readers will see we have correspondents in England, France and Germany. Their letters are worthy of careful reading. Those from France and Germany will prove very interesting reading, and from England we receive the outstretched hand of fellowship from the Amalgamated Carpenters.

—From present indications the result of the general vote on the Endowment or insurance principle of our Brotherhood, is overwhelmingly in favor of maintaining the constitution as it is.

SHORTER HOURS AND EDUCATION.

A public meeting of Carpenter's Union No. 1 of Washington, D. C., was held Feb. 2, 1883, in their hall, to discuss the importance and necessity of taking action in favor of a reduction of the hours of labor. Among the speakers were many advocates of the eight-hour system. The best argument offered during the evening was one advanced by Mr. E. S. Peters, formerly editor of the Washington *Daily Critic*.

He attributed the unsatisfactory condition of workingmen to certain defects in our social and economic machinery—particularly the machinery by which the products of labor are distributed among the different classes of society, and urged that in order to secure a juster distribution, it was necessary for them to discover where these defects lie and how they may be remedied. To do this, they need to study public questions, so that they may know how to use the ballot for the protection of their own interests; and in order to study, they must have more time. Hence the importance of concentrating their efforts to secure a reduction in the hours of labor. A day of eight hours is amply long enough, but if a reduction of two hours can not be got all at once, it should be taken an hour, or even a half hour at a time until the whole amount is gained. If opportunities are rightly used, the reduction of hours can be got without loss of wages even for the time being, while it will bring increased wages after it by promoting an increase of intelligence, which will have the double effect of increasing the efficiency and productiveness of labor, and enabling the workingmen to enforce a fair division of the [illegible] stock of wealth which this [illegible]

It is sometimes argued that workingmen would not improve their opportunities, even if they had leisure for study, but would spend their time in dissipation. The only danger of this would be in the case of the younger, unmarried workingmen and boys in their teens just entered into the industrial occupations. To guard against it in their case, the demand for eight hours should be accompanied by a demand for public evening schools, which should be maintained not merely for a few weeks or months in Winter, but for just as large a portion of the year as the higher day schools are kept open for the benefit of those who are above the necessity of sending their children to work. When such a system of evening schools shall have been established, their will be more truth in our boast that our common school system is a system for the benefit of the masses of the people. At present, the children of the poor are in a great measure excluded from the benefits of our public schools for want of the ability to attend them.

The demand for evening schools would not only meet with favor itself among all who take an interest in public enlightenment, but it would gain a great deal of additional sympathy for the eight-hour movement, winning over to its support many who are now opposed to it. These two things—eight hours and evening schools—should be persistently coupled together, and the whole body of workingmen should unite in battling for them.

BURGLARS IN THE LABOR MOVEMENT.

WASHINGTON, D. C.—The necessity for unification of labor being admitted, I wish for information how to accomplish the task. Must I be compelled to join a conglomerated section of some junk shop and use my best endeavors to break down all other forms of union in order that one may succeed in establishing a sort of an oligarchy? Must my trade lose its individuality and be pinned on as a tail to some other kite?

Must I tacitly admit the labor question is a screaming farce that needs hiding in a secret political organization without a practical sensible measure of relief? The capitalist admits that labor is noble and holy, yet with sacrilegious hands continues to plunder it, and chuckles at the simplicity of men who suppose a preamble and ritual will change human nature. The success of centralized wealth in dominating the legislative power of Government emboldens them more and more.

And while this is going on and we are being crushed, there are men who desire to produce antagonism in Labor's ranks by fighting the trade union movement. These men in many cities openly threaten that if we do not join the Knights of Labor they will "bust us up." That is just what the capitalists want "to bust us up." And now here comes the Knights of Labor, whom we warmed into life in this city, and it says "if you don't let us swallow your union we will bust you up." Well they have tried it and found it a pretty big job "to bust us up." This policy of *burglarizing* existing organizations instead of working in the vast fields of unorganized labor is bound to react to the injury of those who adopt it.

It is not possible for any one order to combine the whole working class, and especially a secret order, because of the difference of opinion among men. Some men like to be taught by signs and symbols; but when they become enlightened they know it to be folly to hide in a secret conclave one of the grandest, noblest questions that ever agitated the human mind, and thus destroy in a measure its power of propaganda. Many men will not advocate a cause that fears to stand the test of public scrutiny. Open organization is not a failure. It can and will accomplish all we desire.

The present movement of labor is a fight for justice,—a step up in the march of civilization, and not for dominion over our fellow workmen who suffer as we do. Life is too short to spend all of it in childs-play and quarrels in the face of an enemy that is seeking every possible means to produce disorder.

Let every labor organization do its own work without antagonism or encroaching on each other. The Knights of Labor have a mission—it is to organize where open and public organizations have failed. Why don't they do it? There is a field for them in New England and wherever open [illegible]

Der Carpenter.

New York, Februar 1883.

Ein Aufruf.

Wir geben hiermit einen Aufruf, welchen der deutsche ... von New York veröffentl... sollte jeder Schreiner ... handeln.

Arbeiter! Brüder ... länger ausbeuten ... die durch Eure ...

gen Anstrengungen der Arbeiter, eine bessere Existenz zu gewinnen, sprechen müssen. Es ist betrübend für jeden Menschenfreund, diesen Zustand der Dinge zu betrachten. Die Organisation der Arbeiter ist ein wichtiger Gegenstand des Nachdenkens für uns. Auf einer befriedigenden Lösung dieser Frage beruht nicht nur ... eigenes Gedeihen, sondern ... die ... r Nation. Wir woll... belehrt durch die sei... n, jetzt einleiten, ... obliegt, und daß ... n, welche ih... munft da...

Wir wollen uns diese Frage etwas genauer betrachten und es tritt uns zuvor die Ursache dieses Uebels vor's Auge.

Zuerst sind wir geneigt, die Ursache dem Monopol in die Schuhe zu schieben, jene aber nennen uns als die schuldtragende Partei; ein Dritter sagt, sie haben beide Schuld. ... sehen. Wir ...

Fortschritt der Arbeiter-Bewegung.

Wohl noch während keines Winters ist die Arbeiterbewegung in den Vereinigten Staaten so lebhaft gewesen wie in diesem, ... lend als ... ng der ... ung ...

YE SLUGGARDS!

...N. Y. The condition of the carpenter and joiner to-day is indeed a sad one. Toiling from week to week, from year to year, for just a bare living, is there one among us who can say that he has laid by enough to live a month without going into debt or to bury him decently when he dies? We know that should a little misfortune of some kind or other throw us behind, those upon whom we are dependent for employment would look down upon us and our families as paupers worthy only of contempt. The spirit of competition among the several contractors has led them into the error of striving to see which could come the closest to financial ruin, without accomplishing the fact, in the hope of driving rivals to the wall. The result is that the poor journeyman has been compelled to suffer a reduction of wages on the pretense of not being able to work more than nine hours a day during the winter months, just as though he were responsible for the seasons or for the incompetency of the contractors to figure a profit out of what they do not own. The cry of the capitalist, the middleman, and the small jobber, is "cheap labor," and the demand for it each year grows stronger, and organized capital has been systematically introducing it from overcrowded Asia. Even the national government of this country has adopted the policy of cheap mechanical labor in giving out contracts to the lowest bidder.

Workingmen, is this right? Do you call this economy? If it is, we will go a step farther in the interest of economy. We demand that the various positions from the heads of the different departments down to the messenger at the capitol, be offered to the lowest bidder. Our public schools, which we once referred to with a feeling of pride, are now termed "The poor folk's school" by the aristocracy, who are striving to institute private schools to be attended by their children rather than have them mingle in the same ...

... that of the rich idler. The toiling millions of the earth are awakening to the grand realization of the fact that no man has a just right to own or control the entire social wealth of the country, and on this and kindred principles they are forming clubs, unions and organizations of their respective trades to batter down, by force of argument the gigantic wrongs oppressing the unhappy toiler and his children.

Fellow workmen, all those evils can easily be remedied, if you but act your part and come into the ranks of the great army of organized labor. The Brotherhood of Carpenters and Joiners of America with its thousands members is co-operating with other intelligent trade unionists, whose interests are identical with our own, that we may through numbers impress the dignity of our just demands on the public and thereby insure the passage of just laws which will enable us to elevate our trade to its proper place among the mechanical pursuits out of the pool of ignorance into which a cursed system of botchery has dragged it. Arouse then, ye sluggards! The social revolution has begun; it is a revolution of the brain; it is a revolution in which radicalism and religion join, and the weapons of their annihilating warfare are a passive resistance to tyranny and the ballot for reform.

M. J. D.

CORRESPONDENCE FROM GERMANY.

BERLIN, Dec. 27.—We have formed an organization of the carpenters of Berlin, upon the basis advocated in your worthy journal. The first work to secure success is to struggle energetically for nine hours a work day in the trade. This demand we have already presented in a petition to the German Parliament. The condition of the building trades in Germany is favorable at the present time, and thus we hope to succeed in case of strike.

The main objects of our Carpenters' Union are; moral public support of the union in all their demands; fixity of carpenters in all their demands; ... employment and proper counsel for all ... fellow craftsmen from far and near. ... propose to organize the entire trade ... as he ...

A HOME-MADE EASY CHAIR.

To one who has been toiling all day, nothing is more welcome on reaching home than a comfortable easy chair. Many mechanics can hardly afford one of the high-priced easy chairs made by furniture makers, hence will appreciate any suggestions that may be offered as to how one

FIGURE 1.

can be constructed at home. Figure 1 gives sufficient detail to enable any ordinary mechanic to construct one for himself. The legs, which cross like a camp stool, should be made of some hard wood, cherry, ash or oak will do, and should be at least 1x1½ inch in size, or, if you choose, a little stouter. The two rails for fastening the seat and back to, should be about 22 inches long in the clear, and 1x2 inches in size; a second rail might be set in the back 6 inches from the top. These rails should be mortised. Small round bolts with nuts on one end can be purchased at any hardware store to secure the legs where they cross each other; a washer should be put between the legs to prevent too much friction.

A strong piece of carpet can be used for the seat and back. Secure both ends well to the upper and lower rail with two rows of tacks, for the strain is great and it ...

FIGURE 2.

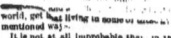

This cut represents a cheaper chair made in the same way as the one above. Ordinary canvas duck can be used for the seat. I have used one of these chairs for five years, and the whole cost was only 68 cents, and that was for material. These chairs can be folded the same as a camp stool and the cloth on the seat and back conforms to the figure of the person when seated, so as to give perfect repose, and make a very handy easy chair.—"*Rivet*" in *Mechanical News*.

Aus Deutschland.

Berlin, 27. Dezember. — Du wirst verzeihen, wenn ich mir erlaube, deine werthe Zeitung zu benutzen, und zwar bin ich im Begriff eine Organisation der Berliner Zimmerer auf Grundlage der vom „Carpenter" verfolgten Richtung zu bilden. Das erste Werk, um einen Erfolg zu erzielen, ist die energische Forderung eines 9stündigen Normal Arbeitstages. Diese Forderung haben wir schon im vorigen Jahre in einer Petition an den Reichstag gestellt.

Die Conjunktur des Baufaches ist z. Z. nicht ganz ungünstig und hoffen wir eventl. im Strikefalle durchzukommen.

Hauptbedingung unserer Bewegung: moralische öffentliche Unterstützung von allen ... (Carpenters) Deutschlands ...

LECTURES ON LABOR.

IV.

LABOR AS AN ELEMENT.

We have seen that there are five elements which enter into the activities of mankind, or rather that these five elements serve as a medium through which the activities of society find their expression, and we have shown that these elements are Land, Labor, Capital, Exchange and Insurance.

Having shown that land is the primary element, and having drawn a distinction between property and possession, we will briefly consider the element *Labor*, which is second in order.

It is very probable that we men and women of the labor movement, who are workers, have conceptions concerning labor which are not entertained by many others, and particularly the political economists; and in order that we may not be misunderstood when we speak of Labor, it is very necessary that we should be explicit in our definition, for it frequently occurs to us—when discussing with our opponents the subject of the labor movement in general to find that the conception which our adversaries have of Labor is so far from being identical with our conception, that confusion rather than clearness arises from the discussion; from the simple fact that our ideas concerning that which is labor, and that which is not labor, are not the same.

I make no hesitation in affirming that mankind can exist on this planet only in one or the other of the following capacities, *to wit:*

As Worker,
" Beggar,
" Loafer,
...

... world, get their living in some of the above-mentioned ways.

It is not at all improbable that, in the near future each man and woman will be placed in their proper category; that each category will be decided to be either moral or immoral, and, as the aspiration of the world at large is to organize society upon a basis of morality, the achievement of that aspiration will necessitate measures which have as yet been contemplated only by the very few.

There are very few among us, I opine, who will object to the correctness of the following simple proposition:

That the four last-mentioned in the above list are parasites upon the body industrial.

There is another class which I will not stop to consider here, which class is subject to subdivision into, first, the imbecile; second, the incapacitated, which latter may again be subdivided. This will come up in the future. I mention it here for two reasons, first, to say that it is not an oversight, secondly, because they must not be looked upon as parasites.

For the general meaning of labor, we can refer all those who inquire to the dictionaries of Johnson, Walker, Webster, and Worcester. There they will find how labor is treated—as noun and adjective, as verb active and verb transitive. But we who have to treat labor as one of the social forces, are compelled to take a much more comprehensive view of the word than our lexicographers ever dreamed of taking, and as it one of the natural forces without which society could not exist, we cannot, I should think, be accused of treating it with too much im...

... other why labor is inherent in man and is truly inseparable from him.

Man is not simple in his nature. He is complex. He is composed of three parts. 1st—the physical, 2d the mental, 3d—the moral. He has a body, he has a mind, he has a heart.

His body requires food, clothing, shelter. He consumes, he ought to produce—hence labor.

His mind requires that he should think, that he should reason, that he should learn, that he should progress—hence science, instruction.

His heart requires enthusiasm, attachment, affection—hence love.

Every man requires all these, and any social environment which deprives him of any of these, is either incom...
Hence we say that to Labor...
to Love is the destiny of ...
does not do all these, he is ...
incomplete; and any sta...
which prevents man from ex...
for which, by the very nat...
within him he was destine...
decline, fall, and become ...

In so far as we deal with l...
to deal with man as a physic...
we take no cognisance of th...
and æsthetic side of his na...
aside the head and the hea...
ment, and deal merely with ...
we say that man is a bundle...
and nervous forces, the exer...
is necessary to his existence ...
ercise of these muscular ...
forces constitutes labor, and ...
labor is a condition of life, ...
labor man cannot live. We ...
bor is a condition of life, ...
porative as eating, drinking, ...
breathing; for if a man refu...

...l, labor is a ...
...ely dies if ...
...dition; for ...
...-food, it ...
...able which ...
...d consumes ...

certain muscular and nerv...
which become superabundant ...
worked ..., ... the body ...
easy, fretful and ...
other words, the food which ...
us strength or generates forc...
superfluous energy, which forc...
long pent up, or if it exists in ...
quantity, causes uneasiness, ...
quires exertion in order to car...

Now this giving off of super...
gy, this exertion necessary to ...
pent-up force, constitutes m...
nervous motion which is ge...
derstood as muscular activi...
employed in the creation ...
thing which is useful, someth...
ministers to the wants, ...
nience or the happiness of man, ...
properly designated as labor. ...
implanted in man the necessity ...
he must have it or die. Struct...
ponds to function, hence he ...
with a physical structure an...
which is provided in abundance ...
that food.

As man cannot continue in health without the exercise of this physical activity, in order to be healthy, he must labor; that is he must expend this superfluous pent-up force.

Now the giving off of this superfluous energy, if conducted into a productive channel, will furnish more than necessary to repair the loss of that energy which is expended in producing. In other words, a man who labors sufficiently to keep himself in health, will produce more than he can consume; or we may say that his power of production is superior to his power of consump...

Here the line of demarcation is distinctly drawn between labor and drudgery.

The compilers of the dictionaries above referred to make no distinction whatever; they confound labor with drudgery, therefore with them they are convertible terms. Not so with us: we define labor to be ennobling, drudgery to be degrading.

Labor calls forth the exercise of the physical powers to the extent of producing a healthy, physical, mental and moral condition in man.

Drudgery carries the exercise of the physical powers to the extent which deranges the physical, mental and moral condition in man.

Hence—Labor is a blessing.
Drudgery, a curse.
Labor is a duty,
Drudgery, a crime.

Drudgery, like idleness, is a parent crime, for it engenders many others.

This acceptation of the meaning of labor is practically entertained by the rich (although theoretically they deny it), as well as by the poor; by the idle as well as by the industrious; by the loafer as well as by the worker. We find the rich, the idler, and the loafer resort to what they call *exercise*, in order to give off this pent-up energy, which makes them feel uncomfortable.

Those who are rich and do not require to work for their food, as also those who are idle and will not work for their food, resort to riding, bowling, fencing, dancing, driving fast horses, playing billiards, etc., (when they do nothing worse), in order to keep themselves in health. Now, we maintain that if the same amount of physical energy were expended in producing something which is necessary or useful, as is wastefully expended on doing that which is useless; that is, if they would expend their energies in productive enterprise, instead of in non-productive exercise, they would produce more than an equivalent for that which they consume.

We consider that if persons consume without giving an equivalent in production for that which they consume, that some other person who does produce, must produce not only an equivalent for his own consumption, but also an equivalent to the consumption of the non-producer; hence the man who does work is compelled to produce double the amount of his consumption, in order that the idler may consume without producing.

Thus the worker has to drudge—and work, which should be a blessing, becomes drudgery, which is a curse.

"Labor," said Franklin, "if you need it not for food, you do for physic."

In the ideas of some, labor is disreputable. The workers should make all efforts to raise it from the low position into which it has been thrust, and make it respected.

Let us assert, with the good men of the 12th century, whose shoe strings their descendants of to-day are unworthy to unloose—

"*Laborare est Orare.*"—To Labor is to Pray.

And say, with the poet—

"Work for thy bread! be it ever so slowly,
Cherish a flower! be it ever so lowly;
Labor! for labor is noble and holy,
And let thy brave deeds be thy prayer to thy God."

BRUTUS.

—General Secretary P. J. McGuire will address carpenters meetings as follows: Boston, Mass., Monday, Feb. 26.—Providence, R. I., Wednesday, Feb. 28.—Hartford, Conn., Thursday, March 1.

—J. B. Johnson of Middletown, N. Y., writes to us as follows: "I am glad to see THE CARPENTER at work. I hope he will

BROTHERHOOD NOTES.

—Carpenters' Union No. 29 of Baltimore is on the upward grade—gaining members.

—Boston Union No. 33 meets now at Caledonian Hall, 43 Eliott str., every Monday evening.

—Union No 15 of Indianapolis has elected Wm. Johnson, President, and W. C. Buddenbaum, Secretary.

—New Orleans Union No. 16 had a well attended soiree lately in their new hall, 287 Rampart street.

—Bro. G. G. Sucilfehn has been elected Financial Secretary of Milwaukee Union No. 30 in place of H. Schomer.

—Kansas City Union No. 13 now meets every first and third Monday at Kumpf's Hall, corner of Main street and Tenth.

—On February 22d, Union 31 of Trenton, N. J., will hold a social gathering or package party; the Union meets every Friday evening at Walkers Hall, Broadway and Factory street.

—Buffalo Union No. 37 is flourishing and is organizing branches in different parts of that city. The carpenter bosses of Buffalo need not think the men are disorganised, or else they will learn otherwise to their cost.

—Bros. Walter Cook, Chas. J. P. Allen, and W. Lonsdale, of Trenton Union No. 31, lost their tools by fire at Bordentown, N. J., not long since. We ought to have a tool insurance as one of the general features of the Brotherhood.

—Patrick Doyle, formerly of Cleveland Union No. 10, will yet have judgment passed upon his doings; and even if a court has acquitted him on a technicality, it does not change the opinion that generally prevails in regard to his character.

—Bro. Whiteside, of Indianapolis, addressed a large meeting of carpenters in Greenfield, Ind., on January 21st, and it was decided to form a local Union under the banner of our Brotherhood. Terre Haute, Ind., is also under way, and so are Bushville, Indiana; Norwich, Conn., and Utica, N. Y.

—The officers of the Executive Committee of Chicago Union No. 21 for the ensuing term are: President, Mr. F. Jones; Vice-President, Mr. D. Schumacher; Treasurer, H. J. Hanson; Financial Secretary, L. E. Schneider; Secretary, W. S. Weeks; Conductor, William Meyers; Warden, Tom Carroll.

—San Francisco Union No. 22 initiates at the rate of fifty a month. Their ball at Irons Hall on January 24th, was the leading event of the season. Bro. Edward Ex-President of the Union, was presented with a handsome gold watch and chain as a testimonial of the appreciation in which he is held by Union No. 22.

—The Carpenter's Union of Providence, R. I., have taken up the question of joining the Brotherhood, and after thorough discussion, in which nearly all favored the move, a committee of four was appointed to arrange the matter, and report on Feb. 12th. This union is doing remarkably well of late and is enrolling members every meeting.

—Toronto Union No. 27 had a live meeting on Jan. 22d. Although the thermometer stood far below zero, two candidates were initiated, and a full attendance was present. It was decided to admit the planing mill hands, or wood working machinists. Bro. John Hanrahan was elected a delegate to the Toronto Trades Council.

—We have received a communication from Chicago, signed "Union Carpenter of Chicago." It is a personal attack on one of our most respected members in that city. We referred it back to the Carpenter's Union of that city, for the reason that we do not care to publish communications from persons who have not the courage to sign their own names.

—It is stated that before Whitney's in-

THE WOMAN'S WORLD.

The spiciest paper with snap and vim that has ever come from the hands of a reformer is Mrs. Helen Wilman's—*The Woman's World.* It is worth every penny of its subscription price, one dollar per year. Here are some extracts from it:

The laborers and producers are not yet enough in earnest. They are not yet enough oppressed. They manage to squeeze through the days and weeks, and live under the wrongs they bear. They know nothing of that impatience that renders even the shadow of a wrong unbearable. This apathy on their part simply delays results. It constantly invites the capitalists to further outrages, which invitation is as constantly accepted; and the point will eventually be reached when the deadest man on this continent will lift his languid eyes in inquiry and raise his heavy hand in blind and dumb resentment;

........Look at the seething, boiling elements of the social and political world. See how high-handed crime stalks through every land under the sun, clothed with invulnerable authority. Then look into the hearts and brains of the people—dull, dead, impassive as they seem,—*thought* is there with its quickening power, and the first lurid gleams of feeling is kindling here a flame and there a flame, to be instantly crushed out of sight. But crushed back as it is, it is smouldering every day and hour to greater purpose, gathering strength and intensity; and presently it will burst with one glaring upward flash into irresistible omnipotence. Its flames shall span the seas at a bound, to find every continent combustible as summer chaff. For the days of the people's wrongs are numbered, and the traitors to the people's hope are doomed.

........The wrongs of the workers are bound to culminate in actual hunger before many years. There is every evidence of this. Capital is not relaxing its hold; it is grabbing more and more; it will never let up. Men and women are being driven to despair and suicide. Humble homes are filled with unwholesome children, gaunt and unnourished with good *blood-making food.* The position of the working men is wretched, and that of the working women indescribably horrible. "God help them!" say some. Let them help themselves, I say. They will help themselves. There is no doubt at all about it. They are on the direct road to that point where they will ask no help but that which comes from themselves.

........Why, what fools we are! It is not the corporations that are starving us; it is we ourselves that are doing it. We are like the beasts of the field—we are unconscious of our own strength, and submit daily to the bit and spur by which we are driven to death. We must wake up to a knowledge of ourselves; we must learn that we are human beings, that there are none with higher privileges than ourselves, if we would but claim them.

Nova Scotia Carpenters.

YARMOUTH, Nova Scotia.—There is very little building here now and twice as many carpenters as there is room for, so they are ready to take anything that is offered. Yarmouth is a seaport town of 7000 population. Good carpenters are working for $1.50 in Summer and in Winter do little or nothing. A few get $1.75, but there is no scale of wages nor likely to be until we are organised. And this I am trying to do.

Masons and painters here get $2.50, plumbers $3 to $5 and work anywhere from 8 to 10 hours and call it a day. If a carpenter is 15 minutes late he is expected to make it up.

Now I ask why is a carpenter's pay less than these other trades? Perhaps the carpenter does not need any brains, no tools, no books, no long years of hard study and training. Oh, of course not! The trouble is this: Boys go to learn the trade and they generally know more than the master to start with, and as soon as they can drive a nail and not break it they are *carpenters*, leave their master and hire for what they can get, so the country is flooded with such carpenters, and workmen are expected to work as low as a botch. So the trade is brought into disgrace and the

HISTORY OF THE AM[illegible] CARPENTERS.

The Amalgamated Society of Carpenters and Joiners was originally formed by a few carpenters and joiners in 1860. Its chief management is conducted by a General and an Executive Council. The General Council is composed of sixteen delegates, elected by the members once every three years; the Society being divided into sixteen districts for this purpose. This General Council is similar to a General Convention. The Executive Council is composed of six members, elected for twelve months from and by the branches situated within a radius of twelve miles from the General Office. A Chairman of the Council is similarly appointed; his duty is to preside over all General and Executive Council meetings. The first rules were drawn up by a committee of four appointed by a meeting of delegates from the Joiners' Societies of London, and were adopted by the same body on April 18th, 1860. The rules have since been revised by delegate meetings and general councils in June, 1866; April, 1869; September, 1871; June, 1873; June, 1874; June, 1877; and June, 1880. Rule 3 was suspended by a vote of the members in 1877, and again in 1878, in order to admit members of other societies on easier terms. The present rules came into operation on the 1st of January, 1881. The first General Secretary, Mr. J. Lea, was appointed at the opening of the Society in 1860. He was superseded in October, 1862, by Mr. R. Applegarth, who resigned in 1871, and was succeeded by Mr. J. D. Prior, who was appointed by the Government to the post of one of Her Majesty's Inspectors of Factories and Workshops, and was succeeded by Mr. J. S. Murchie in April, 1881. The first annual report (1860) contained 24 pages; the last annual report (1881) contained 304 pages. The first monthly report was issued in January, 1863, and contained 4 pages; they have been published continuously ever since. It at present contains 16 pages; they are published at one penny each, and the circulation is 7,500 copies per month. The Society was first registered in the United Kingdom on the 2d of December, 1872. It has since been registered or incorporated under the laws in the State of New York and the Colony of New South Wales.

STRENGTHEN THE UNIONS.

Although we have at present a very flourishing trades union movement, there is much room for improvement in the plan of organization. At present the regular dues of most of them are 25 cents a month, amounting to but $3 per year. This sum is just sufficient to pay stationery expenses and hall rent, leaving nothing or but little over for those struggles in regard to wages which every trades union as yet must expect.

How a trades union can expect to accomplish any permanent good with such trifling dues is a matter of wonder. And yet some men will growl concerning the inefficiency of unionism when they find that 25 cents per month has not increased their wages $1 or $2 per week.

What should be done to strengthen the union, then? Increase the dues to 25 cts. per week instead of 25 cents a month. This will amount to $13 annually. When the member, at the close of the year, will compare the cost of the investment with the return that it has brought him, he will find that it has increased his security as a wage worker, and also the price of his labor. With these dues, the sick and death benefit features, which now flourish in lodges, etc., could be incorporated into the union, where they properly belong.

Experience has shown those unions to be strongest which have taken this path, while those that offer no inducement to a member except, perhaps, the excitement of a doubtful strike, have only a mushroom growth and existence.

Unions should discuss these questions and begin now to take the necessary steps. Bind men to the union by plain, easily understood, material inducements, and the organization is bound to progress. Material interests are stronger ties than

Der Carpenter.

New York, Februar 1883.

Ein Aufruf.

Wir geben hiemit einige Auszüge von einem Aufruf, welchen der deutsche Machinisten-Verein von New York veröffentlichte. Diesen Aufruf sollte jeder Schreiner beherzigen und darnach handeln.

Arbeiter! Brüder! warum laßt Ihr Euch länger ausbeuten? Oder — seid Ihr es nicht, die durch Eure Arbeit einer Handvoll entnervter Faulenzer ein angenehmes Dasein bereitet, während Ihr bei Euren schweren Arbeiten mit Weib und Kind darben müßt.

Sind die Reichthümer Eurer Ausbeuter nicht das Resultat Eurer Arbeit — es ist kurz gesagt: „Euer eigener krystallisirter Schweiß." Als Lohn dafür dürft Ihr Euch von der „Bosses" so lange ausbeuten lassen, als Ihr noch jung und kräftig seid —, wehe Euch aber wenn Eure Kräfte anfangen, nachzulassen.

Seid Ihr alt und ausgepreßt, wie eine Citronenschale, so wirft Euch der kapitalistische Vampyr unbarmherzig auf die Straße. Euer Loos ist langjähriges Siechthum und früher Tod —, wenn nicht Arbeitshaus oder Gefängniß.

Eure Kinder theilen dasselbe Schicksal.

Arbeiter! Ermannt Euch, oder wollt Ihr ewig Sklaven des Capitals bleiben!

Sollen wir noch tiefer sinken! Nein, und abermals nein! Tretet ein in die geschaffene Organisation! Einigen wir uns über die Mittel und Wege, welche zu unserer Befreiung aus dem Joche der modernen Sklaverei dienen können.

Kämpfen wir für ein menschenwürdiges Dasein!

Bedenkt Brüder, daß Ihr als „Einzelner" Euren Ausbeutern gegenüber machtlos seid wenn Ihr nicht mit Weib und Kind verhungern wollt. Gegen die unter uns selbst zu große Concurrenz aller möglichen Arbeitskräfte kann nur eine kräftige Organisation dienen, welche nicht nur das Sinken der Arbeitslöhne verhindert, sondern auch die Arbeitszeit zu verkürzen sucht.

Tretet ein in unsere Union, helfet kämpfen für unsere Befreiung aus dem Joche des Capitals!

Wie die Arbeiter organisiren müssen.

Getrennt sind die Arbeiter machtlos und können keinen wirksamen Widerstand leisten; und diejenigen, welche ihr Brod im Schweiße ihres Angesichts verdienen, werden wie Leibeigene behandelt, anstatt als Freie anerkannt zu werden. Es werden nicht allein ihre Löhne herabgesetzt, sondern auch ihre Arbeiten verkürzt, (siehe das Konspirationsgesetz u. s. w.) Dieses ungerechte Verfahren wird von Seiten des Kapitals mit Vorsicht begonnen und eine Zeit lang mit bewunderungswürdiger Geschicklichkeit und Consequenz durchgeführt. Es wendet gewöhnlich zuerst kleine Gaben an und, obgleich die Pillen bitter und nur mit Widerwillen zu schlucken sind, werden sie doch geschluckt und nur selten trotzig zurückgewiesen. Eine kritische Periode naht bald für den Doctor und für die Patienten! Es müssen stärkere Gaben genommen werden, und zuletzt wird noch der Versuch gemacht, ihnen mit Gewalt den bitteren Stoff hinabzuzwingen. Es wird ihnen bald geschmeichelt, bald gedroht, und die Kur endet mit einem Ausstand, oder mit einer Aussperrung. Schnell vereinigen sie sich wieder zur gegenseitigen Hülfe und Unterstützung. Sie beschäftigen sich eifrig mit der Organisation und kommen oft zur Berathung zusammen. Ihr Magen und ihr Instinkt — wenn sonst Nichts — führt sie zu raschem Handeln. Sie hungern, sie kämpfen, sie dulden —; sie dulden, sie kämpfen, sie hungern —! Das Mitgefühl des Publikums erwacht! man unterstützt sie reichlich nach hartem Streite, und nach langem Leiden ist der Sieg gewonnen oder verloren, oder auch eine beiderseitige Verständigung herbeigeführt, und die Arbeiter kehren zur Arbeit zurück. Werden sie vom Instinkt, vom Naturtrieb allein geleitet, so geben sie nun, nachdem die Gefahr einstweilen vorüber ist, auseinander und lösen ihre Organisation auf, da sie weiter kein Interesse mehr für sie hat. Wenn man derartige Vorgänge auf Seiten unserer Arbeiter beobachtet, muß man da nicht ihre unverantwortliche Gleichgültigkeit in Lebensfragen, welche für sie selbst und für ihre Angehörigen so überaus wichtig sind, beklagen!

Nach ihrem Verfahren zu urtheilen, ist man berechtigt, anzunehmen, daß sie bei ihren Bestrebungen und Bemühungen, ihre Lage zu verbessern, mehr von dem Instinkt als von der Vernunft geleitet werden; oder läßt sich irgend welche Thätigkeit der Vernunft bei der Entstehung und Wiederauflösung so vieler Gewerkschaften der Neuzeit nachweisen? Es schmerzt [illegible] daß wir in dieser Weise von den bisherigen Anstrengungen der Arbeiter, eine bessere Existenz zu gewinnen, sprechen müssen. Es ist betrübend für jeden Menschenfreund, diesen Zustand der Dinge zu betrachten. Die Organisation der Arbeiter ist ein wichtiger Gegenstand des Nachdenkens für uns. Auf einer befriedigenden Lösung dieser Frage beruht nicht nur unser eigenes Gedeihen, sondern auch die Zukunft unserer Nation. Wir wollen hoffen, daß die Arbeiter, belehrt durch die früher gemachten Erfahrungen, jetzt einsehen, welche wichtige Pflicht ihnen obliegt, und daß sie fortan in allen Angelegenheiten, welche ihre eigene Wohlfahrt betreffen, mit Vernunft handeln, indem sie den Beweis liefern, welche Bedeutung Einheit, Disciplin und Ausdauer für ihre Sache haben. Sie müssen nicht, nachdem sie bei dem ersten Zeichen von Gefahr furchtsam zusammengelaufen sind, wieder voneinander laufen, sobald die Gefahr zu schwinden beginnt. Beständige Wachsamkeit, Disciplin und unverbrüchliche Einheit sind die sichersten Schutzwaffen der Arbeit.

(Der Hammer.)

Muße-Stunden.

Es unterliegt keinem Zweifel, daß, wenn wir einen besseren Begriff hätten von der rechten, praktischen und nützlichen Anwendung unserer Muße-Stunden, würden uns mehr derselben zu Gebote stehen, besonders dann, wenn der wahre Nutzen derselben im alltäglichen Leben sich kundgeben würde. Die Folge der praktischen Anwendung dieser Freizeit würde Verkürzung der Arbeitsstunden zur Folge haben. Diese Verkürzung gäbe dann Beschäftigung [illegible], welche unter dem gegenwärtigen System oft unbeschäftigt sind.

Doch über das Achtstundengesetz will ich heute nicht schreiben. Muße-Stunden, wenn recht angewendet, haben einen weittragenden Erfolg, für uns selbst, für unsere Kinder und für unsere Genossenschaft auf der Tribune des Lebens. Sie bieten uns die Gelegenheit zu sittlichen Vergnügen, zur Erweiterung unserer Denkkraft und zur Veredelung unserer geistigen Funktionen. Diese Veredelung würde als natürliche Folge neue Ideen, klarere Begriffe und tiefere Sympathien zum Resultate haben.

Um jedoch den Werth dieser Freizeit recht kennen zu lernen, ist es unbedingt nothwendig, dieselbe zu unserer Ausbildung und zur Kultivirung unseres Denkvermögens recht anzuwenden. Werfen wir einen Blick in die Geschichte und stellen uns die Völker der verschiedenen Zeitperioden vor und wir finden, daß in den Perioden, wo das Volk am unwissendsten, am stärksten litt, daß Bedrückung, Armuth, ja oft Hunger und Elend am häufigsten waren. Doch nicht allein das, sondern auch daß sich Unzucht, Raub und Mord am Gräßlichsten sich zeigten als Folge der Unwissenheit und Armuth. Leset die Geschichte der Spartaner und Athener im philosophischen Griechenland, die Geschichte des Mittelalters, wo Roh- und Unwissenheit gang und gebe waren, da finden wir die Arbeitsklasse sklavisch unterjocht, während die sogenannten Edelmänner in Wollust lebten und das Volk tyrannisirten. Wir blicken in die Geschichte der Neuzeit und wir sehen dieselbe sich wiederholen, wo der Edelmann König auf seinem Gebiete war, der Arbeiter aber unter der strengen Zuchtruthe seines gnädigen Herren (?) seinen Rücken beugen mußte, und je nachdem die Unwissenheit größer oder geringer war, so steigerten sich diese Uebelstände.

Sie erlauben mir wohl obige Abschweifung von meinem Thema, denn sie ist nothwendig zur Erklärung. In gewisser Hinsicht ist dasselbe gerade die Unwissenheit unter der Arbeitsklassen unserer Zeit hervorgerufen; man geht Morgens an die Arbeit, kommt Abends heim, ißt und schläft, um Morgens wieder an die Arbeit zu gehen. Zum Theil ist man mit diesem drückenden Einerlei zufrieden, und warum? weil man glaubt, es müßte so sein, denn es hat ja immer Herren und Sklaven gegeben. Zum anderen begnügt man sich mit Klagen in den Muße-Stunden, daß das Schicksal uns in eine solche Lage gesetzt hat.

Haben Sie, mein geneigter Leser, Ihre Muße auch je dazu verwandt, die Ursache dieses Uebelstandes zu untersuchen und um Mittel zu ersinnen, demselben abzuhelfen? oder sind Sie vielleicht schon zu der Ueberzeugung gekommen, daß Sie selbst Schuld an Ihrem Elend sind? Denken Sie einmal recht darüber nach.

Hier ist ein Gegenstand, auf dem wir unserer Denkkraft Beschäftigung geben können.

Wiederum: Haben Sie je Ihre freie Zeit dazu verwandt, die Ursache zu untersuchen, weshalb der Monopolismus seine Schwingen ungehindert über das ganze Land breitet, die Gesetzgebung kontrollirt, die Stadträthe beeinflußt und die Produktion des ganzen Landes zu seinem Nutzen ausbeutet?

Haben Sie sich auch je in einer freien Stunde mit dem Gedanken befaßt, diesem Uebelstande abzuhelfen? [illegible] ein wenig sagen, sonst würden Sie [illegible] mehr angestrengt haben, um [illegible] zu dieser Abhülfe beizutragen.

Wir wollen uns diese Frage etwas genauer betrachten und es tritt uns zuvor die Ursache dieses Uebels vor's Auge.

Zuerst sind wir geneigt, die Ursache dem Monopol in die Schuhe zu schieben, jene aber nennen uns als die schuldtragende Partei: ein Dritter sagt, sie haben beide Schuld.

Wir wollen sehen. Wir fragen zuerst, was giebt dem Monopol seine Kraft? Wir antworten kurz: Organisation. In diesem einen Wort liegt das ganze Geheimniß.

Was wäre das Eisenbahnsystem, wenn jede Bahnlinie einzelstehend ihre Fracht und Fahrpreise reguliren würde? Competition würde bald die Preise so herabsetzen, daß die laufenden Ausgaben nicht bestritten werden könnten, wie dieses vor einigen Jahren mit den zwischen Chicago und St. Louis laufenden Bahnen geschah. Dasselbe ist der Fall auch auf dem Gebiete aller andern Geschäfte: da sind die Board of Trade, Coal Merchants Association &c. Nun aber haben sie sich durch Organisation verbunden; die Folgen davon sind, daß eine geringe Minorität die große Minorität kontrollirt.

Wir betrachten nun die andere Seite: der Arbeiter steht im großen Maßstabe unorganisirt, das Verhältniß ist, wie oben erwähnt; durch Competition im Geschäft ist einer des andern Schaden. A. arbeitet für \$2.75 per Tag, bis B. kommt und bietet sich an für \$2.50 per Tag und arbeitet mehr als A. C. kommt und übernimmt das Haus auf Stück, so daß er, wenn's gut geht, \$2.00 per Tag (von 12 bis 14 Stunden) verdienen kann. Die Folge davon ist, die Arbeitgeber und Monopolisten zusammen kommen und sagen, da ist Einer, welcher für \$2.00 per Tag arbeitet, wir setzen sie alle herab auf \$2.00 und wer will sagen, daß sie nicht recht gethan haben? Wir würden dasselbe thun. Doch wer ist Schuld an der Herabsetzung? Mein lieber Leser antworte selbst.

Das ist der Arbeiter ohne Organisation und wundern wir uns, daß es ihm schlecht geht? Es geht ihm nicht schlecht genug.

Ich bin der Ansicht, daß der homöopathische Grundsatz auch hier anwendbar ist Similia Similibus Curantum (oder ähnliches mit ähnlichem Curant). Denn hat das Kapital durch Organisation es dahin gebracht, alle Quellen der Industrie unter seine Gewalt zu bringen, zu diktiren, was der Arbeiter für seine Arbeit bekommen soll, die Gesetzgebung dahin zu beeinflussen, Gesetze zu Gunsten des Kapitals und zum Nachtheil des Arbeiters zu erlassen, warum sollte nicht Organisation dasselbe für uns thun? Zählen wir doch zum wenigsten zwei Drittel der Bevölkerung des ganzen Landes.

Kapital in seinen verschiedenen Zweigen erntet den Ertrag des Landes. Wer aber bestreitet die Unkosten desselben, wer bezahlt die Steuern und wer unterhält die Regierung? Statistische Beweise sagen uns, daß es der Arbeiterstand ist, auf dem die Last liegt, während die Anderen verhältnißmäßig frei ausgehen.

Angesichts dieser Thatsache fragen wir noch, warum sollen wir uns organisiren? Prägt sich nicht die Antwort sogleich mit der Frage auf unser Gemüth, nämlich um den Strom der Ungerechtigkeit zu hemmen und unser eigen Recht zu erwerben.

Doch um auf diesem Gebiete Reform zu erlangen oder Reform zu bewirken, ist es nothwendig, zu organisiren, agitiren und gegenseitige Aufklärung, Nachdenken über die Situation, gründliche Untersuchung der Verhältnisse, und wir werden bald dahin kommen, frei und ohne Furcht unser Recht zu beanspruchen und auch zu verlangen.

Zum Schluß erlauben Sie mir noch die Worte des großen Atheners Demosthenes an's Herz zu legen: „Ihr Männer von Athen erwachet zu Eurer Pflicht und wahret Eure Rechte."

Euginus.

Chicago, Jll.

— Eine Convention aller Kohlengräber der Ver. Staaten wird am 1. Mai in Pittsburg abgehalten werden. Es wird beabsichtigt, eine Vereinigung aller Kohlengräber, deren Zahl auf 170,000 angegeben wird, herbeizuführen und dadurch in Zukunft Strikes fast unnöthig zu machen.

— Der Trades und Labor Council von Toronto, Canada, hat kürzlich in einer öffentlichen Versammlung den Carpenter Boß J. J. Withrow wegen arbeiterfeindlicher Gesinnung prozessirt, ihn schuldig gesprochen und beschlossen, daß er geboycottet werden soll. Withrow war angeklagt, im Jahre 1872 gegen die strikenden Setzer agitirt zu haben, ein Feind der Achtstundenarbeit zu sein, Unionmitglieder entlassen und Scabs angestellt zu haben, sich geweigert haben, ein Schiedsgericht anzuerkennen, die Polizei auf die Arbeiter gehetzt und sie verhindert haben, in einer Halle ein Fest zu feiern. Der Angeklagte war mit einem Advokaten und einer Anzahl Kapitalisten vor dem Council erschienen, ließ sich in's Kreuzverhör vernehmen, vertheidigte sich in einer fünfviertelstündigen Rede, wurde aber [illegible] Majorität für schuldig erklärt.

Fortschritt der Arbeiter-Bewegung.

Wohl noch während keines Winters ist die Arbeiterbewegung in den Vereinigten Staaten so lebhaft gewesen wie in diesem, weniger sich in Lohnkämpfen und dergleichen ausdrückend als vielmehr in Verbesserung und Ausbreitung der bestehenden Organisationen und Gründung neuer. Von überall her kommt die Kunde, daß neue Gewerkschaften gegründet wurden; andere bisher vereinzelt dastehende Gewerkschaften schließen sich nationalen Organisationen an oder schreiten, wo diese noch fehlen, zur Bildung solcher; in allen größeren Städten, in denen Gewerkschafts-Centralkörper noch nicht bestanden werden diese ins Leben gerufen, kurzum die Thätigkeit ist eine allgemeine. Erst jetzt scheint sich der amerikanischen Arbeiter im großen Ganzen die Erkenntniß zu bemächtigen, wie nothwendig es ist, daß sie sich gewerkschaftlich organisiren, wenn sie nicht zu gänzlich willenlosen Sklaven herabsinken wollen. Und daß, wenn diese Erkenntniß erst einmal durchgebrochen, es auch in diesem Lande des Dampfes nicht allzu lange dauert, bis man demgemäß handelt, davon legt schon der Umstand Zeugniß ab, daß während der letzten beiden Jahr die Zahl der organisirten Arbeiter Amerikas sich um das Fünffache vermehrt hat. Diese emsige Thätigkeit deutet jedenfalls auf großartige Lohnkämpfe hin, die wir im kommenden Frühjahr und Sommer zu erwarten haben. (Buchdrucker Zeitung.)

Arbeiter-Zeitungen.

Was „Der Hammer", Organ der Metall-Arbeiter, in seiner letzten Nummer sagt, paßt eben so gut für unsere Leser:

Eine Zeitung, wie die unsere, die sich zur Aufgabe gemacht hat, die Gewerks-Organisationen zu fördern, dieselben mit dem wahren Arbeiter-Princip zu beleben, daß jede Lüge und Corruption schonungslos an den Pranger stellen wird, findet leider nur bei wenigen Arbeitern Gehör, weil ihnen die Worte einer „Arbeiter-Zeitung" zu grob an ihre Ohren klingen, da dieselben von Jugend auf den schädlichen Einflüssen der corrupten Presse unterworfen und deren Schmeicheleien gewöhnt, so daß sie selbst die Tatzenhiebe dieser falschen Bestie eher hinnehmen, als ein rauh klingendes Wort einer Arbeiter-Zeitung.

Mitarbeiter! die ihr uns noch ferne steht, eure Unterdrücker wissen es, daß ein Arbeiter des anderen Arbeiters Feind ist, und hierin beruht eure Knechtschaft. Um dieselbe abzuschütteln, schließt euch uns an und wirket thatkräftig für die Verbreitung unseres Organs, damit die Unterdrücker sehen, daß die Arbeiter einig sind.

Mann der Arbeit, aufgewacht,
Und erkenne Deine Macht,
Alle Räder stehen still,
Wenn Dein starker Arm es will!

G. Herwegh.

Gewerks-Notizen.

— In New York und Umgegend sind gegenwärtig viele Zimmerleute arbeitslos.

— In Toledo, Ohio, sind die Löhne für Carpenter, die der Union angehören, \$2.25 per Tag. Die Wilden, d. h. Nicht-Organisirten, bekommen nur \$1.50.

— Die Gewerkschaften zu Middlesborough, England, zogen kürzlich mit vier Musikbanden in die Kirche, um eine Predigt des Erzbischofs von York anzuhören, welcher erklärte, die Gründung von Gewerkschaften sei für das nationale Leben und Wirken der Völker nützlich und nothwendig.

— Am 9. Januar wurde der Bau der neuen Arbeiterhalle zu Chicago in Angriff genommen. Dieselbe wird eine Front von 100 Fuß haben und 212 Fuß tief sein; die Kosten [illegible] auf \$50,000 veranschlagt. Leo P. Dwyer der Painters Union ist Vorsitzer de[illegible] Committees.

— Drei Glasfabrikanten zu Baltimore haben 22 ihrer Arbeiter wegen „Verschwörung" verhaften lassen: 17 der Angeklagten [illegible] Bürgschaft gestellt. Die „Verschwörung" bestand darin, daß die Angeklagte [illegible] Scabs überreden wollten, sich [illegible] der Glasbläser in Baltimore [illegible]

— Der Mayor von C[illegible] ausgestandenen Töpler [illegible] seimacht entgegengeset[illegible] beurtheilt. Den S[illegible] gestattet, sich auf [illegible] Die Proklamation [illegible] Blut erzeugt. [illegible]

— Wo es [illegible] gab, sind [illegible] Besitzer groß[illegible] 1850 einer [illegible] Eigenthu[illegible] [illegible]

CORRESPONDENCE.

TOLEDO, O. We have no fault to find about the progress of Union No. 25, it is growing steadily. Work is fair at $1.75 to $2.25. The car shops are paying $2.05 and steady work.

BALTIMORE, Ind.—Trade is very dull here at present, nearly one half of the carpenters are out of work. The weather for the last 3 weeks has been such as to stop all outdoor work and there is very little of any other work.

Items from Washington.

WASHINGTON, D. C.—Quite a number of carpenters are out of work at present on account of weather; trade is very dull. We have elected new officers: Pres., Geo. Huler; Vice Pres., Wm. Davis; Rec. Sec., W. Ward; Fin. Sec., J. Howard; Treas., John Byler; Conductor, Bro. Chezzom; Warden, H. Humphries; Trustees, Bros. Leahorn, Gregg and Edmonston.

Work and Wages in Oakland.

OAKLAND, Cal.—We have made a very good start here in organizing Carpenters Union No. 36, and we are very careful whom we admit to membership. Wages are from $3 to $3.50, and nearly all our members are employed. Our officers are: President, Richard Stephens; Vice Pres., J. A. J. Davis; Rec. Sec., F. Loveland; Fin. Sec., A. A. Wells; Cor. Sec., Chas. Roesch; Treas., Patrick Maloney; Conductor, N. Prinslow; Warden, O. Vallien.

News from New Orleans.

NEW ORLEANS, La.—Union No. 16 now [illegible] at 667 South Rampart St. On Jan. [illegible] the following roster of new officers [illegible]: President, B. J. Brown; Vice Pres., A. [illegible]; Rec. Sec., [illegible] Dugue; Fin. Sec., W. H. Barnes; [illegible] Sec., J. L. [illegible]; Treas., A. C. Buillard; Conductor, Jos. Marshall; Warden, J. Costley; Trustees, John Jules, L. J. Gillings, Lewis Knight. There is not much work at present; wages down to $1.75 this Winter; weather cold.

Cincinnati Chips.

CINCINNATI, O.—Work was quite plenty [illegible] the late cold snap knocked [illegible] sideways. And at the same [illegible] bosses jumped at the chance, and [illegible] cutting wages wherever they [illegible] a man afraid of them. But the [illegible] men uphold their wages and the [illegible] men take whatever they can [illegible]. There are a great many men idle, [illegible] manage to look out for our own [illegible]. The prospects for Spring are bright.

The Union in San Rafael.

[illegible] RAFAEL, Cal.—Trade good, wages [illegible]. How long it will continue this [illegible] can say. It all depends on [illegible]. There are some good jobs under [illegible] that will take until Spring. The [illegible] is not very bright for the coming [illegible]. The union is growing slowly, and [illegible] account of the indifference of the [illegible] men we are striving to benefit. Some [illegible] curry favor with the bosses while [illegible] are indifferent. But we intend to [illegible] and keep our flag flying. Our officers are good active men.

Trade in Toronto.

TORONTO, Canada.—Trade in this city is [illegible] at present, owing in a great measure to the cold weather—thermometer below zero for weeks. Wages range from $1.75 to $2.25. The bosses have not carried out the agreement entered into last Spring. Although they have not reduced wages directly, yet they have indirectly by discharging men receiving $2.25, and filling their places with cheaper men. But this would not be, were the non-union men only fair enough to join us. There are fully [illegible] carpenters in the city, so that we have a great deal to do to organize them.

Report from Kansas City.

KANSAS CITY, Mo.—We have in this city about 600 carpenters and why more of them do not join us I cannot tell.

[illegible] the day is near at hand [illegible] that kind of stuff those [illegible] The prospects are good [illegible] Bosses are still in line [illegible] our union."

P. J. McGuire will [illegible] as follows: [illegible] 26.—Providence; Union No. 13 and [illegible] 28.—Hartford, Conn., [illegible]

—J. B. Johnson, [illegible] Middletown, N. Y., writes to us as follows: "I am glad to see THE CARPENTER at work. I hope he will use his hammer vigorously until he finds a way to our dull [illegible] and arouses the [illegible] attitude of Labor, thinking and [illegible]

[illegible] National Labor League [illegible] evicted from [illegible] an apartment [illegible] swinging frames [illegible] sashes.

—In a very [illegible] Monthly termed [illegible] and overwhelm[illegible] stifle the great [illegible] and absorbing [illegible] national [illegible]

July last. Our new officers are: Pres., W. Kewly; Vice Pres., R. T. Davis; Rec. Sec., L. P. Dietrich; Fin. Sec., E. R. Loomis; Cor. Sec., J. E. Walton; Conductor, J. H. Bearly; Warden, L. D. Falkerson.

News from Minnesota.

MORRIS, Minn.—Wages last Summer and Fall were $2.75 and $3 in this vicinity. But building is very dull here just now, and on the only work going up the boss wants it let out by piece work, or he says he will pay only 20 cents an hour for 8 hours work by the day. This, of course, is the result of disunion. If the men were united they could demand 30 cents per hour the same as I do. That appeal to carpenters is the "boss" thing. It will wake them up all over. The January number of THE CARPENTER was a grand one; such a journal ought to be in every carpenter's hands. Trade promises to be lively here next Spring.—P. A. MCCARTHY.

Converting Non-Union Men and Bosses.

KENSINGTON, Ill.—We have changed our meeting place to a more suitable hall. Union No. 23 has elected as officers: President, D. N. Wilbur; Vice-President, W. P. Graham; Rec. Secretary, Alex. Munroe; Fin. Secretary, O. K. Wallace; Warden, S. Hershaw; Treasurer, J. M. Stearman; Cor. Secretary, J. Tate.

Your January paper was "a whole team and a yaller dog under the wagon." It was very much liked by non-union men, and it has helped us. Those appeals also have done good. I have circulated them among our enemies. One boss said to me, after he had read our January paper, and also the appeals: "Well, I have always been opposed to all unions, but after reading these little sheets I will always acknowledge the justice of their claims." And mind you, that boss is no small contractor in this town. So you see, the world moves!

San Francisco Overcrowded.

SAN FRANCISCO, Cal.—Wages range from $3 to $3.50 with plenty to do the work, and a large number out of work who have come here under false inducements. They have been told that work was plenty, and hands scarce, and now they go through the streets cursing the sharks who have hoodwinked them to come so far. Very few union men are out of work, as we see that our members are cared for. Initiations still going on, and new officers elected: President, Joseph Saunders; Vice-President, Thomas C. Rowe; Rec. Secretary, J. D. Campbell; Financial Secretary, N. B. Churchill; Cor. Secretary, P. Souter; Treasurer, Thomas O'Neil; Conductor, J. J. Cron; Warden, J. W. Roszell; Trustees, Brothers Uglow, Morgan, Ryan, Whitten and Wandel. At this election we had a very large and harmonious meeting. Bro. Owens declined to run for re-election as President, although many desired him.

What Our Boston Union is Doing.

BOSTON, Mass.—The mass-meeting held here on January 15, by Carpenter's Union No. 33, was a complete success beyond all expectations. Caledonian Hall, on Eliot street, was crowded, and able addresses were made by Bros. Kady, Clasby and Packham. Bro. Packham, of the Amalgamated, and Mr. Shrove, of the Roxbury Curriers, also spoke in favor of labor organization. So we had a very profitable time which resulted in a host of new members. On January 17th, we held our first annual ball, and it was a "rattler." Every one was delighted, and it realized us more than enough to pay expenses. And more than that, it established the fact that the "wood butchers" in the building line of this city can get up something that cannot be excelled for respectability and enjoyment. We have adopted new By-Laws,—one feature of which is a sick benefit of $5 per week for those who are members one year, and $2.50 per week for those who are members only six months. This goes into effect June 1st.

[illegible] of Their Own.

[illegible] Scotia.—Enclosed is [illegible] subscriptions to THE [illegible] the House Joiners Association [illegible] fax, for the use of the [illegible] Union of which we [illegible] THE CARPENTER is very [illegible] here, and our members [illegible] of our most [illegible] We refer [illegible]

—It is [illegible] vention of the co[illegible] work for one hand to clean one [illegible] cotton; whereas Whitney's gin [illegible] and to add to the [illegible] POVERTY is a [illegible]

They say the world's a desert drear, still plagued with Egypt's blindness [illegible] That we were sent to suffer here [illegible]

are always anxious to see it, so we propose to place it in the meeting room of our hall. Our House Joiners Association is only nineteen months in existence, and as the first where, and in that time we have organized three other unions, viz. the Masons, Painters and Bakers. These four unions are united together under the head of the Amalgamated Trades Union. Each man did his part, but a great deal is due to John Saxton and A. C. Lessel. After hard and persistent work, we have a hall of our own with reading-room, meeting-room and other conveniences, all under one roof. Our reading-room is open from 10 A. M. till 10 P. M. We have expended many hundred dollars in fitting up our hall, and never asked nor took a cent of help from any one outside of ourselves. We support this Workingmen's Institute ourselves, because in fighting for our rights we want to stand on our own floors, and defy politicians or capitalists to say they ever gave one cent in support of what we consider a home over the head of every workman in Halifax who becomes a union man.

Some Arguments in Favor of Organization.

RUSHVILLE, Ind. This leads me to say that carpenters should stop and give their condition attention. Carpenters, consider the amount of work you do; put this and your earnings in a balance and you will soon discover which side will be found wanting. Why is this? The answer is easy. Some good workman is a little "hard up" and goes to a boss for a job; perhaps the boss knows his condition and offers him 25 or 50 cents per day less than he is worth. And rather than lose a job the workman consents and goes to work; the boss setting the price, this has been the case too often and is exactly the reason that the carpenters of America are working so cheap to-day.

If we were properly organized all over the country we would be no small power within ourselves. We could regulate our wages and make ourselves respected. Take it as we are, we are looked down upon by capitalists and some of the other trades.

And we are to blame for it ourselves, just because we don't have clean grit enough to get up like men and ask for what we ought to have, and what justly belongs to every carpenter in the land—enough wages to keep us comfortably and respectably, and at the end of the year have something to our credit for a rainy day, or when old age comes and we cannot work at our trade. But at the wages now paid and the price of what we consume there is no man, let him economize ever so close, that can save one penny.

Let us go to work and organize this country thoroughly and demand decent compensation for our labor. All we want to bring this about is for the carpenters to make a little effort and we will get all that we demand, and after we obtain this end, keep it up right up to the top notch and in less than five years you will see the carpenters and joiners of America a different set of men respected and honored in society.

Numbskull's Views.

PHILADELPHIA, Pa.—The month of January has been a very unprofitable one to the majority of carpenters. It has been one of incessant storm, and all outside work must wait the pleasure of milder weather and the union becoming stronger in interest, if not in numbers—stronger in their belief and conviction of the usefulness of organization.

One of our members remarked to your correspondent some time ago, there is no need for a pack of new members to be initiated if the old members would only take hold of the matter as they should. He expresses himself pleased with the results of the union, citing the fact that had it not been for the union we to-day would be getting 50 cents per day less than we are. Besides that the bringing together of men, getting them acquainted, forming new friends, and the fact of one always finding friends and acquaintances on almost every new job—that alone he claims is worth all the dues for a year.

He further says, why cannot men agree to combine? If each one will pick out his man and say: "We propose certain measures, you come with me and help me and I will help you and together we will be able to keep our pay at some decent standard." That is one of the greatest benefits we can secure.

In our home organization the question is often asked; What benefit is the National Organization or Brotherhood to us? Go where you may you find these analyzing skeptics ever ready to pick to pieces everything, out of nothing less than pure cussedness. For the traveling brother who is a member of our B. when he reaches a union on his journey, he finds friends to welcome him, although he is a stranger. When men in your own city have intentions to join your union, the knowledge of your connection with the Brotherhood strengthens their belief in the usefulness of the organization, and they become members. You can never know the condition of work and wages in distant cities without unity through the B.

In a fight for wages you can look for some assistance and sympathy from sister cities while your oppressors are more unwilling to take up the cudgel against you than if you were only a mere local union compelled to stand on your own merits. But I will say this, national organization cannot build up a local union in any city and make it a power, unless there is unity in the union, and the right kind of men before the mast.

Men may become offended at trifling matters in their union and fly off and quit the union and influence others to do likewise. They may even enter another organization and experience just the same difficulty there. I say to you plainly—squarely as a numbskull—that let you be what you may, join any organization you please, if you want to run everything to suit yourself, if you want your highly important self to be the Alpha and Omega of the organization, there is no doubt you will find the organization too small for you and you will have to get out of it. There is no evil in any trade union but which can be corrected in proper time by loyal men. Therefore let every man work on faithfully.

How lamentable it is that the philanthropy of this cold world is not always appreciated! A paper that offers a ton of coal on long time for a year's subscription should certainly have had a prosperous business in these frosty days. But alas! the generosity of *The People* was not appreciated and it has perished—for want of breath—I meant to say money.

Union No. 8 had an interesting lecture on Feb. 12th from Bro. Gompers of the New York Cigar Makers Union. Were it within my power I would be only too well pleased to have taken a full report of it. The practical illustrations, the necessity and value of trades unions were well presented by the speaker. NUMBSKULL.

[illegible] the organization [illegible] to progress [illegible] Material interests are stronger than temporary enthusiasm for an abstract principle.—*New Orleans Workman.*

[illegible] refuse to [illegible] It is to organize [illegible] to enforce a fair division of the [illegible] of wealth which this [illegible] Why don't they do it? There is a field for them in New England and wherever [illegible] belong to [illegible] advance [illegible]

MARCH 1883
ISSUE
MISSING

THE CARPENTER

A MONTHLY JOURNAL FOR CARPENTERS AND JOINERS.

VOLUME III. NEW YORK, APRIL, 1883. NUMBER 4.

OUR HONORED DEAD.

IRA STEWARD, late president of the Boston Eight-Hour League, and for many years president of the National Ten-Hour League, died March 13th, at Plano, Ill., while on a visit to his friends. He will be mourned by the men and women of labor throughout the United States. A machinist by trade, he was one of the few who early took up the cause of the overworked and underpaid wage slaves and worked with the will and energy of an enthusiast, devoting time and money to the cause, without counting the cost, health, and all with the hope that their condition might be bettered. He went about teaching the people the truths underlying the eight-hour movement, writing tracts and a work of 400 pages, entitled "The Political Economy of Eight Hours." One of his most intimate disciples in speaking of this work says:

"His theory included the industry and material welfare of every human being on the earth. The great practical measure in Mr. Steward's argument is a shorter day's work for factory and manufacturing laborers. This leaves out the world's agricultural labor, until its methods are sufficiently absorbed by machinery, capital and capitalists. Then farm laborers will be ready for the legislation necessary to reduce their hours of labor, and still higher wages will follow, through which additional demands will be made upon the industries of other laborers. The occupations thus carried up to wage conditions will increase human progress. Laborers will become more industrious, business prosperity will increase; there will be more knowledge, virtue and freedom, and co-operative conditions will seem nearer than ever."

Like all true reformers, he died poor in purse. Ira Steward will need no monument of stone to remind those who come after him, for he has left his imprint upon the hearts of his fellow toilers.

LITERARY.

We have received a series of pamphlets from F. A. Hodgson, 176 Broadway, New York. These WORK MANUALS, as they are called, are five in number, and cost 25 cents each, or five for one dollar. Each contains from 50 to 75 pages, and is neatly and clearly printed on good paper and well bound.

I. "Cements and Glue," contains 200 recipes for preparation of cements for every purpose.

II. "The Slide Rule and How to Use it," is valuable to all mechanics and saves a world of calculation.

III. "Hints for Painters, Decorators, and Paper Hangers."

IV. "Construction, Use and Care of Drawing Instruments," contains a fund of information for all desirous of becoming draughtsmen.

V. "The Steel Square" is a book which simplifies and solves some of the most difficult problems in carpentry and joinery. It is admirably illustrated and easy to comprehend.

We feel safe in recommending any one of these Work Manuals.

BLACK LIST.

J. A. WALSH, of Brookline, Mass., and formerly conductor of Boston Union No. 33, has been expelled from said union for obtaining and withholding monies due to Union No. 33.

—JOHN GRACE is expelled from San Francisco Union No. 22 for violating Art. 9, Sec. 4, of our constitution, in doing piece work a detriment to the trade.

—C. MUTCHLER, suspended from Trenton Union No. 31 for non-payment of dues.

TRADE NOTES.

—On May 1, Chicago bricklayers will demand $4 per day.

Trade in Cleveland is looking better, although many are out work.

—A union of Carpenters has just been formed in Denver, Col., also in Rushville, Ind.

—A bill limiting street car employes labor to twelve hours per day has passed the Pennsylvania Legislature.

Wages in Norwich, Conn., range from $2 to $2.25 per day. Some of our friends are busy organizing a local union, although it is up-hill work.

—Skilled carpenters in Denver have no difficulty in securing employment, but the "hatchet and saw" class cannot get work carrying a hod.—*Labor Enquirer.*

New York Plasterers' Union have resolved that they will not plaster any building erected by a scab builder. A movement is on foot to amalgamate the building trades.

—The labor [illegible]didates in Toronto polled a very credita[illegible] vote. Bro. S. R. Henkes was the candidate in East Toronto. The candidate in West Toronto came within an ace of being elected.

—A boom in building is expected to take place in Dayton, O., this Spring. A number of large buildings are to be erected. But of what avail is this to Dayton carpenters, if they are not organized?

—Governor Cleveland of New York has signed the Tenement Cigar Bill which goes into effect Oct. 1, next. The manufacturers propose to fight the bill in the Courts. A bill to stop the contract hat making in prisons was also signed.

In Morris, Stevens Co., Minn., carpenters get 30 cents per hour; trade very dull. Carpenters are advised to keep away from that neighborhood this season. A union under our jurisdiction has been formed and a charter will soon be granted.

—The stone-masons of Boston have resolved to demand $4 a day after the 1st of May; the plasterers of St. Louis have agreed to work for $4 per day this season. In Kansas City, Mo., bricklayers wages are $3 per day, and men are asked to stay away from there, as trouble is expected.

From the monthly report of the Amalgamated Carpenters for March, we observe that trade is very dull in England and Scotland, and entirely prostrate in Ireland. In New Zealand and Australia it is improving, and very bad in South Africa. There are 21,013 members in good standing, 1091 out of work, and 522 on sick benefit.

DEATH OF KARL MARX.

Karl Marx died in London on March 14th. As one of the promoters of the International Workingmen's Association, he was detested by all the monarchs, tyrants, monopolists and aristocrats here and in Europe. Born in Germany in 1818, he was exiled from his native land, next driven from France, and found shelter in London. A highly educated man he was one of the ablest of those who dared to take issue with the "orthodox" political economists. His work "Das Kapital" ranks high among scientific men and has been published in all languages, excepting English. The toilers of the world all honor the memory of Karl Marx, for it was he who said: "Workingmen of all countries, unite!"

THE SHORT-HOUR MOVEMENT BEGUN.

In conformity with the orders of our last convention, we have been at work systematically to inaugurate a nine-hour movement among the carpenters of America. Of course we are equally desirous to see the eight-hour system adopted. But as that would meet with more opposition and would require a larger measure of sacrifice from the workmen, we concluded that the better course is to first secure nine hours as a day's work, and in doing this we are instituting the rule, which, thanks to good organization, prevails for many years among the carpenters in Great Britain.

The nine hour movement with our Brotherhood is of more importance than a raise of wages, because it will employ more men steadily and relieve us of the competition of idle men, who will work at any price to get a job. To secure the nine-hour rule will be to not only maintain wages, but eventually to increase them. For all experience shows that that has been the result wherever the hours of labor are reduced. Hence it is not a question of more pay that will concern our unions this season; on the contrary, we are opposed to any further demands for more pay until we have first carried the nine-hour system. We propose to waste no words in advocating the many benefits of reduced hours in our trade. It is universally conceded we are right in our demand.

Now we mean to act! We have argued and pleaded long enough.

The first union to take action on this question is San Francisco Carpenters Union No. 22. At a meeting of that union lately the subject was fully discussed, and by a vote of 237 ayes to 3 nays, it was resolved:

That after the first day of May the hours of labor each day shall be from 7 A. M. to 12 M. and from 1 P. M. to 5 P. M., or nine hours per day, and that a committee of three members be appointed to consult with the architects and bosses to arrange for such a reduction.

So that now the nine-hour movement has fairly begun and we trust it will not stop until it is adopted by every trade in the country.

THE FRENCH WORKMEN AND THE EXPOSITION OF AMSTERDAM.

The National Committee of workingmen of France called a public meeting—which was a complete success—for the purpose of organizing a national visit to their fellow-workers of Holland. At this first meeting no less than 54 trades were represented. A committee was elected to communicate with all trades in the provinces who desire to send delegates to the Amsterdam Exhibition. The matter seems likely to assume national proportions.

The city government of Paris has voted 5,000 francs to send trades union delegates, and other cities will take like action; a proposition is pending in the French Parliament to donate 100,000 francs, but the trades unions have resolved not to take the government assistance, unless they are guaranteed their perfect independence of action and choice of their own delegates.

Stagnation has set in in many industries of France, and thousands are out of work. The Carpenters' Union of Paris called a mass-meeting of the unemployed in the trade on March 9th. It was to be held in the afternoon in front of the *Esplanade des Invalides*, but the police broke up the gathering.

CHIPS.

Sixty thousand persons are said to be out of employment in Paris.

The Governor of New Jersey has signed the bill making labor strikes legal.

Many furniture factories in New York, Chicago and Cincinnati are running only eight or nine hours a day at present.

The labor organizations of Dayton, O., and Hartford, Conn., have handsomely furnished halls leased for a term of years.

—The manufacturers of St. Louis, Mo., have combined to defeat the bill now pending in the Legislature of Missouri for the appointment of a factory inspector.

—Contract prison labor is the great prominent question in the Legislatures of New York, New Jersey, Ohio, Pennsylvania, Indiana and Missouri. Its speedy downfall may be predicted.

—California has created a bureau of labor statistics to appease the organized workers, but the politicians strained every nerve to secure the office of commissioner for some of their lily-fingered gentry—and they succeeded.

—The question of hiring union men or non-union men in the Government Printers was the subject of a [illegible] debate in the United States Senate. It was [illegible] to develop the fact that organ[illegible] has but few friends in that body [illegible]

—Canada has just passed a law ma[illegible] it unlawful for Chinese to enter Can[illegible] without first paying $50 a head. If ch[illegible] labor be an injury to the State, why [illegible] a special law against one kind of che[illegible] labor and none against others? Every cheap labor Caucasian is worse than any Mongolian.

UNION AND DIVISION.

It is a great onward step to organize [illegible] trade into unions; a step that takes work to accomplish, and which can be destroyed within the ranks in much less time than is required in the building. The danger to be most solicitously guarded against does not come from outside, from employers, from opponents of the principle of trades unionism; it comes from the ambition of reckless or unwise men within the organization, who to elevate themselves would wreck the fabric which years of labor have brought into good trim for the betterment of the condition of the members. Beware of the persuasions of men who preach [illegible] subtle art of division of strength. [illegible] nearer a trade is to union throughout [illegible] whole country the stronger it is; w[illegible] perfectly organized at home and [illegible] would be irresistible. We do n[illegible] anything that would please the em[illegible] in a trade where there is a tendency [illegible] pose hard conditions and low wages on [illegible] bor, more than would be the divi[illegible] the trades union of that trade. [illegible] wrecking, let us bend our ener[illegible] lidifying and extending. It [illegible] course promising success [illegible] means defeat on every [illegible] arises.—*Pittsburg Labor* [illegible]

SPANISH [illegible]

The building a[illegible] united and [illegible] the workers [illegible] join the [illegible] eral [illegible] each [illegible]

PUBLISHED [...]
BY TH[E]
Brotherhood of Carpe[nters]
OF AME[RICA.]
Office: 184 William [...]
Terms.—Fifty cents a ye[ar ...] paid.
Send all moneys and com[munications for the] Journal to
P. J. Mc[Guire,]
184 W[illiam ...]

NEW YORK, FEB[RUARY ...]

—THE CARPENTER is wo[rth ...] a year, and all we ask is [...] members to increase our li[st ...] We will give a premium [...] Henry George's "Progre[ss ...] to any one sending us a [...] scribers.

—Another example of w[...] export from the capitalist[s ...] and trial of the Glass Blowe[rs ...] for conspiracy. But in spi[te of ...] sition the workmen have w[...] and influenced the importe[d ...] men to join the union.

—Congressman Upton of T[...] stronger standing army to pu[t down] strikes." Were the capitalist[s ...] ative to pay workmen decent [wages] strikes" would not occur. [...] needs shooting it is not the pe[ople] but the rascals who have d[...] oppressed the workers.

Since 1878, the average wag[es ...] men have increased about sev[...] while the necessaries of life [have in]creased fully twenty-three per [cent ...] still we hear the raving that [...] land of prosperity. So it is for [those] who coin wealth from the flesh [...] and virtue of human beings.

—Some journals speak very fa[vorably of] Gov. Crittenden's message to the [...] Legislature, because he complain[s of the] long hours of street car employ[es ...] Gov. Crittenden was the man wh[o called] out the State Militia in 1881 to sh[oot ...] the street car employes of St. [Louis ...] demanding 12 hours should con[stitute a] day's work.

It is said "Hard times are n[ot ...] !" Well, if they are not, it do[es seem] that the number of idle men i[s ...] [...]g, and that the bankruptcie[s are ...] numerous. The Mercantile A[gency re]ports the failures in the United [States ...] past year number 6,738, as [against] [...]582 in 1881. The liabilities in the [United] States are, for the last year, $101,0[...] as compared with $81,000,000 in 188[1].

—"Strikes are no use; there is n[o ...] in trades unions; we must organiz[e for po]litical action!" This is the talk [...] [common]ly heard from a workman. We turne[d ...] [ro]und and asked him: "Have you a fun[e]ral fund, or a sick benefit, or any such [fe]atures in your union?" And the answer [w]as "No!" Then we calmly said: "Th[en] adopt those benefits before you do anything else, and then you will find some good in your union."

[illegible]

THE CARPENTER.

Entered at the Post-Office in New York, as second-class matter.

NEW YORK, APRIL, 1883.

SIGNS OF PROSPERITY.

FROM THE CHINESE

Where spades grow bright
And idle swords grow dull,
Where jails are empty,
And where barns are full;
Where field paths are
With frequent feet outworn,
Law court yards weedy,
Silent and forlorn;
Where doctors foot it,
And where farmers ride;
Where age abounds,
And youth's multiplied;
Where poisonous drinks
Are chased from every place;
Where opium's curse
No longer leaves a trace;
Where these signs are,
They clearly indicate
A happy people
And a well ruled state.

WORKSHOP NOTES.

—The consumption of mahogany in this country is increasing very rapidly. It is fast becoming the fashion in expensive furniture and for finishing purposes.

—We would advise the oiling of screws or the dipping their points in grease before driving them. This will render them more easy to drive and also to withdraw, and it will undoubtedly retard for a longer time the action of rusting.

—The roof of the Pancras Station, Midland railway, London, has the widest span of any roof, unbroken by ties or braces. It covers ten acres. The length of the roof is 690 feet, with a clear span of 240 feet, making a total area of 165,600 square feet.

—A thorough test of ailanthus wood for furniture has been made, and it has been found hard to work, and fails to retain its shape. This failure is unfortunate in an artistic sense, for the delicate tint and the irregularity of the grain would make rich effects.

—One of the most simple and readiest methods for loosening a rusted screw is [...]ent to the head of the screw. A [b]ar or rod of iron, flat at the end, if [heated] in the fire and applied for a couple [of] minutes to the head of the rusted [s]crew will render its withdrawal easy.

—In sticking large mouldings there is often great waste caused by cutting the moulding direct out of the squared piece instead of first sawing off a triangular corner, from which a smaller moulding may be got out. Cutting direct from the square wastes stuff, time, power, and labor.

—Every man of ordinary intelligence would feel the justice of the laborer's demands, and be ready to acknowledge them, did he not see for himself some spot where he could get an unearned cut on what the laborer produces, and know that through the present social and political inversion of justice he can reap advantages that are not honestly his own.

—A waterproof glue may be obtained by dissolving 10 grams sandarac and 10 grams of mastic in a ¼ liter of alcohol, afterwards adding 10 grams of turpentine. The solution is placed in a water bath, where an equal quantity of a hot solution of glue or isinglass is mixed with the same. Still hot, the mixture is strained through cloth and ready for use. For the gluing of mineral bodies, it is well to add to the above 10 [...] 10 grams of powdered mixture.

HOW TOOLS SHOULD BE KEPT.

An unmistakable evidence of a good mechanic is the manner in which he keeps his tools. Without well kept, sharp tools, no mechanic can do first-class work, nor [is a mecha]nic worth his wages, if he does [not keep] our [...] tools in that condition. With [...] work [...] is a pleasure to work. Many [...] to a trade, often become [...] by being put to work [...] tools. Masters [...] should [...] There [...] can use tools [...] able to proper[...] ously to their [...] chanics and [...] or hire [...] And do [...] follo[w ...]

[illegible]

PIECE WORK AGAIN.

A delegation of San Francisco Carpenters' Union No. 22 appeared recently before a meeting of the Chapter of Architects of that city in reference to the practice permitted by some of the Architects in San Francisco of allowing contractors to sublet the finishing of buildings, in part or as a whole, by "piece-work," instead of having the work done by day labor. The unfairness and injustice of the custom was fully argued by the delegation, setting forth its injurious effects and tendencies as against worthy and capable workmen, many of whom were frequently drawn out of employment by reason of piece-workers offering to "lump" work at prices which would yield current day wages only by slighting the work, crowding in all the working time possible, and rushing it through with but little regard to quality of workmanship, thus debasing and demoralizing the standard of mechanical science and working a common injury upon competent men, and imposing inferior work upon owners.

In reporting this meeting the *California Architect* says:

While the Chapter cannot control and prevent or regulate the questionable practice, the expression of all present disfavored the piece-work system. Many of the members of the Chapter insert a clause in their specifications: "No piece-work will be allowed;" but this is harmless as against contractors who let piece-work when unaccompanied with a contract penalty. The agitation of the matter will, in time at least, induce all reputable architects to incorporate a penalty clause in contracts issued by them. The general sentiment of the members favored the adoption of some practical method calculated to favor the interests of the better class of mechanics. It was suggested to the delegation that the Union, from time to time, inform the Chapter of all cases of piece-work coming to its knowledge.

THE USE AND ABUSE OF SCREWS IN WOOD WORK.

It is an instructive and remarkable fact that our building workmen of a century or two back, in many operations in carpentry and joinery, discarded, as far as was possible, the use of nails or screws, depending more on carefully jointed work, put together by means of mortise, tenon, dovetail, hard-wood dowel, or oaken pin. Their work might have taken a longer time to execute than that done by our present race of joiners and wood-workers, but it was infinitely more lasting, and kept together so long as the timber or wood continued sound. Some years ago the writer examined an old oaken stair case and hand-rail in a college, which work was executed more than two centuries since, and in the construction of which not a nail or screw was used. From time to time, over long years some slight repairs were made, but the workmen during their operations were never able to discover that a nail had been used in the original construction. There were mortises and tenons, grooves and tonguing, wooden pins or dowel work, but no iron fastening of any kind. The writer also examined more than one old roof in which the use of iron spikes, nails and other iron fastenings was dispensed with, and the joining of the timber was effected without their aid. In the hinging of doors and other framework it is necessary to use screws, but unfortunately many workmen will actually drive the screws into the wood two-thirds of its length with the hammer, rather than take the trouble of driving them gradually home with the screwdriver. Hence, if the door be a heavy one, the weight of it will tend to the hinges loosening, and after a time will follow "dragging" and "rubbing" of doors, and their makeshift cure is what is known as "easing" them. A screw that is nearly driven its whole length with a hammer cannot make a regular and corresponding thread or spiral in the wood, and therefore its binding and maintaining power in keeping the hinge in its place is gone.

The *Radical Review* says: "Russian Nihilism, far from being that execrable thing which Americans delight in depicting it, is the salvation of a down-trodden people. We could have only contempt for the Russian people if, lamblike, they submitted to the oppression and the despotism of the czars. Where there is despotism there must be nihilism, if there remains a sp[ark of] manhood in human hearts [...] much of [...] This is very [...] and our members [...]

HALIFAX CARPENTERS AND MILL WORK.

HALIFAX, Nova Scotia. The regular meeting of the House Joiners' Association of Halifax and Dartmouth, held early in March took action in reference to mills furnishing house finish and sending their own hands to finish the same, and the following resolutions passed unanimously:

"*Whereas*, It has come to the notice of this body that mills supplying house finish of their respective kinds and sending their own employees to construct and finish the work, thereby causing a loss to builders and destroying the labor of mechanics employed outside the mills, be it therefore

"*Resolved*, That on and after March 7th all work constructed or otherwise manufactured in establishments known as sash, door, and blind and planing mills shall be subject to the order of the builder herein referred to, and shall be finished by them after completion in said mill, and that any violation of this resolution on the part of mill owners shall be subject to the following: That members of this body shall not put up any work manufactured by the violating party. And be it further

"*Resolved*, That a copy of this be sent to each of the builders, hoping they will sustain us in this cause as one of great importance to them, and trusting they will support us in any cause of justice as we have done in this."

The question of wages was taken up, and on motion it was decided to ask for 20 per cent on all existing rates, and that an advertisement be inserted to that effect giving notice to those requiring mechanical skill, before contracting the coming season.

UNIONISM IN TOLEDO.

TOLEDO, O. Business picking up. Wages average $2.00. Our public meeting on February 28, was well attended—ten new applications. Prospects for summer, good. If carpenters do not improve their chance this season and ask decent pay then they may blame themselves. To say our members are well pleased with THE CARPENTER is to only faintly express our feelings. If it was not for our journal we would have hard work to build up a union in Toledo. There is not a man among us who is a speaker, so we rely entirely on our journal to set our principles and aims before the trade at our public meetings and it works well.

AMUSEMENTS FOR WORKINGMEN.

Steps have been taken in Spain to amuse the workman during his hours of toil, and the plan is said to have been attended by excellent results. "Structural alterations" having been ordered for the Madrid theatres, as (since the burning of the Ring Theatre in Vienna) at so many playhouses in various parts of Europe, the necessary operations were forthwith undertaken at the Theater Royal, but they did not proceed rapidly enough to give the manager any hope of being able to open on the day for which the commencement of the season had been fixed. In his difficulty he selected from a number of workmen, those who had a taste for music, and engaged a portion of the opera band to play to them as they built, joined and painted. Cheered by the strains of a fine orchestra the men labored with such good will that they completed the work in excellent time. And now, according to "Iberia," the question of employing music as an aid to labor is being seriously considered in high places.

A SCAB DEFINED.

The following truthful definition of a "scab" was given by counsel in a conspiracy case in England:

"A "scab" is to his trade what a traitor is to his country; and, though both may be useful to one party in troublesome times, when peace returns they are detested alike by all; so when help is needed, a "scab" is the last to contribute assistance, and the first to grab a benefit he never labored to procure; he cares only for himself, but he sees not beyond the extent of a day, and for momentary and worthless approbation would betray friends, family and country. In short, he is a traitor on a small scale, who first sells his journeyman, and is himself afterwards sold in his turn by his employer, until at last he is despised by both and deserted by all. He is an enemy to himself, to the present age, and to posterity."

NECESSITY OF TRADES [UNIONS].

President Arthur of the Brotherhood of Locomotive Engineers, at the convention of that organization lately at Louisville, Ky., gave the following excellent reasons for labor organizations:

A Trade Union is generally supposed to be organized for the protection of laborers representing any one kind of industry. Protection is not tyranny. If capitalists combine their wealth, time, and talent, to amass fortunes for themselves; to control to monopolize their own branch of industry, even if it necessitates the crushing out of less fortunate concerns, why have not laborers the right to join hands for self protection? In union there is strength, and there is safety in numbers. When the country is rolling in wealth, when all things indicate good times, when stockholders and heads of corporations surround themselves with all that is luxurious, and count their gains in high denominations, then turn and either grind down the men who made wealth possible, or refuse to listen to their cry for a pittance beyond what they have been allowed, is it any wonder that rebellion ensues? Have laborers no rights? People say if they are not satisfied with what they receive as compensation, let them leave and seek it elsewhere; corporations can readily fill their places. That is easily said, but is it so easily done? While seeking labor elsewhere, who will fill hungry mouths at home? Besides he may not be able to better his situation. Go where he will he finds employers all too ready to grind down the employed, and knowing him to be in need of work, will pay but the lowest sum for his services. Without labor there can be no capital; one is essential to the other, and laborers are just as liable to have their demands satisfied in one place as in another. Their association in its ways is quite as strong as the combination of capital. If the one has a right to hold off, hoping to gain its own especial point, so has the other. In the end one or the other must yield. Strikes among the better class of trades unions are not indulged in for the sake of being arbitrary, but only as a last resort. We hold, therefore, that trades unions and similar compacts, though often abused, have on the whole effected signal good. Labor is better paid, and its rights better secured, than otherwise it would or could be. Such being the case, the right of combination should be upheld, not only in theory but in practice. Its surrender would remove the most powerful instrument in the hands of labor to withstand the exactions of capital. It should be cherished as a natural and legal right, as the sheet anchor of prosperity. When employers can justify the position they may take up by facts and legitimate arguments; when they are willing to submit to the principle that every laborer is worthy of his hire; when they will recognize the fact that by fair and liberal treatment to those by whose toil they are many of them building up colossal fortunes, they will not only be benefiting their own workmen but also themselves; when they see they have a higher duty to perform than that of merely paying as little remuneration as they possibly can for as much work in return for it as they can by fair means or foul get out of their workmen; and when, in fact, they more fully enter into the inner life difficulties and requirements of the great labor classes of the country they will, if they are earnest in their wish to use the opportunities placed in their hands in a fair and just manner, find that the advanced, thoughtful and educated portion of workingmen will respond to their efforts in endeavoring to improve the relative position of those who work and those who pay.

A correspondent in Boston writes: A rally of the trade is needed here almost every week to strengthen the weak-kneed and to shame the miserable bounds who are now taking work at prices which will scarcely feed, much less clothe them. The last public meeting of the Brotherhood on Feb. 26, when Secretary McGuire spoke, is considered all around to have been a grand success.

The Toronto Trades Council is contemplating the appointment of an organizer, and Thos. Moor of the Carpenters' Union is mentioned for the place with a fixed salary. His duties will be to look after unorganized labor and bring it within the folds of union. To the cry of the boss carpenters that "Moor must go," the workmen have responded "Moor will stay," and in that the workmen of Toronto have shown signal good sense in standing by a man who has been true to them.

[...] or Plac[e ...]

PLAIN WORDS REGARDING STRIKES.

In discussing the question of strikes the *Cigar Makers Journal* presents the following arguments which are forcibly stated and should be made the rule of action in every trade:

We ascribe the failures of strikes in the past to the following causes:

1. The want of a thorough organization, local, national and international.

2. The low due system and the consequent depleted treasury in time of need.

3. Short-sighted selfishness which could not comprehend the necessity of paying a weekly benefit to the unemployed members.

4. Insufficient knowledge of the conditions of trade, and the inauguration of strikes during the most unfavorable season.

5. The undeveloped condition of the labor movement in Europe, England only excepted.

Without strikes the wages of cigar-makers would be about one-half what they are now. Go to Pennsylvania and visit those places where cigar-makers have never struck, and compare their wages with those places where strikes have most frequently occurred. In one place can be seen a stupid, ignorant, hopeless and over-worked class of cigar-makers; in the other an intelligent, hopeful, energetic and respected class of men.

In England, where the oldest and most powerful trades are to be found, strikes are gained in dull times. We will mention but one instance in 1878-9, the lock-out of the Amalgamated Engineers, Blacksmiths, Pattern-Makers, Millwrights, &c., in London, which lasted over eight months, and ended in a comple defeat of the manufacturers. This was a time when 5,000 members of the organization were out of employment, and trade at a complete standstill. The combined manufacturers insisted upon a reduction of 10 per cent. on the wages, and an increase of the working hours from 54 to 57 per week. But the union had a well-filled treasury amounting to $1,300,000, with a membership of 45,000 extending over the whole civilized world, able to hold out in any emergency. Besides the men on strike they supported the 5,000 unemployed, whom they paid a weekly benefit of $2.50. They have learned the lesson that it is cheaper to support the unemployed, than to allow them to work for low prices and probably become scabs. This is the secret of their success.

Even Wm. M. Evarts, the ex-Secretary of State, in his comment upon the consular reports of Labor in Europe, had to admit that the Trades Unions of Great Britain prevented reductions of wages.

WHAT HAVE WE TO HOPE FROM POLITICS?

The late election shows the weakness of the labor movement on a political basis. How many wage-workers were elected to congress or State legislatures? In the large cities *nobody else* ought to have been elected. Labor can stand by its trade unions, but when it comes into a political fight it throws away its arms and surrenders to the fiction of a "party." It is our parties that divide us, and give us to the common enemy. There seems to be no hope through political action.

As society is constituted, the only real parties are labor and capital, whether in republics or monarchies. It is these parties that are always in conflict, and always will be so long as our social divisions are tolerated. Relief to labor will not come through legislatures, but through universal organization, and a persistent demand on capital for industrial liberty; for it is capital that holds labor in bondage, whether social or political. Compel capital to face the great issue, whether labor shall forever be the serf and hireling of capital or be freed through union and universal partnership. All our voting for a century has had nothing to do with this issue. We have fought against men of straw, represented by parties. And all this time capital has silently plundered us and absorbed our whole accumulations, leaving us as [illegible] in bodies and as darkened in minds as at the beginning.

J. F. BRAY.

Pontiac, Mich.

[illegible] N. Y., [illegible] has been held and it is resolved to [illegible] cents a day. [illegible] demand [illegible] until the car[illegible] ask an ad[illegible]

SMALL BED-CHAMBERS

There is reason to believe that more cases of dangerous and fatal disease are gradually engendered annually by the habit of sleeping in small, unventilated rooms than have occurred from a cholera atmosphere during any year since it made its appearance in this country. Very many persons sleep in eight-by-ten rooms, that is, in rooms the length and breadth of which multiplied together, and this multiplied again by ten for the height of the chamber, would make just eight hundred cubic feet, while the cubic space for each bed, according to the English apportionment for hospitals, is twenty-one-hundred feet. But more, in order "to give the air of a room the highest degree of freshness," the French hospitals contract for a complete renewal of the air of a room every hour, while the English assert that double the amount, or over four thousand feet an hour, is required. Four thousand feet of air every hour, and yet there are multitudes in the city of New York who sleep with closed doors and windows in rooms which do not contain a thousand cubic feet of space, and that thousand feet is to last all night, at least eight hours, except such scanty supplies as may be obtained of any fresh air that may insinuate itself through little crevices by door or window, not an eighth of an inch in thickness. But when it is known that in many cases a man and wife and infant sleep habitually in thousand-feet rooms, it is no marvel that multitudes perish prematurely in cities; no wonder that infant children wilt away like flowers without water, and that five thousand of them are to die in the city of New York alone during the hundred days of the coming Summer.—*The Builder.*

HOW OUR TRADE IS BUTCHERED.

It is generally thought the greatest trouble in our trade is the abolition of the apprentice system. As it is at present in our city a boss will send one good man and 3 or 4 laborers, just left driving team or maybe just finished excavating. Then they strike a job as carpenters when through; they feel themselves competent carpenters and tear along for $1 or $1.50 per day. It is to the advantage of the bosses as they get $1.50 out of the butcher and only 50 cents out of the carpenter. It is an acknowledged fact through the trade that this is the great obstacle in our way of reaping the benefit of our toil, and we are robbed out of the benefits we have served an apprenticeship to gain. Now I think every carpenter should put his shoulder to the wheel and assist in removing this obstacle, which is worse than highway robbery to men who have served time to learn their trade. Then again these butchers are running the trade down by working for the low wages they are working for. It is cutting up the trade and robbing the carpenter of his reputation. Now if our craft will take this hint in this coming spring, I am sure we could remove a great deal of this butchering business. It is not only robbing us but is robbing the capitalist who lays his money out in house property which is put up by these butchers, and the consequence is in a few years they have to be rebuilt and our craft disgraced after being robbed.

I would exhort all carpenters who have not come into the ranks to do so at once. If the bulk will do so immediately we can give this butchering business a death blow. If you neglect to join us you will rue the destruction which will come upon yourselves as well as the men that are fighting your battles. I believe now is the time for the stroke. It can and will be done, the sooner the better, for the longer it goes the harder the task.—*E. B.*

BUFFALO N. Y.

A SOCIAL GATHERING.

On February 22d, Trenton Carpenters' Union, No. 31, held their first annual package party at Temperance Hall. The programme consisted of recitations, addresses, vocal and instrumental music and distribution of packages. Every one attending brought a package of something, tied up so that no one knew what it contained, which were auctioned off and opened at the close of the entertainment, occasioning rare sport. The packages sold for an average [illegible] ized. There were between 400 and 500 persons present, who listened with great satisfaction to brief addresses from C. H. Stimmerman and Victor Drury.—[illegible]

[illegible] them financial [illegible] subscription [illegible] coming [illegible] send to [illegible] consequently

DEGRADATION OF ARCHITECTURE.

Architecture in the United States has been greatly degraded, firstly, on account of a want of artistic and æsthetic culture among the people in general; secondly, on account of the intense selfishness of contractors; thirdly, on account of the pusillanimity of some of the professional architects, who have subordinated themselves to the encroaching avariciousness and the impudent, bombastic money-mongering propensities of the contractors. It is the mission of architecture to elevate the artistic knowledge of a people by presenting to the eye, beauty of form and lines, and by securing to society a refined and proper environment.

It is the selfish interest of the contractors to suppress all the ideas of the architect which will produce these results by *cutting out* all the work he can, or by mutilating the conceptions of the architect in order to make money. To secure this end, the contractor frequently *bribes* the architect to pass work which he should condemn.

So glaring has this corrupting practice become, that some years ago the architects of the United States formed an association for the purpose of discountenancing these fraudulent practices among the less scrupulous of the fraternity.

As workingmen we have been compelled by the grasping spirit of the contractors to *scamp* our work and to suppress the best imagined and most artistic thoughts of the architect, and have been compelled silently to listen to the "*Lie direct*" which the contractor has given to the architect when he has told him that he could not get his "*fools of journeymen to understand the drawings*," when in fact we have been told by the contractor to "put less work in," and to "cut out all we could," and we know as a *fact*, that it was the contractor, the boss, who did not "understand the drawings."

The celebrated architect of the new Grand Opera House in Paris *M. Garnier*, was the first architect who, to our knowledge, recognized the importance of dealing directly with the workmen who were to execute his designs—he kindly received a delegation of stone-cutters, carpenters, modellers, sculptors, fresco painters, ornamenters and artists who offered to execute his work and expressed delight at the prospect of being relieved from the impertinent interference of the contractors, whose only function is the obtaining of a profit upon the labor performed, at the expense of the quality of its execution.

Architecture has always been in rapport with the ideas, the necessities, the development, and the materials,—in fact, with the social environment of a people, and each system and style has responded to the dominant idea of the period which produced it.

It is evidently necessary that science should realize a reformer in the architecture of human habitations—as it has realized reform in the construction of the factory and public buildings—and as it has realized reform in the construction of agricultural implements and railroads.

Therefore, the fancy architects of to-day would do well to study the social requirements which must be met by the architecture of the future—the twentieth century will confide to them the most splendid and gigantic structures which the world has ever seen, which must be in harmony with the industrial and social knowledge, requirements and aspirations of its people, a people emancipated from thraldom and serfdom—a people which is free and has overthrown feudalism in all its phases. For the feudalism of aristocracy has been overthrown, the feudalism of commerce has been overthrown, and within a few years the feudalism of industry will be overthrown, and the people will require an architecture which will respond to its expression of a broader freedom.—*Labor Dictionary.*

A CALL TO ACTION.

No better time could be found than the present to do something for our union. The building season is almost at hand, and before it fairly opens we should have as many as possible of the carpenters of every city with us. With a strong union we can assert and maintain our rights. At present, out of some 5,000 in Chicago, we [illegible] in our union. With [illegible] accomplish much, but [illegible] could were we more [illegible] take [illegible] matter to heart, and do his utmost to induce some non-union fellow-workman to join his union. With such a vast field [illegible]

OUR RECEPTION IN HARTFORD.

On March 1, a labor meeting of over 350 of the best class of workingmen assembled in Talcott & Post's Hall, Hartford, Conn. We leave the Hartford *Examiner* to report the meeting:

On this occasion P. J. Maguire, of the Brotherhood of Carpenters, was the speaker of the evening. Mr. R. C. Baker was called to the chair, and after a short address in his usual earnest and convincing style introduced Mr. Maguire, who spoke for fully an hour and a half to one of the most attentive audiences ever witnessed in Hartford. The gentleman confined his remarks principally to the necessity of organization amongst workingmen, and outside the wages question enumerated the many other advantages derived therefrom.

He took a hopeful view of the situation. Labor had passed over one stage of its destiny, that of feudalism, where the serfs were sold along with the land they tilled; now we were in the waning hours of the commercial stage, where money all potent, enslaves the masses, and next will come the industrial age, when eventually the era of justice will come, when war between man and man shall be known no more. As the speaker would sometimes dive into the depths of his subject, his manner became impassioned and his words grew eloquent, drawing forth the most hearty rounds of applause. His visit to Hartford on this occasion cannot fail of being productive of much good. The hall was filled, and the visitor was well pleased at his reception. After the meeting the Carpenters' Union tendered him a modest banquet, at which he fully explained to the members the benefits and advantages to be gained by attaching themselves to the general brotherhood. All were more than pleased on retiring to their homes during the first of the wee sma' hours of morn.

PRACTICE WHAT YOU PREACH.

Let Union men practice their principles among themselves, and let the world know they profess unionism as a principle and not for selfish convenience; in a word, let them be watchful that they take no unfair advantage of their fellow members, and thus avoid descending to the level of "scabs" in practice when they are so much above them in profession. There are some union men who forget all about their unionism when there is a chance to take unfair advantage of a companion in labor, and who are at the same time loud advocates of union principles. Such men should be taught that true unionism consists in the practice of fraternity as well as profession.

AGITATION AMONG CARPENTERS, CHICAGO.

Branch 9, Carpenters' Union 21, of Chicago, held an open meeting Tuesday evening, March 6th, in Room 20, First [illegible] Church Block, which was well attended. Mr. J. P. McGinley urged the non-union men to join the association, and told of the benefits to be derived. The union paid $5 a week to sick members, $100 in case of accident, and $250 death insurance. W. F. Anderson said, if all the carpenters of Chicago belonged to the Union, they could get $3 a day this summer. L. E. Schr[illegible]der said that they were not trying [illegible] few individuals to benefit themselves [illegible] to benefit the community at large. [illegible] workingmen stand to the capitalists [illegible] eighty to twenty, yet they bow to [illegible] twenty. If they were all organized [illegible] would be otherwise.

—The various labor organizations [illegible] Cincinnati are already making preparations for their annual parade next June. The coming demonstration will eclipse all previous efforts in that line. New York, St. Louis and Chicago will hold similar parades. Out of this will inevitably grow a general labor holiday all over America.

—A State [illegible] was held [illegible] [illegible] Commissioner of State Labor [illegible] A Legislative [illegible] and a [illegible]

And a universal [illegible] labor and ca[illegible] and [illegible]

THE CARPENTER.

PUBLISHED MONTHLY

BY THE

Brotherhood of Carpenters and Joiners,

OF AMERICA.

Office: 184 William St., New York.

TERMS.—Fifty cents a year, in advance, post-paid.

Send all moneys and correspondence for this Journal to

P. J. McGUIRE, Secretary,
184 William St., New York

NEW YORK, APRIL, 1883.

NOTICE TO SUBSCRIBERS.

The March number of THE CARPENTER did not appear, and this number is dated for April. Hereafter our paper will appear on the first of each month, and in order to do this, we have had to omit the March paper. This will be made good to all subscribers.

—From Germany we have received a letter from the carpenters union of Berlin, which informs us that on March 15th they would demand an increase of wages, and in case it was refused they propose to strike and at the same time demand nine hours shall constitute a day's work.

—Our visit to Boston, Providence and Hartford has had fruitful results. It encouraged Boston Union No. 33, and has led the Hartford Union to join us, which will make it Union No. 43. The Providence Union has given evidences that it will become Union No. 44. In this number we publish reports of these meetings.

—We must send out Organizers this spring to wake up backward cities! The past circulars we sent out have stirred up a live interest that needs to be followed up. Let us raise a fund to send out organizers. It can be done! Let each union arrange some festival or sociable at once this spring and devote the proceeds to an Agitation Fund. Which union will be the first? Let us see.

—The "Lectures on Labor" are eagerly relished by our readers, and so much are they appreciated that now they are finding their way into the labor papers of the country. Of all that has ever been written on political economy these lectures are [illegible] almost and yet the most comprehensive. They prove conclusively that it is possible for a workingman to make the "dismal science" radiant with hope for our class.

—New York has lately had a surfeit of events that indicate with what lightning-like speed we are approaching a social convulsion. The pompous honors paid by [illegible] gangs at the funeral of Jim Elliott, [illegible] prize-fighter, and at the bier of Mc[illegible] the murderer, is only worthy of a [illegible]ization that produces a Vanderbilt [illegible] for the display of stolen millions. A [illegible]em of society that perpetuates the [illegible] empires of human industry is only mo[illegible] enough to pay homage to prize-fighters and murderers.

AROUSE, AND DO YOUR DUTY.

A long and protracted winter has delayed building operations this spring. But our [illegible] when work does open there are every evidences that there will be a great rush and an abundance to do for a few months.

In many cities the past winter has been a [illegible] one for carpenters; [illegible] have had but little to do, and [illegible] the existence of our Brotherhood [illegible] wages would have been reduced to [illegible] way to [illegible] of some bosses [illegible] thinking and [illegible] concluded to let wages alone this winter. Whether that will be the case next winter depends entirely on the carpenters themselves!

If we neglect to extend our organization this coming season, if we fail to strengthen our unions, to increase our dues and add to our benefits there is no doubt we will find ourselves powerless to uphold wages.

Mere talk and pretence of organization will avail nothing. The only thing that counts is a strong fund in every local union a well-filled treasury. This it is that makes the Amalgamated Carpenters and Engineers the powers they are in England; it is that which enabled the Locomotive Engineers to lately face Jay Gould and the Railroad Kings in this country.

Instead of placing faith upon chance results, let us imitate the examples set us by trades that command no greater craft skill, yet by virtue of better organization secure better wages. Our Brotherhood has become a permanent institution. It has stood the storm of false friends on the inside and secret enemies on the outside. It has proved its usefulness and will live to see all its enemies humbled. In it we have no room for adventurers, place-hunters nor politicians.

We want men of honor, of principle, men who are willing to make some little sacrifice of time and money to uplift their class. Such are the men who make every great movement, and we are proud to find them in our ranks.

This movement is no child's play: it is earnest and real and must be agressive. It needs that every man shall attend the meetings, pay his dues, and bring others to join. It needs that men shall work with devotion and enthusiasm for its success. Then, brothers, let us be up and doing! The coming spring should more than double our membership and double the number of our local unions. Will you help us to do it! The future of our trade depends upon each one of you. We advocate no strikes for more pay this season; better confine our efforts to a reduction of the hours of labor. That will be of more benefit and will pay every man in the end.

GAMBON'S SPEECH.

At the farewell banquet given by the French workmen to the English trades unionists, during the recent visit of the latter in regard to the Channel Tunnel, the speech of M. Gambon is worthy of all attention.

When the moment arrived for the toasts, M. Gambon, member of the National Assembly, rose to drink to the friendship of England and France, and to the union of laborers of both countries. He begged to salute the real ambassadors of England; the repesentatives of English labor; the creators of England's wealth. They had been received in Paris by a man of commanding genius, Victor Hugo, and by the entire heart of the French people. He wished to dispel an error. It had been said that they were revolutionists for revolution sake. They were, on the contrary, moderate, as all true Liberalism is moderate. If they had been thought violent, it was because the oppression from which they had suffered had been violent. If they had made revolutions, they were discounted on the morrow. Was it not Republican France that proclaimed the rights of man and spread the principle all over the world? By the side of this good there was the evil; there was Bonaparte, who dragged us through all the capitals of Europe. Again, in 1848, the Constituent Assembly at once proclaimed the liberty of Italy, of Poland, and the union of all peoples as the fundamental policy of the French Republic. But again the good seed was destroyed, and this time by Napoleon III., whose influence had proved more fatal than that even of the First Empire. Then came 1870, when Napoleon wanted to re-open the era of wars. In vain the people rose to protest; they were at once arrested. But surely, when 400,000 French soldiers surrendered, this might be taken as evidence that the heart of France was not in favor of war. At the same time, on the other side of the Rhine, the organized workingmen of Germany sacrificed their liberty in their efforts to [illegible] the annexation of Alsace and Lorraine. This showed that the peoples, even when apparently most divided, [illegible]

UNIVERSAL BENEFITS, UNIVERSAL DUES, AND EQUALIZATION OF FUNDS.

In THE CARPENTER for February there is an account of the formation of the Amalgamated Society of Carpenters and Joiners. I presume few know the origin of that society, and as it will interest the readers of THE CARPENTER, I will try as near as I can remember to give it to them.

I was an apprentice boy at the time of the formation of the society in 1860, at that time the carpenters of London were in about the same fix as the carpenters of Chicago are to-day, at the foot of the ladder in the building trades; to-day they are the leading trade in London. They received five shillings ($1,25) per day of 10 hours, and worked till 4 o'clock on Saturdays, and indeed, some shops (like some here in Chicago) kept them full time on Saturdays; over time was very much abused. In some shops the old hands used to think trade was slack if they did not work one-quarter day over time every night, and piece work was the general rule.

In order to rectify these abuses and to establish 9 hours as a day's work, the carpenters of London resolved to strike. They let their bosses and the world know of their intention beforehand, had lots [illegible] talk before they struck, and the men of Messrs. Trolope & Sons shop (very large builders in those days) struck first. Hereupon the boss builders had a meeting, and resolved to have a *general lockout* of all the Building Trades, and formed what is known to-day as the Master Builders Association. Then commenced a mighty struggle. The bosses introduced what was known as the "document." Each man was required to sign a document which bound him not to belong to any combination of men, and recognized the rights of employer and employed to make their own individual agreement as to wages. In fact, I do no not remember all it contained. I do know it was very humiliating, and against the "document" the men made a *vigorous kick*. The strike lasted six months, thousands of families were in a starving condition. At last it was settled by the bosses withdrawing the "document" and the men returned to work on the hour system. They worked 56½ hours per week at seven pence per hour, or ten hours per day for 5 days and 6½ hours on Saturday, and their wages averaged $1,37 per day. So you see they gained something.

Now in those days trades unions were illegal in England, and the carpenters and joiners were *dis-united* in a lot of local societies. They were taught a very severe lesson by that strike. Hence the delegates of the various locals met and formed the Amalgamated Society of Carpenters and Joiners; that is, an amalgamation of all the unions. That was a generation ago, and I have lived long enough to see the Amalgamated the pride and boast of an English joiner.

I have given you the sketch of the origin of the Amalgamated, because we of the Brotherhood are precisely in the same fix to-day that the London joiners were in 1860—only a lot of disunited locals. The London carpenters started out right, they commenced with *high benefits, high dues, and equalization of funds*, and upon that they have built up a mighty union. And in order to show that that is precisely what the Brotherhood of Carpenters and Joiners of America will have to do, if they ever expect to build up a *National Union* in America, is the object of this letter.

Now, our Brotherhood has been in existence nearly two years. Last year we had a very costly convention (it cost Chicago $195) and did the delegates give us a good National Union? I say, with all courtesy, *No, they did not!* The delegates met, some from the East, and some from the West, North and South, and one did not know what the other wanted, and it has occurred to me that we may arrive at a better understanding through the medium of THE CARPENTER before the next convention will meet, and let us see if we can't make a fresh start at that convention and do as the London joiners did, *start right*. I will therefore give you my views, and I hope some other brother will answer this in the next CARPENTER, and give us his views. Thus we will be more likely to arrive at a better understanding. I am not in favor of cheap articles, they are generally expensive ones in the end, and that is just my idea of a *Cheap Union*.

Now I claim we can never expect to build up a national organization unless we start out with three cardinal points to work upon: *universal benefits, universal dues, and equalization of funds*, that is to say, let [illegible] and without [illegible] these three principles we can never be united. And unless we are united in the truest sense of the word, we might as well give up trying to get up a national organization. We will find our Brotherhood dwindle away till there is nothing left of it. It will take very little argument to prove that high dues and high benefits are more likely to get and *retain* members than a "cheap" affair. Chicago immediately after the last convention adopted 50 cents per month dues and has more than doubled its membership since.

Now, my experience as Financial Secretary of our Branch 9 of Union 21, I find the great trouble is that members join the union and soon after will have to travel to some other city in search of work; they will never think of applying for a traveling card and joining the union in the city where they are going to, and if they did the union would have no sick benefit (as at present constituted) or would charge a new entrance fee, so that where a member leaves the city, that, as a general rule, is the last of him, and he is lost to unity forever. Well, now, if we had an "Equalization of Funds," how simple we could manage that. All the brother would have to do would be to go into the Local where he goes to and keep on paying his dues, and it would be the business of the corresponding secretary of the Union he goes to, to notify the Union he had left, and thus hundreds of members yearly would be saved to the Union that are now lost. Now, again, when Vanderbilt and other great railroad magnates find they are working against each other, what do they do? Why, they adopt the equalization plan; *viz*: they pool their earnings, and then they find it pays; why cannot we do the same?

Again, in regard to the death benefit. When a brother dies, his widow (if he leaves one) will want the benefit at once to do her any good, and it can't be paid under six months under our present plan. If we had an "equalization" the benefit could be paid out of the Local to which he belonged before the funeral.

In fact, the arguments in favor of "Equalization" are so many I cannot see how anything can be said against it. In my next letter I will try to show how a high price union is more likely to retain members, than a cheap one. In the meantime, I hope some other brother will answer this, give me a chance to "talk back," and so we will understand each other before the convention meets at Cincinnati next August.

Let us be united, brothers, for there is a big field here in America for a big National Union, and it is badly needed. L. J. B.

IMPORTANCE OF EMPLOYMENT BUREAUS.

One of the orders of business in our Brotherhood is asking the question, "Is there any employment standing or bosses wanting help?" which is answered by any brother who knows of such. We also have another method, which we call a dummy employment office. By these means we are able to keep most of our brother union men at work. But, carpenters and joiners, we want a more effective method; we want an employment bureau in the center of the city, to which all bosses wanting help will apply for men. Now, let us consider the benefits we would derive from such a system. Instead of starting on a week's, and in many cases a month's hunt, for a job, we would only have to report to the employment bureau that we were open for the first job that came in, which we would get in our turn, then go home and enjoy the company of our family, fix up our tools, make a tool chest or a piece of furniture, and by so doing pass our time pleasantly and profitably. But in order to bring about such a state of affairs, it is necessary for every resident carpenter to belong to the union. But at present when we are out of a job, how are we going to get one? It is a bitter cold day in mid-winter; after meeting our partner at the appointed place, we commence our hunt; go to a new building, ask the man in charge if he wants any more help? "Not at present." Next house same reply. We keep it up that week with no better results; but it is the only method we have for getting a job. With an employment office of our own, conducted by a man of our own choice, what a change for the better would be the result!

CHICAGO, Ill.

—We understand [illegible] organizations have [illegible] on foot to have do it? There is a field for Louis go on [illegible] England and wherever [illegible] belong to [illegible] their [illegible] they obtained an advance [illegible]

[illegible] Labor League [illegible] evicted from [illegible] swinging frames [illegible] sashes.

POVERTY is a [illegible]

They say the world's a desert drear, still plagued with Egypt's blindness! [illegible] We demand [illegible] God of the Eight [illegible] "winding"—the only remedy is to plane [illegible]

BROTHERHOOD NOTES.

—Union No. 15 of Indianapolis donated 0 to the Ohio river flood sufferers.

—On February 24, Union No. 14 of St. uis held a very successful ball at Apollo ill.

—Trenton Union No. 31 is growing and ows signs of good promise for the ring.

—St. Louis Union No. 6 now meets at E. corner 5th street and Morgan every turday evening.

—Carpenters' Union No. 39, of Rush- lle, Indiana, has been granted a charter. ork brisk in Rushville; wages low.

—Union No. 40 has been formed in Mem- is, Tenn., and Union No. 41 is under y in Morris, Minnesota. And so the od work goes on.

—The wood working machinists of To- nto have a union, and they propose to nnect themselves with the Brotherhood. e bid them a hearty welcome.

—Bro. Geo. G. Newberry, of St. Louis ion No. 6, who fell some time ago and oke his ankle, is now on his feet again, d has resumed his duties as Recording cretary of Union No. 6.

—Carpenters' Union No. 33, of Boston, s adopted a sick benefit of $2.50 per ek for those who are six months in mem- rship, and $5 per week for those twelve onths; the benefit to extend thirteen eks.

—The dues of each local Union should at least 50 cents per month. This cheap hn kind of unionism that asks only 15 25 cents a month does not bind men to e union. High dues means larger bene- s and funds to pay them.

—St. Catherine Union No. 38, has a rong membership, and prospects of ubling it this month. Carpenters come om villages three or four miles distant attend the meetings. This shows the ry spirit which is bound to win.

LECTURES ON LABOR.

V.

FRIENDS.—We considered labor from e physical side of the question only. ut we must not overlook the fact that in- llectual faculties of men are engaged in roduction, and therefore to restrict the nsideration of labor to his mere physi- al capacities, would be to ignore his men- al power, which plays, perhaps a much reater part in production than even phy- cal power.

We may say that labor is the expression f the sum total of all the forces, physical, ntellectual and moral, which are centered n man and which result in production. roduction is the result of labor.

Above all other animals, man is born eeble and without the power to secure hose things which are indispensable to is preservation, as well as to the satis- action of his wants.

But he is born with hands and with in- elligence; that is, with the faculty to cre- te all he wants.

It is labor that procures him shelter, ood and raiment. It is labor that has uilt cities, canals, railroads, steamships and telegraphs.

It is to labor that man owes the discov- ry of the forces and the laws of nature; he invention of machinery, which enables im to utilize these forces, and even to ubjugate the elements.

Labor is so essential to life that if men ease to employ their time in useful em- ployment they are driven to expend their ctivity in brutal orgies, vice and degra- dation.

All wealth, all riches, are the product f labor. Nature grows and ripens the ruit upon the trees, and yet they must be athered before they become useful. The ery act of gathering is labor, and no one an enjoy the useful properties of fruit, no [illegible]

[illegible] a union man, but in [illegible]

The water which flows in the river can- not be utilized until labor has been ex- pended, in order to bring it to the spot where it is required for use.

Therefore, upon such things as nature has furnished in the most complete form, labor in some degree must be expended in order to give to it its full sum of utility.

The products of the land must be supple- mented by labor before a thing is suffici- ently useful to be ready for consumption.

The forces of nature, aided by the land, produce the wool on the back of the sheep. In the raw state it is practically useless to man; but when it is spun, woven and man- ufactured into garments it becomes of the greatest utility to him, and it is labor, and labor alone, which gives this utility. But in its passage from its primitive condition of wool to its ultimate condition of a gar- ment, it has passed through a numerous series of manipulations, in which have been employed tools, implements and ma- chinery, which are the result of centuries of discovery, invention and perfection. This machinery itself represents an incal- culable amount of labor, both mental and physical, which past generations have performed.

Labor, then, is the application of our strength and our intelligence upon the ma- terials which are furnished by nature.

It does not create wood, stone nor metals; it only fashions them, gives them shape and utility. It does not create or invent steam or electricity, it only dis- covers and applies them. It does not cause the grains nor the fruits to grow— it merely aids the productive forces of the land.

It would, perhaps, be proper to recog- nize only one industry. To give shape to a stone or to give shape to the intelligence of a human being, are analogous opera- tions, in each case we apply our strength and intelligence to modify things which are already in existence, but in no case are the materials upon which labor is ex- ercised created by that labor.

Men should, before all other things, know how to labor, how to produce. Scien- tific and professional education should be accessible to all. Any state of society which condemns a portion of its population to ignorance and misery, commits an act of suicide.

The more theoretical and practical knowledge a man has, the more can he contribute to the progress of industry, science and art. In a word the greater is his power of production. Such a man is useful to society, while the ignorant and degraded are a burden to themselves and to the community.

There are, unfortunately, certain periods in which men, however well disposed to produce, are not able to apply their power by reason of causes brought about by panics, etc., similar to the one which brought about such vast suffering in 1873.

Since we see that man exercises his ac- tivity upon a fund furnished by nature, and which is common to all, since it is not of human creation, it should be accessi- ble to all; consequently, the land and all the natural agents should not be unjustly monopolized by the few, but should be in the possession of those who increase, through their agency, the wealth of the world and the comforts of society.

The word "Labor" is so diversely under- stood that when the workers speak of it the capitalists will persist in giving to the term certain significations which we do not intend to convey, and which we do not ever imply. It will, therefore, greatly aid our cause when we can insure a definite in- terpretation of the word, and when we say labor, I think we mean the applica- tion of man's powers (his physical, mental and moral powers combined), to the pro- duction of something which administers to the wants or increases the [illegible] ity, or, the [illegible] would defra- [illegible]

called into play by the performance of la- bor. A little reflection will convince us that they are. Were it not so we should not see people labor to produce that which they, themselves, cannot live to enjoy.

We have seen old farmers at the age of seventy-five years, and who expected to die from season to season, carefully plant- ing, budding and grafting fruit trees, the fruits from which to a moral certainty, they never expected to enjoy; they had no children or grandchildren, neither kith nor kin, nor were they compelled to do so from want; they had all [illegible] hoped for, and yet they lab[illegible] cently gave as a reason for [illegible] the impossibility of reaping [illegible] results of their labor wa[illegible] them, that "future generati[illegible] joy them."

There are those who deny [illegible] faculties are in any way stim[illegible] junction with labor; to such I [illegible] consider well, ere you deny it. [illegible] Humphrey Davy think as [illegible] not he should be paid for h[illegible] he applied himself to the [illegible] the safety lamp, etc.

He was prompted by his m[illegible] to save the lives of the [illegible] slaughtered miners. Consid[illegible] and you will find innumera[illegible] The great base of human na[illegible] did and selfish—it is only th[illegible] social pyramid which is g[illegible] the greed of gold.

* * * *

When the silk-producing [illegible] France were threatened with [illegible] by a disease which attacked t[illegible] Pasteur, the celebrated Fre[illegible] gave his skill, knowledge, ge[illegible] bor to the discovery of the [illegible] their remedy. He worked wi[illegible] or hope of reward or gain. [illegible] were prompted solely by his [illegible]

He saw the [illegible] and [illegible] the destruction of the [illegible] caused, and would further [illegible] homes of thousands of the F[illegible] antry; the sight of that mis[illegible] heart bleed, and with that lov[illegible] ocity which can be awakened [illegible] finer examples of human na[illegible] to the rescue, prompted by a [illegible] of humanity. His patient [illegible] labors were crowned with suc[illegible] stands to-day, as he ever wi[illegible] evidence that morality is a f[illegible] sum of labor

"One touch of nature makes the who[illegible]

The same may be said of [illegible] who labored so earnestly in th[illegible] of antiseptics while engaged [illegible] hospitals of Paris.

All men are not prophets i[illegible] land, it is true; and the value [illegible] were unrecognized, even by th[illegible] until, having been practiced w[illegible] in the hospitals of London, [illegible] was recognized in Paris in the [illegible] ing.

While pursuing the experim[illegible] sary to the discovery of the an[illegible] mind was never, for a momen[illegible] pied as to whether reward or [illegible] follow; he never once asked [illegible] selfish question, "Will it pay?"

To deny that the moral fa[illegible] called into play in the performa[illegible] bor is to restrict the idea of lab[illegible] ulous limits, and we claim th[illegible] moral as well as mental and [illegible] labor.

It is necessary to take into [illegible] tion the difference between usef[illegible] less labor. The banker, the broke[illegible] us that they work very hard. [illegible] But is it useful labor? The burg[illegible] hard to rob a house; a whole gal[illegible] will work very hard, both ph[illegible] the carpenter does, and mentall[illegible] the bank[illegible] the landlord, or the [illegible] and [illegible] [illegible] building

felter labors both mentally and physically to manufacture and pass counterfeit coin; yet this is all useless labor, nay, worse than useless, so says the banker. Certainly so, Mr. Banker, we workingmen admit that. But we also conceive that when you receive a bill drawn upon goods which never existed, from one of your confederates, and when you endorse that commercial bill and get it discounted, that your labor in so doing is useless, worse than useless, as you say. In fact, we look upon it as a counterfeit, which it is, and we demand that if the law (misnamed justice), punishes the one by state prison for his useless labor, that the law should also punish you, Mr. Banker, for *your* useless labor. It is this difference between useful and useless labor which makes the difference between misery and prosperity, for if all who are now engaged in working hard at that which is useless, were to expend the same amount of labor in producing that which is useful, there would be less of poverty and of want; and when we speak of the "organization of labor," we imply a correct and good use of all the forces which are now expended partially in an incorrect and improper manner. As an illustration of non-productive labor, I have visited prisons, arsenals, etc., where prisoners have been condemned to hard labor, and I have seen them under the superintendence of a paid overseer move a pile of building stones from one position to another, and then replace them in the original position. I have seen the same thing done in another prison with a pile of cannon balls.

Here is an example of the good sense of so-called government, and an illustration of the "majesty of the law!" If self-conceited jurists cannot distinguish between useful and useless labor, let us not, as workingmen, follow in the footsteps of their blind and fossilized errors, and expend our forces upon that which is useless.

It would perhaps be well to consider before closing with the element "Labor," the difference which we make, or rather the distinction which we draw between labor and drudgery.

It has been shown that the food which we consume generates nervous and muscular force, which, if not expended, renders the body fretful and uneasy. This expending or giving off of, this superabundant force, when applied to that which is useful, constitutes labor.

To a properly educated and well-balanced person this labor is a pleasure, because it contributes towards keeping the body in health and renders life enjoyable. But when this force is once fully expended, and repose and food are necessary to recuperate the totally expended strength, to continue to labor at the same kind of employment is at first irksome, it next becomes painful, and eventually it becomes insupportable, and at this point ceases to be labor, and is, in fact—drudgery.

There are two things which will destroy men and nations—Drudgery and Idleness. The drudges overworked and underfed, the idlers overfed and underworked; rickets and phlegm among the workers, scrofula and gout among the idlers.

Every advanced industrial nation has these two cobras stinging it at each extremity.

England, which claims to be the first in the race, presents more pointed evidence of this than any other nation. The decline in the physical development of the industrial population in her manufacturing districts is evident, even to the casual observer; as is also the low maudling examples of the effete and scrofula-eaten portion of her aristocracy.

Nothing but the labor of a nation can secure its greatness, its progress and its continuity; the preservation [illegible]

of statesmen at the direction of affairs. Unfortunately nations have nothing better than politicians to direct them.

Under our present system of industry, to speak of avoiding drudgery may appear far too Utopian, but we may profitably look upon such a possibility in the far future, and by keeping the possibility in sight, work for the means which will enable us to avoid drudgery.

It is a well recognized fact that there is a point beyond which it is not profitable to continue labor, and that if it be continued beyond that point it ceases to give a remunerative result.

The statistical investigations which the present factory system of industry so greatly facilitates, will no doubt lead to a knowledge of what those limits really are in the various industries.

Unfortunately, the "right of private property," steps in and prevents the state from collecting such information as would lead to a positive knowledge of certain industrial phenomena, for manufacturers will not permit the labor bureaus of the States to look into their factories and their books, and by comparing them arrive at results. Such little, however, as is known, demonstrates certain facts.

In factories (cotton) where the operatives have worked thirteen hours a day, it has been found that all the fabrics woven during the last hour were not so good as those woven during the previous hour, and that a loss occurred from the imperfection of the work done.

Here, then, is one fact which demonstrates that there is a limit to the powers of labor, but it does not demonstrate what that limit is.

Some time ago in the public offices at Washington, where the work of the clerks is calculating and adding figures, it was discovered that the errors made during the last hour of their work, took more than an hour to correct on the following day. Here, then, is another confirmation of the fact that labor may be prolonged beyond a profitable point, and our effort should be to ascertain what that point is in all industries and in all kinds of labor.

We see plainly that it applies to mental labor equally as well as to physical labor. The weaver's labor may be classed as physical, the clerk's as mental labor, and neither of them can be carried on beyond a certain point without becoming drudgery.

It would be interesting to follow the subject farther and see the result which labor and drudgery have upon the human frame and the human mind; how the one ennobles a man—how the other degrades him.

It would, however, not be to our purpose here. It is sufficient that we have called attention to the fact, for it must not be ommitted when we treat of the element "Labor."

It is upon the integral development of the moral, mental, and physical faculties of mankind that progress—the development of the race—depends.

We hope that it has been made clear that land and labor are naturally the two first elements of production.—Brutus.

Der Carpenter.

New York, April 1883.

Correspondenz aus Chicago.

Die deutschen Zweige Nr. 2 und 7 der Local-Union Nr. 21 von Chicago, der Bruderschaft der Bauschreiner von Amerika, sind dahin übereingekommen, fortan jeden Monat einen Artikel an die „Carpenter-Zeitung" einzuschicken, um den deutschen Brüdern und Kameraden, welche der englischen Schrift und Sprache noch unkundig sind (und solcher haben wir in Chicago allein nicht wenige) etwas mehr deutschen Lesestoff bieten zu können. Möge unser Unternehmen von jedem deutschen Carpenter und Schreiner [illegible] unterstützt [illegible] Vollständiges erzielen. Daß unsere deutschen Kameraden in Chicago bald anfangen einzusehen, daß es sich mit der Union nicht gerade um etwas ganz Gewöhnliches, wie z. B. um „einen Korb saurer Aepfel" handelt, beweist die Thatsache, daß Zweig Nr. 2, welcher im verflossenen Frühjahre circa 70 Mitglieder zählte, bis jetzt auf beinahe 2?0 angewachsen ist. Dasselbe Verhältniß ergiebt sich bei Zweig Nr. 7: derselbe löste sich im vorigen Frühjahr von dem englischen Zweige Nr. 3 mit 1? Mann ab und gründete den Zweig Nr. 7: derselbe zählt jetzt beinahe 100 Mitglieder. Erfreulich ist es zwar, selbiges unseren Brüdern mittheilen zu können, aber so lange wir nicht die Majorität in unserer Organisation haben, läuft der Eine oder Andere Gefahr, daß es ihm mit seinem Carpenter-Handwerk geht, wie es vor kurzer Zeit einem gewissen Bildhauer, Heinrich Witt mit Namen, ergangen ist. Derselbe arbeitete für John Moore & Co., an Desplaines und Fulton Str. Er hatte auf Stückarbeit $2.35 verdient, am Zahltag gab es aber nur $2 mit dem Bemerken, daß dieses genug für 8 stündige Arbeitszeit sei.

Das Comite.

Arbeitslosigkeit.

Am vergangenen Donnerstag fand hier eine Arbeiter-Massen-Versammlung statt, wo P. Grottkau ein Referat über die Ursache der zunehmenden Arbeitslosigkeit hielt. Redner sagte: Die Ursache der zunehmenden Arbeitslosigkeit liege in der Trennung der Arbeitsmittel von der Arbeit. Wir finden in der heutigen Gesellschaft zwei Klassen. Die eine dieser Klassen, und zwar die minder zahlreiche, sei im Privatbesitz des Grund und Bodens, der Maschinen, der Rohstoffe, der Communikationsmittel, kurzum im Besitz aller jener Güter, welche zur Erzeugung neuer Güter resp. zur Arbeit erforderlich sind. Die andere Klasse, und zwar die bei weitem zahlreichere, sei besitzlos, sie lebe aus der Hand in den Mund; sie habe nichts zur Verfügung als ihre Arbeitskraft. Die besitzende Klasse arbeite selbst nicht, sondern sie stelle nur die Besitzlosen zur Arbeit an. Die Besitzlosen erhalten für ihre Arbeit, unter dem Namen Lohn, nur einen Theil des Werthes, den ihre Arbeit erzeugt. Dieser Theil ist aber von den Besitzenden so knapp berechnet und bemessen, daß er kaum ausreicht, die Arbeitenden vor dem Verhungern während der Arbeit zu schützen.

Redner erwähnt unter anderm, die Arbeitslosigkeit in der Gegenwart entspringe nämlich aus dem Uebel der Ausbeutung der Masse durch die Besitzer der Arbeitsmittel. Weil die Masse noch nicht einmal die Hälfte des durch ihre Arbeit erzeugten Neuwerthes erhält, deshalb kann sie für die gesammte Summe ihres Lohnes auch nicht die Hälfte der erzeugten Güter zurück kaufen. So verschwenderisch nun auch das Nichtsthuer-Gesindel lebt, so kann es vermöge seiner geringen Zahl doch nicht alle erzeugten und dem arbeitenden Volke abgenommenen Güter selbst consumiren. Diese Güter häufen sich in den Speichern, Magazinen und Läden an; die Armuth der Ausgebeuteten macht es diesen unmöglich, die Dinge, nach denen sie allerdings Verlangen haben, zu kaufen, und die Geschäftsstockung mit ihrer Arbeiterentlassung ist fertig. Die Ausbeuter haben die Früchte der Arbeit der Ausgebeuteten aufgespeichert, der zu große Fleiß der Ausgebeuteten macht sie also arbeitslos. Dieser Zustand ist wahnsinnig, weil total vernunftwidrig. Und es ist auch nicht zu hoffen, daß er jemals beseitigt wird, wenn das betrogene arbeitende Volk ihn nicht selbst beseitigt.

Als Linderungsmittel gegen die Arbeitslosigkeit giebt es nur Verkürzung der Arbeitszeit, Beseitigung der Kinderarbeit und eine starke Beschränkung der Frauenarbeit. Um dieses zu bewerkstelligen, dürfen die Arbeiter bei irgend einer Wahl, überhaupt bei irgend einer Legislaturwahl, die Hände nicht müßig in den Schooß legen und mit zusehen, sondern selber Hand ans Werk legen, um Leute in den gesetzgebenden Körper zu schicken, die Willens sind, mit aller Kraft für die Interessen der Arbeiter einzuschreiten und zu wirken.

Als radikales Heilmittel gegen Arbeitslosigkeit und Uebervortheilung durch Ausbeuter gibt es nur die Beseitigung des Ausbeutungssystems überhaupt, indem die gesammten Arbeitsmittel und das Land für gemeinschaftliches Eigenthum erklärt und die bisherigen Faulenzer zur Arbeit angehalten werden, und wenn sie nicht arbeiten wollen, ihnen nichts zu essen gegeben wird.

Diese große, nothwendige Aenderung der gesellschaftlichen Einrichtung kann nur durch die arbeitende, bisher ausgebeutete Klasse herbeigeführt werden.

Da der Einzelne zu schwach ist, irgend etwas Bedeutendes zu vermögen, so ist die Organisation der Interessirten nothwendig. Organisation gibt Macht. Was den Ausgebeuteten fehlt ist nur Macht. Deshalb organisirten wir uns, um die alte, vernunftwidrige, brutale, ungerechte, niederträchtige, culturfeindliche Ausbeuter-Ordnung zu vernichten und an ihrer Stelle eine freie und gerechte Gesellschaft zu etabliren, [illegible] Redners in dieser Beziehung wollen wir hier nicht weiter eingehen.

Chicago, Ill.

Das Comite von Union Nr. 21.

Berlin, März 10, 1883.

Der geehrten Redaction von „The Carpenter."

Am 3. December 1882 ernannten die Zimmerleute Berlins eine Commission und beauftragten dieselbe mit der Regulirung der Lohn- und Arbeitsverhältnisse für das Jahr 1883.

Diese Kommission trat Ende December mit der Forderung eines Minimal-Lohnes von pr. Tag Summa 4 „vier Mark" vom 15. März cr. ab zunächst an die Innung „Bund der Bau-, Maurer- und Zimmermeister zu Berlin" heran. Dieselbe erkennt laut Zuschrift des Vorstandes vom 15. Januar cr. vollständig die Unzulänglichkeit des bis jetzt gezahlten Lohnsatzes an, glaubt jedoch, wie im Jahre 1881, als nicht maßgebend auch nicht bestreiten zu können; und dürfte somit die Zeit hingezogen werden, um unsere Forderung resp. Stellungnahme zu vereiteln und abzuschwächen durch Organisirung der Arbeitgeber, durch Vorkehrungen und Vorsichtsmaßregeln betreffs der übernommenen Arbeiten, durch Heranziehen von Massen-Arbeitskräften aus den Provinzen, kleinen Städten ic., um dann zur geeigneten Zeit einen Gegendruck auf die Gesellen-Bewegung ausüben zu können und deren Forderungen abweisen, event. für spätere bessere Zeiten unter dem bescheidenen Vorwande zu verweisen, daß die Verhältnisse eine Lohnerhöhung nicht gestatten.

Obwohl wir den guten Willen unserer Meister und Arbeitgeber nicht ableugnen und verkennen wollen, sind wir doch moralisch gezwungen, die größtmöglichste Vorsicht zu beobachten, um nicht im entscheidenden Augenblick unvorbereitet und rathlos, entblößt von moralischer und pekuniärer Unterstützung dazustehen und mit unserer, durch die ungünstigen gesellschaftlichen Zustände, die wohl Niemand abzuleugnen vermag, uns aufgezwungenen, sowie auch berechtigten, mäßigen Forderung Fiasco zu machen.

Die Schilderung unserer bedrängten Lage dürfte wohl jeder Handwerker, resp. Arbeiter aus eigener resp. allgemeiner Erfahrung zu beurtheilen in der Lage sein, umsomehr, da der Bauhandwerker durch die Winterjahreszeit periodisch zur Arbeitslosigkeit verurtheilt, die traurige Lage desselben begründet und eine Selbsthülfe daher für uns unmöglich ist.

In Anbetracht dessen sehen wir uns genöthigt, an alle Kameraden und Brüder der Arbeit mit der Bitte behufs einer moralischen und pekuniären Hülfe für die von der Arbeit ausgeschlossenen Zimmerleute vorzusprechen, sollen wir energisch unsere Forderung durchsetzen.

Im solidarischen Interesse für die Berliner Zimmerleute J. A.: Marzian.

Sollte uns diese Forderung nicht gestattet werden auf gütigem Wege, dann treten wir im Falle eines Strikes mit der Forderung des neunstündigen Normal-Arbeitstages heran.

Vereinigung ist Macht!

Klassenbewußtsein, Zusammengehörigkeitsgefühl muß unsere Brust beseelen, Proletarier, denn einzeln sind wir nichts, vereinigt Alles! Der Geldsack kennt seine Interessen, vereinigt tritt die Ausbeuterzunft für dieselben gegen uns Arbeiter ein, und wir sollten kurzsichtig Gewehr bei Fuß zusehen, wie ein Theil unserer Brüder vom Geldsack bedrängt wird? Nie und nimmermehr, Genossen! Zeigen wir der beutehungrigen Ausbeutersippe, daß unsere Erkenntniß gewachsen und daß wir uns als Ganzes fühlen, daß wir den Ruf: „Proletarier aller Länder vereinigt Euch!" begriffen und beherzigt haben.

Arbeiter! Wer will uns widerstehen, wenn wir ohne Unterschied des Berufs und der Nationalität gemeinsam unser übereinstimmendes Interesse wahren? Niemand! Wohin gelangen wir, wenn wir nicht einig, als Klasse vorgehen? An den Bettelstab, zu noch schamloserer Ausbeutung, als sie heute existirt!

Die Befreiung der Arbeiter muß durch die Arbeiterklasse selbst geschehen, es kommt uns kein Messias von Oben! Wohlan denn, Proletarier, vorwärts zur Bethätigung als Klasse! Zögern bringt uns Verderben, Kleinmuth vermehrte Knechtschaft! Die Macht, welche Berge durchbohren, reißenden Strömen ihr Bett weisen kann, welche der Natur die Schätze abringt und alle Werthe schafft, diese Macht sollte auch im Stande sein, sich selbst zu schützen, sich gegen end- und gewissenlose Ausbeutung zu wehren. Doch wo keine Vereinigung ist, ist auch keine Macht, kein Recht und kein Erfolg!

(Arbeiter-Stimme.)

— Die [illegible], welche die [illegible] von [illegible] [illegible] erzielt, hat [illegible]

[illegible]

Literarisches.

Ferd. Lassalle's Reden und Schriften.

Verlag von Wolff und Höhne, 330 E. 4. St., New York.

„Möge, wenn ich beseitigt werde, irgend ein Rächer und Nachfolger aus meinen Gebeinen erstehen!"

Die von uns zum Motto erwählten Worte waren es, die Ferd. Lassalle in seiner Ronsdorfer Rede den Tausenden von Arbeitern zurief, in Vorahnung seines tragischen Lebensendes; und wenn je ein prophetisches Wort in geradezu überwältigender Weise in Erfüllung ging, so war es die oben aufgegriffene Sentenz. — Wohl ist der treue Kämpfer nun bald 20 Jahre im Schooß der Erde, seine heroische Gestalt ist in das All aufgegangen und der feurige Hauch seiner Worte entflammt nicht mehr, wie einstens, die Herzen seiner Jünger, aber trotzdem sind seine Grundsätze und seine erhabenen Lehren von der Gleichberechtigung alles dessen, was Menschenantlitz trägt, für uns erhalten geblieben, — zahlreiche Rächer sind aus seinen Gebeinen erstanden und hinausgegangen in alle Welten, zu allen Völkern, und haben seine Lehren verbreitet unter den enterbten und entrechteten Menschenkindern. Zu Hunderttausenden sind seine Nachfolger angewachsen, und kaum wohl dürfte es einen gebildeten Arbeiter geben, der nicht mehr oder weniger von dem phänomenalen Geistesschatz Ferd. Lassalle's etwas profitirt hätte. — Immerhin aber hat die große Masse, das auf der Stufe tiefster menschlicher Knechtung stehende Proletariat, den Werken eines seiner begabtesten Anwälte noch nicht genügende Aufmerksamkeit geschenkt, resp. schenken können; einestheils sind ja hauptsächlich die traurigen ökonomischen Verhältnisse der Proletarier mit ein Hauptgrund, anderntheils aber darf nicht unbeachtet gelassen werden, daß die schriftstellerischen Arbeiten des großen Apostels der Freiheit bis vor kurzer Zeit in Folge verschiedener Umstände nicht vollständig zusammengestellt veröffentlicht wurden und die Beschaffung in Folge des Verbots derselben in verschiedenen Ländern mit außerordentlichen Schwierigkeiten verbunden war. Auch diesem Mißstande ist nun seit Jahresfrist abgeholfen. Das Verdienst, Lassalle's Reden und Schriften in richtiger Reihenfolge gesammelt und in wohlfeilen Lieferungen à 10 Cents dem [illegible] lenden Volke zugänglich gemacht zu ha[illegible] den obengenannten Verlegern zu. [illegible] Höhne, beide selbst schlichte Arbeiter, [illegible] nicht um ein Geldgeschäft als vielmehr [illegible] zu thun ist, ihren Mitarbeitern durch die Beschaffung einer solchen Lectüre die Mittel zur Bekämpfung des Alles unterdrückenden heutigen Gesellschaftssystems an die Hand zu geben, haben denn auch ihre Aufgabe richtig aufgefaßt, und liegt bereits der erste Band dieser Heiligen Schrift des Proletariats elegant ausgestattet mit dem Golddruckbildniß Lassalle's vor uns, während in nächster Zeit der zweite Band beendigt sein wird. Daß den Unternehmern bei solchem Wirken nicht unerhebliche Kosten entstehen, ist klar, und ist es Sache der Arbeiter, nun durch zahlreiches Abonnement der Vollendung dieses Werkes die nöthige Unterstützung angedeihen zu lassen, was um so leichter ist, als die Lieferungen je nach Wunsch wöchentlich oder alle 14 Tage bezogen werden können. — An jener Stelle, wo die alte verrottete Ausbeutergesellschaft ihre Bibel, Gebetbuch und und Tractätchen aufbewahrt, dort muß der Arbeiter seine Arbeiterschriften und nicht zum Mindesten Ferd. Lassalle's Reden und Schriften haben.

Das Ganze wird 4 Bände geben, und wird der Band elegant gebunden zum Preise von 1.75 von obiger Firma versandt.

Mitgefühl für Bruder John Mathiesen.

Da wir die traurige Kunde erhielten, daß Ihnen durch den Tod Ihre theure Gemahlin weggerafft wurde, so sei es im Namen der Carpenter Union No. 14,

Beschlossen, daß wir Ihnen unsere innigste Theilnahme an dem schweren und unersetzlichen Verlust durch den frühzeitigen Tod Ihrer geliebten Gattin hiermit kund thun.

Ist es ferner

Beschlossen, daß wir als Committee Ihnen unsere innigsten Mitgefühle durch diese Zuschrift mittheilen.

Und ferner sei es

Beschlossen, daß diese unsere Beschlüsse in dem „Carpenter" publicirt werden.

Das Committee: Joseph Weber, Johann Tawitzki, Johann Reinke.

St. Louis, Mo.

— In der Gesetzgebung von [illegible] ist ein Gesetz angenom[illegible] für Kinder [illegible]

Ein Wort über Recht und Unrecht.

Ich hörte neulich einen „Arbeiter" sagen: „Die organisirten Arbeiter verlangen mehr, als recht ist. Den Lohn um so und so viel erhöhen, oder die Arbeitszeit um zwei Stunden zu verkürzen; damit kann der Arbeitgeber nicht bestehen; der muß doch auch Etwas für seine Mühe und sein Risiko haben." Das ist aber ein großer Irrthum und eine ganz falsche Sentimentalität.

Der Vortheil der Arbeitgeber geht uns durchaus garnichts an. Wenn es sich für die Herren nicht mehr bezahlt, „Boß" zu sein, so laßt sie das Werkzeug in die Hand nehmen und selber arbeiten. Wenn die Arbeiter auf den Vortheil der Boße sehen wollen, so müssen sie für den denkbar niedrigsten Lohn die denkbar längste Zeit mit der größtmöglichen Anstrengung arbeiten; denn was darüber hinausgeht, geht von dem Vortheil der Boße ab. Und wenn dieselben bei einer Lohnreduktion nicht den vollen Unterschied in die eigene Tasche stecken, so haben sie das nur sich selbst und der Konkurrenz, die sie sich einander machen, zu danken. Von so sentimentalen Ansichten, daß die Arbeiter auch Etwas für ihre Arbeit haben müssen, um menschlich leben zu können, ist bei den Boßen verteufelt wenig zu spüren. Sie sagen einfach: Ich kann die Arbeit um soviel billiger gemacht bekommen, wollt ihr sie dafür machen — gut; wenn nicht — so nehme ich andere Leute, die es dafür thun. Ob ihr damit auskommt oder nicht, das ist nicht meine Sache. Und der Boß, der so spricht, hat von seinem Standpunkte aus, als Boß, ganz recht. Warum sollen wir Arbeiter es nun anders machen und nicht Alles fordern, was wir bekommen können?

Das Befinden der Boße geht uns doch nicht mehr an, als sie das unserige. Wenn wir uns um den Vortheil oder Nachtheil, den die Boße von unserem Thun haben konnten, bekümmern wollten, so wäre das gerade so, als wenn im Kriege die schwächere Partei einen Vortheil erringen könnte und sagte, nein, das thun wir nicht, denn das verursacht unserer Gegnern zu viel Schaden. Eine solche Krieg führende Partei hätte wegen ihrer Dummheit doch verdient, ganz vernichtet zu werden.

„Darum sollen uns Arbeiter nicht so [illegible]

„Macht ist Recht und Recht ist Macht."

Da nun die Kapitalisten faktisch im Besitze alles Rechtes sind, so sind sie demnach auch im Besitze fast aller Macht. Alles, was man durchsetzen kann, ist Recht, und Unrecht sind alle Forderungen, die man nicht nöthigenfalls erzwingen kann. Setzen die Boße es durch, daß die Arbeiter billiger arbeiten müssen, so haben sie Recht; setzen die Boße es aber nicht durch, so haben sie Unrecht. Zwingen die Arbeiter die Boße, mehr Lohn zu zahlen, so ist auch das ein Recht.

Mit dem übrigen Gefasel von Recht und Unrecht will man nur den Arbeitern Sand in die Augen streuen, damit dieselben den wahren Sachverhalt nicht sehen sollen, daß Macht Recht ist und Recht Macht; denn dann würde die Masse den Wenigen die Macht nehmen und mit dieser auch das Recht. Wenn die Kapitalisten die Macht nicht hätten, uns auszubeuten, so hätten sie auch kein Recht dazu. Die allgemeinen Rechtsanschauungen ändern sich mit den Machtverhältnissen und Unrecht ist nur, was denselben entgegen ist.

So war es im Jahre 1770 noch Recht, wenn England Amerika beherrschte; aber ein paar Jahre später, wie Amerika stärker wurde, schlug es sich frei — und das war auch Recht. Vor dem Bürgerkriege war es noch Recht, daß mit Menschen gehandelt wurde, wie mit Vieh, auf offenem Markte. Wollte Jemand das heute versuchen, so wäre es das größte Unrecht und derselbe könnte dafür streng bestraft werden. Heute ist es Recht, wenn die Kapitalisten und Monopolisten die Arbeiter so aussaugen, daß dieselben kaum nothdürftig das Leben fristen. Man nehme diesen Aussaugern die Macht — und sie haben ihr Recht verloren. Vor 30 Jahren war es noch Recht der Boße, die Arbeiter 14 bis 16 Stunden sich abrackern zu lassen; heute ist es ein Unrecht, selbst wenn einzelne Boße die Macht dazu hätten, denn im Allgemeinen haben sie die Macht nicht. So wäre es auch ein Unrecht, wenn die Arbeiter in einer Stadt den Lohn auf $10 per Tag festsetzen wollten, auch dann, wenn sie es für den Augenblick durchsetzen konnten; denn im Ganzen und Allgemeinen haben sie nicht die Macht dazu, und nur das, wozu im Allgemeinen die Macht ausreicht, ist Recht.

Aber Macht ist auch Recht, das sieht man deutlich an der Entstehung und Entwickelung der bürgerlichen Kapitalherrschaft, die in Amerika ja schon in einem ziemlich hohen Entwicklungsgrad [illegible] Europa eingeführt wurde und sich hier noch [illegible] als in Europa entfaltet. Im Anfange [illegible] Recht die große Mehrzahl, um den [illegible] unbeschränkte Alleinherrschaft zu [illegible] ein recht deutliches Beispiel bald- [illegible]

Städte, welche fortwährend im Kampfe mit dem Adel waren, bis sie zuletzt durch Ueberzahl und Reichthum sich und der besitzenden Klasse überhaupt die Mitherrschaft errangen. Es halfen dabei freilich noch viele Umstände, so z. B. die Erfindung des Pulvers und der Buchdruckerkunst; aber die Ueberzahl that doch das Meiste. Als dieselben zur Macht gelangt waren, machten sie natürlich Gesetze zu ihren eigenen Gunsten und fingen an, ihre Rechtsanschauungen dem Volke mit Gewalt aufzudrängen, bis sich dieselben so fest im Volke eingewurzelt hatten, daß es glaubte, jene Rechtsanschauung sei die einzig richtige. Nun konnte sich schon die Zahl der Machthaber verringern, was auch durch die Konkurrenz geschah, indem die minder Reichen und minder Schlauen den Reicheren und Schlaueren unterlagen, so daß die Zahl der Herrschenden heute eine sehr kleine ist und noch immer kleiner wird. Diese kleine Zahl kann nur noch durch das so hergestellte Recht über die große Masse des Volkes herrschen indem sie immer größere Reichthümer ergaunert und in die Hände Einzelner aufhäuft — auf Kosten des Volkes. Wenn es z. B. nach den heutigen Rechtsbegriffen kein Unrecht wäre, den Reichen ihren Besitz und damit die Macht zu nehmen, so möchte ich sehen, wie ein Vanderbilt oder Gould ihre Reichthümer vertheidigen wollten. Wir sehen also, daß Recht auch Macht ist.

Wenn sich die Arbeiter erst ihrer Macht, die in ihrer Zahl liegt, bewußt werden, so werden auch andere Gesetze gemacht und andere Zustände werden eintreten und dadurch auch die Ansichten über Recht und Unrecht ändern, aber nicht früher.

Um dieses Macht- und Rechtsbewußtsein unter den Arbeitern zu fördern, müssen wir bei allen Forderungen genau prüfen, ob wir sie durchsetzen können, und in solchem Falle auch Alles fordern, was zu erreichen ist. Haben wir das und können später mehr thun, so ist es dann Zeit, aber nicht früher, damit wir kein Unrecht begehen; aber auch nicht später, damit wir nicht unser Recht verlieren. Ein jedes Unrecht würde sich bitter an uns selber rächen.

St. Louis, Mo. J. W.

Die Arbeiterbewegung Deutschlands.

[illegible] Gewerbe[illegible] der An[illegible] Arbeitsbücher [illegible] ganz dazu [illegible] wirklichen Sklaven zu machen. Hiergegen haben besonders auch die Tischler durch ihre Fachvereine in zahlreichen Versammlungen energisch protestirt und zwar nicht ohne Erfolg.

Die Fachvereine der Tischler agitiren auch ganz besonders für die Abkürzung der Arbeitszeit, und wird in Hamburg in vielen Werkstellen 9½ Stunden täglich gearbeitet. Eine Petition an den Reichstag für Feststellung eines Normal-Arbeitstages erhielt in Hamburg 32,840 Unterschriften.

In einer kürzlich in Frankfurt a. M. abgehaltenen zahlreich besuchten Versammlung der dortigen Tischler wurde erklärt, daß man diese Petition, da sie nicht weitgehend genug sei, nicht unterstützen könne. Die Statistik habe ergeben, daß in Frankfurt von hundert Schreinern bei durchschnittlich 11stündiger Arbeitszeit beständig zehn außer Arbeit seien, weshalb man den 8stündigen Arbeitstag einführen müsse.

Carl Marx.

Die Nachricht vom Tode dieses Mannes wird mit tiefer Trauer empfunden werden, so weit es Arbeiter giebt, welche gegen die bestehenden drückenden Verhältnisse kämpfen. Er hat dem unterdrückten Arbeiterstande gezeigt, wo die Axt an die Wurzel der Uebel, unter welchen die Welt seufzt, gelegt werden muß. Die Arbeiter können diesem Manne ihre Dankbarkeit nicht besser bezeugen und sie können sein Andenken nicht besser ehren, als wenn sie seinem Rufe folgen, welcher lautet: „Arbeiter aller Länder, vereinigt Euch!" (Möbelarb. Journ.)

Besuchst Du die Versammlungen Deiner Union regelmäßig? Nimmst Du thätigen Antheil an den Verhandlungen derselben? Bezahlst Du Deine Steuern pünktlich? Wenn Du diese Fragen mit Ja beantworten kannst, dann hast Du ein Recht, die Handlungen der Union zu kritisiren; mußt Du sie aber mit Nein beantworten, dann hast Du kein Recht, Dich über das zu beschweren, was in den Versammlungen gethan wird. (Detroit Unionist.)

Um Eisen oder Stahl dauernd in Holz zu befestigen, also z. B. Thürpitzen im hölzernen Pfosten, tropft man in die vorgebohrte oder geschlagene Oeffnung des Holzes eine geringe Menge von einer starken Lösung salzsauren Ammoniaks (Salmiak). Diese Flüssigkeit erzeugt [illegible] da, wo sie mit dem Eisen oder Stahl in [illegible] rung [illegible] starke [illegible]

Klassifizirung der Vereins-Mitglieder.

Es giebt drei Klassen von Vereinsmitgliedern und es ist wahrlich keine schwierige Aufgabe für den Beobachter, diese drei Klassen zu bestimmen. Die erste Klasse besteht aus den intelligenten Mitgliedern des Vereins. Sie besuchen die Versammlungen, nehmen regen Antheil an Allem, was von Interesse für den Verein ist, sie lassen sich zu Beamten erwählen, bieten ihre Dienste als Komite-Mitglieder an und verrichten alle zur Aufrechterhaltung und zum Gedeihen des Vereins nothwendigen Arbeiten. Sie wissen in allen Vereinsangelegenheiten guten Bescheid; ohne sie könnte ein Verein gar nicht bestehen und da sie auch sich dessen vollauf bewußt sind, deshalb sind sie auch hochherzig genug, ihre Dienste der Sache zu widmen, da eine Auflösung des Vereins nicht nur ihnen selbst, sondern auch der Majorität der Mitglieder, welche die anderen beiden Klassen bildet, Schaden verursachen würde. Diesen Mitgliedern gebühren mit vollem Recht alle die Ehrenbezeugungen und Unterstützungen, über welche der Verein zu verfügen hat. Leider aber ist es nicht selten der Fall, daß diese braven Männer für all' ihre Mühe und Opfer nur Undank und Mißgunst ernten.

Die zweite Klasse möge als die „sorglose Menge" bezeichnet werden. Die zu dieser gehörenden Mitglieder sind nicht von Natur aus schlecht; sie würden es ungern sehen, daß der Verein nicht gedeihe oder gar sich auflöse, sie sind jedoch so bequem, daß sie nur ungern in jedem Monat einmal einige Abendstunden den Interessen des Vereins widmen. Sie statten wohl während des Jahres dem Vereinslokal ein- oder zweimal einen Besuch ab, um ihre „Beiträge" zu entrichten, sind aber stets sehr bereitwillig, sich aller anderen Pflichten und Obliegenheiten zu entledigen. Einer Vereinsversammlung beizuwohnen, verursacht ihnen „ungeheure" Mühe, und viel lieber würden sie statt dessen sich zu einer Partie „Skat" oder „Sechsundsechzig" niedersetzen. Werden sie aufgefordert, an einer monatlichen Versammlung Theil zu nehmen, dann ist es geradezu erstaunlich, was für Ausreden sie haben. Nicht allein allerhand „wichtige" Ereignisse in der Familie, auch imaginäre „Business"-Angelegenheiten, persönliche und „sehr [illegible] andere Verbindlichkeiten, die sich „un[illegible] [illegible] schieben lassen, u. dergl. m. werden [illegible] sich „drücken" zu können. [illegible] „so sehr beschäftigt", [illegible] Abend im Jahr zu ihrer [illegible] Und doch glauben sol[illegible] Vereinsmitglieder [illegible] es einige wenige — näm[illegible] gehörigen Männer giebt, [illegible] allen Pflichten und Obliegenheiten [illegible] und sie gelangen schließlich zu der Ueberzeugung, daß sie „ihrer" Pflicht vollständig Genüge geleistet haben, wenn sie regelmäßig ihre Beiträge bezahlen.

Der Rest oder die dritte Klasse rekrutirt sich aus der vorhergehenden. Für solche „Vereinsmitglieder" ist es eine wahre Qual, auch ihre Geldbeiträge dann einzuzahlen, wenn sie dazu aufgefordert werden. Sie gelangen zu der Ansicht, daß das Geld eigentlich viel angenehmer in Kneipen, Kegeln, Billard u. s. w. angelegt werden kann. Es ist daher auch nichts Seltenes, daß solche Mitglieder, falls sie auf wiederholte Aufforderungen hin ihre Geldbeiträge dennoch nicht einzahlen, aus dem Verein ausgestoßen werden. Nun, solche Leute mögen wohl einige Tage lang unangenehm hiervon berührt sein, schließlich sagen sie aber doch: „Was geb' ich darum!"

Es muß in der That befremdend erscheinen, daß, obgleich alle Vereinsmitglieder ein und dieselben Pflichten und Interessen haben, obgleich sie alle, je nachdem der Verein stark oder schwach ist, Vortheile oder Nachtheile genießen, dennoch zwei Drittel derselben auch nicht ein oder zwei Stunden im Monat ihrem eigenen Wohle widmen können.

Die drei Klassen können mit je einem Worte bezeichnet werden: 1. Intelligenz, 2. Eigenliebe, 3. Rohheit. Wer sich getroffen fühlt, möge sich das selbst zuschreiben. (Cigar Maker's Journal.)

Je weniger ein Arbeiter eines bestimmten Industriezweiges verdient, je länger er täglich arbeitet und je tiefer er in seiner Lebenshaltung gesunken ist, desto schwerer ist er für eine Gewerkschaft zu gewinnen, weil die unvernünftigste Selbstsucht seine Triebfeder ist. Daher kommt es, daß die Mitglieder der Gewerkschaften nicht nur bessere Arbeiter, sondern auch bessere Bürger sind, als jene, und sollten sich deshalb von jedem Gemeinwesen unterstützt und nicht chikanirt werden, wie es jetzt der Bundessenat der Setzer- und Druckergewerkschaft versucht, indem er anzuordnen beabsichtigt, daß in der Regierungsdruckerei auch Scabs beschäftigt werden sollen. Freilich, was ist von einer [illegible] schaft zu [illegible], deren Erwählung [illegible] der direkten [illegible]

CORRESPONDENCE.

ST. LOUIS, MO.—We have experienced a very severe Winter—one of the severest in many years. And the signs of an early Spring are not very promising. Men are walking around idle by the hundreds, and they begin now to think of coming into the union.

SAN FRANCISCO, Cal.—Everything favorable for Summer. We expect 9 hours a day after May 1st, and anticipate no trouble whatever in getting it. We expelled John Grace for violating Art. 9, Sec. 4, of our Constitution.

Chicago Matters.

CHICAGO, Ill.—Times are very dull for carpenters, and a great many men are out of work. Wages range all the way from $2 to $3 per day. Carpenters' Union No. 21 held a ball on March 28, which was a success in every sense. The prospects of work this coming season are pretty fair, but there will be no scarcity of men, for just as fair weather opens, carpenters then flock to the city from every point of the compass. Union No. 21 is in a healthy condition financially and numerically. We are carrying on the case of the widow Anderson, whose husband was a member of our union, and was killed by a falling scaffold through the negligence of his employers. Union No. 21 is ready to advance $2000 to aid the erection of the Workingmen's Hall in this city.

What Cincinnati is Doing.

CINCINNATI, O.—The floods of the Ohio river submerged the lower part of the city, and the consequence was everything was at a standstill the past month; no business, no work and countless numbers out of work; but the result has been that when the waters subsided, there was a rush of work, as many buildings were damaged by the flood. The outlook for the season is encouraging. If carpenters will only look out for their own interests and join Union No. 2, of this city, and if those who have left will come back and pay their dues, in order to make a strong union, the result will be an increase of wages this summer.

The stone-masons have asked an increase of 50 cents per day over last year's wages, which makes their wages $3.50 per day—one dollar a day more than carpenters are receiving. Why is this? Simply because they are well organized, every one of them belongs to the union, and they have a strong union to back them. Just as long as carpenters are backward in belonging to their organization, just that long they will receive low wages.

Home from Oakland.

OAKLAND, Cal. Union No 36 is improving: we have taken in a score of good members every week and still a good prospect ahead for us. There are a good many here who are on the "fence," and some who are afraid of their own shadow. Wages in Oakland are from $1.00—$3.50 per day and work is picking up very rapidly, but no great demand for carpenters. The cost of living in Oakland is in some regards more expensive than in San Francisco; the only thing that keeps our men here, is, because the most of them own a little property and some would like to sell if they would only get a chance. I would not advise any carpenter to come here for the present, for if we don't have rain soon there will be dull times this season.

Our Cleveland Letter.

CLEVELAND, O.—I am sorry to have to inform you that Bro. John Madden, a member in good standing almost since the first organization in this city of Union No. 11, died last Thursday night. He was buried on Sunday last, March 11th. Members of our union attended his funeral in a body. You, of course, will remember Bro. Madden, as he was our delegate to the Philadelphia Convention in August last and a good true union man of the right grit. We will miss his counsel in Union No. 11 very much. He leaves a widow who I think from what I can learn has not much means; he left some children also; he has been sick all of the past winter and the two hundred and fifty dollars death benefit [illegible] our deceased brother will be a great [illegible] to his widow.

We are initiating a few new members [illegible] along; it looks a little brighter for [illegible]

we find some of our old members that dropped off and left our union after the strike in April last now show a disposition to come back. Those who are pretty good workmen we will take back, but we have a good many marked that we would not take back if they wanted to come ever so bad, for the reason that they would injure us more than they would benefit us, they are poor mechanics and have no grit or backbone to stand up and assert their rights like men.

Something for All to Read.

INDIANAPOLIS, Ind.—Ask yourself: Has my union done its whole duty to its members and to the Brotherhood during the year that has past? Have its beneficiaries been promptly cared for; its business done in a business-like way; its reports promptly made, and all its machinery kept moving smoothly along? If not, why not? Who has been to blame? Have you been in your place every lodge-night when your presence was not imperatively required elsewhere? Have you been ready with the word of counsel and admonition, and thus aided the officers and your brethren in the discharge of their duties? These are questions which you must answer to your own conscience. Even though you decline to answer them affirmatively, you are, to a certain degree in proportion to your dereliction, responsible for whatever may not be just right in your union. If, in the past, you have been derelict, resolve now, as you read these lines, to be more faithful in future; do not refuse to work lest you may seem too forward, or perchance may, now and then, make some mistake. Better make a mistake, once a in while, than be an idler and a careless observer in the Lodge-room. Better for a time be censured for trying to run the union (what a childish charge!), than to let the union run itself, or not run at all. Time will remedy whatever of harm so puerile a charge as this may do you, and your brethren as they become infected with your interest and zeal will retract whatever of harsh judgment they may have passed upon you. Wake up, then, and help us all make 1883 the grandest year in the history of our Brotherhood!

Condition of Trade in Hamilton.

HAMILTON, Canada.—A statement was made in one of our city journals that carpenters wages for the coming season would be from $2 to $2.75 per day, causing a false impression to go forth. There is no doubt that it was put in for a purpose, as if we had let it go unchallenged undoubtedly our city would have been flooded with carpenters expecting to get $2.75 per day. We acted promptly in the matter and caused the following to be published in all the daily papers here.

THE CARPENTERS' UNION AND WAGES

A statement has appeared regarding carpenters' wages for the coming season which may be the cause of some uneasiness in the building trade of this city, and as we know not by what authority that statement was made, the members of local union No. 18, Brotherhood of Carpenters and Joiners of America, at our last regular meeting authorized me to make the following announcement as concerns our union.

1. That the standard wages for the coming season, we are determined, shall not be less than twenty cents per hour for union men.

2. We will not demand more than 20 cents per hour as the standard wages for union men for the coming season.

3. We will accept, and will expect our employers to give us a raise of wages, providing the state of trade will allow it.

4. We will discountenance any and all moves that are likely to cause uneasiness in the building trade in this city as far as our trade is concerned.

5. We propose that our employers work a little more in unison with us and each other so by so doing we would not have occasion to take the public into our confidence as we are now obliged to do, and they would also be able to pay better wages and leave themselves a larger margin of profits at the end of the season.

THOS HAYLEY, Cor. Sec'y.

MARCH 6th, 1883.

The standard union wages is $2.00 per day of 10 hours for union men. A few out of work, but all will be busy when the severe weather is passed. Board $3.50 to $4 per week with lodging. We are firmly established in Hamilton, and are growing slowly but surely. In our meetings the best of brotherly feeling prevails; an unkind word has not been spoken to each other for months past. We have as manly a lot of members as you could wish to associate with, always ready to help each other in difficulty and distress. Of course, there are some that are not very punctual in attendance at our meetings; this fault prevails, I would suppose, nearly everywhere, [illegible] rings and jealousies are unknown [illegible]

From the "Land of Cakes."

GLASGOW, Scotland.—It is of the utmost importance to the labor cause throughout the world that good feeling and fraternity should exist between the various unions, and I shall only be too glad if I can in any degree contribute to that result. Unionists have too much to do in their contests with non-unionists or blacks to waste time and energy in quarrelling with each other.

I have carefully looked over the copies of THE CARPENTER you sent me, and am highly pleased with the spirit, tone, and ability with which it is conducted.

Shipbuilding is still in a healthy state, and little prospects of falling off as yet, but housebuilding is still dull throughout Scotland, and no appearance of any great improvement. WILLIAM PATTERSON.

General Secretary of the Associated Carpenters and Joiners of Scotland.

Points of Interest From Detroit.

DETROIT, Mich. Some men want to know what Carpenters' Union No. 10 is going to do about wages this Spring. They seem to think a spasmodic effort every year is all a union is good for—to throw in 25 cents dues for one month, and expect a few to take all the abuse, while the others howl for a strike and stand in the shade and take all the benefits without any effort on their part. That is the class we have to deal with here. They are such a contented lot that while they have the name of a job, that's all they want. Trade is pretty good here; there are not many men out of work. Wages ranged from $1.50 to $2.25 this Winter. They would have been higher had the men joined Union No. 10 and helped it on. Quite a good bit of work will be done here this Spring. The new Post Office and Depot and some good houses are talked of. No doubt this will bring an influx from other cities. But men had better not come here, as wages are too low now.

Buffalo Building News.

BUFFALO.—The Bricklayers and Plasterers are preparing to demand nine hours and 50 cents a day more pay this Spring; the Stone-Cutters and Plumbers will join in the movement very likely. A certain boss builder who was brought to his senses last Spring by the work of the Carpenters' Union, lately said he would hire none but the poorest mechanics and charge an exorbitant price, and do nothing but day-work to show the public that our union compels him to pay the mechanic and botch the same wages. The Builders' Association had an election of officers this season, and elected the most bigotted and most heartless and overbearing set of fellows that could be chosen.

A New Civilization Wanted.

WASHINGTON, D. C.—The outlook in Washington is favorable for a good season. Union No. 1 has improved in many respects, though not in any great extent in attendance. But there seems to be a deeper interest manifested in discussing the best method of improving our condition. We have been debating for several weeks past the possible advantage of working less hours, its effect in increasing the demand and the wages.

The law of supply and demand is not a natural law, above the control of human will. The exchanges of commerce control it to a great extent, and why may we not use the same skill and foresight that has been shown in other occupations? Simply because we have not held together long enough to educate the selfish instincts of our own numbers in the value of investment of time to produce a certain result.

The practical value and necessity for shorter hours becomes more apparent each year as labor saving machinery improves. The exclusive use of machinery is granted to private individuals by laws protecting the inventor. But the economic question does it inure to the benefit of the masses, has never been fully considered. True, it cheapens the production, so also does it cheapen human energies and limits the power of many to gratify lawful desire, while the benefit is reaped by those who have already the power to more than gratify lawful desire who constitute a minority. Governments reduce taxation when there is shown an excess of income over expenditure, to relieve the burdens of that taxation. So also should society emancipate labor of its burdens, when the [illegible] tion is increased to such an ex[illegible] produce consequent idleness [illegible] in surplus. If society ignores th[illegible] and competition is intensified [illegible]

class follows another in its fall, who is left to guard capital from the raids of a pauper majority? If we are reduced to extreme poverty with our intelligence to understand where and how we have been robbed, will we not become extreme communists? We don't want any one to divide their wealth with us, but "by the eternal," we do want them to stop dividing ours among themselves under the cunning device of "regulating commerce"—granting public domain to railroads to develop the resources (of our pockets), and exemption of a class of property from taxation that ought to bear its just proportion. Besides many other enactments of a similar character all having for its object to make labor produce as much as human endurance will permit for the lowest amount of the coarsest fare possible. What for? To develop the resources of our country, we are told. Who, what is the country? The land, trees, &c.? For whose benefit? Why should we care a continental for developing a country that grinds our lives out to make luxuries that we don't enjoy? This Roman civilization is about played out, and the time to map out a new one seems close at hand.

The principle difficulty in establishing shorter hours lays in the selfish greed of our own numbers who are not willing to make any sacrifice of wages to accomplish this result. They rather expect to get it by a *strike* and preserve wages. Suppose it could be accomplished after one month's idleness, would we gain as much as if we accepted a reduction? One month's wages lost would be equal to the pay of one hour for 260 days a $3.00 per day, while by making the sacrifice ourselves, the increased demand would enable employers to demand better prices and consequently support our efforts. G. EDMONSTON.

In Memoriam.

On March 9, we lost one of our most active members—a man of conscience and spirit, one who was universally beloved by all his associates, for no better man ever lived than our lamented brother, John Madden. He was President of Cleveland Union No. 11 for several years, and we had the benefit of his mature counsel as a delegate to the Philadelphia convention. His illness lasted many months and at last he fell a victim to consumption. An old and respected citizen of Cleveland, his remains, were followed to the grave by an immense concourse of friends and relatives. Let us do the duty we owe his widow and orphans; let us pay the funeral benefit of $250 without delay.

CARPENTERS UNION NO 33.

Meets every Monday Evening at Caledonian Hall, 43 Eliot St., Boston, Mass.

Non-union men are cordially invited to come and join, and thus lend a hand to uplift our craft. Don't stand back like a coward and a slave! Come work in unity with us.

RICHARD CASSADY, Pres.

T. F. PARSHAM, Rec. Sec.

W. J. SHIELDS, Cor. Sec.

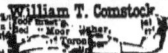

THE CARPENTER

A MONTHLY JOURNAL FOR CARPENTERS AND JOINERS.

VOLUME III. NEW YORK, MAY, 1883. NUMBER 5.

PREPARE MASS MEETINGS.

On May 20, General Secretary McGuire will start out on an extended trip throughout the United States and Canadas. His mission is to strengthen the unions wherever he goes and to organize new unions where they do not now exist. He will visit the following cities and address Carpenters Meetings:

NEW YORK. — Albany, Troy, Syracuse, Utica, Rochester, Buffalo, and Erie.

CANADA. — St. Catherines, Hamilton, Toronto and Guelph.

OHIO. — Columbus, Cincinnati, Dayton, Cleveland, Toledo and Sandusky.

INDIANA. — Indianapolis, Rushville and Evansville.

MICHIGAN. — Detroit, Lansing and Jackson.

ILLINOIS. — Chicago, and Kensington.

Also Milwaukee, Wis. — St. Louis Mo. — Louisville, Ky. — Wheeling, W. Va — Pittsburgh, Pa. — Washington, D. C. — Baltimore, Md. and Philadelphia, Pa.

Our friends in these cities will be informed by letter as to the date and arrangements. During the absence of the General Secretary from this city, his business will be attended to and all correspondence will be answered, so that the Brotherhood will still continue in working order.

TO PHILADELPHIA MEMBERS — Take notice that the address of the Secretary of Union 8. is W. F. Eberhardt, 2046 North 20th street, Philadelphia, Pa. He has removed from Cambridge Str.

EUROPEAN LABOR NEWS.

SWITZERLAND. Johann Philip Becker, the veteran economist and revolutionist recently celebrated his 75th birthday in Geneva, amid the congratulations of workingmen's societies all over Germany and Switzerland. His hair is as black and his step as vigorous to-day as it was 25 years ago. He played no small part in the revolution of 1848 against the German monarchy.

SPAIN. — The coach-painters of Madrid are on strike; they are well sustained by the other trades.

FRANCE. The metal workers are making preparations to hold a Congress for the purpose of combining all branches concerned in metal working. This will give France an organization similar to the Amalgamated Engineers of England.

STRIFE AMONG THE KNIGHTS OF LABOR.

In the daily press of this city and also in the *Irish World*, the following appears: Secretary Layton, of the Knights of Labor, has issued a circular calling District Master Workman Rankin to account for misrepresenting the work of the Order. He charges Rankin with stirring up strife and bringing discord into the ranks and allowing petty spite to enter into the official work of the district. Layton says the district is fast nearing the end of its usefulness under Rankin's management. Local assemblies have ceased to work and membership has fallen off over fifty per cent. Out of thousands of dollars spent the only good that has been done has been one victory of thirteen chainmakers at Beaver Falls. The circular causes much comment and excitement among the Knights of Labor. A prominent member of the Knights says the charges against Rankin are false and will ultimately result in Layton's removal. Grand Master Workman Powderly, of Scranton, has called a district meeting to be held in Pittsburg, at which the charges [illegible] discussed.

SHAVINGS AND CHIPS.

—Cigar makers have been making a general movement the past month to raise wages so as to obtain some of the benefits the manufacturers have obtained through a reduction in the internal revenue.

The Glass Workers National Union have distributed over $50,000 to their striking members in their present fight with their employers, and every cent of this has been raised in their own trade organization.

—We regret to chronicle the death of John G. Mills, late of Washington, D. C. and formerly of Philadelphia. He was a zealous worker in the Eight Hour movement and was deeply interested in the advancement of the working class.

— Furniture Workers Int. Union has a funeral fund that pays $250 on death of a member, and $100 on death of the wife of a member. None over 50 years of age are entitled to benefit. It is raised by taxing each member 25 cents on the event of a death.

—The State Legislatures of New York and of Wisconsin have passed Labor Bureau bills. The Wisconsin governor, like that of California and Missouri, has appointed a small *fry* politician. We await to see if Gov. Cleveland will do any better. Later.—And he has done no better.

— Union No. 46, of Guelph, Canada, has started with a large roll of members and has been granted a charter. The new union organized on March 16, and meets every second and fourth Friday. Initiation fee one dollar and monthly dues 30 cents. (The dues ought to be 50 cents; it will pay the members to have high dues.)

Gov. Crittenden has appointed a backwoods, "mossback" politician named H. A. Newman, to the office of Labor Commissioner in Missouri. And in plain violation of the law which says the commissioner shall be "some suitable person *identified with the labor interests*. This is the way Governors and politicians enforce labor laws.

The Executive Board of the Brotherhood in conjunction with the Trustees and General Secretary met in Philadelphia, April 25th, 1883. The books and accounts of Secretary McGuire were examined and found correct and in good order. Other business of an important nature was transacted which will be made known by private circulars to the unions.

CHICAGO BRICKLAYERS STRIKE.

Since the first of April, over 3,000 bricklayers have been on a strike in Chicago for $4.00 per day. Some of the bosses have granted the advance of fifty cents, but the bosses who are members of the Master Masons Association are a unit against the men and have resolved not to hire any union men. The men are firm and well organized and are well supported by all the trades. The carpenters donated $1,000 and the Plasterers $050 to assist the Bricklayers.

— The artists and decorators employed on the scenery for the coming music festival in Cincinnati, Ohio, struck recently in defence of their honor. The manager had said that they were drunkards, and worked too slowly. They did not return to work until the same manager furnished them a champagne supper and had withdrawn the insult.

NINE HOURS VICTORIOUS.

By telegram from San Francisco dated May 2, we are informed that the Carpenters of that city have gained their demand for nine hours as a days work, and full pay. Many firms granted the demand even in advance of the time, while the others seeing plainly that there was no possible chance to defeat the men yielded on May 1 so that a complete victory has been gained. Union 22 is worthy all praise for the noble work she has accomplished and after her will now follow Oakland and San Rafael. The movement has spread all along the Pacific Coast, and will embrace Sacramento, Portland etc., so that the general adoption of the nine hour system will be the rule before long. Last Fall the carpenters in these cities established the eight hour system on Saturdays. This rule will remain in force.

One fact must be remembered that the success of this movement in a great measure is due to the patience, moderation, restless activity and untiring devotion of Brother Edward Owens. His vigorous pen was freely used until the entire press of the city was ranged on the side of the movement, and in all his efforts he was ably seconded by all the brave workers of Union 22. The architects were enlisted in support of the agitation and their organ — *The California Architect* rendered every service in aid of the cause. Mass meeting after mass meeting was held and "No Surrender" was the unanimous cry of the men. Conferences with the bosses took place and all was done to convince the public that nine hours as a day's work was no more than just and reasonable. So well was the campaign conducted that non-union men were as enthusiastic as union men. And the result is a sweeping victory all along the line. The arrangement now is that the men will go to work at 7.30 A. M. and quit 5.30 P. M.

Now one word of advice to carpenters everywhere. We say to you keep away from San Francisco for some time to come, or if you go there you will only reduce wages and bring the men back to ten hours slavery. No doubt glowing inducements will be sent broadcast, as in former years advising men to go on to San Francisco that there they can get four or five dollars a day and plenty of work. Whenever you see such report stamp it as a lie! It is intended simply to flood the labor market of the Pacific Coast and thus cut wages to $1.50 per day. There are enough men there now for all the work. And when more are wanted we will tell you. Stay where you are and fight for nine hours at home!

THE STRIKE IN NEW YORK.

In a mass meeting of the trade held on April 12, the carpenters of this city resolved to strike on the following Monday for the same demands they made last year, viz.: $3.50 per day; double pay for overtime and legal holidays; eight hours as a full day on Saturdays, and that when sent to work out of the city the employer should pay their expenses. At this meeting the "Lumping" system or piece work was denounced. One of the speakers, S. Gompers, remarked that it was a strange proceeding that they should have to strike again to carry out the same demands they obtained last season. He recommended they should join the Brotherhood and no longer work as an isolated union. On April 16, the date appointed, the men struck against all bosses, [illegible] the union terms, and the abolition of [illegible] strike was [illegible] employers and [illegible] ing union men, [illegible] of capital and la[illegible] employing [illegible]. And a universal [illegible] labor and capital [illegible] and more [illegible]

TRADE NOTES.

—Work in Florida is very dull and the weather warm.

—Stair Builders of New York [illegible] to move for higher wages.

—Marble Cutters of Phila[illegible] mand nine hours as a day's [illegible] cents a day more pay.

Carpenters get from $1.[illegible] Indianapolis, Ind., and from [illegible] per hour in Morris, Minn.

The Iron Molders' [illegible] Union pays $100 death benefit on [illegible] cease of a member.

—John Young, President of [illegible] Molders' Union of Schenectady, [illegible] has been elected Mayor of that [illegible] large majority.

—Carpenters at Waterville [illegible] Utica, N. Y., after a short strike [illegible] cured an advance of 25 cents a [illegible] this season. They now get $2.[illegible]

—Building is reported to be [illegible] the South, and the planing mills [illegible] respondingly busy. Wages for [illegible] in the Southern States range from [illegible] $2.75 per day. In most instan[illegible] the rule.

—The carpenters of Jersey C[illegible] on April 23, demanded an inc[illegible] $2.75 to $3 per day, and got it in [illegible] cases after a few days trouble. [illegible] carpenters are also agitating for [illegible] advance as the Jersey City men.

The Detroit Stone Cutters struck [illegible] for nine hours as a day's work, with [illegible] ent pay. After a day's idleness the [illegible] ter was settled by the men agreeing [illegible] work 10 hours a day to May 1, when [illegible] pay is to be $3 for 9 hours.

—The *Journeyman Builder*, organ [illegible] Bricklayers National Union, says [illegible] latest issue;

> The Brotherhood of Carpenters are turning [illegible] attention strongly toward a reduction of the [illegible] of labor, instead of demanding higher wages, [illegible] go hand in hand with them.

$20,000 have been paid out in [illegible] benefits by the Iron Moulder's [illegible] tional Union during the last four [illegible] and yet that body has thousands of [illegible] lars in its treasury. And this has all [illegible] done through high dues and wid[illegible] organization. Surely this does [illegible] as if *Trades Unions are failures!*

—On April 1, the carpenters of [illegible] N. Y., struck for $3 a day—an advance of 50 cents. After two weeks struggle the men compromised on $2.75. Some of the bosses at first were willing to grant the full $3, but were influenced to stand against the men. Now let our Albany brothers keep up the union and join our Brotherhood.

—The quarterly report of the German House Joiners' Union of New York for the past quarter shows receipts $[illegible], expenses $4,776, and a surplus on hand $3,822. During the quarter 35 new mem[illegible] bers were admitted, while 16 memb[illegible] were disabled by accident, and two dea[illegible] occurred. The union resolved to stand its rate of $3 per day this season.

—Philadelphia Brickla[illegible] Union [illegible] heavy treasury, and [illegible] vest it in the erec[illegible] This is what the [illegible] did years ag[illegible] selves, for [illegible] dollars [illegible] [illegible] could only be established b[illegible] [illegible] to each of the [illegible]

THE CARPENTER.

Entered at the Post-Office in New York, as second-class matter.

NEW YORK, MAY, 1883.

A LEAF FROM THE HISTORY OF UNION NO. 22.

In retiring from the office of President of San Francisco Union No. 22, Bro. Edward Owens delivered the following address, and it is worthy of place in the history of our Brotherhood, as it demonstrates the growth and struggle of unionism:

"The initial steps for the formation of this Union were taken in the month of January, 1882. A few carpenters who were convinced of the necessity that existed in this city for some organization of our trade, determined to call a public meeting of our fellow-craftsmen, and endeavor to induce them to join us in founding a Carpenters' Union.

We issued an address through the columns of the press, setting forth in brief the evils which want of Union had produced among us, and attempted to outline the good results which should and would follow a thorough organization of the carpenters and joiners of San Francisco.

We believed the time had arrived for action on their part in their own behalf, and in conclusion reminded them that our trade is our property, and it was our duty to protect it; he who will not, deserves to be cheated, for he encourages others to rob him of the fruits of his toil.

In answer to this and subsequent appeals quite a number of carpenters attended our preliminary meeting, but at first the project was regarded with apathy, and our efforts disregarded by those who should have an equal desire with us to improve their condition.

We were not disheartened, however, but stuck determinedly to our task. Some of the older members will no doubt remember the up-hill struggle we had in the early days of this Union. They will remember the secession of one of the first eleven men who signed the call for a charter, also the long wrestle over the adoption of the first local constitution. Slowly our fellow-craftsmen awoke to the advantage of union. They began to think that [illegible] might possibly do some good. Some of the [illegible]dest determined to give the Union a trial, and our membership commenced to increase. Thus our purpose was accomplished.

What we wanted, was to set them thinking, and the rapid growth of Union No. 22 within the last four months, proves that the carpenters and joiners of San Francisco now think that the founders of this Union were right, for in organization lies their only hope of redressing any grievances which they labor under, or of protecting themselves against injustice and fraud.

A SPICY LETTER FROM OUR EX-PRESIDENT.

One question that carpenters ought to consider well is: Have we as a trade enough intelligence to build up a National Organization that will eventually assert the position of our craft, or shall we tack on as a tail to some other kite?

The cigar-makers have built up one of the best working International Unions in America, and why may not we take advantage of their experience and do likewise. The secret of their success was what L. J. B. advocates in the April number of THE CARPENTER, viz: Equalization of funds and high dues.

A rooster that hasn't sand enough in its craw to crow on its own dung hill, is too weak to scratch for its own worms. So also is an organization with no money in the treasury powerless for aggressive warfare, and compelled to lean up against some other body for support.

How is it we lose members when we ought to retain them? Because men selfishly imagine they have received all the benefits to be derived from organization [illegible] they get the highest wages and take [illegible] further interest in its welfare. This we [illegible] provide for by death benefits, etc. [illegible] a different inequalities of workmen [illegible] two hundred [illegible] [illegible]. There can be [illegible] our deceased brother a slow, inferior [illegible] to his widow. The same pay [illegible]

We are initiating a fewer to scab him [illegible]; it looks a little [illegible] to make [illegible] them for [illegible], or per[illegible] [illegible] men at [illegible]

The following resolutions seem to me the fit thing, for bosses to adopt:

Whereas, Under the demands of our present civilization *excessive labor* is limited merely by the maximum amount necessary to sustain human life.

And whereas, the utter extinction of individual liberty, and the growth of the passive virtues is necessary to perpetuate the power and glory of a divine few and must depend on dietic measures therefore,

Resolved, In the interests of peace, and in obedience to the law of self-preservation, we offer the highest honor in the gift of American freemen, to the scientist, or inventor, that will discover a method by which the life sustaining elements may be extracted from air and water at a nominal cost to replace the present expensive food required to keep bone and muscle in good working order.

G. EDMONSTON.

WASHINGTON, D. C.

THE HOLLOW FORM OF LIBERTY.

There is a law in Connecticut which makes it a penal offence to employ children over fifty-eight hours a week; but at a legislative hearing the other day it was shown, on the testimony of cotton and woolen manufacturers, that the hours of labor for men, women and children alike are from eleven to eleven and a half a day, or from sixty six to sixty-nine hours a week. The newspaper paragraph in which we find the above information concludes as follows;—"No operative was heard, it being understood that one who appeared in favor of such a measure might as well have his goods packed ready to move into some distant State." To those who are continually boasting that "this is a free country," this must be extremely refreshing; but it reminds us of the old saying that

"Walls do not a prison make,
Nor iron bars a cage."

We may be slaves without having a paper constitution to declare us such, and we may be prisoners without "walls" or "iron bars." The great trouble with these people is that they confound the hollow *form* of liberty with liberty itself. Legally and politically we in this country are *freemen*; socially and industrially we are *slaves*.—*Irish World.*

PUT THIS IN YOUR PIPE.

Workingmen, you are beaten at every turn. Sharpers over-reach and rob you, do it while your eyes are wide open, and laugh in your face and despise you. Why? Because you everlastingly sit down for some one to help you, for wrongs, somehow to get righted, for something to turn up. Things never do turn up of their own notion; and you can lay it to heart as an imutable fact, that if you do not spring to action and make things more to the best of your own welfare, scheming men will twist them to your eternal detriment.—*Labor Gazette.*

HISTORY OF SAWS

The Egyptians were the first to use saws. They made them of bronze metal, and applied them to cutting out planks from logs. The saw was single handed, and the log to be cut was set on its end, and secured to posts in the ground.

In Greece, the inventor of the saw was deified under the name of *Talus*, or Perdix. The saws used by Greek carpenters were similar to the straight frame ones of modern times. The block of wood to be sawed was clamped down to the bench, and the sawyers stood opposite each other.

The French knew the use of the saw propelled by machinery as early as the thirteenth century, and in Germany as early as 1322. One was known to exist in the island of Madeira in 1420, and another in Norway in 1530. The Dutch were one hundred years in advance of the English in the use of saws. Then a Hollander was the introducer of it, with a mill built near London in 1663, and it proved a failure through the opposition of the hand sawyers; and in 1767, the one erected by the Society of Arts, at Limehouse, was destroyed by a mob. American colonists were more sagacious, and began the erection of saw-mills as early as 1663; the first of these was built at the falls on the Piscataqua, this was followed by three others, erected by the Dutch West India Company in New York, to be worked either by water or wind; at our [illegible] early Dutch settlers, [illegible] I would suppose, not soon carried the [illegible] and jealousies the Delaware, [illegible] William Penn [illegible]

Lumberman.

THE INJURY AND MISCHIEF THAT SOME PEOPLE DO.

The order of Knights of Labor is a noble one, doing a grand work in reclaiming humanity from poverty and subsequent crime, misery and degradation. In elevating men to a higher plane of civilization, and procuring for them more of the comforts of life, it fills a long-felt want, as it brings within the folds of organization unskilled as well as skilled labor, and to effect this it has a noble band of skirmishers scattered over every part of this broad country as organizers, who, with commendable zeal and energy, are ever alert to add to the rapidly increasing numbers of the order and thereby gain additional strength for it in its battle for the rights of the down-trodden of mankind. So far so good.

They have a power that involves responsibility; but when they assume it with ardor, and their zeal and ardor burns to such an extent, that with intent and by artful wiles they seek to seduce avowed union men from their fealty and loyalty to their brethren; when they so far forget the courtesy extended that grants them admission to the meeting of a union working under a charter from a National organization, and paint in glowing colors with fervid language the beauties of that which they represent, and misrepresent, and so far forget the noble principles of their order as to advise men to desert their comrades in arms and to renounce their allegiance to their colors, that have braved the battle and the breeze of many a hard fought contest for the rights of man, then, indeed, are they doing the base work of a traitor to the cause of labor by inculcating and advocating treason, and sowing the seeds of discord that set workingmen by the ears and make them an easy prey for their enemies.

They undo the good work of years, and in gaining additional strength for their order they more than counterbalance it by the enmity which they create. The warfare waged by greed and avarice is severe enough, without dissensions created in the ranks of labor to make a tool of it for its own subjection.

We are well aware that the order does not proclaim or advocate any such policy, yet such acts should not be winked at, as many who do not know otherwise hold it guilty and responsible for the acts of its agents. Already deep growls and mutterings of indignation come from more than one quarter, and are heard in more than one International organization.

It is our firm opinion that it is the wise and proper course to pursue for all branches of labor to make common cause together as firm allies with the one purpose in view — the complete emancipation of labor. But as a distinct class of workmen we have interests which can be best subserved by the distinct and complete unification of our trade from one end of the continent to the other, a stronger and more lasting bond of friendship, cemented by mutual sympathies, which would be entirely lost were we merged into a general whole and our identity as a separate trade organization swept away. And therein lies a safeguard for the perpetuity of unionism in which no blow ever so severe can be struck that will demoralize labor to the extent of requiring generations to pass away before it can recover. Trades unionism has not outlived its day, but is entering on a brighter career of usefulness than ever was dreamed of in the past.—*Journeyman Builder.*

FRENCH WORKINGMEN'S POLITENESS

Two working mechanics, house-joiners by trade, who were largely instrumental in getting up the recent demonstration of carpenters lately in Paris, and which was suppressed by the police, having received a summons to appear before one of the police magistrates, whereupon these workmen wrote that functionary a letter in the following terms, *i. e.*—

"Monsieur, we have the honor to acknowledge the receipt of your summons, but regret we cannot avail ourselves of the pleasure it would give us to attend at the hour therein mentioned. We have just got work, and we have been too long idle to afford the loss of half a day, or perhaps dismissal, and the risk of being again thrown on the streets of Paris without employment. Should 6 o'clock in the afternoon suit your convenience we shall be happy to appear before you. Accept, Monsieur, the assurance of our most distinguished consideration.

"M. CARDERLA.
"G. GAUTIER."

This is a specimen of how politely our French brothers know how to treat police judges. They are not at least craven and cowardly enough to cringe and cower before the [illegible] of a police judge.

AMALGAMATED CARPENTERS

The Twenty Third Annual Report of the General Secretary of the above society has been sent us from Manchester England. It is for the year 1882. They have opened fifteen new branches during the year—eight in England, one in Ireland, one in Scotland, two in the United States, one in Canada, and two in South Africa. They admitted 3,432 into membership, and excluded 1,592; the net increase being 1,857 and a total of 376 branches. The net income for the year was $225,815 an increase of $24,245 on previous year. The expenditure was $219,670 being $27,140 less than the income. The buildings and other property is valued at $200,590 or $12.50 per member.

The Society have expended $73,670 for persons unemployed, as against $95,910 last year. In sick benefits they expended $61,280. The compensation for tools lost by fire, water, or theft, cost $6,080; accidents, $8,250; superannuation, $5,150; In benevolent grants to distressed members was $3,815, and in grants to other trades, $175. In what is called "trade privileges" an item covering strike pay, conciliation, arbitration and law expenses, expenses of the management of all trade movements; they expended $11,285.

The wages of members have improved in 28 different towns the past year. During the past year work in the building trades has been better than in 4 years previously. The Amalgamated has spent during the last 23 years the sum of $2,072,325 in benefits or $195 for each member. Let us work to establish our Brotherhood on as solid and enduring basis.

WORK AND WAGES IN FLORIDA

SANFORD FLORIDA.— After a six months trip through this "land of flowers" I wish to give a few points of interest to your readers. I came from New York to Fernandina on the Steamer Carondelet of the Mallory line, and although we had been promised good treatment, we had miserable sleeping accomodation, and at meal time our table was the forehatch. From Fernandina I went to Jacksonville by rail. Building trade dull in that city; carpenters wages $1.75 to $2.50. Colored men are the principle mechanics in the building line. I next took a steamer to Sanford. It is not my desire to disparage this country, but I must say as a traveller who has seen much of America and of Europe, that this country down here is very much overrated by interested land speculators. The scenery is monotonous, a constant panorama of swamp lands and palmetto trees thickly covered with heavy moss. I visited various cities on my route. And at last came to Sanford and found work. Wages for carpenters in this vicinity average $2.50. In Orlanda $2.75 for good men. But this State is so overrun by carpenters that many work for even $2.00 a day. The climate here is fine rarely going beyond the seventies in Summer and in Winter not lower than twenty-five degrees. The soil is poor and needs great care and a liberal use of fertilizers; farms sell for from $5.00 to $150 per acre. But there is a great deal of malarial fever among strangers. I would advise workmen to stay away from Florida for a few years, as the labor market is overdone here.

A federation of all the furniture trades was effected by the Parisian workers during last month. A reduction of the hours of labor is the first line of action decided on.

BOOK NOTICES.

CAMERON'S PLASTERER'S MANUAL is a handy neat book, not only of interest to the novice in plastering, but it also contains numerous recipes, tables of reference, etc., of value even to the experienced. It treats of tools, materials, and gives rules for ornamental and difficult work. W. T. Comstock, 6 Astor Place, New York, are the publishers. Price 75 cents.

EXTRACTS FROM CHORDAL'S LETTERS.—John Wiley & Sons, 15 Astor Place, New York, is the publisher of these extracts, and it is a very interesting volume, especially for machinists. It comprises the choicest selections from a series of articles which have been appearing for the past two years in the columns of *The American Machinist*. Written in a quaint, humorous vein, and admirably illustrated it furnishes a text book of value to all interested in machine shops. Price $2.00.

SAW FILING, by Robert Grimshaw, published by John Wiley, 15 Astor Place, New York. Price $1.00. This practical treatise in popular form deals with sharpening, gumming and setting of all kinds of modern saw teeth.

HINTS ON BUILDING, by J. H. Carpenter, Architect and Constructing Engineer, [illegible] street, Hartford, Conn. Price [illegible] copy.

CHANGES RECOMMENDED IN THE WORKINGS OF OUR BROTHERHOOD.

In my last article I advocated *universal dues, universal benefits, and equalization of funds*, and I will now explain what I mean by this.

Our Brotherhood must be universal to be successful, that is we must be united in the truest sense of the word; we must be one. We must all pay like dues, and all receive like benefits. I don't believe in one union adopting three dollars initiation and fifty cents dues and a sick benefit, and another union adopting one dollar initiation and twenty-five cents dues, and no sick fund. Or one union adopting the Branch System, and another the Central System for large cities; nor do I believe in any union being allowed to adopt laws which apply only to that Local; I believe in *all being subject to the same Constitution and By-Laws*, and all paying the same dues, and receiving the same benefits, and that is universal benefits and universal dues.

I will try now to explain the workings and some of the benefits of equalization of funds. Without universal benefits and universal dues, we cannot have equalization. Now, equalization does not mean that all the money from the Locals should be centred at one point and kept by one person, as some imagine. But it means simply that once a year, say at New Years, the General Secretary shall reckon up just how many members and how much money there is in all the Locals, and so find out how much per member in good standing there is in the Brotherhood. The unions that have an excess in their treasury will have to remit to the unions that have not enough, sufficient to make them all equal. For instance, if there were 100,000 and 100,000 dollars in all the unions, that would be one dollar for each member, and if Chicago had 1000 members and $1,500 in the treasury, and New York had 1000 members and only $500 in the treasury, then Chicago would have to remit to New York $500 to place in its treasury, and then they would both be equal.

Now, the Financial Secretaries of the Locals should be obliged under a heavy fine to send to the General Secretary on the first week in every month a report of their Local, also quarterly and yearly balance sheets audited. The General Secretary must then print a quarterly statement, showing how many members and how much money in each Local, expenses and receipts, also number of members in good standing, number suspended and admitted. Then as many of these quarterly statements are printed, as there are members in the Brotherhood, and one given to each member.

In like manner each local Financial Secretary will draw up a yearly balance sheet at the end of each year, and transmit the same to the General Secretary who will cause to be printed a yearly report, which contains the balance sheet of each Local in full, the names of all the members that have been suspended or expelled during the year, and for what cause. He shall have as many of these quarterly reports printed as there are members, and distributed to the members the same as the quarterly reports. The yearly report also contains the financial report of the General Secretary, and also a list of which Local will remit money to another Local, and how much.

Such is the mode of working the "Equalization of Funds." Brothers, you will see at once the great advantage of the plan. We are now only a lot of disunited Locals. Under the universal plan and equalization of funds we would be one grand Brotherhood. If we had, say only 100,000 members and three dollars per member in the treasury, that would make $300,000 in the funds. Now, I feel quite sure, if the carpenters of Chicago were to make any demands, and the bosses knew that they had $300,000 at their back, the bosses would grant the demand without a strike.

Hence we should adopt the Universal and Equalization plan. It would then be a very short time until

8 hours work,
8 hours play,
8 hours sleep, and
4 dollars a day

would be a general rule in the United States.

Another argument in favor of Equalization is the fact that one Local helps another; the strong will help the weak. I hold that a Local in a small town with 20 members does as much good as a local in a large city with 3000 members, because the most evil in large cities ... the Publ... carpenter Lake front, than the ... to competition Building most ... work "cheap." Now, if there was a Local of the Brotherhood in every town and village, it would be otherwise; no small Local, however, can live without the Equalization plan.

Now, so much for the "Equalization Fund." I think all will see its advantages and understand its workings. I will now take the stand that high dues and high benefits are more likely to make and *retain* members than low dues and no benefits. I am in favor of paying 30 cents per week all over and of having the following benefits: A sick benefit, a funeral benefit, an accident benefit, an out of work benefit, a tool benefit, a strike benefit and a superannuation benefit, also benevolent grants in cases of distress. Now I say, I am in favor of all these benefits, and if they were adopted would I claim, not only establish a strong union, but would *retain* every member we make. But I am not sanguine enough, however, to hope that such a radical change will be adopted all at once. What I hope to see adopted soon is that the dues be 60 cents per month, and a sick benefit of five dollars per week, for 26 weeks, $100 death benefit, $500 accident benefit, and a tool benefit and a strike benefit; also a scale of entrance fees according to age. That would not be so radical a change.

Some of the Locals have now a sick benefit and fifty cents dues, and I see others falling in line. It is a fact that those Locals that have a sick benefit and 50 cents dues have been successful in the past year and have added to their membership, while the cheap Locals have all, or nearly all fallen behind. We ought to try 60 cents dues and the benefits I have named for one year, and, if successful, adopt the higher dues the next year.

I may explain why I have put the funeral benefit at $100, and the accident benefit at $500. Because it appears to me that if a man meets with an accident, and is disabled for life, he will need more assistance than his relatives will to bury him.

Now, I am not giving ideas of my own that have been lately formed, I am giving the result of 18 years experience, since I became a member of a trades union. I will mention two of them in order to prove my point. In the years 1865 and 1866 I was a resident of the city of Brisbane, Queensland, Australia, and I helped to form a carpenters union there. It was a cheap affair, no benefits and low dues, and of course, isolated from the other Australian unions. But in a few years they saw that the "cheap and isolated plan" did not succeed, and adopted *high dues and high benefits, and equalization of funds*, and are to-day in a flourishing condition. 1866, 1867 and 1868 I was a member of the Progressive Society of Carpenters and Joiners of Sydney, New South Wales, and we paid low dues and received no benefits. If some member introduced a measure and could not carry his point, he would get mad and leave the union. There was nothing to bind members. I see that union also has found the "cheap plan" did not answer, and they have adopted high dues, high benefits and equalization of funds. See the city of Chicago. For 3 years they tried the disunited and cheap plan (the old Locals 3 and 4), and did not succeed, and a little less than a year ago tried the "high dues and united plan", and are now on a fair road to success. I will take up this subject again next month.

In the mean time I would like every brother to consider, not what suits his own individual Local, but rather what will be most likely to establish a good National Union with a firm basis.

L. J. B.

CHICAGO, Ill., April 22d, 1883.

CARPENTERS ON STRIKE IN GERMANY

From all reports the carpenters of Berlin, Germany, struck on May 1, for an increase in wages and a reduction in time to nine hours per day. Over 2000 men take part in the movement. On April 16 the bosses offered the the terms after July 1 and to last until Oct 15, but the men want an agreement for a year. They have formerly been getting 21 Marks ($5.50) per week. The union has resolved to pay the strikers 15 Marks ($3.75) per week. They have 1500 Marks ($1150) in their treasury and will require $5,000 to carry on their strike, assistance has been sent them from Hamburg, Lubeck, Kiel, and other cities. A national union of carpenters in Germany depend on the s... of this movement. They appeal to ... therhood to give

AN IDEA THAT SHOULD BE ACTED ON IN EVERY UNION.

There is one proposition which I wish our local unions would carefully consider. And that is the idea of not holding any Convention of the Brotherhood this year (1883). Annual Conventions are not so necessary while we have a journal of our own through which we can communicate with each other.

The Amalgamated Carpenters hold their Conventions once every three years, and have thousands of dollars in their treasury. Several leading unions in this country, such as the Granite Cutters, Cigar Makers, Iron Molders, Engineers, etc., no longer hold annual sessions. They find that annual sessions have been too expensive and have not resulted in any good. Hence they have adopted the practice of biennial sessions, or leave the calling of a convention an open question to be determined whenever a convention is absolutely necessary. And yet those unions that hold conventions only once every two years, instead of falling to pieces, are better off financially, and do not fritter away much money for delegates, railroad fares and expenses of conventions.

Now, suppose our Brotherhood try this plan for awhile. The experiment can't injure us, and surely it will save a good deal of money to each local union. If we sum up the expenses of each local union to send delegates, it will make a total cost of fully $2,000 for the next convention. If even half this sum were devoted to sending out a couple of energetic organizers, it would be of more profit than a convention. It would build up many a union, and thereby add to the strength of our Brotherhood. And besides that the unions would not be strained as they are each year to send delegates to a convention. Some do not get over the strain for many months.

Then there is another fact. In conventions business is generally hurried through without sufficient deliberation, so that delegates can return speedily to their homes.

If we discontinue holding a convention each year, and only hold one at least every two years, we can do our business just as well and far more deliberately by a general vote of the members.

This principle of a general vote must be recognized in our Brotherhood. It gives each member his full voice in the affairs of the Brotherhood; it allows the members to rule and does away with the autocratic power of delegates; it consults the judgment of every member and gives us the ripest and best legislation. This principle of a general vote is truly democratic and republican in the proper sense of those terms. Why should we not adopt it?

Therefore I suggest that some union should take up this matter and frame a resolution to cover it, and if two more unions second the motion, then let it be printed in THE CARPENTER, so that every member can read the propositions and vote on them. Or let the Executive Board take the initiative. But the two points should be: 1st.) No convention in 1883; 2d) The adoption of the principle of a general vote.

Let there be no delay on these matters, as they are very urgent.

PHILADELPHIA, Pa. ARGUS.

Class Distinctions and the Servitude of Labor.

PONTIAC, MICH.—There is only one idea as a foundation for all labor organizations, and that is the abolition of the servitude and dependence of the wage-workers upon the capitalists. Combinations for the mere amelioration of this servitude amounts to nothing, especially if engineered by politicians. The last election shows that the workers are not yet prepared for decisive political action. They run after the old political gods. We have not yet crystallized together on one idea; are divided by mere policies. The wage makers are numerous enough to capture and control the government of every large city in the union, and sweep away the abuses and vast taxations that help to impoverish them. But we merely blow our trumpets, and set up a few of our friends and then—knock them down. I have never had any faith in political action, except locally, in large cities. And no political success will liberate labor from the dominion of capital. It seem... that the battle must be fought ... unions, actuated everywhere by ... class dist...

means, because this is a matter t... be freely discussed, and its adv... and disadvantages pointed out. ... involves no breach of law, and calls ... governmental interference. For w... be sure that our capitalistic govern... will always take sides with capital a... labor. I have been hammering at t... sue for a long time. It ought to b... cussed by every labor paper in the ... try, and this would force its discuss... the enemy. Labor desires more wag... fewer hours and more liberty, and bett... conditions, and it has been striving for these by attacking effects, without going to causes. And it is plain that the cause ... of wrong lie in our class divisions, and ... absolute dependence of labor upon capi... ists for work and bread. There is no ho... for labor under these class divisions, whi... generate all political and social wrong... and will destroy every popular politi... government that can be ... lished. As yet no trade union or labor ... ganization stands on this idea, but we sh... do nothing effective until we give ... tives, and stand face to face ... on this plain issue: "Do you, ... ist, affirm that Labor was ... your hereditary serf; yes ... should come down to an issue ... be dodged. Every man shou... where every other man stand... of the industrial liberty or ... vitude of labor, for this class ... hereditary as proved by all hi...

BRAY.

Encouragement from the ...layers.

NEW YORK.—I would be gr... to see every trade as well or... the bricklayers at the present ... see no reason why this cannot ... one and all, will only make a... will build up an organization ... bined capital can destroy. ... to all carpenters and joiners ... of their notice, and I hope th... penter or joiner will conside... what ground he is standing. ... to himself: "I have been doi... not joining the Carpenters ... so doing I have retarded man... that they are engaged in ... know my duty. I will go lik... perform it, and to make up ... shortcomings I will urge my ... do likewise." If this feeling ... animate the carpenters am... would not be long before th... cure a just remuneration fo... Their labor is just as nece... bricklayers or other crafts. ... my brothers in Labor, and i... time you will like it so well th... urge others to join with you. ... from year to year until you ... most needed for success—a p... ization. In regard to the eig... tion I can say but little, alth... under discussion for nearly a ... our Bricklayer's Convention, ... definite was arrived at other ... mmendation to the unions ... where there might be a chanc... its adoption. But where it ca... fully put into force is more th... Nine hours, in my opinion, w... easily gained than eight. Bu... our trade will not listen to an... ment. They say when the ti... action it will be eight hours f... is enough for any man to w...

O. COLE, Pres. Bricklaye... Union.

STAIR BUILDERS ORGANIZE!

STAIR-BUILDING has become a separate branch of carpentry in Baltimore, as it has long been in other cities. Those who f... low this skillful branch of industry, nearly every part of the country, formed themselves into a Union. ... years ago many of our best stai... here, those who worked for ... refused to follow their regu... and took jobs as house-c... why? Because having ... being thus disunited, ... powerless, they could n... deemed equivalent to ... business, having to ... and necessarily info... having no organiz... united, and conse... business was run... sarily inferior ... would ...

... of conducting the business of the collectivity, or, in ordinary parlance, would defra... ... Our last lecture we observed ... ould only be establish... ...ing to each ... a union man, but in ... connection with us at all. ... cent. of the ... is also against ... rikes. The building ...

THE CARPENTER.

PUBLISHED MONTHLY

BY THE

Brotherhood of Carpenters and Joiners,

OF AMERICA.

Office: 184 William St., New York.

TERMS.—Fifty cents a year, in advance, post-paid.

Send all moneys and correspondence for this Journal to

P. J. McGUIRE, Secretary,
184 William St., New York

NEW YORK, MAY 1883.

—San Francisco Union No. 22 initiates now from 25 to 40 new members each night.

—Smoke no scab cigars; ask for "Union Label." If you can't get it in one store then go where you can get it.

—Now is the time prescribed by our constitution to propose all changes you may desire in the laws of our Brotherhood.

—From latest indications the bricklayers of Chicago have won their strike. All honor to them for the determined stand they have made!

—We thank the Pittsburgh *Labor Tribune*, Buffalo *Truth*, and other papers that have lately given such flattering notices to our humble journal.

—Twenty-eight assemblies of the Knights of Labor have lapsed in the Pittsburgh District during the last quarter. The expenses of the central office of the K. of L. will amount to fully $25,000 for the year ending next September.

—The main questions now for our Brotherhood are: Shall we have a Convention this year and waste money; shall we stand by the autocratic idea, or shall we introduce the principle of a general vote in our unions?

—Wherever our members travel let them be missionaries in our cause. Each travelling brother should feel it his sacred duty to organize a carpenter union as he journeys along. Be enthusiastic and show your devotion to our principles and you will inspire others to nobler action.

—The cowboys in the Pan Handle district of Texas are the ones to strike terror to "scabs." They recently demanded an increase in pay and were refused, whereupon they quit work, and well armed with rifles, they threatened to take the lives of any who dared to take their places.

—Several very lengthy communications [illegible] been sent us this month. Our cor[illegible]ents should remember that our [illegible] very limited, and that short art[illegible] the ones most likely to be read. [illegible] spondence by all means, but [illegible] write only on one side of [illegible]

[illegible] does protect Labor; [illegible] a different [illegible]? The iron manu[illegible] hundred [illegible] and the West pro[illegible] our deceased [illegible] to his widow. [illegible] per cent. on [illegible] We are initiating a [illegible] Society re[illegible] it looks a [illegible]

SHALL WE HAVE A CONVENTION THIS YEAR?

Our Philadelphia correspondent this month makes some very appropriate and worthy suggestions that involve the dearest interests of our Brotherhood. They should not be thrown aside, nor scoffed at. On the contrary, they betray a spirit of statesmanship and good sense that would be well to encourage.

The main points pressed by our correspondent are:

1st. No Convention of the Brotherhood until 1884.

2d. Adoption of the principle of a general vote, as part of our constitution.

The arguments he presents are convincingly in favor of both measures, especially the point he urges that the money for a convention could be spent to better purpose, sending out organizers to build new unions.

The reasons he presents in favor of a general vote are very forcible. We believe firmly in the principle of popular sovereignty and see no reason why it should not be introduced into our organization. It affords an excellent means to inform our members thoroughly in all the workings of our Brotherhood. And any trade organization that fails to recognize this principle, is doomed to early destruction. Autocracy, no matter if it triumph for awhile in some societies, is bound to fall before the desire of the people to rule themselves.

PETER COOPER.

In the death of Peter Cooper we all mourn the loss of a man, who was a brilliant and single example among all the capitalists of America. His gift of Cooper Institute was made at a time when he was worth not much more than $100,000—only half of what it cost Vanderbilt for one night's jamboree lately. No man in his life was more respected, nor in death more lamented than Peter Cooper. And it was not that his fame had been gained on the battle field or in the affairs of government. He was neither soldier nor politician. But his fame was in that he had administered his wealth as a social trust, and in so far as he could, he had used it to advance the condition of his fellow men. We well remember his language on his ninetieth birthday when he said in a public meeting:

"The production of wealth is not the work of any one man, and the acquisition of great fortunes is not possible without the co-operation of multitudes of men; and, therefore, the individuals to whose lot these fortunes fall, whether by inheritance or the laws of production and trade, should never lose sight of the fact that, as they only hold them by the will of society expressed in statute law, so they should administer them as trustees for the benefit of society as inculcated by moral law."

Did A. T. Stewart with his countless millions ever feel that he had a social responsibility for the wealth he had gained; did he ever realize that his wealth was social in its origin and perforce must be social in its administration? Do the Vanderbilts, Goulds, Fields and their tribe realise that fact to-day? The thought is vile to them. And so they heap up their millions, forgetful that there is a social recompense after all, and if they fail to pay the penalty in their lifetimes, they are apt to do it in their graves. Where are A. T. Stewart's bones to-day? He who had thousands of acres in life has not even seven feet of ground in which his bones can rest. The millions he had in life did not buy even common respect for his carcass after death! And as it was with him so it may be with the Vanderbilts and all the plunderers of Labor. But come what may no one will ever desecrate the grave of Peter Cooper!

OUR NINE HOUR AGITATION.

San Francisco has succeeded. By wise and cautious action Union No. 22 has obtained the nine hours for non-union as well as union men. Had there been no union the men would still be working 60 hours a week where now they work only 53 hours, and their wages are $6 per week more now than when they had no union. In the face of these facts who will say that trades unions are no benefit.

Inspired by the success in San Francisco, other cities on the Coast are moving on for Nine Hours as a day's work.

[illegible] that in our trade the high pressure system of labor—the intense hurried, driving system of work—prevails in America threefold more than anywhere in the world. Human life is prematurely worn out and destroyed! Men who ought to be in the prime of sturdy manhood, at 40 years of age, are either in their graves or bent and decrepit by overwork. The severe, laborious and heavy character of our work demands shorter hours of toil. The progress of the age demands that our burdens should be lightened, and that inventions and machinery should not condemn us to exhaustive hours of toil, nor should they consign multitudes of our class to walk the streets idle for want of work.

We ask shorter hours that we may have more of the comforts of life, more time for mental improvement, social enjoyment, and recreation. Have the workers no justice in these demands? Must we forever toil early and late with no hope of advancement, no pleasure in life—to be mere machines at the command of the Almighty Dollar? The united voice of organized Labor answers No! Then let us work to reduce the hours of labor.

We all agree. Eight Hours is long enough for any man to work. But before we can reach that point we must move forward to secure Nine Hours. We advocate that as the most practical. The result has been successful as we see in San Francisco. Now let other cities take up the question: discuss it and be prepared to act; but dont strike until the word is given for your city to move.

If dull times should come the bosses will attempt to resume long hours. But sooner than yield to this better suffer a reduction of wages. For once the hours of labor are reduced there is better chance of maintaining wages. Remember by all means hold the hours!

BUILD YOUR OWN HALL.

In Brooklyn the workingmen have a splendid hall of their own known as the "Labor Lyceum," and in Chicago, the trades unions secured a plot of land, and were at work building a hall when stopped by an injunction. New York, St. Louis and other cities have been discussing the subject. The bricklayers of Cincinnati have a hall of their own on Central Ave. and have netted thousands of dollars from their investment. In Millville, N. J., the glass workers also have their own hall under way.

Every leading city where unions exist should have a hall of their own. We pay enough rent for our weekly meetings to cover the cost of a hall in seven years, and are always in constant fear of eviction at the hands of landlords. But if we had a hall of our own we could have four or more lodge rooms on the upper floors for union meetings. These might be so arranged by having a movable partition that would convert the lodge rooms on one floor, into a large hall for mass meetings. We could have a reading room and library and a general labor bureau as a resort for unemployed union men. On the ground floor stores could be rented which would go far toward paying expenses of the hall.

Of course all union men agree we need such an institution in each city. But the question arises: "How can it be done?" And to this let us say, there is no way to do it only to undertake it ourselves! We need not expect capitalists or politicians to either donate the money or give us the land. Hence we must raise the means among ourselves to buy the land and materials. Many of our unions have funds enough on hand that could find this project a better investment, than to trust to the tender mercies of savings banks.

From among the idle labor in the building trades enough men could be selected in dull season, who would be willing to do the work of their respective trades on the building. They could be paid a small part of their wages in cash, and the balance in *labor notes* or notes of credit, with say a low rate of interest and redeemable within a certain specified time. Consequently, only a small amount of money would be required to hire labor. The only thing of importance is to get the money to buy land and materials. Of course, the organization to conduct this business should be incorporated, and it should be further provided never to mortgage or deed away this hall. It should be held in perpetuity for the working class. The working class need never hope to command public respect until they have a Trades hall of their own looming up in every city. That will demonstrate they are able to manage their [illegible]

LIVELY WORK IN CHICAGO.

Chicago Union No. 21 has gained over 200 new members this month through lively agitation by public meetings. Bros. McGindley, Schneider, Jones, Henderson, Boyer, Pake, Dixon and others are out every night in the work and at work in various quarters of the city where mass meetings are held. Our unions in other cities should follow the example of Chicago and stir around among the craft more publicly. Printers' ink and mass meetings will work wonders in gaining new members.

A good carpenter certainly ought to receive as good wages as a good bricklayer, and the chances are that he would if carpenters would all enroll themselves on the union lists. Let every carpenter who would have his pay at least equal to that given in other trades unite with his brethren in the effort to obtain it.

The initiation fee at present in Chicago carpenters Union No. 21 is $3 and monthly dues 50 cents. On and after June 1, the initiation fee will be $5.

WHAT STRIKES HAVE DONE

In an address recently issued to the public, T. V. Powderly takes occasion to speak of strikes in the following terms:

I can say nothing on strikes that I have not already said. "A strike cannot change the apprentice system, a strike cannot remove unjust technicalities and delays in the administration of justice, a strike cannot regulate the laws of supply and demand, for if it cuts off the supply it also cuts off the demand by throwing consumers out of employment, thereby curtailing their purchasing powers. A strike cannot remove or repeal unjust laws, for at best the strike secures but temporary relief; it may result in an advance of wages but if so it is a dearly bought victory, and at the first available opportunity another reduction is imposed. The strike is the weapon of force and 'who overcomes by force hath overcome but half his foe.' If the men who willingly lose one, two, three or six months' time in a strike would continue to work and set apart the money thus spent for the purpose of creating a co-operative fund, and if the men who contribute to their support would set apart the money they advance for the purpose of adding it to that fund, they would soon amass a sum sufficient to erect the mills or shops large enough to give employment to their idle brethren. But I fail to see any lasting good in a strike." *They have done more injury to labor than they can ever make amends for.*

In no spirit of carping criticism do we take issue with the above statements. But so many well meaning men are led away by the same delusion, that we think it high time to cry halt to this wholesale denunciation of strikes. Gen. Francis A. Walker, an economist of high rank, and whose experience as Superintendent of the Census in 1870 and again in 1880 qualifies him as an authority has written a book entitled "Work and Wages." He lays no claim to being a labor reformer, yet we will place his argument on strikes against that of Mr. Powderly's. It reads:

"Strikes are the insurrections of Labor. They are, of course wholly a destructive agency. They have no creative power, no healing virtue. Yet as insurrections have played a most prominent part in the political elevation of down trodden people, through the fear they have engendered in the minds of oppressors, or through the demolition of outworn institutions which have become first senseless and then pernicious, so strikes may exert a most powerful and salutary influence in breaking up a crust of custom which has formed over the remuneration of a body of laborers, or in breaking through combinations of employers to withstand a legitimate advance of wages, where the isolated efforts of individuals, acting with imperfect knowledge, with scanty means, and under a dread of personal proscription, would have proved inadequate.

Doubtless even more important than the specific object realized by strikes has been the advantages resulting from the permanent impression produced by these insurrections of Labor upon the minds and tempers of both employers and employes. The men have acquired confidence in themselves and trust in each other; the masters have been taught respect for their men and a reasonable fear of them.

Nothing quickens the sense of justice and equity like the consciousness that unjust and inequitable demands or acts are likely to be promptly resented and strenuously resisted. Nothing is so potent [illegible] clarify the judgment and sober the [illegible] in questions of right and wrong [illegible] that a [illegible] to a [illegible] Labor"

BROTHERHOOD NOTES.

—A new union is organized in Guelph, Canada, and will be known as Union No. 46.

—Indianapolis Union No. 15 is holding outside public meetings of the trade with success.

—Toledo Union No. 25 reports trade improving; wages $2.50; union holding its own and gaining strength.

—Charters have been granted to Union No. 41, of Morris, Minn., and to Union No. 43, of Hartford, Conn.

—Union No. 22, of San Francisco, Cal., will have its second annual excursion and picnic to Belmont, on Sunday, July 15.

—Our Endowment Fund is now established beyond doubt. All the local unions now recognize its importance and benefit.

—General Secretary McGuire has for some time lately been very ill with pleurisy, but now he is well and regaining his usual vigor.

—Baltimore Union No. 29 promises to soon double its membership the way it is now increasing. It has also raised its initiation fee and dues.

—Union 41 of Morris, Minn., had an enjoyable and profitable ball and supper on April 19th, in Phœnix Hall. This Union takes great interest in the Brotherhood.

—A correspondent in Dayton, O., says: The carpenters of this city need organizing badly. Yet, in my opinion, it will be a difficult thing to do, as there are so many wood butchers here.

—Why does not the Stair Builders Union of Cincinnati join our Brotherhood? They certainly have as much to gain by it as have the carpenters. Our Brotherhood extends them a hearty welcome.

—The three carpenters' unions of St. St. Louis have been discussing the question of consolidating in one union, but no decision has yet been reached. We think it better, if they were consolidated.

—Union No. 45 has been organized in Seattle, Wyoming Territory with a strong membership. Bro. J. R. McKell of San Rafael Union No. 35, was the organizer, and is worthy all honor for his work.

—Chicago Carpenters' Union No. 21 has donated *one thousand dollars* to aid the striking bricklayers of Chicago. Many members of Union No. 21 are also paying $3 a week from their wages into the Bricklayers' strike fund.

—Branch Secretaries of Chicago Union No. 21 should be prompt in making out and sending their monthly statements to the Executive Council in that city, or else it will complicate matters.

—A public mass meeting of the carpenters and joiners of Buffalo was held at Market Hall, April 18th, under the auspices of Union No. 37. The objects of the National Brotherhood, its affiliation with the trade in Europe, the working of the endowment fund, and other kindred topics were discussed and many new members gained.

—Business in San Antonio, Texas, is booming, and wages run from $2.50 to $3.50 per day. Board $4.50 to $6 per week. Lumber $22 to $60 per thousand. Nails and hardware away up. July and August will be dull on account of hot weather. Good prospects for coming Fall and Winter. Our correspondent is at work organizing a union in San Antonio.

—The dues of Union No. 9, Cincinnati, O., have been increased to 50 cents per month, to take effect May 1, 1883, and to continue for six months in the year. The balance of the year—in dull season—the dues will remain at 25 cents per month. Union No. 9 hopes that every member will pay up promptly, so as to have funds on hand to sustain their benefits.

—Judge Moran has granted an injunction against the trades unionists of Chicago erecting their Trades Hall on the Lake front. The objections are raised that the [illegible] It they can't have [illegible] ment any [illegible] the Lake front, then the Publ[illegible] all [illegible] Exposition Building must

THE LABOR QUESTION.

LECTURE VI.

CAPITAL.

We have considered the first two elements through which the activities of Man manifest themselves in the production of utilities, which are—first, Land; second, Labor.

We have said that the total number of these elements are five, hence there remains to be considered the other three elements in their natural order.

We have seen that without *Land*—the first element; *Labor*—which is the second element—would be impossible. It now remains to be seen that the joint action of these two elements, Land and Labor, are necessary, nay, indispensable to the formation of the third element—*Capital*. Therefore, we may promulgate as an axiom, that *without Land and Labor the formation of Capital is impossible.*

The question naturally arises, What is Capital? A very simple question in appearance, and not a difficult one in reality to answer, and yet it cannot be answered in a single sentence; for Capital itself exists, not in a simple and single form, but in complex and numerous forms.

We cannot better convince ourselves of the difficulty of replying to the question, "What is Capital!" in a trite sentence, than by looking over the works of the economists from Turgot down to Thornton, and observing the variety of their opinions upon that point. It will be seen that the terms money, wealth, riches, etc., have been used as synonymous with Capital by these authors: we shall find, also that they have divided capital into various kinds; such as fixed capital, floating capital, productive capital, non-productive capital, landed capital, merchandise and moneyed capital, etc., all which has contributed more to mystify the people than to enlighten them.

Later on they have defined Capital to be "accumulated labor;" still later on they designate as Capital "all that aids in the production of wealth," and, at this point, we can begin to agree with them.

Capital has never been created without labor, pain or effort, although there are values which are not the result of labor, and yet they aid labor to produce; such as the solar heat, terrestrial magnetism, the force of the wind, water power, etc.

Capital, then, is the accumulated results of labor applied to production; and the collective capital of the world, or social capital, is composed of all the products, tools and machinery, the physical power and acquired knowledge of mankind, and all and everything which contributes in any way to the increase of production, the formation of wealth, or to the creation of utilities.

All that which is an auxiliary to labor, the sum total of all the human forces and faculties, every tool or instrument, every means which is employed by industry or which can assist in the production of utilities, everything that can be appraised, estimated, or valued, bought or converted into an instrument of labor, or become an object of reproductive consumption is Capital.

It may be said that the action of exchange makes Capital differ from the product, according to the manner in which it is employed, or according to its destination.

For example, wool, when it is made into yarn, is the product of the spinner; when it is purchased by the weaver it becomes capital for him, for he makes it into cloth; it is reproductively consumed. The cloth [illegible] penter; just as the steel, which was a product in the hands [illegible] the steel founder, became capital f[illegible] saw-maker [illegible]

Now it will be clearly seen that capital and product are, in reality, one and the same thing, and that they take to themselves different names according to their destination.

There is, then, but one kind of capital, and in the industry of the world up to the present time (with the exception of two or three very noble examples), it has always been made to perform the same function, to play the same part, to wit, it has been used to increase wealth when employed by the worker. When employed by the capitalist it has been used to exact house-rent, interest, ground-rent, annuities, farm-rent, profits, income, dividends and premiums; in a word, it has been made to take from the laborer a net profit in return for its pretended services to industry; it has been loaned at usury on mortgage, it has been made to shave notes, discount bills and spoliate industry in innumerable ways, while persuading the laborers that it rendered to labor an incalculable benefit; and capital, which, from its very nature, should have been an assistant to the worker, has been, in reality, converted into his oppressor, from the fact, that through its agency the proprietors of capital, who are called capitalists, have confiscated a part of the results of his labor, and have monopolized that which, in justice, belonged to the worker; hence, capital has been an instrument in the hands of the capitalist which has been used to the detriment of the worker; and capital and capitalists have been used as interconvertible and *synonymous* terms.

Capital is matter, and is subject to modification only in a restricted degree.

The capitalist is a compound of matter, mind and morality, and in a much higher degree is subject to modification.

It is evidently impossible to engraft any sentiment of morality upon Capital; it may however be possible to inculcate a sentiment of morality in the capitalist.

The element of morality cannot therefore be developed in capital and modify it.

It may, however, be developed in the capitalist and modify him.

It is this absence of moral development in the Capitalist, as well as the short-sighted, intellectual perception common to all men, which makes him an enemy to the Laborer.

The question as to whether or not the capitalist can be made amenable to moral influences is a most important one, as it decides whether or not the labor problem is to be solved by peaceable and moral means or by physical and warlike means.

Having seen what Capital is, we may look to see how it is formed.

Capital is formed by the combined action of Land and Labor. Land, which is of a purely material character; Labor, which is of a purely immaterial character. Or, it may be said that Capital, which is, itself, one of the elements of production, is composed of two minor elements, the first of which is labor bestowed upon the second element, which is the *substratum*, or the product of the land, in the sense in which we use the term, and which we developed in former lectures, and it is this *substratum* which we contend has cost neither pain, labor nor effort to any man, and, consequently, it is a value given gratuitously by nature to man—*to society as a whole*—and, therefore, should not be monopolized by individuals, but should exist as nature intended it should exist, as the collective possession of society for the benefit of mankind, and not for the exclusive benefit of the privileged few.

And we further contend that this sub- [illegible] of conducting the business of the collectivity, or, in ordinary parlance, would defra[illegible]

If, then, the definition of capital [illegible] we here present be correct, it necess[illegible] leads us to the correction of a grave [illegible] into which have fallen many of the ex[illegible] ents of the labor movement, who [illegible] that "Capital is an enemy of Labor[illegible] assertion is manifestly false, and [illegible] that those who make the assertion [illegible] ficient in the power of analysis. [illegible] they say that capital is an enemy to [illegible] they merely mean that the propri[illegible] capital, *i. e.*, the *capitalist*, is an en[illegible] the laborer.

Between the capitalist and the la[illegible] enmity, that is, non-identity of in[illegible] may and does exist; but between c[illegible] and labor there can be no enmity [illegible] interest are identical, and necessari[illegible] for they are one and inseparable; the [illegible] of to-day is not only capital to-da[illegible] the unconsumed product of the la[illegible] to-day becomes the capital of the f[illegible] The comprehension of this simple [illegible] is very necessary to enable us to se[illegible] distinction which is to be drawn betw[illegible] the *capitalist* and *capital*.

Capital is non-consumptive and aids [illegible] duction; capital is, therefore, the gr[illegible] est friend to labor, in fact, it is part of [illegible] bor itself.

The capitalist is a consumer, and [illegible] quently prevents production, in which [illegible] the capitalist, may, in truth, be called [illegible] enemy of the laborer.

Let this difference not only be well [illegible] fined and understood, but let it be defi[illegible] ly stated by all those who engage in [illegible] defence of the workers. The confus[illegible] which arises from the misapplication [illegible] terms is frequently very detrimental to [illegible] cause; we must not let our feelings ov[illegible] come our judgment; the heart must [illegible] balanced by the head if our battle is to [illegible] favored by victory.

We have shown that capital consists [illegible] raw materials, machinery, tools, etc. [illegible] us not forget that the tools belong to [illegible] workers. The fact of these being mono[illegible] *lized* by the *capitalists* is another reason wh[illegible] capital has been called the enemy of labo[illegible] such enmity, however, does not exist [illegible] the raw materials, machinery, etc., but [illegible] the fact of monopoly; hence, *capital* shou[illegible] be made *accessible to labor* and not be mono[illegible] polized; it should be placed at the dispo[illegible] tion of the worker, in order th[illegible] he m[illegible] freely exercise his power of pr[illegible] tio[illegible] and it should not be under the exclusi[illegible] control of the capitalists, who, animate[illegible] by his own personal interest or his capric[illegible] can prevent the laborer from producing.

To accomplish this would appear an [illegible] most hopeless task, but we will attemp[illegible] show the possibility of its accomplishm[illegible] when we come to speak of Insurance a[illegible] Machinery.

As Capital is one of the elements in [illegible] production of wealth, a portion of [illegible] wealth produced should, in all justice [illegible] to capital as its reward. What shoul[illegible] the portion? How should it be de[illegible] mined?

As we have admitted that much [illegible] and misery comes from the la[illegible] given to some of these elements [illegible] share than they merit, justice [illegible] done by giving a mathematical and [illegible] able portion to each. Capital, then, [illegible] have such a portion as is necessary [illegible] safe keeping and to its replacement [illegible] worn out, that is, an equivalent to its [illegible] and tear.

Let it not be supposed when we sp[illegible] the replacement of capital, that [illegible] look the necessity of providing fo[illegible] crease. We believe, however, that th[illegible] crease of capital is to be provided for [illegible] [illegible] our last lecture we observed [illegible] should only be establish[illegible] ing to each [illegible] ith, an equitable portion to each of elements, according to the proportion in which they have contributed to its ...ation. Capital, then, should have ...h a portion as is necessary to its re...cement when worn out or consumed, ...d to its preservation or safe-keeping; or equivalent to its wear and tear.

As the economists have confounded cap...al with the capitalist, and have asserted that capital should have its reward, which we do not deny, they have claimed that the reward of capital should not only be sufficient to replace the capital when worn out or destroyed by fire or other accidents, ...ut that it should also extend to the pro...iding of a fund which shall enable the ...apitalist to increase his capital; for argue ...hey, if no surplus remains to capital other ...han will replace it, it is evident that capi...l would never be increased; in other ...ords, in an established industry, no pro...on would be made for an increase in ... material and machinery, etc., which ...uld give employment to an ever increas... population or labor force.

...he fact of this argument being used ...as proof that they have never yet ana...sed industry, or divided it into its prim...ry elements and several functions, as we ...re now doing, and, therefore they have ...aimed as a reward for the element "Cap...al," that which in truth and logically, ...ould go to the element "Insurance." If ...e require a further proof of this want of ...nalysis, or failure to distinguish between ...e elements which contribute toward the ...rmation of wealth, we shall find it in an...ther very closely allied instance. They ...y that the capitalist should be rewarded ...r the care and trouble which he takes in ...aning his capital to parties who are solv...t; in other words for the talent which ... has in discerning between a probable ...ilure and a probable success, in order to ...avoid either a non-productive employment ...f his capital or a total loss.

Now, the fact of his employing his time ...r devoting his energies to this superin...ndence of his capital constitutes labor, ...nd, therefore, the reward for his personal ...ervices should be called what it really is ...a reward for labor performed or services ...endered and therefore again we say that ...n this case, as in the other, the portion ...hould not be awarded to Capital, but to ...nother element, which, in this case, is ...abor; as in the last instance cited it ...hould be awarded to Insurance.

Let us boil down the teachings of the ...conomists on this point and investigate ...em briefly. It will do us no harm to ...ecisely know them. On the contrary it ...ill fortify us in our own position.

The employment of capital in commerce ...d industry, they assert, gives rise to ...rofits, which profits are divided into three ...tinct elements or parts.

...st. Rent, which the landlord receives ...he remuneration for the use of the land.

...d. Wages, which the laborer receives ...s reward for the amount of work done.

...d. Profit, which capital receives as a ...muneration or reward for abstinence.

...ere, then, we see that their position ...hat the employment of capital gives ...to profits, and that profit is one of the ...nts of those profits.

...w, the economists would present an ...tance of this kind. Suppose a farmer ...s land and employs a given capital, ... at the end of a year, he obtains $5,000 ...et profit. To obtain this he must have ...ven his time and knowledge; he must ...ve run all risk of failure, etc. Therefore, this $5,000 must be divided into three ...rts, and thus distributed:

... A reward for abstinence, which is ... interest on capital.

... Compensation for risk of loss.

... Wages of superintendence.

...w, in the first instance given, we find ... [illegible]

would appear to be necessary to show that the economists have not understood the primary elements of industry. And yet they are clearly on the road of discovery, and will eventually succeed, with the help of the workingmen, if their pride, and the intellectual arrogance for which the whole fraternity of the *professeurs* is famous, does not prevent them.

It is evident that which they claim as rent, and which should go to the landlord, is a recognition of the fact that a portion of the total product created by labor, should, in justice belong to the element which we designate as Land, and which is our first element.

It is also evident that when they demand that a certain portion should be set apart as a compensation for risk of loss, that they begin dimly to discern our fifth element, which is Insurance. But they have evidently no comprehension of it as one of the constituent elements proper in the creation of wealth.

When, again, they speak of the wages of the laborer and the wages of superintendence, they clearly prove that they have no rationally defined and well formulated comprehension of labor, and that they do not regard it as one of the integral factors in the sum total of human activity. Therefore they have demanded for capital a proportion which is disproportionate to the service which it renders, and this has been the cause of depriving the elements Labor and Insurance, most directly, and the other elements indirectly, when it has not been in alliance with them—of their just proportions.

Instead of dividing labor into useful labor and useless labor, and attempting to draw, as distinctly as possible, the line of demarcation between them, which would be a real benefit to the world, and in doing which the political economists would render an undoubted service—they have divided, or rather confounded, mental labor with manual labor; the labor performed by the man who has money, with the labor performed by the man who has none. The one, according to them, being wages for labor, the other the reward for superintendence and the reward for abstinence at the same time.

So with capital; instead of analyzing the processes of the formation of wealth, and discovering the primitive elements which enter therein, they have claimed for capital a part of that which should go to insurance, and a part of that which should go to labor, as also a part of that which should go to exchange. Hence, they have permitted and encouraged injustice, without attempting to secure a more harmonious condition of society by the investigation of industrial phenomena, which will alone enable us to discover the natural laws which should govern the distribution of wealth. Enough has been said to give a general idea of what we mean by Capital; in a more exhaustive investigation, which we will shortly present in the form of a treatise, we will enter into more minute particulars.

Dirty Work By Sneaks.

BUFFALO, N. Y.—We have our eyes on some persons who claim to be union men and are going around trying to undermine our carpenters union. They find out where our men are getting $2.50 and they offer to work for $2 or $1.75, and after being hired they never show up on the work. They are going around all the shops doing this. And we know perfectly well the persons who instigate this; and if they don't stop it and some more of their tricks, we will publish their names broadcast to the world. C. Chaplo, a leading boss in this city, advanced his men some time ago and now reduced them on all on account of this.

—Fowler Bros, Kansas City, Mo, and the Chicago North Western R. R. have issued orders that they will discharge any workmen found using intoxicating drinks or ... whether at work or not. This is a ... San Francisco, ... are moving on for ...

HOW TO MAKE A PLUMB AND LEVEL.

Many who are engaged in mechanical pursuits often desire to use a plumb or level, yet do not have enough use for one to invest two or three dollars in a spirit level and plumb such as is used by carpenters and builders. The sketch which I give will enable any ordinary mechanic to construct one in a short time at very little expense.

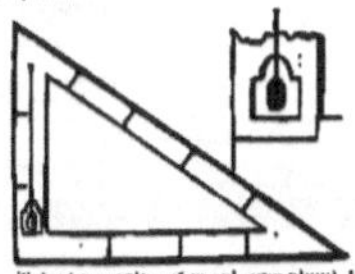

Take two strips of wood, one about two inches wide and two feet long, the other the same width and one foot six inches long, and halve them together at one end, so that when they are put together they will be flush on either side. Having done this, lay a steel square on the bench and place the two pieces of wood on the inside of the square, with the ends already prepared lapped together. See that both strips touch the square, then with short screws or small nails secure the ends at the corner of the square. If you have hot glue at hand use that, and fasten with screws or nails afterward. This accomplished, take a longer strip of wood about the same width, placing the outer edge at each outward corner of the two pieces already fastened together. With a sharp knife mark on the inside of the two pieces first laid down, the angle made across them by the third piece. With a saw cut the two right-angle pieces half in two, and with a chisel cut away the wood, making a rabbit on each piece. After having cut these out true, place the third strip back again and turn the whole over, being careful not to move the joint first made. Then with a knife mark along the edge of the two first pieces the shoulders to be made on the last piece. Saw down the shoulders and remove half the wood, so when all is put together it will be flush all around. Secure with glue if you have it, finishing with small screws or nails. Lay it away to dry if you use glue. When the glue is thoroughly hard, saw off the projecting ends and finish up with a plane, so that it will fit closely the inside of the square. With a gauge mark a line parallel with the outer edge of the short arm of the triangle. At the lower end, with a centerbit, bore an inch-and-a-quarter hole through about in the position shown in the cut. Then with chisel and knife it can be enlarged, as shown in the diagram in the upper right hand corner. Suspend a small plumb bob with a string from the upper end of the short arm. Your plumb and level is thus complete and ready for use. The short arm represents the plumb, while the horizontal end represents the level. The line and bob will show you when the article is plumb or level, as you desire.—*Mechanical News.*

Der Carpenter.

New York, Mai 1883.

Die Ursachen der Niederlage.

So oft „gute Zeiten" eintreten, oder um sich richtiger auszudrücken, so oft eine lebhaftere Nachfrage nach Arbeit sich kund thut, da tritt auch die „Periode der Strikes" ein und zugleich mit der Niederlage ertönt auch der gewöhnliche Ruf: „Habe ich Ihnen nicht immer gesagt, daß die Strikes ein Humbug sind?"

Doch nach den Ursachen forscht Niemand. Der Regel nach wird selten blindlings „gestrikt", so lange die Geschäfte flau und die Zeiten „hart" sind. Auch wird in einer solchen Zeit selten den Gewerk-Vereinen Aufmerksamkeit geschenkt. Sobald jedoch sich die Geschäftslage zu bessern beginnt, sobald die Preise für alles Andere, nur nicht für Mensch-Arbeit erhöht werden und es dem Arbeiter schwieriger wird, seinen Lebensunterhalt zu verdienen, da tritt auch ein Wechsel ein. Der Arbeiter sieht bald ein, daß er unter solchen Verhältnissen sich nicht „über Wasser" halten kann und er ist gezwungen, höheren Lohn zu beanspruchen. Er strebt danach, — gleichgültig ob er einem organisirten Verein angehört, oder nicht — von seinen Arbeitgebern höheren Lohn zu erzwingen.

... oft im Anfange ... die Arbeitgeber bilden auf solche „Strike" ...

mit „Herablassung", wenn nicht gar — um einen schärferen Ausdruck zu gebrauchen — mit Geringschätzung und weisen ihre berechtigten Forderungen in schroffer Weise zurück.

„Warum?"

Weil die „Bosse" genau wissen, daß es nur eine kurze Frage der Zeit ist, um diese Arbeiter, die ohne Organisation und Geldmittel dastehen, durch die zwischen ihnen früher oder später ausbrechende Uneinigkeit und Hunger zu zwingen, sich den von den „Bossen" diktirten Bedingungen zu unterwerfen. Dieses Schicksal hatten die New Yorker Frachtverlader, die Cohoes Weber und Spinner, die Lawrence Spinner, die Maryland Kohlengräber, die Boston Werftarbeiter und andere betroffen, die, trotzdem sie zu ihren Ansprüchen vollauf berechtigt waren, dennoch unklug genug gewesen sind, sich mit ihren leeren Taschen und leeren Magen gegen die Geldprotzen des Kapitals aufzulehnen.

Hätten sich jedoch diese Strikers in entsprechende Vereine organisirt und als solche Vereine sich anderen Gewerkvereinen angeschlossen, hätten sie die Organisation der Arbeiter ihrer betreffenden Berufe so vervollkommnet, daß jeder ihrer Mitarbeiter genöthigt gewesen wäre, dem Vereine anzugehören; hätten sie gewartet, bis sie Geldmittel genug in ihrer Kasse hatten, um für Fälle der Noth gerüstet zu sein und ihre Schwester Vereine im Stande gewesen wären, ihnen die nöthige Unterstützung angedeihen zu lassen, dann würden wir von der traurigen Aufgabe, diese Thatsachen anzuerkennen, behoben sein. Wie aber unausgebildete Rekruten, die ohne Waffen und Ausrüstung blindlings sich dem Feuer einer geschulten Artillerie aussetzen oder gegen eine wohlbefestigte Schanze des Feindes stürmen, unbedingt dem Tode verfallen, so müssen auch die Arbeiter unterliegen, falls sie erst striken und sich dann erst zu organisiren trachten.

Schreiner! Ziehet eine Lehre aus diesen Niederlagen! Rüstet euch in Zeiten des Friedens für etwa bevorstehende Kämpfe!

Wenn ihr euch gehörig organisirt, dann werdet ihr nicht nöthig haben, zu striken, denn Strikes werden euch nur dann aufgedrungen, wenn die Bosse wissen, daß ihr uneinig, arm und hilflos seid!

Sehet euch z. B. die „Amalgamated Engineers" und die „Stone Cutters of Great Britain" an. Diese Vereine haben auf Grund ihrer Einigkeit („Unions") und ihrer wohlgefüllten Kassen, bisher stets ihre den Arbeitgebern gestellten Bedingungen aufrecht erhalten und seit Jahren keinen Strike gehabt. Die einzige Ursache aller in den letzten Jahren hier zu Lande in Scene gesetzten, aber mit einer Niederlage der Arbeiter beendigten, Strikes ist Desorganisation und Uneinigkeit.

P. J. McGuire.

Gewerbs-Notizen.

Die Marmorschneider in Philadelphia fordern jetzt 8stündige Arbeitszeit und 50 Cts. mehr per Tag.

— In Indianapolis, Ind., bekommen die Zimmerleute $1.75—2.50, und in Morris, Minn., per Stunde 20—25 Cts.

Die Zimmerleute von Jersey City, N. J., forderten am 23. April eine Lohnerhöhung von $2.75 auf $3 per Tag und erhielten sie auch in den meisten Fällen nach mehrtägigen Bemühungen bewilligt. Auch die Brooklyner Zimmerleute agitiren für die gleiche Lohnerhöhung, wie ihre Kameraden in Jersey City.

Die Philadelphiaer Backsteinleger Union hat eine große Kasse und will diese Organisation ihre eigene Arbeiter-Halle bauen. In Cincinnati hat die Union schon seit mehreren Jahren ihre eigene Halle. Mit den Backsteinlegern sollten die Bauschreiner Hand in Hand gehen und in jeder Stadt ihre eigenen Arbeiterhallen bauen.

— $20,000 sind von der Internationalen Union der Former in den vergangenen 4 Jahren für Begräbnißbeiträge ausbezahlt worden und doch hat die Körperschaft noch Tausende von Dollars in ihrer Kasse. Alles das wurde geleistet vermittelst hoher Steuern und weitverzweigter Organisation. Dies sieht gewiß nicht darnach aus, als ob Gewerkschaften Fehlschläge seien.

Die Executivbehörde der Brüderschaft in Verbindung mit den Verwaltern und dem General-Sekretär versammelte sich am 25. April in Philadelphia. Die Bücher und Rechnungen des Sekretärs McGuire wurden geprüft und richtig, sowie in bester Ordnung befunden. Noch andere Geschäfte wichtiger Natur wurden erledigt, die den Mitgliedern durch Privat-Cirkulare bekannt gegeben werden.

— Am 1. April strikten die Zimmerleute in Albany, N. Y., für einen Lohn von $3 täglich — eine Erhöhung von 50 Cents. Nach zweiwöchentlichem Kampfe ließen sie sich mit $2.75 abfinden. Einige der Prinzipale waren Anfangs willens, den vollen Betrag von $3 zu bewilligen, wurden aber dahin beeinflußt, daß sie gegen die Arbeiter Stellung nahmen. ...

... until they ... looming up ... of right and wrong ... because they are able to manage their own affairs in a business-like manner. ... that a man ... fight" ... will lead to a ...

Die Carpenter von San Francisco führen die 9stündige Arbeitszeit ein.

San Francisco, 3. Mai. Die Carpenter in hiesiger Stadt legten am 1. Mai die Arbeit nieder, um die Einführung der 9stündigen Arbeitszeit bei vollem Lohne einzuführen. Die größeren Firmen bewilligten die Forderung sofort, während die übrigen nach kurzem Sträuben sich ebenfalls fügten, so daß heute ein vollständiger Sieg zu verzeichnen ist. Die Union No 22 der „Brotherhood of Carpenters" setzte die Agitation für Abkürzung der Arbeitszeit in's Werk und es folgen den hiesigen Carpenters nun die in Oakland und San Rafael. in ersterer Stadt ist der Ausstand auf den 1. Juli festgesetzt; in letzterem Orte wird ein solcher schon früher ausbrechen. Die Bewegung dehnt sich auf alle Städte der Pacific Küste aus, so daß man der allgemeinen Einführung der 9stündigen Arbeitszeit dort in der nächsten Zeit entgegensehen kann. Im vergangenen Spätjahr setzten die Carpenters der genannten Städte die Regel durch, daß an Samstagen nur bis 4 Uhr Nachmittags gearbeitet wurde; diese Regel bleibt bestehen, so daß die wöchentliche Arbeitszeit thatsächlich nur 53 Stunden beträgt.

Zimmerer-Ausstände in Berlin.

Berlin, 13. April. Wir sehen uns genöthigt, einige Zeilen direkt an Dich zu schicken, und zwar müssen wir Dir mittheilen, daß nun endgültig beschlossen ist, im Falle, daß die Meister die Lohnforderung von 4 Mark per Tag nicht bewilligen, die Arbeit am 1. Mai d. J. einzustellen. Ob wir unsere Forderung, den 9stündigen Arbeitstag, zur Verwirklichung bringen, hängt von der uns zufließenden Unterstützung ab. Ueber 2000 Bauschreiner sind in diese Bewegung eingetreten. Der Geist unserer Kameraden ist ein sehr guter, aber, wie Du weißt, fehlt schließlich die Ausdauer, wenn der Hunger zu sehr peinigt. Unsere eigenen Mittel sind beträchtlich und unsere Kameraden in Hamburg, Lübeck, Wandsbeck, wie auch die Schiffszimmerleute in Kiel und mehrere Kameraden an anderen Orten haben uns ihre Unterstützung zugesagt.

Der Voranschlag der behufs Ausführung unseres Strikes nöthigen Geldsumme beziffert sich auf 15,000 bis 20,000 Mark, und da wir vernommen, daß von unseren Brüdern jenseits des Oceans bedeutende Summen für die Ueberschwemmten am Rhein gesammelt sind, so hoffen wir, daß sie auch ein Scherflein für die hungernden Carpenters in der deutschen Metropole [illegible] solidarischem Interesse opfern werden.

[illegible] besonders ermahnen wir die deutschen Carpenters, ihre kämpfenden Brüder in der alten Heimath nicht zu vergessen. Wir empfehlen, Sammelbogen für dieselben aufzulegen und an P. J. McGuire, No. 124 William Str., New York, zu senden.

Mit Brudergruß und Handschlag

Der Vorstand
des Berliner Zimmermanns Vereins.

Warnung.

„Branch 2 Union 21 B. of C. and J. of A." warnt hiermit einen Jeden vor einem gewissen F. Hube, wohnhaft Cornell, Town Jefferson; derselbe stellt als Carpenter-Boß Leute in Arbeit und bezahlt ihnen dann ihren Lohn nicht. Mit sühen Reden hielt er die beiden Zimmerleute Karl Wille, 24 Kenan Str. und Fritz Wille, 250 Augusta Str. wohnhaft, so lange in Arbeit, bis er einem 20, dem andern 47 Dollars schuldig war. Nehme sich ein Jeder dies zur Lehre und arbeite nicht für einen solchen Menschen, um schließlich um seinen sauer verdienten Lohn beschwindelt zu werden.

Wm. Krause,
Chicago, Jll. Kor. Sekr.

Handwerker und Arbeiter.

Hiermit warnt „Branch 2, Union 21 B. of C. and J. of A." alle Arbeiter vor einem gewissen John Dunphy, jetzigem Stadt-Schatzmeister, sowie seinem Vormann John Wood. Dieselben sind Kontraktoren für Bauten, und [illegible] solche stellten sie vor einigen Wochen die Zimmerleute Christ. Gohrt und Wilh. Wegner [illegible] Commis und Congreß Str. in Arbeit. [illegible] legten, da sie kein Geld erhielten, die Arbeit nieder, und erst, nachdem sie mehrere Tage darnach gelaufen, erhielten sie dasselbe. Man hüte sich vor diesen Menschen!

Wm. Krause,
Chicago, Jll. Kor. Sekr.

[illegible] In Betreff des Kampfes der Arbeiter [illegible] die Kapitalisten äußerte Karl Marx [illegible] Wahrheit, als [illegible] haben nichts zu verlieren. [illegible] Ketten [illegible]

Brüderschafts-Notizen.

— Die Indianapolis Union Nr. 15 hält mit Erfolg öffentliche Gewerksversammlungen im Freien ab.

— Unser Endowment-Fond ist jetzt vollkommen sichergestellt. Alle Local Gewerkschaften erkennen seine Bedeutung und seine Vortheile an.

Die Toledo Union Nr. 25 berichtet, daß das Gewerbe sich bessert. Der Lohn beträgt $2.50; die Union hält sich aufrecht und gewinnt an Stärke.

Der General Sekretär McGuire war jüngst eine Zeit lang an Pleuresie erkrankt, ist indeß jetzt wieder hergestellt und wird bald seine gewöhnliche Arbeitskraft erlangt haben.

— Die Baltimorer Union Nr. 29 verspricht, wenn sie sich im jetzigen Verhältniß weiter vermehrt, ihre Mitgliedschaft bald zu verdoppeln. Auch hat sie ihr Eintrittsgeld und ihre Beiträge erhöht.

Diesen Monat hat unsere Brüderschaft folgenden Lokal Gewerkschaften Charters bewilligt: 41, Morris, Minn. — 43, Hartford, Conn. — 45, Seattle, Wyoming Territorium. — 46, Guelph, Canada.

— Die Untersekretäre der Chicagoer Union Nr. 21 sollen in der Ausarbeitung und Einsendung ihrer monatlichen Berichte an die Exekutiv-Behörde in jener Stadt pünktlich sein, sonst werden die Geschäfte verwickelter.

— Die drei Bauschreiner-Gewerkschaften von St. Louis haben eine Diskussion über die Frage der Verschmelzung zu einer einzigen Gewerkschaft gehabt, sind aber noch zu keiner Entscheidung gekommen. Wir halten es für besser, wenn sie sich vereinigen.

— Die Chicagoer Zimmermanns-Union Nr. 21 hat eintausend Dollars zur Unterstützung der streikenden Backstein-Maurer Chicago's gespendet. Viele Mitglieder der Union Nr. 21 zahlen außerdem $1 wöchentlich von ihrem Lohn in den Strike-Fond der Backstein-Maurer.

— Die Steuern der Union Nr. 2, Cincinnati, O., sind auf 50 Cents per Monat erhöht worden. Es gilt dies vom 1. Mai 1886 an und bleibt 6 Monate des Jahres in Kraft. Während der übrigen Zeit — in den flauen Monaten — werden die Steuern 25 Cents monatlich nicht übersteigen. Die Union Nr. 2 hofft, daß jedes Mitglied prompt bezahlen wird, so daß sie Fonds zur Unterstützung der Mitglieder zur Verfügung hat.

— Die Geschäfte in San Antonio, Texas, gehen sehr lebhaft, und die Löhne steigen von $2.50 auf $3.50 per Tag. Ebenso steigt der Board von $4.50 auf $6 per Woche. Desgleichen das Bauholz von $22 auf $30 das Tausend. Nägel und Metallwaaren kommen sehr hoch. Der Juli und August aber wird des heißen Wetters wegen flau sein. Dagegen günstige Aussichten für den kommenden Herbst und Winter. Unser Correspondent ist gerade daran, eine Union in San Antonio zu organisiren.

Französische Nachrichten. In Frankreich ist es von lange her Sitte, daß der Staat oder auch die Gemeinden bei größeren Industrie-Ausstellungen Mittel zur Entsendung von Arbeitern nach den betr. Ausstellungsorten bewilligen. Da nun demnächst in Amsterdam eine große holländische Industrie-Ausstellung stattfindet, so hat bereits der Gemeinderath von Paris 5000 Franken zu diesem Zweck bewilligt, andere städtischen Collegien sind ihm gefolgt, und in der Kammer ist ein Antrag auf Bewilligung von 100,000 Franken eingebracht worden. Die Pariser Arbeiter-Syndikats-Kammern (Fachvereine) haben bereits mehrfache Besprechungen über diesen Gegenstand gehabt und beschlossen, die Ausstellung zu beschicken, die Unterstützung aber nur anzunehmen, wenn keinerlei Bedingung daran geknüpft wird. Die Delegirten sollen lediglich von Fachvereinen ernannt werden, — ein Beweis, wie eifersüchtig die französischen Arbeiter auf die Wahrung ihrer Unabhängigkeit bedacht sind.

In vielen Industriezweigen herrscht zur Zeit große Geschäftsstille. Tausende von Arbeitern laufen beschäftigungslos herum. Der Fachverein der Bautischler hat daher die Initiative zur Abhaltung einer Versammlung aller arbeitslosen Collegen unter freiem Himmel ergriffen, aber es ward von der Polizei vernichtet.

„Gerechtigkeit benachtheiligt Niemand," ist ein guter, alter Grundsatz der englischen Gewerkschafts-Bewegung, den wir niemals vergessen sollten.

— Die Internationale Union der Möbelarbeiter hat einen Sterbefond, aus welchem $250 beim Tode eines Mitgliedes und $100 beim Tode der Gattin eines Mitgliedes bezahlt werden. Niemand über 50 Jahre hat auf diese Summe Anspruch. Dieselbe wird durch Besteuerung jedes Mitgliedes um 25 Cents [illegible]

Krieg der Dummheit.

Friedrich v. Schiller, glaube ich, hat den Ausspruch gethan: „Gegen Dummheit kämpfen Götter selbst vergebens!"

Wie oft hat dieser Ausspruch als Trost für einen aufgeklärten Arbeiter gelten müssen, der sich Jahrelang vergeblich abgearbeitet hat, seine Kameraden auf einen höheren Bildungszustand und zu einer verbesserten materiellen Lage zu verhelfen. Elende Verläumder und Lügenmäuler sind oft im Stande, die Frucht jahrelanger Arbeit einer Anzahl braver Männer, die mit Aufopferung ihrer Kraft für die Verbesserung der gesammten Arbeiterklasse gewirkt, zu vernichten und die Arbeiter zur Machtlosigkeit zu verdammen.

Und was ist schuld daran! Nichts als die Dummheit der Arbeiter selbst! Sie besitzen nicht Urtheilskraft genug, um die charakterlosen Verläumder zu entfernen und den wirklich ehrlich Kämpfenden zu unterstützen. Der Ehrgeizige verfolgt seine eigenen egoistischen Zwecke und der brave, der wirkliche Kämpfer hat nur das Beste der Gesammtheit im Auge. Er tritt offen und aufrichtig vor die Versammlung hin und legt seine Gründe dar, weil die Masse der Arbeiter aber leider ihr eigenes Bestes sehr langsam begreifen, so hat er nur die aufgeklärtesten auf seiner Seite und unterliegt oft so der Dummheit seiner Kameraden.

Der Ehrgeizige aber hat seine Pläne schon vorher gesponnen und in kurzer Zeit hat er die Majorität auf seiner Seite, und benutzt so die Dummheit seiner Kameraden zu seinem eigenen Vortheil.

Seit des Bestandes unserer Union sind schon oft solche Fälle vorgekommen, die wenigstens eine Schwächung der Union zur Folge hatten. Dann zuletzt kommt der Fuchs zum Loch heraus und dann sehen selbst die Einfältigsten den Fehler, den sie begangen haben. Ich sage daher: Ewiger Krieg der Dummheit! Sie theilt und schwächt die Arbeiter, sie verdammt den Gerechten und belorbeert den Falschen; sie erhält die Arbeiterklasse in Armuth und Elend; kurz, sie ist unser grimmigster Feind!

Wie ist sie aber zu verbannen! Die Millionen, welche alle Jahre geboren werden — wer soll sie gescheidter machen! Alle Schulen sind in den Händen unserer Feinde, den Kapitalisten. Die kapitalistische Produktionsweise herrscht überall und zieht die Dummheit absichtlich groß in den Köpfen der Arbeiter. In allen religiösen Schulen wird das Gift des Aberglaubens schon früh gesäet; in den öffentlichen Schulen lernen die Kinder höchstens das Buchstabenmalen und wenn's weit geht, die vier Species, aber wahre Geschichte und die Grundlage der verschiedenen Wissenschaften bleiben den Kindern der Arbeiter unbekannt. Die Ungleichheit der Erziehung und die mangelhaft ausgebildete Geisteskraft der Arbeiterklasse ist die Ursache der Uneinigkeit der Arbeiter untereinander.

Warum lassen die Arbeiter sich nicht Mann für Mann in die Union aufnehmen? Weil ihr Verstand zu schwach ist, um begreifen zu können, daß nur durch einmüthiges Handeln etwas erreicht werden kann. Die Unionleute selbst, heißt es dann, sind sich ja nicht einig. Nun, dies mag bei untergeordneten Fragen wohl vorkommen; aber in dem einen Punkte sollten alle Mitglieder einig sein: daß die Union der einzige Schutz ist, den die Arbeiter heutzutage haben. Ist dieser dahin, dann ist der einzelne Arbeiter seinem Arbeitgeber gegenüber machtlos und muß deshalb Fußtritte hinnehmen, die er mit Hülfe der Union hätte abwehren können.

Ich bin jetzt in einer Stadt, wo keine Union ist und wo trotz aller Mühe es nicht gelang, eine solche zu gründen.

Wie traurig ist die Lage aller Handwerker! $1.75 bis $2.25 ist der höchste Lohn, und jetzt hat die Eisenbahnkompagnie noch um 20 Proz. den Lohn reduzirt, was selbstverständlich den Lohn in der ganzen Stadt nieder drückt. Die Arbeiter sind verdummt und versklavt, sie lassen sich alles gefallen, und doch könnten sie mit einer nur halbwegs organisirten Kraft diesem Drucke leicht widerstehen.

Möge jeder Leser sich bemühen, unser Organ, den „Carpenter", zu verbreiten, denn er sendet Licht in die dunkle Kammer des Gehirns und verjagt daraus unsern grimmigsten Feind — die Dummheit!

Topeka, Kansas. G. L.

Bauschreinerarbeit in Florida ist sehr flau.

— New Yorker Treppenbauer machen Vorbereitungen, um einen Ausstand für höhere Löhne in Scene zu setzen.

— Die Steinhauer Detroits waren in ihrem Ausstand für 9stündige Tagesarbeit und vollen Lohn siegreich.

— Das Baugeschäft in den Südstaaten ist sehr gut und die Löhne variiren zwischen $1.75 und $2.75, in meisten Fällen $2.25.

[illegible] Arsenal, Utica, N. Y. [illegible]

Allerlei.

— Im Orden der „Knights of Labor" sind Zwistigkeiten zwischen den höchsten Beamten ausgebrochen, welche der gedeihlichen Entwickelung dieser Organisation sehr gefährlich werden können. Allem Anschein nach ist die ganze Angelegenheit nur auf eine Eifersüchtelei zurückzuführen.

— Was sich gewisse Arbeitgeber ihren Arbeitern gegenüber bereits herausnehmen, wie sie dieselben auch während ihrer freien Zeit kontrolliren wollen, zeigt sich so recht deutlich an einem Ukas, welchen die Firma Fowler Bros., in Kansas City, Mo., sowie der Betriebs-Direktor einer Abtheilung der Chicago & Northwestern Eisenbahn in Madison, Wisc., erlassen haben, dahin gehend, daß die von ihren Angestellten, gleichviel ob sie sich im Dienst befinden oder nicht, bei Strafe sofortiger Entlassung keine berauschenden Getränke irgend welcher Art genießen dürfen. Was wohl das Nächste sein wird?

— Auch einen Künstler-Ausstand haben wir zu verzeichnen, der zwar nicht eine Folge verweigerter Lohnerhöhung, sondern beleidigter Ehre war, aber sehr bald, weil sich keine Scabs fanden, zu Gunsten der Striker entschieden wurde. Die Künstler und Dekorateure nämlich, welche die Scenerien für das Musikfest in Cincinnati herstellen, legten kürzlich ihre Arbeit nieder, weil die dramatischen Leiter des Unternehmens gesagt haben sollten, die Künstler seien Trunkenbolde und arbeiteten langsam. Sie nahmen die Arbeit erst wieder auf, nachdem man ihnen ein feines Souper mit Champagner gegeben und die Beleidigung zurückgenommen hatte.

— Von Ausständen in den Bauhandwerken hört man in diesem Frühjahr lange nicht soviel, wie gewöhnlich um diese Jahreszeit. Die Backsteinleger in Chicago sind noch im Ausstand, und scheint das Ende desselben zum Besseren nahe zu sein. Die Arbeitgeber haben ihre Absicht kundgegeben, die Union zu sprengen, was ihnen aber doch schwer werden dürfte, da dieselbe als eine der stärksten in der Stadt gilt und außerdem die übrigen dortigen Gewerkschaften hinter sich hat.

Erfolgreicher waren die Bauschreiner und Anstreicher in New York, welche mit ihrer Forderung auf $3.50 Tagelohn in sehr kurzer Zeit in fast allen Werkstätten durchgedrungen sind.
(Buchdr. Ztg.)

— In der vierteljährlichen Versammlung der Vereine der Zimmerleute von New York und Umgegend, welche am 2. April abgehalten wurde, wurden die folgenden Geschäfte abgewickelt:

Ueber den für diese Saison festzustellenden Lohn in diesem Sommer keine Aenderung eintreten zu lassen, hingegen soll darauf gesehen werden, daß der Unionspreis unter allen Umständen bezahlt werde. Ferner soll in den Vereinigten Baugewerken auf eine Verringerung der Arbeitszeit hingewirkt werden. Der Finanzbericht für das verflossene Vierteljahr ergab an Einnahmen $1,455.50, Ausgaben $4,776.30. Das Gesammtvermögen des Vereins beträgt $1,825.03. Im letzten Vierteljahre wurden 35 neue Mitglieder aufgenommen. Es verunglückten in dieser Periode 18 Mitglieder, von denen zwei mit Tod abgingen.

Gewerks-Nachrichten über Löhne und Arbeit.

Für diesen Monat kommen die folgenden Berichte:

Hartford, Conn.: $2.25–3.75. Geschäft flau.
Baltimore, Md.: $1.25–3.00. Annehmbar.
Allegheny, Pa.: $2.50–3.00. Annehmbar.
Chillicothe, Mo.: $1.50–2.50. Flau.
Trenton, N. J.: $1.25–2.50. Flau.
Wilmington, Del.: $2.[illegible]–2.35. Annehmbar.
New Orleans, La.: $2.00. Sehr flau.
Rushville, Ind.: $1.50–2.50. Eine gute Union.
Newark, N. J.: $2.25–2.75. Meistens Accordarbeit.
Boston, Mass.: $2.50. Aufblühendes Geschäft.
Topeka, Kansas: $1.80–3.00. Sehr flau.
St. Catharines, Canada: $1.75–2.25.
Cincinnati, O.: $2.50. Geschäft langsam.
Milwaukee, Wis.: $2.50. Mittelmäßig.
San Rafael, Californien: soll bald in Ausstand kommen für 9stündige Tagarbeit. Jetzt arbeiten die Mitglieder 9 Stunden nur am Sam[illegible]
Oakland, Cal.: $3.00–3.50. Werden am 1. Juli streiken für 9stündige Tagarbeit.

— Die Hoffnung der Arbeiter beruht o[illegible] [illegible], Organisation und Erziehung.

— Der Mann, welcher den ein[illegible] Anspruch auf Beschäftigung abge[illegible] [illegible] Mann. [illegible]

from $1.50 to $1.15, and the same proportion of reduction has been made in the skilled branches of labor. Carpenters get from $1.80 to $2 per day. There are six carpenters for one job, although business is picking up considerably.

St. Catharines' Union Making Healthy Progress.

ST. CATHERINES, Canada. Trade fair: every union man employed; wages $1.75 to $2.25. Day work prevails—no piece work. Cost of living averages $8 per week for a family of five. Rent from $5 to $10 per month. Union No. 38 is increasing every meeting, members coming from all around the district and prospects of larger numbers. Some are hanging back to see how we succeed and then jump in and join us if we do well. But the mass of men are with us. I do not like to say anything against any labor society, but it is my conviction that the Knights of Labor, the way they are managed now, are working to absorb the trade unions, and if not able to do that, then break them down.

News from Cincinnati.

CINCINNATI, Ohio.—The meeting of Carpenters Union No. 2 on March 27th was the largest since the strike last spring. It made us all feel good to see so many faces that had been so long absent. The object of the meeting was to increase the dues to 50 cents per month. All the members were invited to attend, and many in bad standing came forward and paid their dues like men. The increase of the dues went through with a "hurrah" that has put courage in us all. The combined Trades Union Picnic, June 3 4 in this city, will be a success as in former years. Each union pays $10 to the arrangements and all tickets sold by each union goes into its treasury, and if any surplus is left, each gets a dividend.

Milwaukee Matters.

MILWAUKEE, Wis.—The carpenters of this city seem to dislike organization. Union No. 30 has done all it could to induce them to join, but they always have the same stale excuses. They say they once had a union and it did not last long, and that will be the way with us. They seem to have no interest, only work for whatever the bosses will give them, and many are afraid to join us because their bosses are opposed to us and we would be discharged. This city is a perfect Babel of different languages and nationalities, and they don't and it seems won't understand each other, nor will they associate with each other as they ought. Wages for best carpenters are $2.50, but the majority are working for less than $2. Trade is middling. Union No. 30 had a ball on March 31st and had a jolly time with their friends.

Moving for Nine Hours.

SAN RAFAEL, Cal.—Union No. 35 has unanimously resolved to inaugurate the 9 hour movement in San Rafael. A public meeting was held on April 20, to discuss the question with the bosses, which had a splendid result. Our union is booming ever since we instituted the 8 hour ruled on Saturdays, but we are very particular whom we admit to membership. The boys all jump to get THE CARPENTER, when it comes to the meeting.—On the first Saturday in April all the union carpenters of this city demanded that work should stop at 4 P. M. on Saturdays - eight hours work for that day and full pay. This was done by order of Union No. 35. Some of the bosses thought to oppose us, but we showed them we were ready to take the work on contract ourselves and employ none but union men, for we have the best men in town.

BLACK LIST.

Owen Anderson, formerly a member of Indianapolis Union, No. 15, has been expelled from said union for non-payment of dues and for conduct unbecoming a brother.

Words of Cheer From Hamilton.

HAMILTON, Canada.—In your last quarterly report I see that you are cramped for funds to carry on the legitimate work of the Brotherhood. And all this trouble and embarrassment is caused by the dullness of the past Winter and the failure of a number of unions to do their duty. Do these unions expect you to carry on the business of the Brotherhood, get out our journal and pay all expenses, and do it without money? We find no difficulty paying all our just debts and dues, we assist our sick members, we insure each member's tools against both fire and theft, we have money in the bank and owe no man anything, except good will to all brethren. Brothers, why do you allow our Executive to be embarrassed? If you will only exert yourselves we will be entirely relieved from debt. Allow me to suggest that a strong treasury is the main pillar in our superstructure, either for the Locals or the Brotherhood; let us all do our duty both as individuals, and also as unions.

THOS. BAYLEY.

An Interesting Letter from Oakland.

OAKLAND, Cal.—We intend to go to Alameda, Cal., soon and give our brethren carpenters there a call and have them organize.—We have notified the carpenter bosses of this city that on and after July 1, 1883, we will work no more than 9 hours for a day's work, and so far we have heard of no great opposition. It was at first our intention to start from May 1, but as we considered it would take the bosses at a disadvantage we have been fair enough to fix the date for July 1, 1883. Now let us see if the bosses will be fair enough to grant our demand. We are getting from 6 to 12 new members every meeting. We have more than doubled the past month. The increase has been so great that we had to get a larger hall and now meet on every Monday evening at Knights of Pythias Hall, 1058 Broadway. Members all at work: $3 to $3.50 per day. Work fair since we had rain. We will soon have all the good carpenters in the city in our union. All our best bosses favor the nine hour system, only a few bulldosers oppose it. But we don't intend to work for them; they can leave town, as one of them had to do lately.

The greatest frauds on the Pacific Coast are the Emigration Bureaus. They swindle and dupe workmen to come here from the East to get work. They picture everything in a rosy light to get men here. They claim wages are high and work plenty, and then when the working people get here they find this no better than the East - in fact they find they have been duped to pay big railroad fare and put money in the pockets of the railroads, only to swell the crowd of men who are now looking for a chance to work. There are plenty of men here in California now for all there is to do plenty of carpenters—no matter what lies are told you in Eastern papers about how well we are off here. Many months we are out of work and things promise soon to come to a crisis, then what is the use of moving around to make bad worse. We advise our Eastern brethren not to fall into the hands of the emigration sharks. We are perfectly willing to give full information about this country to any one who thinks of coming to the Coast. I would advise no carpenter to start for California unless he is a union man, or else he will find a hard time to get a job. Otherwise he may fall in the hands of some of the bosses here who never pay their men. One of these bosses ran for School Director last week and got beaten. It would have been better if he paid his men first before he run for office.

Organization Needed in Newark.

NEWARK, N. J. — At present there is very little else than jobbing going on in the city, and future prospects are not very encouraging. Wages run from $2.25 to 2.75, most shops pay by the hour, half the year counts little more than five days; and in Summer only fifty-nine hours per week.

As to the "Carpenters Union" there is such a thing in this city but it is a misnomer, as its proper title "Carpenters disunion" was somehow omitted. Individualism is the order of the day in this city as each one is better than everyone else in his own estimation. But there is a time when the bosses make them all equal by cutting down wages all around thus making them if not entirely equal, at least proportionally equal, as of course when wages are cut down it very generally takes

THE CARPENTER

A MONTHLY JOURNAL FOR CARPENTERS AND JOINERS.

VOLUME III. NEW YORK, JUNE, 1883. NUMBER 6.

NOTICE TO READERS AND MEMBERS.

P. J. McGuire, our General Secretary, is now on the road, and will not return until July 5th. Hence, the next number of this journal may be delayed a few days, and for this we ask the indulgence of our friends. During this month the General Secretary will have his "headquarters in the saddle," nevertheless all letters sent to 184 William street, New York, will be promptly forwarded to him and receive his personal attention.

CHICAGO CARPENTERS.

A mass meeting of the trade will be held at Ulrich's Hall, cor of Kinzie & North Clark Sts., Chicago, Ill., on Monday evening, June 11th, 1883, at 8 P. M.

On the following evening (June 12) at 8 o'clock a general meeting of Union No. 21 will be held. P. J. McGuire will attend both meetings. Let every man attend and bring his friends. Business of importance.

ATTENTION, MEMBERS OF BUFFALO UNION NO. 37.

Every officer and member of Union No. 37 is requested to turn out and attend the meetings of the union regularly. On Thursday, June 21, 1883, P. J. McGuire of New York will address a mass meeting of carpenters in this city. Arouse every man of you, and let there be one more grand rally of the trade. It is time for action. We can't afford to sleep any longer. So come forward, and do your share.

COMMITTEE OF UNION No. 37.

AN EIGHT WEEKS STRIKE ENDED.

When we last went to press, information was given us that the Chicago Bricklayers' strike had succeeded. But it happened that the arrangements then entered into failed through the unfairness of the bosses. Hence the strike was further prolonged until now at the end of eight weeks it has been brought to a close, resulting in a victory for the men. The strike was for $4 per day or 50 cents a day advance, and this is now granted to the men on condition that they modify some of the rules of the Bricklayers' union. These terms have been accepted by the men. Further it is agreed on both sides that all difficulties hereafter shall be settled by arbitration, and should the arbitrators not agree then the matter shall be submitted to any Judge of the United States Supreme Court who may be agreed upon by both sides.

This is [illegible] one of the hardest strikes of the season, and the success of the strike has demonstrated what thorough union will accomplish, when backed up by determination and vigor. The solidarity of the building trades in Chicago was proven in this strike by the practical aid in money given by Carpenters' Union No. 21 and other building trades. Let us hope that a League of the building trades will be now formed in Chicago.

Wages in Buffalo $2.25 to $2.75. [illegible] of Union No. 37 [illegible] [illegible] full of "rats" [illegible] [illegible] projected by speculative [illegible] Builders' Association [illegible] are [illegible] [illegible] [illegible] threat [illegible] against the [illegible]

SPLINTERS AND SHAVINGS.

San Francisco Painters have emulated the example of the Carpenters and won the nine hours.

The Stair Builders of Baltimore, Md., organized a union on May 24, and purpose joining our Brotherhood. Let other cities take a like course.

Horseshoers' unions from 17 cities met in National convention last month and formed a National Union of 11,000 members, with $53,000 in the treasury.

Brass Workers in New York city are agitating for a Saturday half holiday and to that end they have called a convention of the various trades. A nine hour movement would be more likely to succeed and would be more beneficial in every respect.

A great evil among carpenters in New York city is the practice of semi-monthly pay day the men have to wait two weeks to get their wages. Furthermore instead of being paid on the job they must go down to the shop after quitting time and hunt up the boss to pay them.

—A delegation of ship carpenters and caulkers, who arrived at Camden, N. J., from Rockland, Me., to take the places of the strikers, refused to go to work when acquainted with the condition of affairs, and concluded to return home. The strikers cared for them and paid their fares home.

Carpenters get $3 per day in Mobile, Ala. Men are in demand at St. Paul, Minn. Wages are low in Winnipeg, Manitoba. Knights of the saw and plane get only $2.00 per day; the bosses offered false inducements of high pay until there are now ten men for one job.

The San Francisco [illegible] pays a sturdy tribute to Union No. 22 of that city. It says:

[illegible]

This is what the [illegible] organ of the Bricklayers' International Union, says of us:

[illegible]

We appreciate the compliment of our sprightly contemporary, and we shall labor on hoped that we shall [illegible] to merit its good favor.

NEW YORK CARPENTERS.

A well attended mass-meeting of Carpenters was held in Jefferson Hall, [illegible] street and Third avenue, New York, on May 25th. It was held under the auspices of Lodge No. 2, of the U. O. American Carpenters. Addresses were made by Peter Burke, P. J. McGuire, James Lynch, Victor Drury and others. The advantages of the Brotherhood, as well as its aims and constitution were explained by Secretary McGuire and the meeting was very favorably impressed with our plan of organization.

H. [illegible], of [illegible], Indian Territory, has [illegible] the [illegible] the [illegible] of the carpenters in Indian Territory.

[illegible]

A VICTORY OVER VICTIMIZATION.

That system of persecution which capitalists generally use to follow up employes, and victimize them, has last month received a severe blow in the City Court at Trenton, N. J.

Mary E. Slattery a minor entered suit through her father against the American Crockery Company of that city. The testimony shows that she left the employ of the American Co. to find work in another concern known as the Union Pottery Co. Mr. Pliny Fisk, President of the American Co., procured the discharge of the girl from the latter place. This was done in accordance with an agreement among the boss potters of Trenton, not to employ any one working for another firm unless said person can produce a "release" from the previous employer. Mary Slattery left Fisk's employ without such "release" and for this alone she was discharged. The Operative Potters Union took this up as a test case and the result was that the jury gave a verdict of $[illegible] damages in favor of the girl, the full amount of damages claimed for wages lost through this interference. This victory should be followed up everywhere that bosses try to uphold such fugitive slave agreements.

VALUE OF ORGANIZATION.

On April 30th, the stone-cutters of Washington struck for nine hours and got it without any great trouble. They have also established eight hours as the [illegible] on Saturdays. Previous to the organization of the Stonecutters' Union in Washington a year ago, wages were only $2.50 per day, now they get $3.50. Where they formerly worked 60 hours a week, now they work only 53 hours. So through union these trades get one dollar a day more pay, and seven hours per week less work. And all within one year. Surely this proves [illegible] [illegible] [illegible]

AN ARGUMENT FOR SHORTER HOURS.

During the recent nine hour agitation in San Francisco, Rev. Edward Owens made the following very forcible argument:

At a [illegible] of intelligence [illegible], the question of reduction of the hours of labor far ahead of the question of wages. Carpenters should have time for study and association with their families. With reduced hours of labor men at 50 will be straight and strong instead of bent and worn by reason of having drawn too heavily upon the bank of life. With inanimated matter a test of its bearing power is made and no heavier burden than it will bear is placed upon it. But with man it is different. As great a burden as he can stagger under is piled upon him, and should he fall by the wayside the boss does not care for he is only looking to his profits. As long as the carpenters bore an injustice without complaining, so long would they have to bear it. No redress would be had until they rebel and demand their rights.

Baltimore Union No. 29 has raised initiation fee to $2 and [illegible] this dues to 35 cents, formerly the fee was $1 and the dues 25 cents.

Whenever society becomes [illegible] [illegible] true principles of [illegible] [illegible] [illegible] man who stood [illegible] [illegible] [illegible] [illegible] to his fellows, will be looked on as an enemy of his race, and forced into the ranks of honorable toil.

TRADE NOTES.

Toledo, O., trade slow at $2.50.

Trenton, N. J., trade brisk, wages same as last month.

A Labor Bureau Bill has passed the House in the Michigan Legislature.

Carpenters of Troy, N. Y., have organized a union with 200 members and are doing well; wages $2.50 to $3 per day.

- Carpenters are warned to keep away from San Francisco for the present. There are more than enough men in that city for all that there is to do.

The carpenters of Detroit, Michigan, will hold a meeting on June 7, to discuss trade matters, and to arouse an interest in Union No. 40.

Carpenters of Dallas, Texas, recently demanded an increase from $2.50 to $3 per day and got it. But they won't keep it long if they are not organized in a union.

- There are eleven branches in Chicago Union No. 21, and every one of them is active and prosperous. There is a red-hot agitation all over the city, and new members are rolling in from all quarters.

Correspondence from Charlottetown, Prince Edwards Island, reports wages of carpenter's average $1 to $1.25 per day, and work scarce. The men are so poorly off they have no desire for a union.

In Rochester, N. Y., a meeting of carpenters was held May 10th, in favor of $3 per day; the action of this meeting was afterwards reconsidered, and it was resolved to demand an advance of 10 per cent., and to quit at 5 P. M. Saturdays.

The stonecutters of New York, Philadelphia, Brooklyn and Boston, work eight hours a day, while those of Washington and Baltimore work nine hours a day and eight hours on Saturdays. Wages in their trade range from $3.50 to $4 per day.

In Norwich, Conn., business dull; wages $1.75 to $2.25. In New London, Conn., business fair, wages $2 to $2.50. In Norwich very little to do. They had an isolated union there three years ago, and it is [illegible]. Somewhat [illegible] [illegible] [illegible] to start.

ACROSS THE SEA.

Australian carpenters and mechanics generally work only eight hours per day.

- In Berlin, Germany, 3500 carpenters are on strike for 4 marks per day and nine hours as a day's labor. In Frankfort, Grossenhain and Leipzig strikes of various trades are now pending.

The carpenters of London, England work from 6 A.M. to 6 P. M. with three hours of an interval in this time, and a half holiday on Saturday, thus making 56 hours per week. The other building trades average the same.

According to Ex-Secretary Evarts' report [illegible] Belgium, Denmark, Germany, Spain, Austria, Holland and [illegible] average [illegible] $4.50 per week, while [illegible] $6.10. Switzerland $[illegible], Ireland $7.[illegible] Scotland $8.12. [illegible] Great Britain $8.2[illegible] [illegible] [illegible] [illegible] from [illegible] [illegible] [illegible] [illegible] [illegible] is best [illegible] [illegible] pay. Yet [illegible] [illegible] that [illegible] [illegible] come [illegible] Evarts in the [illegible] [illegible] [illegible] are a [illegible]!

[illegible]

THE CARPENTER.

Entered at the Post-Office in New York, as second-class matter.

NEW YORK, JUNE, 1883.

NEW SUBSTITUTES FOR WOOD.

At the very moment when the most intense discussion was going on in the Lumber trade journals as to the growing scarcity of lumber in America, then it was that science came to the front with Straw Lumber as a substitute, and now this is still surpassed by the introduction of Terra Cotta Lumber. A great deal is to be said in favor of both these new materials, but the test of time may show some undiscovered objection to their popularity.

A large straw lumber factory is located at Lawrence, Kansas. Three thousand tons of straw will make 1,000,000 superficial feet of inch slabs. At present it cannot be made as cheaply as pine, but it is considered equal in value to hard wood. It will warp unless used when damp. The boards can be made no longer than 13 feet long and 3 feet wide, but of any thickness. They cannot be split, but otherwise may be sawed and worked the same as ordinary lumber. When finished the material has a streaky appearance caused by the fibers of the straw, is hard, saws quite cleanly, and admits of nails being driven without cracking, splitting or tearing. It has no grain and may, it is asserted, be worked up, finished, polished and decorated in all respects as well and easily as wood. It is nearly fire and waterproof. Floors and ceilings have been made of it. For some uses the fact that the straw lumber is heavier than wood will be a considerable drawback. Tests of the strength of the new material show that a slab 3-4" thick will bear up a weight under which a pine board 1 inch thick will give way.

The second material named, Terra Cotta lumber, is made of a cheap black clay, worthless for any other purposes, and mixed with sawdust in the proportion of three parts of sawdust to two parts clay. It is mixed and ground in mills and then run into molds to any size desired. It is cheaper than wood, and can be sawed and planed, and worked the same as lumber. It is entirely fireproof and extremely light and desirable and fills all the requirements of brick or stone. At a recent meeting of the Franklin Institute, Philadelphia, a gentleman said of it: "We will undertake to produce joist, scantling, cornice or square logs at the rate of 30,000 feet per ten hours."

CONTINUED ACTIVITY OF UNION NO. 21.—NON-UNION MEN COMING INTO THE FOLD.

Union 21, Brotherhood of Carpenters and Joiners of America, is certainly doing faithful and effective work, for the union cause in Chicago. The union numbers among its members many active, intelligent, and whole-souled men, who are laboring zealously and constantly and with splendid results for their organization in this city. Probably two hundred or more new members have been added to the union during the past few weeks, apparently all good men, and among them some of the best mechanics and best known carpenters in Chicago. This has been accomplished mainly through the untiring energy and efforts of the different officers of the union, including President Jones, Vice President Schumacher, Bros. L. E. Schneider, L. J. Boyer, T. H. Blair, J. P. McGinley, W. L. Weeks, W. T. Henderson, William Myers, L. E. Pake, Thos. Carroll, John McCartney, and others who have co-operated and labored with them. The good work still goes on, and it is hoped that it may continue vigorously until all the carpenters of Chicago stand solidly together as brothers, with one purpose in view—to secure the greatest possible good to the whole.

Branch meetings are held all over the city, and every effort is made to thoroughly arouse the trade and bring it within the folds of organization.

ENDOWMENT PAID.

The Endowment or Death Benefit of $300 due to the family of Frank Sanderhaus, deceased, formerly of Cincinnati Union No. 2, has been paid by our General Treasurer.

The endowment due to the family of Bro. John Madden, deceased, formerly of Cleveland Union No. 11, is now next in order.

BALTIMORE BUILDING LEAGUE.

At a regular meeting of Union No. 29, Carpenters and Joiners of the City of Baltimore, the following preamble and resolutions were adopted:

Whereas: It has become a self-evident fact that the organization and combination of interests are the only safeguards workingmen have against the steady encroachments of capital and monopolies in the building line, and

Whereas: We believe that organization of all trades unions connected with the construction of houses, or buildings of any kind in the State of Maryland would be beneficial to all concerned, and

Whereas: There are quite a number of trades unions, as stonemasons, bricklayers, tinners, painters, carpenters, and others connected with building, whose interests are identical with each other, and, therefore, a combination would be of great interest to all, and

Whereas: It has been suggested by some of the members of the different unions, that some steps be taken for self-protection of all the parties in any way connected with the building of houses or property of any kind, so that grievances may be adjusted by arbitration instead of law suits, and

Whereas: The "Mechanics Lien Law," as it now stands on the Statutes, is of no practical use to the workingman who labors by the day, as the trouble, time and expense of collecting by lien is of more than the amount collected, therefore, be it

Resolved: That the members of this union use all honorable means to bring about a combination of all the trades unions in any way connected with the building interests of this State for self-protection and mutual benefit.

Resolved: That we, as members of Union No. 29, believe that the interest of every workingman lies in organization and combination of common interests, so that each association can help to protect the interests of the other.

Resolved: That we recommend that a committee of one member of every organization connected with building in any way be appointed to draft a suitable "Lien Law" for the protection of the different workmen employed in the construction of buildings. Said committee to have the same ready for presentation to the next Legislature for adoption.

Resolved: That a committee of five members of this union be, and are hereby appointed to visit the different trades unions and recommend a like committee on conference of the different interests with a view to organization. Time and place to be appointed by the various committees when appointed.

(Signed) COMMITTEE.

OBITUARY.

ADOLF JOHNSON, aged 35 years, born in Sweden, died April 12, 1883—member in good standing of Chicago Union No. 21, and entitled to benefit. Union No. 21 has paid the widow of our late brother $150 on account of endowment fund.

FERDINAND KOCH, aged 28 years, born in Germany, died April 28, 1883, member in good standing of Chicago Union No. 21, and entitled to benefit. Union No. 21 has paid Mrs. Koch $100 on account of endowment fund.

PRACTICAL CARPENTRY.

The above is the title of a book just published by Fred. T. Hodgson, 201 Broadway, New York. Price one dollar.

This is the most complete book of the kind ever published. It contains about 300 fine illustrations, showing the various methods of obtaining the lines for Roofs, Hoppers, Angle Bars, Raking Mouldings, Curved Rafters, Splayed Work, and hundreds of other things useful to the practical workman. The work also contains a Treatise on Carpenters' Geometry, written in a style so plain that any ordinary workman may easily understand it. The book is thorough, practical and cheap, and gives as much matter and as many engravings as can be found in mechanical books costing $5. Mr. Hodgson, the author, is a man of practical experience in the trade and is the author of "The Steel Square and its Uses," as well as many other valuable works. This new work "Practical Carpentry" should have a large sale.

THE NEXT CONVENTION.

I agree with Amos that annual conventions are very expensive, but to my mind the next convention is settled, and must [illegible] be held this year, and any change from annual conventions must be made at next convention held this year. If a selected number are to meet and deliberate, and the result of such deliberation to be set aside after such great cost and before any meeting of convention, what is the use of conventions?

Although opposed to continual alteration of the constitution, the suggestion of L. J. B. in respect to funeral benefits meets my view. In fact, I have frequently advanced in our Union No. 27, that the figures ought to be reversed and to be: disability $250, death $100, and have been waiting for the convention to take action upon it. In fact, I think that such radical changes, as suggested by L. J. B. show the necessity for a convention this year, so that, if possible, the constitution may be fixed upon a good, sound basis that will not need continual tampering with.

I hope that the result of this will be the adoption of all the changes suggested.

Yours, J. B.

TORONTO, Canada, May, 21, 1883.

THE USE OF WORDS.

Too much care cannot be taken in the use of words. We often hear the terms "capital" and "capitalist" used for the same thing, when in fact there is a vast difference. Capital is necessary for the carrying on of business in the present minute division of industry, but the controller of capital, the capitalist, is a tax on labor that could be dispensed with. There is no antagonism between capital and labor; it is between the capitalist and the laborer. Don't mix the terms.

The word "profit" is oft-times made to do duty for interest, rent and labor. Profit is something for nothing; interest is something for the use of some other thing; rent—for land—is something for the use of that which no man created, of which no man should hold exclusive possession, and to charge for which is robbery; labor is—well labor is the sleek kine, its udders swelled with rich milk for the capitalist and monopolist to squeeze dry, save merely the drippings for the laborer. *Detroit Unionist.*

LABOR STATISTICS.

Miles S. Humphreys, ex-Chief of the Pennsylvania Bureau of Labor Statistics, writes to us as follows: "Our annual reports are distributed *pro rata* among members of the State Legislature for distribution among their constituents. The members complain that the reports as well as those of other departments accumulate on their hands for want of applicants. I have not the least doubt but what the Legislature would take more interest in the Labor Bureau, and aid in making it more efficient, did the people only make a personal demand for the reports and take an interest in them."

This should be sufficient to demonstrate that workingmen, if they wish to support labor bureaus, they should demand the reports.

TROUBLE AVERTED IN THE IRON INDUSTRIES.

The magnanimous bosses in the iron and steel industries, have saved themselves the sufferings of another ordeal such as they went through in the spring of 1882. It is the custom of the workmen to make an agreement each spring as to wages for the year. This is then submitted to the Iron Manufacturers Association for their action. When the scale was submitted this year the bosses proposed a reduction in wages. The Amalgamated workmen would listen to no such proposition, and maintained a bold front. After six weeks of consultation and discussion, the bosses found themselves divided and on May 31st, they yielded to the men and signed the scale for the ensuing year without any reduction. This defeat of the Pittsburg bosses demoralized their confreres in Wheeling, Chicago, and elsewhere, so that the Amalgamated have beaten the bosses, completely and along the whole line! This saves a lockout which would have thrown over 250,000 men into idleness. And all this is due to the cohesion, discipline and power of the Amalgamated Association of Iron and Steel Workers. Long life to it!

BLOOD OF THE WORKERS SPILLED BY SOLDIERS.

For many weeks difficulties have occurred in the coal districts of St. Clair County, Illinois, especially in Belleville. The operators or bosses wanted the men to work for slavish pay. The men refused, whereupon the mines were filled with "blacklegs," who afterwards ran away. When things came to this pass the wives of the miners, as well as the miners themselves were aggravated by sight of soldiers, brought there by orders of Gov. Hamilton, who was only too willing to serve the will of the coal operators. When the soldiers reached the scene they did not delay in firing into the people. The result was over 500 shots were fired; only a few of the miners being armed, they along with their wives were compelled to retreat. Two workmen were killed and several wounded. Twenty-six miners were made prisoners, and afterwards released on their own recognizance. One of those killed was our friend Hoffmeister, who was a true and faithful worker in the labor cause. The Deputy Sheriff commanded the militia to fire upon the people. Now, what strikes us most forcibly in this whole affair is that the authorities recognize their own guilt and that they are the real offenders, or else why did they allow these twenty-six miners to be released on their own mere promises? It is about time that militia were kept from being used to settle the quarrels provoked by capitalists. If Government must be called in on such occasions then it should first insist that the capitalists should do justice to the workers, or else leave them to fight their own battles.

SCABS USING DYNAMITE.

Of all the subterfuges that scabs have ever resorted to in order to gain public sympathy, the latest one surpasses all. The news comes from Troy, N. Y. Some non-union iron moulders were quartered together in a certain building in that city, and one morning not long since it was discovered the building had been undermined, and several excavating tools laid around in the tunnel. At once the cry was taken up, that arrangements had been perfected to blow up the building with dynamite. Of course, this was calculated to arouse prejudice and public indignation against those "horrid" trades unions. It worked very well and the scabs were delighted, but on closer investigation it is now revealed, that the entire scheme was planned and contrived by the scabs themselves to manufacture sentiment against the union men.

BROTHERHOOD NOTES.

Kansas City reports trade good at $2.50 to $3 per day; average $2.50.

Hartford Union No. 43 takes in members every meeting. Meets every first and third Thursday.

—Mr. F. Dunn, Financial Secretary of Union No. 31, Trenton, N. J., has started into business as a builder. We wish him every success.

—On a very stormy night last month, President Stephens and Secretary Busch of Oakland Union No. 36, proceeded to Alameda, Cal., and organized Carpenters Union No. 47.

—Late Spring in Toronto; trade extremely dull; wages forced down last Winter. Those getting high wages were discharged and could not get work only at reduced rate.

Gustav Luebbert, formerly of Topeka, Kansas, has removed to Milwaukee, Wis., and Union No. 30 will find in him great assistance both as a speaker and writer in English and German. He has not fully recovered from his long illness.

New Orleans, La.

Our members here should be more active. They should work to get new members. It is not enough simply to hold the members we have; we must gain new ones continually. Every man in Union No. 16 should see to it that he takes a deep interest in our meetings and in the growth of our union. No lot one and all be up and doing. Business is lively, work brisk, wages $2.50—$3 per day; average mostly $2.50. Plenty of small pox in the city.

THE CARPENTER.

PUBLISHED MONTHLY

BY THE

Brotherhood of Carpenters and Joiners,

OF AMERICA.

Office: 184 William St., New York.

TERMS.—Fifty cents a year, in advance, post-paid.

Send all moneys and correspondence for the Journal to

P. J. McGUIRE, Secretary,
184 William St., New York.

NEW YORK, JUNE 1883.

—Keep away from San Francisco, and advise all carpenters to do the same.

Stop "rushing" each other to satisfy the demands of the bosses. Do an honest day's work. No more; no less.

—Our whole strength should be centred on a reduction of the hours of labor. Let nine hours be our objective point until it is firmly established in our trade all over America.

—In 1879 after 19 weeks strike the Amalgamated Machinists of Great Britain gained the nine hour work day. Yet American workmen in the vast majority of cases are content to work ten hours a day. And some even cringingly beg the bosses to let them work overtime when they ought to have the manhood to organize and get enough pay for eight or nine hours a day, not to work any longer.

CHICAGO STRIKE.

From latest information sent us from Chicago, we learn that the bricklayer bosses have been dishonorable enough to violate the agreement already entered into with the men. Consequently, the strike is now renewed in its fiercest form. And the result is doubtful to predict, as many conflicting rumors prevail.

IMPORTANT TO LOCAL UNIONS.

Whether there is a convention or not this year, it is now time that the local unions sent in to the General Secretary this month (June) all changes, amendments or alterations they may desire to have made in the constitutions and laws of the Brotherhood. This is necessary in order to have them printed in next month's (July) journal. The constitution requires they shall be sent in this month.

BERLIN CARPENTERS OUT ON STRIKE.

BERLIN, Germany, May 1, 1883. A few days ago 3000 carpenters assembled in Tivoli Hall, and amid great enthusiasm decided to make a general strike to-day, inasmuch as the bosses have not granted their demand for a few cents a day more. To-day the strike started, and now it has assumed gigantic proportions. The unmarried men are pledged to leave the city sooner than surrender. Those who get the advance are to pay to support those on strike. This morning 42 bosses acceded to the men, while there are about 200 bosses still holding out. Strict rules have been laid out for the conduct of the strike and all the men need, is a little financial assistance. They are full of courage.

(The writer of this letter appeals to our Brotherhood to assist the strike. And we second the motion. Each local union should do something to aid our brothers in their brave struggle. Our trade has one common interest the world over. Information as to where money can be sent will be furnished from this office. P. J. McGuire, 184 William street, New [illegible]

HOW A GENERAL VOTE CAN BE TAKEN.

In considering this question, we have before us the examples of a score of trades unions, national and international, scattered all over the globe. Some of our members say "A general vote can't work in the Brotherhood. It is too complicated and slow."

Look at the Amalgamated Carpenters with 22,000 members in good standing! They are scattered all over Europe and this country, also in Australia, New Zealand and South Africa, yet the system of a general vote on officers and changes in their laws is carried out with the greatest satisfaction. The same rule is in force among the Engineers, Blacksmiths, Coal Miners, and all the leading Trades Societies of Europe.

In this country the Cigar Makers with 15,000 members and over 300 unions, make all changes in their laws by a general vote. So do the Granite Cutters with 8000 members. The German Printers, Cabinet Makers, Iron and Steel Workers, and Iron Molders do the same. Now if these International Unions can carry out this plan, why can't the carpenters? Are we inferior to the other trades in point of intelligence, or do we love more to be ruled by delegates and officers than to rule ourselves?

What is there about the plan that is impracticable? All that makes some men oppose it is simply that, it is novel and unknown to them. Well so were railroads and telegraphs opposed in their time; the electric light and the telephone were ridiculed when first projected. But all these improvements have become firmly established and are now benefitting even those who opposed them.

Men who have become accustomed to the rule of delegates and political bosses, imagine that the same rule should apply in trades societies. That is all there is in it. And when men once understand the method of a general vote they will be heartily in its favor.

Let us examine its workings. Suppose it is discovered that some change is required in our laws, we have to wait now until a convention makes the change. But under the system of a general vote the change can be made at any time required. Whether an amendment or an addition, it is first proposed by some union, and then printed in our journal for the information of each and every member. In the mean time the motion is sent out in circular form to every union by the E. B. of our Brotherhood. At the end of say six or eight weeks, the yea and nay vote of each union on the question must be sent into the officers of the Brotherhood and the vote of each union is then announced in the journal. It is plainly evident that this is certainly a fairer and better plan than to permit a few delegates to make laws just as they please.

A BUILDING PLAN.

Messrs. Palliser, Palliser & Co., of Bridgeport, Conn., the well known Architects and Publishers of standard works on architecture, have lately issued a sheet containing plans and specifications of a very tasteful modern eight-room cottage with tower, and also with the necessary modifications for building it without the tower, and with but six rooms if desired. In its most costly form, the outlay is estimated at $3,000; without the tower it has been built for $2,500; and if only six rooms are included, the cost may be reduced to $1,700 or $2,000. Details are given of mantels, stairs, doors and casings, cornices, etc. The publishers have found it the most popular plan they have ever issued, and state that it has been adopted in more than five hundred instances within their knowledge. The same firm issue specifications in blank adapted for frame or brick buildings of any cost; also forms of building contract, and several books on modern inexpensive, artistic Cottage plans which are of great practical value and convenience to everyone interested.

THE BRANCH SYSTEM OF ORGANIZATION. POSTPONING THE CONVENTION.

Since my last communication to the *Carpenter*, I see there has been a meeting of the Executive Board of the Brotherhood and that body has shown it is not a figure head. The proposition to postpone the next convention this year meets with my hearty approbation, and the plan of electing officers and making changes in the workings of the Brotherhood by popular vote, was one of the points I intended to make in a future communication. By that means every man will have a chance to vote as he pleases, whereas in the convention plan it is very expensive and left to a few men.

I am glad to see such an important step made in the right direction. The plan of general vote ought to be adopted by our local unions by acclamation, and then with the adoption of the equalization and universal plan, and the election of a General President, who would be an organizer throughout the United States and Canada, we would commence business in earnest, and in one year from now our Brotherhood would grow so fast that its best friends would not know it.

In regard to the third recommendation relative to remitting of the endowment-fund direct to the Treasurer of the Brotherhood, that would not be necessary, if the equalization plan is adopted, for then the benefit could be paid direct from the local of which the brother was a member, but I am in favor of all moneys being remitted direct to the Treasurer of the Brotherhood, and all bills being paid by that officer in the usual way. I hope the proposed changes will be put to a vote and carried without delay.

Now I would like to say just a word in favor of the branch system being adopted in large cities, in preference to the centre of city system. I take it that our Brotherhood will have to be firmly established in all the principal cities of this continent, before we can make any headway in the smaller towns, that is to say, it will have to control the trade in any city where a local exists, by that I mean that two thirds of the carpenters in the city will have to be members in good standing in the union to control the trade in the city. So you see the sooner the locals that are already started get strong, the sooner will our Brotherhood become a power in the land. The question arises which is the best system to adopt in order to strengthen the local unions. I say the branch system and it will not take me very long to prove it.

The battle has been fought and won here in Chicago only a little over a year ago. We were "like a house divided into itself." We [illegible] two local unions, one having the branch system and the other the opposite way. I by accident happened to join the one that had no branches although I was then as now strongly in favor of the branch system. Many of my friends differed with me in that regard, those brethren after one year's trial of the branch system are to-day its strongest advocates; that is a very strong argument in its favor. Well, as I said, we were divided, one local pulling at one end of the rope one way, and the other in the opposite direction, after creating a great deal of ill will against the leading members on both sides. With the aid of General Secretary McGuire we came together, adopted a different number and transacted our business in branches through the medium of an Executive Council. At that time I don't believe both locals together could muster more than 200 good members, although they claimed more than that number. That, as I said, was but one year ago, and now look at us, we have 11 branches in full blast and 1000 members, initiated about twice as many, and if our Brotherhood had been in better shape we could have *retained* a very great many more. Now, supposing we had only one meeting place, and had abolished the branches, do you suppose we would have made such headway as that?

No local has done so well as Chicago (Union No. 21) in the past year, excepting San Francisco (Union No. 22), but they had a live President, Bro. E. Owens. We have German branches, Scandinavian branches, and a Bohemian branch, and the constitution printed in the different languages; how do you suppose we could transact our business in one meeting place?

Another point in favor of my plan is the fact, that by establishing branches you can have meetings of the union, convenient to the residences of all the brothers. You cannot expect every man to inconvenience himself to attend every meeting, when he will have to go 3 or 4 miles to the place of meeting, but if the meeting hall is located within a few blocks of his residence, he will attend every meeting and become a good member. Also I have noticed as a rule, just as soon as a member gets into office, then he becomes a worker for the union. Every branch has so many officers and they, consequently, so many workers for the union.

There are a great many more points I could mention in favor of the branch system if space and time permitted. I will close with the advice to the locals in cities, where there are a thousand or more carpenters working at the trade to try the branch system, and you will find you will succeed beyond your most sanguine expectation.

L. J. B.

CHICAGO, May 27, 1883.

AN EXPLANATION.

The following appears in the *Lowell Sunday Advertiser:*

We can't see the wisdom of THE CARPENTER in persistently growling at the Knights of Labor. We opine that a majority of its readers do not approve its course.

We beg to state that THE CARPENTER does not "growl" at the Knights of Labor. Those who view our remarks in that light mistake the spirit in which they are presented.

THE CARPENTER has always, and persistently recommended, urged, and practically performed the organization of labor.

Where, however, it perceives that some, misconceiving the objects and purposes of the Knights of Labor, proceed on such a course as is likely to result in labor's disorganization, then THE CARPENTER considers it within its province to call attention to the fact.

And in this we are sure our course is approved by our readers and by all fair-minded men.

FROM OUR GENERAL PRESIDENT.

I desire to call your attention to some few facts that perhaps many of you have heretofore recognized and then dismissed from your minds. But facts are stubborn things and should always be held in mind in preference to false ideas. Our organization being young and inexperienced in the proper methods to pursue to ultimately bring us to the goal of our aspirations, makes it vitally necessary that one and all interested in our movement should consider well and wisely all questions placed before them for their consideration.

Snap judgment which generally prevails where experience is not master, places almost every question or proposition whether for weal or woe to the organization, entirely at the mercy of the inexperience and temper of the majority of those who compose the organization. Hence the passage or rejection of any resolution, question or proposition is susceptible to a condition of temper or judgment where cool and deliberate consideration and experience does not rule.

Therefore the necessity of your carefully considering all new propositions, or amendments to our laws, and all important changes in our laws as well as every question submitted to you that has an equal bearing on all unions, before you adopt or reject them.

Be not hasty in condemning or in ratifying any question. But first consider it carefully from every standpoint of view, always remembering that the solidarity and longevity of any institution or structure solely depends on the perfection of its foundation. If the foundation be inadequate to sustaining the superstructure, the mass must fall in shapeless ruin. Let us give such thought and attention to the perfecting of the objects of our young organization, that no imperfections of an unsound nature will ever overtake us through the stress of times that may come to us in after years.

The circular of the Executive Board issued to you in May is neither [illegible]—changes necessary to make the working of the Brotherhood more perfect as viewed by us. It is for you to take the matter up and use the suggestions as you think proper.

The postponement of the convention is a question that is of vital importance to you, as we can only see it in one light—that it is an outlay of money needlessly expended when greater results can be gained with half the money, expended for agitation and organization. The system of popular vote is to my mind the only rational method that can be established to give voice and vote to all who compose the Brotherhood. For the practical determination of that greed and of the prescription of reason and justice, must be left to those interested, with the rational certainty that the judgment of the majority will be safest. Beyond these limits any one who is subject to the control of another without voice or vote in the government, is the essence of tyranny and should be put down. Popular vote does away with bossism and leaves our members the masters.

Let us look at our beneficial features for a moment. It has been claimed by one of our unions that benevolent features in trade unions were injuring its protective principles, and that the two could not be maintained together. It looks very much like an oversight, for a union that is strictly protective is literally beneficial in finding work for its members at higher rates than can be obtained through disorganization. If a high rate of wages could be maintained and financial crises forever deterred, if men could be taught that only through protective organization is the realization of decent competence possible, if the selfish greed, the niggardly disposition to outrun his fellow man could be thrown off as we do an old coat, then there would be no need of paying benefits. But until such results are achieved something more binding than the mere protection of wages is necessary for the establishment of a lasting organization among the carpenters of America.

In conclusion I say to you make your endowment features stronger and better, more possible of fulfillment, for in that portion of your organic law lies the success of your organization. So far we have been a benefit, let us continue our work. Don't let stupidity or greed blind us or cause us to do that which will discourage our trade, but let us inculcate friendly feelings that will give universal hope for the perpetual establishment of our Brotherhood.

Respectfully

J. D. ALLEN, G. P.

PHILADELPHIA, PA., June 1, 1881.

INDUSTRIAL GEMS

(BY HELEN WILMANS.)

The animals live; but man who is the roof and crown of things is exiled from life. Cramped and dwarfed by laws not of his making, tethered to exhausting and yet precarious toil, debarred of hope, confused with fears, his existence wastes itself in sluggish pain. From the cradle to the grave it is a lingering death.

The future of the race whether man shall descend again to be a savage or ascend to be a god, depends upon his ability to solve the problem of how to satisfy his animal needs without toil so severe as to be exhaustive of his mental qualities. Once freed from the never ending curse of a struggle for bread, the race would be masters of Nature's forces within a generation.

Society has always proven itself equal to the task of protecting itself when left to itself. And if the so-called courts of justice were abolished, and all laws relating to the conduct of the individual were repealed, there would, as I firmly believe, be less crime than there is to-day.

GOOD INFLUENCE OF FAIR WAGES.

Evil influence of depressed wages. The example of such individuals, or bodies of individuals, as submit quietly to have their wages reduced and who are content if they get only the mere necessaries of life, ought never to be held up for public imitation. On the contrary, everything should be done to make such apathy be esteemed disgraceful. The best interests of society require that the rate of wages should be elevated as high as possible that a taste for the comforts, luxuries and enjoyments of human life should be widely diffused, and if possible, interwoven with the national habits and prejudices. A low rate of wages, by rendering it impossible for increased exertions to obtain any considerable increase of comforts and enjoyments, effectually hinders any such exertions from ever being made, and is of all others the most powerful cause of that listlessness and apathy that contents itself with what can barely continue animal existence.—McCulloch's *Political Economy, Part III., Sec. VII.*

— It is stated that the Count de Chambord has been issuing free bread tickets to the poor in Paris. If he and the rest of the brigand aristocrats and money robbers will take their thieving clutch off the productions of labor, poor people would be able to buy their own bread. — *San Francisco Truth.*

THE LABOR QUESTION.

LECTURE VIII.

EXCHANGE.

We have attempted to show in previous lectures that the first three elements through which the activities of mankind manifest themselves in order to produce wealth, are land, labor and capital.

We have now to consider the two remaining elements, which are Exchange and Insurance.

If we can demonstrate that Exchange is one of the elements which aids in the production of wealth, and that the exchanger is one who should simply perform an industrial function, and if we can give a clear conception of the service which that function performs, we shall show that the element "Exchange," performs a useful function, and that it merits a certain compensation.

If, again, we can show that exchange has had an inequitable share in the distribution of wealth up to the present time, and can point out a means by which the function of exchange can be performed with greater advantage to society in the future, we shall have rendered a service to the cause of labor in general and to every worker in particular.

Labor, that is, the activities of humanity, which are purely immaterial, operating upon the products of the land or material objects, results as we have seen in the formation of capital.

When capital is formed, the fourth element, "Exchange" enters upon the scene of human relations in its natural order, as one of the five elements of production.

In the prosecution of the various branches of industry, it has been found advantageous to practice the subdivision of labor, by reason of which one man by his labor produces much more of one particular thing than he requires for his own consumption; and of many other things which he requires, he produces none. It is this simple fact which gives rise to the element "Exchange," and makes it equally as important as the other four elements, but certainly not more so.

In order to show the necessity of exchange, it would, perhaps, be well to illustrate more fully the above paragraph as a correct understanding of the subdivision of labor, giving rise to the necessity of exchange, is very important when treating of the labor movement.

We will presume, for the sake of clearness, that a farmer, with a family of five, cultivates a farm of fifty acres, from which he produces wheat, oats, rye, corn, potatoes, meat, butter, and all kinds of vegetables. He evidently produces much more of these things than his whole family could possibly consume. He requires, boots, shoes, hats, coats, furniture, linen, etc., but he does not produce any of these articles.

In precisely the same way the shoemaker makes more than he requires of shoes, the hatter makes more hats, the tailor makes more garments, the carpenter makes more tables, the weaver makes more linen &c.

But neither of these last-named five men produce any wheat, corn, potatoes or vegetables, and yet they all require these things. It is evident, therefore, that the farmer will gladly give part of his corn, &c., to the shoemaker for part of his shoes, and that the shoemaker will just as gladly give the farmer part of his shoes for a part of the farmer's corn. It is equally evident that the farmer will act in the same way with the hatter, tailor, carpenter and weaver, who, in their turn, will reciprocate.

This act of giving part of what the one has in over-abundance for a part of that which another has in over-abundance, thereby furnishing each other with what neither of them before possessed, which is a mutual benefit to both parties, constitutes what we call "exchange."

Exchange may, therefore, be considered as the distribution of wealth, or that which is produced by labor. Or it may be called the exercise of labor in the transportation of capital from a place where it is not in demand to a place where it is demanded.

It is not difficult to perceive that exchange is one of the elements in the production of wealth, just as labor is, and that it is an element equally as useful, for without its exercise men could not procure those things which are necessary to satisfy their wants or minister to their enjoyment, no more than they could enjoy these benefits without the exercise of labor.

It is here necessary to call the attention of the reader to certain definitions which are used by the economists, many of whom define political economy to be "the science of the production, distribution and consumption of wealth," and hence they speak of the producer and consumer as though they were entirely separate, the one from the other.

Now it is evident that the two terms, producer and consumer, are interconvertible, and cannot be separated, for the producer is at the same time a consumer, not only of part of that which he himself produces, but also of part of that which is produced by many others. When they say that the interest of the producer and consumer are opposed to each other, they fail to see the identity of interests which exists between all men.

Because labor and exchange are two distinct functions, it has been supposed that the interests, of the producers and consumers, were opposed to each other, for labor seems to represent production, while exchange would appear to represent consumption. It is this appearance which has enabled the economist to deceive, while appearing so plausible.

It arises from a want of power of analysis. They do not see the difference between the labor of the producer and the labor of the exchanger, both of whom are producers and consumers, and their interests are mutual. Both are laborers, whose labors are directed to different ends.

In precisely the same way as we saw when treating of the element "capital," many have confounded the element "capital," with the capitalists; and as the capitalists had committed enormities against the laborer, they declare that capital is an enemy to labor, making no distinction between capital and the capitalist, labor and the laborer. In fact, displaying a want of the power of analysis.

When wealth has been produced through the instrumentality of the land, labor and capital, exchange becomes possible, and is effected by various means or through various agencies, the two most important of which are transportation and money, or currency. Transportation is effected by railroads, canals, high-ways, and the various vehicles used upon the different kinds of roads. The railroad is to-day the most important of all these agents. In fact, it may be termed the high-way of the nineteenth century. Money is also an important agency, as it is or should be, a representative of wealth, which wealth, being itself a product and consequently a representative of labor, money should be a representative of labor or service performed.

It is evident that if these agencies or mediums of exchange are monopolized, thereby preventing the free exercise of exchange in the interest of a few, and to the detriment of the many; if the function of exchange is performed by a few in their own exclusive interest, it is equally evident that this element, "exchange," obtains for itself a larger share of the wealth produced than in equity belongs to it, and therefore injustice exists, since one or some other of the elements, if not all of them, obtain less than they should, and either land or capital or labor is robbed of its just portion.

In order to secure an equitable distribution, it is necessary to place all the producers of wealth who desire to make exchanges in direct communication with each other by the proper organization of exchange, and to abolish all unnecessary intermediate agents, traders or middlemen, who, because they perform exclusively the function of exchange, and, by virtue of monopoly, can control markets, have arrogated to themselves the power of determining not only the reward which shall go to the element of exchange or to themselves, but also to all the other elements.

The division of labor, which causes men to devote themselves, exclusively to one particular branch of manufacturing industry, leads others to devote themselves exclusively to exchange, and the merchants, by continually teaching and preaching, have succeeded in making the world believe that their own function of exchange is of vastly greater importance than the function of the laborer or producer, and, by virtue of this belief, have preyed upon the workers and have established the present system of commercial feudalism.

It is evident that production and exchange are two separate social functions, and that the separation is advantageous to all; for if the man who devotes himself to labor were compelled to find a market for his production — in other words, become also an exchanger — it would necessitate loss of time, etc., thereby reducing his capacity for production; while, on the other hand, the exchanger, if he were to occupy himself with production, would necessarily be unable to occupy himself with exchanging. It will be necessary to provide for the exchange of labor as well as the exchange of commodities, this has been perceived by the French workmen who are building a labor exchange in Paris.

The exchanger by means of monopoly, has become virtually the proprietor of the products of labor, and from that fact, instead of performing his functions honestly by facilitating the exchange of the products of labor, has really become the means of preventing the facility of exchange.

In the first place, by monopolizing the railroads; secondly, by a partial monopoly of the currency, which is a medium of exchange; thirdly, by monopolizing the products of labor by "cornering" the markets &c.; fourthly, by controlling the express and carrying companies, which have been compelled, through the influence of monopoly, to combine for the purpose of preventing the legitimate extension of the business of the post-office.

The Adams Express Company interfered with the mail by lobbying at Washington, when it was proposed to carry packages over four pounds in weight. The post-offices should logically extend its operations to all kinds of carrying and transportation. If it is legitimate to carry four pounds, why not five or six pounds? Where is the limit? Are the express companies to decide what the limit is to be, or is the decision to remain with the directors of the United States Post-Office, who represent people?

The railroad companies pretended to dictate terms to the post-office, and interfered with the regulation of that establishment, when they refused to contract with the post-office to carry mail matter on their fast trains. In fact, by defying the government, they asserted that corporations were not subject to the government, but that they were the government and could govern it.

The railroads are permitted to practice extortion upon the producer by regulating the price of the transport according to their caprice, without any reference to the cost of transportation, thereby levying blackmail upon industry.

The State of Massachusetts is the only one in the Union which has asserted the supremacy of the State over the power of railroad corporations, by the establishment of a Board of Railroad Commissioners, who, in their report of 1871, determined the actual cost of transportation to be eight cents per hundred miles for each passenger, at the same time admitting that the railroads of that state were loosely and wastefully administered. The report of that commission is fully corroborated by the investigations made upon the management of the railroads of England, France and Belgium, which shows that in those countries it only costs five cents to carry a passenger one hundred miles.

This feature of monopoly will continue until the people become cognizant of the fact that the railroads and telegraphs are instruments of exchange, and should be run in the interest of production and the people, instead of being run in the interest of an individual or a corporation. As currency is an instrument of exchange, and is based upon gold, and as that gold is monopolized, the banker steps in and prevents the facility of exchange by reason of that monopoly.

The monopolists who control the telegraphs interfere with the freedom and facility of exchange. The consolidation of the various companies, is accomplished simply for the purpose of robbing the public. The total capital invested in the telegraph lines of the United States is about $30,000,000 but by the watering of stocks it has been raised to about $80,000,000.

The governments of England and Belgium have purchased the telegraphs of those countries and have placed them under the management of the post-office. It is not at all unlikely that the government of the United States will follow the example set by other countries.

The question will naturally arise as to whether the government shall purchase them at the actual cost or whether they shall pay for the watered stock, and thus offer the patronage of the government as a premium for swindling.

Between the actual cost of establishing those lines and the sum which they represent in shares of stock, there is a margin of some $50,000,000, which the people should take care to see is not put into the pockets of lobbyists, speculators, monopolists and swindlers.

The practice of forestalling and cornering the markets is so detrimental to the interest of the people at large, that we may well wonder why those who practice it have not been punished as they merit. An example of this practice will show its villainy. While in the winter of 1873-4, the miners were digging coal for 30 cents per ton, the exchangers of New York, the monopolists combined, were making the poor pay at times from $15 to $20 per ton; and yet these men have made the people believe that they confer a benefit to labor by taking care of Exchange. It is well that the workers should determine to recognize exchange merely as an industrial function, of no greater importance than Labor, meriting its due reward, but unworthy of the lion's share of the wealth produced.

When exchange becomes organized, it will not be found necessary to make profits off the products which are delivered to the consumers, but merely to cover the cost of operating the exchanges, or, in other words, to pay those who take charge and care of them, and place them at the disposition of the consumers. The present commercial methods, with their antagonisms and deceits, will be eliminated.

The Eastern States are full of wares and manufactured goods; the Middle States are glutted with iron and coal; the South is overflowing with grain and cotton; the West has corn and meat in superabundance; and yet East, West, North, and South people are dying of starvation. Why? On account of a restricted distribution of wealth, caused by the monopoly of the means of exchange.

Der Carpenter.

New York, Juni 1883.

Gewerbe-Nachrichten über Löhne und Arbeit.

Cincinnati, O.: $2.50–2.75. Geschäft gut. Union 2 hat am 1. Mai ihre eigene Vereinsfahne bekommen.

Moberly, Mo.: $1.50–2.25. Geschäft flau.

Utica, N. Y.: $1.75–2.50. Mittelmäßig.

New Newport, Mass.: $2–2.25. Lebhaft. Eine Union steht in Aussicht.

Wheeling, W. V.: $2.25–2.75. Geschäft nicht so gut, wie vor zwei Jahren. Bald kommt eine Union hier zu Stande.

Lancaster, Pa.: $1.75–2.00. Auch in dieser Stadt sind Schritte zur Bildung einer Union gethan.

San Rafael, Cal.: $2–3. Flau, der Arbeitsmarkt ist überfüllt.

St. Catherines, Canada: $1.75–2. Annehmbar. Uebrigens agitiren wir für 9stündige Arbeitszeit am Samstag.

New Orleans, La.: $2.50–3. Annehmbar. Die Blattern grassiren stark in der Stadt.

Oakland, Cal.: Unsere Neunstunden Agitation macht schöne Fortschritte. Viele neue Mitglieder sind gewonnen.

Cleveland, O.: $2.25–2.75. Annehmbar. Unsere Meister wollten gerne einen Lohnabzug in Scene setzen, sind aber zurückgetreten.

Jeffersonville, Ohio: $1.25–2. Viel zu thun, aber wir müssen unsere Zustände durch Organisation verbessern.

Ron. N. Y.: Unsere Union besteht schon seit zwei Wochen, und das Geschäft ist sehr annehmbar.

Toledo, O.: Eines von unseren alten Mitgliedern ist jüngst gestorben. Er war indeß mit seinen Beiträgen im Rückstande und dadurch verliert seine Familie die Begräbnißgelder.

Boston, Mass.: $2.50 sind hier jetzt leichter zu bekommen, als im letzten Jahre, und das ist nur der Macht unserer Organisation zu verdanken.

Washington, D. C.: $3. Wir haben ein Unions Nachweisungsbureau errichtet.

Toronto, Cannada: $1.75–2.25; meistens $2. Einwanderer haben den Arbeitsmarkt überfüllt.

Newport, N. J.: $2–3. Geschäft annehmbar. Eine Union steht in Aussicht.

San Francisco, Cal.: Die 9stündige Arbeitszeit ist vollständig durchgeführt; es sind aber mehr Zimmerleute hier, als das Geschäft braucht.

Baltimore, Md.: $2.50. Geschäft annehmbar. Unsere Massenversammlung am 2. Mai war sehr erfolgreich. Redner war P. J. Mc Guire.

Die Kapitalisten-Presse und die Arbeiter.

Wer in den letzten Wochen einen Blick in die täglichen Kapitalistenblätter geworfen, wird darin verschiedene Artikel über Strikes gefunden haben. Dieselben hatten meistens den Schlußsatz, daß die Arbeiter Unions schuld daran seien. Allerdings, behaupten sie, gibt es auch harte „Brodherren", welche die Arbeiter drucken, aber deren Zahl ist nur klein, die meisten wollten das Wohl ihrer Arbeiter befördern, aber die Großmäuler und Wühler in den Unions verführten die Arbeiter zum Strike und zur Unzufriedenheit, wovon schließlich die Bosse den größten Vortheil hätten etc. Besonders sind es die deutschen Kirch[illegible], welche ihren gläubigen Schaaren solche Baren aufbinden, die dann von den übrigen deutschen Denk- und Schreibfaulen Zeitungsschreibern im Lande nachgebetet werden.

Sie kommen meistens mit der Phrase: „Jeder Arbeiter ist seines Lohnes werth," aber sie sollen die Freiheit der Arbeiter aufrecht erhalten, indem der fähige und tüchtige Arbeiter einen höheren Lohn verdiene, als der ungeschickte und faule, die Unionleute verlangten aber gleichen Lohn und das sei eine Tyrannei. Diese ganze Schwätzerei ist nur deshalb in Scene gesetzt, um den Fortschritt der Arbeiter Unions zu verhindern, damit die Unternehmer und Fabrikanten einen größeren Profit von den Arbeitern ziehen können. Deshalb versuchen diese Schreiberseelen den Arbeitern den Kopf zu verdrehen und ihnen falsche Ansichten über ihre Interessen beizubringen. Viele sind aber auch so polizeiwidrig dumm, daß sie die Interessen der Arbeiter mit denen der Brodherren für gleich halten.

Heut zu Tage ist es kein Geheimniß mehr, daß nur durch Arbeit neue Werthe und Güter entstehen, und daß daher die Arbeiterklasse der Brodherr der Kapitalistenklasse ist. Es mag allerdings der einzelne Boß auch mit arbeiten und seinen Lebensbedarf selbst erzeugen, aber für die Arbeiter schafft er das Brod nicht. Er beschäftigt die Arbeiter nur, um Gewinn von deren Arbeit zu ziehen, nicht aber um Geld zuzusetzen oder dem Arbeiter mehr zu geben als er verdient. Diese altertümliche Phrase vom Brodherrn spukt nur noch in den Köpfen verkommener Zeitungsschreiber, alle halbwegs civilisirten Menschen lassen sich nicht mehr davon übertölpeln.

Was nun die Freiheit der Arbeiter anbetrifft, welche diese Herren meinen, so wissen wir gut genug, daß sie darunter verstehen, einem jeden Arbeiter den Lohn so viel wie möglich herunter zu drücken, daß der Arbeiter dann, durch die äußerste Noth gezwungen, annehmen muß. Wo eine gute Union existirt, da wehrt sich der Arbeiter gegen die Herabsetzung des Lohnes und weiß, wenn es zum Strike kommt, daß seine Kameraden ihn unterstützen. Durch Zusammenhalten der Arbeiter ist oftmals eine Kraft, welche der geldmächtige Boß nicht brechen kann. Diese Blutsauger wollen die Arbeiter wehrlos zu ihren Füßen liegen haben, damit sie dieselben aussaugen können, wie der Wolf das Lamm. Deshalb ihr Wuthgeheul gegen die Männer, welche sich der Mühe unterziehen, Arbeiterorganisationen und Trades Unions zu gründen und zu erweitern.

Durch unsere Unions erhalten wir mehr Macht und durch Macht mehr Rechte, Freiheit und Brot.

Daß nun auch die Zunft der Gottesgelehrten gegen uns heult, ist sehr natürlich. Sie wollen keine selbstdenkende, nach Freiheit und Rechten strebende Arbeiterklasse haben, weil diese viel besser ohne die Pfaffenzunft vorwärts kommt, denn, sie wollen Herren und Diener, Reiche und Arme haben, damit es immer genug Lämmer gibt, die ihren Säckel öffnen, um den Herren Gelegenheit zu geben, sich einen Schmeerbauch anfressen zu können. Sie sehen, daß durch die verbesserte Organisation der Arbeiter ihnen dasjenige davonfliegt, was sie so lange ungestraft gerupft haben.

Heute glauben allerdings immer noch Arbeiter ihren Seelenhändlern, aber je mehr die Arbeiter ihre eigene Klassenlage erkennen, desto mehr verlieren sie an Gewicht, was nur zum Besten unser Aller sein kann.

Uns aber sollte die Thatsache immer mehr anspornen, für die Erweiterung und Verbreitung unseres Organs und aller anderen wirklichen Arbeiterzeitungen zu wirken, damit wir die Lügen der Mammonsknechte überall aufdecken und unschädlich machen können. G. L.

Die St. Louiser Bau-Schreiner wollen ausstehen.

In der Central Turnhalle hielt eine sehr zahlreich besuchte Massenversammlung der Carpenter eine Berathung ab, um über die Lohnfrage zu einem Beschluß zu gelangen.

St. Louis besitzt gegenwärtig drei Carpenter Unions, welche eine Stärke von 225, [illegible] resp. 115 Mitglieder haben.

Die Versammlung war von der Union No. 2 einberufen.

Nachdem die Versammlung zur Ordnung gerufen, wurde Herr Caspar [illegible] zum Vorsitzenden gewählt. Herr Glute führte das Protokoll.

Die Schreiner erhalten gegenwärtig $1 per Tag.

In Anbetracht der hohen Löhne, welche andere Handwerker erhalten, und in Erwägung der vielen und großen Arbeiten, welche die Bauunternehmer zur gegenwärtigen Zeit an Hand haben, beschlossen die zu Unions gehörigen Arbeiter, eine Lohnerhöhung von 50 Cents zu verlangen, so daß den Arbeitern von einem noch näher zu bestimmenden Termin $2.50 per Tag bezahlt werden soll.

Die Unions streben nun danach, sämmtliche Carpenter von St. Louis und Umgebung in den Strike zu ziehen. Sie wollen eine Carpenter Association gründen, und um dies anzubahnen, wurde die Versammlung anberaumt.

Das Thema wurde des Längeren besprochen und man kam zu dem Beschluß, eine weitere Versammlung abzuhalten, um die Organisation einer Verbindung sämmtlicher Schreiner von St. Louis zu vollenden.

Es wurde berichtet, daß ein gewisser Hackett, früheres Mitglied der Union, sich bei dem Bauunternehmer Stewart als Sub-Kontraktor hat anstellen lassen; Hackett habe Leute engagirt und ihnen $3 per Tag versprochen. Einige der Arbeiter hätten ihr Geld erhalten, doch nicht von jenen kleinere Beträge angeboten wurden, andere hatten gar nichts bekommen, bis sie nachher von Stewart ausbezahlt worden waren.

Man beschloß, gegen Hackett das „Boycott Verfahren" anzuwenden und vertagte sich dann.

— Die New Yorker Zimmermanns Union hat unseren Generalsekretär P. J. McGuire eingeladen, vor einer ihrer Logen zu sprechen; sie hat damit im Auge, das Wesen und die Thätigkeit unserer Brüderschaft kennen zu lernen, damit sie sich uns anschließen kann.

Zur Lohnbewegung der Berliner Bauarbeiter

wird aus Berlin vom 1. Mai geschrieben: „In auf Tivoli stattgehabten, von etwa 3000 Berlinern besuchte Generalversammlung der Zimmerer Berlins hat definitiv beschlossen, von heute (Dienstag) ab allgemein die Arbeit niederzulegen, wenn die Meisterschaft nicht den geforderten Minimallohn von 4 Mk. pro Tag bei 10stündiger Arbeitszeit zu zahlen sich verpflichtet. Das mit dem heutigen Tage in Kraft tretende Strike Reglement der Zimmerer enthält folgende Bestimmungen:

„1. Die Arbeit wird überall da niedergelegt, wo man die Forderungen der Gesellschaft nicht bewilligt.

2. Es ist Ehrenpflicht eines jeden Zimmerers, der unverheirathet oder familienfrei in Berlin lebt, während der Dauer des Strikes, wenn ihn nicht dringende Verhältnisse zum Bleiben zwingen, Berlin zu verlassen.

3. Die Pflicht derjenigen Gesellen, welchen event. die Arbeit gegen Erhaltung bis zu Lohnes wieder aufzunehmen von der Strike Kommission gestattet wird, ist es, die auf Weitere eine wöchentliche Unterstützung für die strikenden Kollegen zu zahlen.

4. Die den Strikenden zu gewährende Unterstützung von 12 M. pro Kopf und Woche wird von Anfang der zweiten arbeitslosen Woche nach Einstellung der Arbeit an gezahlt.

5. Jeder strikende Zimmergeselle ist verpflichtet, die Arbeit da wieder aufzunehmen, wo ihn die Kommission hinweist.

6. Jeder Platz Deputirte hat sofort nach Niederlegung der Arbeit dem Bureau davon mündlich oder schriftlich Kenntniß zu geben und erhält dann binnen 24 Stunden weitere Verhaltungsmaßregeln. Er hat ferner über die Strikenden seines Platzes genaue Kontrolle zu führen und dem Bureau jeder Art von den Vorgängen Bericht zu geben. Das Bureau führt zu diesem Zwecke eine Gesellenrolle.

7. Behufs Kontrolle findet vom 1. Mai ab allvormittäglich während der Dauer des Strikes eine öffentliche Versammlung in einem bestimmten Lokal statt mit der Tagesordnung geschäftlicher Berichterstattung.

8. Jeder Zimmerer ist gehalten, während der Dauer des Strikes strengste moralische Disciplin zu beobachten, um in keiner Weise bei Publikum oder Behörde Anstoß zu erregen, und so die Lohnbewegung der Zimmerer in Ehren durchzuführen.

Die Generalversammlung der Maurer im [illegible] ebenfalls [illegible] Theilnehmer auf.

Die strikenden Zimmerer Berlins haben folgenden Appell veröffentlicht:

[illegible]

Mit [illegible]

Die Zimmerer [illegible] Berlin.

— Einen weiteren Strike wollen die Buch- und Schuhfabrikgesellen am 5. d. M. eintreten lassen, falls die Meister dieser Branche nicht bis heute ab einen Normal Lohnsatz von 4 M. pro Tag eintreten lassen wollen und demgemäß am Sonnabend auszahlen.

Zehn Tage später, am 15. d. Mts., werden auch die Maler die Arbeit einstellen, wenn ihre Forderungen, 24 M. Wochenlohn bei 10stündiger Arbeit, von den Meistern nicht bewilligt werden.

Werth der Organisation.

Am 30. April streikten die Steinhauer in Washington für 9stündige Arbeitszeit und erhielten dieselbe ohne viele Umstände. [illegible] haben sie 8 Stunden für den Samstag als [illegible] gefordert. Noch vor einem Jahre, bevor die Organisation der Steinhauer Gewerkschaft in Washington bestand, betrugen die Löhne $2.50 täglich; jetzt werden $3.50 bezahlt. Arbeitete man früher 60 Stunden wöchentlich, so arbeitet man jetzt nur 53 Stunden. So bekommt also durch die Union dieses Gewerbe $1 mehr bezahlt und braucht 7 Stunden weniger die Woche zu arbeiten. Und das Alles in einem Jahre! Jedenfalls beweist dies, daß Gewerkschaften manches Gute leisten können.

Blumenlese in der Arbeiter-literatur.

Von Hugo Miller.

Der Gewerkverein ist das Capital des Arbeiters. Harrison.

Wie das Verlangen nach materiellen Verbesserungen der Lage stets mit Denen begann und beginnen wird, welche derselben am wenigsten, nicht mit Denen, welche derselben am meisten bedurften, so wird auch die Lösung der heutigen socialen Frage von den bessergestellten Arbeitern, den gelernten, betrieben.... Nur unter denjenigen Arbeitern eines Gewerbes, deren Lohn überhaupt eine Verminderung zuläßt, d. h. unter den besseren Arbeitern, können Gewerkvereine bestehen. Brentano.

Ich halte nicht viel von Nichtgewerkvereinlern, und meinem Dafürhalten kann man denkende Arbeiter nie überreden, daß es nicht in ihrem Interesse liege, sich gewerkschaftlich zu organisiren. Mundella.

Das dauernde Bestehen eines Gewerkvereins bringt nothwendig mit sich, daß er die Masse der besten Arbeiter des Gewerbes umfaßt; denn nur der fleißige Arbeiter kann ihn durch seine Beiträge erhalten; nur der intelligente ihn vor Verschwendung seiner Mittel in unbesonnenen Kämpfen bewahren.... Jedoch ist es unzweifelhaft wahr, daß in beinahe jedem Gewerbe einige der vorzüglichsten Arbeiter, [illegible], außerhalb des Vereins bleiben. Und nichts ist natürlicher. Selbstverständlich ist das Zusammenbinden der menschlichen Stäbe ein nicht allen angenehmer Proceß. Diejenigen, welche sich für zu kostbar halten, oder für zu hart, oder vielleicht für zu geschmeidig, um gebrochen zu werden, können wohl beanspruchen, draußen zu bleiben. Die größte Vollkommenheit der Arbeit, welche Dem, der sie erreicht hat, eine stetige Nachfrage nach seinen Diensten sichert, macht die Coalition für ihn unnöthig.... Stark ausgeprägter Individualismus hält einen Anderen zurück. Ludlow.

Die Statistik ergibt unwiderleglich, daß lange Arbeitszeit und geringer Lohn stets zusammen fallen, und daß durch ungünstige Verhältnisse an solchen Orten vorkommt, wo das Wesen der Gewerkvereine wenig vorhanden wird. John Prior.

Weitere Schritte zur Reform der Gesellschaft sind niemals mit irgend einer Aussicht auf Erfolg durchzuführen, wenn nicht zuvor der Arbeitstag beschränkt und diese vorgeschriebene Schranke streng erzwungen wird. A. T. Sanders.

Die weltweite Entfernung, welche die theuersten und die billigsten Arbeiter voll Europas trennt, schrumpft zusammen in demselben Maße, in welchem der Unterschied ihrer Löhne zunimmt. Es ist also eine Grenze vorhanden, über welche die Löhne eines Landes nimmer steigen können, bis etwas gleichen ist, und das Niveau der Preise, welches in den schlechtest bezahlenden Ländern der Welt herrscht, zu heben. Ira Steward.

Die politische Freiheit kann keine gleiche sein, wenn ökonomische Ungleichheit existirt. Der ökonomisch Bevorzugte wird stets einen moralischen Druck auf den schlechter Situirten ausüben.... Was nützt dem Arbeiter die ganze politische Freiheit, wenn er dabei hungert, wenn seine Lage sich nicht verbessert, er nach wie vor der vom Kapitalisten ausgebeutete Mensch ist, der sein ganzes Leben lang sich plagen und arbeiten muß, um schließlich elend zu Grunde zu gehen! Bebel.

Fürwahr, wer leugnen wollte, daß die englischen Arbeiter ohne Arbeitereinrichtungen sich heute nicht in der günstigen Lage befinden würden, in der sie sich (anderen europäischen Ländern gegenüber) befinden, würde damit nur seine gänzliche Unkenntniß der Geschichte der englischen Arbeiter dieses Jahrhunderts beweisen. Brentano.

In England haben die Arbeitseinstellungen regelmäßig zur Erfindung und Anwendung neuer Maschinen geführt und so durch die Anforderung des Unternehmers einen ununterbrochenen Einfluß auf die Entwicklung der Industrie ausgeübt.... Doch hätten die Gewerkschaften auch keinen andern Erfolg, als das Maschinenwesen herangerufen und so das Lugengewebe des harmonischen Interessen zu zerreißen, würden sie uns dennoch größere Dienste leisten, als alle jene politischen Charlatane, die mit Geringschätzung auf dieselben blicken, je meist zu leisten im Stande sein werden. Carl Marx.

Die Zeit der Gewerkvereine ist so lange nicht vorbei, als es noch Lohnarbeiter gibt. Gewerkschafts-Zeitung.

Aus dem Süden.

Im südwestlichen Arkansas sieht es für unser Geschäft und für die Arbeiter im Allgemeinen noch recht schlecht aus. Der Lohn für Zimmerleute und Schreiner steht von $1.25–$2.50 per Tag; ein Jeder nimmt Kontrakte an, wenn er sie bekommen kann. Da die meisten aber auch nicht annähernd berechnen können, was eine Arbeit werth ist, so wird denn nach Gutdünken darauf los gerathen, und der niedrigste Bieter erhält den Kontrakt. Es war z. B. in dem Platze, wo ich war, eine Office zu bauen, ein kleines Ding; die höchste Forderung von $1.. , die niedrigste $.., während die Arbeit wenigstens $20 werth war. Das Material wurde geliefert. Das zeigt, wie gut die Leute rechnen können. Die Arbeit, die da aber auch durchschnittlich geliefert wird, ist auch darnach. Die Leute sind es dort ebenso gewöhnt, ihre Arbeit bald umsonst gemacht zu bekommen, daß selbst die paar guten Arbeiter, die dort sind, Pfuscharbeit liefern müssen, um mit den Preisen auszukommen. Der Taglohn für Handlanger beträgt $1 bis $1.25, dabei wird für Kost und Logis $12.50 per Monat gefordert. Ein Mann mit Familie muß alles doppelt bezahlen. Die Miethe für eine elende Bretterhütte beträgt im Durchschnitt 7 bis 10 Dollar per Monat, wo die ganze Hütte höchstens 50 bis 60 Dollars zu bauen kostet und Sonne und Mond durch Dach und Wände scheinen.

Es gibt dort noch Häuser, die weder Thür noch Fenster haben, sondern blos an jedem Fenster ein Loch; wenn der Wind vom Süden kommt, so wird das Loch am Südende mit Brettern zugestellt, und kommt er vom Norden, so wird mit dem Loch am Nordende ebenso verfahren. Ist ein Schornstein vorhanden, so steht derselbe nicht im, sondern neben dem Hause; es werden jetzt aber doch schon ganz nette Wohnhäuser gebaut. Das Klima ist dort sehr gut. Auch kein Winter im Ausgang März und Anfangs April blühen die Rosen. Auch ist es nicht so ungesund mit Ausnahme der sumpfigen Niederungen. Der Boden ist zwar nicht reich in den höher gelegenen Gegenden, aber bei guter Bearbeitung wäre doch eine gute Ernte zu erzielen. Gegenwärtig wird fast nichts wie Baumwolle gebaut, weil das nicht viel schwere Arbeit erfordert und leichte leicht zu verkaufen ist.

Die Bevölkerung ist aber leider zur Zeit der Sklaverei aufgewachsen und hat die Arbeit ganz nicht schätzen gelernt, und sein Kinder werden ebenso so erzogen. Auf es was ihr dort wenn er nicht muß, und ein Jeder will sein Leben mit leichter Arbeit machen. Es hat wohl der meiste Schuld daran, daß es dort noch so wild aussieht.

Von Organisation kann man dort fast gar nicht sprechen ohne ausgelacht zu werden, die armen Leute [illegible] damit, daß sie lieber Gott und [illegible] noch bis zum Niederwerden zu bringen. Beständig kann man nur zu einem Theil denjenigen sprechen, welche vom Norden oder Osten daher gekommen sind. Wenn die Einwanderung dort erst starken wird, werden sich die Zustände auch zum Bessern wenden. Gegenwärtig möchte ich keinem Carpenter rathen, dahin zu gehen, obgleich es ziemlich viel Arbeit ist, denn fast Niemand ist dort [illegible]. J. M.

Hope, Arkansas.

Louisville, Ky., 27. Mai. Dein Aufruf ist mir zugekommen. Aber so gerne ich für Organisation der Carpenter sowohl wie für die anderen Geschäftszweige bereitwilligst mithelfen möchte, so sehe ich doch bei den hiesigen Hinterwäldlern die Erfolglosigkeit ein.

Ich gab mir kürzlich alle erdenkliche Mühe, die Möbelschreiner zu organisiren durch einen Aufruf zu einer Massenversammlung, hoffend, dieselben aus ihrer Lethargie aufzurütteln, allein es war nutzlose Mühe und weggeworfene Opfer. Die Möbelschreiner hier sind zu tief gesunken und ebenso die Carpenters und ich kenne keine drei, die für Organisation einen „Schuß Pulver“ werth sind.

Es wird sehr viel hier gebaut, besonders einige große Geschäftshäuser und, was Du wohl schon wissen wirst, das Southern Exposition Building, was sehr viele fremde Carpenter herzog. Da dieselben nicht organisirt sind, so verdient auch der größte Theil nur einen Hungerlohn von $1.25 bis $2.25, was ganz gute Carpenters sind; es gibt sogar einzelne Ausnahmen, die es auf $2.50 per Tag bringen. Die Hausrente sowie Lebensmittelpreise sind im Verhältniß zum Verdienst hoch.

John Lips.

Mögen die Knights of Labor manches Gute bewirken und auch am Platze sein, so sollten es doch national organisirte Gewerkschaften nicht so eilig mit einem Anschluß an den Orden haben, der sich wohl zum großen Theil aus Lohnarbeitern zusammensetzt, aber auch eine ganze Menge anderer Elemente in seinen Reihen birgt. Die nationalen Gewerkschaften und deren Verband vermögen die K. of L. vorläufig noch nicht zu ersetzen.

Gewerbs-Notizen.

Toledo, O. Geschäft langsam. Verdienst $2.50.

Trenton, N. J. Geschäft lebhaft, Löhne dieselben wie vergangenen Monat.

Zimmerleute von Troy, N. Y., haben eine Gewerkschaft mit 2.. Mitgliedern organisirt und stehen gut; die Löhne betragen $2.50 bis $3 täglich.

Die Zimmerleute sind aufgefordert, von San Francisco vorläufig fernzubleiben. Es sind in dieser Stadt mehr Leute als hinreichend für die vorliegenden Arbeiten.

Die Zimmerleute von Dallas, Texas verlangten jüngst eine Lohnerhöhung auf $3 statt $2.50 täglich, und erhielten sie auch. Sie werden sie indeß nicht lange behalten, wenn sie sich nicht als Gewerkschaft organisiren.

— Zuschriften aus Charlottetown, Prince Edwards Island, berichten, daß sich die Löhne der Zimmerleute auf $1 bis $1.25 täglich belaufen und die Arbeit spärlich ist. Die Leute sind so ärmlich gestellt, daß sie kein Verlangen nach einer Union haben.

Die Steinhauer von New York, Philadelphia, Brooklyn und Boston arbeiten acht Stunden täglich, während die von Washington und Baltimore neun Stunden täglich und nur Samstags acht Stunden arbeiten. Die Löhne in diesen Geschäften schwanken zwischen $3.50 und $4 per Tag.

— In Rochester, N. Y., fand am 10. Mai eine Versammlung von Zimmerleuten zu Gunsten eines Taglohnes von $3 statt. Das Vorgehen dieser Versammlung wurde aber später in Wiedererwägung gezogen und man beschloß, eine Erhöhung von 10 Proc. zu fordern und am Samstag um 5 Uhr Abends aufzuhören.

In Norwich, Conn., ist das Geschäft flau, die Löhne belaufen sich auf $1.50 bis $2.50. In New London, Conn., ist das Geschäft leidlich; die Löhne betragen $2 bis $2.50. In Norwich sehr wenig Arbeit. Man hatte dort vor drei Jahren eine stolze Gewerkschaft, die aus dem Leim gegangen ist. Manche möchten wieder eine haben, fürchten sich aber den Anfang zu machen.

Brüderschafts-Notizen.

Bleibt weg von San Francisco und rathet allen Zimmerleuten, dasselbe zu thun.

Kansas City berichtet, daß das Gewerbe gut ist und sich auf $2.50 bis $4 per Tag stellt. Durchschnitt $2.50.

— Die Hartforder Union No. 43 nimmt in jeder Versammlung Mitglieder auf. Sie versammelt sich jeden ersten und dritten Donnerstag im Monat.

Hr. J. Lunn, Finanzsekretär der Union No. 31 in Trenton, N. J., hat ein Geschäft als Baumeister eröffnet. Wir wünschen ihm allen Erfolg.

Die Philadelphiaer Union No. 8 hat neuerdings mehrere gute Agitationsversammlungen gehabt und durch dieselben viele neue Mitglieder gewonnen.

Die Baltimorer Union No. 29 hat das Eintrittsgeld auf $2 und die monatlichen Beiträge auf 35 Cents erhöht; früher betrug das Eintrittsgeld $1 und die Beiträge 25 Cents.

In einer sehr stürmischen Nacht vergangenen Monats gelangten Präsident Stephens und Sekretär Kirch von der Oaklander Union No. 36 nach Alameda, Cal., und organisirten daselbst die Zimmermanns Union No. 17.

In Toronto später Frühling; Gewerbe höchst flau; die Löhne im vergangenen Winter herabgedrückt. Diejenigen, welche hohe Löhne bekamen, wurden entlassen und konnten selbst zu erniedrigtem Lohnsatz keine Arbeit finden.

Br. Whiteside von Indianapolis verwendet sich dafür, daß ein General Organisator ausgesandt und für seine Dienste bezahlt werde. Er glaubt, daß sich dies für die Brüderschaft lohnen würde und daß die Lokal Gewerkschaften die Frage in Erwägung ziehen sollten.

— Gustav Lübkert, früher in Topeka, Kans., ist nach Milwaukee, Wis., gezogen und die Union No. 30 wird an ihm als englischen und deutschen Redner und Correspondenten großen Beistand finden. Er ist noch nicht ganz von seiner langen Krankheit genesen.

— Das Sterbegeld von $250, das der Familie des verstorbenen Frank Sunderhaus, seiner Zeit Mitglied der Cincinnatier Union No. 2, zukommt, ist von unserem Generalschatzmeister bezahlt worden. Nun kommt zunächst das für die Familie von John Madden, ehemals Mitglied der Clevelander Union No. 11, fällige Sterbegeld an die Reihe.

— Eine Anzahl Schiffszimmerleute, die am 16. Mai aus dem Westen in Camden, N. J., ankamen, um die Stellen der Strikenden zu besetzen, weigerten sich, als Scabs zu fungiren, nachdem sie von der Sachlage Kenntniß erlangt hatten. Die Striker bezahlten ihnen das Fahrgeld nach dem Westen, und sie reisten wieder dorthin zurück.

Die Union No. 21 von Chicago macht wunderbare Fortschritte; sie hat ein Zweigvereine und ein starkes Agitatorenkorps. Vergangenen Montag kamen zwei Todesfälle in dieser Gewerkschaft vor und die Familien dieser verstorbenen Brüder hatten auf eine Unterstützung von $250 Anspruch, von der ihnen die Union No. 21 bereits einen Theil ausbezahlt hat.

In Buffalo betragen die Löhne $2.25 bis $2.75. Vier Fünftel der Union No. 9 arbeiten für $1.75–$2. Die Tagesblätter wimmeln von „Carpenters verlangt“, welche von spekulativen Unternehmungen in der „Baumeister-Association“ ausgehen, damit sie sehen, wie viele beschäftigungslos sind und so Gelegenheit haben, den Arbeitern das Messer an die Kehle zu setzen.

Zur Lohnbewegung in Deutschland. In Berlin, in Frankfurt a. M., in Großenhain und Leipzig, kurz an den verschiedensten Orten Deutschlands finden augenblicklich mehr oder minder große Kämpfe der Arbeiter um bessere Arbeitsbedingungen statt. In Berlin sind es namentlich die Bauarbeiter — Maurer, Zimmerleute, Tischler, Maler, Stuckateure rc. — welche mit Eintritt der Bausaison den Kampf aufgenommen haben, und zwar, wie wir mit Freuden berichten können, nicht ohne Erfolg. Der Geist, der unter den Arbeitern herrscht, ist ein ganz vortrefflicher, tägliche Versammlungen, die von Tausenden besucht werden, sind an der Tagesordnung, und die Fachvereine nehmen stetig an Kraft und Ausdehnung zu. Der Lohnkampf der Zimmerleute ist bereits so gut wie gewonnen.

Die Kohlengräber von Pittsburg.

Herr Flannery, der Sekretär der Kohlengräber Union, hat die neue Distrikts Konstitution vollendet und es wird eine Konvention zusammenberufen werden, um dieselbe zu ratificiren. Dies muß aber vor der am 1. d. Mts. stattfindenden Konvention geschehen. Die auf Ausstände bezüglichen Punkte der Konstitution lauten folgendermaßen:

In keiner Grube soll wegen einer allgemeinen Beschwerde die Arbeit eingestellt werden, ohne daß dieser von einer Distrikts Konvention genehmigt wird.

Die Distriktsbehörde soll alles Mögliche versuchen, um übereilte und unnöthige Lokalausstände zu verhüten. Sie soll ferner die Ursachen von Mißhelligkeiten zwischen Arbeitern und Arbeitgebern untersuchen, die beiderseitigen Angaben entgegennehmen, und wenn die Behörde die Streitigkeit nicht in zufriedenstellender Weise schlichten kann, soll sie eine Versammlung der betr. Grubenarbeiter einberufen und dieselben von dem Resultat der Untersuchung in Kenntniß setzen.

In keiner Grube soll zu einem Ausstande geschritten werden, ehe die Arbeiter sich an die Distriktsbeamten um Rath gewandt haben, oder bis zwei Drittel der in der betr. Grube angestellten Kohlengräber sich für einen Ausstand erklärt haben.

Die Abstimmung über einen Ausstand soll mittelst Ballotirens geschehen. Keine Grube soll Unterstützung erhalten, wenn die vorstehenden Regeln verletzt werden. Wenn in einer Grube in Uebereinstimmung mit den obigen Regeln ein Ausstand inscenirt wird, dann sollen die Beamten das Recht haben, während der Dauer des Ausstandes wöchentlich jedem Kohlengräber der betr. Grube $1 aus dem Distriktsschatz zu zahlen, vorausgesetzt, daß besagte Grube innerhalb dreißig Tagen vor Einstellung der Arbeit alle fälligen Beiträge und Assessments bezahlt hat. Wenn sich zehn oder mehr Arbeiter zu gleicher Zeit im Ausstande befinden, dann ist der Distrikt nicht angehalten, die wöchentlichen Beiträge zu zahlen. In solchen Fällen mögen Gruben Fonds aufbringen zur Unterstützung hülfsbedürftiger Kohlengräber. Es soll ein Ausstand-Fond gegründet werden, gleichbedeutend mit einem Dollar per Kohlengräber. Die Distriktsbeamten sollen von Zeit zu Zeit den einzelnen Gruben ein Assessment auflegen, um den Schatz wieder aufzufüllen. Jeder der beiden Theile soll wenigstens eine Woche vorher Notiz gegeben werden von einer beabsichtigten Lohnreduktion oder von einer verlangten Lohnerhöhung.

THE SCAB'S DEATH.

The bells tolled forth a mournful peal,
Which told another soul had fled,
No tears burst forth and no one sighed
In loving memory of the dead.

No noble deed had marked his life,
No noble action had he wrought,
He lived an outcast and a slave,
And let his soul with gold be bought.

He lived [illegible], debased and scorned,
By even those whose feet he kissed;
And died a wretch, despised and cursed,
Whom no one mourned, whom no one missed.

And when his loathsome corpse was cold,
In Potter's pauper field it was laid,
No stick nor stone to mark the place—
A dog he lived, a dog he died.

And when the golden gate he reached,
He read this legend, bold and grim,
"No scab at all from earth below,
Among the blest shall enter in."

JOHN SMITH.

CORRESPONDENCE.

CINCINNATI, O. Trade booming, men in demand at $2.50–$2.75. Union No. 2 got its new flag on May 21st, and held an entertainment on May 27th. We are in favor of no convention this year, provided it is held in this city next time.

MOBERLY, MO. Building trades slack so far this season; prospects better later on. Carpenters get from $1.50 to $2.25 per day.

UTICA, N. Y.—Trade middling, wages from $1.75 to $2.50.

HARTFORD, Conn.—Work is not very rushing, yet all our union "chips" are at work. Wages $2.25 to $2.75. A good many buildings will be put up this season. We are initiating new members steadily.

NEWBURYPORT, Mass.—A Carpenters' Union is possible here. Wages $2–$2.25, plenty of work. The bosses here make prices to suit themselves, and the men ought to organize and have their say about wages.

Wheeling, West Virginia.

We need a Carpenters' Union here, and steps will be taken to organize one. Wages are from $2.25 to $2.75. Trade not as good as it was two years ago, but nevertheless fair. No building of any account going up.

Lancaster, Pa.

Carpenters of this city mean to organize and will take hold of the matter. Work good at present, and promises to be so all through. Two large market houses at $20,000 each, and a large hall at $20,000, and 200 dwellings are going up. Wages are too low. Good men get $1.75 to $2 per day of ten hours; wood butchers $1.50.

San Rafael, Cal.

We postponed our eight-hour move until later in the season when trade is better. Bad weather now makes work very scarce and many of our men are out of work. Wages from $2 to $3. Some bosses are importing men from Europe to use against us and keep us out of work. But that does not discourage us.

St. Catherines, Canada.

Trade continues fair. One sign that our union is now beginning to be recognized is that when men are wanted, inquiry is always made of our officers. Some of our members, however, are out of work. The agitation for an eight-hour quit on Saturdays is making fine headway here. Wages $1.75 to $2.00.

Boston Mass.

Although we have up-hill work here in this city of "culture," yet we take in some every night. What we want, is a little more agitation, and we are going to have it. Business fair. All carpenters seem employed. Wages average $2.50, and we find it a great deal easier to get it this Spring than it was last Spring, no doubt on account of being organized.

Jeffersonville, Ohio.

We have six contractors and about thirty hands in the trade. Wages run from $1.25 to $2. We favor a Carpenters' Union here to better our condition, for two dollars a day is no pay, considering what we have to pay for the necessaries of life. We can't keep our families on such wages. Trade busy, and season promises to be good.

Troy, N. Y.

We have a carpenters union of two hundred members just started. Business is good, wages low. The union here ought to join the Brotherhood for a complete organization of the carpenters of America is needed, and our trade can accomplish more organized in the Brotherhood than in any other way.

A Lesson. Pay Up Your Dues.

TOLEDO, O. One of our oldest members died suddenly last Monday, May 21, but unfortunately for his family he was behind-hand with his dues, and consequently his family loses the $250 which they would otherwise get, had the dues been paid up. This affair has stirred up some of our delinquents, and they are rushing up to pay their dues.

Louisville, Ky.

Carpenters in this city work for prices ranging from $1.25 to $2.25 per day, a few get $2.50. Trade is very busy, but the men are too slavish to organize. The city is full of strange carpenters from other cities who have come to work on the Exposition Building and other large jobs.

Oakland, Cal.

Our membership is increasing at the rate of eight to twelve every meeting, and we hold very interesting meetings. The nine-hour movement we have made will undoubtedly be a complete success in this city. It will go into effect July 1st. Nearly all of our bosses are favorable, excepting two or three, and they will have to fall into line when the time comes. We have organized Alameda, Cal., and we hope soon to have this whole Pacific coast well organized, as far as carpenters are concerned. Wages hold the same as at last report, and work is fair. We are holding public mass meetings on the nine-hour question and arousing all the craft.

Cleveland, Ohio.

The Spring season has been cold and backward, hence trade has been very slow. Union No. 11 is raising its head and new members are now joining us. The demand for carpenters is pretty fair; the standard wages for good men $2.50 per day, and many at $2.25, extra good men get $2.75. It was rumored here this Spring that the Builders' Exchange would make a strong effort to have the wages at most $2.25 this season, but this movement of theirs seems to have collapsed. We are contemplating a picnic some time in July when we will dedicate a banner for our union. For the purpose of buying the banner we are now raising funds. We trust all our sister unions will help the Brotherhood out of all embarrassment.

Washington, D. C.

Wages $3 per day. Carpenters' Union No. 1 has established an intelligence office here and had postal cards printed. When a member gets out of work, he goes to our Financial Secretary, and if in good standing, he will get a card and address it with his name and residence. Then any boss wanting a workman will sign his name and mail the postal. At present trade is good, and instead of men coming to our bureau for work, we find the bosses are after us for men.

Toronto, Canada.

We had a month's strike last Spring to increase our wages, in which we succeeded to a great extent. The wages were to be $2.25 per day for standard workmen, according to agreement with the bosses in settling the strike. The bosses at once began to discharge $2.25 men, and would employ none at that rate if possible. So wages now range from $1.75 to $2.25, a few old hands at the latter figure. Others have to take whatever they can get, owing to the lateness of the season. Work is backward, and this city is flooded with immigrants "dumped" here to crowd every branch of trade.

Baltimore, Md.

Work is a little brisker with an abundance of hands. One would wonder where they all come from. On May 14th, the carpenters of this city demanded $2.50 per day as the minimum wages, and most of the bosses conceded it at once, and the rest soon followed after a few days' trouble. Within the past month Union No. 24 has more than doubled its membership, and the increase still continues. We have also raised our initiation fee to $2, and our monthly dues to 35 cents. The mass meeting we held here on May 28, in Castle Hall, under the auspices of Union No. 24, was well attended. P. J. McGuire of New York was the principal speaker.

Newport, R. I.

The appeal from your Brotherhood has aroused the carpenters of this city, and steps will be taken to organize a union. Plenty of work here and all employed, and any one who can do a decent job can get work. The outlook for the year is good, many houses under way, and plans are out for quite a number. Many contractors are here from other cities, and they have brought their men with them, so there are more strange "chips" here than ever before.

Wages from $2 to $3 per day; only a few good men get the latter figure. Work, ten hours a day. Carpenters are not by any means paid as high as other trades, considering expenses for tools. I also favor eight hours as a day's work, so as to have more time for recreation, study, &c. If man is to be worthy of his hire and Labor to stand on an even footing with Capital, mechanics must be educated up to the times, and by making a stand throughout the country, cannot only shorten their hours of labor without reduction of wages, but can gain time for improving the mind, lifting themselves to a higher standard in society with credit to themselves and to their trade.

San Francisco, Cal.

There are only a few jobs going up at ten hours. Our union decided to make the hours of work from 7 A.M. to 12 M., and from 1 P.M. to 5 P.M., but some of the contractors want from 7.30 A.M. to 5.30 P.M., but no union men will work on these jobs, so these jobs are filled with non-union men, but working nine hours. The nine-hour movement was a decided success. On one job, 25 non-union men quit on the 1st of May at 5 P.M., and thus gained their early quit as well as ourselves. Union No. 22 is booming now, from 25 to 50 new members every meeting. Our initiation fees now raised to $2.50. There is not a single job in this city run on the ten-hour system; all are running on the 9 hours. Wages run from $2.50 to $3.50 per day. There are 1500 carpenters here, and that is enough for all the work and more too. So carpenters better stay away till word is broken.

WHY IS IT?

The *Labor World* of Philadelphia is said to be one of the most successful labor papers in the United States. While other journals have struggled along for a while in the noble fight for the rights of the people, and then reluctantly given up for lack of support, the *Labor World* has had smooth sailing, and has with each issue shown marks of continued prosperity. Why is this? We do not ask this question in a spirit of jealousy or envy, but in justice, and because we are half inclined to the belief that we have hit upon the reason.

Good, newsy papers, conducted by honest, noble, self-sacrificing men and women, have labored hard and unrewarded, and have had to succumb to necessity. The rule has been that those which have suspended for lack of support have been the most uncompromising champions of the poor and toiling classes, free from mediocrity.

But to return to the case of the exceptional successful labor paper: In the last issue of that paper in an editorial boasting of its great successes, appears the following: "We have been recognized not only by labor but by capital, as the champion, fearless and unbiased, of truth and justice whether on the side of employer or employee."

Can it be on account of this recognition by capital that the *World* is enabled to move into "new and commodious quarters?"

Now, we fully understand and realize that there is no antagonism between legitimate capital and labor, but between the unscrupulous capitalists and the oppressed and poorly paid laborer of to-day there is not one kindred thought; and while the so-called labor journal that is continually ringing in its readers ears the sweet consolation that labor is receiving too large wage, and has no hope through its organizations, may be enriching its publishers, we are disposed to look upon it as a traitor.

As to how much it deserves the confidence of laborers it boasts of, we leave our readers to judge from the following extracts made from the last issue: "Cooperation is no good. Several recent failures have been announced. Labor is blindly rushing here and there lending something to lead it out of the slough. There is no escape. The strongest organization is unable to stand up against the laws which control trade and commerce." "The Amalgamated Association smells defeat in the air. The scale is based on 2½ cent rates. Iron now sells at 2 cents, a 20 per cent reduction in wages is considered a fair compromise."

In conclusion, we desire to warn those of our readers who are subscribers to this professed friend (and there are several) against being influenced by anything they may read in its columns. We know a great many unjust reasons will be assigned to us for this article, and probably some of our exchanges will be ready to side against the course, but we don't care three straws. Traitors in our ranks have ever been one of our greatest curses, and now is a pretty good time to commence the weeding out process. We have been surprised that no more has been said on this subject long ago by some of the bold and honest advocates of the cause. The San Francisco *Truth* is an exception, as it keeps the name of the *Labor World* standing in its columns, under the head, "Journals Pretending to be 'Friends of Labor.'"

From Denver Labor Enquirer.

NO ISSUE

JULY 1883

CARPENTER

MONTHLY JOURNAL FOR CARPENTERS AND JOINERS.

NEW YORK, AUGUST, 1883. NUMBER 7.

CHIPS AND SAWDUST.

The strike of ship-carpenters in Cam-en, N. J., has been won by the men.

—The Trunk Makers have a National rganization with local unions in thirteen ities.

—The Bricklayers' Union of London, ngland, have just opened a fine society all of their hall worth $34,000.

—Even Chinamen will strike. Three undred Chinese shoemakers in San 'rancisco struck lately for 20 cents a day ore pay.

—*Denver Labor Enquirer* says: "*The Car-enter* is better than ever and contains a and of valuable information for the raft."

—In Troy, N. Y., there are 11 Trade nions" represented in the Trades Assem-ly, out of 14, with a total strength of ,500.

—The Spinners National Union is in a etter financial condition than it ever was. he fund in the bank is $6,000 larger than t any previous time.

—The Printers in their International onvention at Cincinnati, Ohio, last onth, discussed the founding of a union ome for aged printers.

—I. B. Dyer, the efficient General Se-retary of the Granite Cutters Internation-. Union, has been reelected to that osition for the third term.

—A Trades Assembly has been formed Montreal, Canada, consisting of fourteen cal unions representing 15,000 men. A milar organization is being formed in artford, Conn.

—Harness Makers delegates from Tor-nto, Chicago, Cleveland, Louisville, St. ouis, New Orleans, Cincinnati and New ork, met in Cincinnati to form a National nion of their trade.

Chief Arthur states in his report that e Brotherhood of Locomotive Engineers ow numbers 280 subdivisions, whose embers constitute nine-tenths of the best comotive engineers in the country.

—Various trades unions in New York ty have combined together, and formed "Short Hour League" to agitate for a aturday half holiday and for a general ovement to reduce the hours of labor.

—William Martin, Secretary of the malgamated Iron and Steel Workers of e United States is urged for the position President of said association to succeed arrett. Brother Martin has been Secretary the body for the past five years.

—Boss Sleicher of the Mallable Iron orks, Troy, N. Y., armed the scabs in s employ with deadly weapons and of-red $15 reward for every union molder lled. Naturally the result was one union an murdered, another mortally wounded d a third badly shot.

—Ship laborers of Quebec refuse to ork longer than eight hours a day. That the only way to establish shorter hours, workmen wait for legislatures and po-ticians to give them the eight hours they ill wait in vain. The only way is to get for themselves—to work no longer than ey agree upon, be it eight hours or nine.

STRIKING AGAINST NON-UNION MEN.

Carpenters Union No. 35 of San Rafael decided against working with non-union men, with the result of gaining the strike. The union men had coaxed the non-union men long enough, and finding no other course left, took this method of forcing them into the ranks of organized labor. Just as soon as the union carpenters an-nounced this plan of action, the bosses succumbed without further trouble, so that now non-union men in San Rafael will have to either join the union or seek some other city. There is no more work for scabs or non-union men in San Rafael.

REDUCING THE HOURS INCREASES THE PAY.

The nine hour-system is the rule among printers in England and Scotland. And as an evidence to prove that reducing the hours increases the pay we will cite a few facts. The printers of Glasgow in 1860 received 25 shillings per week, working 60 hours, and in 1877 they worked nine hours a day or 54 hours per week and got 32 shillings and 6 pence. In Greenock in 1860 printers worked 60 hours per week for 20 shillings, while now they get 30 shillings and 6 pence for 54 hours work.

WHY NOT ORGANIZE?

Carpenters, you have spent years to learn your trade; you have to furnish many tools; you lose a great deal of work-ing time; you are continually subject to perils of life and limb, and to the exposu-res of climate. Is your severe labor worth no more than a bare existence? Should you have naught but a beggarly pittance? It is a shame to think that carpenters in some cities have to work for $1.75 or $2 a day. If the carpenters were organized and banded together all over the country they would command more consideration.

A CORRECTION.

In our last number an item appeared from Buffalo, N. Y., which stated that four-fifths of the members of Union No. 9 were working for $1,75 to $2 per day. During our visit to that city we took particular care to inquire into this statement, and with pleasure we desire to announce that it is not entirely verified by the facts. We make this correction in justice to the members of Union No. 9, and we hope that they will see that *The Carpenter* is al-ways ready to make amends for any error that may appear.

SUPPORT YOUR OWN PRESS.

Other organized trades, such as the iron molders, cigar makers, granite cut-ters, locomotive engineers, and a host more, have their monthly trade journals. Why should not the journeymen carpenters have a monthly devoted to them? It is true that there are several monthlies published in the interest of the trade, but no one of them touches the question of most concern to us—the question of or-ganization, more pay and shorter hours.

Athletes are on strike on the railroads

TRADE NOTES.

—Wages in Ogden City, Utah, $4.50; Portland, Oregon, $3.50 to $4.00.

Workingmens' Unions in Muskegon, Mich., are building their own hall.

—Paterson, N. J., $1.50 to ... for carpenters, and no interest in ... zation.

—In Payson, Utah, building is ... carpenters' wages 25 cents per hour. Glenwood, Minn., $2.50, trade fair.

—Work in Mississippi is dull at ... wages of carpenters $2.50 to $3.... of the journeymen are colored.

—The Associated Carpenters ... ers of Scotland has a total of ... bers out of a total of 10,623 carpe... the country.

—J. S. Murchie, General Secre... the Amalgamated Carpenters, ... re-elected General Secretary of the ... ty by an overwhelming majority.

—Brooklyn carpenters are agita... a permanent rate of wages, as the... are in the habit of reducing wag... $3.25 down to $2.50 per day in ...

—In Scotland the union car... in over hundred cities work on... hours a day, and a half holiday on... day, making as a rule 51 hours pe...

—The Carpenters' Union in Germany, has just issued an official ... —a monthly—*Zeitschrift der Zim...* published at 50 Skalitzer St., ... Germany.

—Carpenters are as thick as flies ... in Denver, and receive but $2.50 ... per day. Common board in that cit... from $6.00 to $7.00 per week. So sa... *Denver Labor Enquirer.*

—The new census for the ten year... ing 1882 show that 3,544,458 immi... came to the United States. In the ... occupations carpenters take the lea... ing 51,000 on this immigrant list.

—The Painters in Paterson, N. J., ... reorganized and repulsed an attem... reduce wages. What is the matte... the carpenters of that city? Are th... well off that there is no room to im... their condition at all by organization...

—The conventions of the Amalga... Carpenters are held every three ... and the meeting is called the Ge... Council and consists of one delegate ... each district. A General Council wa... this year from June 11, to June 22, ... great deal of valuable business was ... acted.

—Report of Amalgamated Carpe... for July shows 382 branches with 2... members. Trade is very dull in Lon... Manchester and all the large citie... England, the same in Ireland, and ... rately good in Scotland, dull in New ... and and South Africa, while goo... Australia.

... to all stair builders.

THE CARPENTER.

Entered at the Post-Office in New York, as second-class matter.

NEW YORK, AUGUST, 1883.

WORKSHOP NOTES.

—Sharpen your tools properly, and you will husband your strength.

—Hit the nail straight upon the head, and you will save many crooked blows.

—Glaze your sashes with putty if you will, but make your mitres and other joints without it.

—The workman that makes the most noise will be often found doing the least work, and doing it badly.

—To remove rust from steel, cover it with sweet oil well rubbed on, and after two days take a lump of fresh lime and rub till the rust disappears.

—Paper doors composed of pressed sheets of paper board, are coming into use. It is claimed for these that they are free from liability to shrink, swell or warp.

—Contrary to the old saying, "a carpenter is known by his shavings," he is known by the character of his work; and the state of his tools may be judged by the same standard.

—In making out building quantities do not overrate them too much, for you may calculate too liberally for your own good, as well as estimate by guess-work too lowly for your own and others loss.

—The trusses of the old part of the Basilica of St. Paul, at Rome, were framed in 816, and were sound and good in 1814, one thousand years. These trusses are of fir. The timber work of the external domes of the church of St. Mark, at Venice, is more than 840 years old, and is still in a good state.

ACROSS THE SEA.

ENGLAND.—An error occurred last month in our statement as to the hours of labor of the carpenters in London, England. The working hours are from 7 A.M. to 6 P.M., not from 6 A. M. to 6 P.M; nevertheless the hours of labor are only 50 hours per week, while we work 60 in free America.—Carpenter work is very dull in great Britain, bad in South Africa, and fair in New Zealand and Australia, also in Scotland.—A branch of the Amalgamated Carpenters in Sunderland, England, propose the society offer a prize for an essay on *Profit*.—Seven friendly societies and eight trades unions in Great Britain spent $6,600,000 among their members in the year 1881. This is a practical evidence of the value of labor organizations. —The strike of the North Staffordshire miners against a reduction of 10 per cent. in wages is becoming formidable. It involves 15,000 men. The men have not acted hastily, and have had several interviews with their employers with a view to conciliation. The engineers of Cleveland are also moving against a five per cent. reduction.

SCOTLAND.—All over this country a general movement was made by the carpenters on May 1, for an advance of one-half penny an hour. In Edinburgh, Glasgow, Dundee, and Dunfermline the advance was granted with but very little trouble. In Ayr the matter was compromised on one farthing more an hour.—The Associated Carpenters of Scotland have their own trade union hall in Glasgow.—The machinists of Glasgow are on strike for a-half penny advance per hour.

GERMANY.—The carpenters all over Germany are making every effort to perfect a National Union of their trade, as can be noticed here and elsewhere in our columns.—The carpenters' strike in Berlin in the main is successful. The stone masons and the painters of Berlin also struck for an advance and got it.—In Cologne carpenters demanded 20 per cent. increase early in June, and on the first day 18 employers acceded, thus leaving scarcely 250 men on strike with the final result of a complete victory for the men, who not only got the wished for increase, but also a reduction in the hours of labor from 12 to 9½ hours per day.—In Nurnberg, Bremen and Frankfort, the carpenters have likewise made movements for more pay and 9½ hours as a day's work, and gained their demands.—Mosaic weavers in [illegible] have won their strike against a reduction.—The masons in Hamburg have organized a strong trade organization and are now preparing to issue their own [illegible] [illegible] rules [illegible] Carpenters' Union [illegible] for two delegates [illegible]

SWITZERLAND.—The trades unions and labor societies of this country will hold a National Convention this coming September to secure legislation in their interests and to bring their organizations into closer unity with each other.—After a very severe struggle in 1872, the carpenters of Zurich and all other leading cities of Switzerland established the ten hour system. On June 19, this year, a prominent carpenter boss in Zurich demanded that his employes should work eleven hours a day, and in this movement he was sustained by several other bosses. Whereupon the carpenters Union of Zurich held a mass-meeting of the trade, nearly 500 men present, and they unanimously resolved to stand by the ten-hour system.

HUNGARY.—In Pesth several strikes are now pending. The tanners want higher wages, and 200 of them have quit work. 500 bakers are now out for more pay, and the leaders of the strike have been arrested. This reminds us somewhat of the fashion now coming into vogue in America whenever strikes take place.

ITALY.—In Rome the journeymen bakers are on strike for higher wages. The police have sided with the bosses and have supplied them with bakers taken from the army. The Prefect has threatened any journeymen bakers who do not prove that they can support themselves with expulsion from Rome. This interference seems a violation of individual liberty, and the press of every color is strong against the measure. The newspapers say that as the bosses have been supplied with men, the journeymen bakers ought to be supplied with ovens.

THE LOGIC OF SHORTER HOURS.

Did wage workers generally understand that their wages are not regulated by the number of hours they work, nor the amount of wealth they produce, it would then be much easier for them to understand the logic of shorter work hours. The wages of laborers under the present system is regulated ultimately by the rate of living to which they accustom themselves. If they are satisfied to work for just enough to buy the coarsest food and clothes, that will be their wages. The negro slaves of the South before the war were satisfied with little—their rate of life was low—and in consequence their wages were low. It made no difference to the chattel slave whether he worked six hours or twelve hours a day, he got no more than what would support him in the rate of life to which he had accustomed himself. The reason the Chinaman works for less wages than the native American is because centuries of tyranny coupled with the believe in the doctrine that by saving his wages he could better his condition, has reduced his rate of life far below that of the American workman. He has lived cheaply so long that he has himself become cheap—the cheapest workman in the world; and the workmen of the world despise him for it. We hate the effects of cheap living, and yet teach it and practice it in the hope of elevating our condition. Vain hope! If every worker in America resolved to-morrow to work fifteen hours a day, his wages would not increase, but on the contrary would decrease, because his wants would not only be lessened, but his crowding two days into one would crowd the labor market and the competition among the workers would reduce wages to that point at which they would be content to live. By reducing the hours of labor the opposite effect is inevitable.—*Detroit Spectator.*

PROGRESS OF THE CIGAR MAKERS.

The last semi-annual report of the Cigar Makers' International Union shows benefits have been paid out as follows:

To traveling cigar makers......	$10,722 60
For sick benefits..............	16,043 73
For death benefits.............	1,569 25
Total..........................	$27,935 58

The amount expended for strikes has been $50,621, while the sum of $39,905 has been added to the general fund, thus doubling the amount on hand at previous report.

—A convention of journeymen tailors will be held in Philadelphia, Pa., beginning September 15th, next, to form an International Tailors' Union. The objects are various, among which are: the [illegible] tion of a monthly trade [illegible] up for them [illegible] and death benefits, [illegible] [illegible] for co-operation [illegible] [illegible] to [illegible] [illegible] wo. [illegible] om. On May four [illegible]

CINCINNATI, OHIO.

Trade booming and about six of the largest firms have raised their men 25 cents per day, so that men getting $2.50 are now receiving $2.75 and those getting $2.75 now have $3. The scabs think the bosses are getting kind but we can not see it in that light. The bosses have been kept in continual hot water by Union No. 2 this year for fear of a strike and they think we will strike yet. That is the reason we think the bosses have for being so kind to their men. The affairs of Brother Sunderhaus, deceased, have been settled very satisfactorily and the following notice of thanks has been inserted in all the daily papers:

NOTICE.—THANKS TO THE LOCAL UNION No. 2, of the Brotherhood of Carpenters and Joiners of America, for the $250 death benefit of Frank Sunderhaus, deceased, received by B. BENKEMEYER.

On May 27th, there was a large gathering of carpenters and their friends at Workmen's Hall, at the entertainment given by the lady friends of Carpenters' Union No. 2. The entertainment consisted of music, recitations, tableaux, and the presentation to the union of a new flag by the ladies.

More than 1,000 people, or as many as the large hall and commodious galleries could accommodate, were present.

In the opening address Mr. John Stuhlfauth impressed upon his hearers the necessity and advantages of unionism, and urged them to combine and banish from the city the "saw and hatchet men," thus elevating their craft. He spoke very ably and to the point. He showed how Union No. 2 had withstood the storms and trials of the past and in spite of all had fixed itself on a firm basis, and this festival was a good evidence of its prosperity.

The flag was presented at about 10 o'clock P. M. Miss Lou Ellick made the presentation on behalf of the other ladies in a neat little address in which she hoped the union would prosper under its new banner and might carry it many years. John Vallirus received the banner as a member of the union, and responded appropriately to the young lady's remarks. The flag is of heavy silk, on one side the American flag, on the other side a blue field with the emblem of our Brotherhood in gold. At the conclusion of the following programme, tables and chairs were removed and a ball was inaugurated until an early morning hour.

Overture—Opera Selections
........................Kohlbrandt's Orchestra.
Opening Address............John Stuhlfauth.
Song....................Cincinnati Glee Club
Harmonica Duets.
Cohn and Bosh, Members of the Adrian Club
Song [illegible]................S. L. Sprague
Selections on the Zithern......Mr. John Gosel
Accompanied by C. P. Bischoff with Guitar.

Tableau 1.

Carpenters' Accident

Recitation in German......Miss Matilda Riehr.
Presentation of Flag by the Ladies.
Recitation................Alexander Rumpler

Tableau 2.

Out of Work, No Money, and not Organized.

Duet on Guitar.
Cohn and Bosh, Members of the Adrian Club.
Selection on Violin Zithern......Mr John Gosel
Accompanied by C. P. Bischoff with Guitar.
Song.................................Alert Club.
Recitation..................Miss Matilda Riehr.
Song........................Cincinnati Glee Club

Tableau 3.

Well Organized, Good Wages and Happiness.

Tableau I. — "Carpenters' Accident" was a truthful and accurate representation of an incident of daily occurrence in our trade. A carpenter had fallen from a high scaffold and lay in a disabled condition surrounded by a group of his fellow workmen.

Tableau II. — told the simple story of a carpenter out of work, no money, and without an organization, his family around him hungry and crying for bread.

Tableau III. — was the reverse of the 2nd. All three tableaux were recalled several times amid storms of applause.

A regular meeting of Union No. 2, held July 3d, elected officers with the following result:

President—John Stuhlfauth.
Vice-President—Gus Miller.
Recording Secretary—Rob't Hammond
Financial Secretary—Gus Brethauer
Cor. Secretary—Charles Rumpler.
Treasurer—Joseph Leininger.
Sergeant-at-Arms—Jno. Schreckenboeller.
Trustees—Henry Barnard, Robert Le[illegible] [illegible], John Valerius, Joseph Stein and Al [illegible] [illegible]

IN MEMORIAM.

The following resolutions have been adopted by Local Union No. 33 of Boston;

Whereas, The Great Ruler of the Universe in his infinite wisdom has removed from our midst our worthy and esteemed Brother DANIEL SIMPSON.

Resolved, That this sudden removal of Brother Simpson from our Union, of which he has been a respected member, leaves a vacancy and casts a shadow that will be deeply realized by all members of this union and by his friends, and will prove a grievous loss to this union and to his family.

Resolved, That in deep sympathy with the afflicted relatives and friends of the deceased, we express our earnest hope that even so great a bereavement may be overruled for their highest good.

Resolved, That this heartfelt testimonial of our sympathy and sorrow be printed in the *Daily Herald* and *Globe*, and a copy sent to his family and THE CARPENTER by the Secretary of the meeting.

Per order,

W. G. SHIELDS,
JOSEPH CAHILL,
WM. T. MCCORMACK,
Committee.

J. J. SMITH, Cor. Sec'y.

A LETTER FROM GERMANY.

BERLIN, July 25, 1883. All over Germany wages uprisings are now the order of the day. The tailors of Frankfort and Berlin, the shoemakers of Frankfort, and the weavers of Grossenhain have gained an advance in pay and other concessions.

The most important movement is the strike of the carpenters all over the Empire. In Köln and Nürnberg they demanded 20 per cent. advance and 10 hours a day, also no overtime or Sunday work. And in this they succeeded after a sharp struggle. In Stuttgart a strike was made against one carpenter boss for ill treatment of his men, whereupon all the other bosses joined with him, and locked out their employes to the number of 1,200. Then the men demanded 10 to 20 per cent. more pay which was granted after a fight of a few days.

In München the carpenters made a similar move to that of Köln and Nürnberg, and with success. Carpenters' Union of München now numbers 600. In Berlin there are over 1,000 carpenters, and of these nearly 3,000 are members of the union. When we struck on May 1, there were 280 out of 350 bosses who yielded at once. But on May 30, the strike was declared closed with eight bosses still determined to hold out. When the strike closed the Berlin Union had $750 in their treasury. Carpenters formerly worked here from 10 to 11 hours per day, but now, through union, we have given the men a reduction of hours. On June 1, the cabinet makers of Frankfort instituted the plan of 9½ hours per day. The cabinet makers of this city want 9½ hours a day and 10 per cent. advance. A national convention of carpenters will be held in Berlin on August 18-20, to perfect a national union in Germany.

Toronto, Canada

I am glad to inform you, we are increasing in number; 8 initiated last meeting and more for next night. We have decided to raise dues to 40 cents per month in future, and to revise our local By-Laws and increase the benefits, the revision being considered by a committee. A joint committee of, or at least a committee from Amalgamated and Brotherhood are about discussing the conduct of the bosses in reducing wages last winter, and, if possible, to prevent the same being done next Winter. The demonstration of the trades council was a great success as regards number and spectators; the line of march being densely packed, and when the press intimates that Unionism is powerful and gave us credit for showing steady determination and also ordering, I take it for granted that the public will conclude we are a power. I trust that we shall be fully organized so that our power may be felt.

—We thank the Paterson *Labor Standard* and the Pittsburg *Labor Herald*, as well as other labor journals for their kind appreciation of the work of our Gen'l Secretary and for their flattering notices of our journal. Whatever our General Secretary has done he considers simply his duty, and all he asks is that all workingmen shall do theirs, by organizing and working for the advancement of our common cause.

St. Catherines, Canada.

Trade quiet, no men out of employment, wages $1.75 to $2, a few at $2.25. On June 2d, we started the eight-hour system on Saturdays, so as to quit at 4 P. M., and the result is we gained it with but very little opposition from the bosses. At first only one boss paid full time, but after two weeks all the bosses dropped into line and paid full time for Saturdays. When we made our demand for eight hours on Saturday, we raised no question about wages, so the bosses have given the wages of their own accord. And this would never have been, were it not for our brave Union No. 38. We are steadily increasing in membership, and very few now outside of our union. One of our members, Robert Bald, aged 64, native of Scotland, died June 2. He was engaged from earliest youth in the building trade, at one time a leading boss, but more latterly a journeyman. He was a staunch union man and highly respected as an upright mechanic. Union No. 38 turned out in a body to attend his funeral.

On all sides we hear praise of P. J. McGuire's lecture. Every one was pleased and instructed with the able and forcible manner in which he showed the benefits of organization. McGuire's visit here is bearing fruit. We have five or six new members next meeting, and the only boss who was holding out against the 4 o'clock quit on Saturday, was obliged to throw up the sponge last week, and he told his men he was willing to give them the hours and full pay.

San Francisco, Cal.

The Carpenters' Union of this city is making huge progress, and members are coming in rapidly—41 in one meeting, and a total of 92 new members for May. The meetings are extremely interesting. Work is fair, and wages hold the same as last month. Men enough here for all the work. All our members are working; union men preferred in most cases; non-union, as a general rule, are inferior workmen. We are constantly gaining ground. The nine-hour rule is a great success; only three carpenter firms working ten hours one of these a mill, and there is no doubt all three of these will soon have to succumb. We wish to state that to Bro. P. J. Wellen is due the credit of starting this grand movement here among the carpenters, and in this he was ably seconded by Bro. Owens and a host of others. To our President J. S. W. Saunderr is due the honor of the eight hours on Saturdays. We have hosts of good material in our union. Our union appointed a committee of three to confer with a similar committee from the building trades, so as to form a Building Trades League. All the unions have answered. Painters, Carpenters, Gasfitters, Bricklayers, Metal Roofers, Stair Builders, Lathers and Plasterers are represented. We have formed a temporary organization by electing Bro. Farley of the Stair Builders as Chairman, and J. W. Maher of Carpenters' Union No. 22 as Secretary. Union No. 22 has the credit of starting this league. The picnic of Union No. 22 was held on July 15, and was a grand affair. Lumber men are increasing the price of lumber and building materials are going up, which may have a tendency to take some work out of the market. We have raised our initiation fee to two dollars, and still they come in.

Omaha, Nebraska.

I have canvassed the sentiment of a majority of carpenters and find quite a difference of opinion. I find a number who without consideration or justification unhesitatingly predict the failure of any effort to organize the carpenters, one of their arguments being, "There are too many saw and hatchet men in the business." But a larger number are in favor of an organization for mutual protection, claiming that they know the advantages and benefits to be derived from a close union of their craft. They would like to see such a one effected and managed judiciously. [illegible] would be [illegible] I am a [illegible] Bricklayers [illegible] subordinate [illegible] Bricklayers [illegible] efforts t[illegible] ized and became a part of the [illegible] tional Union almost three years ago. We are now in a prosperous and flourishing condition. I wish I could s[illegible] as much for the carpenters. Wages of carpenters [illegible] per diem; fore[illegible] range from $1.80 to $2.2[illegible] [illegible] $2.50. The $1.80 [illegible] not an isolated case by any means. In order to show you the value of unorganized skilled labor in this section of the continent, I will inform you that hod carriers are getting $2 per day, and are not required to furnish a chest of tools in order to get work. Compare rates with unorganized carpenters.

As an illustration of what organized labor, whether skilled or unskilled, can do, I will state that a little over a year ago I organized the Omaha Laborers' Protective Union, when common labor was being paid at the rate of from $1.10 to $1.25 per day, the same labor is now paid from $1.75 to $2, and they were mainly instrumental in having an ordinance passed by the city council, reducing the hours of labor from 10 to 9 hours for city employes.

E. WALSH.

HOW THE CZAR WAS CROWNED.

A recent dispatch from London states: "Mr. George Augustus Sala, the English journalist and renowned travel-writer, has returned from Moscow. He says that the real story of the coronation pageant has not been told. The mobs cheered by order of the police. The officials simulated a confidence they did not feel in the loyalty of the people, but were actually in constant dread. All the telegrams sent were carefully scrutinized and adapted. The newspaper dispatches were opened and doubtful passages obliterated." For the honor of the Russian people we are glad to note these remarks.

ARE WORKMEN DRUNKARDS?

The following is a sample of the wholesale lies generally indulged in by the capitalistic press. We take it from a leading journal:

"In paying out $700 in wages to his workmen a manufacturer, at Marseills, Ill., privately marked all the bills. Within two weeks $342 of it was deposited in the local bank by saloon keepers."

From the above the kind charitable bosses argue the workmen get more pay than they need, hence wages ought to be reduced. If the $342 above mentioned got into the hands of the saloon keepers is it not as likely that it got there through storekeepers and others with whom the workmen traded? If there is any degree of dissipation to which workmen are addicted, it is largely due to the system of overwork, long hours, poor pay and the discouraging conditions consequent upon poverty. The best remedy is to shorten the hours of labor, encourage workmen to organize for that purpose and to improve their condition. Then drunkenness and intemperance will have less cause to exist.

DETROIT CARPENTERS REORGANIZING.

At well-attended meeting of the carpenters and joiners a new union was formed, and by the looks of determination which animated the countenances of a majority of those present, we have great hopes for the future. Detroit carpenters are "all broken up," as regards wages. The men have been continually cutting each others' prices, undermining each other; and they have now about concluded to stop such foolishness and establish a minimum rate of wages below which they will not work.—*Spectator*.

—Ex-Congressman Thompson J. Murch of Maine appeals to all trades unions and labor societies to render him all financially in his charges against James G. Hill, Supervising-Architect of the Treasury. He proposes to show fraud, corruption, favoritism and incompetency in the erection of public buildings, and that the public are robbed of large sums that go into the pockets of thievish contractors and corrupt politicians. He predicts this investigation will result in doing away with contract work by the United States Government and that it will lead to the enforcement of the 8 hour system.

WORKINGMEN AS FACTORY INSPEC-

[illegible] rotary. This is the third [illegible] has been selected within a few yrs from the ranks of trades unions [illegible] Britain. J. D. Prior, General Sec[illegible] of the Amalgamated Carpenters, was first.

SUCCESS OF THE BUILDING LEAGUE IN NEW YORK.

Scarcely three months ago the delegates of all the trades in the building line in this city met together and formed what is known as "The Amalgamated Building Trades Union." Every building trade in the city is represented. It is the custom in this city for each union in the building trade to have a "walking delegate," as he is termed, whose business it is to go around and visit the various jobs, and see that the members of the union comply with the rules, and that they are not in arrears. In the Building Amalgamation these walking delegates of each trade combined together form the Executive Committee.

Whenever complaint is made that scabs or non-union men of any trade are at work on a building, then this Executive Committee notifies the contractor that he must get rid of these scabs or non-union men or compel them to join the union. In the event of a refusal, then the union men of all trades on the building quit work until the boss yields.

The first strike in which all the trades employed in the building line participated began owing to the fact that Mr. Corr, a contractor, who is building two large houses at Seventh avenue and Fifty-eighth street, had at work a number of non-union derrickmen. The walking delegate of the Derrickmen's Union informed the delegates of the other unions, and, as the "scabs" refused to join the union, a demand was made on Mr. Corr to discharge them. This he refused to do, and the plumbers, laborers, bricklayers, carpenters, laborers, bricklayers, roofers, framers and steam-fitters employed on the job, to the number of 200, quit work at once.

After a few days the boss sent for all hands and notified them that he would not employ any more "scabs." Since then similar strikes occurred on a score of buildings, and always with success. The most prolonged strike of all was against Lynd Bros., which lasted nearly three weeks. The strike demanded that the non-union laborers should become members of the Laborers' Union, and that $2.50 should be paid to those men instead of $1.70. It ended to the advantage of the union men.

Lately a notice as follows has been inserted in the New York dailies:

NOTICE TO ALL BOSSES CONNECTED with the Building Trade.—You are hereby notified to employ none but society men.
By order of the Executive Committee of the Building Trade.

This advertisement has occasioned considerable uneasiness among builders, and its terms have been complied with in several instances by bosses who were employing non-union men. Strikes are now pending on the New Opera House, 200 men having thrown down their tools against non-union men. The same has been done at the Produce Exchange by 120 men on account of non-union plumbers. Also by 50 men at Eigthy-sixth street and First avenue, on account of scab stone masons, and in another place on account of scab stone cutters.

A WRONG COURSE.

We clip the following from the Detroit *Spectator*:

"The Furniture Workers' Journal gives the details of some trouble that has occurred between the furniture workers and carpenters of Troy, N. Y. The former are connected with the F. W. I. U., and the latter with the K. of L. The furniture workers wished to form an alliance with the carpenters, recognizing each other as good union men; but this the carpenters refused to do, unless the furniture workers should become knights. We consider the course of the carpenters wrong. There is no antagonism between trades unions and the assemblies.

Newport News, Va.

Not long since the carpenters employed on elevator work here struck for an ad-[illegible] [illegible] Framers Union of New York [illegible] at s[illegible] our places and thus [illegible] [illegible] out. This action of [illegible] treachery and [illegible] [illegible] rld.

THE BUILDING LEAGUE IN CHICAGO.

Carpenters Union No. 21 has been foremost among the building trades of Chicago in organizing them all into one solid league for their mutual protection. And as there is so much of interest connected with this movement we will here give a brief outline of the work.

The first step was to issue the following circular to all the building trades in Chicago.

The growing importance of labor is the issue of the future. Among the many ideas put forth by different societies and wage-workers of the country, we see now a clear way to to settle the labor questions that arise in the different trades. Namely, for all trades in the building line to be united in one body, thus making the grievance of one trade the concern of all. One trade alone is like a ship at sea with no rudder, left to the mercy of the wind. So it is with one trade; it is left to the trade concerned to fight its own battle, and very often proves a failure. By the amalgamation of all the trades, the thing is changed for one trade must assist the other, and no one trade can go on a strike without the consent of all the concerned. The advantage that will come from it will increase the strength of all trades, for the non-union men will have to quit or join the union. For example: A carpenter can't work on a building where there is a non-union man, let him be a plasterer or a bricklayer or of any other trade. He has to quit work or join the union, and for this purpose the carpenters have appointed a committee to confer with the different trades for the purpose of forming a building league. The committee has waited on the plasterers and bricklayers and these two unions have notified the committee that they are with us. We hope that other trades will follow their example.

Immediately after Union No. 21 had issued the above appeal Mr. Geo. C. Prussing, of the "Master Masons' and Builders' Association" is reported to have said:

"That the carpenters, who had started the movement, were probably the worst paid men in the building trade, and had also been heavy sufferers by the late bricklayers' strike. They were undoubtedly actuated by the best of motives in their undertaking, and it could not be denied that the proposed amalgamation might be instrumental in doing a great deal of good. But it was to be feared that the concentration of power which the amalgamation would bring would be abused by the ignorant and vicious, and that the best interests of the workingmen would not always be served if the men who might obtain control of the proposed organization. He had not given the matter any special thought, but was not disposed to look upon the movement as intended to be inimical to the employers, and did not think it would hurt anybody to have the experiment tried."

Whereupon the *Progressive Age* makes the following comments:

It is a fact, as Mr. Prussing states, that the carpenters are the worst paid men in the building trade, and it is also true, as he states, that in their efforts to form a building league in this city they are actuated by the best of motives. There is no disposition to disguise the objects which they seek to accomplish, for they are such as must commend themselves to all reasonable, fair-minded men. They seek to reduce the hours of labor, secure better pay, and prevent strikes and disturbances of every kind and character in the building trades. Who then will say that the movement is not a commendable one, and worthy of unqualified success? The union carpenters of Chicago not only stand foremost among the best of organized workingmen, but they rank as high in all that constitutes true manhood as any other class of citizens, no matter what their occupation or calling. While maintaining their own distinct organization for the consideration and regulation of all matters concerning only themselves, they wish to unite in one grand organization with those who are identified with their interests, the bricklayers, stonemasons, plasterers, painters, plumbers, tinners and others to guard against other dangers which constantly menace workingmen, and prevent the disasters which so frequently overtake them in consequence of injudicious and ill-advised action, and secure to the whole the great advantages to be gained from the combined wisdom, intelligence and experience.

BOOK NOTICES.

HINTS ON ESTIMATING.—A Handbook for Builders, published by Chas. D. Lakey. Price 10 cents. This little pocket pamphlet will prove an invaluable help to thousands who desire a few hints on estimating in the building line.

HAND SAWS, THEIR USE, CARE AND ABUSE, how to select and how to file them, by Fre[illegible]

[illegible]

[illegible] to be a union man, but in [illegible] connection with us at all. | bosses. This is the third season that they have demanded [illegible] $3.50 per day [illegible] | that scarcely more than 5 per cent. of the [illegible] there have been few strikes. The | [illegible] is also against [illegible] building

THE CARPENTER.

PUBLISHED MONTHLY

BY THE

Brotherhood of Carpenters and Joiners,

OF AMERICA.

Office: 184 William St., New York.

TERMS.—Fifty cents a year, in advance, post-paid.

Send all moneys and correspondence for this Journal to

P. J. McGUIRE, Secretary,
184 William St., New York

NEW YORK, AUGUST 1883.

—Nearly 800 delegates are assembled at the Convention of the Amalgamated Iron and Steel Workers, now in session in Philadelphia. General Secretary McGuire addressed the convention by invitation.

—Why not work only nine hours all the year round? We have to work short time in Winter owing to the short days, and by a little effort, we can establish the system the rest of the year.

—Before you strike for more wages or less hours, form building leagues. Then strike against "scabs" and non-union men, and force them into the union for their own good and our's. After that we can accomplish greater results.

—During the nine-hour agitation in our trade in San Francisco, the bosses offered an advance of 50 cents a day for the men to keep on at ten hours. But the men stood firm and took the nine hours in preference to an advance in wages. This shows they had le.el heads.

—Had our San Francisco brothers waited for the California Legislature to give them a nine-hour law, they would have a long wait. But they have got it themselves, and you can bet it will be enforced too. For it does not depend on the will of Governors, nor a President, nor any politician.

—If workingmen want a reduction in the hours of work, they must not wait for Congress or State Legislatures to pass a law on the subject. Such laws are never enforced. Workmen must make the law themselves in their Unions, and thus organized they can enforce any eight or nine-hour law they enact.

—What use is a National Trade Union—What use is our Brotherhood? This is a question often asked. The use of such an organization is not only the benefit in case of strikes, death, accident, etc., but also if the member pays dues into one union and is forced to move, he finds a union in another city ready to receive him.

PRACTICAL RESULTS GAINED BY OUR BROTHERHOOD.

Oakland carpenters struck on July 2, and gained the nine-hour system; on July 15, San Rafael did the same and was successful, so that now the carpenters of San Francisco, Oakland and San Rafael are working nine hours a day, and are also getting at least 50 cents a day more pay than they did 18 months ago when they had no organization and were working 10 hours a day. They also work only 8 hours on Saturday, so that they have gained seven hours a week more for themselves and at least $3 a week more pay. And this has been accomplished [illegible] through our Brotherhood [illegible] but the Pale[illegible] [illegible]

BUILDING TRADES LEAGUES.

In Chicago, Baltimore, San Francisco, and other cities, active efforts are being made to form combinations of the various trades in the building line. Delegates from these trades meet together, and by a closer unity of action, they are able to effect measures for their unions that can not be so well done if separated and distinct from each other.

In daily labor, the carpenter is thrown into contact with the stone-cutter, mason, bricklayer, painter, etc., and work on the same building. For want of a definite understanding, a union carpenter frequently works on a job with "scabs" of the other trades, and *vice versa*. But by federating these trades, this can be avoided. They can be of wonderful help to each other in getting rid of scabs and non-union men. They can also render each other immediate financial aid in case of any trouble with employers. And best of all, the date of strikes will be arranged without one trade coming into conflict with the other.

This plan is now effectively at work here in New York, and with beneficial results. Every Union in the building line, bricklayers, laborers, plasterers, framers, carpenters, stair builders, stone-cutters, masons, lathers, plumbers, derrickmen, tinners, roofers, etc., are all in one league together. Through the power of this union they have forced non-union men away from their jobs, as is noted elsewhere in our journal. And thus they have aided each other. For if a building boss can get non-union men of one trade, it will not be long until he will extend the system to the other trades on the building.

Naturally the unions of all these trades should be united, as the same contractor in many cases is the employer of all the various trades on the same building. Hence their interests should be in harmony with each other. Then again, through this league, they can form an employment bureau for the information of bosses seeking workmen. There is a vast field of work for these leagues, and they should be extended to every city.

The formation of building trade leagues dates back earlier than the present day. A confederation of the various building societies of Germany was formed in 1452 by Dotzinger, chief master at the building of the Strasburg Cathedral, and was organized with four central lodges at Strasburg, Cologne, Vienna and Zurich. From the earliest date of trades unions, we find the building trades have been the advance guard in promoting a fraternity of interests among the workers. And so powerful were they that the government made them the subject of repressive legislation in Great Britain in 1350. In France the building trades formed the "Compagnonnage," and for centuries it existed among the workmen in those trades.

—The Coal Miners have held a national convention in Pittsburg, Pa., and formed the Amalgamated Association of Coal Miners of the United States and Canadas. The plan is mainly similar to that of the Iron and Steel Workers' Association.

—The Saturday half-holiday movement has apparently fizzled out. By act of the Board of Aldermen of New York, the city laborers were granted th. .turday half-holiday over the veto of the Mayor. But when the appointed day came to enforce it, the laborers themselves kept on working the full ten hours for fear they would lose a half day's pay. While workmen are so craven as not to stand [illegible] what better can be expected than [illegible] the boss in their [illegible] made [illegible] by [illegible]

A GIANT STRUGGLE.

We have too long obeyed their orders,
Bowed to their caprices, sweated for them
The wearying summer's day—wasted for them
The wages of our toil; fought for them,
Conquered for them, bled for them—
Still to be trampled on, and still despised.
When shall we break our chains?

SOUTHEY'S *Wat Tyler*.

These stirring words now find full expression in the hearts of the working people the world over. At one time they are murmured in the steppes of Russia and in the workshops and streets of Europe; another time in the coal mines of Pennsylvania and in the cotton mills of New England. But yesterday they were uttered in the great strike of 1877 and to-day in the noble stand of the telegraphers. Yes when shall we break our chains? The chains of poverty and hunger, the chains of low wages and long hours, the chains of servitude, political and social, bound around us by our monied taskmasters! Are we to forever bow the knee and bend the head at the bidding of the Jay Goulds and the Vanderbilts and Fields; are we to sweat and toil and slave and work to be crushed to the earth by their giant power? No! Then let us rise in our might and array our scattered battallions under the banner of organization.

The Telegraphers to-day are making a spirited fight not only for themselves but for all classes of labor. Arrayed against them are not only 80 millions of money in the Western Union, but the countless millions of all the millionaires of the land. Their fight is for eight hours as a days work, and against starvation wages and other evils. At a single moment from Maine to the Pacific they broke the iron fetters that bound them to Jay Gould and launched defiance in his face. They stood arrayed in the majesty of organized power, and as they did the world stood aghast and wondered!

For over a month with heroic fortitude the battle has been waged — empty stomachs against well filled purses, — the men and women of labor against the men of millions. And the result is yet in doubt. Up to their rescue with funds have come the trade and labor unions of the land. While all the forces of duplicity and deception, corruption and bribery, police and detectives, are in the company's service to demoralize the strikers. Was there ever such a struggle, waged as it is by strikers peacefully and orderly, depending solely upon moral weapons for success? *Such a strike if lost is no failure!* It will teach the myriad hosts of labor that they must perfect their organizations first before they can cope successfully with the Capitalists. It will teach the bosses that if they would avoid loss of dividends and injury to business they must do justice to Labor. And the economic education alone that has come to the men and women engaged in this strike is worth more than all the money lost. Honor to the Telegraphers and Linemen of 1883! They have compelled the N. Y. *Herald* and the leading papers to say that trades unions are necessary institutions in America. They have proven the hypocrisy of the N. Y. *Sun* and other papers — pretended "friends of the workingmen." They have cried "*Halt*" to the insolent arrogance of Jay Gould. They have prepared the world for the impending giant struggle which will never end until Labor is emancipated from all bondage to Capitalists!

TRUSTEES REPORT.

PHILADELPHIA, AUG. 13, 1883.

To the Officers and Members of all Local Unions:

We have examined and audited the books, receipts and vouchers of General Secretary P. J. McGuire, for the months of April, May and June — the last financial quarter and also for July, 1883, and find the same to be correct and that all monies have been duly and properly accounted for.

Signed,

W. F. EHRHARDT, } Trustees
JAS. UHRICH,

REDUCE THE DEATH BENEFIT.

Our last convention "bit off more than it can chaw." It has provided an Endowment Fund that whether we have 1,000 or 10,000 members, will take 15 cents a month instead of 10 cents. The death rate is 7 per 1000, according to all insurance statistics. 7 deaths at $250 would amount to $1.750, and at 10 cents per member each month, it would be $1.20 a year or $1,200 revenue for 1,000 members, which would leave us $550 in debt, on every 1000 members, or on 3,000 members we would be in debt $1,650. Now tell us, where can we [illegible] this deficiency, and how in honor can we promise the sum of $250 when we can not get the money and can't get it at ten cents per month? But we can pay $100 at 10 cents per month, and besides establish a sinking fund to provide in case a pestilence, *viz:* small pox, yellow fever, etc., came to any one city and increased our date rate.

But there is one sure fact, we can't pay $250 on ten cents a month. We can do it for a few months and no longer. The figures given prove it. And it is on the strength of these facts that Washington and other cities object to the Endowment. They favor $100.

ARGUS.

OUR GENERAL SECRETARY ON HIS TRAVELS.

Owing to the crowded condition of our columns this month, we can only give a brief summary of the June trip of our General Secretary. At all points he was met by large and attentive audiences of carpenters, and his remarks had the effect of strengthening the local unions visited, and of placing the nature of our Brotherhood and its workings properly before the public.

He addressed meetings in the following cities: Cincinnati, Rushville, Indianapolis, Chicago, Milwaukee, Detroit, Toledo, Sandusky, Cleveland, Erie, Buffalo, Hamilton, Toronto, St. Catherines, Syracuse, Albany. There were several other cities he visited on his route and talked to the men at their jobs of the necessity of forming unions; but he found it impossible to arrange meetings in those cities at the time. While in Cincinnati, by invitation, he addressed the Printers' International Convention, and thus solidified the chain of solidarity between the types and our Brotherhood. In Rushville he discovered that Carpenters' Union No. 39 had secured their own hall and fitted it up to lease to other societies.

And here let us mention that in Cincinnati some members of Union No. 2 have formed what is known as "The Mutual Aid." It consists entirely of members of Union No. 2, and none other can join. It is limited to 30 members, and whenever it exceeds that a new branch is formed. It is a sick benefit society and pays $6 a week on the plan of weekly assessments when a death is reported.

Milwaukee proposes to form a German branch, and the union was greatly strengthened by the mass-meeting. Chicago members have adopted a Brotherhood pin, which is simply the official emblem—a rule and compass as seen on the title page of this paper.

The meetings in Toledo, Cleveland and St. Catherines were extremely fruitful. During his stay in Buffalo our General Secretary endeavored to reconcile the differences between Union No. 9 and Union No. 31, with the result of securing the appointment of a conference committee from each union to adjust the difficulty.

In summing up, we can safely say that the results of the trip are plainly evident in an increased membership of the Brotherhood this month. Owing to this trip and others since then, our journal has been delayed. But we are sure our readers will be content when they know that our General Secretary has been by no means idle.

—We want equal dues and equal fees, and then equalization of funds so that we will keep every union we have, and carry out the principle of Brotherhood — that the strong help shall the weak.

—Bro. Henry Warne, a member in good standing of San Francisco Union No. 22, died of Pneumonia recently in Seattle, Washington Territory. He leaves a boy 17 years old and a girl 11 years. His family are entitled to the Death Benefit.

—What our Brotherhood needs is to be one in fact as well as name. We want equal initiation fees, equal dues, — the same in one city as another, and the initiation fee to be at least $2, and the dues at least 50 cents per month.

—At a recent national convention of Plasterers, it was resolved to confer with all plasterers' unions in the United States and Canadas as to the advisability of adopting the eight hours per day for eight hours pay, beginning December 1st, next, and continuing it forever after.

—Cleveland Carpenters' Union No. 11 has demanded 8 hours as a day's work on Saturday and put it into effect on July 21, regardless of the wages. The annual picnic and excursion of this union will take place at Congress Lake, Aug. 13. Tickets $1.00. A day of [illegible] recreation can be well [illegible]

BROTHERHOOD NOTES.

—Victoria, British Columbia, has organized Union No. 48.

—Boston Union No. 33 held a large public meeting on July 30, to agitate the nine hour question.

—The House Joiners Association of Halifax, Nova Scotia, contemplates joining our Brotherhood.

—Cleveland, trade dull as usual in July nevertheless all union employed, no raise in wages this season.

—Work and wages in Trenton, N. J., same as last month. Union No. 31 increasing in members every week.

—N. B. Heakes, formerly President of Toronto Union No. 27, has gone into the boat building business in Toronto.

—Hartford Union No. 43 gaining briskly and will hold a picnic or excursion at Savin Rock, Conn., in middle of August.

Send in to the General-Secretary your nominations, amendments, changes or alterations to the Constitutions of the Brotherhood.

—Union No. 47, Alameda, Cal., is doing very well and has a body of devoted men who are determined to organize the carpenters of that city.

—St. Louis Union No. 6 has removed its meetings to 22nd St. and Franklin Ave. A few noble fellows are doing their utmost to swell its' membership.

—Union No. 14, St. Louis: President, Aug. Overbeck; Vice-Pres., John Reinke; Rec. Sec., Aug. Doiel; Fin. Sec., T. P. Blattner; Treasurer, H. Lindhorst.

—We want a sick-benefit of at least $5 per week in each and every union and under equalization of funds the smallest union can pay it as well as the largest.

—Baltimore Union No. 29 is at last making very satisfactory progress—17 new members in the past month shows there is some vitality and action in the union.

—A Carpenters' Union with over 25 members has been formed in Kirksville, Mo. There are some good live workers in the union and they contemplate joining the Brotherhood.

—Indianapolis Union No. 15, has initiated many new members in May, and Secretary McGuire's visit last month has wakened up some of the outsiders so that the union is growing more rapidly.

The Carpenters' of Utica, N. Y., have formed the nucleus of a union and although they have a mountain of apathy to move, still they have the pluck and energy to do it, though few in numbers.

—Philadelphia Union No. 8 is agitating the 8 hour movement and has held several very successful meetings on the subject. A branch has been organized in Germantown and a German Branch is in course of formation.

—A man pays dues into one union, for several years, then leaves that city and upon entering another city joins the union there, ought to feel that the dues he has paid give him full rights and benefits wherever he goes.

—Chicago Union No. 21 reports trade picking up since the bricklayers trouble is settled. Wages average $2.75 per day. The Building League is creating a favorable impression not only in labor circles but even among business men.

—Toronto Union No. 27 has elected the following officers: President, John Hanrahan; Vice-Pres., B. Crombie; Rec. Sec., Alex. Edgar; Fin. Sec., P. Menton; Cor. Sec., J. Bedford; Conductor, Bro. O'Brien; Warden, Bro. Falconer; Treas., Robert Lee.

—Oakland Union No. 36 has elected: President H. A. Thompson, Vice-President C. E. Nichols, Recording Secretary E. Wland, Financial Secretary A. A. Wells, Corresponding Secretary Wm. Winnis, Treasurer W. H. Finney, Conductor J. T. Francis, Warden C. H. Scott.

—Bros. Schneider and Fake of Chicago Union No. 21 have formed a partnership and gone into the business of contracting. [illegible] shop is at No. 3723 South Lasalle [illegible] Chicago, Ill. [illegible] and faith[illegible] union men and [illegible] [illegible] is no doubt [illegible] will be successful [illegible] enterprise.

THE LABOR QUESTION.

LECTURE IX.

INSURANCE.

We have demonstrated in our previous lectures that Land, Labor, Capital and Exchange are four of the elements through which human activity operates in the formation of wealth. We have now to show that the fifth element is Insurance; and that Insurance is equally as important an element as any of the others, and therefore, in the distribution of the wealth which is created conjointly by these five elements, insurance has a right to an equitable part, which should be allotted to it. It is necessary, however, to remark that we do not use the term "Insurance" in the restricted sense in which it is generally used, and yet we can't find no better term to convey our meaning. We therefore retain the word while we extend its application and broaden its significance until it includes Security in all things and against all accidents, or a guarantee against all unforeseen circumstances, however remote, which may bring suffering or evil upon an individual or society, and which may be averted by the exercise of forethought and provision. It is, therefore, well understood that when we speak of Insurance, we mean something very different from what is ordinarily understood by that word.

Before showing what it should be, let us show what the practice of insurance, in the ordinary acceptation of the word, has been up to the present time, and how, like all other commercial schemes, it has fleeced and robbed the people.

The abuses which have been practiced by insurance companies are almost beyond belief. The legislature of the State of New York has instructed a committee to inquire into the management of insolvent insurance companies and savings banks, the receivers of which were proven guilty of the most flagrant delinquencies. The report of that legislative committee was read before the Assembly on the 23d of May, 1878. A few extracts will show the incompetency of the present organization of insurance.

Among other things, the report says: "Originating in the necessities of commerce, its application tends to free competition from its harder features and to protect highly-organized societies against the stress of financial vicissitudes and the severer hardship of natural catastrophes. Its essence is the spirit of true democracy, and in its development it lends stability to those institutions of the republic which are based upon equity and the community of interests."

In 1858 the total number of policies in the United States amounted to 43,000. We may judge of the development which the principle of insurance has made in the United States by comparing these figures with the following citation from the report of the legislative committee: "The corporations organized under our laws, i. e., the laws relating to insurances of the State of New York, have outstanding 260,000 policies, amounting to over $800,000,000, while the amount of existing policies of all companies doing business within the State more than equals our entire interest-bearing national debt."

This statement gives us an idea of how generally the principle of insurance is recognized by the people at large. Let me call your attention to one or two paragraphs from this same report to show how sadly the principle is misconceived and abused. The report says:

"Of the thirteen companies considered by this committee, only one can be claimed to have been decently conducted during its declining years. The others afford a spectacular exhibition of varied phases of incompetent, unscrupulous, irresponsible and unchecked misconduct. In place of the simple contract of life insurance, fantastic diversions in the nature of policies were introduced. Of many of the companies it may be said that swindler succeeded swindler, company swallowed company, until the last fell into the hands of swindling receivers."

It is a fact which should be noted in the memory of every American citizen that those receivers were appointed by a judge (Westerbrook) of the Supreme Court of New York. There was a time when the belief was current that the Supreme Court —at least—was free from the taint of financial and party political corruption. Since 1876 that belief no longer obtains, and for obvious and just reasons.

The report further says: "Tried by Judge Westerbrook's own tests, the manner in which these appointments were made, must be condemned, and if a proper effort had been made in each case to ascertain that the appointee possessed due qualifications, these trusts would have been administered by other men, and with better results."

"This year the Senate committee has caused to be prepared a table, and it forms a part of their report, which contains an analysis of the accounts of the the receivers of eighteen insurance companies. This table is divided into accounts of receipts, expenditures and differences. In the case of the American Popular, of which Mr. E. D. Lawrence was the receiver, there came in his hands available assets amounting to $203,255.85, for every dollar distributed he spent $2.40 for expenses. In the case of the Continental, of which Mr. John P. O'Neil was the receiver. The percentage of expenditures to dividends was 82 per cent.; that is, for every $100 he distributed to the policy holders it cost $82."

Mr. Kiernan, chairman of the committee, stated as follows: "I may say, generally, that the whole system is an extravagant one; but if you want a gross example of extravagance take the case of the Guardian Mutual, of which Mr. Henry B. Pierson was the receiver. The total expenses were $55,912.88 for a dividend amounting to $3169.46. In other words, for every dollar distributed he spent $17.44 for expenses. An item of over $26,000 went for legal expenses."

Not only are workers swindled by the insurance companies when they attempt to secure themselves against unforeseen accidents and the contingencies of poverty, but also by the savings banks, where they deposit their surplus earnings in order to provide against a "rainy day." The first sworn report of the receivers of the defunct savings bank institutions was laid before the B. superintendent of the State at Albany, on February 26th, 1872. This report is a very mild expose of the villainy of these institutions. Of 18 institutions reported, the sum of $9,585,838 was due to depositors alone at the date of closing. This sum does not include debts to other creditors. The bulk of these depositors are men who work for a living, and the sum represents their savings.

We have but to watch the newspapers to see frequent appeals for information from the poor victims who are swindled by these fraudulent institutions and still more fraudulent directors.

The workers are called "dissolute, thriftless and careless," etc., and that even by the shining lights of the pulpit, who should know better, and who, were they wise, would pay more attention to mundane affairs and try to inculcate a little more morality among their flocks, which are composed so largely of bank and insurance directors.

Let me now give an instance of the application of the principle of insurance where it is conducted more honestly; it shows the tendency of modern society to apply it rationally and justly.

The Postmaster of Great Britain calls the attention of the public to the following advantages offered by the post-office, with government security for [illegible], safety [illegible]

1st. For investing savings and small sums of money.

2d. For insuring life.

3d. For making provision for old age by means of an annuity.

A savings bank account may be opened with twenty-five cents, and money can be paid in or taken out at any post-office savings bank in the kingdom, no matter where the account may be first opened. Interest at the rate of two and a half per cent. is paid upon deposits. Women and children can become depositors. Lives may be insured for any amount between $100 and $2500; the premiums can be paid either in one sum or in periodical amounts of not less than fifty cents.

An annuity, immediate or deferred, of not more than $250, may be bought for any person not under ten years of age. In case of a deferred annuity—that is, an annuity which is payable at some future period—the payment may be made periodically in small sums instead of in one single amount.

There are post-office savings banks in every town and in most villages; and at most savings banks there is an insurance and annuity office. Printed papers, containing the rules of the post-office savings bank and of the insurance and annuity offices, can be obtained at any post-office, and if further information is needed, it can be obtained by application (the postage of which need not be paid) to the general post-office, London.

This institution has been established by the British Government for years past. The workers have a well-guaranteed security for their savings. In Canada, also a similar institution is in successful operation. We, on the contrary, in America, are robbed, plundered and swindled daily, and are still fruitlessly demanding the post-office department to do the same thing for the workers of th[illegible] [illegible]. We find ourselves periodically [illegible] our savings, and we have no redress.

The principle of insurance has been fully recognized in the domain of political economy, and forms one of the three elements of profit, which the professors of that so-called science have determined as belonging to Capital, viz.: "Insurance against risk of loss." I will not here stop to show that this risk of loss, as claimed by them, is of two very distinct characters; I will [illegible] say that the amount or value of this risk has been calculated to a great nicety, and is known by the rates which are charged by the various companies for insurance under the present system.

The owners of capital have also recognized the existence of this principle, and they transfer this "risk of loss" to insurance companies as a general thing. The amount of this risk is indeed very small, much smaller than was generally supposed and the exact knowledge we have upon the subject is in no way due to the political economists—whose business it was to have ascertained it—but to the Boards of Underwriters of the various nations of the world, and the computations they have made after a series of close and careful observations.

I will incidentally mention the fact here. One of the most entertaining, and, at the same time, instructive investigations which the student of social affairs can make, is that which relates to the manner in which Insurance has been instituted, as it fully follows the three necessary conditions of the establishment of a science, viz., observation, comparison and experiment. The Northampton tables, which serve as the basis of life insurance, are marvels of careful observation and comparison of [illegible] and a reliance upon the evidence [illegible] tistics.

The post-office and the bureau [illegible] the [illegible] tration of births and deaths [illegible], and on [illegible] perhaps, [illegible] [illegible] system. [illegible] articles of organization on the history of the labor and [illegible] in California.

by the number of letters which will be returned to the dead letter department next year. With equal certainty can it be foretold how many letters will be misdirected, how many will have no address at all, how many will contain money which will be unclaimed, &c.

In relation to deaths, not only can it be foretold the number who will commit suicide in a given year, the respective ages and condition of the suicides, but even the means by which death will be self-ministered; and the number in each month of the year can be foretold—so many by drowning, so many by suffocation, so many by firearms, &c., and all with such a degree of correctness that the power of prevision becomes no longer a matter of doubt or wonder.

(To be continued.)

REPORT FROM BRANCH 4 OF CHICAGO UNION.

At the regular meeting of Branch 4 Union 21 of Chicago, the nomination and election of officers took place; the following were elected:

President—Tom Jones.
Vice-President—John Wallace.
Recording Secretary—C. McRae.
Financial and Corresponding Secretary—L. J. Boyer.
Treasurer—W. T. Henderson.
Warden—James Fitzpatrick.
Conductor—James Ballentin.
Delegates to E. C.—L. J. Boyer, W. T. Henderson, John McCartney and William Meyers.

After the meeting adjourned the friends of Bro. James Fitzpatrick assembled to congratulate him on his election to the office of Warden, and to present him with a nosegay of flowers. Bro. Thomas Carroll made the presentation speech, in which he alluded to the valuable services rendered to the union and the brotherhood by Bro. Fitzpatrick in the past, and of the high esteem in which he is held by his brother union[illegible] and [illegible] the name of the company [illegible] congratulated him on [illegible] to the office of Warden, and [illegible] him with the nosegay of flowers as a mark of their esteem.

Bro. Fitzpatrick replied in a neat speech, in which he congratulated the brothers on the consolidation of the two Branches, Four and Nine, and predicted a glorious future for the united branch. He hoped all would work heart and hand for the good of union 21 and the brotherhood, and that they would all live and die true and loyal union men.

After three hearty cheers for the newly-elected Warden, the company dispersed.

Tulsa, Indian Territory.

On my journey from Ritchie, Mo. to this place I noticed that there were lots of new buildings in course of construction, and a good deal of repairs — more than I have ever seen in the South West for many years. Wages for carpenters $1.50 to $2.50. Bridge builders $3.50 per day. There are about 25 carpenters at work here from all parts and I am passing around your papers and appeals among them. I hope to get them stirred up and set them thinking so that when they go home after this bridge across the Arkansas River is finished, they may do something in favor of organization among carpenters. In South West Missouri, carpenters are scarce, jacklegs and botches plenty; very little day work; all contract. Wages in Ritchie, Mo., $1.50 – $2. — Granby, Mo., the same. — Neosho, Mo., $1.50 — $2.25. — Vinita, Indian Ter., $1.75 — $2.50.

—One of the most common errors is to organize and imagine, that a union with small dues can be efficient. The true way is to have dues high enough to accumulate a fund able to sustain any fight you make.

—New Officers for Chicago Union No. 21: President, I. B. Blair; Vice-Pres., F. Leibenguth; Rec. Sec., C. McKee; Cor. and Fin. Sec., L. E. Schneider; Conductor, [illegible]Grandy; Warden, J. Carroll.

[illegible] three St. Louis unions should be [illegible] under one charter, and if three [illegible] are necessary then three [illegible] be organized. But it will [illegible]. For want [illegible] city all [illegible] have [illegible]

Der Carpenter.

New York, August 1883.

Berlin, 16. Juli 1883.

Geehrter Freund und Handwerksbruder!

Meinen herzlichsten Dank im Namen der Zimmergesellen Berlins für Euer gütiges Wohlwollen im Interesse der deutschen Brüder.

Ein unserer Tendenz entsprechendes Blatt wurde am 28. December 1882 unter dem Namen „Berliner Arbeiter-Zeitung" herausgegeben, mußte jedoch nach sechswöchentlichem Bestehen wieder einschlafen. Gründe sind beschränkte Schreibefreiheit in Folge des Socialistengesetzes, demgemäß ein interessanter Arbeiter-Lesestoff unmöglich ist, und hieraus dürfte die Abonnentenlosigkeit zu erklären sein, wiewohl auch die allgemeine Erwerbslosigkeit der letzten Jahre eine Schuld an der Muthlosigkeit trägt. Wir hatten wenig über 3000 Abonnenten, das Blatt erschien alle Tage, Abonnementspreis konnten wir nicht höher nehmen, wie jene, welche 20,000 Abonnenten haben.

Ferner übersende ich eine in München erscheinende radikale (jedoch noch nicht verbotene) Arbeiter-Zeitung die „Gerichtszeitung" und den „Süddeutschen Postillon".

Außerdem theile ich mit: Wie bekannt, übersendet ich im Herbst 1882 ein Cirkular „Die Petition der Gewerkschaften Berlins an den deutschen Reichstag" nebst Motiven — ich fand einen Artikel darüber im „Carpenter", jedoch von München handelnd, ob dieses Irrthum ist? — Gründer der Zeitung sind wir 30 Leiter der verschiedenen Fach- und sogenannten Interessen-Vereine für die einzelnen Corporationen auf Vergehen gegen das Vereinsgesetz vom 11. März 1850 mit einer 29 großen Bogen (Akten) Seiten langen Anklage bedacht worden. Zusammen sind gegen uns drei verschiedene Anklagen gestellt, die erste vom 16. Juni 1880, Dietrich und Genossen, zweite vom 15. Februar 1881, Ewald und Genossen, dritte vom 9. Juni 1881, Lüdke und Genossen.

Die zweite Anklage wirbelte einen großen Staub auf und macht Aufsehen in allen Kreisen. Wir schreiten muthig weiter — wie es kommt, muß es getroffen werden. So jedoch verfährt man hier mit uns — die hiesige Organisation ist keine leichte Aufgabe, denn man ist bemüht, uns der Reaktion gegenüber unschädlich zu machen, und wenn man einen hängen will, findet man auch einen Strick — (Strang) a.

Die Lohnbewegung dauert in Wirklichkeit fort; mit der neunstündigen Arbeitszeit können wir erst dann durchdringen, nachdem eine bessere Organisation in Deutschland aufgebaut ist und uns mehr Kapital als gegenwärtig zur Verfügung steht.

Wünschenswerth wäre es, wenn von den amerikanischen Brüdern einmal ein tüchtiger Aufruf zur Organisation an die deutschen Arbeiter — Zimmerleute — gerichtet würde. Ich bitte sehr darum, aber ja nur auf ökonomischem Gebiete, auf streng politischem Gebiete verfällt er dem Ausnahme- (Polizei-) Gesetz und würde in Beschlag genommen und keinen Nutzen haben.

Auch beabsichtigen wir, im Monat August einen Congreß — „Deutscher Zimmerer-Tag" — abzuhalten und werden die nöthigen Vorbereitungen dazu getroffen.

Der Handwerkertag der deutschen Zimmerleute soll am 18. und 20. August in Berlin stattfinden. Das Programm enthält u. A. folgende Punkte:

Hebung der materiellen Interessen der deutschen Zimmerleute auf Grund einer gewerkschaftlichen Konstitution (politisch parteilos) durch

a) Gründung eines Verbandes deutscher Zimmerleute.
b) Die möglichste Lohnaufbesserung allerorts.
c) Die Regulirung der Arbeitszeit gegenüber der heutigen Maschinenproduktion.
d) Gebstmöglichste Einschränkung der Sonntagsarbeit.
e) Erstrebung eines Schutzes gegen Zahlungsunfähigkeit des Arbeitgebers (Garantie des Arbeitslohnes).
f) Schutz des Zimmermanns gegen Unfall: 1. durch Errichtung einer gesetzlich garantirten Unfallskasse, 2) durch Rechtsbeistand im Falle des Verschuldens dritter Personen, 3) durch öffentliche Klarstellung der technischen und praktischen diesbezüglichen Fragen.
g) Die Errichtung einer wirklichen Vertretung der Gesellschaft im Meisterrathe, bezüglich Gesellen-, Arbeits- und Lohnfragen, sowie auch des Lehrlingswesens.
h) Allgemeiner Rechtsschutz durch dauerndes Engagement eines tüchtigen Verbands-Rechtsanwalts.
i) Gegenseitige technische, praktische und moralische Belehrung in Wort und Schrift zur allgemeinen Vervollkommnung.
k) Die [illegible] der Ehre des Handwerks und des [illegible] [illegible]

[illegible] Ray [illegible]

[illegible], Berlin N., Greifswalderstraße, baldmöglichst zu senden.

In Erwartung, daß auch von jenseits des Oceans einige moralische und pekuniäre Mittel geboten werden, zeichnet in gegenseitiger Brüderlichkeit

A. Marzian.

Zur innern Organisation.

Schafft eine Krankenkasse.

Stimmt für die Urabstimmung und schafft das Basthum ab.

Stimmt für Abhaltung unserer Konvention alle zwei Jahre.

Indem unsere Brüderschaft nirgends in große Kämpfe nach Außen verwickelt ist, so ist es um so mehr an der Zeit, die inneren Angelegenheiten gründlich zu studiren und zu verbessern. Es hat sich herausgestellt, daß es viele Kameraden giebt, die nicht durch das Prinzip der Union, unsere gesammte Klassenlage zu verbessern, zum Festhalten an unserer Fahne bewogen werden können, sondern es muß ein bestimmter Vortheil sein, der sich ihnen darbietet, um der Sache treu zu bleiben.

Schon vor zwei Jahren habe ich im „Carpenter" darauf hingewiesen, daß eine gut eingerichtete Krankenkasse ein gutes Bindemittel sei, um unsere Kameraden zusammen zu halten. Ferner sollte der Beitrag zur Union im ganzen Lande gleich sein, ebenso das Umstands- und Krankengeld, so daß, wenn ein Kamerad von einer Stadt zur andern reist, er niemals sein Recht zur Kasse verliert. Wenn an einem Orte nicht Geld genug vorhanden ist, um die nöthige Summe auszahlen zu können, so muß der Sekretär solche Union zur Aushülfe beordern, wo mehr in der Kasse ist. Hierdurch können auch in kleinen Orten Unions aufrechterhalten werden. Das Krankengeld sollte meiner Ansicht nach auf $5 per Woche gesetzt werden. Das Sterbegeld scheint jetzt viel zu hoch zu sein. Hundert Dollars wären auch genug. Das Invalidengeld dagegen könnte $200 sein. Selbstverständlich muß demgemäß der Beitrag erhöht werden und zwar so hoch, daß alle Ausgaben damit bestritten werden können. Die Statistik der Krankenkassen zeigt, daß, wenn wir $5 per Woche Krankengeld auszahlen wollen, wir $5 per Jahr einzahlen müssen, weil ungefähr 2 Prozent Kranke vorhanden sind. Dies macht ca 42 Cents per Monat. Nehmen wir an, daß auf Tausend Mitglieder 10 Sterbefälle kommen, so macht das ungefähr $1 per Jahr, also 8½ Cents per Monat, hierzu 10 Cents Invalidengeld, so giebt das schon 60 Cents per Monat. Nun kommen noch die Ausgaben der Union und Strikekasse hinzu, so daß wir auf 80 Cents Beitrag per Monat kommen oder 20 Cents per Woche. Dies ist meiner Ansicht nach durchaus nicht zuviel für die Vortheile, welche jedes Mitglied hierdurch genießt. Mit Zahlen kann man keinen Humbug treiben und man kann keine $5 aus einer Kasse nehmen, wenn nur $3 darin sind. Sollte sich herausstellen, daß wir nicht so viel Geld brauchen, können wir den Beitrag für die drei Wintermonate niedriger stellen oder ganz aufheben, wie es in Deutschland an vielen Orten bei den Zimmerleuten eingeführt ist.

Wenn dieser Artikel im „Carpenter" erscheint, ist die Abstimmung über das Abhalten einer diesjährigen Convention bereits geschehen und wird hoffentlich bis auf's nächste Jahr verschoben sein. Die Gründe hierfür brauche ich nicht anzugeben, weil die Exekutive dieses bereits in einem Rundschreiben gethan hat, und ich erlaube mir, noch einige Punkte hervorzuheben. Nach der ersten Konstitution entscheidet die Konvention, also die Delegaten, welche die verschiedenen Unions gesandt haben, über alle Angelegenheiten der Brüderschaft, und die Mitglieder haben nichts mehr zu sagen. Anfangs ging das nicht anders; jetzt aber, nachdem wir fest organisirt sind, sollte jedes Mitglied Gelegenheit haben, seine Ansichten selbst auszudrücken, um die Gleichheit in unserer Organisation vollständig herzustellen. Dies geschieht dadurch, daß alle Gesetze und Beschlüsse in Hinsicht der Brüderschaft jeder Union zur Abstimmung unterbreitet werden, und dann die Ansicht der Majorität zum Gesetz erhoben wird. Hierdurch wird verhindert, daß unsere Brüderschaft für das Interesse einzelner Männer geleitet wird, sondern das Interesse der Gesammtheit stets im Vordergrund steht. Durch unsere Organisation ist es möglich, einen Gedankenaustausch der Mitglieder herzustellen und diejenigen Kameraden, welche mit den neuen Vorschlägen nicht einverstanden sein sollten, nicht versäumen, ihre Gründe dagegen zu veröffentlichen. Es handelt sich nicht darum, daß dieser oder Jener Recht hat, nein, es handelt sich darum, das Beste für uns Alle herauszufinden.

Viele Mitglieder werden Anfangs den Beitrag für zu hoch halten, sie vergessen aber, zu [illegible], daß wir [illegible] Organisation nicht wie [illegible]

bensunterhalt abzwacken müssen, nein, die Erfahrung lehrt uns, daß wir es den Bossen von ihrem Profit abtrotzen können, indem wir dann stark genug sind, um höheren Lohn zu erringen oder die Arbeitszeit verkürzen können. Ohne eine gute Union arbeiten wir vielleicht durchschnittlich für $2 per Tag und haben keine Krankenunterstützung; mit einer guten Union erhalten wir leicht $3 per Tag und haben eine gute Krankenunterstützung.

Der Beitrag zu einer guten Union ist daher das einzige Geld, welches der Arbeiterklasse gute Zinsen trägt. Je früher dieses von allen Kameraden erkannt wird, je besser ist es für uns Alle.

Milwaukee, Wisc.

Gustav Luebkert.

Spähne und Sägmehl.

— Die Koffermacher haben eine nationale Organisation, mit Lokal-Gewerkschaften in 13 Städten.

— In Troy, N. Y., sind 11 Gewerkschaften unter 14 in der Gewerbekammer vertreten, mit einer Totalstärke von 3500 Mitgliedern.

— J. B. Dyer, zur Zeit Generalsekretär der Internationalen Granitschneider-Gewerkschaft, ist zum 3. Male für dieses Amt wiedererwählt worden.

— Die Drucker diskutirten vergangenen Monat auf ihrem internationalen Convent zu Cincinnati, Ohio, die Gründung eines Gewerkschafts-Heims für betagte Drucker.

— Die Nationale Spinner-Gewerkschaft befindet sich in einer besseren finanziellen Lage, als je. Der Fond auf der Bank ist um $6000 stärker als zu irgend einer früheren Zeit.

Die Gelchirrmacher-Delegaten von Toronto, Chicago, Cleveland, Louisville, St. Louis, New-Orleans, Cincinnati und New-York traten in Cincinnati zusammen, um eine nationale Verbindung ihres Gewerks herzustellen.

— Chef Arthur theilt in seinem Departement mit, daß die Brüderschaft der Lokomotiv-Engineers gegenwärtig 200 Unterabtheilungen zählt, deren Mitglieder sich aus 9 Zehnteln der besten Lokomotiv-Engineers des Landes zusammensetzen.

— In Montreal, Canada, ist eine Gewerbekammer gebildet worden, aus vierzehn Lokal-Gewerkschaften bestehend, welche 15,000 Mitglieder repräsentiren. Eine ähnliche Organisation ist in Hartford, Conn., im Entstehen begriffen.

— William Martin, Sekretär der „Vereinigten Eisen- und Stahlarbeiter" der Ver. Staaten, wird für die Stellung eines Präsidenten der genannten Verbindung, als Nachfolger Jarrett's, in Vorschlag gebracht. Bruder Martin ist seit 5 Jahren Sekretär dieser Körperschaft gewesen.

— Schiffsarbeiter von Quebec weigern sich, länger als 8 Stunden täglich zu arbeiten. Dies ist der einzige Weg, kürzere Arbeitszeit zu Stande zu bringen. Wenn die Arbeiter warten, bis ihnen Legislaturen und Politiker die Achtstunden-Zeit gewähren, können sie bis an's Ende der Tage warten. Das einzige Mittel ist, dieselbe auf eigene Hand zu erringen — indem sie nicht länger arbeiten, als von ihnen vereinbart ist, sei es nun acht oder neun Stunden.

— In San Francisco waren in einer Schuhfabrik 200 Chinesen ausgestanden, weil eine Forderung, die sie gestellt, ihnen abgeschlagen worden, und wurden die Plätze der Strikers mit weißen Arbeitern besetzt.

— Die Bewegung für Verkürzung der Arbeitszeit breitet sich immer mehr aus, und wir müßten uns sehr irren, wenn nicht daraus das ganz bestimmte Verlangen der Arbeiter auf Einführung des 8stündigen Normal-Arbeitstages entspränge und dieses Verlangen bis zum nächsten Frühjahr greifbare Form annähme. Die Short Hour League in New York arbeitet rüstig weiter und findet immer mehr Ermunterung durch Beitritt neuer Vereine.

— Unsere Organisation liefert so recht einen Beweis für die Nützlichkeit, die absolute Nothwendigkeit der gewerblichen Organisationen. An ihr können jene Zaghaften und Kleingläubigen in anderen Gewerken es erkennen, daß doch die Gewerkschaftliche Organisation die einzige ist, welche die Lage der arbeitenden Klassen zu bessern vermag und nicht eine Organisation, gemischt aus allen möglichen Elementen der Bevölkerung. Freilich würden sie dann auch ersehen, wie eine gewerkschaftliche Organisation beschaffen sein muß, wenn sie ihren Mitgliedern Nutzen bringen soll, und daß sich dies mit seinem Monatsbeitrag von 10 Cents nicht erreichen läßt. Unsere Mitglieder aber wissen gut genug, daß ihnen jede weiteren 5 Cents Wochenbeiträge [illegible] [illegible] einen Dollar [illegible] eintragen, [illegible] zahlen sie [illegible]

(Rochd. Z.)

Arbeiterliteratur.

Von Hugo Miller.

Was ist der Arbeiterstand? Nichts! — Was sollte er sein? Alles! Abbé Sieyes.

Arbeit schuf das Kapital, ehe das Kapital die Arbeit beschäftigen konnte. X.

So, wie in der Naturwelt alles Große von unten, aus der Erde herauswächst, so geht auch in der Geschichte jede große Bewegung, jeder große Fortschritt der Civilisation von der Masse des Volkes aus. Hildebrand.

Kapital sind diejenigen von der Arbeit geschaffenen Werthe, durch deren Benützung die Arbeit neue Werthe schafft. Marx.

Die menschliche Arbeit ist keine Waare. Arbeitskraft in dieselbe Kategorie mit Roheisen, Holz u. zu stellen, ist ein verfluchtes Verbrechen gegen die Natur und gegen die Menschlichkeit. H. J. Wales.

Das Kapital ist nur ein Frachtmittel, dienend zur Ueberlieferung begehrter Güter von einer Person zur andern. Hermann.

Der Hauptbeweggrund zur Versklavung von Menschen war der, ihre Arbeit oder die Frucht derselben umsonst zu bekommen, und mit der Sklaverei ist diese Neigung nicht abgeschafft worden. Ira Steward.

Die Geschichte ist ein Kampf mit der Natur, mit dem Elend, der Unwissenheit, der Machtlosigkeit und somit der Unfreiheit aller Art, in der wir uns befanden, als das Menschengeschlecht im Anfang der Geschichte auftrat. Die fortschreitende Besiegung dieser Machtlosigkeit — das ist die Entwicklung der Freiheit, welche die Geschichte darstellt. Lassalle.

In geschlossenen Reihen, als Macht, müssen die Arbeiter auftreten, um die Hebung ihrer sozialen Stellung durchzusetzen; denn wer im Besitze der Macht ist, der politischen wie der wirthschaftlichen, theilt sie unfreiwillig und räumt nur Denjenigen, die gleichfalls als lebensfähige Macht auftreten, eine Stelle neben sich ein. Schulze-Delitzsch.

(D. A. Buchdr.-Ztg.)

Legalisiren der Gewerkschaften.

Während vieler Jahrzehnte wurden in England die Gewerkschaften als ungesetzlich und ihre Handlungen als Verschwörungen betrachtet. Aber die Beschränkungen, welche diesen Gesellschaften durch die Regierung auferlegt waren, wurden eine nach der andern durch die überwältigende Kraft der Unions niedergebrochen, so daß zuletzt nicht nur ihr Recht, sich zu organisiren, anerkannt wurde, sondern sie wurden auch unter dem Gesetz registrirt und dadurch rechtskräftig gemacht und ihre Ausdehnung befördert.

Im Jahre 1871 nahm das englische Parlament das „Gewerkschafts-Registrirungs-Gesetz“ an, welches unter Anderem folgende Bestimmung enthält:

„Die Zwecke irgend einer Gewerkschaft sollen nicht auf den bloßen Grund hin, daß sie dem Gewerk einen Zwang auferlegen, als ungesetzlich erachtet werden, um irgend ein Mitglied einer solchen Gewerkschaft, als verbrecherisch, einer gerichtlichen Verfolgung zu unterwerfen.“

Das Gesetz bestimmt ferner, daß solche Gewerkschaften Kontrakte machen und daß die Mitglieder unter sich Verabredungen treffen können in Bezug auf Lohn, Arbeitszeit, Arbeitgeber, Arbeitsregeln und Vereinsstrafen, und daß solches Verfahren nicht als ungesetzlich betrachtet werden soll. Ferner können die Unions Grundeigenthum und Vereinseigenthum besitzen, sie können Beamte verklagen, wenn sie Gelder veruntreuen und haben alle Rechte, welche in Amerika kapitalistischen Corporationen zugestanden sind.

Daraus geht hervor, daß die organisirten Arbeiter Englands weit mehr gesetzliche Anerkennung errungen haben, als man unseren Gewerkschaften in Amerika gewährt. Während das englische Gesetz behauptet, daß Gewerksverbindungen als ein Gewerks-Zwang nicht ungesetzlich seien, haben ein Dutzend Staaten dieser Republik immer noch Conspirations-Gesetze, die das zum Verbrechen machen, was in England gesetzlich ist.

Dies ist eine Schmach für Amerika! Man bedenke: Von einer Monarchie müssen wir uns in dieser Hinsicht beschämen lassen. Daß dem so ist, ist unsere eigene Schuld. In demselben Augenblick, in welchem wir vereinigt und entschlossen den Versuch machen, die Freiheit der Vereinigung — die Freiheit, uns zur Verbesserung unserer Lage zu verbinden — zu erringen, in demselben Augenblicke werden wir jede Staatsgesetzgebung zwingen, sich unserem Willen zu beugen.

Wir wollen die Legalisirung unserer Gewerkschaften, damit unsere Fonds sicher gestellt sein mögen. Wir wollen unsere überschüssigen Fonds in Land und Eigenthum anlegen können. Es bezahlt sich für Kapitalisten, ihr Geld in Grundeigenthum anzulegen, und wir haben Fonds, welche eben so gut angelegt werden können, als wie auf die Bank gebracht, damit sie Andere anlegen. Wir wollen unsere eigenen Gewerkschaftshallen bauen, wir wollen gegebenen Falles Arbeitskontrakte übernehmen und unsere Geschäfte ohne das Eingreifen Anderer verwalten. Um all' dies zu vollbringen, muß unser erster Schritt sein, unsere Gewerkschaften rechtskräftig zu machen, wie es in England geschehen ist.

Die Bestrebungen zur Abkürzung der Arbeitszeit.

Die Nothwendigkeit einer Abkürzung der Arbeitszeit für alle industriellen Arbeiter ist so einleuchtend, so leicht zu beweisen und tritt in der fortwährend zunehmenden Brachlegung von menschlicher Arbeitskraft in allen Industriezweigen durch neu erfundene und verbesserte Maschinen so klar zu Tage, daß Vertreter aller Klassen und aller Stände sich gezwungen sehen, dieselbe zuzugestehen. Wenn also Fabrikanten dieses Zugeständniß gemacht haben und, wenn einzeln befragt, fortwährend machen müssen; wenn Nationalökonomen, Professoren, Gesetzgeber und Politiker aller Schattirungen, kurzum ein großer Theil derjenigen Leute, welche gewissermaßen die Oberaufsicht über unsere ganzen gesellschaftlichen Einrichtungen führen und die Macht in Händen haben, dieselben jederzeit zu ändern, — wir sagen, wenn alle diese Leute zugestehen, daß ein Beibehalten der jetzt üblichen Arbeitszeit bei unseren sonstigen gesellschaftlichen Einrichtungen einen Theil des Volkes in immer größere Armuth, Abhängigkeit und materielle und geistige Bedürfnißlosigkeit treibt und daß dies schließlich dem ganzen Volk und der ganzen Civilisation zum Verderben gereichen muß — und die Abkürzung der Arbeitszeit macht dennoch in der Praxis so langsame Fortschritte, so mag dies sonderbar erscheinen, ist aber sehr erklärlich. Diese Leute haben unzweifelhaft die Macht, eine Abkürzung der Arbeitszeit herbeizuführen oder doch zu beschleunigen, aber — haben sie auch ein Interesse, dies zu thun? Sofern als das Wohl des ganzen Volkes in der Zukunft dadurch gesichert werden kann, haben sie allerdings ein Interesse daran; aber wo ist der Fabrikant, der Gesetzgeber, der Staatsmann oder der einflußbesitzende Gelehrte, welcher sich heutzutage um so fernliegende Dinge kümmert? „Jeder für sich!“ ist so lange der leitende Grundsatz in der Gesellschaft gewesen, daß jeder Gemeinsinn und der vernünftige Egoismus, welcher auch für die Zukunft sorgt, fast abhanden gekommen ist. Die Leute, welche heute die Macht in Händen haben, die gesellschaftlichen Einrichtungen und damit die Reichthümer der Nation zu beherrschen, ahnen es, daß mit jeder halben Stunde Arbeitszeit, welche den Arbeitern erlassen wird, ein Stück ihrer Macht und Herrschaft über die Arbeiter verloren geht. Da also ihr unmittelbares Interesse in Frage kommt, so sind sie gegen die Abkürzung der Arbeitszeit, nach einem weiteren Grundsatz handelnd, welcher sich nach und nach bei ihnen ausgebildet hat und welcher lautet: „Nach uns die Sündfluth.“

Wir ersehen daraus: Wenn eine Abkürzung der Arbeitszeit durchgeführt werden soll, so muß es durch Diejenigen geschehen, welche ein unmittelbares Interesse daran haben, — durch die Arbeiter selbst. (Möbel-Arbeiter Journal.)

Chicago-Union 21, 25. Juli.

Unsere Union 21 hat seit der zweiten Hälfte April drei neue Zweige gegründet, und unsere Organisation steht im Begriff, groß zu werden. Gegenwärtig haben wir 1500 Mann und 12 Zweige; bei jeder Versammlung treten neue Mitglieder hinzu. Das Geschäft für Carpenter ist hier seit dem 15. Juni fast flau. Der Lohn für die Inside-Shop-Bauschreiner beträgt von $1.75—2.50 und für auswärtsschaffende Carpenter $2.50—$3 per Tag bei 10stündiger Arbeit.

J. A. Pohl,
Pr. Sek. von Zweig 10.

— Neue Beamte für die Chicagoer Union No. 21: Präsident, J. B. Blair; Vicepräsident, P. Leibenruth; Prot. Sekretär, E. McKea, Corr. und Finanz-Sekretär, L. F. Schneider; Geschäftsführer, M. Casaby; Aufseher, J. Carroll.

— Die drei St. Louiser Gewerkschaften sollten unter einem Charter organisirt sein und wenn drei Versammlungsplätze nothwendig sind, dann könnten ja drei Zweigvereine gebildet werden. Es wird aber niemals angehen, drei Gewerkschaften zu haben. Aus Mangel an Einigung unter eine gemeinsame Leitung herrscht bei allen drei Gewerkschaften dieser Stadt seit über einem Jahre nahezu Stillstand. Brüder von St. Louis, tretet zusammen und verbindet Euch zu einer Gewerkschaft!

Brüderschafts-Notizen.

— In Victoria, Britisch Columbia, hat sich die Union Nr. 48 organisirt.

— Die Hausschreiner-Assoziation von Halifax, Nova Scotia, beräth sich über den Anschluß an unsere Brüderschaft.

— Arbeit und Löhne in Trenton, N. J., dieselben wie letzten Monat. Union Nr. 31 wächst jede Woche an Mitgliedern.

— Union Nr. 33 in Boston hielt am 20. Juli eine große öffentliche Versammlung ab, um für die Neunstunden-Frage zu agitiren.

— Union Nr. 43 in Hartford wächst lebhaft und wird Mitte August ein Pic Nic oder eine Excursion nach Savin Rock, Conn., veranstalten.

— Sendet dem Generalsekretär Eure Nominationen sowie Eure Zusätze, Aenderungen oder Verbesserungen zur Constitution der Brüderschaft ein.

— Das Gewerbe in Cleveland flau, wie gewöhnlich im Juli — trotzdem ist die ganze Gewerkschaft beschäftigt; in dieser Saison keine Lohnsteigerung.

— Union Nr. 29 in Baltimore macht endlich befriedigende Fortschritte — 17 neue Mitglieder im vergangenen Monat zeigen, daß noch Lebens- und Thatkraft im Vereine steckt.

— Union No. 47, Alameda, Cal., steht sehr gut und hat eine Körperschaft hingebender Männer, welche entschlossen sind, die Zimmerleute jener Stadt zu organisiren.

— Union Nr. 14, St. Louis, Präsident Aug. Overbeck; Vice-Präsident, John Reinke; Protokoll-Sekretär, Aug. Dodel; Finanz-Sekretär, T. P. Blattner; Schatzmeister H. Lindhorst.

— Wir wollen eine Kranken-Unterstützung von mindestens $5 wöchentlich in jedweder Gewerkschaft, und als Ausgleichung des Fonds das Niedrigste, sowohl wie das Höchste, das eine Gewerkschaft bezahlen kann.

— Union Nr. 15 in Indianapolis hat im Mai viele neuen Mitglieder aufgenommen, und der Besuch des Sekretärs McGuire im vergangenen Monat hat viele Außenstehenden aufgerüttelt, so daß die Gewerkschaft nun rascher wächst.

— Union No. 8 in Philadelphia betreibt die Achtstundenbewegung und hat mehrere sehr erfolgreiche Versammlungen in dieser Sache abgehalten. In Germantown ist ein Zweigverein organisirt worden und ein deutscher Zweigverein ist im Entstehen begriffen.

— Die Zimmerleute von Utica, N. Y., haben den Kern einer Gewerkschaft gebildet und obgleich sie noch einen Berg von Gleichgültigkeit zu überwinden haben, so besitzen sie auch den Muth und die Energie hierzu, trotzdem sie wenige an Zahl sind.

— Wir sind für gleiche Steuern und gleiche Gebühren und alsdann für Begleichung der Fonds, damit wir jede Gewerkschaft, die wir haben, behalten und das Prinzip der Bruderschaft — daß der Starke dem Schwachen helfe — ausführen können.

— Union Nr. 21 in Chicago berichtet, daß das Gewerbe sich macht, seit der Trubel der Backsteinmaurer beigelegt ist. Löhne durchschnittlich $2.75 per Tag. Der Bau-Verein macht einen günstigen Eindruck, nicht nur in Arbeiterkreisen, sondern auch bei Geschäftsleuten.

— Ein Mann, der mehrere Jahre Beiträge an eine Gewerkschaft bezahlt, darauf die Stadt verläßt und beim Betreten einer anderen Stadt sich der dortigen Gewerkschaft anschließt, sollte fühlen, daß die von ihm gezahlten Beiträge ihm volle Rechte und Vortheile geben, wohin er geht.

— Bruder Henry Warno, ein gutstehendes Mitglied der Union No. 22 in San Francisco, ist jüngst in Seattle, Wyoming Territorium, verstorben. Er hinterläßt einen 17jährigen Jungen und ein 11jähriges Mädchen. Seine Familie hat Anspruch auf die Sterbe-Unterstützung.

— Was unsere Brüderschaft bedarf, ist, eine Brüderschaft in der That, ebenso wie dem Namen nach zu sein. Wir wollen gleiche Eintrittsgebühren, gleiche Beiträge — in einer Stadt wie in der andern, und die Eintrittsgebühr soll mindestens $2, die Beiträge mindestens 50 Cents per Monat betragen.

— Die Clevelander Zimmermanns-Union No. 11 hat den achtstündigen Arbeitstag verlangt und am 21. Juli durchgesetzt, ohne Beeinträchtigung der Löhne. Das jährliche Picnic nebst Excursion dieser Gewerkschaft wird am 18. August am Lake stattfinden. Tickets $1. Es steht ein Tag des Vergnügens und der Erholung zu erwarten.

Praktische Erfolge unserer Brüderschaft.

Die Zimmerleute von Oakland strikten am 20. Juli und setzten das Neunstunden-System durch; am 15. Juli thaten die in San Rafael das Gleiche, und ebenfalls mit Erfolg — so daß jetzt die Zimmerleute von San Francisco, Oakland und San Rafael neun Stunden täglich arbeiten und dabei mindestens 50 Cents per Tag mehr bekommen, wie vor achtzehn Monaten, wo sie keine Organisation hatten und zehn Stunden täglich arbeiteten. Auch arbeiten sie Samstags nur acht Stunden, so daß sie wöchentlich sieben Stunden für sich selbst und mindestens $3 wöchentlich mehr Lohn errungen haben. Und dies wurde erreicht vermittelst des Gewerkvereins, durch unsere Zimmermanns-Brüderschaft. Und nicht allein das — auch die Anstreicher und andere Baugewerke sind unserem Beispiele gefolgt und haben gleichfalls die neun Stunden errungen.

Zimmermanns-Notizen.

— In Paterson, N. J., $1.50 bis $2 täglich und kein Interesse für Organisation.

— Die Arbeit in Missisippi ist gegenwärtig flau; die Löhne der Zimmerleute betragen $2.50 bis $3. Die meisten Arbeiter sind Farbige.

— Die „Vereinigten Zimmerleute und Schreiner Schottlands“ haben im Ganzen 4050 Mitglieder unter 10,626 Zimmerleuten dieses Landes.

— J. S. Murchie, Generalsekretär der „Vereinigten Zimmerleute“, wurde mit überwältigender Majorität abermals zum Generalsekretär dieser Gesellschaft erwählt.

— Die Zimmerleute sind in Denver im Juli so zahlreich wie Fliegen und bekommen nur $2.50 bis $3 täglich. Die gewöhnliche Kost in dieser Stadt beträgt $5 bis $7 wöchentlich.

— In Schottland arbeiten die Gewerkschafts-Zimmerleute in über hundert Städten nur neun Stunden täglich und haben Samstags einen halben Feiertag — was durchgängig 51 wöchentliche Arbeitsstunden macht.

— Die Zimmermanns-Gewerkschaft in Berlin, Deutschland, hat jüngst ein offizielles Journal — vorläufig monatlich — erscheinen lassen, „Zeitschrift der Zimmerleute“, herausgegeben in No. 50 Stalitzer Str., Berlin, Deutschland.

— Der neue Census-bericht für die mit 1880 abgelaufenen zehn Jahre zeigt, daß in dieser Zeit 2,544,458 Einwanderer in die Ver. Staaten kamen. Auf der Liste der Handwerker stehen die Zimmerleute oben an, indem 54,000 dieser Einwanderer zu ihnen gehören.

— Die Convente der „Vereinigten Zimmerleute“ werden alle drei Jahre abgehalten; die Versammlung wird der Generalrath genannt und besteht aus einem Delegaten von jedem Distrikt. Dieses Jahr wurde ein Generalrath vom 11. bis zum 22. Juni abgehalten und sehr viele wichtige Angelegenheiten erledigt.

— Der Bericht der „Vereinigten Zimmerleute“ für Juli weist 382 Zweigvereine mit 21,488 Mitgliedern auf. Das Gewerbe in London, Manchester und allen großen Städten Englands ist sehr flau, ebenso in Irland und nur mittelmäßig ist es in Schottland, flau in in Neu-Seeland und Süd-Afrika, gut dagegen in Australien.

— Die Treppenbauer-Gewerkschaft in San Francisco strikte für eine Lohnerhöhung von 50 Cents täglich — von $3.50 auf $4 — und hat nach den neusten Berichten den Strike verloren. Die Ursache ihres Unterliegens besteht darin, daß sie keine Verbindung mit Treppenbauern anderer Städte hatten — was zu bewerkstelligen wäre, wenn sie sich nur unserer Brüderschaft anschließen würden. Die Pforten unserer Brüderschaft stehen allen Treppenbauern offen.

— Warum nicht blos neun Stunden das ganze Jahr über arbeiten? Wir haben im Winter eine kurze Arbeitszeit wegen der kurzen Tage — und mit etwas Anstrengung können wir dieses System auch im übrigen Jahre einführen.

— Wozu nützt uns ... Winn, a well-known resident, one of the 1849 pioneers of ... died recently in Sonoma, Cal., ... was a contractor and builder ... for years identified with the labor movement on the Pacific Coast, and an ... advocate of the Eight-Hour system. ... time ago we published some articles ... his pen on the history of the labor movement in California.

THE C

THE OLD CARPENT

CORRESPO

THE CROSS AND THE CROWN.

Raise your wages as you will, [illegible]
Still will fortune [illegible]
To shorten hours [illegible]
[illegible] the way to wear the crown.

[illegible]
Which will be the greater [illegible]
While higher wages [illegible]
Ever shall we bear the cross.

If to-day our wages rise
We pay more for goods to monied men,
And we find with grief [illegible]
No load is lifted from our sorrow.

If we but reduce the hours,
There's more work for every man.
[illegible] won't rise [illegible] power,
Can raise the [illegible], do all they can.

Long enough we've born the cross,
We've raised the wage, they've pulled it down.

To us has always come the loss,
Strike for less hours and wear the crown is [illegible].

CORRESPONDENCE.

Kearney, Neb.

Wages for carpenters $1.50—$3.00 per day. Twenty buildings erected since March. Others under headway. Will agitate for a union.

Detroit, Mich.

Through the activity and strenuous efforts of Bro. C. F. Smith, Union No. [illegible] of this city is again brought into life. Night after night he has gone around pasting bills and announcing meetings, thus making every effort to stir up the sleepy headed carpenters of this city.

Burlington, Iowa.

Carpenters in this city are considering the matter of organizing a union. Wages $2.25—$2.50, business dull. In Des Moines there is a lively demand for carpenters at $3 per day. At Ottumwa $2 $2.50, mostly repair work. Building trade slack.

New Orleans, La.

Union 16 is in good cheer, plenty of work, weather hot. An abundance of rain has somewhat delayed work. Wages average $2 per day. Some parties are trying to adopt piece work system, but it has very little hold here so far. If carpenters know their own true interests, they will never allow piece work at all. There is plenty of sickness in the city, chiefly small pox and fever. The painters and their bosses are at war about wages.

Cleveland, Ohio.

Union No. 11 has voted against holding a convention this year. Trade brisk; wages $2.25—$2.75. No difficulty for good men to get at least $2.50. New officers are: President, D. F. Sleeper; Vice Pres., Robert Johnston; Rec. Secretary, G. G. McFarland; Cor. Secretary, A. L. Pellew; Treasurer, D. McIntosh; Warden, A. Brown; Conductor, W. B. Kiringham; Financial Secretary, F. Freeman.

Chillicothe, Mo.

Trade is not very brisk at present. There are not many new buildings going up; mostly repairs and alterations. Wages $1.50 to $2.50. Those appeals you have sent out have done some good here. The men are now talking about forming a union and establishing a scale of prices. We had a meeting and organized a union to join the Brotherhood.

Boston, Mass.

Union No. 33 has had an election of officers. Richard Cassidy has been reelected President; W. J. Shields, Vice-President. [illegible] of the officers are new men. The balance [illegible]. Our union still keeps filling up rapidly; initiating from six to eight members every meeting. Wages average $2.50 per day, with a great many union men at $2.75.

[illegible]

[illegible] a day. They also [illegible] Saturday, so that they [illegible] hours a week more for them. [illegible] pay. [illegible] by union [illegible] their [illegible] have [illegible] ty hands in [illegible] $1.25 to $2. We favor [illegible] ample [illegible] here to better our [illegible]

Fort Wayne, Ind.

Carpenters' wages in this city are $1.50 $2.00 per day, with plenty of work this season. But the contractors have everything their own way. We are now arranging to form a carpenters' union and then we will be able to command more respect when we have a union, and our wages will be better. There are 75 men ready to join the union.

Fall River, Mass.

The great trouble in this city is that if a man can hew down a tree or whittle a stick, he considers himself a carpenter. This class of wood butchers work cheap and cut down pay. The state of trade is bad; very little new buildings. Wages for carpenters $1.50 to $2.50. A union is difficult to establish here on account of the hostility between nationalities, and yet a union is greatly needed and these national prejudices should stop.

San Rafael, Cal.

At a largely attended meeting of Union No. 35, it was decided by an unanimous vote that it is not necessary to hold a convention this year, and we approve of the principle of a General vote. We do not favor an increase of the monthly allowance for endowment from 10 cents to 15 cents, nor do we favor sending on the 10 cents per member each month to the Gen. Treasurer. It is better to carry out the law as it is, so that the General Treasurer always has one endowment on hand. We are in favor of always having the headquarters in some fixed place, without shifting it around every year. Bro. Edward Owens of San Francisco visited us recently, and he warmed up some of our skinflint bosses. We are now working nine hours per day, and work is quite dull all season until a few weeks ago.

Washington, D. C.

In regard to the Endowment Fund it does not suit the members of our union. They are nearly all in some endowment fund now and they are taxed about as much as their wages will afford to support these endowments. If the Endowment fund in the Brotherhood was a separate degree so as to let those join who want to, it would work better with our members. Trade is very good; men all at work, wages $3 per day on the average. Our new officers are: Pres., Thos. Galloway; Vice-Pres., G. W. Backman; Rec. Sec., W. A. Ward; Fin. Sec., Patrick O'Brien; Cor. Sec., G. W. Heldy; Treasurer, J. T. Soter; Conductor, David Gregg; Warden, Sam Maloy. Bros. [illegible] and Helsly have gone into business for themselves. Our union is growing splendidly.

Oakland, Cal.

We are very busy now initiating new members; we have nearly doubled our strength the past month. Members are coming in pretty lively, at the rate of 25 to 30 every meeting. We have more than a majority of the carpenters of Oakland, and our men stood shoulder to shoulder and have gained 2 hours on a day's work. Work is fair, wages $3 to $3.50 and plenty of men for all the work. Our members are all working on the nine-hour plan. On July 2, we instituted the system and had no trouble whatever. Our members are all at work and non union men are not allowed to work with us any longer in this city. We will have 200 members before two weeks more. We hope that some of the Eastern unions will fall in line soon and we think they can get the nine-hours. Within a year every mechanic in California will work only nine hours a day. This movement of the carpenters in the two cities of San Francisco and Oakland has awakened a wide spread interest among all other trades.

Baltimore, Md.

Our carpenters mass meeting here on May 28, was well attended and has resulted in an increase in membership. The members of Union No. 29, proceeded from their hall and paraded the streets headed by a band of music. The meeting was held in Castle Hall, and our General Secretary in a very able and skilful manner explained the principles and benefits of our noble brotherhood. The newly elected officers are: Pres., J. W. Pugsley; Vice-Pres., Jas. Chadick; Preceptor, J. Walsh; Treasurer, J. W. Bentley; Rec. and Cor. Sec., J. B. Aylsworth; Fin. Sec., Geo. H. Striewig; Conductor, Chas. [illegible]; Warden, C. G. Davis; Trustees, Geo. Wooden, D. Whitney and C. O. N. Woods. The union is in a very prosperous condition, having quite a large surplus in the treasury, while new accessions are being added in the way of membership. We will have to get a larger hall. The initiation fee has been raised from $1.00 to $2.00. Our excursion on July 28th was a success.

Brownsville, Mo.

Sometime ago I received a card from you requesting that I should send for blanks and all papers necessary to establish a Carpenters' Union at this place. I have talked to some about it, who admit that it might do well here and I send to you, to send the papers and full particulars, instruction etc. and some of your appeals to carpenters. The carpenters here are not united by any means and I believe a Union is badly needed. Wages are only moderate; too many botch mechanics who go to contracting after a few months' journey-work. Wages range from $1.50 to $3.00 per day. I enclose 50 cents for the *Carpenter* and will get more subscribers. There is more matter in your little paper that interests me than in many large sized costly Journal.

Toledo, Ohio

The visit of our General Secretary has done us more good than anything that has come to pass in this city among carpenters. His talk is endorsed in every shop. It looks now as if we will double our membership before the Summer is over. We propose now to raise our dues and initiation fee, and have a sick benefit. Our newly elected officers are: President, Charles Murphy; Vice Pres., John O'Neal; Rec. Secretary, R. L. Herbold; Financial Secretary, John Kluster; Cor. Secretary, M. J. Thompson; Treasurer, Simon Zirale; Conductor, M. F. Kied; Warden, John Adams; Trustees, J. Thompson, J. B. Young, F. Adams.

P. J. McGuire's lecture has had a good effect, as shown by the class of men making application for membership. For although they are some of the best in the trade, and always in sympathy with union, they were afraid to trust our organization lest it fail, as all other attempts at organization in the past. But they are now becoming satisfied after what they heard at the lecture, and the way the union is carried on. They now see there is a good foundation, and the union is going to stand.

Charleston, S. C.

We have received your documents and have a union in this city which is called "The Carpenters' Protective Union of Charleston, S. C." It is a chartered body under the laws of the State, and we protect our brother members in sickness, and aid in case of death, and protect each other in wages and equal right to work. Eight months ago our union numbered 300 members, but now we have fallen down to 155 in good standing. We desire to be united with the Brotherhood of Carpenters, as that will help us to build up again. Work is good, wages very low, from $1.50 to $2.25 per day. There are from 50 to 60 new buildings going up besides lots of jobbing. Of course, there are plenty of men for all there is to do.

Rushville, Indiana.

Union No. 22 is still alive and gaining strength. We elected and installed our new officers for the coming term. On June 27th we cast an unanimous vote for no convention this year. This is what we think every local Union in the B. ought to do, thereby saving to our fund the money that must necessarily be paid out for railroad and hotel fare, to say nothing of other expenses. Croakers will say, "I told you so; you are not of enough importance to support a convention played out, etc., etc." But they don't know it all. Our debts must be paid, our future looked to, and in course of time, when we shall have attained a position among the old trade unions of the world, our conventions will then be in keeping with them. For some time our attendance has been small on account of bad weather, but not enough so to discourage us in the least. Our membership is growing.

At present work is slack. Harvest is at hand, and that stops country work, and work in town is in no haste. Wages range from $1.50 to $2.25 per day. New chips coming in all the time. Board $3.50 to [illegible] per week. We all make an extra 10 or [illegible] day and quit at 1.30 and 5 on Saturday. Rent here is high. Any kind of a shell or hut brings $5 per month. We have five building associations that have helped many a poor man to a good home, and houses are going up every day out of their funds.

Hartford, Conn.

Union No. 43 has adopted the nine-hour system on Saturdays, and all hands have gained it. The bosses in nearly all cases pay us for the hour. Many non-union men joined in with us for this point, and the result is, we have got many new members, and we keep on bringing them in every meeting. Business rather dull at present, many idle. Wages same as last report. Our union has voted to a man against holding a convention this year. We voted in favor of a general vote to elect officers, and that the endowment fund remain as it is and be left in hands of local unions, and to send same in advance when called on for same.

List of officers of Union No. 43, Hartford: President, Philip H. Fagan; Vice President, Mallory Tabor; R. S., P. J. Brooks; F. S., J. F. Egan; T., John B. Cosgrove; C. S., James A. Robertson; Conductor, John Mulcahy; Warden, Daniel Healey; Trustees, David Geddie, P. J. McCann, James Brennan, Charles Warrender, Louis Labadie.

CHICAGO ITEMS.

Non Union Carpenters in Chicago had better join Union No. 21 now at once while the initiation fee is small, as it will soon be doubled and then all the harder to pay.

— Branch 11 held a very successful public meeting, July 16, corner of 35th St. and Cottage Grove Ave. This branch is a live aggressive one and is making good headway.

— Bro. Schneider reports that the proposed Building League is already having a favorable effect upon the different trades concerned and upon the building community at large.

— We hope each branch Secretary in Union 21 will send us news direct to this office as to the doings of the branch each month. We want to make these reports interesting.

— A committee has been appointed by the E. C. to secure the opinion of the branches as to a picnic to be held this summer. The prospects are that a picnic will be held at an early date.

Union No. 21 has been the projector of the building trades league in Chicago and we are proud to note that a convention of the various building trades was held July 25th, and was well attended by delegates from the trades interested.

— The *Progressive Age* says: "The election of Thomas B. Blair as President of Union 21 was a well-merited compliment to a very worthy gentleman. Mr. Blair is an earnest, intelligent worker, who has the courage of his convictions, and it is safe to predict that Union 21 will continue to make progress during his term of office.

— At the last general meeting of Branch 12 the following officers were duly elected: President, J. Theisen; Vice-President, J. Hildebrand; Recording Secretary, J. Heltz; Financial and Corresponding Secretary, J. Thone; Treasurer, C. Sper; Conductor, J. Schmitz; Warden, J. Weber. Branch 12 is a German Branch and meets every Monday evening at 2235 Wentworth Ave.

THE CARPENTER

A MONTHLY JOURNAL FOR CARPENTERS AND JOINERS.

VOLUME III. NEW YORK, SEPTEMBER, 1883. NUMBER 9.

ACROSS THE SEA.

GERMANY.—The strike of the joiners in Stuttgart has ended favorably to the men; the men were firm and well supplied with funds from their trade in all parts of Europe.—The National Convention of journeymen carpenters, held in Berlin, August 19, was an immense success. Delegates were present from all quarters of Germany, and the convention was preceded by a street parade.—In Munich the labor movement is marching forward with rapid strides. The Cabinet Makers' Union in a month has grown to number 1000 members, the carpenters 400, the masons 382, while the shoemakers and others are organizing rapidly. Since 1876, there has been no trade union movement in Munich.

ENGLAND.—In York, the carpenters were reduced ½ d. per hour in 1879, and the same again in 1880. This season trade has improved, and the men are now on strike since July 21, for an advance of ½ d. per hour.—The strike of the weavers at Ashton is very firm and spreading; it is against reduction in wages.—At Sheffield, the file-grinders and cutters have been beaten in their strike against a reduction of ten per cent., and it was all for want of organization.—On September 10th, the Trades Union Congress began its session at Birmingham.

FRANCE.—The delegates of the French Trades Unions to the Holland Exposition at Amsterdam have arrived there, and have been warmly greeted, and the workers of Holland fraternized with the representatives from France in the heartiest manner.—A delegation of twenty trades unionists from Paris are now on their way to America to attend the Boston Exhibition now in progress.

STRIKE STATISTICS.

Adolph Strasser, the President of the Cigarmakers' International Union, in his testimony before the Senate Committee on Labor a few days ago, made the statement that during the last eighteen years there were 363 strikes of cigarmakers, of which 157 failed and 204 were successful. The cost of these strikes was $280,444, but they had added $1,800,000 a year to the wages of the strikers and had prevented reductions estimated at $500,000. Here is an incontrovertible statement that should set workmen thinking and put an end to the false statements of the capitalistic press.

NATIONAL TRADE UNIONS.

A National Union of Journeymen Tailors has been formed in convention at Philadelphia with ten cities represented. The Constitution covers a sick benefit and a strike benefit of $10 per week, and a death benefit of $25. The question of eight hours as a day's work is to be one of the main objects. The Car Painters' National Association with 150 delegates met in Baltimore on Sept. 17. The Hat Makers' National Union opened its convention on Sept. 17, in Brooklyn; 42 delegates present; action was taken against contract convict labor, as it seriously affects the hat trade. The Varnishers have formed a National Union and held a convention in Indianapolis. The Stationary Engineers met in convention at Chicago, October 24. In Cincinnati the Boiler Makers held their convention, and the Wood Carvers will hold theirs in that city on Oct. 16.

SAWDUST AND SHAVINGS.

Trades Assembly has been formed in Akron, Ohio.

—The State Trades and Labor Congress of New Jersey will meet in Trenton, N. J., on October 1st.

—Coopers met in Convention in Peoria, Ill., and formed an International Union with good prospects.

—Boiler Makers' and Ship Builders' Society of Great Britain has 28,943 members and an annual income of $350,105.

—In place of John Jarrett who declined to serve another term, Wm. Weihe has been elected President of the Amalgamated Iron and Steel Workers. William Martin, the former efficient Secretary, has been re-elected.

—It now looks as if we will have a National Labor Bureau of Statistics passed by act of the next Congress. The political parties are incorporating the idea into State platforms. This is the result of the labor movement.

—The Hat Finishers' Association of Newark, N. J., passed resolutions condemnatory of Ben Butler for renewing the hat contract held by John T. Waring & Co., which called for 300 convicts to be employed by that firm in Massachusetts.

—The Cigar Makers' International Union is now holding a convention beginning Sept. 17, at Toronto. In 1877 this society was so weak it could only send 7 delegates to its convention, in 1880, 32 delegates, and this year they will have 87, a twelve-fold increase in six years.

—The Trades and Labor Congress adopted some very wise measures and carved out a lot of work that, if carried out, will do much to benefit the industrial classes. We hope every National and International Trade union will join the Federation of Trades, and help on the good work.

—Brotherhood of Locomotive Engineers has paid during the last fifteen years insurance benefits amounting to $1,362,411.80, an average of $2,620.08 on each claim, at a cost per member of $33.33⅓ per year. The Brotherhood pays for the loss of a hand, arm, limb or eyesight, the same amount as for death.

AN ACT OF TREACHERY.

For many years no movement in this city was ever started with better prospects of success than the Building Trades League; strike after strike was gained and it was generally conceded that it would soon make the union of the building trades a giant power. And all went well until at a very fatal moment the Framers Union of this city committed an act of treachery that consigns its members to disgrace forever in the labor movement. A strike was ordered on a row of buildings on West 73d street against some scab plasterers that were working for the Clark Estate. The Framers along with the other unions ordered their men out and indorsed the strike, by that act. After standing out two weeks, just at the moment of victory, the Framers returned to work by orders of their union without waiting to consult the other trades or even informing them. The Framers Union was formerly Union No. 5 of our Brotherhood and in the same perfidious manner withdrew from us illegally owing us to this day a large sum of money for journals and supplies. Their President John Ritter is receiving some very severe censure from all quarters for the action of the union in scabbing it against the other trades.

TRADES UNION TYRANNY.

The despairing wail of the *Evening Post* and other capitalistic mouth pieces in this city, about "Trades Union Tyranny" is indeed distressing and painful. Now that the building trades of New York have formed a league to assist each other, the servile curs of the press snap and bark about the "tyranny of trades unions." It was all right while the contractors and boss builders had their own way, when they could browbeat men, defraud them of their hard earnings and screw them down to pauper pay. But for the workmen to now combine and perfect their combination by alliances with sister unions in the building line is, according to these capitalistic scribblers, an act of "arrogant dictation, and will leave the contractors at the mercy of the workmen."

Oh! How we pity these poor, helpless contractors! They are certainly in a very bad situation: we ought to, of course, have some consideration for them, they have had so much regard for us. They have been charitable enough to employ us, and we ought to be forever humbly grateful, even if we have to wallow in the dust to lick their feet. Workmen should never be base enough to organize for their own common interests—that is a right the bosses alone should possess, and for workingmen to organize the same as bosses do, is a step that ought to be discouraged and combatted.

This is the language that would suit our bosses. But workingmen are not any longer to be trifled with and in the Building League the workmen in the building trades have found a formidable weapon to make non-union men become union men, and unfair bosses are brought to terms without much delay. The bosses have talked of refusing to hire union men hereafter. But they discover that such a rule will not work, because they can find but few outside the union, and these are mostly inferior workmen.

Meanwhile the work of the Building League progresses; strike after strike succeeds; non-union men are taken into the various unions by the score at every meeting. The treasuries of these unions have been increased by over a thousand dollars in some cases, which is the sum paid in for initiations and dues. Thus the ranks of Labor are strengthened and solidified. The constitution of the Building League is to be found in another column of this journal, and we hope to see this constitution made the basis of a league in every city.

THE RIGHT TO COMBINE AND STRIKE.

The New York *Herald*, the great enemy of workingmen, says: "They (the telegraphers) have not only a right to strike; they have a right to combine and strike in a body; and all talk about secret and oath-bound societies is rank balderdash. The great capitalists who employ labor in this country have their organizations also, and by united efforts stop production in order to raise prices to consumers, and employ lobby agents at Washington to secure legislation injurious to the great mass of the people for their own joint benefit.

—Fred Turner of Philadelphia has been elected General Secretary of the Knights of Labor. Fred is the right man for the place and knows full well the intent of the Order. Under his administration we expect a spirit of fraternity and reciprocity will be established with all trade and labor societies.

TRADE NOTES.

—Wages in New Orleans $2.50—$3.00. Plenty of work in city and adjacent country; fever still prevalent.

—Wages in Buffalo, N. Y., have fallen to $2 per day since the men have become so indifferent as to neglect their union.

—Trade in Indianapolis is only moderately brisk, and not by any means very flattering; prospects for the Fall are fair. Union No. 15 gaining rapidly in membership.

—Toledo Union No. 25 is doing handsomely; it is now one of the liveliest unions under our jurisdiction, with its membership nearly doubled since the visit of the G. S. last June.

—The Baltimore carpenters have a system which compels all men applying on a job for work to show their clear cards, and the "scab" who is unable to show up, finds himself discounted at every turn.

—The eight-hour system in Australia was first established by the stone masons on March 24, 1856, and became general in the building trades on April 21, 1856, and was soon after adopted by all classes of labor.

—The parade and demonstration of the Central Labor Union of New York, on September 5, brought fully 20,000 men into line, and aroused a live interest not only in this city, but throughout the whole country.

—On September 1, the Western Union Telegraph Company granted a reduction in the hours of service and an increase in pay equal to about $10 per month. Had there been no strike, the company would not very likely have been so generous.

—The *Telegraphers' Advocate* is a 12-page journal, published semi-monthly at 78 Cortlandt street, New York; Tallavall & Mitchell, publishers. It is full of good, sound advice to the telegraphic fraternity, and is doing loyal service in upholding the banner of labor organization.

—Every capitalist who has been on the witness stand of the Senate Committee on Labor has shown the cloven foot and horned head of devilish antagonism to labor organization. Dr. Green, Jay Gould and John Roach all united in denouncing trades unions and in chanting the glories of monopoly.

—From the September report of the Amalgamated Carpenters, just at hand, trade is improving in England, and at best is only moderate; in Ireland it is in most cases good, and in Scotland poor; while in New Zealand, Australia and South Africa trade is very bad and overstocked with men.

—The St. Louis *People's Advocate* says: A scheme is on foot to unite the three Carpenters' Unions in this city. If this is done, and a few of the loud-mouthed "stinkers" who have disgusted the fair-minded men, are forced to occupy seats in the back row of chairs, the result will be one of the liveliest and most efficient Labor Unions in the city.

—Gen. A. M. Winn, a well-known resident, and one of the 1849 pioneers of California, died recently in Sonoma, Cal., aged 73. He was a contractor and builder and was for years identified with the labor movement on the Pacific Coast, and an ardent advocate of the Eight-Hour system. Some time ago we published some articles from his pen on the history of the labor movement in California.

CORRESPON

8

THE OLD CARPENT

'Tis many years I've ha
My weary hand now gr
What weary hours did
From Monday's sunrise
Both you and I are
And I too shall be c
To die and perish in
Of the poor workma

Both you and I have wo
And brightness of our y
The temper of the meta
Our edge and teeth are
Both you and I are
Together we've not
Our boss will turn
Together, on some

You; dull and senseles
I—cursed with life—can
You tire not, I've "not
Will he have human fee

To think if we woul
I, perhaps, may be
Both you and I are
To be worn out and

CORRESPO

HARTFORD, Conn.—
tinting new member
4 every meeting. W
wages $2.25 to $2.75.

BALTIMORE, Md.—
prospect for second
son, but not so good
Wages $2.25 to $2.50
creasing.

TRENTON, N. J.
enough for what is
$2.25 to $2.50. Ste
members; we never
we started.

CHILLICOTHE, Mo.
not flattering; only
Wages from $1.50 to
chips" here work fo
or take small jobs fo
for.

ALLEGHANY CIT
wages $2.50 to $3
Plenty of saw and
around; first-class
penters' Assembly of
out, owing to trouble

WILMINGTON, Del.
ters union in Wilming
very much. Your
into the hands of som
among eight or ten
It is stirring the "C
Wages $2 to $2.35 a
only trouble is the
and single handed th

From the C

NEW ORLEANS, La.
of work in architect
valence of small
Plenty of sickness
average $2 per day;
higher. Union No.
good prospects ahea

Items fror

...VILLE, Ind.
union started
...ts for increase
...nty of work and
to do it. Wages $1.5
to put our shoulder
uplift our down trod
man in the Brother
we will become a p

What is Going

BOSTON, Mass.—
erage pay $2.50;
the way of new me
old members would
in getting non-union
a District Sick Co
working order with
sick list. On May
lecture in Tremon
auspices of the Bost
Labor Union.

Topeka

...KA, Kansas
here is
1st. A
...s, 2d.
the publ
...r unions other

THE CARPENTER.

Entered at the Post-Office in New York, as second-class matter.

NEW YORK, SEPTEMBER, 1883.

SIGNING THE DOCUMENT.

A Reminiscence.

The action of the Western Union Telegraph Company in compelling the returning strikers to sign a document, which binds them to keep clear of connection with any labor organization is not the only instance of its kind.

Such cases have been very common. This case however calls to mind a reminiscence which will serve to illustrate the results of "signing a document" by workmen, both in regard to the treatment they receive in consequence of the act from their fellow-workmen, and from the masters whose purposes were served by it.

In 1842 or '43 I obtained a job in the carpenters' shop of one of the largest and best building establishments of London, with the apparent prospect of steady employment for one or more years. Seven years previous to that there had been a prolonged builders strike which ended in the bosses requiring the men to sign a document—but the men sturdily refused to do so and returned untrammeled, only after they had secured the discharge of every man who signed the document.

One morning a strange man applied for work at the foreman's office. After he left the office an old workman named Pugh went immediately and inquired of the foreman if he had given this man a job. Receiving an affirmative reply, Pugh told the foreman that the new applicant was a "document man," and if he came into that shop he (Pugh) would leave. The foreman endeavored to compromise the matter with Pugh by saying that the man better be allowed to go to work for the balance of the week, and at its close he should be discharged. Pugh was unrelenting. "No! He must not be allowed to work in that shop for even a day."

The workmen were not aware at the time what was transpiring in the office, nor for some time afterward. By and by Pugh wrote a simple statement of the facts upon a sheet of sandpaper: "Mr. Ward has given a document man a job. As soon as he brings his chest into the shop I shall stop work," and signed his name. This was sent to the man working at the first bench in the shop. This man just added: "We shall all stop work at the same time. Joe Mathews." The paper was passed to the next bench, signed, and so on through the shop until every man had signed to it his name. This shop method of obtaining signatures is called a "round robin."

The foreman, after the interview with Pugh, would have taken means gladly to prevent the new man from coming to work, but he had no knowledge of his whereabouts. A union man could easily be found through the society, but a "document man" was an outlaw afraid to be discovered.

On the following morning at seven o'clock the document man, assisted by an expressman, came through the shop door carrying his chest of tools. At a preconcerted signal—three distinct blows with the hammer on the bench the stout active arms of nearly a hundred men were stilled in a moment; their gaze directed intently upon the office. The poor devil of a "document" stood as if rivetted to the floor, and near him stood the foreman, while the shop was silent as the dead. From the opposite entrance walked in the "Master," as was his usual custom at this hour in the morning. He was a white-haired benevolent-looking man, between sixty and seventy years of age. His practical experience helped him immediately to an understanding of the scene and situation. He knew the attitude of his men indicated a strike. He walked hastily through the shop to the office, where stood the foreman and the doomed document man. "What's the matter, Mr. Ward?" he said, addressing the foreman, who at once explained the matter, stating that he was himself ignorant of the fact that the man he had engaged was a document man. Thereupon the usually pleasant face of the master assumed a savageness of expression. He fairly glared at the poor, shrinking, shivering creature (who had, by the way, signed the document in this same office not ten feet from where they now stood) and roared out, "D— the document man, pay him for a day's work and send him away. I'll not have my shop curled by a d— document man."

I have seen many strikes since that time. Some of these have become historical, but none of them ever gave evidence of more quiet determination and of more deepseated hatred of the cause of a strike. Each man felt and acted on that occasion as if the victim of their wrath was, "tainted with the moral leprosy." His chest and himself were removed without loss of time; then each workman quietly resumed his place at the bench and went to work.

The instigator of the strike, Pugh, had been in the employ of this firm upwards of forty years, and had at the time a son who was thirty-five years old, and had there learned his trade. These two men left this shop at the time of that strike when the document originated. They had remained idle for months after having refused to sign it, and returned to work only after every document man had been driven away. It would be well for some people to institute careful comparisons before tossing up their hats and hurrahing for this free and glorious republic, and bemoaning the slavery of the English wage-workers. What does it show when American workmen sign away their independence on degrading contracts, as our telegraphers have recently done, but that they are slaves? Will American masters be less consistent than was my genial, generous, old "Boss" to the "document man?" Probably not. Succumbing to the pressure of a prolonged strike, that poor fellow performed an act that outlawed him from his natural associations, but at the same time fortified his master in the stronghold of prosperous security, and for which the thanks were only kicks and curses.

The end is not yet, and we shall see what future consequences await the signers of the telegraph masters' "document."

JACKPLANE.

HINTS ABOUT SCREWS.

Where screws are driven into soft wood and subjected to considerable strain, they are very likely to work loose, and it is often difficult to make them hold. In such cases the use of glue is profitable. Prepare the glue thick; immerse a stick about half the size of the screw and put it into the hole; then immerse the screw and drive it home as quick as possible. When there is an article of furniture to be hastily repaired, and no glue is at hand, bore a hole, insert a stick, fill the rest of the cavity with pulverized resin, then heat the screw sufficient to melt the resin as it is driven in. Where screws are driven into wood for temporary purposes, they can be more easily removed by dipping them in oil before inserting.

POLITICS IN TRADES UNIONS.

During the past few days, workingmen in different parts of England have been receiving a great deal of advice, some of it disinterested, no doubt, but a good deal of it very cheap and gratuitous. It was a little premature on the part of Mr. Bradlaugh, for example, in speaking at the Dean Forest miners' demonstration, to urge introduction of politics into all trades unions. Such advice, if acted upon by working men, would be most mischievous, and would result in breaking up trades unions. It would take away the attention of working men from the objects which are nearest their interests—the rate of wages, the state of trade, the fluctuations of prices, and the conduct of employers. These are objects enough and important enough for any society or organization to look after and to keep steadily in view, without mixing them up with politics. Nothing, we believe, would please the employers better than to see trades unions introduce politics into their programme. While workingmen would be discussing the franchise, the law of entail, perpetual pensions, the land laws and other kindred topics—all very important no doubt, and worth any amount of discussion the masters could be manipulating the markets—the bases of sliding-scales, and lining their pockets with gold at the expense of their workmen. Let workingmen study and discuss politics by all means, but let them do so outside their trades union organizations.—*Reynold's Newspaper.*

—One of the most common errors is to organize and imagine that a union with small dues can be efficient. The true way is to have dues high enough to accumulate a fund able to sustain any fight you make.

SUPPLY AND DEMA

Every time we attempt to ... union or make a demand fo... are confronted by the cry: ... demand will fix your wages ... unions can't stop it!" This t... of the "dismal science" ho... scarecrow for the political ec... frighten workmen into subm... theory these sophists advan... *work is plenty and labor scarce, ... high; and when work is scarce an... wages will be low.*

Let us examine this theo... "law of supply and demand... labor is subject to the same... regulate the price of pork, cot... articles of commerce. The pr... commodities rise and fall eac... portion to the supply. By th... *the price of labor should rise and...* in accord with the demand, a... price would be nicely adjuste... very first stagnation in busine... at once reduced; but who eve... corresponding advance on th... good times?

Even the capitalists have ... combinations to affect price... supply and demand. This so-c... and immutable law has agai... been set aside by boards of ... exchanges, and like organiza... members are loudest in conde... unions, and pronounce our ... We may ask till doomsday fo... in wages, and wait for a h... thereafter for the operation o... demand, and we will never ge... wages without organization. ... how much the increase in ... high the cost of living, indi... demands will be unheeded ... ganize and collectively compe... lists to yield all that we justly...

TECHNICAL SCHOO

This is what the *Southern Lu...* in regard to technical sch... are a great many old-fashion... have and will still resist th... idea of educating the laborin... art, but they cannot maintai... tion against the facts.

In conversation recently ... telligent mechanic, the writer ... gratified to notice that he h... subject earnest consideratio... said he, "I was brought up a ... and wagon builder, but I cann... trade now, because the m... undersells hand-made, and ... every article I might name."

"But does this fact not ... mechanical trades?"

"It does in the few instan... who really learned their tra... entirety, and who still begi... rough material and finish the ... by hand. Of course they can... against the work of machin... they make a support if certa... did not still think that han... was the only kind worth buyi...

"What do you think is the ... likely to benefit the working ...

"Either establish one or ... technical arts schools in eve... town in the country, or add ... course of these studies to the ... our public schools, and, wh... still better, teach the indust... applied to mechanics, mining ... and chemistry practically. I ... a portion of each day or ... actual manipulation of the m... in subjects taught. Thus the ... the working classes who atten... schools would learn to work; ... lose all taste for it during the... devote to other studies; b... they learn is of but little use ... far as their future labors in ... cerned."

RITTER DENIES SENDING ... NEWPORT NEWS

John Ritter, President of ... Framers' Union of New York ... brage at our statement last m... sent house framers down to Ne... Va., to take the places of me... He claims that in June last, a ... Chas. Smith came to the labo... the New York Framers and ... He wanted house framers to ... folk, Va., at $3 per day to wor... summer hotel. Ritter furnis... for the job, but the men at ... week discovered that the boss ... every Saturday whereupon th... to this city. This is Ritter's s...

CONSTITUTION OF THE BUILDING LEAGUE.

By the recent amalgamation of twenty of the most powerful trade organizations in the building line in this city the journeymen have been enabled to win every strike which has been inaugurated under its guidance, with the exception of two which are still pending. A few important trades organizations, however, have not joined, and the question as to whether they shall co-operate in the movement or act on their individual responsibility is the subject which forms the most important topic of debate at their meetings. The idea of amalgamation is for the trades unions to act concertedly for the general good. Without this plan of proceeding it is held to be impracticable to regularly compel the employers to pay the desired rate of wages, and to prevent them from placing restrictions upon the workmen. Strikes which occurred heretofore involved great expense, whether successful or not, as they generally lasted some time when conducted by trades unions individually.

The strikes which were inaugurated under the plan of amalgamation have continued but a short time, involved little or no expense and resulted in victories. Amalgamation is held by its advocates to be the best method of improving the affairs of the workman, by inducing all non-society men to become trade unionists, and thus completely organizing labor.

The following is the constitution which was adopted by the Executive Council of the Building Trades:

CONSTITUTION.

ARTICLE I.

SECTION 1. This organization shall be known as the Executive Council of the Building Trades of New York City.

SECTION 2. This council shall be composed of delegates duly chosen from all societies in the building trades, who shall, before being admitted, produce credentials signed by the president and recording secretary of their society, and shall have the seal of their lodge attached.

SECTION 3. In case of a secret society, the seal of their lodge attached will be a sufficient guarantee of their genuineness.

SECTION 4. The officers of this council shall consist of a chairman, vice chairman, recording secretary, corresponding secretary, financial secretary, treasurer and sergeant-at-arms.

SECTION 5. The chairman and vice chairman shall be elected at each meeting, and shall be nominated from delegates of different societies, nor shall the chairman sit in judgment on any case affecting the union he belongs to.

SECTION 6. The recording secretary, corresponding secretary, financial secretary, treasurer and sergeant-at-arms shall be elected quarterly; the recording secretary shall receive such salary as this council shall deem advisable.

ARTICLE II.

SECTION 1. The executive functions of this council shall be vested in the officers and delegates while in session, and in such committees as this council may find necessary to conduct its business under this constitution.

SECTION 2. The objects of this council shall be to centralize the united efforts and experience of the various societies engaged in the erection and alteration of buildings, that they may form one common council, and with common interest to prevent that which may be injurious, and properly perfect and carry into effect that which they may deem advantageous to themselves and for the common good of all.

SECTION 3. All trade and labor societies represented in this council, when desirous of making a demand for either an advance in wages or an abridgment of the hours of labor, shall, though their delegates, report the same to this council, prior to the demand being made, when, if concurred in by a two-third vote of all the societies present, at any stated meeting, the action shall be binding. This section shall not prevent any society from acting on their own responsibility.

ARTICLE III.

SECTION 1. No trade shall be entitled to more than three votes on any question that directly affects the material interests of any trades society.

SECTION 2. All trades or societies represented shall be entitled to three delegates.

SECTION 3. Any society having two branches shall be entitled to two delegates for each branch.

SECTION 4. Any society having three or more branches shall be entitled to one delegate for each branch.

ARTICLE IV.

SECTION 1. Any trade society represented in this council that may desire material aid shall state their case to this council, and if approved by the delegates shall bring the matter before their respective organizations for immediate action.

ARTICLE V.

SECTION 1. It shall be the special duty of this council to use the united strength of all the societies represented therein to compel all non-union men and scabs to conform to and obey the laws of the society that they should properly belong to.

SECTION 2. It shall be the duty of any trade or labor society to use every lawful means to induce all non-union men or scabs to become members of their respective unions, and any trade society failing in their just efforts shall bring the matter before this council through their delegates, with all the facts in the case, with the names of the men, if possible, where employed, and the name of the employer, the same to be presented in writing with the signature of the president of the society affected, when this council shall take immediate action in the matter, and, if deemed advisable, this council may, by a two-thirds vote of the delegates then present forming a quorum, order a withdrawal of any or all trades or societies who may be on any building where said non-union men or scabs may be employed. This order shall be carried into effect through the agency of the delegates of the various societies.

ARTICLE VI.

SECTION 1. All societies represented in this council shall pay the sum of two dollars per month.

ARTICLE VII.

SECTION 1. On demand of a union represented, a general strike shall be ordered to reinstate a member or members who have struck and are refused employment on the job that was struck.

SECTION 2. Any walking delegate or delegates of any society ordering a strike without the consent of this council, the trade he represents shall be held responsible for the wages of the men on strike. This shall not prevent a delegate from ordering a strike of the members of the society he represents to adjust its own internal affairs without the assistance of this council.

SECTION 3. Members of a union seceding from a parent organization and forming a separate union shall be excluded from this council.

SECTION 4. All branches of a union shall demand the same wages and the same hours of labor.

ARTICLE VIII.

SECTION 1. When the members of two unions represented in this council work at the same trade, it shall be unlawful for one to take the place of the other on strike.

ARTICLE IX.

SECTION 1. No society or branch of a society shall be allowed to strike more than one employer at a time, unless there are two or more employers on the same job.

ARTICLE X.

SECTION 1. Two-thirds of all the trades represented in this council shall form a quorum.

SECTION 2. It shall take two weeks notice of motion and two-thirds majority to alter or amend any article of this constitution.

Every union man should attend the meeting of his union; the irregular attendance and negligence of members have been the downfall of many unions. When men realize that the union depends upon their attendance, then the first step to power has been taken. Let us be as attentive to our own interests as the bosses are to theirs.

—Let union-men always help each other to get employment. If you know of a job open don't run after a non-union man nor tell him where it is. Look around and get a union man to fill it. Cling to each other and be faithful to one another. Let "scabs" take care of themselves!

— In some cities it is a common practice for bosses to hire carpenters for outdoor work, and after weeks of labor in the hot sun, when the in-door work is to be done, they hire men at cheaper rates and let the others go. We must remember such bosses.

REASONS FOR SHORTER HOURS OF LABOR.

Michael Clarke, late of Glasgow, Scotland, now of New York, for many years prominent in labor circles in Scotland, has made the following very sage observations in an interview with an *Irish World* reporter:

Strikes are of rare occurrence in Scotland for the reason that workingmen there are thoroughly well-organized. Their unions are numerous, well supported, and strong financially, a circumstance which makes the employers exceedingly slow to encroach too far upon the rights of workmen. In fact, the employers do not — unless driven by absolute necessity, such as an enormous fall in the price of manufactured goods—attempt to cut down wages, because they know well that the men would resist, and that they have the means to "hold out" in case of a strike being decided on. The British workingman is now much more intelligent, better educated, and more comfortable than he was twenty or thirty years ago. Thirty years ago he was nothing more than a slave—little better than a machine. Working all day and every day without relaxation, he had no taste—no culture—no education—no opportunities of improvement. His house was a wretched hovel—his children and himself in rags. The few hours that he was not working or sleeping he spent in the whiskey shop which was his only place of recreation. He had not an idea on politics, and if he had, he had no time to give them thought, development or practical effect, and therefore the "big people" had all the game of Government to themselves, and we know how well they played it in their own interests. They excluded the workingmen from the franchise and kept his voice from being heard within the walls of Parliament, until the workingman got time to read and inquire and look into the matter. He very soon began to see where and why things were wrong, and he very soon and very resolutely began to put them right—did put a great many things right, and is at the good work still, although to go-ahead and free American republicans he may seem somewhat slow in his movements. He could have done nothing, however, if he did not get his hours of labor shortened. I regard the success of the Short-Hour Movement in Great Britain as of more value to the people of that country than any other reform obtained within a hundred years. Had that movement failed, three-fourths of the reforms, political, social and educational, since wrung from a reluctant and resisting aristocracy, would certainly never have been effected.

It may be said that a cheap press would have done the work. There would be no press worth mentioning in existence, if the people had not leasure to read. Before the short-hour agitation there was no popular press, no social or political organizations among the people, and carried on by the people, no agencies by which popular rights could be asserted, urged and secured. Thirty years ago the workingman of Scotland was as low and degraded as it was possible for a human being to be. Although there is still much to be done, he is to-day infinitely better, socially, morally, educationally, better housed, better fed, and better clad.

BUILDING IN NEW YORK.

The New York *Mail* says it is probable that the number of buildings in that city at the end of this year will be 100,000. The number erected last year was 2,561, and the indications are that a larger number will be put up this year. The amount expended in this way in [illegible] was nearly $45,000,000, and it is thought this year it will be $70,000,000. The value of real estate is higher than ever before. A lot at the corner of Broad street and Exchange Place was recently sold at the rate of $15,000,000 per acre. The best land on Broadway is worth $2,000,000 an acre.

Every strike lost proves the power of those who possess the means of labor—the Capital—over those who are without those means — without Capital — and shows plainly that that power—Capital—must be taken from out the hands of irresponsible private individuals and placed under the collective control of the workers. The more strikes the better as it seems that the people learn faster that way than by being told these things; they like bitter experience as a teacher.

REPORT OF DELEGATE TO TRADES CONGRESS.

To the Officers and Members of all Local Unions.

BROTHERS:—I beg leave to submit the following report of my action as delegate to the Third Annual Trades Congress, which met at New York City August 21st, 1883. The Congress lasted five days; 23 delegates present, representing 140,000 men. I had the honor to submit two important measures for the consideration of that body, which were favorably received and passed. One for the object of the unification of labor, the other to demand from political parties a plank in their platforms in favor of the enforcement of the Eight-Hour law, the incorporation of national trades unions, and the establishment of a National Bureau of Labor Statistics.

Allow me to digress for a moment. The necessity for unification becomes more apparent each year in view of the fact that combinations of capitalists become bolder and more aggressive, as they discover their power, and the inability of society to protect itself against their demands. The power that brought the telegraphers to their knees is at present master of the situation, and has given a sister organization its death blow. Shall we accept their defeat—the defeat of a skirmish line—as a Waterloo, or shall we bend our energies toward more perfect organization, better preparation and systematic action? The present disjointed movement of labor invites defeat in detail, and can only be excused on the ground of inexperience. Therefore we must strive for a more perfect unity.

But now to resume my report. The Trades Congress selected your delegate for a position of honor the ensuing year that may better enable him to carry out your wishes and to protect the best interests of the Brotherhood. I have been chosen one of the Vice Presidents of the Federation, which makes me a member of the Legislative Committee.

The work of the Congress was in every way worthy of its high character as the representative body of the workers of this country. Some of its most notable works may be briefly summarized: Favoring arbitration; demanding the enforcement of the eight-hour law on government work; asking the passage of a law limiting the dividends of corporations to ten per cent. and dividing the balance among the employes; demanding of conventions of political parties plain declarations of their position on the labor question; favoring a government telegraph; initiating a movement looking to the unification of labor organizations throughout the entire country; recommending trades unions to have higher dues and attach benevolent features to their plan of organization, and directing the presentation of a bill to the Congress creating a national department of industry and statistics, and the incorporation of trades unions.

The Congress condemned the iron-clad oath of the Western Union Telegraph Co., and sent its President to the Senate Committee to protest against it. A movement to reduce the hours of labor in all trades this coming year was recommended and steps are to be taken to organize the mill and factory operatives of New England. A prize of [illegible] is offered for the best essay on "Trades Unions and Strikes."

A resolution was adopted providing that a committee should be appointed to confer with the Knights of Labor and other kindred organization, with a view to a thorough unification and consolidation of workingmen throughout the country, and holding that as there are many thousands of organized associations of laboring men scattered throughout the land, that ought to be centralized that no one has a right recognized by the others to monopolize the absolute control and government of the whole body of laborers.

The General Secretary of our Brotherhood P. J. McGuire was called on to address the Congress, and in his remarks he proposed the above resolution, and also suggested the following change in capita tax, which was adopted, so that now the dues are not so heavy and the Federation is better likely to embrace a larger number of organizations the coming year. Organizations of 1000 or less are to pay $10; 1,000 to 4,000, $20; 4,000 to 8,000, $25; 8,000 to 12,000, $40; over 20,000, $50.

The Congress adjourned to meet in Chicago on the third Tuesday in October, 1884.

G. EDMONSTON, *Delegate.*

[illegible] Washington, D. C., Sept. 14, 1883.

THE CARPENTER.

PUBLISHED MONTHLY

BY THE

Brotherhood of Carpenters and Joiners,

OF AMERICA.

Office: 184 William St., New York.

TERMS.—Fifty cents a year, in advance, post-paid.

Send all moneys and correspondence for this Journal to

P. J. McGUIRE, Secretary,
184 William St., New York

NEW YORK, SEPTEMBER, 1883.

—We are slaves without the advantages of slavery.

—Two-thirds of the wealth of the United States is in the hands of one-fifth of the people. Remember that!

· Why should Labor fill the world with plenty and live in want and abject misery? There is something wrong when those who do the most get the least.

—Read the constitution of the Building League of New York, and consider it well. It ought to be made the basis of action for the building trades in every city.

—The time will come when no man will have the right to be worth a million, when that milion is composed of what 10,000 workingmen earned and were deprived of.

The subdivision of labor, the increase in machinery and the high pressure system of work have rendered ten hours labor to-day far more exhausting than 14 hours work years ago.

—Less hours means higher wages; and that is just what the capitalist knows and fears. It increases the wants, and the wants increase the demand, and the demand stimulates trade.

—Man is not on earth to be a slave; he has a social, moral and intellectual nature to provide for, as well as for his physical, therefore he should have all the comforts of life he works for and the leisure to enjoy them.

—Horace Mann, America's great Patron of Education, said: "Although we have doubled and quadrupled the products of labor by the ingenuity of the American mind, we have not made one single step toward a fairer distribution of those products.

—We want stringent lien laws in every State, and the collection of judgment without long stays of execution or other unnecessary delays. A claim for wages should have priority over the claims of all creditors or mortgagees. Workmen have a right to be protected in their earnings.

—Capitalists talk about the risks of capital, as if Labor had no risks at all. Are the constant risks of workmen in life and limb and bodily health, from the perils of their daily labor of no value? If they are, we will never get any recompense for them, unless we organize and amalgamate our forces.

—Down with piece work in the carpenter trade! It is a fraud upon the public by leading to botch work and scamping—it is dishonest. It is an injury to the workmen by intensifying the competition among them, reducing wages, and increasing the hours of labor—it appeals to the greedy and selfish, and is a curse to the trade.

THE PHILOSOPHY OF STRIKES.

The following paper was presented by P. J. McGuire in his evidence before the U. S. Senate Committee now investigating the labor question:

A strike is a movement of the workers against some imposition of the employers, against a reduction in wages, or an increase in the hours of labor; on the other hand it may be for an advance in pay, or for a shortening of the hours of toil.

But no matter what may be the nature of the difficulty, strikes are indications of a class war between the capitalists and the laborers, and are an evidence of growing intelligence among the workers as to their class condition. They are a passive form of resistance to the aggressions of capitalists and a protest against the social system that adds millions to the wealth of the millionaires and keeps the workers in poverty and subjection. In a word, a strike is a revolt against the class rule of the capitalist. Such revolts, although sometimes organized, are oftener unorganized. And just in proportion as Labor becomes better organized in trades unions and labor societies, that far are strikes less indulged in by the workers.

Well-organized bodies of workmen are not so apt to strike: they command the consideration of their employers, hence their demands are respectfully considered, and in most cases granted. Bosses are not likely to provoke a conflict with a body of men that they know are financially prepared to stand out for an indefinite time. Hence, to diminish the number of strikes, all that is necessary is to promote and encourage labor organizations, and protect them and their property by legalizing their existence the same as in England and in France.

No strike is a loss or a failure to the workers, even if the point sought is not gained for the time being. If naught else, they at least teach the capitalists that they are expensive luxuries to be indulged in. Consequently we find it proven by facts that in trades where strikes have been most prevalent in the past, the employers are now more ready to listen to the demands of their employes. Very few employers who have passed through the agonies of one or two strikes ever care to enter into any further struggle, and this is a warning to employers generally. Were it not for fear of strikes, employers would be far more exacting than they are. Hence every strike is a *success* to the workers, and is effective in advancing the social interests of the working class.

Viewing the question from another standpoint, we find, the result of a strike, if not satisfactory in gaining the point at issue, instead of dampening the ardor of the men, only demonstrates all the more forcibly the importance of organization beforehand and the necessity of accumulating funds to sustain them. More than that, they are an education to the working classes in showing us what we have to expect from the government, when it uses its police and soldiers at the instant bidding of the capitalists to imprison us or to shoot us down.

In proof of my point that wherever strikes have occurred, employers in those occupations are more inclined to treat with their employes. I will cite an instance: Over a year ago Jay Gould attempted to reduce the pay of his employes on the railroads centering at St. Louis. As soon as the proposition was made, the railroad engineers and firemen took organized steps to resist, and as Jay Gould already knew what a power was behind the Brotherhood of Locomotive Engineers, he yielded sooner than provoke a struggle that he feared might prove only too disastrous to him. He recognized the Brotherhood of Locomotive Engineers, while he refused to treat with the Brotherhood of Telegraphers, because they had not yet power. But if ever similar trouble occurs again in the telegraphic interests of the country, the capitalists will be far more ready to meet the employes than go over the same experience.

THE SAFEST POLICY FOR BUILDING LEAGUES.

If the Building League in New York fails it will because of the Framers perfidy, and because the proper policy of the movement has been reversed. The League should not have entered into any struggle with the larger bosses until next spring. As long as it confined its action to movements on the smaller jobs it was successful and that policy should have ben continued. But when it came to ordering two or three strikes of the same trade at the same time, and also striking against the leading bosses the Building League has discovered the magnitude of the task. The safe road for success is a few strikes at a time and on the smaller jobs first; after that then the larger bosses can be encountered safely.

A RECOMMENDATION.

To the Readers of THE CARPENTER.

In another place in this issue of THE CARPENTER you will see the advertisement of the Derby Bit Co. I can highly recommend these bits. I have had a full set of them from Mr. Condron, the agent of the Company here, and they are the best bits I have ever used.

I can recommend Mr. Condron as a very fair dealing man, he has been supplying the members of Union No. 21 with these bits for the past six months, and has given general satisfaction. I should advise all those who want a good article from a very good man to deal with Mr. Condron; he will give our members the bits 20 per cent. less than published prices.

L. J. BOYER.

CHICAGO, Ill., Sept. 10, 1883.

RIENZI, THE ROMAN TRIBUNE.

What Cola di Rienzi, the last of the Roman Tribunes and leader of the working people, said in 1300, A. D., is entirely apropos of those rascally politicians who in 1883, A. D., swarm in our labor organizations ready to sell us out any amount to the highest bidder:

"The patricians would gladly advance the fortunes of some among us—but how? by some place in the public offices, which would fill a dishonored coffer by wringing yet more sternly the hard-earned coins from our famishing citizens! If there be a vile thing in the world, it is a plebeian advanced by patricians, not for the purpose of righting his own order, but for playing the panderer to the worst interests of theirs. He who is of the people, but makes himself a traitor to his birth if he furnishes the excuse for those tyrant hypocrites to lift up their hands and cry, 'See what liberty exists in Rome when we, the patricians, thus elevate a plebeian!' Did they ever elevate a plebeian if he sympathized with plebeians? No, brothers, should I be lifted above our condition I will be raised by the arms of my countrymen and not UPON THEIR NECKS."

ASHTORETH.

TAKE NOTICE!

Postal Notes can be had in any Post Office of the United States for sums of money less than $5. They cost only three cents each and are cheaper than money orders for sending subscriptions or any amount of money less than $5 to this office. After October 1. the postage on letters will be only two cents instead of three.

—The right of each generation to the soil is older than statutes and constitutions.

—A workman's capital is the result of abstinence and self-denial.

A rich man's capital is the result of other peoples labor.

—Statistics in England show that during 15 years of long hours in 2,500 cotton mills with 400,000 operatives, the productiveness of labor increased only 28 per cent., while during 17 years of short hours it increased over 35 per cent. Reducing the hours does not decrease production.

POSTAL TELEGRAPHS.

The Telegraphers' strike has been made the occasion for hundreds of daily papers to advocate that the government shall institute a system of postal telegraphs under its own control and management. Upon close investigation, the only objection that can be reasonably offered against the proposition, is that it will place more powers in the hands of the government, and increase the political patronage of the administration, thus adding to the number of voters in the interest of whichever party may be in power. And this, it must be admitted is an objection that is a very serious one.

We favor a postal telegraph and are opposed to the system which allows corporations to take possession of public franchises and monopolize a business to the injury of the public and to the degradation of the employes. But in establishing this postal telegraph, we should do so without placing it entirely under the control of political office holders. Our system of civil service examinations as now conducted, is a farce, because it is conducted by politicians. What folly it would be for men outside of the telegraphic profession to pass upon the qualifactions of an applicant for a position as telegrapher!

Hence we contend that the first step is for the government to legalize the incorporation of the Telegraphers' Brotherhood. After assuming a legal existence, the Telegraphers' Brotherhood might be empowered to select a Civil Service Commission from among the members of the Brotherhood, and such commission could be the parties properly qualified to pass upon the applications of persons desiring positions in the telegraph service. This would remove the telegraph beyond the influence of politics and decentralize the powers of the government in that respect.

The history of the Ancient Guilds furnishes precedents enough to show that to the respective trades were granted "royal" favors, and to them the government intrusted many of its functions.

CONCESSIONS GRANTED.

Some may contend that labor organization has not accomplished much. But on this score we have a few instances of results achieved worthy of consideration. For example, the Kinney Bros., cigarette manufacturers in this city, not long ago provoked a strike by refusing the demand of their employes for a trifling advance. After a vigorous struggle, the employes who were mostly women and girls were forced to return defeated. The goods of the Kinney Bros. were boycotted during this strike and afterwards by the trades and labor unions everywhere. This made quite an inroad on the income of the Kinneys. And now, to offset boycotting and ingratiate themselves in public favor, the Kinneys have increased wages ten per cent.

The same way with the Lorillards, tobacco manufacturers. When this firm subjected their employes to the indignity of searching their persons as they left the factory door each evening, the trades and labor men of America took action against the sale of Lorillard's tobacco. The wrong of searching the persons of employes, and they mostly women, branding them as thieves, was an insult to all classes of labor, and they soon made the Lorillards feel they could resent it. The injury done the Lorillards by boycotting was incalculable, and the sales of their tobacco fell off very largely. Taught this costly lesson the Lorillards have repealed the odious rule, and last New Years presented each employe with a week's extra pay, which in all amounted to $15,000. Who for a moment will say that the Lorillards would have done this, were it not that they were forced to it?

We could go on enumerate many other instances; but the most striking case of all is that of the Western Union Telegraph Company. Since the strike it has practically increased the wages and reduced the hours of labor.

—A lockout of the Window Glass Workers is threatened by the manufacturers.

—As a rule when men search for work, they only ask the boss: "Do you want a man?" and when pay night comes they get whatever the boss pleases to pay them. The first question should be: "How much do you pay?" And if the union wages are not paid avoid that boss the same as you would the small-pox.

BROTHERHOOD NOTES.

—Seattle Union No. 45 proposes to organize a new union at New Tacoma, Washington Ter.

—It has been intimated that if the death benefit were reduced to $100 it would satisfy Washington Union No. 1.

—Bro. David Farren, of Philadelphia Union No. 8 has lost several fingers on his right hand by accident in a planing mill.

—During the telegraphers' strike our local unions everywhere rendered not only moral, but financial aid to the strikers.

—A carpenters' union has been just organized in Paterson, N. J., and it promises to be a thrifty society. Another one is under way in Richmond, Va.

—Without any authority, Chas. Mason, of St. Louis Union No. 6, published a statement in the St. Louis *Union* that Union No. 6 had withdrawn from our B.

—The second annual report of the General Secretary has been transmitted to all local unions, and it shows an encouraging growth both in members and the number of new local unions.

—The official circular with a list of the nominees for general officers of the Brotherhood has been sent out to all local unions. Act on it at once and make a full and speedy return of the votes cast.

—Baltimore Union No. 29 now meets at Rechabite Hall, corner Frederick and Fayette streets. It held a very well attended meeting on August 20, and the union is making great strides in increased membership.

—Our Ex-President G. Edmonston, Washington, D. C., acted as our delegate to the Trades and Labor Congress, held in this city last month, and he has donated his expenses for time and travel to the benefit of the B. Such generosity will be remembered.

—High dues should be the rule in our local unions; a trade society based upon 25 cents a month is one that will only serve for mere amusement. And this fact is recognized by many of our unions, and they are now increasing the dues to 50 cents per month.

The custom of the majority of trade unions in paying a death benefit is this: Suppose the benefit be $250, in the case of a married man the benefit is divided into two parts one part, say $100, is paid for the burial of his wife—the other part $150 is reserved until the death of the member.

—ROBERT ABERNETHY, died after one day in the hospital at Toronto, Canada. Death resulted from injuries received by falling from a scaffolding at Wooderham & Wort's distillery. His ankle and pelvic bones were broken. Bro. Abernethy was one of our most faithful members in Toronto Union No. 23.

—A tool insurance is as of much vital importance to our Brotherhood as any benefit we can inaugurate. It need not cost more than a trifle, and the benefit might be fixed at say $30 at most, which would be sufficient to replenish a working kit for all ordinary purposes. In case of fire or other accident, a tool benefit would be a blessing to many who would otherwise be in distress to replace their tools.

Victoria, British Columbia.

Union No. 48 is making very good progress and we have a majority of the carpenters of Victoria already in it and hope soon to have them all. Trade is good in Victoria, the wages will average about $3.00 per day all through; board is from $5.00 to $7.00 per week, clothing is very high and unless a man is able to get $3.50 per day here he is no better off than he is back East at $2.50 per day.

—George Howell in advocating trades unions and the right of laboring men to dictate their own terms, uses the following powerful argument: "Labor, we are told, is a commodity, and as such is governed by the same [illegible] modities. But in [illegible] *conditions, it is the* [illegible] *fixes the price.* If [illegible] the same position [illegible] labor, it is brand[illegible] their part, and [illegible] are the sellers of labor, which is their only commodity."

SAN FRANCISCO, CAL.

The following officers have been elected by Union No. 22: Pres., J. S. W. Saunders; Vice Pres., J. McDonald; R. S., J. Tierney; F. S., J. C. Rowe; C. S., J. W. Maher; Treas., P. Connor. We do not work 8 hours on Saturdays; since we adopted the nine hours we have made that the rule for every workday in the week. Our initiation fee is $2.50. *The Carpenter* gives us a great deal of information and is eagerly sought for by all our members.

The non-union carpenters working for the United States on the Presidio Reservation in this city have to work 10 hours a day while we work only 9, and the U. S. law says that eight shall be the rule. On this same reservation union carpenters are asked to work only 9 hours a day on producing their certificate as members of Union No. 22.

Peter R. McIntyre, the champion pedestrian and runner of the Pacific Coast, is a member of Union No. 22.

P. M. Wellin, the father of the nine hour resolutions in our union, is an ex-member of the late constitutional convention held in this State. Two other members of that convention are on our rolls.

Bro. W. J. Simon, Assemblyman from the 9th district was the proposer of the bill in the State Legislature last spring creating a Bureau of Labor Statistics in this State.

Under our new by-laws we have adopted an accident benefit of $10 per week until $50 are paid beyond which no further accident benefit is paid. Union men are not allowed to work with non-union men who violate our nine hour system.

Trade is fair; wages hold their own. Union No. 22 is still moving forward and will soon have a thousand members. Our picnic resulted very profitably in every respect—netting nearly $400 clear—and the games were a very interesting feature. Bro. Jas. Mooney lost a little girl of 4½ years on the picnic grounds and all efforts to find the child since then have proved ineffectual. Union No. 22 promptly offered $150 reward, Bro. Mooney $50, and the Catholic Arch-Bishop $200 for her delivery to her father. But not the least clue has been so far discovered.

California has a great floating population and a large number of our members have gone into the interior of the State, also to Oregon and the Territories, and wherever they go they will be missionaries to organize new carpenters unions.

Bro. L. Larsen a native of Norway died Aug. 4, 1883 after a brief illness. He was not long enough a member to entitle his family to death benefit. We have three members on our sick list drawing $10 per week for accident benefit.

This city is not by any means behind the times in the way of strikes. Coopers were out for some time and came out the victors. Union printers on *Morning Call* and *Evening Bulletin* are on strike against non-union men. The labor societies are boycotting these papers and with good results. Our union has donated $100 to aid the printers. The Telegraphers had a theatre benefit at the hands of the trades unions and netted several thousand dollars.

I observe Denis Kearney has been parading himself through the East. He has not a corporal's guard of followers. He claims 2000 men elected him to go East. I passed the meeting when he was elected and there were at most 30 persons present. From conversations I have had with him and his public utterances, I know that he is a deadly enemy to trades unions. I suppose for the reason that if the masses organize and educate themselves the days for men like Kearney will be gone. He never did represent or advocate the social elevation or educational advancement of the working class. Everything was politics from first to last. He drew in his wake a set of so-called reformers whose only argument and policy was to obtain political power and delude their followers into the belief that after them would come the millenium. The policy that unites mechanics and workman for self protection and social power he always opposed and despised, but that era of political frenzy is past in California and a new era of rational, practical work has begun. Kearney can [illegible] and has a good roll of me[illegible] with. We w[illegible]

THE LABOR QUESTION.

LECTURE X.

INSURANCE.

Insurance is the element which gives to every person in society the benefit of security; it guarantees every individual, in his capacity of unit in the collectivity, against accident, want, insecurity and evil, which may arise in a thousand unforeseen and unexpected ways. All institutions of provision in favor of infancy, old age and infirmity, all things of necessity or utility of which society profits, or might freely profit, are of this nature. The farmer may have his crops destroyed by storm, blight, fire, etc.; a workman may, by accident, lose his life in the performance of his work; any person may lose his house by fire; children may lose their parents by death; persons may lose their lives while traveling; a community may lose home, family and possession by inundation. The total failure of crops in a district will bring starvation to the inhabitants. The loss of a limb from accident by machinery will frequently incapacitate a man from supporting his family. During a voyage a ship may be wrecked, and a loss of life and wealth may ensue. By reason of a long-continued sickness or chronic malady the father of a family may be prevented from supporting his wife and children. A child, brought up in ignorance, never having been taught to satisfy his wants by labor, is compelled to steal his food. This ignorance is a very dangerous cause of insecurity, against which society should be insured.

In order to secure the community against destruction by epidemics which are engendered in our large cities by filth and uncleanliness, it is necessary to drain and otherwise provide the necessary sanitary precautions; the rural districts must be similarly treated, according to requirement.

To treat sickness and accidents it is necessary to build hospitals or provide in some way against the loss to the community which occurs from one of its members becoming incapacitated to produce, by reason of sickness.

All these, and innumerable other examples which cannot here be given, are so many proofs that accidents and evils do occur in society against which all men should be guaranteed; that guaranty should be mutual and universal; and it is the correct application of the principle of insurance which will make it so, since it will have its part in the distribution of wealth when the general interests shall be equitably administered.

We know from experience that when disastrous accidents occur that they are but local and partial, that while they ruin the individual or the community which is afflicted by them, if the loss which they occasion is equally distributed among all people, so that the loss, *pro rata*, may fall upon the whole of society, the amount is so insignificant as to be not felt by any individual, and, therefore, many kinds of suffering by reason of accident is easily and entirely abolished.

It has already been shown that the existence of man upon the planet depends upon his power of producing by labor all that is necessary to sustain life. If he does not possess these things his productive power is destroyed; hence, insurance, if scientifically considered; signifies also the guaranteeing of man against deterioration or death from the effects of the elements or the inclemency of the weather; and, therefore, it should include the securing to man of a shelter as well as food.

We may go further and say that man [illegible] instruments of labor; [illegible] ...ared se[illegible] permanently be[illegible]

ed upon peace and harmony, this must be done. And it is this broad conception of insurance which trades unions should propogate and practice.

The father who teaches his boy a trade exercises insurance; he provides for the future existence of the boy by insuring to him the means of providing his food. The father who makes a fortune to leave to his sons, or who gives a marriage portion to his daughters, only insures them against want and poverty. When a father cultivates a field, raises cattle on his farm etc., he only *insures* his family against hunger; when he drains his fields and cleanses his stables he does so to *insure* himself and family against disease. Of course we do not suppose that these acts are accompanied by a conscious conception of their effect, but the ultimate result is there nevertheless. Why, then, should insurance be confined to the individual and the family—why should it not be extended to society in general?

It is gratifying to those who study the question to observe the gradual, yet extensive, application of insurance which is made by the trades unionists. We find that they cover accidents, out of work, sickness, loss of tools by fire, burial and superannuation. Doubtless life insurance will soon be added to this list, and made to extend to wife and children.

All trades unions do not insure against all these things, but each is insured in the majority of the unions. Some insure against three or four of these features; others, against one or two only. None, I believe, cover the whole list; while some unions do not practice insurance in any way. In those unions where insurance remains unrecognized as a principle, and, consequently, unorganized, we find, nevertheless, under the title of "benevolent grants," "trade privileges," etc., large items in the expenditure of their funds.

The feeling of security against want—that is, the actual necessaries of life—will no doubt be insisted upon by the workers of the world as soon as an enlightened knowledge of the economic possibilities of production shall have spread among them.

The old economists, philosophers and moralists have very highly praised want and necessity; they have considered them the motive-spring of all incentive to action, and, consequently, to production. But we workers know from experience that want acts in a greater degree as a preventive to production. The economists point with pride to the known number of naturally robust men, favored with strong physical organizations, who have surmounted the difficulties of want and poverty and have achieved success; but we workers point with pity and with the same amount of conviction to the unknown number whose more sensitive mental and moral organizations, and more delicate frames, have been crushed by this demon of Want, and, consequently, prevented from producing, although, perhaps, they have possessed a higher order of genius than the successful. They can count their Tennysons; we cannot count the number of our Chattertons.

If, however, they were to apply the principle of insurance, and in so doing, were to make use of the same methods which insurance companies and their agents have employed up to the present time, in all probability they would fail to accomplish the end desired, for, be it well understood, the application of old methods will never produce anything but old results, and as inequity and injustice have followed the old methods, we are not likely to establish equity by continuing [illegible] into such a conduct of public affairs in which the societary interests shall be considered and legislated for, the administration of public affairs will be probably conducted in the future by a commission of surveillance rather than an executive power; it will, therefore, be necessary to furnish the means for furthering their work.

Whether for obtaining the protection of society against a personal injustice or aggression, or for the elevation or instruction of youth—in order to secure a healthy, robust and intelligent population—or to develop the natural resources of the country—we must build schools, canals, roads, bridges, and keep in good condition our rivers, harbors, ports, and all that contributes to securing against loss, deterioration and destruction, all that has been produced by the combined action of land, labor, capital and exchange, the cost of all of which must naturally be paid, and it is the amount of this cost which should determine the amount to be applied to the element, Insurance.

DRURY.

Newton, Missouri.

Here in this region of South Western Missouri, carpenters are scarce, but jack legs and botches are plenty. Very little day work, all contract. I got it from a man who saw one of our botches put up some stairs, that there were no two steps or risers of the same width or height. And the reason I write of this circumstance is that I have grounds to believe it. I worked with the botch on a house last Winter, and I am sure that he don't know the first principle of carpentry. The house we worked on last Winter was day work and 1½ story, 14 foot studs, and he wanted to put in joice overhead in the upper story. I asked him what for, he replied, to support that hip roof we have to put up. I inquired: How are you going to make a two-story house out of one and a-half story, or out of 14 foot studs? He answered: I don't know, but we will have to throw joice across there to support that roof, and lower the second floor joice until we have got room above. I just told him that we were building that house for a white man and not for a Chinaman. That his style would suit a Chinaman well enough, for they like low ceilings, but I didn't think that it would suit a white man. Such is a sample of the carpenters we have to contend with. There is one sure thing that these fellows are no good for organization at all, and as far as getting any of that class of men to subscribe for any building journal, it is a matter of impossibility, as they already know more than all the books and journals can tell them—that is in their own estimation.

Morris, Minnesota.

Wages $2.50 per day, board $3.50 and $4 per week; work fair; enough men for what there is. In Sauck Center, Minn., the union carpenters struck for an increase of wages, and a lot of non-union men went to work on the job and the union men ordered them off, but they would not go, so the union men took the scabs' tool boxes and carried them off with them, and made the owners go with them. The union men came out ahead. Why would it not be a good idea to have the Brotherhood incorporated with power to have all its subordinate unions to be a body incorporate as soon as charters are granted to them by the Brotherhood? Such is the way that the Ancient Order of United Workmen do in this State. The Statutes of Minnesota are very liberal to incorporations. If no other State will allow such incorporation I think Minnesota will.

(REMARKS OF EDITOR.—We favor the national incorporation of our Brotherhood. For years the Iron Molders' Union of North America has applied to Congress asking for a special act of incorporation that would cover all local unions under their jurisdiction. But the measure has just as often been defeated by the Congressional enemies of trades unions. A bill on this subject was introduced in the House by Congressman March, and in the Senate by Senator Blair during the last session. The Blair bill stands good chances of passing in the next session, owing to the mass of evidence in its favor before the Senate Committee now investigating the labor question.)

Der Carpenter.

New York, September 1888.

Was unseren Gewerkschaften fehlt.

Bei dem großen Strike der Telegraphisten machte sich der Mangel einer gesetzlichen Anerkennung der Arbeiter-Organisationen besonders fühlbar. Unter „gesetzlicher Anerkennung“ wollen wir nämlich keineswegs nur die bloße Duldung der Gewerkschaften verstanden wissen, sondern wir begreifen darunter gewisse gesetzliche Rechte, Korporationsrechte und Machtbefugnisse, welche dem eigentlichen Zwecke der Gewerkschaften angepaßt sein müssen. Die Western Union Telegraphen-Kompagnie weigerte sich, mit dem Exekutivkomite der Brüderschaft der Telegraphisten zu unterhandeln, erkannte das Exekutivkomite nicht an. Es hatte ihr gegenüber angeblich nicht Autorität genug.

Man verlangte, daß, wenn man einmal mit dem Exekutivkomite der Brüderschaft in Unterhandlung treten würde und dieselben zum Abschluß gelangen und gewisse Forderungen und Bedingungen von beiden Seiten formulirt und angenommen würden, die kontrahirenden Theile auch dafür gesetzlich haftbar gemacht werden könnten, daß alle ihre Mitglieder strikt die eingegangenen Verpflichtungen erfüllen. Eine solche Macht, nöthigenfalls selbst zwangsweise Erfüllung der eingegangenen Verbindlichkeiten durchzusetzen, hat das Exekutivkomite der Brüderschaft der Telegraphisten ebensowenig, wie solche Macht jetzt irgend einer der übrigen Gewerkschaften des Landes eigen ist. Es wird aber Jedermann leicht begreifen, daß es viel besser für die Gewerkschaften wäre, wenn sie Korporationsrechte, und zwar solche, wie sie dem besondern Zweck der Gewerkschaften entsprechen, besäßen.

Man wird uns einwenden: Nun, die Gewerkschaften können sich ja ganz einfach unter den bestehenden Staatsgesetzen incorporiren lassen! Ein solcher Einwand würde nur die Unkenntniß der ganzen Gewerkschaftsfrage seitens Desjenigen verrathen, der ihn erhebt. Erstens können die Einzelstaaten nur Korporationsrechte für ihr eigenes Gebiet verleihen, die Gewerkschaftsorganisationen müssen aber national und international sein und dennoch ein einheitliches Recht und einheitliche Statuten haben. Zweitens aber braucht die moderne Arbeiterorganisation für ihre großartigen und vielseitigen Aufgaben auch besondere Rechte und Befugnisse, welche nur durch spezielle Gesetzgebung verliehen werden können.

Man hat Kirchengesetze, Handelsgesetze, Militärgesetze, Reglements für die Advokaten, kurz für alles Mögliche, aber man hat noch keine Arbeitergesetzgebung, welche den Gewerkschaften, also den Arbeiter-Korporationen, besondere Befugnisse einräumte. Und doch müßten gerade diese das Recht haben, selbstständig Klagen zu erheben gegen kapitalistische Korporationen, welche die Landesgesetze in Bezug auf Arbeiterschutz gegen Unfälle, wegen Kinderausbeutung, wegen Uebervortheilung der Arbeiter in irgend einer Richtung, z. B. durch Anwendung des Truck-Systems &c. verletzen.

Die Gewerkschaften müßten Kontrakte abschließen können, sie müßten das Recht haben, durch ihre offiziellen Vertreter Fabriken und Bergwerke zu inspiziren und dort Anordnungen zu treffen, sie müßten Zeugen vernehmen, zwangsweise vorladen und beeidigen dürfen. Sie müßten die Beantwortung ihrer statistischen Fragebogen unter Eid erzwingen können. Sie müßten Eigenthum erwerben und ihre Mitglieder gesetzlich zwingen können, ihre offiziellen Beschlüsse durchzuführen, das heißt, sie müßten ihre Mitglieder zwingen können, das zu thun und zu lassen, was sie selbst vorher in ordnungsmäßiger Weise beschlossen haben.

Zu diesen Zwecken reichen die bestehenden Incorporationsgesetze, welche für ganz andere Zwecke, nämlich nur für die bessere Profitmacherei der Ausbeuter, gemacht wurden, nicht aus; sie können daher auch den Gewerkschaften nichts nutzen, sondern sie hindern nur deren Entwickelung. Hier ist wieder einmal der Beweis gegeben, daß auch die Gewerkschaftsbewegung eine politische ist, denn ohne politische Bethätigung, ohne eine zweckentsprechende Arbeiter-, resp. Gewerkschaftsgesetzgebung, werden die [illegible]

[illegible]

Die Solidarität der Arbeiter.

Die Thatsache, daß alle Arbeiter gemeinschaftliches Interesse haben, wird jetzt wohl überall erkannt, und die Zeit ist vorbei, da die Arbeiter eines Gewerkes mit Neid und Mißgunst oder auch mit Stolz und Hochmuth auf die Arbeiter einer andern Geschäftsbranche blickten. Aller Orten erkennt man, daß die Arbeiter Schulter an Schulter kämpfen und sich gegenseitig unterstützen müssen, um ihr Recht zur Geltung zu bringen.

Die Trades Assemblies der einzelnen Städte haben nicht wenig dazu beigetragen, diese wichtige Lehre zu verbreiten. Hier sind Delegaten der verschiedenen Gewerke vereinigt, um gemeinsam ihre Lage zu besprechen, über die zahlreichen Uebel und Schäden zu berathen, die den gesammten Arbeiterstand bedrohen und Mittel und Wege für deren Abhülfe zu treffen. Gewerke, die sich früher kaum dem Namen nach gekannt, treten in rege Berührung zu einander und lassen erkennen, daß ihre Interessen gemeinschaftlich sind und ein Uebelstand in einem einzelnen Gewerke auch alle anderen mehr oder weniger berührt. Bauarbeiter und Schriftsetzer, Schuhmacher und Schneider, Zimmerleute und Buchbinder &c., sie alle treten ein für Abschaffung der Tenementhaus-Arbeit, oder für Verbot der Gefängnißarbeit, oder für Beschränkung der Kinderarbeit, oder für Abkürzung der Arbeitszeit in irgend einem oder allen Gewerken, je nachdem Zeit und Umstände es für passend erscheinen lassen. Selbst die direkte finanzielle Unterstützung bei Strikes ist schon oft durch die Trades Assemblies geregelt worden, und die Zeit wird wohl nicht mehr ferne sein, wo jede Trades Assembly durch einen geringen monatlichen Beitrag aller ihrer Mitglieder eine Strikefond ansammelt, stark genug, um irgend ein Gewerk im Falle eines Strikes kräftig zu unterstützen. Sobald dieses geschieht, werden die Strikes zu den Seltenheiten gehören, denn jeder Arbeitgeber wird sich wohl hüten, den Kampf mit seinen Leuten aufzunehmen, wenn er weiß, daß alle anderen Arbeiter ihnen durch Geldunterstützung beistehen.

Wo immer also eine Trades Assembly besteht, sollte auch die Zimmerer-Union ihr angehören, und sind in einer Stadt mehrere Gewerkschaften und noch keine Assembly, so sollte sie versuchen, eine solche zu gründen.

Ein imposanter Zug.

Am 3. September fand hier die zweite jährliche Arbeiter-Parade der „Central Labor Union“ statt, an welcher sich 15 Gewerkschaften betheiligten, welche, nach den verschiedenen Schätzungen zu urtheilen, 10–12,000 Mann repräsentirten. Der imposante Zug mit seinen Fahnen und Mottos und 16 Musikbanden bewegte sich von der unteren Stadt bis zur 42. Straße, woselbst er sich auflöste, und die Theilnehmer sich nach dem Pic-Nic-Platz in der 92. Straße (Wendel's Elm Park) begaben, wo sich englische und deutsche Arbeiter bei Gesang und Spiel und die Bedeutung der Demonstration feiernden Reden der allgemeinen Festesfreude hingaben. Außer den verschiedenen Mottos, welche den Forderungen und Bestrebungen der Arbeiter Ausdruck gaben, erregten besonderes Interesse eine Anzahl Transparente, welche die sociale Frage in Wort und Bild in grellen Contrasten darstellten.

Gewerkschafts-Statistik.

Sekretär Howard von der Spinner-Union giebt in seinem letzten Circular über Trades Unions und Strikes folgendes statistisches Material, nach welchem die Cigarrenmacher während der letzten 18 Jahre 361 Ausstände hatten, von denen 204 erfolgreich waren und 157 verloren gingen. Diese Strikes kosteten $288,414, brachten aber den Cigarrenmachern $1,800,000 an erhöhten Löhnen per Jahr ein und verhinderten Reductionen zum Betrage von $500,000. 1866 gab es in Amerika und England 300,000 Mitglieder von Gewerkschaften, und 1870 war die Zahl auf 800,000 gestiegen; 1874 betrug die Anzahl 1,000,000, und jetzt wird sie auf 1,500,000 geschätzt.

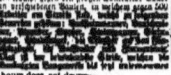

— Die Vereinigten Baugewerke von New York fahren in ihrem Guerillakriege gegen die Kontraktoren von Bauten, welche Nicht-Unionleute neben Unionleuten beschäftigen, fort und sind in den meisten Fällen erfolgreich. Augenblicklich führen sie einen hartnäckigen Kampf gegen den großen Kontraktor Tuder an verschiedenen Bauten, an welchem gegen 200 [illegible]

Die englischen Trades Unions und die Landfrage.

Ueber den Beschluß des National-Kongresses der englischen Gewerkschaften hinsichtlich der Landfrage schreibt der „Al. A.“:

Welche Bedeutung die Landfrage in Großbritannien bereits erlangt hat, zeigt die entschiedene Stellungnahme der Gewerkvereine zu derselben. Die englischen Gewerkschaften sind bekanntlich eine Macht und haben schon manches Gesetz vom Parlamente erwirkt, obwohl die britischen Arbeiter nicht einmal den Vortheil des allgemeinen Stimmrechts haben. Doch selbstverständlich befaßten sie sich bisher ausschließlich mit Angelegenheiten, welche die besonderen Interessen des Fabrikarbeiterthums berühren. Da sie keine eigentlich politischen Vereine sind, sondern lediglich Schutzverbände, so begnügten sie sich damit, Arbeiterforderungen, die nur durch staatliche Einmischung erfüllbar schienen, der gesetzgebenden Körperschaft mit Nachdruck zu unterbreiten. Im Uebrigen kümmerten sie sich nicht um die Politik, sondern überließen es jedem einzelnen Mitgliede, nach seiner Ueberzeugung zu den Parteien Stellung zu nehmen.

Jetzt aber hat der in Birmingham tagende Gewerkschaftskongreß Beschlüsse des Inhalts angenommen, daß es Pflicht des Staates sei, die wüsten Landstrecken im Königreich dem Ackerbau zugänglich zu machen und zu diesem Zwecke nöthigenfalls mit Beschlag zu belegen. Mit anderen Worten heißt das, daß die Torf- und Heidemoore und Thierparks in Irland und Schottland, welche die Kerbe der Cultur theils nicht zuführen lassen, theils sogar wieder entzogen haben, aus Tummelplätzen für den sportlustigen Adel in Fruchtfelder für das nahrungsbedürftige Volk von Staatswegen umgewandelt werden sollen. Die englischen Arbeiter verständen, daß der Adel nicht das Recht hat, große Landstrecken lediglich für Jagdzwecke einzubehalten und dem „Pöbel“ zu entziehen. Sie stellen den revolutionären Grundsatz auf, den Herbert Spencer, John Stuart Mill und andere Denker neuer Richtung wissenschaftlich begründet haben: daß es ein unbeschränktes Eigenthumsrecht am Grund und Boden nicht geben darf, die organisirte Gesellschaft vielmehr das Recht haben muß, die Benutzung und Ausbeutung des Landes zu regeln.

Von welchen Folgen diese Erklärung der englischen Gewerkvereine begleitet sein wird, läßt sich allerdings nicht bis in die Einzelheiten vorher sagen, doch sind wenigstens einige der unmittelbaren Wirkungen unschwer zu erkennen. Zunächst müssen die parlamentarischen Führer der ehemaligen irischen Landliga erkennen, daß sie im Bunde mit den englischen Arbeitern ungleich mehr erreichen können, wie als eifrige Verfechter des irischen Nationalismus. Eine Verständigung zwischen den Pächtern auf Irland, vielleicht auch Schottland, und den industriellen städtischen Arbeitern Englands wird auf dieser Grundlage leicht zu erzielen sein, und eine in der Landfrage radicaler vorgehende Regierung könnte auf größeren parlamentarischen Anhang rechnen, als gegenwärtig Gladstone. Mittels des allgemeinen Stimmrechts, dessen Verleihung nicht mehr lange wird verzögert werden können, dürften die fortschrittlichen Elemente die Oberhand gewinnen und den letzten Ueberbleibseln des Feudalismus ein Ende machen. Mit dem Landbesitze steht und fällt der britische Adel, und es ist wahrscheinlich, daß er in Kurzem fallen wird. Dann aber wird Großbritannien wahrscheinlich auch nicht einmal dem Namen nach Monarchie bleiben.

— In München macht sich gegenwärtig eine lebhafte Arbeiterbewegung geltend. Der vor einigen Wochen gegründete Fachverein der Schreiner zählt bereits über 1000 Mitglieder. Unmittelbar nach den Schreinern gingen die Maler mit Gründung eines Fachvereins vor, und ihnen folgten die Zimmerer, deren neu gegründeter Verein auch schon circa 400 Mitglieder zählt. Dann hielten die Maurer eine Versammlung ab, die von ca. 1000 Mann besucht war, und als deren Resultat sich gleichfalls die Gründung eines Fachvereins ergab, zu dem sofort 342 Mann ihren Beitritt erklärten. Hierauf wandelten die Schuhmacher ihre „Innung“ in einen Fachverein um, und kürzlich beschlossen die Schneider in einer gut besuchten Versammlung, ebenfalls einen Fachverein zu gründen. Diese Regsamkeit in Bezug auf gewerbliche Organisationen ist hier um so bemerkenswerther, da seit 1867 Organisationen dieser Art in München nicht mehr bestanden haben, nachdem die früheren Gewerksgenossenschaften theils durch finanziellen Krach, theils, wie bei den Schuhmachern und Schreinern, durch Massenverurtheilungen der Mitglieder zur Auflösung gebracht wurden.

Theils und [illegible] ist der Wahl- [illegible] Grunde schären [illegible] den [illegible] und arbeitende Volk, in [illegible] Gruppen [illegible] Ums es aus- [illegible] Narrenseile geführt und desto weiter von seinem wahren Ziele abgeleitet werden.

[illegible] the hours does not decrease …

Angebot und Nachfrage.

Noch immer, wenn ein Versuch gemacht wird, eine Gewerkschaft zu organisiren, oder die Löhne zu erhöhen, begegnen wir dem Ausspruch „Angebot und Nachfrage reguliren die Löhne, und kein Gewerkverein kann hieran etwas ändern.“ Dieses schaurige Gespenst einer Pseudo-Wissenschaft ist das Schreckniß, mit dem die politischen Oekonomisten die Arbeiter in fester Knechtschaft zu erhalten suchen. Die Theorie dieser Sophisten lautet: Wenn viel zu thun ist und das Angebot von Arbeitern gering, sind die Löhne hoch; ist wenig zu thun und das Angebot von Arbeitern groß, sind die Löhne niedrig.

Laßt uns diese Theorie ein wenig näher betrachten. Ist dieselbe richtig, so sind die Arbeitslöhne denselben Bestimmungen unterworfen, die die Preise von Lebensmitteln oder von Kleidungsstücken oder von allen andern Waaren reguliren. Diese Preise aller dieser Waaren steigen oder fallen mit jedem Tag, je nach deren Bedürfniß oder Ueberfluß, mithin müßten auch die Arbeitslöhne an jedem Tage verschieden sein, je nach lebhafterem oder flauerem Geschäftsgang. Gewiß ein netter Zustand! — Wir sehen allerdings, daß bei flauerem Geschäftsgang die Löhne sofort reduzirt werden, doch wer hätte je gehört, daß eine Erhöhung der Löhne gleich schnell stattfindet, sobald das Geschäft sich hebt?

Selbst die Kapitalisten gebrauchen allerhand Mittel, um die Löhne festzustellen und Angebot und Nachfrage zu controlliren. Wie oft ist das sogenannte „eherne ökonomische Lohngesetz“ durch Handelskammern, Kohlenbörsen oder ähnliche Verbindungen von Großfabrikanten über den Haufen geworfen worden. Und doch sind gerade diese Leute am lautesten in der Verdammung der Gewerkschaften und erklären deren Bestrebungen für unnütz. Und wenn wir bis zum jüngsten Tag um eine Erhöhung der Löhne bitten wollen, und dann noch hundert Jahre weiter warten auf eine Regelung durch Angebot und Nachfrage, wir werden nie einen gerechten Lohn erhalten, sofern wir nicht organisirt sind. Ganz gleich, wie hoch Wohnungsmiethe oder Lebensmittel steigen, unsere persönlichen Bedürfnisse werden nicht berücksichtigt werden, so lange wir nicht organisirt sind und gemeinsam die Arbeitgeber zwingen, unsere gerechten Forderungen zu bewilligen.

Zur Lohn- und Arbeiterbewegung. Der Strike der Stuttgarter Schreiner ist im Großen und Ganzen beendet, und wenn die Arbeiter ihre Forderungen auch nicht in ihrem vollen Umfange durchsetzten, so ist doch der Sieg ihnen geblieben. Vom Ausschluß ist natürlich gar keine Rede, mit diesem Plan sind die Herren Fabrikanten gründlich hereingefallen. Sie haben vielmehr alle wesentlichen Forderungen der Arbeiter bewilligen müssen. Gestrikt wird nur noch in der Fabrik von Georg Schöttle, und sind noch 55 Mann zu unterstützen. Die Strikekommission ersucht indeß mit Rücksicht auf die großen Geldsendungen, die von auswärts eingelaufen sind, von weiteren Geldsendungen vor der Hand abzusehen, dagegen ist es noch immer dringend erforderlich, Zuzug fernzuhalten!

„Kollegen! Arbeiter!“ schließt der letzte Aufruf der Strikekommission, „Herzlichen Dank für die uns so zahlreich zugewendete Unterstützung; wir wissen, was wir in ähnlichen Fällen Euch schuldig sind.“

„Ein Tramp.“ Mit dieser Unterschrift erhielt das in New York tagende Senats-Komite einen schwungvoll und geläufig abgefaßten Brief, den der Vorsitzende Blair verlas. Der Brief des „Tramps“ besagte, daß der Schreiber ein eingeborner Amerikaner sei, der eingesehen habe, daß die heutigen Zustände unhaltbar seien. Diejenigen, welche Alles produziren, hätten Nichts, und Diejenigen, welche Alles hätten, produzirten Nichts. Das müsse anders werden. Er entschuldigte sein Schreiben mit dem Schamgefühl, das über ihn komme, seine Ansichten persönlich denen von Millionären und Staatsmännern gegenüber gestellt zu sehen. Wenn er an den Kontrast zwischen seinem aus 32 Cents bestehenden Vermögen und den $100,000,000 des Hrn. Jay Gould denke, so komme er zu der Ueberzeugung, daß heutigen Tages noch dasselbe System des Erwerbes bestehe, wie zur Zeit William Penn's, der für $10 und einen Schnaps von den Indianern den Staat Pennsylvanien kaufte. Das Land-Monopol und das Zinsennehmen müßten abgeschafft werden, wenn die Zustände besser werden sollen: 95 Prozent des Reichthums dürften nicht länger in den Händen von 3 Prozent der Bevölkerung bleiben. Zum Schluß erklärte der „Tramp“, daß er kein Trunkenbold und Faullenzer, wie die Herren vom Komite sich vielleicht einbildeten, sondern einfach arbeitslos und ohne Geld sei. [illegible] daß die [illegible] des Herrn „Tramp“ [illegible] Er solle nur kommen.

Die Senats-Komite-Untersuchung in Neu-England.

Während zwei Mitglieder des genannten Komites in New York thätig sind, haben zwei andere Mitglieder desselben in Fall River, Mass., eine Untersuchung eingeleitet. In Begleitung des Spinnereibesitzers J. G. Stevens, H. C. Flenner, Schatzmeister der Slade'schen Spinnereien, und Robert Howard, dem Präsidenten des Spinnervereins, besuchten die Senatoren Aldrich und George die den verschiedenen Spinnereien gehörenden Tenementhäuser. Zuerst wurden die zur Bourne'schen Spinnerei gehörenden Tenementhäuser besucht, und man fand, daß dieselben ziemlich komfortabel sind. Die einzelnen Wohnungen (Flats) bestehen fast durchgängig aus vier Schlafzimmern, einer Küche, einem Speisezimmer und einem Parlor. Einige dieser Wohnungen waren jedoch von zu vielen Leuten bewohnt, da viele der Miether Kostgänger annehmen. In einem dieser Flats waren vier Zimmer von 12 Erwachsenen bewohnt. Die zur Shove'schen Spinnerei gehörenden Tenementhäuser sind nicht so gut als die Bourne'schen; die einzelnen Flats bestehen aus vier Schlafzimmern und einem anderen Zimmer. Diese Flatwohnungen werden zu 5 Dollars monatlich vermiethet. Für Kost und Logis wird 3 Dollars wöchentlich für Frauen und 4 für Männer gerechnet. Die Spinner erhalten einen durchschnittlichen Wochenlohn von 8 Dollars. Die zu den Slade'schen Spinnereien gehörenden Tenementhäuser schienen die schlimmsten von allen zu sein, indem sie auf aufgefülltem Grund gebaut sind und die Drainirung schlecht ist. Eine Anzahl der in den Spinnereien beschäftigten Arbeiter ward verhört. Einer derselben, ein französischer Canadier, sagte, er könne hier besser leben, als in Canada; dort könne er nur hin und wieder Fleisch bekommen, hier aber jeden Tag. Eine alte Spinnerin meinte, die Lage der Spinner sei hierzulande eine viel schlechtere als in England. (Balt. Journ.)

Löhne und Geschäftsstand der Zimmerleute.

Albany, N. Y. — $1.75 bis $3. Geschäft flau.

Harper, Kansas. — $1.75 bis $2.25. Geschäft mittelmäßig. Steinmaurer bekommen $3 bis $3.50, Gypser (Plasterers) $3.

St. Catherines, Canada. — $1.75 bis $2.25. Die Bosse wollen die achtstündige Arbeitszeit am Samstag abschaffen, aber unsere Mitglieder standen fest und haben gesiegt.

Grinnell, Iowa. — $2.50 bis $3. Arbeit lebhaft.

Victoria, British Columbia. — $2.75 bis $3.50 für 10 Stunden Arbeit.

Toledo, Ohio. — Geschäft angemessen.

New Orleans, La. — $2.75 bis $3. Das Eintrittsgeld beträgt jetzt $5, Krankenunterstützung wird gewährt.

Der Arbeitgeber nimmt die Arbeitskräfte da, wo er sie am billigsten und zweckmäßigsten finden kann, ohne in der Regel nach dem Geburtsorte des Einzustellenden zu fragen. Der Fabrikant verbindet sich mit anderen Fabrikanten ohne Unterschied der Nationalität, sobald es die Wahrung des Berufs-Interesses so erheischt. Wir Arbeiter aber sollen so wählerisch in der Wahl unserer Kampfmittel sein, daß wir in Folge des Wählerischseins unsere Interessen gar nicht kräftig wahren können! Wir sollen, weil wir Zimmerer sind, uneinig vorgehen, sollen uns nicht verbinden dürfen mit anderen Arbeitern! Ist das nicht unsinnig? Nur unsere gemeinsamen Feinde, die ausbeutungssüchtigen Herren, haben einen Vortheil von solchem Vorgehen, das arbeitende Volk aber hat den größten Schaden davon.

Ueber die Arbeiterverhältnisse in Sachsen wird von dort der „Voll. Ztg.“ unterm 26. August berichtet: „Die jüngsten Strikes in der Weberbranche haben für die Arbeiter wenigstens in einigen Gegenden eine dauernde Verbesserung der Arbeitslöhne zur Folge gehabt. So besonders in Meerane und Umgegend. Die von dem dortigen Fachverein herausgegebene Lohntabelle weist im Vergleich mit dem im Dezember vorigen Jahres aufgenommenen Verzeichniß eine durchschnittliche Lohnzunahme von 15 Proz. nach. Auch in Glauchau sind die Weberverhältnisse etwas bessere geworden, doch hört man ab und zu bei den Fabrikanten Klagen, daß das Absatzgebiet der Waaren sich nicht erweitere, wodurch sie gezwungen seien, schon jetzt wieder vielfach auf Lager arbeiten zu lassen. Dieselben Klagen verlautet man aus Crimmitschau, so daß man [illegible] „etwas bessern Zeiten“ [illegible] Geschäfts- und Arbeitskräfte [illegible].“

Der Handwerkertag der deutschen Zimmerleute zu Berlin.

Am 19. August Begrüßung der Delegirten durch Herrn Marzian. Nachdem ordnet sich der Festzug folgendermaßen: 1. Marschallstab; 2. Musikcorps der Garde Pioniere; 3. der Festzugführer mit dem großen Zollstock des Berliner Zimmerhandwerks; 4. das große Gewerksbanner der Berliner Zimmerleute begleitet von 4 Mann mit geputzten Winkeleisen; 5. ein Zug Gesellen mit Aexten und geputzten Winkeleisen; 6. das große Kuppelmodell des Berliner Handwerks; 7. Hamburger Stadtwappen, Reichsadler und Berliner Stadtwappen; 8. die große Bremer Fahne; 9. die Charlottenburger Fahne, derselben folgen der Delegirte und Gewerkschaftsmitglieder Charlottenburgs; 10. eine große Schrotsäge mit Inschrift „Es lebe das deutsche Zimmerhandwerk“; 11. der Senior des Zimmerhandwerks (der alte Zimmermann Kühne trägt einen „Willkomm Humpen“ aus dem Jahr 1734); 12. der werktätige Geselle mit Axt, hohem Hut und Schurzleder; 13. die Königsberger Fahne (Königsberg i. Pr.), dieser folgt der Königsberger Delegirte. Mit dieser Begleitung und den betreffenden Delegirten folgen nun: 14. die Stettiner Fahne; 15. Frankfurt a. O. Fahne; 16. Magdeburger neue Fahne; 17. Wolmirstädter Fahne; 18. Neustadt-Magdeburger Fahne; 19. Breslauer Fahne; 20. Ein Riesen-Bärenschild (Symbol Berlins); diesem folgen die Lehrburschen mit hohen Hüten, Aexten, blanken Winkeleisen und Schurzleder; 21. Fahne des Beerdigungsvereins Berliner Zimmerleute, dieser folgen sämmtliche Vorstandsmitglieder der verschiedenen Vereinigungen der Berliner Zimmerleute; 22. sämmtliche in Berlin geschriebene fremde Zimmergesellen mit Stubenschild; 23. Braunschweiger Fahne; 24. das Magdeburger Gewerksschild; 25. die Hannover'sche Fremden-Fahne; 26. die alte Berliner Gewerkschaftsfahne von 1748, dieser folgen die Berliner Delegirten, in deren Mitte der Berliner Altgeselle (Marzian) mit dem alten Ausklopfhammer des Berliner Zimmergewerks; 27. ein Zug Berliner Gesellen mit Aexten und geputzten Winkeleisen; 28. alle übrigen Zimmergesellen, welche am Festzuge theilnehmen, denen kein Extra-Platz angewiesen werden konnte (über 1000 Mann). Den Schluß bildete ein Zug Gesellen mit geputzten Winkeleisen. Jede Fahne war von zwei Mann mit Aexten oder geputzten Winkeleisen begleitet.

In dieser Reihenfolge bewegte sich dieser imposante Zug, überall von dem zahlreichen Publikum auf's Freundlichste begrüßt.

Gegen 10 Uhr eröffnete der Vorsitzende, Zimmermann Marzian den Handwerkstag und brachte ein Hoch auf das deutsche Zimmergewerbe aus. Hierauf hielt Zimmermann Schönlein die Festrede.

Der Festrede folgte die Prüfung der Mandate. Am Abende fand ein großer Festball statt.

Montag den 20. August, früh 8 Uhr, begann der eigentliche geschäftliche Theil des Handwerkstages. Die Präsenzliste zeigte neunundzwanzig Delegirten von Berlin, Braunschweig, Breslau, Bremen, Charlottenburg, Cassel, Düsseldorf, Frankfurt a. O., Hamburg, Hannover, Halberstadt, Kiel, Königsberg i. P., Leipzig, Liegnitz, Landsberg a. W., Mannheim, Magdeburg, Nürnberg, Ohlau, Spandau, Stettin und Wolmirstedt.

Nach Erwählung des Bureau's bildete den Hauptgegenstand der Tagesordnung: „Die Gründung eines allgemeinen deutschen Zimmerverbandes.“ In mehrstündiger Debatte wurde von den Rednern die Nothwendigkeit eines solchen Verbandes betont. Die traurige materielle Lage der Zimmergesellen erheische dringend, daß die Zimmerer Deutschlands eine feste Organisation schaffen; nur solchergestalt sei es möglich, eine Besserung der Verhältnisse herbeizuführen.

Es wurde hierauf einstimmig die Gründung eines „Allgemeinen deutschen Zimmergesellen-Verbandes“ beschlossen. — Alsdann wurde in die Statuten-Berathung des zu gründenden Verbandes eingetreten. Als Zweck des Verbandes wurde in die Statuten aufgenommen: „Wahrung der Ehre, Hebung und Schutz der Interessen deutscher Zimmerleute auf gewerkschaftlichen Grundlagen, a. durch eine möglichste Lohnaufbesserung, b. durch Regelung der Arbeitszeit, durch Beschränkung der Ueberstunden- und Sonntagsarbeit, c. durch Erstrebung eines Schutzes gegen Zahlungsunfähigkeit der Arbeitgeber, d. durch eine wirkliche, direkte Vertretung der Gesellschaft im Meisterrathe bezüglich der Gesellen-, Lehrlings- und Lohnverhältnisse, e. durch Errichtung eines Schutzes des Gesellenhandwerkzeuges gegen Diebstahl und Feuersgefahr.“ — Die weitere Berathung des Statuts zog sich bis in die späte Abendstunde hin.

Dienstag, den 21. August, früh 8 Uhr, wird die Berathung der Statuten von den Delegirten wieder aufgenommen. Die Zeitschrift des Zimmerhandwerks wird als Organ des Verbandes [illegible] in Städten, die durchschnittlichen Lohnsatz bis zu 3 Mark haben, 30 Pfg., Städte bis 4 Mark Lohn 40 Pfg. und bis 5 Mark Lohn 50 Pfg. Die Zahlung der Beiträge geschieht jedoch nur während der Monate März bis incl. November, also neun Monate lang.

Die Rechte der Mitglieder sind nach § 6 folgende: a. Jeder Verbandsgeselle hat Sitz und Stimme in allen Verbands-Versammlungen der Gesellschaft; b. desgleichen Anspruch auf Rechtsschutz und Sachverständigenbeistand in allen vorkommenden Streitfällen; c. Anspruch auf Gerichtskostenvorschuß und Nachzahlung desselben, sobald der Anspruch vom Verbandsrechtsanwalt für begründet erachtet wird; d. jedes Mitglied bezieht allmonatlich die Verbands-Zeitschrift in den Lokalversammlungen durch den Ortsschreiber; e. der Rechtsschutz beginnt bei Ablauf einer dreimonatlichen Mitgliedschaft. In allen übrigen Punkten geben die in nächster Zeit im Druck erscheinenden Statuten Auskunft.

Noch wollen wir bemerken, daß in allen Orten Deutschlands, wo sich über 25 Zimmerleute zusammenfinden, ein Lokalverband gegründet werden kann.

In später Abendstunde, nachdem der Sitz des Vororts (Berlin) bestimmt war, wurde die Haupt-Vorstandswahl vorgenommen. Als 1. Vorsitzender wurde Herr Marzian, als Verbands-Cassirer Herr Dietrich (Berlin) gewählt. Mit einem Hoch auf das deutsche Zimmergewerk schloß der Handwerkertag.

Die Wirren unter den Baugewerkschaften.

Das Special-Komite der New Yorker Central Labor Union, welches die Wirren untersuchen soll, die infolge des Ausstandes an den Dakota Flats unter den Baugewerkschaften entstanden, hielt eine Sitzung, an welcher John Ritter und Delegaten der Zimmerleute-Union und der übrigen Baugewerkschaften theilnahmen. Es wurde zuerst festgestellt, daß die Baugewerkschaften vor drei Monaten den Strike besprachen und es den verschiedenen Delegaten überließen, zu bestimmen, wann der Strike begonnen werden solle. Vor drei Wochen begann der Strike. Am Donnerstag nach Annahme des Beschlusses ließ Delegat Franklin von den Bricklayers seine Leute zu arbeiten aufhören und Ritter beorderte die Zimmerleute erst am Samstag zum Strike, weil er von dem Beschluß der übrigen Delegaten vorher nichts gewußt hatte. Der Boß Schwedenberger beeinflußte die an den Gebäuden in 73. Str. arbeitenden Zimmerleute, in ihrer Union für eine Beendigung des Ausstandes zu stimmen und zu drohen, daß sie die Union verlassen wollten, falls der Strike nicht beendigt würde. Die Zimmerleute beschlossen deßhalb die Beendigung des Ausstandes, und indem Ritter seinen Leuten gebot, an die Arbeit zurückzugehen, gehorchte er nur den Befehlen seiner Organisation. Hierauf wurde konstatirt, daß keine Organisation der Ver. Baugewerkschaften das Recht habe, einen Strike ohne Erlaubniß vom Exekutiv-Komite zu beendigen. Einer der Zimmerleute erklärte, Delegat Franklin sei mit Ritter für die Beendigung des Strikes gewesen, weil durch denselben doch nichts erreicht werden könnte. Delegat Gallagher erklärte, Ritter habe selbst für den Beginn des Ausstandes an den Gebäuden in 73 Str. gestimmt, Ritter aber stellte dies in Abrede, ebenso, daß in der Union der Zimmerleute keine Bosses geduldet würden. Das Komite hielt hierauf eine Exekutivsitzung ab, und es war ihre Entscheidung, daß Ritter und die Union der Zimmerleute beide schuldig seien und aus der Central Labor Union ausgestoßen werden sollten.

Arbeiter-Verhältnisse in Montreal, Can.

Das Klima ist hier rauh, der Winter anhaltend und streng; die Bauarbeiter haben deßhalb hier eine viel längere Winterpause. Ueber die Löhne habe ich Folgendes in Erfahrung gebracht: Schneider durchschnittlich $6 per Woche, Handlanger $6—7; Dock-Vormann $2 per Tag; Vormann bei dem Bau von Stadt-Barges $1.60; Zimmerleute und Caulkers $1.60; Maschinisten $1.35; Vormann in einer Sägemühle $9.60 und $10 per Woche; Arbeiter bei Eisenbahnbau $1.35 per Tag; Schmiede $9.60 per Woche; Painters $1.25—1.50 per Tag. Etwas billiger sind die Lebensmittel allerdings; ordentliches Board kostet auch hier $3.50 per Woche und der Durchschnitts-Canadier lebt nicht so kräftig wie der Amerikaner. Ja, mit „Biers“ und dergleichen Quark kann man hier zu Tode gefüttert werden. Sonntags ist hier fast jede Kneipe geschlossen und die heimlich offengehaltenen [illegible] Kirchen und Kapellen [illegible] der Arbeiter ist [illegible] Die französischen Canadier [illegible] Demuth vor ihrem „Herrn“, und [illegible] H. L.

DEATH BENEFITS.

ROBERT ABERNETHY, Toronto Union No. 27, died from injuries received while at work.

S. SORENSON, San Rafael Union No. 35, died July 23, 1883. Cause of death not stated.

JAMES THOMPSON, Philadelphia Union No. 8, died of consumption, Sept. 4, 1883.

BLACK LIST.

PETER WILLIAMS has been expelled from San Rafael Union No. 35, for violation of the constitution.

THOMAS JOHNSON, expelled from Chicago Union No. 21, for vile conduct and slanderous language.

CORRESPONDENCE.

Toledo, Ohio

Trade fair; but lots of tramping carpenters. Union No. 25 is flourishing with 8 to 12 new members every meeting.

New Orleans, La.

Work plentiful, wages $2.75—$3. Small pox still raging. New members joining. We have just raised our dues to 50 cents per month, beginning Sept. 1. Initiation fee $5, and sick benefit $2.50 per week.

Victoria, British Columbia.

Union No. 48 is making very good progress. There are only between 60 and 70 carpenters in this place, and we have the majority of them. The hours of labor are 10 hours per day; wages $2.75 to $3.50. Trade in general is good with none unemployed at present.

Boston, Mass.

We had a good mass meeting on August 7, in favor of reduced hours. Admitted 8 new members, also donated $50 in aid of telegraphers and agreed that each member pay 10 cents per week until the strike was ended. At our mass meeting speeches were made by Sherman Cummins, F. K. Foster, F. Newburns, John Wilson and others.

Albany, N. Y.

Work is dull and wages range from $1.75 to $3 a day; very few getting the latter. Since our strike last April, our union has not made much progress, the members are indifferent, and it will be useless to try to rouse them, until the bosses find out that there is no union, and then cut down wages. Very likely the men will then flock to the union like sheep in a storm. Better if they would do so now than when too late.

Hartford, Conn.

Our excursion to Savin Rock, Aug. 16, was a complete success, resulting in making a surplus of a few dollars. We had a turnout of over 500, and spent a jolly day at the seaside. Trade good, all employed. Wages same as at last report. We have appointed delegates to act with other trades in organizing a Trades Assembly in this city. Eight new members this month, and they still keep coming in every meeting.

Rushville, Ind.

There is still plenty of work and good demand for hands. Our village has become a city, another railroad has promised to locate here, and everything is promising for the future. Now, if something will cause the scales to drop from the mechanics eyes and cause them to band themselves together, all will be well.

I received an official report from Gen'l President Allen in which he speaks of our endowment. Now, we had a big talk on that subject last Wednesday night. Not one of us favored any reduction of that fund, $250; we don't care what it costs, in fact, we all favored making it $1000. Now, why can't we have an Endowment rank the same as the K. P.; or the Widows and Orphans' Fund, like the Knights of Honor? We have members of both organizations with us, and they think that we can just as well carry $1,000 as $250.

THE CARPENTER for August was full of good and interesting news that was read closely by every one of us.

Alameda, Cal.

Our union meets every second and last Friday of the month. Since our strike of August first, for nine hours, the boys have got somewhat scattered through the city, but we are doing well considering the bitter opposition we meet with. The principal bosses in Alameda are Gilbert & Co., real estate and building firm, for whom most of us were working for years previous to our strike of Aug. 1st, and the planing mill of Alameda. They have been trying to break up our movement from the very start. But we have gained the nine hours in spite of them, and all small contractors obey the rule. Gilbert & Co. have a number of inferior men, mostly from Oakland, working 10 hours. All that keeps the firm from conceding to the men is their wounded pride. The plasterers have resolved to not work on any house where carpenters work ten hours.

Toronto, Canada.

Trade fair; none unemployed at present. The joint committee of our union and the Amalgamated have requested the employes of Barber and Singley's shop to quit work, until they get $2.25 per day, the price agreed upon at termination of our strike last year. They are good workmen and both unions will sustain them. We propose to make this case a test one.

In some cases we have already been successful, in one shop entirely. We are gaining new members.

Seattle, Washington Territory.

Although under headway but a few months, our union is growing very rapidly. We have located our meetings in Masonic Hall, and we will soon have the cream of the trade in our ranks. The population of Seattle is a trifle over 10,000. Work plenty at present but in Winter it is generally very slack here, and consequently we would not advise any one to come here until after Winter. Wages are usually cut down in the cold season to 35 cents per hour and only eight hours work. At present they range from $3 to $3.50 for 10 hours work.

Harper, Kansas.

A Carpenters' Union is very much needed in this place. This is a new town, scarcely a half dozen years old, and growing very fast. It is the terminus of a very prominent railroad, and there are new comers every day. The workingmen are all strangers to each other, and I think that a union would be a great help. Wages are very low, carpenters only getting from $1.75 to $2.25 per day, whilst we have to pay $4.50 and $5 per week for board. There is a great deal of building going on, some very nice 2-story stone buildings, a good brick opera house, and a great many nice residences. All other trades, except the carpenters get very good wages, stone masons from $3 to $3.50 per day, plasterers $3.00, hod carriers and common laborers from $1.75 to $2.

St. Catherines, Canada.

Some bosses here are busily at work endeavoring to take from us the eight-hour rule on Saturdays, and force us back to ten hours. We have been accustomed to getting 10 hours pay for Saturdays ever since we adopted the eight hours, and the first intimation we had of their action was when we received our wages lately minus two hours pay. And with it some bosses gave notice that the hours of labor should be either 12 o'clock, 3 or 6 P.M. But our men have determined to uphold the four o'clock quit, and would sooner give up the two hours pay than take and work ten hours. But it is not the hours the bosses are striking at, it is unionism they are fighting. We have arranged to have a conference with the bosses who have formed a society and meet secretly. Trade is not very brisk, but our men are finding employment jobbing for themselves, and all that keeps them from conceding to the men is simply their wounded pride. The plasterers have resolved not to work on any house where carpenters work ten hours; that seems to worry the bosses more than anything else. Wages $1.75 to $2, not many $2.25.

We have suspended James Hunter for non-payment of dues.

LATER.—Our Committee has met the bosses, and the latter have conceded the eight hours on Saturday, but we are to lose 40 cents—the pay for two hours—or 20 cents an hour. We do not know whether all unions take the same interest in THE

CARPENTER that we do; if t
I think it could soon be be
If our union could afford, we
organize Brantford, Chatham
and Galt. They are growing

Grinnell, Iowa

This is a lively town, and
booming. Wages for good m
from $2.50 to $3 per day.
finishing up the West Colleg
cost when completed about $
Central College walls are up (
roof timbers; the building,
pleted, will cost about $1
there are several dwellings b
which will cost from $8,000 to
a good many smaller ones co
to $2,600, although the town
last year by a very destruct
destroying over 100 building
over 40 persons. It is built u
a finer and much better class

Hamilton, Cana

A grand labor demonstrat
here in the Crystal Palace o
which proved a success financ
a labor movement has never l
here. Since our picnic we r
our membership very rapid
new additions are of the righ
men are beginning to work
better for the cause of unio
various jobs. Our picnic wa
success.

The carpenter trade is on
only a few good jobs on hand
ing a rush of carpenters to th
false representations of trade
is fear of a cut in wages. Uni
working hard to prevent suc
initiated 15 new members du
month. In May, during the
strike, one mason worked un
through the strike up till a f
he started to work on the Ar
sle job. As soon as it was k
had started work, both bri
carpenters struck; it lasted
he being discharged immed
is a specimen of how non-u
treated, and showing the ne
ing a union man in Hamilton

Chicago, Ill.

Trade in Chicago is picking
few now out of work. Un
making splendid progress and
are holding very interesting
adding to their membership
week.

THOMAS JOHNSON has been
Union No. 21 for slanderous
becoming conduct. He wa
the union against his will a
the spirit of a man. He is a
first water.

The Branch Secretaries sh
trade news and reports of m
to this office.

All of the Branches in this
ing excellently and there w
active movement this fall. L
arise and stir himself so that
against non-union men and
nine hours.

THE CARPENTER

A MONTHLY JOURNAL FOR CARPENTERS AND JOINERS.

VOLUME III. NEW YORK, OCTOBER, 1883. NUMBER 10.

PRISONER ROBINSON'S SPEECH.

"When your term expires it is to be hoped you will lead a different life," Judge Elcock of Philadelphia said, after he had sentenced James Robinson to three years in the Eastern Penitentiary. Robinson, who had been convicted of conspiring to make off with three cases of linen goods from a dray, retorted after the sentence: "I worked three years in your State Prison making shoes, and I know as much about shoemaking as I do about watches. They taught me in your prison to be dishonest. My principal work was to paste leather and pasteboard together to make a thick sole to impose on the public. The man who had the contract was a Christian, a member of a church, and at the time I called his attention to the pasteboard business he was foreman of the Grand Jury.

A NEW UNION IN CHARLESTON, S. C.

Wages range from $1.50 to $2.25; all it needs is a more thorough union among the carpenters of this city and we can then do something for our elevation. We have formed a union and connected ourselves with the Brotherhood of Carpenters and we intend to do our utmost to spread its principles, for in them we believe is the salvation of the trade.

CIGAR MAKERS' CONVENTION.

The convention of the Cigar Makers' International Union at Toronto was largely attended. This Union does not hold annual conventions, but leaves the matter to be decided by the general vote of the unions whenever a convention may be required. At the late convention it was decided to place a general organizer in the field, and that the International Union shall be incorporated. The weekly dues were fixed at 20 cents and the death benefit was increased to $40 and sick benefit $5 a week. The matter of an "out of work" benefit was favorably considered and referred to the next convention.

FROM FOREIGN LANDS.

FRANCE.—A congress of workingmen was held in Paris on Sept. 30, and another has just been held in Roubaix.

SPAIN.—The workingmen's organization have held their congress in Valencia, Oct. 1.

SWITZERLAND.—At the labor congress in Zurich, 172 delegates were present and a plan of organization was perfected.

ENGLAND.—The Trades Council of London has 14,864 accredited members. In Glasgow, Scotland, the Trades Council has nearly 12,000 members, in Edinburgh 8,000, in Manchester 6,000, and in Bolton 6,500. Of the women's trades unions in England there are the Bookbinders, 262 members; Dressmakers of London 51; Power Loom Weavers of Huddersfield 2,000; Tailoresses of Westminster, 100; Women Trades Council of London, 376; Upholsterers, 86; and the Womens Protective Society, 73. A great demonstration of over 50,000 men took place Sept. 22, at Newcastle, to demand reforms in the franchise.—Agitation among the railway servants for higher pay and shorter hours still continues.

Union No. 46, of Guelph, Canada, is [illegible] busily at work. The Stone Masons' [illegible] [illegible] Layers' Union, and Moulders' [illegible] [illegible] city are working in unity [illegible] [illegible] unions. A movement is on [illegible] Building League.

TRADE JOTTINGS.

— In Dakota Territory, Carpenters get $3.50 a day and are in demand but the cost of living is extremely high.

— The Carpenters strike on the elevator at Newport News, Va., still continues and all are warned away from there.

— Copies of the Constitution and By-Laws of the Central Labor Union of this city can be had by applying to this office.

— Under the new tramp law of Wisconsin, a man in Milwaukee has just been sentenced to the Penitentiary for 10 months at hard labor.

— Many of our exchanges are very fond of taking items from this humble journal without any credit. Of course it costs very little labor to clip these items, but it costs much more to write them.

— Send us your subscriptions for *The Carpenter*—50 cents per year. This a live trade journal and the one that every Carpenter should read. Subscriptions can be sent by Postal Notes to be had at any Post Office in the United States for 3 cents.

— Don't go to Cape Town, South Africa. A correspondent of the *Granite Cutters' Journal* writes from there that Europeans cannot get work, because Malays are so much cheaper as mechanics, and Kaffirs and Zulus do laborers' work for a mere pittance.

— According to the Census of 1880, there are 373,143 Carpenters in the United States. This is a large field to work in, but we have "put our hand to the plow" and don't propose to turn back. The Carpenters must be organized. And our Brotherhood will do it.

— There is great necessity for authorized representatives of Trades Unions to be located at Castle Garden and acquaint immigrants with the rate of wages and conditions of the various trades in this country. Then those people would not be used so readily against us.

— Technical or industrial education is a subject that we gave considerable attention to at all times in this journal, even from the first number. Now we are pleased to note that it has become a leading public question endorsed by the vast majority of witnesses before the Senate Committee.

— W. H. FOSTER, late secretary of the Federation of Labor, has removed from Cincinnati to Philadelphia. No doubt before long we will hear of a first class Trades Assembly in Philadelphia. It was largely due to Foster's efforts that the Cincinnati Trades Assembly attained its prominence.

ELECTION ECHOES FROM OHIO.

The organized workingmen in various districts of Ohio have elected members of the Legislature.

A. D. Fassett, a member of the Iron Molders Union is elected State Senator from Trumbull and Mahoning Counties. Eight trades unionists have been elected members of the Assembly as follows:

Cleveland—James Mooney, Wm. Roche, and John P. Haley.

Cincinnati—J. B. Menke, Wm. Post, and Peter F. Stryker.

Stark County—John McBride.

Lucas County—Wm. Beatty.

L. Watermann, the candidate of the Cincinnati *Volksfreund*, a "rat" sheet, was defeated, although all other candidates on its ticket were elected by large majorities.

WAGES IN CANADA.

From the report of the Legislative Committee of the Toronto Trades Council we glean the following facts: With regard to carpenters and joiners it may be remarked that notwithstanding wages have ranged higher in Toronto during the past year than at any time for years previous, the yearly average has been only about $583.40, or $1.80 per working day of ten hours. Wages in country places range from $1.50 to $1.75 per day. As Toronto is unquestionably a "jumping off" point, it results that the supply at all times is much in excess of the demand, and tends in the direction of low wages. On considering the above rate of wages the fact must not be lost sight of, that this is in a great measure due to organized effort on the part of those immediately interested, and is at least from ten to fifteen per cent higher than prevail outside of Toronto. The cost of necessaries of life, clothing, house rent, and fuel, are on the whole at least thirty per cent. higher than in Great Britain.

ORGANIZATION AND COOPERATION.

By organization and co-operation, the industrious ant accomplishes tasks that have caused it to be pointed to by philosophers as worthy of man's emulation; by organization and co-operation the busy bee weaves its most wondrous cell and extracting sweets from every bloom accumulates its wintry store; by organization and co-operation, the persevering beaver fells the monarchs of the forest, and by a system of engineering peculiarly his own, constructs of them most wonderful dams, that in their powers of resistance to the force of surging billows, would do credit to the ingenuity and power of man; by organization and co-operation the artisans of the world are enabled to enforce their demands for living wages, for fair work; by organization and co-operation, the master mechanic and his force of co-workers present to the admiring gaze of the passer-by, structures so beautiful in design and so stupendous in the magnitude of their construction, as to inspire their beholder with the feeling that some power more than human must have prompted their origin; by organization and co-operation Wall street gamblers who assume the more respectable title of members of the Exchange, so control the prices of the necessary commodities, as to say to the producer so much shalt thou have for what thou makest, and to the consumers, so much tribute shalt thou pay now before thy wants can be supplied; by organization and co-operation the lawyers who comprise not more than one thousandth part of the population, monopolize at least two thirds of all legislative, judicial and executive office, and so manage to mystify and multiply the laws of the country to render the vocation, to unscrupulous and designing members, the most profitable, least useful, and most distress—producing occupation known to a sin cursed World. And all that is left to the workers is to organize and cooperate together for their own social emancipation.

—Letters from every section of the country from the telegraphers bring tidings of satisfaction with the results of their strike. And by no means does a feeling of dejected defeat possess them. And on this the *Telegraphers Advocate* says: "Our wrongs have not been righted and the Brotherhood of Telegraphers still thrives, and so it will always while [illegible] [illegible] [illegible] [illegible] corporations and monopolies

STRAY CHIPS.

— A very spicy and neatly edited paper is the Cincinnati *Unionist*, and our members of Union No. 2 are helping it along.

— The question of contract prison labor will be voted on by the people of this State in the coming November election.

— The Denver workingmen are agitating a reading room, and employment bureau under the management of the trades unions.

— Philadelphia trades unions are moving to organize a Central Labor Union modeled somewhat after the manner of the one in New York.

— Thomas Burt, the coal miners representative in the British Parliament, is on a visit to this country and is now on a tour through the Western states.

— Joseph Joyce, President of the Utica, N. Y., Trades Assembly, a life long trades unionist and a devoted friend of our Brotherhood, has been nominated for the State Legislature.

— An ad-valorem duty on foreign labor is advocated by the New York *Post*, to keep down European competition in the labor market here and to keep up the tariff on foreign products.

— For years we have favored the Inter-State organization of coal miners all over this country. Now at last it has been accomplished in the formation of the Miners National Association.

— We regret to hear of the death of Chris. H. Siemon of St. Louis, a cigar maker by trade, staunch in his union principles, true to the interests of all laborers, we felt proud to call him our friend.

— Canada will have a labor congress in December which has prospects of being well attended. The Missouri Labor Congress at St. Louis, Mo., met on October 2, and was well attended.

—The call for a Labor convention to be held in Philadelphia, January 12th, next, to form a Labor Party, is a fraud and emanates from a New York clique of political strikers, with Denis Kearney to back them.

—In New York City the journeymen bakers have made a vigorous movement against Sunday work, and procured the arrest of several boss bakers for violating the Sunday law, and secured their conviction.

— New York manufacturers of tenement house cigars are fighting the law against manufacturing cigars in tenement houses. The first case in the courts has gone against them and they have now appealed to a higher court.

— At Trenton, N. J., the Fifth Annual State Labor Congress was held with 41 societies represented and 70 delegates present. A permanent plan of organization was adopted and an abundance of good work prepared.

— John G. Warwick, Democratic candidate for Lieutenant Governor of Ohio was defeated because he had called out the militia to shoot down the coal miners of Massillon, Ohio, in 1876. He ran fully 20,000 votes behind his ticket, while it was elected.

—The Belgian glass-worker[illegible] come to this country under [illegible] of their own volition, are go[illegible] home again, under the pressure [illegible] offer of $130 per month in go[illegible] [illegible]. Meanwhile the trouble [illegible]

THE CARPENTER.

Entered at the Post-Office in New York, as second-class matter.

NEW YORK, OCTOBER, 1883.

THE GRINDSTONE.

Mr. J. E. Mitchell, of the *Journal* of the Franklin Institute, says about the grindstone: "All nations use it, and it is perhaps withal the one piece of mechanism that bears the same form and is the same in principle. More or less directly it takes part in the greatest modern material enterprises; it has no doubt assisted to fashion the implements of many of the lost arts, and is still needed in many of the requirements of the arts of the present day."

NEW YORK'S TALLEST BUILDING.

Inspector Esterbrook of this city has under consideration an application for the construction of an apartment house at the corner of Seventh avenue and Fifty-seventh street to be 182 feet from curb to line of roof. The building will be 15 stories high and cost $650,000 and will have a cupola forty feet high on top of the building, making the peak 222 feet above the curb line, or only sixty-two feet lower than the spire of Trinity Church. The height of the Colossus of Rhodes, which was reckoned one of the seven wonders of the world two and a half centuries before Christ, was but 127 feet. Ancient wonders are but the common things of modern times.

THE NOTTINGHAM TRADES CONGRESS.

The sixteenth annual Congress of the Trades Unions of Great Britain and Ireland opened in Nottingham, England on Sept., 10th and was six days in session. There were 134 Societies represented, covering all parts of the United Kingdom with 165 delegates, 7 of them women, and a constituency of 552,681 an increase of 42,000 over last year's numbers. Among the leading societies present were: The Agricultural Laborers Union, 20,000 members; Boiler makers 29,000; Cotton Spinners 17,600; Carpenters, 22,500; Engineers and Machinists, 50,000; Iron-Founders 11,563; Laborers Union 12,500; Stone Masons, 12,000; Miners (all branches) 50,100; Weavers 21,500; Tailors 17,658; Printers 8,200.

After the election of officers the Report of the Trades Unions Parliamentary Committee was read. It dealt with the various and many labor issues that had been acted on by the British Parliament during the year, at the instance of the committee. It mentioned the growth of the Trades Union movement in America, and in words of the kindest nature spoke of the Trades Unions of America and France.

On the second day the President, Thos. Smith, a lithographer of Nottingham, delivered his address, which reviewed the work of the past year and was very encouraging to Trades Unions. After that the report of the parliamentary committee was discussed at length and adopted. On the subject of amending the Employers Liability Act it was stated that in Lancashire alone no less than 40,000 workmen were forced by their employers to contract themselves outside of the Act. And in Staffordshire and elsewhere this plan was extending. An amendment to the Act is asked for by the Congress to prevent this power of contracting out of the Act and also to extend its provisions to Seamen.

Mr. Frederick Harrison read a paper on the work of the Trades Unions during the past 16 years. He said: The most common idea of a trade union is that it is an organization of workmen designed chiefly to give their support in strikes against their employers. Mr. Harrison shows that, so far as English unions are concerned, this is an error. They have more than doubled their numbers and incomes during the past sixteen years. Five of the principal unions, which did not in 1867 number in all 60,000 members, now have an aggregate membership of 125,000. During the same period they have doubled their incomes and their reserve funds. Trade in England suffered severe depression during these years, and the strain upon the unions was very great. Seven of them spent within six years nearly $10,000,000 in support of men out of work and for other charitable purposes, drawing upon their reserve funds for nearly $1,000,000, yet now they have an aggregate balance on hand of $1,800,000. The Engineers' Union alone paid $780,000 to men out of work in the year 1879, and during five years the same society paid for the same object $1,225,000. During the hard times in 1879 more than 46,000 persons were wholly supported by the funds of five unions, which in the same year spent $5,000,000 in aiding the sick, paying insurance on tools and lives, and for other purposes. Out of the total expenditure of $10,000,000 in six years, only $800,000 was spent in settling strikes and trade disputes of all kinds; and during the last year, when their aggregate income was $1,650,000, and their aggregate resources $3,450,000, they spent only $21,000 in settling disputes, or less than 1 per cent of their resources.

Mr. Crompton spoke on the codification of the Criminal law and action was taken in its favor. Resolutions were adopted on the following subjects; engineers certificates, sub inspectors of Mines, inspection of factories, the Paris International Trades Congress, recovery of wages; inquests of mine accidents, extension of franchise, Cooperation, labor representation in Parliament, employment of females in forges, local trades councils, infectious diseases, wages in the cotton trade, education, and other important matters.

The attention of the Government was called to the necessity of a law to regulate the hours of labor of all workers in the employ of the State, and by all chartered companies, so that eight hours at most shall be a days work.

A very exciting debate took place on the land question. Last year the Congress by a large vote indorsed the Nationalisation of the Land. In this session Joseph Arch of the Farm Laborers Union introduced the following resolutions: "That considering the large number of acres of waste lands capable of cultivation, as well as large quantities not more than half cultivated, this Congress is of opinion that radical changes in our land system are immediately required so that the land may be cultivated for the benefit of the entire community." Mr. Rowland of the London Cab Drivers contended that Mr. Arch's resolution did not go far enough nor deep enough, and he favored that the Congress should reaffirm last years resolution that "nothing will be considered complete, short of nationalization of the land." The result of the vote was in favor of Arch's resolution and against reaffirming the nationalization of the land.

After electing a Parliamentary Committee one of whom is J. S. Murchie of the Amalgamated Carpenters, the Congress adjourned *sine die*.

VENEERING.

A correspondent of the London *Cabinet Maker* writing on this subject speaks as follows regarding the veneering of large panels, etc.: A great many engaged at the bench are aware of the irritating difficulties of preventing the veneered side going hollow as the glue sets, in fact, many tedious methods have been devised to avert it, such as jointing end in several places, veneering on both sides, the one to counteract the other, and fixing round, before and after veneering. The method I have strictly observed for over 20 years has the two great advantages of being simple and inexpensive regarding material and time. In the preparation of the surface for veneering, many workmen damp or swell the heart side or face side of the board and the side on which the veneer is to be placed. This I consider radically wrong; the very reverse is the correct mode. Let any one try the experiment on, say, a wardrobe end of pine, and 6 feet by 1 feet 9 inches. After preparing the heart side for veneering, swell the other side by placing a layer of damp sawdust on it over night; it will in the morning be about three-quarters of an inch hollow on the face side; then size the face side, keeping the back damp until the size is sufficiently dry for the cold, and it will be observed, on coming from the cold, to be round on the face or veneered side, and may be kept nearly so by placing the veneered side against a flat board, or the two veneered sides face to face, to dry gradually. Of course after trying this experiment it will be necessary to know how long the article will require swelling. Considering the pine fairly seasoned and the veneer well dry, one night as a rule is sufficient.

— Wood Carvers National Union met in convention at Cincinnati, Oct. 15.

— In New South Wales, Australia, an employers liability act has been passed and also a law to legalize trades unions.

TO WORKING GIRLS AND WOMEN.

The Federation of Trade and Labor Unions of the United States and Canada makes to you the following appeal:

There is to-day, in this most civilized country on the face of the globe, a vast multitude of girls and women condemned to struggle for very existence. They are doubly handicapped by poverty and by sex. Neither sentiment or humanity counts in the race for gain. The weaker become the prey of the stronger when the labor market is glutted, and keen competition disposes of the products of labor at the lowest market price. The toil of our seamstresses, shop-girls and factory-operatives is exploited by hard taskmakers and soulless corporations.

Thousands of tragedies are daily enacted, where virtue falls a victim to want and shame springs from social needs. It is the mission of the labor movement to shield and protect those who cannot defend themselves. It is the creed of the labor movement that labor should be fairly paid for, that the laborer should be more than a passive factor in the contract that disposes of his labor. It is further the creed of the labor movement that equal amounts of work should bring the same price, whether performed by man or woman. In other words that the value to the purchaser, not the necessity of the seller, should fix the standard of a day's wages.

In the carrying out of this belief there is needed the hearty co-operation of all interested parties. The working-women of the land should array themselves under the banner of united labor. It is the hope of the Federated Trades to assist in bringing about this much-needed result. Those who desire to form labor societies will be supplied with all necessary information, by applying to the Secretary, and will be either furnished with an organizer or directed to the proper source from which to obtain one.

We solicit your correspondence, and pledge you our support.

Fraternally.

LEGISLATIVE COMMITTEE FEDERATED TRADES.

FRANK K. FOSTER, Sec'y,
10 Wendell st., Cambridge, Mass.

A PROTEST AGAINST RACE LINES.

Fred Douglass, the eloquent champion of his race in a speech at the colored men's convention in Louisville, Ky., said: "The colored man is an oppressed and abject race in the United States. Trades unions refuse him admission. Mechanics refuse him as an apprentice, and even when he dies the same old contempt and spite follows him. He is spurned from the cemetery gates and compelled to seek a resting place of his own. If he applies for admission to colleges or aspires to education and profession, the race line is again drawn. That is what we are here for to raise this line and make us the equal of the whites. The cause lies more in the diseased imagination of the Americans than in firm belief.

LORD MACAULEY'S OPINION.

In the British Parliament, during the discussion on the reduction of the hours of labor, Lord Macauley made a speech from which we extract these splendid sentiments: Rely on it that intense labor, beginning too early in life, continued too long every day, stinting the growth of the body, leaving no time for healthful exercise, leaving no time for intellectual culture must impair all those high qualities, which have made our country great. Your overworked boys will become a feeble and ignoble race of men, the parents of a more feeble and ignoble progress, nor will it be long before the deterioration of the laborer will injuriously affect those very interests to which his physical and moral interests have been sacrificed * * * Never will I believe that what makes a population stronger, and healthier, and wiser, and better, can ultimately make it poorer. You try to frighten us by telling us that in some German factories the young work seventeen hours in the twenty-four; that they work so hard that among thousands there is not one grows to such a stature that he can be admitted into the army; and you ask whether, if we pass this bill, we can possibly hold our own against such competition. * * * If ever we are forced to yield the foremost place among commercial nations, we shall yield it, not to a race of degenerate dwarfs, but to some people preeminently vigorous in body and in mind.

AN ATTEMPT AT DISORGANIZATION REBUKED.

WASHINGTON, D. C. I defy the United States or Canada to produce an organization of workmen that contains better material than Local No. 1, Brotherhood of Carpenters of this city. I am prouder of my connection with them than I am with a membership in any other order, although connected with several.

A call was advertised, for a meeting of carpenters for the purpose of forming an assembly of Knights of Labor, [illegible] the same column with one of our [illegible] notices for a public meeting of [illegible]. The members of Local No. 1, [illegible] indignant, held an informal talk and concluded to sustain the call, in view of an oft-repeated assertion that there was a number of non-union carpenters anxious to form an "assembly of carpenters" that would not join the Brotherhood. They also concluded that it was better [illegible] themselves to sustain two organizations than allow dissensions to creep [illegible] our trade.

The meeting was totally devoid of non-union carpenters, while the presence of plasterers and painters suggested [illegible] materials to form an assembly of carpenters to deceive the public, and our trade in particular, and for the sinister motives of a few designers. The Union carpenters took in the situation at a glance and quietly captured the meeting, without disorder or a single unkind word. Their display of forbearance with ignorant stupidity, was marked by that gentlemanly deportment which characterizes known superiority over blind fanaticism.

While we contend for the autonomy of our craft, we are not ashamed to [illegible] and before the public and declare our purposes.

It is a mistaken idea that the carpenters forming the Brotherhood are opposed to the Knights of Labor. We glory in their successes and deplore their defeats as a part of the same army that claims us as a division. And it is to be regretted that men will allow their imprudent zeal to run away with their judgment. We think our Union cannot be beat, and are not willing to try experiments with something else when we known we have a good thing.

Washington, D. C.

The Brotherhood of Carpenters held a large and enthusiastic meeting at their hall, corner Thirteenth-and-a-half and E, Oct. 1 President George T. Suter in the chair. The meeting was addressed by G. Edmonston, Thomas Galloway, Joseph Billingsley, David Gregg, Mr. Williams and others. The speakers tried to impress on the non-union carpenters the advantages of organization in protecting wages and the injury they were doing to the craft by their indifference to the efforts of the brotherhood. This was said to be giving a decided advantage to cheap bosses who employ cheap labor to gain an advantage over those, who have been always willing to pay fair living wages in a market already depressed in point of an intense competition. In answer to a call for new members about forty new names were enrolled, besides several delinquent members, who came forward and paid up their dues. This organization is in a flourishing condition, and is somewhat more liberal in their dealings with non-union men than the ordinary trades union. For some time past we have been annoyed in this city by a body of men who seem bent on disorganizing every trade union [illegible] summit of their audacity was reached when on Oct. 5 they called a meeting to form an Assembly of the Knights of Labor.

In answer to the advertised call a gathering met at Red Men's hall, nearly two-thirds of which were carpenters, the balance of other trades. A chairman and secretary were elected and invitation extended for carpenters to sign their names, but only eight responded. The failure to obtain the required number to constitute an "assembly" the meeting adjourned subject to the call of the chairman.

— The cigarmakers have at present thirty thousand members in good standing and a capital of $7.49 per member in their treasuries or in all $251,800.

—The strike of the Telegraphers [illegible] has done no more it has at least cr[illegible] halt to future reductions of wages and increases in the hours of labor. But it has accomplished more. It has gained a concession of more pay and shorter hours for the employes and cheaper rates for the public.

FULFIL YOUR OBLIGATIONS.

Th[illegible] ...bles of business are: Fulfil your ...ns. The common-sense and sub...siness man, or firm, before giv...amount of credit to a customer ...deavors to ascertain: "Does he ...obligations?" Of course, it may ...imes, that a customer who has ...fulfilled his obligations, may ...unforseen disappointments and ...tly cannot carry them out. But ...common-sense business man is bent ...ascertaining the true position of affairs ...and if he finds the person honest in his statements, a little good sense pre...vails on him from pressing for a fulfil...ment of obligations.

To ...your obligations means character ...integrity. As the character of the ...ual is established by carrying out his ...ions promptly, so is the society ...fulfils all obligations. And if the ...rhood desires to enlarge its forces ...solidify its prospects, it must do ...se. It must endeavor to fulfill its ...ions, and do it promptly. It is the ...great essential necessity for ...ing up a harmonious and strong Brotherhood. Such a Brotherhood that com...respect from the better class of our employers, as well as from the general public.

Character implies honesty of purpose ...ed with intelligence. It should find ...y into all the local Unions of the Brotherhood, and remand carping ambi...to the back seats, and all its best men ...places of trust. To elect our best ...into places of trust means confidence ...ong the rank and file of the B. An in...gent confidence is the knowledge that ...the B's. officers are known as men of ...ability, those who are known to do ...r duty faithfully and energetically.

This is my ideal Brotherhood. Is it attainable? The aim is high, perhaps too high for some. But my good feeling prompts me to work for it. The best of us are imperfect in some respects, and the worst of us may have some good quality in him. Let us endeavor to crowd down the bad in us, aye, and in the Brotherhood, and let our good qualities have the foremost place. Let us endeavor to fulfill our obligations. That should be the watchword of our Brotherhood. Let us endeavor to find out what a hitch here and a jar there, and a little tantalizing ambition cropping out somewhere else mean to the B.

The summit of our hope is to be men! Be brothers! Endeavor to carry out the business in the local Unions with integrity and with judgment, and may I say with a little forethought, a little forethought that will provide for the proverbial "rainy day." The rainy day is sometimes very gloomy. When the cloud or the gloom hangs over the household, it is sometimes not pleasant to the inmates. Brothers, endeavor to dispel the cloud, or the gloom not only from the household, but from the B. Dispel it from the home of sickness and from the house of mourning. Dispel it when it hangs over the brain-rest of the officers of your local Unions, and of your Executive, and particularly of your General Executive. Dispel it, brothers, by endeavoring to fulfill your obligations promptly. To dispel the cloud or the gloom means, in full, to dispel *mistrust*, to check disintegration, to save the Brotherhood.

Brothers, I hope you see the aim of this letter. Fulfill your obligations promptly, it will instill confidence into one and all.

Enough from an humble Canadian carpenter whose desire is international good will to our American brothers. But you must acquit yourselves as men, and fulfill your obligations, thus showing yourselves worthy to be called great in character as well as geographically great.

W. H. STEVENS.

TORONTO, Oct. 6th, 1883.

WOMEN AS CABINET-MAKERS.

The woman who indulges in cabinet makers' work seldom does much harm. She contents herself with trying to drive nails into the wall, and with experiments with mucilage. She drives her nails with great caution, and when she has loosened an inch or two of plaster, she becomes alarmed, and resolves to let her husband assume the responsibility of inflicting further injury on the wall. She has a profound faith in the value of mucilage as a substitute for glue, and hopefully attempts to mend china and furniture with it; but mucilage is as harmless as it is inefficient, and it is only on the rare occasions when it is used to mend the wheels of the clock, that it does any permanent injury to anything. It is doubtless the timidity of woman which restrains her mending instincts. She dreads the saw and the chisel as treacherous tools that inevitably inflict wounds on the user, and she dislikes hot glue owing to its proneness to burn unwary fingers. Moreover, she can never grasp the difference between a nail and a screw, and regards the latter as an absurd variety of nail which can not be driven with a hammer unless the wielder of the hammer has the muscles of a man. Thus, for one reason or another, cabinet makers' work, as practised by women, is harmless and inexpensive, and she knows nothing of the remorse to which the man who owns an amateur tool chest and is not wholly hardened, is a prey.

IN MEMORIAM
OF BRO. STEPHEN SORENSON.

WHEREAS, The dread messenger of death having visited the peaceful home of our worthy Bro. S. Sorenson, and with a ruthless hand suddenly torn from his wife and family a brother and beloved husband and a dear father; therefore be it

Resolved, That in sundering the links which bound him to our Union, this Union has sustained the irreparable loss of one of its most honored and loved members, one who was eminently endowed with all the kindly, manly, Christian graces, and his wife has lost an affectionate and faithful companion.

Resolved, That in this hour of her sad bereavement, the members of this Union tender to Mrs. Sorenson their heartfelt sympathy and sincere condolence; therefore be it

Resolved, That these resolutions be spread in full upon the minutes of this Union, that they be furnished to THE CARPENTER for publication, and also that a copy be transmitted to his sorrowing wife.

B. C. SAMIS,
J. W. McLEAN,
E. N. KELLOGG
Committee.

COMMUNICATIONS.

Baltimore, Md.

If all the local unions would do as we do, there would be no trouble to get the money needed to pay off every endowment in a few days after being notified. We lay aside, according to the Constitution, 10 cents per month for every member. So, when we are called on, we have the money ready. We are initiating two or three members, sometimes more, every meeting. The Building League here is growing and contemplates soon holding a public meeting. We do not hold any mass-meetings in Raines' Hall hereafter, because it belongs to the owner of a "rat" paper: *The Correspondent*. We patronize no "rat" paper editors. We can do without them.

Trenton, N. J.

Union No. 31 was lately visited by our General Secretary and with good results to the Union and the Brotherhood. In the meeting room of Union No. 31 the emblem of our B is hanging on the wall, and it is a feature that might with profit be adopted in all our unions. The emblem consists of a compass and quadrant square with a plane in centre. The emblem we speak of is 3 feet in length and in due proportions, and made of white maple and walnut. The ground work is walnut and the tools are maple with the letters "Labor Omnia Vincit" in walnut. The initiation fee of the Union has been raised to $4 and the Union is thriving steadily.

Toledo, Ohio

Union No. 25 is going right along; it looks as if the carpenters of Toledo, are getting their eyes open to the situation of the trade, for, although there is more work here than ever before, still there are lots of carpenters out of work. The town is full of strangers—we might say tramps—for very few of them are mechanics, but they serve the bosses to keep wages down, and already some are beginning to cut wages, but union men generally hold their wages, none working for less than $2.25; the tramps are working for anything they can get, some of them are working for $1.50, and indeed, they are not worth that. I noticed in the journal an article on the Endowment Fund, signed "Argus," which I was about to answer when I received your annual report and found that each member was supplied with a copy. I thought it unnecessary, for, if "Argus" is a member, he can see by the statement of the Endowment Fund that he is mistaken about the B. not being able to pay $250.

Union No. 25 has received a State Charter under the laws of Ohio, and our Treasurer and Trustees are under bonds accordingly. Trade is slacking; wages $2.25.

Victoria, British Columbia.

Union No. 48 is still growing; there were five new members initiated last night, and several applications. I think by the way we are going on that we shall have every carpenter of Victoria in our union by next Spring. We have been discussing the nine-hour movement of late, and we have decided not to work more than nine hours per day after the first of April next.

Trade keeps very steady here, and we have every prospect of having plenty of work all through the Winter. We meet every first and third Monday of each month, and charge fifty cents per month dues and one dollar initiation. We are busy making our By-Laws.

Portland, Oregon.

Union No. 50 met on October 5th, and formed a permanent organization, and elected officers. We start with a strong membership, and many applications are coming into us. Bro. Whitten, of San Francisco, organized us in good shape and installed our officers. Building has been brisk the past season, but now it is quite slack owing to the rainy season coming on which will last until next June; very little outside work can be done in the Winter and Spring. The supply of carpenters is equal to the demand, and far in excess at times. The wages vary from $3 to $3.50 per day, and carpenters work harder and faster than any place I was ever in. Cost of living is high.

Hartford, Conn.

MATHEW FLANNERY, of Union No. 43, a member in good standing, died Sept. 11th, of brain fever. He was not long enough a member to be entitled to Death benefit. Nevertheless our Union furnished six pall bearers to attend his funeral which took place at New Britain, Conn., many miles from here. The following resolutions were passed by our union:

WHEREAS, In the world of labor to-day we find men who are true to their fellow men, and in organization together they establish the strongest ties of solidarity, and

WHEREAS, By the death of our late Brother, Mathew Flannery, we lose not only an active and staunch member of Carpenters' Union No. 43, but also one who has been worthy of all esteem and honor, and in his loss we mourn the death of a beloved companion and member, therefore be it

RESOLVED, That we deplore the death of Mathew Flannery, and with his family we mingle our regrets that his life has not been spared for the useful work he had designed.

RESOLVED, That we send six pall bearers from this Union to attend his funeral, and that we drape our charter for 30 days in honor of his memory.

Signed: PHILIP H. FAGAN, P. A. BROOKS, ANTHONY DONOVAN, *Committee.*

From The South West.

RYCOBEY, Mo.—There has been a great deal of work going on here since the first of August. First-class hands are scarce; we are getting $10 per week on a certain job, but wages are from $1.55 to $2 per day for work on a job that lasts for a week or so. But when you get a job for a month or more it is by the week they hire. There is about as much building going on in this country as there is in the United States, and I saw a great many new buildings going up both in Missouri and in the Territory, and there is a great deal of building going on here at present. Sarcoxie, Jasper Co., Mo., is booming, and Pierce City is building rapidly. Neosho, Mo., the county seat, is building a college and a large school house, besides a great many dwellings and store houses.

I have been a reader of THE CARPENTER ever since the first number was published, except this Summer when I was travelling; it seems like I have lost something valuable when I don't get it. I would not do without it for double the price of subscription.

J. H. AVERY.

San Francisco, Cal.

Members still joining; got 17 new ones in one meeting night last week. R. Whitten, one of our trustees, is rousing the men north of this city. He has organized Portland and Victoria. Our Union pays a fraternal visit to Oakland Union No. 36, on the 15th, inst. A. A. Cohen, of San Francisco, a capitalist and lawyer, appeared before the Congressional Labor Committee, and made statements in regard to the condition of carpenters in California which are *false*, and we will take steps to contradict them immediately. Trade and wages are same as last month. Prospects fair for the Winter season. The Printers are making a desperate fight against the morning and evening papers the *Call* and the *Bulletin*, on which they are locked out. The entire sympathy and material support of the unions are with them, and we have cut very heavily into the subscriptions and advertising patronage of these papers. The *Call* lost 1500 in circulation the first week. Our Union netted $340 from its picnic.

Ansichten des Predigers R. Heber Newton über die sociale Frage vor dem Senats-Comite.

Die öffentlichen Schulen seien äußerst mangelhaft, einseitig und die Folge davon sei, daß die Jugend sich immer weniger für ein ehrliches Handwerk interessire, eine Tendenz, die für das Gemeinwohl sehr verderblich wirken müsse. Mit den öffentlichen Schulen sollten deßhalb Werkstätten verbunden werden, in denen die Schüler zu praktischer Arbeit angeleitet werden könnten. Ein weiterer Faktor, der auf die Gesellschaft schädlich wirke, sei der Mangel am Interesse der Arbeiter an ihrer Arbeit, welche durch die Arbeitstheilung zu einförmig und geisttödtend geworden seien. Der Mangel an Gefühl seitens der Arbeitgeber, den Arbeitern gegenüber, sei ebenfalls zu erwähnen; derselbe sei nicht durch Antagonismus, sondern durch den maschinenmäßigen Gang des heutigen Lebens herbeigeführt worden. Daß die Arbeiter zu ihren Arbeitgebern nicht mehr in näherer Beziehung stünden, vermehre die Feindseligkeit Beider gegen einander. Die Arbeiter kamen nur noch mit ihren Aufsehern, die früher selbst Arbeiter waren, in Berührung und Niemand sei hartherziger, grausamer, als Vorleute in großen Fabriken, die Korporationen gehören. Die mehreren National-Oekonomen, welche der Ansicht sind, daß die Arbeit nur eine Waare im Markte, seien ebenfalls hartherzige, grausame Menschen. Um den Kampf zwischen Arbeitern und Kapitalisten zu mildern, sollten Beide mit einander kooperiren und die Arbeiter sollten am Gewinn theilnehmen. Es seien großartige Mächte an der Arbeit, die Kluft zwischen Arbeitern und Kapitalisten fortwährend zu vergrößern, und die Gesellschaft sei verpflichtet, diesen Mächten entgegenzutreten. Jeder, der die Zunahme der Maschinenarbeit und der damit verbundenen Arbeitslosigkeit großer Massen ... beobachte, müsse ... z. B. die enorm...

THE CARPENTER.

PUBLISHED MONTHLY

BY THE

Brotherhood of Carpenters and Joiners,

OF AMERICA.

Office: 184 William St., New York.

TERMS.—Fifty cents a year, in advance, post-paid.

Send all moneys and correspondence for this Journal to

P. J. McGUIRE, Secretary,

184 William St., New York

NEW YORK, OCTOBER, 1883.

— A single ton of coal converted into steam and operating machinery can now do the work of 8,000 men.

— Our war is not against men but against the inhuman system that permits capitalists to take the lions share of our wealth.

—Saving is the result of acquisitiveness. The trouble with the workmen is not that they do not save enough, but that they can not *spend* enough.

-- Labor can never get the full result of its work under the present system of industry. Competition must be superseded by cooperation.

Every labor saving machine should help the whole world. Every one should tend to shorten the hours of labor and relieve the burdens of toil.

— It matters not whether our substance is stolen from us under the lash of the law, or under the lash of the slave master, the principle is the same and we are slaves.

— How is it your Astors, Scotts, Goulds, Belmonts and Vanderbilts possess hundreds of millions worth of the labor of others, and all they ever did was to stand between producer and consumer in the transit of wealth.

— The English trades union congress held its annual session this year in Nottingham and as usual transacted some very important business, a report of which will be found elsewhere in our columns. Frederick Harrison's paper on Trades Unions was a masterly effort and deserves the closest attention of all trades unionists.

— This great hydra of monied interests and corporate powers owns our Legislatures and Congress—being virtually the master of the laws, of the courts, the military, police and municipal forces, corrupting the press, subsidizing and degrading all whom it can buy, and crushing all who will not serve its interests.

REDUCE THE HOURS.

In the world of labor today we work too long.

We are not paid any more wages the longer we work.

Mr. Frederick ... longest hours the the work of the Trades ... and are the past 16 years. He said: The ... mon idea of a trade union is that it is an organization of workmen designed chiefly to give their support in strikes against their employers. Mr. Harrison shows that, so far as English unions are concerned, this is an error. They have more than doubled their numbers and incomes during the past sixteen years. Five of the principal unions, which did not in 1867 number in all 60,000 members, now have an aggregate membership of 125,000. During the same period they have doubled their incomes and their reserve funds. Trade in England suffered severe depression during these years, and the strain upon the unions was very great. Seven of them spent within six years nearly $10,000,000 in support of men out of work and for other charitable purposes, drawing upon their reserve funds for nearly $1,000,000, yet now they have an aggregate balance on hand of $1,800,000. The Engineers' Union alone paid $760,000 to men out of work ...

of these civilizing agencies. Ten hours labor today is more exhaustive than fourteen hours labor in the past. The high pressure system of labor that now prevails is destructive to human life, and unless something is done, it means the downfall of our race. But we have hope, yes, confident are we, that the time has come when the hours of labor must be reduced.

And if we can't get the eight-hour system, let us move on for nine hours. No matter if wages are reduced for awhile on account of the shorter hours. That need not be if the men are united. The main thing is to reduce the hours, after that the wages will rise before long. If 1,000 carpenters drop off one hour's work a day—work only nine hours a day—this will be 6,000 hours work less in the week, which will require 111 more men to do it.

The employment of this extra force relieves the labor market of a large surplus now out of work and takes away the element that is now used to reduce wages.

Why should we not reduce the hours of labor? In the words of a gifted poet we want:

> The leisure to live,
> The leisure to love,
> The leisure to taste our freedom.

CHANGES NEEDED.

There are some few points in our Brotherhood constitution which need amendment. We can do this very well and very satisfactorily, by means of a general vote the same as we elected our General Officers. In that way the wishes of the members are consulted and their judgments called into exercise.

For instance, the Endowment Fund needs to be more secure, and certain provisions should be attached to it not only to make it secure but also prompt of payment. Furthermore it should be only granted to members one year in our B. And in cases of married men, where the death of the wife occurs, a certain part of their $250 claim should be set aside subject to be called upon by the member entitled. This would make the Endowment Fund a veritable Insurance for the families of our members and would make the wife feel interested just as much as if she were a member. This would be no wrong to the single members, as their $250 would remain intact for whomsoever they would will it. The married men might have say $100 out $250 in case of the wife's death.

We might also institute a Tool Insurance of say $30 just sufficient to cover a working kit. It would be a blessing to many and would make our members doubly interested and bring many backward ones up to join us.

Think over these suggestions.

AN ARGUMENT IN FAVOR OF OUR ENDOWMENT FUND.

In the August CARPENTER I see that "Argus" finds a great deal of fault w... ... of the General Convention the face side; then size the face ... keeping the back damp until the size is sufficiently dry for the cold, and it will be observed, on coming from the cold, to be round on the face or veneered side, and may be kept nearly so by placing the veneered side against a flat board, or the two veneered sides face to face, to dry gradually. Of course after trying this experiment it will be necessary to know how long the article will require swelling. Considering the pine fairly seasoned and the veneer well dry, one night as a rule is sufficient.

— Wood Carvers National Union met in convention at Cincinnati, Oct. 16.

— In NEW SOUTH WALES, Australia, an employers liability act has been passed and also a law to legalize trades unions.

50, and working at a very healthy business, and he will find by statistics that mortality is not more than from 3½ to 4 to the thousand, and no high salaried officers and canvassers to pay.

I cannot see why there should be such a hue and cry about the Endowment until it has been fully tried. My opinion is that it will work very well; and if by some sad accident we should happen to lose more than the usual quota of members, which might take a little more than is in the Endowment Fund, how easy it would be to call on our regular fund for a small assessment to meet the extra call. Now, as Treasurer of one of our local Unions, I have a good chance of information. Our Union has complied with the law to the letter, laid aside the proper amount monthly, and paid all assessments promptly on notification, and still we have a large sum to the credit of Endowments, fully enough to pay ten more assessments at the same rate of the last that we paid. Now, I am sure this does not look like going behind, and I hope it will not be changed until our treasuries become depleted by an extra draw on them. Then it will be time enough to change.

Now I would like to ask the few Locals that are making such a time about this fund, if they have complied with the law. If so, tell us how it is they have not plenty of funds to meet all assessments and a nice balance left for future calls?

I also see by your correspondent from Washington, that the Endowment as it stands, does not meet with the general approval of the members of Union No. 1. It seems to me that they have made more complaint about it than any other Union in the Order. He gives as a reason that most of the members are in some other Endowment, and therefore, to suit them, those that are not connected with other like funds ought to give way. In the name of common sense, what kind of an argument is it, that many thousand members not prepared as these are, should bow to them and to their will? I would like to ask those members where they get the funds to pay premiums in other organizations if it is not from their labor and from the benefit they gain from the labor organizations of the present day?

If it were not for labor unions we would have a very small surplus to pay premiums on life insurance. My opinion is that labor organizations are the foundation of all societies, and are the best and most beneficial of all. I have been a member of all the benevolent and beneficial societies of the present day. I have now ignored them all, and pay strict attention to labor unions only. I have found out to my satisfaction that I receive a double benefit by getting acquainted with all the members of my craft, and by combining against reduction in pay, and by trying to teach my fellow laborers that eight hours is a fair day's work.

If mechanics and laborers would establish their institutions on the same basis as the Odd Fellows, or Red Men or other societies of the same kind, they would find it greatly to their advantage to keep their dues well paid up in their unions, and if there is any surplus left, pay to the other societies. And if they can't keep up in both, then stand by the labor societies first of all, as they are the very foundation of the rest. If we can obtain the same feeling of union among us as exists in other beneficial and benevolent institutions, there is no danger of failure.

Raise the initiation fees and dues to the same as others and pay the same b... and endowment—say five ... than and six dollars ... draw from ... and w...

... a close ... only way that ... in a solid unit.

J. T. B.

BALTIMORE, Md.

— Our new blanks for "Notice of Arrears" are convenient for every Union to have.

—On October 1st, the tenement house Cigar Manufacturers started out to violate the law, which went into effect that day against the system of tenement factories. Yet capitalists pride themselves on being law-and-order people.

—Endowment papers in the death of the late Bro. Stephen A. Sorenson, deceased, of San Rafael Union No. 35, have been sent us, and they show death has occurred from consumption. The family are entitled to benefit.

GENERAL OFFICERS ELECTED.

The general vote for election of general officers of the Brotherhood is now closed and the result determined. A private circular with the details of the vote will be sent to all unions. The cost of a convention has been dispensed with, and too many unions have been spared from drawing upon their funds to send delegates. As but few changes in our constitution are requisite and these can also be effected by general vote, the Brotherhood is now on a fair road to success the coming year. All that is necessary is for each and every union and every member to give his ... services and all his efforts to aid our newly elected officers. The general officers elected are:

GENERAL PRESIDENT—J. P. McGinley, Chicago, Ill.

GENERAL SECRETARY—P. J. McGuire, New York.

1st VICE PRESIDENT—Thos. Blai... Chicago, Ill.

2d VICE PRESIDENT—Gus. Bre... Cincinnati, Ohio.

3d VICE PRESIDENT—John ... Boston, Mass.

4th VICE PRESIDENT—R. Stephens, Oakland, Cal.

5th VICE PRESIDENT—Thos. W. S..., Hamilton, Canada.

6th VICE PRESIDENT—Chas. Armstrong, Toronto, Canada.

7th VICE PRESIDENT—James O..., Philadelphia, Pa.

8th VICE PRESIDENT—Thos. J..., Chicago, Ill.

THE DESIRE FOR INDEPENDENCE.

The desire for independence and a better condition which comes with education, brings the laborer into conflict with the opposing conservatism of the past; and as men will not freely yield power or privileges once enjoyed, so it happens that employers and the public have been slow to recognize the increasing strength and intelligence of the workingman who is disposed to encroach on their prerogatives.

But capital is no longer the master of labor. And, though strikes are not to be encouraged, yet as political revolutions have frequently forced more liberal and progressive ideas on governments, so, we believe, these labor conflicts have been largely the means through which labor has attained its present social recognition. Strikes, therefore, only result from unwillingness to adopt more rational means of adjusting differences and settling disputes. The mission of trades unions is to supply better and more peaceful methods, and it is a fact, well attested, that where the workmen are disciplined by organization, disputes between employer and employed are infrequent. Indeed, many of the largest manufacturers of this State no longer seek to destroy the unions, but admit their advantages. This is especially true in some of the New Jersey glass factories, where the workmen receive higher average wages than those of any other trade.

SPECIAL NOTICES.

BROTHERHOOD NOTES.

Boston Union No. 33 will have its ... Annual Ball, Oct., 24th.

Cincinnati Carpenters Union No. 2 is ... for a Winter Nights Festival ...

... Union No. 33 has made ar... to form a Union in Lynn, ...

... Union has been chartered ... of Nashville, Tenn. May it ... prosper.

... in Hamilton, Canada, is dull; ... the prospects will be brighter ...

... more Union No. 29 has had a lot of ... badges manufactured similar to those of the Chicago Union.

The money for the Endowment Fund ... be kept separate from all other funds ... Unions.

... No. 18 of Victoria, British Co... is growing rapidly indeed; the ... fifty cents monthly.

... Financial Secretary of To... Union No. 27 is an admirably prompt ... Would that others were like him.

St. Catherines Union No. 38 proposes ... its monthly due. They pro... to organize Galt. Bro. Andrews is ...

In Hartford business is good, and all union men at work. All the Unions in ... city have voted to form a Trades Assembly.

Pay the endowment quota quickly whenever called on, for we can not tell what moment an appeal may have to be made for the death claim of any one of us.

— When members start out to travel they should take travelling cards with them or else they will have trouble in many places and be looked on as "scabs."

—The Independent Carpenters' Union of Cincinnati has been disbanded, and the funds have been turned over to the Bethel. Thus all trouble in Porkopolis is settled.

In the Cincinnati Trades Assembly two members of Carpenters Union No. 2 are officers. Gus. Brethauer is Recording Secretary and John Valerius is Sergeant-at-Arms.

In small towns like Rushville, Ind., complaints are made about the excess charges of grocers. The only remedy is for the members to club together and buy their provisions on the cooperative basis somewhere else.

We can not understand why the St. Louis *Union* makes it an object to continually report the dissolution of some of the carpenters unions of that city? It would be better for that paper to do something to organize the working classes than to disorganize them.

We want every member of our Brotherhood who travels to be a missionary in our cause. They should be filled with the fire and zeal of enthusiasts, and as they go from place to place they should leave a Carpenters Union organized behind them. Organize Unions wherever you go.

San Francisco Union 22 initiated 110 new members during the past three months and has a good sized bank account to its credit and that is what every Union ought to have. But they can't have it unless they have at least 50 cents per month as dues — even more would be better.

A correspondent from Cincinnati advises that Union No. 2 shall take action against piece work on buildings in that city. He states that on several buildings in that city piece work is the rule and that the system is spreading. A move should be made against this wrong. And Union No. 2 will do it.

— Jacob Wasmleker and Chas. Seleseman of Cincinnati Union 2 suffered severe injuries by falling. A picnic for their benefit on Sept., 15th, arranged by the Union netted $61,00 each for the families of these two men. The committee and the union deserve great credit and have been publicly thanked through the press.

— From the best of sources we learn that [illegible]

Homestead Law.

CHICAGO REPORTS.

BRANCH 6. I have to report the death of H. KRETCHNER, August 15, (of typho-malarial fever), a member of Branch 6, in good standing. He died at Hammond, Ind. I have written for death and burial certificates 5 weeks ago, but as yet have heard no more from the family.

I am much pleased with THE CARPENTER, will distribute it in Branch 6 to-night. Trade is fair, wages $2.75 to $3; lots of building, and plenty of non-union men.

GENERAL REPORT. Business is pretty brisk just now in this city, and fair prospects for the Winter. But we would not advise any one to come here, for they will find it uphill work as strangers to get employment. Only union men are wanted, and even then it is better for them to stay where they are than ramble about. Wages are $2.75-$3 per day. Our Building League has had its Summer vacation and is now springing into renewed life. The Trades Assembly has taken up the subject and is pushing it.

NEUTRAL ON TARIFF VS. FREE TRADE.

Frank K Foster of Cambridge, Mass., the newly elected Secretary of the Federation of Trades has issued an open letter to John Jarrett, Ex-President of the Amalgamated Iron and Steel Workers. In his letter Foster sets at rest the charge that the Federation had declared in favor of free trade as intimated by the iron workers. And on this point he says: "The proceedings of the Cleveland session of the Federation, to which you refer, contain no "censures on tariff." It was the unanimous desire of the delegate composing that convention that the Federation should remain unpledged upon this vexed question, and protectionists as well as free-traders voted for the motion to place the Congress upon a neutral footing in this matter. It was believed that the tariff was a *political issue*, and one upon which men equally honest in the labor movement might always differ. It was thought best, therefore, while so large a field for harmonious and united action remained open for trade unionists, that the tariff plank should not be forced upon those who could otherwise subscribe to our platform of principles."

A CIRCULAR FROM OUR RETIRING GENERAL PRESIDENT.

TO ALL LOCAL UNIONS.

PHILADELPHIA, Pa., Oct. 15, '83.

Brothers,

In accordance with my duty as General President, it affords me great pleasure to declare the following named brothers as General Officers of the B. for the ensuing year. This is based upon the report made to me this day by the General Trustees who have compiled the votes as returned by your respective Unions, and they find the following have received the highest vote for the respective offices and are consequently elected;

John P. McGinley, Gen'l President.
P. J. McGuire, Gen'l Secretary.

Thos. Blair,	1st	Vice President.
Gus. Brethauer,	2d	"
John Clasby,	3d	"
R. Stephens,	4th	"
Thos. W. Scott,	5th	"
Chas. Armstrong,	6th	"
James Orrick,	7th	"
Thos. Jones,	8th	"

The Executive Board for the ensuing year will consist of:

John P. McGinley, of Chicago.
Thos. Blair, of Chicago.
Gus. Brethauer, of Cincinnati.

By reference to Official Circular No. 2, you will find the authority delegated to me to make this announcement.

By virtue of my office, I hereby decide that on Monday, Oct. 29, 1883, the newly elected officers of the Brotherhood shall assume the duties of their respective offices to serve until their successors are duly elected and installed.

In retiring from office, let me say I trust you will ever remain faithful and obedient to the laws and usages of our organization, and that you will strengthen the hands of your officers by your confidence in them and appreciation of their ability. [illegible]

B., and for health, strength and long life to our new officers, and success to their efforts, I thank you for your many tokens of respect to me in the past, and I hope that my acts shall always be such as will merit a continuance of your good will.

Fraternally yours,

JOHN D. ALLEN,
Gen'l President.

THE LABOR QUESTION.

LECTURE X.

If the previous lectures have been of service in pointing out the elements which enter into the formation of wealth, they have done no injury. If they have resulted in inspiring a desire to become more fully acquainted with the nature and importance of these elements, they have done good. If they have determined some few of our members to seek for the fundamental causes of of the present unhappy and impoverished condition of the workers, and to lay a secure foundation for the means to avoid poverty and misery in the future, then our object in presenting them will have been fully accomplished.

If we look at all that has been attempted in the past, we shall be compelled to admit, in all justice to the workers, that they have made many noble and self-sacrificing efforts to better their own condition and that of their fellow laborers. It cannot, therefore, be charged that it is a want either of desire on their part to alleviate themselves or of sympathy for their fellows, which has prevented them from elevating their brothers.

It is not their hearts that have failed, but their heads; not the desire to do, but the knowledge *how* to do; not ignorance of the end, but ignorance of the means. In fact, the whole history of the workers proves that their objects have been worthy, noble and holy; but but their *methods* have been inefficient or incorrect. The aspiration through the sympathies has constantly been present; the knowledge through the intellect has been absent. They have not failed by reason of their hearts, they have failed by reason of their heads. They have failed, not because they could not *feel*; they have failed because they could not *think*. Their aspirations, their feelings, their sympathies, have been generous and sublime; their knowledge, their thoughts, their reasoning, have been puny and impotent.

Seeing that the workers have not succeeded in extricating themselves from the suffering attendant upon poverty in the past, what then, remains to be done? To *know* correctly certain things, to think correctly about certain things, to reason correctly about certain things; that is, to analyse and synthesise that which we know, that which we think, and that which we feel, and to practice that which we feel by reason of the knowledge which we possess; in other words, to correctly establish our premises, and as correctly to draw our conclusions therefrom.

Now, all that has been done in these lectures hitherto is to establish premises, no attempt has been made to draw conclusions. It is useless to go further until these premises be examined—if faulty, corrected; if false, rejected. It therefore remains with you to examine, and either to correct or improve, to reject or approve. That is the business—I may say duty—of our members, to whom these lectures have been presented; as an individual member I have performed mine in presenting them.

Let me, then, ask you one or two brief questions and give briefly the reply.

We have already accepted as axioms—

1. Labor creates all wealth.
2. Wealth belongs to those who create it.
3. The productive capacity of society is superior to the consumptive capacity of society.

We confine ourselves to the possible, and do not care to sophisticate. The economists assert that the power of consumption is limited only by mans power of production, and, in order to prove this, they assert that the imagination can create wants which are ever increasing in a greater ratio than his power to supply them. We cannot admit that all the desires of the imagination can be construed to constitute a want. If the imagination prompts a man to want the moon, of course the labor of all men could not supply such a want. To supply the demand which might spring from the imagination of one or two patients [in] a lunatic asylum, all the labor of a [world] might not suffice.

If the first and second axioms are correct, which they certainly are, the laborer should not be in poverty, since it is the laborer who makes all the wealth, and yet it cannot be denied that he is poor.

Why, then is he poor?

Simply because he is ignorant of the laws which regulate industrial, economic [and] social phenomena; and he is also [illegible] in subjection to the crafty, subtle, cunning [illegible] although perfectly their [illegible] funds are pursued to subject yet [illegible] have all a portion of the hand [illegible] 000. alone [illegible] 000 to[illegible]ion is correct, poverty should not exist upon the face of the earth, and yet it cannot be denied that it does exist.

Why does it exist?

Because there exist two *classes* in the world the *Producers* and the *Non-Producers*.

Because part of that which is produced by the workers is taken from them by the idlers.

Because the workers have not the knowledge necessary to prevent the idlers from securing a part of that which the workers produce by their labor, and that part the greater part.

These are the reasons.

It then becomes our business, as well as our interest, and our duty, to inquire through what agencies the laborers are deprived of the fruits of their toil.

Let us not forget to bear constantly in mind that the five elements of production are, Land, Labor, Capital, Exchange and Insurance. Now from the proceeds of Industry—

The Landlord takes Rent
" Banker " Interest.
" { Capitalists, Employer, Exchanger or Merchant, } takes Profit

Therefore, to Rent, Interest and Profit goes the lion's share of the proceeds of Industry, leaving to the laborer enough food in times when trade is good and he is in health; only want and hunger in dull times; charity, the almshouse, the hospital and starvation when he is sick, old and worn out.

How does this fact of rent, interest and profit agree with our five fundamental elements?

Rent	goes to the	Landlord,
Interest	" " "	Capitalist
Profit	" " "	Exchanger,
Wages	" " "	Laborer.

And we might show that Insurance is divided among the three first mentioned.

Therefore we may naturally conclude that four-fifths of the total product go to those who own land and capital, perform exchanges and employ labor, while but one fifth goes to the laborer as wages.

Now it will be seen that as land and capital are in the hands of those who employ labor, perform the function of exchange and rent the land, four-fifths of the wealth of the world go to one class of men, who are principly non-producers or idlers, while but one-fifth goes to another class of men, who are the producers—the workers.

I know that the landlord, the capitalist the exchanger and the employer, are not frequently found combined in the same person. To make a complete analysis of them, although it would be proper to an economic treatise, would be out of place in a series of brief addresses such as these; I therefore pass it by with mere mention, and will treat it later on more fully.

But whether the laborer is compelled to relinquish four-fifths of his production to one man, or whether three or four men divide it among them, the result of the laborer is precisely the same, viz., he is deprived of four-fifths of the result of his labor.

Now let us remark, that while profit which goes to the exchanger may be secured to the laborer by organization—which is the object of societies of consumption—it affects the problem in but one-fifth of its totality; the problem being to give to labor all that labor creates or produces.

Further, let us remark that while the elementes, Land and Capital, hold their predominant sway, rent and interest, represented by the landlord and capitalist, will be able to extort this one-fifth, belonging to exchange, from the laborer, with as great facility as exchange, represented by the merchant, extorted this one-fifth from the laborer; the only difference being that it will take a little longer time to accomplish the feat; in other words, the profit which went to the merchant or exchanger will find its way into the pockets of the capitalist and the landlord.

Hence we see that the resolving of the one-fifth of the problem has but a momentary result, that it is not permanent; in fact, that eventually it resolves nothing.

Tis, therefore, we are treading the rounds of a vicious circle, and always returning to the same point; never starting off in a direct forward line from the centre to the circumference. Like the weary traveler on the plains, desirous of quickly reaching his journey's end, he walks all night in the dark, and when daylight appears he finds himself footsore, weary, disappointed and exhausted at the place from whence he started, having lost his time and expended his forces going blindly in a circle, while thinking he was proceeding in a straight line. So it is with the vast energies which the workers have deployed in times past, it has brought them round to the same point of the vicious circle, although at each struggling attempt the circumference has been enlarged.

Suppose we do give to the laborer that portion which now goes to the exchanger, are not the landlord and capitalist still there ready to retake it? Even though we do eliminate the exchanger, what is its economic significance? Simply that we increase the purchasing power of wages, which means that we reduce the cost of living.

It may be argued that you will, at the same time, increase the consuming power by increasing the culture and intelligence of the workers, but you cannot *increase* intelligence as quickly as you can *decrease* wages; the capitalist would be first in the race, having the benefit of the start. Labor is always the under dog in the fight.

What regulates the rate of wages under the present industrial system?

The cost of living!

Ergo—reduce the cost of living under the present system and you reduce the rate of wages and the power of Land and Capital is there, ever potent, ever cruel and ever ready to enforce this economic effect, and this power, this cruelty will ever be exercised against us while we confine our efforts to the single element of Exchange.

So it is with capital, (I use the word in its fullest meaning); if we confine our efforts to control capital and become our own capitalists, the element "Land," represented by the landlord, will be ever there to defeat us, and will forever swallow us up. No matter how great the amount of capital possessed, it cannot be used or made fruitful without the use of the land, and if all those who hold capital to-day were to invest that capital in land, and thus release or relinquish their capital—and if we, the workers, hold all this capital to-morrow, the landlords could and would so increase the rent of their land as to extort back or re-obtain the whole of their capital again in two, five, six, ten or twenty years; the amount of time it would take to do so would not alter the fact or its influences one iota.

After they had accomplished this end the condition of the laborer would be precisely what it is to day, the only difference being that instead of being deprived of four-fifths of that which he produces, by four different men under the name of landlord, capitalist, merchant and employer, in the shape of rent, interest and profits, he would be deprived of four-fifths of the total products of his labor by the one person named, the landlord, who would control the one element, Land.

This brings us back to the starting point—the *Land*. If the attention of the workingmen is to be turned in any one direction, it should be to the land—that is the bank into which to place their savings. The land—that bank has never been a defaulter, has never "busted" it is in that bank that the greatest interest is returned, whether the laborer invests his money or his labor.

We hope that we have said sufficient to make it clear that the whole of human activities find their expression through five elements—

1. Land.
2. Labor.
3. Capital.
4. Exchange.
5. Insurance.

And next that this is the logical and indisputable order of their existence. We do do not pretend to have made a complete analysis of these five elements, or mediums through which society expresses its activities. We are aware that they are subject to a further sub-division which we will give more in detail when we come to take up each of the elements in a more exhaustive essay. We do not claim that the one is superior to, or of more importance than, the others; but we do claim that neither the third, fourth or fifth element can be successfully controlled until we have control of the first element. In other words, no matter how well we may be able to control Capital, Exchange and Insurance, if we cannot also control the land, our situation, although it may be momentarily alleviated, can never be permanently improved.

DRURY.

—Das Achtstunden-System wurde in Australien zuerst von den Maurern am 24. März 1856 adoptirt und wurde am 21. April auch bei den übrigen Bauhandwerken eingeführt. Bald darauf wurde es von allen Arbeitszweigen angenommen.

Der Carpenter.

New York, Oktober 1883.

An alle Bauschreiner und Zimmerleute.

Gewerksgenossen! Wie lange wollt Ihr noch warten, bis Ihr Euch entschließen könnt, Euch zu organisiren, oder glaubt Ihr, daß sich Eure Lage von selbst verbessere? Solltet Ihr das Letztere abwarten, so werdet Ihr im Laufe der Zeit finden, daß Ihr Euch geirrt habt, denn Ihr könnt von dem heutigen Gesellschafts-System nichts erwarten. Die Säulen, auf welchen das heutige System ruht, sind Personen, welche Euch ausbeuten und knechten, Haß und Hader in Eure Familien bringen, Eure Kinder von den Schulen fern halten und in die Fabriken ziehen, damit sie billige Arbeitskräfte erhalten. Die Träger des Systems sind Raubthiere in Menschengestalt, die Euch ihre Dienste aufbürden, welche Euch glauben machen von der großen Vorrathskammer mit all den schönen Genüssen, welche über den Sternen sein soll. Die Euch die politischen Drahtzieher der allen Parteien bestimmen, welche Euch als Stimmvieh fangen sollen, es sind die, welche bestimmen, welchen Beamten Ihr zu wählen habt, damit diese wieder für Jene, die Gesetze machen und ausführen, um Eure Ausbeutung noch ungehindert weiter betreiben zu können; und daß sie dieses wollen, beweisen die Aussagen von Jay Gould und John Roach, Letzterer Schiffsbauer in Chester, Pa., vor dem Senats-Kommittee über die Lage der arbeitenden Klassen. Wollt Ihr Eure Lage verbessern, wollt Ihr die Produkte Eurer Arbeit selbst genießen, so müßt Ihr Euch organisiren in Gewerkschaften, oder als Mitglieder in schon bestehende eintreten, dann müßt Ihr dahin wirken, das heutige ungerechte System zu stürzen. Das System ist der Wille der Machthaber, erhalten durch Militär und Gesetzgeber. Es erhält Euch in Sclaverei, es schafft Euer Elend, erhält Euch in hündischer Demuth und verkürzt Eure und Eurer Kinder Lebensdauer. G. H.

Englische Gewerkschaften und Strikes.

Ein Herr Frederic Harrison in London beschäftigt sich mit der Statistik der Gewerkschaften Großbritaniens und sucht ihnen politische Freunde zu machen. Ein Vortrag, welchen er zu diesem Zwecke neulich in London gehalten, beabsichtigt, den Leuten die Vorstellung zu benehmen, als seien die Gewerkschaften blos zum Behufe von Ausständen gegründet und wirksam. Dies sei in Betreff der britischen ein großer Irrthum. In den letzten sechs Jahren hätten sieben davon zusammen zehn Millionen Dollars ausgegeben, wovon nur $800,000 zur Unterstützung Ausständiger, also kaum ein Zwölftel sämmtlicher Ausgaben. Alles Uebrige sei für verschiedene gegenseitige Unterstützungs verwendet worden (Kranken-, Sterbe-, Invaliden- und andere Kassen) und trotzdem, daß die Zeiten sehr traurig gewesen seien, zumal im Jahre 1879, da fünf von diesen Gewerkschaften allein 40,000 Mann ganz aus diesen Kassen hätten unterhalten werden müssen, was 5 Millionen Dollars gekostet habe. Diese fünf, die ältesten Gewerkschaften, hätten von einer gleichzeitigen Einnahme von $1,650,000 und aus angesammelten Fonds von $1,850,000 nur $25,000, also noch nicht 1 Procent zu Ausstands- und Schiedsgerichts-Zwecken verausgabt. Dies beweise schlagend, daß die Gewerkschaften, je älter und besser organisirt und je größer ihre Fonds seien, desto weniger zu Ausständen griffen und desto mehr der gegenseitigen Unterstützung lebten, also den Gemeinden viele Armenversorgung ersparten und dem Lande selbstständige Bürger heran erzögen.

Wir haben die Wahrheit von dem Allen zu bezweifeln keinen Grund, müssen jedoch bemerken, daß diese Gewerkschaften so viel wechselseitige Unterstützungskraft entwickeln konnten, blos weil sie durch „Strikes" ihre Ausbeuter nachgiebig gemacht hatten. Die „Strikes" waren auch deswegen überflüssig geworden, seitdem der kurze Werktag, die Beschränkung der Frauen- und Kinderarbeit und andere Verbesserungen ihrer Lage durch Gesetze erreicht waren. Wenn die Gewerkschaften in anderen Ländern nicht so viel auf Unterstützung unter einander verwenden, so kommt dies weniger von ihrem Belieben her, als von weniger günstigen Umständen, sowie besonders daher, daß die Organisation noch so jung, während sie in England so alt ist. Auch ist es gerade kein Ruhm zu nennen, daß die Gewerkschaften den Gemeinden Armen-Unterstützung ersparen; eher möchten wir es einen Ruhm nennen, daß sie den Profit der Arbeitgeber auf ein bescheidenes Maß durch Lohnsteigerung herabgedrückt haben. Im Uebrigen bestätigt Herr Harrison Alles, was wir von den britischen Gewerkschaften gesagt haben. (Volkszeitung.)

Ueber die Gewerkschaftsbewegung

sagte Dr. Douai vor dem Senats-Committee Folgendes: Zu Anfang des 19. Jahrhunderts betrug die tägliche Arbeitszeit 14—16 Stunden. Die Gewerkschaftler wurden als Verschwörer angesehen und ihre Versammlungen verfolgt. Als die Maschinen in den Fabriken aufkamen, zerstörten die Gewerkschaftler dieselben. Sie standen aber davon ab und kamen zu der Ueberzeugung, daß die Maschinen wohlthätig wirken würden, wenn sie Allen gehörten. Die Verschwörungsgesetze gegen die Gewerkschaften seien schließlich abgeschafft worden und es hätten sich gegenseitige Unterstützungs-Gesellschaften u. dergl. gebildet. Besonders in England florirten dieselben. Die Gesellschaften hielten Jahres-Congresse ab und übten einen großen Einfluß auf die Gesetzgebung aus, um die Lage der Arbeiter zu bessern. Es seien Gesetze gegen Frauen- und Kinderarbeit, zur Inspection der Fabriken und Bergwerke erlassen und das Wahlrecht ausgedehnt worden. Es bildeten sich auch Cooperativ-Vereine, welche produciren und consumiren. Durch die Gewerkschaften seien die Beziehungen zwischen Arbeitern und Kapitalisten in vereinzelten Fällen angenehmer geworden; Zeuge kennt selbst Kapitalisten, welche bekennen, daß ihre Arbeiter nicht genug vom Arbeitsertrag erhalten. Im Allgemeinen sei die Lage der Arbeiter hierzulande eine elende und sie werden sehr schlecht behandelt. Wo die Arbeiter sich organisiren, mildere sich der Kampf zwischen Kapital und Arbeit. In den Ver. Staaten erhalte der Arbeiter im Durchschnitt nur 17½ Prozent vom Arbeitsertrag und der Kapitalist 19 Prozent; dies werde durch den Census bewiesen. Wenn die Löhne der Arbeiter z. B. um 20 Prozent erhöht würden, mache das auf die Waare nur 3 Prozent. Durch die Lohnerhöhung verliere der Kapitalist stets am Profit, aber die Masse der Produkte werde vermehrt, weil die höheren Löhne einen größeren Consum bedingen. Da die Arbeiter den größten Theil ihres Lohnes für Rente und Lebensmittel ausgeben und die beim Hausbau und der Production von Nahrungsmitteln angestellten Arbeiter nur einen Antheil vom Product in geringen Löhnen erhalten, würde eine Lohnerhöhung für alle Arbeiter dem Consumenten nicht besonders oder gar nicht fühlbar werden. Bei fast jeder Waare, die zu den Nahrungsmitteln und der Wohnung gehören, bilde das Rohmaterial 80 bis 90 Prozent des Werthes, und aus diesem Grunde schon treffe eine Lohnerhöhung den Consumenten weniger, als allgemein angenommen werde. Die Gewerkschaften streben eine Verbesserung der Lage ihrer Mitglieder an; dies geschehe durch Lohnerhöhung oder Verkürzung des Werktags, und aus Erfahrung wüßten sie, daß Alles, was dem Lohne zuwachse, dem Kapital abgezogen werde, und umgekehrt. Das Endziel der Arbeiterbewegung sei die vollständige Beseitigung des Profitnehmens.

Correspondenzen.

Toledo, O.—Union No. 25 im schönsten Wachsen begriffen, massenhafte Tramp Carpenters in der Stadt und viele Leute außer Arbeit. Einige Bosse möchten den Lohn gern herabdrücken. Unionleute bekommen $2.25, die Tramps arbeiten für $1.50. Wir haben unter dem Staatsgesetz einen Charter erwirkt.

Trenton, N. J.—Unsere Union hat die Aufnahmegebühr auf $4 erhöht und die Mitgliedschaft nimmt stetig zu.

Washington, D. C.—Die „Knights of Labor" versuchten neulich, Union No. 1 zu disorganisiren, es gelang ihnen aber nicht. Sie beriefen eine Versammlung ein, um eine Carpenters' Assembly zu gründen, unsere Leute aber ließen sich darauf nicht ein und blieben der Brüderschaft treu.

Wilchey, Mo.—$1.25 bis $2 per Tag.

Sarcopia, Mo. — Sehr viel Arbeit; Löhne niedrig.

— Union No. 22 in San Francisco hat während der letzten drei Monate 110 neue Mitglieder aufgenommen und in der Bank hat die Union eine hübsche Summe Geld — und so könnte jede Union es haben; dann müßten aber die Beiträge auf 50 Cents erhöht werden — je höher, desto besser.

— Bei der Convention der Internationalen Union der Cigarrenmacher, welche letzten Monat zu Toronto stattfand, wurden die Wochenbeiträge auf 20 Cents, das Sterbegeld auf $40 und die wöchentliche Krankenunterstützung auf $5 festgesetzt. Die Frage, ob bei Arbeitslosigkeit Unterstützung ausgezahlt werden soll, wurde den Unionen zur Entscheidung überwiesen und beschlossen, einen General-Organisator durch das Land zu schicken. Diese Organisation hält nur Conventionen ab, wenn die [illegible] Unionen es durch Abstimmung verlangen.

Gewerbs-Notizen.

— Union No. 50 ist in Portland, Oregon, organisirt worden.

— Eine Carpenters Union ist soeben in Paterson, N. J., gegründet worden und sie verspricht das Beste für die Zukunft. Eine andere bildet sich in Richmond, Va.

— Hohe Beiträge sollten in unseren Central-Unionen an der Tagesordnung sein; eine auf 25 Cts. per Monat basirte Gewerkschaft ist die reinste Spielerei. Und diese Thatsache wird von vielen unserer Unionen anerkannt, denn sie beginnen ihre Beiträge auf 50 Cents per Monat zu erhöhen.

— Unser Ex-Präsident G. Edmonston, Washington, D. C., fungirte als Delegat bei dem Gewerkschafts-Congreß, welcher im letzten Monat hier abgehalten wurde und er hat seine Ausgaben für Reisespesen &c. der Brüderschaft nicht angerechnet. Wir werden ihm das nicht vergessen und ihm seiner Zeit dafür dankbar sein.

— Nieder mit der Stückarbeit im Carpenter-Geschäft! Das Publikum wird damit betrogen, denn sie führt zur Pfuscherei und zur Bummelei — sie ist einfach unehrlich. Sie bringt den Arbeitern Schaden, indem sie die Concurrenz unter ihnen vermehrt, sie macht den Arbeiter habgierig und selbstsüchtig und ist dem ganzen Handwerk ein wahrer Fluch.

— Wir verlangen strenge Haftpflicht-Gesetze in allen Staaten und fordern, daß alle Zahlungs-Urtheile, die Arbeiter gegen Bosse erwirkt haben, unverzüglich vollstreckt werden. Lohnansprüche sollten allen anderen Gläubigerforderungen oder Hypothekenansprüchen vorgezogen werden. Die Arbeiter haben ein Recht, in ihren Ansprüchen auf das Resultat ihrer Arbeit beschützt zu werden.

— Eine Werkzeug-Versicherung ist von größerer Wichtigkeit für unsere Brüderschaft, als irgend eine andere Einrichtung, die wir treffen können. Sie braucht nur ganz wenig zu kosten und das Benefit könnte auf $30 beschränkt werden, damit für alle gewöhnlich vorkommenden Fälle das Werkzeug wieder angeschafft werden könnte. Bei Feuer oder anderen Unfällen würde eine Werkzeug-Versicherung eine Wohlthat für Viele sein, welche sonst in Verlegenheit sein würden, wie sie ihre Werkzeuge ersetzen sollen.

Spähne aller Art.

— Die Gewerkschaften von Philadelphia sind im Begriff, eine Central-Labor-Union wie die in New York zu organisiren.

— Die Frage betreffs Abschaffung der Gefängniß-Contract-Arbeit wird bei der nächsten Herbstwahl dem Volke dieses Staates zur Abstimmung vorgelegt werden.

— Die Union-Carpenter in Schottland arbeiten neun Stunden per Tag und feiern einen halben Tag Samstags, also arbeiten sie 51 Stunden per Woche.

— Die Bäckerei-Arbeiter von New York haben eine Bewegung gegen die Sonntagsarbeit in's Leben gerufen und ein Boß ist bereits verhaftet und bestraft worden.

— Die New Yorker Tenementhaus-Cigarren-Fabrikanten bekämpfen das neue Gesetz, durch welches die Cigarren-Fabrikation in Tenementhäusern verboten wird.

— Die belgischen Glasbläser, welche hierher importirt wurden, um als „Scabs" zu dienen, gehen nach Belgien zurück, wo ihnen $130 in Gold per Monat geboten werden.

— Seit Jahren haben wir die Organisirung der Kohlengräber im ganzen Lande befürwortet. Dies ist jetzt endlich durch die Begründung der Miners' National Association geschehen.

— In Toronto, Canada, wird im December dieses Jahres ein Arbeiter-Congreß für alle Theile der Dominion abgehalten werden, dessen Zweck es ist, eine in Aussicht genommene Volksgesetzgebung gründlich zu besprechen.

— Der Strike der Schreiner in Stuttgart ist im Großen und Ganzen beendigt und die Forderungen der Arbeiter sind in der Hauptsache bewilligt. Mit dem Ausschluß sind die Fabrikanten gründlich hereingefallen.

— Der Aufruf zu einer Arbeiter-Convention, die am 12. Januar in Philadelphia gehalten werden soll, um eine Arbeiter-Partei zu gründen, geht von einer Clique politischer Schnorrer in New York aus, hinter die sich der berüchtigte Denis Kearney gesteckt hat.

— John G. Warwick, demokratischer Vice-Gouverneurs-Candidat von Ohio, ist bei der Wahl durchgefallen, weil er im Jahre 1876 die Miliz herausbeorderte, um die Kohlengräber von Massillon, Ohio, niederzuschießen. Er erhielt 20,000 Stimmen weniger, als die übrigen Candidaten seiner Partei.

Ein Arbeiter-Congreß.

Der sechszehnte Jahres-Congreß der Trades Unions in England trat am 15. September in Nottingham zusammen. Es waren 131 Vereine durch 160 Delegaten vertreten, welche 552,000 Mitglieder repräsentirten. Unter den betheiligten Vereinen waren fünf Vereine von Möbelschreinern mit einer Mitgliederzahl von 4,500 durch fünf Delegaten vertreten. Ferner waren vertreten 4 Vereine von Bauschreinern mit einer Mitgliederzahl von 22,500 durch 4 Delegaten. Einer der wichtigsten Gegenstände, über welche verhandelt wurde, war das Haftpflichtgesetz, welches seit zwei Jahren in Wirksamkeit ist.

Das Gesetz wurde seit seiner Einführung auf verschiedene Weise zu umgehen oder illusorisch zu machen gesucht. Vielfach werden die Arbeiter von den Arbeitgebern gezwungen, Contracte zu unterzeichnen, wodurch sie der Entschädigung bei einem Unfall verlustig gehen.

Ein Delegat berichtete, daß in Lancashire nicht weniger als 40,000 Arbeiter gezwungen wurden, solche Contracte zu unterzeichnen und daß in anderen Distrikten dasselbe geschehe. Der Delegat führte Fälle an, bei welchen Arbeiter ihr Leben verloren und von den Arbeitgebern keine Entschädigung erlangt werden konnte, weil solche Contracte vorhanden waren. Das Parlaments-Committee hat schon längst eine Bill vorbereitet, um diesem Zustand gesetzlich ein Ende zu machen, doch berichtete der Vorsitzende desselben, daß sie bis jetzt in dieser Hinsicht im Parlament noch keinen Erfolg hatten. Es wurde eine Resolution angenommen, welche dagegen protestirt, daß die Arbeitgeber noch länger ihre Gewalt über die Arbeiter benützen dürfen, um auf diese Weise das Gesetz zu umgehen. Der Congreß dauerte 6 Tage.

Brüderschafts-Notizen.

— Die Independent Carpenters' Union zu Cincinnati ist aufgelöst worden.

— Union No. 61 von Victoria in British Columbia wächst stark; die Beiträge sind 50 Cents per Monat.

— In Hartford geht das Geschäft gut und alle Unionleute haben Arbeit. Es ist dort eine Trades Assembly gegründet worden.

— Die Carpenters' Union No. 2 zu Cincinnati ist mit den Vorbereitungen für ein Winternachtsfest und einen Ball beschäftigt.

— Union No. 20 zu Baltimore hat sich Brüderschaftszeichen ähnlich denjenigen der Chicagoer Union machen lassen.

— Wenn Mitglieder auf Reisen gehen, sollten sie Reisekarten mitnehmen, sonst dürften sie Trubel haben und als „Scabs" angesehen werden.

— In der Trades-Assembly von Cincinnati sind zwei Mitglieder der Carpenters' Union No. 2 Beamten. Gus Breihauer ist Protokoll-Sekretär und John Valerius Sergeant at Arms.

— Bezahlt Eure Sterbegelder, sobald es von Euch verlangt wird, denn man kann nie wissen, wann es nöthig sein wird, das Benefit für irgend einen von uns, den der Tod erreicht, auszuzahlen.

— Die Durchschnittslöhne der Carpenters in Toronto, Canada, beliefen sich während des vergangenen Jahres auf $993.40, oder $1.80 per Tag, während in anderen Theilen von Canada der Durchschnitt per Tag $1.50 bis $1.75 beträgt.

— Wir können nicht begreifen, weshalb die Zeitung „Union" zu St. Louis fortwährend über die Auflösung dieser oder jener Carpenters' Union in jener Stadt berichtet. Es wäre besser, wenn jene Zeitung dabei helfen wollte, Gewerkschaften zu organisiren, statt sie zerstören zu helfen.

— Wir wünschen, daß jedes Mitglied, welches auf Reisen geht, als Missionär für unsere gute Sache wirke. Sie sollten Alle voll Eifer und Enthusiasmus sein und überall, wohin sie gehen, sollten sie Carpenters' Unions zurücklassen. Organisirt Unions, wohin Ihr auch gehen möget!

— Aus kleinen Ortschaften, wie Rushville, Ind., kommen Klagen über betrügerische Grocer, welche für ihre Waare zu viel Geld verlangen. Dafür giebt es ein Mittel: die Mitglieder sollten zusammenlegen und ihre Waaren im Großen einkaufen, nach Art eines Cooperativ-Geschäfts.

— Jakob Wasnicker und Chas. Scharman von Union No. 2 in Cincinnati haben durch Fallen schwere Verletzungen erlitten. Bei einem Picnic, das am 15. September von der Union für sie veranstaltet wurde, erzielte man $41.00 für jede Familie der Verunglückten. Das Committee und die Union verdienen dafür gelobt und durch die öffentliche Presse bedankt zu werden.

Gewerkschafts-Neuigkeiten.

Der Carpenters Strike am Elevator zu Newport News, Va., ist noch nicht beendigt. Vor Zuzug ist zu warnen.

— Im Dakota Territorium bekommen Zimmerleute täglich $3.50 und es ist eine starke Nachfrage nach Arbeitern, aber das Leben ist dort sehr theuer.

— Unter dem neuen Tramp-Gesetz von Wisconsin ist ein Mann in Milwaukee vor Kurzem auf 10 Monate zu schwerer Arbeit in die Penitentiary geschickt worden.

Schickt Eure Beiträge für den „Carpenter" ein—50 Cents per Jahr. Er ist das beste Gewerkschafts-Organ und jeder Carpenter sollte ihn lesen. Die Beiträge können auch per Post-Note eingeschickt werden, die in jeder Postoffice der Ver. Staaten für 3 Cts. zu haben sind.

Nach dem Census von 1880 giebt es 373,143 Zimmerleute in den Ver. Staaten. Das ist ein großes Feld für uns, aber wir müssen die Hand an den Pflug legen und wir werden nicht aufhören, bis das ganze Feld bearbeitet ist. Die Zimmerleute müssen organisirt werden und unsere Brüderschaft wird es thun.

— Es ist sehr nothwendig, daß autorisirte Vertreter von Gewerkschaften in Castle Garden stationirt werden, damit sie die Einwanderer mit der Höhe der Löhne und den Arbeitsbedingungen in den Ver. Staaten bekannt machen können. Wenn dies geschähe, könnten die Einwanderer nicht als Scabs gegen uns benutzt werden.

Europäische Nachrichten.

— Am 4. October wurde zu Valencia in Spanien ein Arbeiter-Congreß abgehalten.

— Ein National-Congreß französischer Gewerkschaften fand am 30. September zu Paris statt. Es waren 304 Organisationen durch mehr als 100 Delegaten vertreten.

— Ein internationaler Congreß englischer und französischer Gewerkschaften wird Ende dieses Monats in Paris stattfinden, um die internationalen Beziehungen der Gewerkschaften zu diskutiren.

— In der Schweiz, und zwar in der Stadt Zürich, fand am 9. September eine Delegirten-Versammlung sämmtlicher Schweizer Arbeiter-Vereinigungen statt. Der Zweck dieser Versammlung war, einen Bund zu schaffen. Mehr als 170 Delegirte waren anwesend und war die Versammlung vom besten Erfolge gekrönt.

— Der 16. Jahres-Congreß der englischen Gewerkschaften fand am 10. September in Nottingham statt und dauerte 6 Tage. Es waren 134 Vereine durch 160 Delegaten vertreten, von denen sieben Frauen waren. Die Anzahl der vertretenen Mitglieder betrug 592,000, d. h. kaum die Hälfte der organisirten Arbeiter England's, und doch war es eine Zunahme von 40,000 gegen das vorhergehende Jahr.

Berichte von den Unions.

— Die Löhne in Philadelphia sind $2.50 bis $2.75; Geschäft geht ziemlich gut. — In New Orleans $2.50 bis $3.25. Bruder A. J. Johnson von New Orleans starb am 17. September. — Die Union von Rushville, Ind., wächst; Arbeit nicht besonders. — In Hartford, Conn., starb Matthews Flannery am 11. September; 6 Bahrtuchträger unserer Union gingen nach New Britain, Conn., zum Begräbniß. Eine neue Union wird in Nashville, Tenn., gegründet. — Den Carpenters in Troy gefällt unser Journal. — St. Louis Löhne $2 bis $3 per Tag. Union No. 11 ist dort die einzige Union, welche die Brüderschaft anerkennt. — In Toronto, Canada, wird im Frühjahr 9 Stunden gearbeitet werden; Toronto zahlt wöchentliche Krankengelder von $2.50 aus und zwar für 13 Wochen. — Baltimore, Md., organisirt eine Baugewerkschafts-Liga.

Chicago, Ill.

Die Löhne in Chicago sind $2.75 bis $3 per Tag. Viel Arbeit und viele Non-Union Leute.

Kretschmar, ein ehemaliges Mitglied von Branch No. 6, starb am 15. August.

Die deutschen Branch-Sekretäre von Union No. 21 sollten ihre Berichte jeden Monat direct an unsere Office senden.

— Unsere Union zu Boston organisirt die Carpenters in Lynn, Mass.

— Aus [illegible] kommen Klagen über das Umsichgreifen [illegible] Stückarbeit. Wir rathen, daß allenthalben [illegible] die Stückarbeit agitirt werde.

DEATH BENEFITS.

A. J. JOHNSON, New Orleans Union No. 18, died September 17, 1883. Assessment No. 9.

H. KRETCHNER, Chicago Union No. 21, died August 15, 1883, of typho-malarial fever. Assessment No. 10.

CORRESPONDENCE.

Philadelphia, Pa.

Business here is the best it has been for years. Every mill is full of work; some of them have orders ahead for the next twelve months. Small houses in great demand. Wages $2.50 to $2.75. Had the carpenters fully organized this season they could now be getting $3 per day and 9 hours. Prospects are brilliant for a busy Winter.

New Orleans, La.

Bro. A. J. Johnson died Tuesday, Sept. 17, 1883, and was a member in good standing at time of death. He leaves a family to be provided for. Union No. 18 turned out in full force to attend his funeral, also a benevolent society of which he was a member. Work fair; wages, $2.50 to $3; weather cooler, plenty of small pox.

Rushville, Ind.

Work is still good, and it seems that as long as it continues, Union No. 39 can make no impression. But let work get slack, and the bosses will cut prices, and then you will see these outsiders will rush to us to help them out. A largely attended public meeting of carpenters under auspices of Union No. 39, was held here, October 17. J. K. Whiteside, of Indianapolis, was the speaker.

A New Union in Nashville, Tenn.

We have had a good meeting of Carpenters, elected officers and organized Union No. 51 of the Brotherhood. There is every prospect of having a prosperous union which is very badly needed in this city. Wages are very low, indeed.

There is a vast amount of building under way in Nashville; wages range from $1.50 to $2.50; hours of labor 10 to 10, hours per day. The Printers, Engineers and Bricklayers have Unions in this city. Union No. 51 has still a very prosperous outlook. We are trying our utmost to make it a success, and expect many new candidates this month.

St. Catherines, Canada.

All union men employed; trade quiet; no change in wages. We keep moving along; the situation is fair.

Troy, N. Y.

I am very well pleased with your valuable paper. Our Carpenter Assembly is doing very well, and THE CARPENTER has many friends in Troy. We are forming a club, and shall do all we can to help along the good cause. Business is first class.

A. J. B.

St. Louis, Mo.

Carpenters here seem to be afraid to belong to any organization that will revolt, if trampled upon. There are too many that would work for a dollar a day rather than be idle. There are some members that do big talk, but are the poorest when money is wanted for their dues. Union No. 14 is reorganizing, and promises to become strong. After this we will have only one union in this city with branches like Chicago, if necessary. The existence of three unions was a source of continual trouble. Wages are from $2 to $3 per day, very few at the latter figure.

Toronto, Canada.

Trade is only middling; union doing well. The sentiment here is very strong in favor of nine hours as a day's work the year round. We have adopted some new rules. We will now set aside 10 cents per month for a sick fund, and pay $2.50 per week for thirteen weeks, and $1.25 per week for the next thirteen weeks thereafter. This goes into effect February 1st, 1884. We also set aside 5 cents per month for a contingent fund to relieve distressed brothers, and also other trades in trouble. ... expenditure of the ... position of surplus, ...

FROM OUR FRENCH CORRESPONDENT.

PARIS, Oct. 1, 1883. An International Trades Union Congress will be held in this city at the end of this month and in which the English trades unions will be represented by three delegates, elected by the late Trades Congress and others from local unions. The Paris Congress will discuss international legislation on the condition of labor, the hours of work, sanitary condition of shops, factories etc.; secondly, the conditions under which workmen, especially mechanics, are able to work in countries other than their own; and thirdly, the measures to obtain in each country, the abrogation of those laws which place obstacles in the way of permanent international relations between the Trades Unions.

The invitation for this Congress emanated from the National Committee of the Possibilistes of France, which is composed of more than 150 labor societies federated in six districts, including Algeria. And this great force has been organized in France during the past few years that freedom of meeting and speech has been tolerated. The National Committee is the only recognized body representing the workmen of France. It was through it that the French Government provided the money for, and selected, the delegates to the Amsterdam Exhibition, and it did the same in sending the delegates to the Boston Exhibition.

It is expected that the International Trades Union Congress will be one of the most influential gatherings of workmen that has ever been convoked. Able labor advocates from both sides of the channel will be present, and while the French will do well to adopt some of the orderly, systematic and practical ideas of our English brothers, yet on the other hand the English in return will find it beneficial to imbibe in some degree the intensity of fervor and broadness of opinion that characterize the French.

A National Congress of French Trades Unions was held in this city on Sept. 30 at which over 100 delegates were present.

The National Printers' Union of France met in convention at Paris, August 23, 25, last; 27 cities represented. Delegates from Spain and Italy were present. The French Printers' Union consists of 62 Unions with over 6,000 members and 11,300 francs in the treasury. It has an official trade journal known as the *Typographic Journal*. A system of traveling benefits and other reforms were adopted.

JEAN PROLETAIRE.

BENEFITS PAID.

Death benefits have now been paid by our Brotherhood for six assessments out of eight, leaving only two to be paid, and these are for the benefit of the families of S. Sorensen, late of San Rafael Union No. 35, and Robert Abernethy, late of Toronto Union No. 27. These will soon be paid, as all the Unions are now taking a live interest in the Endowment Fund. All that is needed is a little more promptness in sending on the assessment.

THE CARPENTER

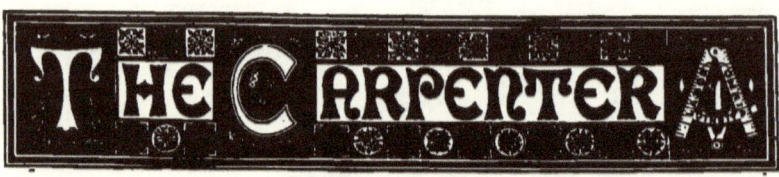

A MONTHLY JOURNAL FOR CARPENTERS AND JOINERS.

VOLUME III. NEW YORK, NOVEMBER, 1883. NUMBER 11.

NOTICE TO OUR READERS.

We have been compelled to put a large amount of our matter into small type this month, owing to the pressure of advertising space upon our columns. If it keeps on, we will soon have to enlarge to twelve pages.

ACROSS THE SEA.

SWITZERLAND.—The tailors of Zurich are obtaining large accessions to their union; the carpenters and cabinet makers are doing likewise.

ENGLAND. The coal miners in Yorkshire are demanding 15 per cent. increase in wages. This will involve 41,000 men.—1100 men were on strike in the Darlington Iron and Steel works against a large reduction; the matter was compromised by arbitration. A monument to Alexander McDonald, the miners' late representative in Parliament, is to be placed in Miners' Hall, Durham.

FRANCE.—The chair makers (*chaisiers*) of Paris are on strike against a reduction of 25 per cent. in pay from 6 francs down to 4½ francs. The Chair Makers' Union established the wages at 6 francs in 1852, and since then have never allowed any reduction.—The strike of the *Verriers* at Grenoble after two months' struggle ended in victory for the bosses. At Montceau-les-Mines where there was trouble last Spring, the stockholders of the mining companies are now agitating another reduction in pay, and of course they will then have the police and soldiers on their side "to preserve order." Well, who is disturbing order, if it is not these capitalists? The pay of the miners is only three francs per day.

GERMANY. The carpenters of Braunschweig have a union of 110 members, and have joined the Carpenters' National Union of Germany.—In Berlin, at a general meeting of the local Carpenters' Union, it was unanimously resolved to join the National Union. The union sharply criticized the action of a few carpenter bosses who have lately attempted to reduce wages, although they with other bosses had agreed upon a fixed scale until October 1.—The *Zeitschrift der Zimmerleute* is the monthly organ of the Carpenters' National Union of Germany, and is doing very good service in the cause. As a warning to the carpenters of Germany it has published many articles from our journal, but the most effective one is that which showed the immense emigration of carpenters to America.

THE POWER WHICH ELEVATES THE WORKERS.

In a work on Trades Unions, Stanley Jones, a famous writer on such subjects says: "Trades-unionism in England is an established fact, and a power which, although many politicians try to shirk or avoid it, it is best to openly admit. The unprejudiced observer must allow that, in England, trades unions have raised workingmen morally and intellectually, and have taught them a higher sense of their responsibilities. They have increased the prices and shortened the hours of labor; have educated workingmen to a knowledge of their common interest and common duty, and in every sense have raised the character of English workmen." Another eminent English authority quoted on the same page (222), the *British Quarterly Review*, says: "It appears pretty clear that unionism by its influence has, by slow degrees, altered for the better the circumstances [illegible] British workmen."

TRADES UNION AGENTS AT CASTLE GARDEN.

Our proposition to have trades union agents at Castle Garden we are glad to notice is indorsed by the *Iron Molders Journal*, the official journal of all the iron molders unions in America. This same question should be discussed in all the leading National and International Trades Unions, and then through the Federation of Trades the work could be properly accomplished. The agents should be competent men able to speak the leading European languages; and we have no doubt that by this means we could offset the work of the capitalistic immigrant agents, who are deluding immigrants by the thousand. For the present we will not add anything further, but here will we give the opinion of the *Iron Molders Journal*, which we heartily indorse:

It is about time that the trades unions of this country should place an agent at Castle Garden, New York, to prevent mechanics coming from foreign countries falling into the hands of agents of unscrupulous employers, who are always on the lookout for cheap labor to take the place of mechanics who may be out on strike or locked out for refusing to work at starvation wages. Four or five of the national organizations could employ one man to look after their interests. The expense would come light.

It would be a very easy matter to keep an agent informed where trouble existed in the different trades. We are satisfied that much good would result from such a movement.

Employers resort to this plan to secure cheap labor and to break down trades unions, and why not trades unions take steps to prevent it. The expense would be but a trifle compared with the amount of good it would do.

FORCED TO SPEAK WELL OF TRADES UNIONS.

Commenting on the statements made by Frederick Harrison before the recent English Trades Unions Congress, the New York *Evening Post*, one of our wealthiest and most conservative dailies, says: "As the unions increase in power and wealth the number of disputes between employers and laborers diminishes. The reasons for this are not far to seek. The strength of the unions not only makes employers more cautious about provoking them, but has a restraining influence upon the unions themselves. They have more to risk, and are in consequence less inclined to risk it. Their large reserve fund represents the labor and self-denial of many years and many men, and they will hesitate long before risking its sacrifice in what may be an unsuccessful strike. This is in accordance with an old familiar law. The man who has nothing is always more ready to accept risks than the man who by self-denial has saved something. By gradual development the trades unions of England have become great mutual benefit associations, which, by improving the condition of their members, have increased the proficiency of their labor, and thus added directly to its value to their employers".

—Our friend Joseph Joyce, of Utica, N. Y., a trades unionist of many years' standing, is elected as an Assemblyman of this State by 565 majority.

—Robert D. Layton, retiring Secretary of the Knights of Labor, is now acting as short-hand reporter for the great monopoly, the Standard Oil Co.

SHOT GUNS AGAINST STRIKERS.

We observe lately that capitalists are more and more prone to invoking the use of shot guns to settle the labor question. When strikes break out, scabs are often armed with rifles or pistols and instructed by their bosses to shoot down any union man upon sight. The Ida Hill tragedy at Troy, N. Y., this early Summer, when boss Kielcher, of the Troy Malleable Iron Co., played his murderous part, is still fresh in memory, and also the Belleville, Ill., coal miners affray. But more recently we have the news that in the strike of the coal miners in Bradford, Pa., an armed band of 100 men — Pinkerton's detectives — were brought into play against the strikers. And these detectives, well armed with Winchester repeaters and revolvers, were instructed to shoot down the 600 half-starved miners. Then again in the switchmen's strike at St. Louis, last month. The scabs were sworn in as Deputy Sheriffs, fully equipped with rifles and revolvers and aided to arrest the leaders of the strike under the old dodge of "conspiracy." On October 22, last, at Oswego, N. Y., the vessel loaders to the number of 250 were on strike, and scabs were imported and armed which lead to a deadly shooting between them and the strikers.

And so this carnival of blood goes on! And so it has been for many years. Clubbing, shooting, arresting, and incarcerating strikers. But that will not solve the question. It will only arouse bad blood, which may lead to fearful sanguinary results. Workmen are not likely to stand by many more years and see their comrades butchered by orders of the capitalists and monied kings. They are human and have sympathies and may pay back "an eye for an eye, and a tooth for a tooth." All they ask is fair treatment, the means to live, and the right to a full share of the wealth they produce. And they are organizing to obtain it, simply because they see plainly that without organization they are powerless. The bloody hands of hireling police, detectives, or soldiers can not stop them nor stay this movement. They will overwhelm everything that obstructs their liberty to organize and demand a better existence.

We are not alarmists. But we say to the capitalists and to the government: Keep your shot guns and armed men out of sight. And woe unto those who place too much trust in them! We propose to settle this question by better means. And when worst comes to worst we have the secrets of the laboratory at our command.

CENTRALIZATION OF UNION FUNDS.

Thomas Burt, of England, who has had over thirty years' experience as a trade unionist, and who is still one, says that the centralization of their funds has been a standing menace against strikes, and has done more to prevent them than all other things combined. The miners' unions of the counties of Northumberland and Durham have a reserve fund of over half a million of dollars. Let carpenters remember, that and see that our Brotherhood adopts the same plan. Centralization of funds does not mean centralization at one point or city. No! It means centralization of interests in the funds through universal dues and equalization of funds, with equal benefits and equal rights for all. That is what the miners of England have accomplished.

—The operatives in cotton and woolen mills of this State work 11 hours and 15 minutes a day.

STRAY CHIPS.

Convict contract labor has been defeated at the polls in this State by a majority of over 250,000. This means death to the prison contract system.

New York Plasterers have decided to work only nine hours a day with full pay and carried it out without a strike. That is the result of organization.

—Carpenters in Richmond, Va., are lukewarm and indifferent. They had an organization already under way and then let it fall to pieces; so was it the same in St. Paul, Minn.

—By act of the California Legislature an amendment to the State Constitution has been adopted, which does away with the prison contract system, beginning January 1, 1887.

—Printers' Union No. 3, Cincinnati, O., proposes that a law be passed, making it a felony for employers to demand or receive any pledge from their employes to keep them from joining trades unions.

—Kimball & Co., the boycotted cigarette manufacturers, Rochester, N. Y., have yielded to the labor organizations, and conceded the wished for advance in wages and reinstated all employes who were discharged for union principles.

—Contractor Nieber, carpenter and builder, has been censured by Carpenters' Union No. 2, of Cincinnati, O., for not paying the hospital expenses of Mr. Wosnick, who fell from a building while in the former's employ.

John G. Warwick, candidate for Lieutenant Governor of Ohio, was not defeated in the October election, but came mighty near it. He ran 20,000 votes behind his ticket, because he had the brutality to call out the militia to shoot down the coal miners of Massillon, Ohio, in 1876.

—The magnificent victory of Typographical Union No. 6, of this city, in its late movement for a uniform scale and higher pay, is due entirely to able management and to keeping their plans and counsels to themselves, until they were prepared to act. They gave no extended notice to their employers so as to flood the city with men.

—Typographical Union No. 101, Washington, D. C., is boycotting Stilson Hutchin's paper, the *Washington Post* for employing non-union printers and paying less than union prices. This is not the first time Hutchins had to go through the same ordeal for the same crime. His sad experience on the St. Louis *Times* ought to have taught him how costly it is to play with organized labor.

—There are fears expressed that the boss builders of this city will make a general reduction in wages this Winter.

These are stirring times in New York; twenty six hundred carpet weavers are on strike in this city against a reduction of 10 per cent; 1000 cigar box makers are locked out to break up their union; the silk weavers are striking for payment of their unpaid labor in repairing their looms and the book binders are out in one [illegible] while many other strikes are pending.

Detroit, Mich.

[illegible] per day. [illegible]

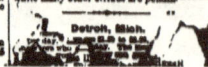

THE CARPENTER.

Entered at the Post-Office in New York, as second-class matter.

NEW YORK, NOVEMBER, 1883.

THE LABOR QUESTION.

LECTURE XI.

Our former addresses may appear to have been critical, aggressive and negative; they are so only in appearance; in the future they will be more positive and constructive.

It is not alone necessary to tear down an old shanty when we require to build a palace upon the spot of land where the shanty stood; we should have the conception, design and plan for the palace before we remove the shanty, however old, dilapidated and leaky it may be.

So with social institutions; it is not sufficient to tear down the old, the worn out and the rotten—that is a work of destruction and easily accomplished—it is necessary to know what we are to put in the place of the institutions which we are to remove; that is a work of construction, and much more difficult of accomplishment.

In fact, we may say that the world has never seen but two forms of civilization—the Constructive and the Destructive.

The military or warlike, the industrial or peaceful.

The military, warlike and commercial methods which have obtained in the past, represent the destructive periods and forms of civilization.

The peaceful, associative and industrial methods, to which society at present aspires, and which will, doubtless, obtain in the near future, will represent the constructive period and form of civilization.

Progress may be said to be the net result of the struggle for supremacy between these two forms of civilization, and advancement may be defined as that part of the struggle in which peace and construction have been victorious in the struggle, and have overthrown war and destruction by becoming parts of the social system, having become practically incorporated into the habits and customs of the people.

As it is much easier to critically depict the errors of the past than to present a possible future devoid of error, or to indicate means to gradually eliminate error, we may probably not be more successful in our constructive work than others who have preceded us, and yet, having constantly before us the lessons which the experience of the past is able to teach, we may arrive at simple practical beginnings in the immediate, which may lead us to complex achievements in the remote, if we can but refrain from being drawn too far into the seductive theoretical.

It has been our object to show that society exists by virtue of industry, and to reduce industry to its most simple elements, in order that it may be fully comprehended.

We have said that industry, i. e., human activity, manifests itself through five elements—Land, Labor, Capital, Exchange, Insurance.

Let us now express a concise idea of our broad meaning of these words, and what we intend to convey when we use them; until it comes to be expressed in more concise language we may use the following formulas:

Land is the element which furnishes all the material objects upon which man bestows labor, in order to create capital (or utilities), and comprises all that is below the surface of the earth down to the centre of gravity; all that is above the surface, up to the outer circumference of the terrestrial atmosphere.

Labor is the exercise of the physical, mental and moral forces of the man, singly or combined, in any way that administers to the wants or increases the happiness of mankind.

Capital is the accumulated, unconsumed product of the joint action of the two elements, Land and Labor, which aids the present to produce further Capital for future consumption.

Exchange is the exercise of labor, or of the physical, mental or moral forces of the man, applied to the transportation or distribution of capital from places and [illegible] where it is required.

[illegible] is the exercise of the faculty [illegible] for the sake of provision. We [illegible] that calamity will [illegible] provision [illegible]

Any definitions more complete or more concise will be readily and cheerfully accepted by us. We wish to eschew all the inconsistencies of the political economists, and to conserve all that which contains good; we cannot look upon political economy, as at present established, as being a science. When it has been placed upon a more rational basis, political economy will perhaps be called the art which teaches us to employ Land, Labor, Capital, Exchange and Insurance to the best possible advantage; and in such a way as shall secure the happiness of all who labor, and eliminate from society all the loafers.

When we get something like the foregoing definition of political economy accepted by the professors, we shall be making progress in the world.

In Lecture X. we showed how futile would be the results of attempted emancipation of the workers until they could control the land.

We now say that *labor* or production must be controlled in the interest of industry by securing to all the laborers the *instruments* and the *means* of labor.

Exchange must be controlled in the interests of the laborers to prevent *profits* from going to non-producers.

Capital and credit must be controlled in the interest of the laborers to prevent *interest* from going to brokers, capitalists and non-producers.

Land must be controlled in the interest of the laborer, to prevent *rent* from going to the lazy, the loafer and the landlord.

This brings us back again to the land, and to the point where we must definitely treat this element as being of the most primary importance, although of no greater importance than any other of the five elements.

The land is the element to be first controlled.

How, then, are we to regain or reconquer this element which has been unjustly taken from us?

The present proprietors of land have obtained it only by one of three methods—by cultivation, by purchase, or by conquest.

Purchase and cultivation mean peace; conquest means war.

I know of no other means of obtaining control of the land, either as proprietor or possessor.

If we wish to re-obtain the land, we have, therefore, no alternative: It must either be *peace or war*. We must fight for it or we must purchase it.

It is not necessary to our purpose to show here that territorial acquisition by means of conquest is historically on the decline; it is sufficient to mention it as a fact.

If I were to listen to the dictates of my own inclinations, I should say to the workers of the world—Take it by war! Do not purchase it by peace! Foul means have been used to deprive you of it; use the same means to regain it; for I feel with the poet, who said—

> "We're weary of waiting the help of heaven,
> And the battle goes still with the last."

Injustice and suffering have been your portion while being deprived of your inheritance; inflict injustice and suffering upon those who have deprived you of that inheritance.

But, as a careful scanning of history shows us, that victory is not always on the side of justice, that the issue of war is uncertain and treacherous, although it may occasionally be rapid and decisive; that the methods of peace are always effectual, although sometimes of very slow results, I feel it my duty to condemn all warlike attempts and to recommend peaceful methods.

The chances of war can never be calculated, but the results of the methods of peace can be calculated to a nicety, admitting, always, that time is a factor which we do not pretend to include in our calculation.

It is therefore incumbent upon us to adopt the proper methods without inquiring the time it will take to accomplish our ends, or whether or not we may live to see the full fruition of our works and the attainment of our aspirations.

If we establish correct methods we may rest assured that the growing intelligence of our fellow-workers and the increased knowledge, in relation to the labor question, which is fast permeating the sons and daughters of toil, will accelerate the general application of such methods.

We will, therefore, consider it as an accepted proposition, that we must first control the land, and indicate a way to accomplish it.

We, in the city, deal with the land for manufacturing and distributive purposes, as an instrument of general production and exchange, and not as an instrument of agricultural production.

The Trades' Unions are organized for the cities, the agricultural laborers must be organized for the country; this latter work has been commenced by the Patrons of Husbandry, or Granges. Every Trades Union may begin the work by becoming the possessor of its own meeting hall. For this purpose it should purchase a few city lots in some back street, not too far from the centre of the city. As it would be difficult for each trade to do so, since all trades have not sufficient funds, several or all of the Unions in a locality or city, could combine to do it together. For this purpose every Union must become chartered by the State; they must be legalized and recognized as a constituent element of the Republic.

When rooms for meetings have been secured, the next step would be to secure a few acres of land in the suburbs of each city for the purpose of building a retreat for aged members who are past work. This would furnish labor for the various trades in dull seasons. A small percentage of the funds of each Union would be set apart in order to accomplish this. As time rolled on, larger tracts of land would be secured and worked as farms, the produce of which would be consumed by the workers.

The principle of coöperation is becoming extensively practised; a store could be opened at every hall, and a part of all profits made should be devoted to this purpose.

Let each Union call upon every member of the Order to aid it in their individual capacity to the best of his ability, with any sum as a loan without interest, repayable, from ten cents to ten dollars.

Let Unions organize and give social gatherings, tea parties, lectures, concerts, &c., at a small cost, the proceeds of which are to be devoted exclusively to the *Land Fund*, and to no other purpose.

Let them organize lotteries and give prizes of such works and articles as the members and friends may please to give which will, doubtless, be some product of their labor—the hatter should give a hat, the tailor a vest, the shoemaker a pair of shoes, the cabinet-maker a box, table or what-not, &c. It would be instituted in no spirit of gambling. Let it be always fully and unequivocally understood that all these sums from all these and various other resources, are to be devoted to the *Land Fund*, and that under no circumstance can they be used for any other purpose or object.

Now, I believe fully that if this association has only a dozen members who are equally imbued with the importance of the subject of these five elements which we have considered, and will give themselves the trouble to become intimately acquainted with them as I am myself, and if this dozen men will form themselves into a lecturing corps, confining themselves to this subject, and devote themselves to the elucidation of the five elements, and then explain the necessity of first becoming possessors of the element Land, and will visit all assemblages of labor and ask them to assist in the work, that this dozen men will be able to accomplish the object, aided by individuals and Unions, if the individuals and Unions are thoroughly prepared for a full comprehension of the method.

But let us well remember this! It is not likely to be accomplished in a day, a week, or a year; time is not a factor which should enter into our calculation. Let us consider that it has taken this association more than three months to consider the subject and to get so far on the road as we are to-night, and that with a ready ear to listen and a desire to learn. How would it be with those who turn a deaf ear and have no desire to learn? Do not let our enthusiasm run away with our judgment: we have a thankless task before us, and we are more likely to be dismayed than encouraged. The importance of the work is so great, however, and its ultimate results upon the condition of the workers so vast, that we ought to feel ourselves nerved to the performance of the task.

It may be asked, why go into a back lane or a by-street; why not purchase a house upon one of the principal thoroughfares?

Why not rent an imposing store, &c.?

We should not rent meeting-rooms or stores, because rent eats up profits, and we must first emancipate ourselves from the landlord. Again, we do not require meeting-rooms on a principal thoroughfare to begin with; but many have failed who have attempted this; and further, we want to go into the back streets and the poor parts of the city for more than one reason.

1. The poor live there, and we want the poor, in order to do good and increase in numbers and usefulness.

2. In by-streets and back lanes, land and houses are comparatively cheap, and consequently, more easily obtained.

3. If we get one house in a back street, we shall—by working diligently, silently and cautiously—soon be able to buy the houses on both sides of it, and so on until we have purchased our way through to a front street, and shall be on a "principal thoroughfare" as possessors, but not as tenants.

Again, if we are in a back street we are surrounded by the workers, and we can go into their homes, talk to them and make members of them. Our own members can then make apostles of themselves and call on their brother workmen in the neighborhood. We can get them and their families to come to our meetings, perhaps on the first floor of our house, where we could institute weekly or semi-weekly lectures; and thus get the whole neighborhood indoctrinated. We might, then, feel sure of our work, and go to another neighborhood to do a similar thing.

This would give the Order "a local habitation and a name" in every State of the Union, and would be the first very simple step toward forming what we so much require—a central point, a central home, a labor exchange bureau, library, reading-room, club-room, meeting-rooms, &c., around which all may rally, always sure of finding it in the same place, without any fear of moving or change of locality.

We all know the inconvenience and loss which fall upon a man in private business if he changes his place of business frequently; in fact, it is impossible to successfully conduct business under such conditions. How, then, can the business of a collectivity succeed if we are not stationary?

It is impossible to calculate the expenditure and income of such an enterprise without making an estimate upon a basis of supposition. It would, however, vary in every locality. As this address is sufficiently lengthy, I will reserve it for future consideration.

I may say, however, that this subject was presented to the workingmen of New York city some fifteen years ago, and to those of Philadelphia as far back as 1872. Unions were then paying from $1 to $4 per night for meeting-rooms. The Unions had from $150 to $7,000 in their various treasuries. These sums were deposited in savings banks, some of which "busted", and thus the *improvidence* of the workers was made manifest. Had they invested their savings in the land and built a hall, the result would have been different. Had it been begun then, the workers would now have their hall, and not be to-day asking *charity* from politicians. If the workers begin now, in a few years they will own their hall; if they never begin, they never will possess it, but continue to pay rent to landlords who oppress them.

Recently, however, sufficient interest has been awakened upon this fundamental question to incite the erection of workingmen's halls and lyceums in Chicago, Millville and Brooklyn. In Paris, the municipal council is erecting a building devoted to the wants of the workers in the central part of the city, the cost of which will exceed 2,500,000 francs.

DAVEY.

CLEANING SCREWS FROM RUST.

Rust can be removed from small screws, etc., that are too small for holding against an emery-wheel, by attrition. Take, say, 1 pound of screws, and place them in a box; a cigar-box will do. Put a small quantity of oil on them, and shake for another minute or so, and then sift the sawdust from the screws in a fine sieve, when the screws will be found to be as good as new.

AN APPEAL TO CARPENTERS.

The following appeal has been issued by Milwaukee Carpenters' Union No. 30 and is an ably written document which is equally pertinent for the carpenters of every city.

FELLOW CRAFTSMEN:

The Carpenters of this city have tried at different times to form a strong Union of their trade which failed for lack of the cooperation of the majority of our comrades. The present Union has therefore resolved to try again to unite us all, and to form German branches on the South and North Side, and asks all English speaking carpenters to join the old branch, which meets every second and fourth Wednesday at Casino Hall, cor. 7th and State streets.

If the Carpenters of Milwaukee had been united during last season, they could have had $4 a day as well as their comrades in Chicago, St. Louis, and other places. To not unite is the great fault of the working class in general. Most of them do not comprehend the fact that a workman has to ask the boss for work, and has to offer his labor for sale, and as hunger and starvation face him, if he don't work, he is often compelled to take the lowest price for his labor. Thus the boss is master of the situation.

The labor market is generally overcrowded, and if you don't take the terms of the boss, his answer is: "If you don't want to work for that, I can get plenty of hands who are glad to take it." Thus the boss uses his advantage over a poor fellow who has to submit.

Now we have the same right to sell our labor as high as possible, as every merchant does his goods and every doctor his skill. They all put up their own price. Let us do the same and say: we want 30 cents per hour, and no less, and those bosses who don't want to pay it, let them do their work themselves. We can easily gain this if we unite. What we neglected this season, let us not miss the next. Let us form one brotherhood — this is the first step to better our condition. Let us form a protective union with sick benefit, that in case of need we have help on hand. Our comrades in New York, St. Louis, and other places are ahead of us in this respect.

Five years ago the wages in New York ranged from $1.50 to $1.75. This low rate compelled the carpenters to form a union, and they now pay $5 sick benefit and $[illegible] endowment to members, and $5 a week to any union man out of work, and they raised their wages up to $3 and $3.50 per day. All this was gained by union and a weekly payment of 15 cents. Without a union their earnings were from $9—12 per week, and no help in case of sickness, or when without work. With the union they now get from $18—21 per week and have $5 benefit in case of need, and all that for a contribution of 15 cents per week, which leaves a gain of [illegible] per week. This shows clearly that a union is the best savings bank for working men.

Certainly such a union cannot be completed in one week. Experience teaches us that working men always had some money for some sort of amusement with which the capitalistic class is blinding their eyes, but seldom they show the courage and vigor to take steps for their own interests and the carpenters, on the average, are like all working men they don't seem to care for their own good.

Fellow craftsmen, let us quit this shiftless condition, and let us act manly. Look at our brothers in California, they broke up all piece work and established a new system of labor, whereby they accomplished more within two years than was expected. They secured 9 hours as a day's work, and raised their wages the same time 20 to 25 per cent. There is work enough here for the same, but 30 or 40 men cannot do it. We have to be one solid body with one principle, to do this we need the help of all. The crisis and panic have set in, and will soon be upon us, then the time for improvement has passed; but if we unite now we can gain a great deal and guard against hard times.

The bricklayers, firemen, and engineers did so during the last panic. The bricklayers' union in Cincinnati held their $4 a day, while in Pittsburg and Allegheny City the bricklayers had to work for $2—2.25 per day, because they had no union.

Some of our comrades may think our bosses will not pay $3 a day. This is true, as long as we do not ask it. They will not offer the carpenter 50 cents more a day, though this would be to their interest. Naturally, some bosses believe they make more profit by low wages. The hard competition between these forces this idea into their minds. Each of them is trying, by low bids to obtain more work, and to make up for his loss by cutting the wages of his men. If the men consent, another boss will do the same, and in a short time wages are reduced all over town. But bosses are not aware of the evil effects of such condition on the entire business. Low wages cripple the purchasing power of the working class, thus creating a shrinkage in every business. If the majority of the people—and that is the working class—has got no money, the consumption or purchase of a good many articles ceases, warehouses fill up, factories stop, real estate drops in prices, and the bosses feel the loss heavily, and a good many have to break up because the building trade is also paralyzed.

High wages make business flourish, low wages depress it.

Now, if we carpenters in this city stick together, and let the bosses know that next Summer we want 30 cents per hour for our work, they can make their figures accordingly. The bosses have not to pay for this increase, but squeeze it out of the pockets of the money lords, and this is a benefit for all, because more money gets into circulation.

We believe most of the bosses will not object to our purpose, if they have the assurance that every boss has to pay the same scale. The standard of competition will be the same as it is now, and none of them can get the best of each other by cutting wages.

To accomplish this, is our duty, is your duty, and we offer our helping hand to every carpenter in this city. We have been wasting our strength and nerve long enough, let us use our brains now for the benefit of our ourselves and our families.

We invite you to come to our meeting places. A public meeting is held every fourth Wednesday at Casino Hall, corner State and 7th streets, West side, at 8 o'clock P. M.

The South side German Branch meets every first and third Saturday of each month at Mechanic's Hall, corner Grove and Park streets, at 8 o'clock P. M.

For Milwaukee Union No. 30,
THE COMMITTEE.

PALLISER, PALLISER & CO.

It is only seven years since a member of the above firm was a journeyman carpenter in Bridgeport, Conn. [illegible] at 1877, the business of this firm [illegible] and they won a number of competitions by submitting fine designs that were practical and could be built. [illegible] Palliser, Palliser & Co. were the successful ones. This firm consists of five brothers, three carpenters and two masons, practical mechanics, who have become architects by dint of hard study and natural talent. Born in England, they there received a very thorough training as mechanics, and in their schools they were taught drawing in school, and followed it up in evenings, making many fine drawings and being always proficient in that art [illegible] Geo. Palliser, [illegible] one of the firm, when a lad of 18 years, in Leeds, England, built a small steam engine in all its parts, [illegible] And 10 years ago he made drawings for [illegible] railway, published by *Frank Leslie's* [illegible]

The Pallisers win every time, except where political or other influences have been used against political [illegible] Recently 17 architects competed and sent in designs for a High School building in Elizabeth, N. J., the firm of PALLISER, PALLISER & CO. were the winners of the premium of $100 for the best design with instructions to prepare full working plans and all details, and to superintend the building. [illegible] Also the county Court House, [illegible] Fla., and the High School, Deep River, Conn., and many other buildings within a year past. This firm is a reliable, trustworthy concern, composed of practical, straight-forward men.

San Francisco, Cal.

Trade holds good. Wages range from $[illegible] to $[illegible] per diem, mostly at the latter figure. Union men all employed and prospects fair. On October 15, the Carpenters' Union of this city paid a fraternal visit to Oakland Union No. [illegible], and we discovered to our surprise that they had resolved to allow men employed in building shops and sheds for the Central Pacific R. R. to work ten hours per day, while the remainder of the union worked only nine hours a day. Of course, we gave them our sentiments in opposition to such action. The painters are still making a heroic war against the *Call* and *Bulletin*, and the unions are aiding them liberally. Several large firms have dropped their advertising and donated money to the strikers. There is now quite a rush from the country of botch carpenters, but they meet with very poor success with our union boys, for we have this city pretty well in hand, and "scabs" and non-union men get a wide berth and no quarter. Our union will pay a fraternal visit to the Alameda Union, on November 15. Union No. 22 is now a power in this city, and if all our members will hold steadfast and true to our Brotherhood, we can make our craft much more respected.

Seattle, Washington Territory.

Our union is growing rapidly; we initiated seven members at our last meeting, and had quite a number of proposals. Most of carpenters are at work, and business is pretty good at present, but will certainly slack off before Spring. Strangers coming here now find it very difficult to get work, and we would advise no one to come here during the Winter months. Wages are from $3 to $3.50, and a very few get $3.75. Cost of living is very high. Men working on unsheltered buildings can't make more than half time on account of the rain.

THE CARPENTER.

PUBLISHED MONTHLY

BY THE

Brotherhood of Carpenters and Joiners,

OF AMERICA.

Office: 184 William St., New York.

TERMS.—Fifty cents a year, in advance, post-paid.

Send all moneys and correspondence for this Journal to

P. J. McGUIRE, Secretary,

184 William St., New York

NEW YORK, NOVEMBER, 1883.

A SUMMARY OF THE SITUATION AMONG CARPENTERS.

Reports from all the various cities show that carpenter work has been fairly busy up to date, with a tendency to slack off as the cold weather is felt more keenly. Wages hold firm; very few cities are reducing the day's pay on account of the shorter hours of Winter. The membership of our various Unions is increasing; a livelier interest is taken in the meetings; the dues are all coming up to one standard of 50 cents per month with $2 initiation fee. Sick benefits of $4 per week are being introduced, also accident benefits; while the matter of a tool insurance as a general institution in our Unions is talked of very favorably. Our Death Benefit is looked upon by many as one of the features upon which our Brotherhood will thrive, while others favor its partial reduction to embrace other benefits as well. New unions are being formed; the number of non-union men is diminishing, and the work of organization is progressing splendidly. Our members are educating each other in the principles underlying this great movement, so that before many years we will all be proud to have been pioneers in this glorious work.

WHY REDUCE WAGES IN WINTER?

Frost and snow are now at hand! The [illegible] season of cold and stormy weather [illegible] short days has made its advent. And with its advent the carpenter bosses in a few places declare that carpenters must work cheaper, that they must be paid only for the hours they work.

Why is this?

Is it the fault of the journeymen carpenters that they can not work more than eight or nine hours a day, is it their fault that the days are dark so early? When the heat of Summer makes the day's work tiresome long before quitting time, when men can not do as much work in the day as they can now, when their energies are comparatively prostrated and weakened, what boss carpenter then proposes to pay men by the hour? Why, if we then asked for eight or nine hours as a day's work, some of them would almost faint away at our "supreme cheek?"

But now when Winter has come, when every man "pulls out for all he is worth," so as to keep warm, the bosses have the audacity to propose in some places to reduce wages. And yet in a short day of Winter every honest workman can do more work [illegible] he can on a hot day in Summer. [illegible] the [illegible] of proof on nearly all [illegible] work. Why then should there [illegible] in pay; do the bosses [illegible] the benefit of it to their customers, [illegible] that would be too much like [illegible]

[illegible] must always be the [illegible] of the short days [illegible] bosses want to [illegible] of the fruits [illegible] that we are [illegible] been able to [illegible] of organi- [illegible] try [illegible]

Man's wants are greater now than at any season of the year. It costs more for fire, food, clothing and all the necessities of life, and more are consumed on account of the severity of the weather. How then can carpenters submit to or afford a reduction of wages? Let them organize and stop it.

CONTRACT PRISON LABOR.

For years and years the organized workingmen of this State and of other States have agitated against the evil of contract prison labor. They have petitioned State Legislatures, they have held public demonstrations, they have spoken in no uncertain tones in favor of removing the contract system from our prisons and penitentiaries. Not that the workers want the convicts maintained in idleness at public expense, but they are desirous that the convicts shall work and support themselves without being a dangerous source of competition to outside industries.

The contract system of labor in prisons is degrading to the dignity of the government and the majesty of law. It has the most pernicious influence upon the convict, causing him naturally to think that crime is simply a vehicle of profit and wealth for favored contractors. It is antagonistic to the aims and ends of a prison—constantly interfering with the rules and discipline of the prison, and thus obstructive to the reformation of the convict. It is a cruel wrong to the working classes of the whole nation by placing their labor in competition with that of criminals.

This system it is said is the best paying system! That is the main argument in its support. But prison statistics show that of all those sentenced for crime 75 per cent are amenable to reform, provided the prison is a *penitentiary* in the true sense of the word. Yet barely 25 per cent of those who serve their terms engage in honest pursuits—a clear loss of 50 per cent. Does this pay; is it for this that the huge machinery of the law, the courts, and all the paraphernalia of police and constabulary are supported by the people? We supposed the main purpose of incarceration was not alone to protect society from the prisoner, but also from his further depredations by liberating him a reformed man.

This is not done. And how can it be done while ruffianly keepers and favored contractors have charge of the prisoner and make him the object of exploitation, brutality and persecution? Where is the attempt to reform under the prison contract system? None at all. The prisoner is given a task, and if not completed, the dark cell, the shower bath or the paddle is his punishment. Where is the system of credits and awards to stir him to interest and excellence in his work? What provision is there for the dependent family of the convict to keep them from crime? Where is the bonus to be placed in the hands of the prisoner upon liberation to lead him away from his old haunts and associates?

These measures of reform are not thought of. No! Our prison system is as brutal and inhuman as is our whole industrial system. The only thing thought of is how to make *profit*. What wonder then that the convicts should leave prison with their hearts full of hatred and animosity against the community that maintains such a system. If the people in each State would diminish crime they must break down this villainous contract system. It is maintained simply that certain contractors in a few industries can hire labor at 35 or 60 cents a day to compete with outside manufacturers, who are paying $2 to $3 per day for the same work. In this State alone 1652 convicts are engaged in the boot and shoe trade, 1255 at iron moulding, and the balance of over 5,000 prisoners at harness-making, tailoring, etc. And yet only a small percentage of these ever learn a trade, as the work is so subdivided that they only learn a small part. In addition to this there are over 25,000 inmates of Reformatories, Houses of Refuge and Penal Institutions of this State who are engaged under the same conditions.

The people of New York in the late election have proclaimed by over 100,000 majority that this convict contract system must go! And the statesmen to put in its place the public [illegible] indicate a way which will keep the p[illegible] supplies for the [illegible] deal with the land for agement of [illegible] and distributive purposes.

OUR [illegible] LETTER.

PARIS' Nov. [illegible], 1883. The International Labor Conference held here, which opened on October 29, has terminated very satisfactorily. The delegates were chiefly from England and France; Italy and Spain likewise having representatives. The proceedings were dispassionate and indicated that at least the workingmen of England had common ground of action upon which they could co-operate with the workmen of the Continent. An address was adopted, expressing the sympathy of the conference with the interests of the workingmen of all countries, and recording its protest against wars.

Henry Broadhurst, Secretary of the British Stone Masons' National Union, and member of Parliament, was elected Honorary President of the conference. In opening the meeting he pointed out the importance of workmen of all nations being in constant communication with each other. He guaranteed in behalf of the English trades unions their cordial support to the trades union movement all over the Continent.

The best means of furthering a permanent understanding among workingmen's societies of the different countries was then discussed by the delegates. The Italian and Spanish delegates advocated parliamentary agitation, popular propaganda and universal suffrage. A French delegate spoke in favor of resort to force, as nothing could be gained otherwise. Other delegates, especially those from England, vigorously protested against such ideas. General applause was elicited by this declaration. A motion, advising popular agitation for the purpose of preserving liberty of association was adopted. The following resolution was accepted: "That the conference records its opinion that the principal end to be pursued is to limit the hours of labor. This is attainable in two ways, namely: Legislation for the protection of the weak against corruption and the organization of workingmen, who should be united and disciplined. It is the duty of workingmen to direct their efforts against unjust laws which render the organization of labor impossible and hinder international legislation, which is so necessary to ameliorate the condition of the working classes.

Before adjourning the conference unanimously adopted the resolution that emigrants should accept the conditions of local trade organizations and not undersell each other's labor.

In the evening session 100 delegates were present. It was suggested that it was possible to establish international legislation, especially for the protection of children. The speakers urged the French workmen to devote more attention to business and less to politics, and to organize trades unions. Various delegates advocated the formation of unions in France similar to those in England. Mr. Peronese, French delegate, maintained that the unanimity shown by the conference foreshadowed the organization of the Internationale. Signor Costa, Italian delegate, announced that the next conference would be held at Turin, in 1884, and invited foreign delegates to attend. The conference expressed a desire for more congresses.

—A. J. Johnson, formerly a member of New Orleans Union No. 16, died Sept. 17, 1883, of congestion of the Kidneys. The notice of assessment was published in our last Journal.

NEW PUBLICATIONS.

THE DOMINION MECHANICAL AND MILLING NEWS, a monthly journal, published in Toronto, Canada, is a new entry on our exchange list, and is a handsomely illustrated, finely printed, and a very instructive journal. It is devoted principally to the milling interests.

THE CRAFTSMAN, Washington, D. C., is the new official organ of the International Typographical Union, and takes the place of [illegible]. Not only is it devoted to the interests of printers, but in its columns the labor movement of Washington finds an able representative.

HOW TO BECOME A GOOD MECHANIC. By an old apprentice, published by the Industrial Publication Co., 294 Broadway, price 15 cents. A small pamphlet, full of good suggestions.

ARCHITECTS' AND BUILDERS' POCKET COMPANION AND PRICE BOOK. In this work our readers will find a short but comprehensive Epitome of [illegible], with tables of U. S. Measures, sizes, weights, strengths, etc., of Iron, Wood, Stone, Brick, Cement and Concretes, Quantities of Materials in given sizes, and Dimensions of Wood, Brick and Stone. And full and complete Bills of Prices for Carpenter's Work and Painting. Also Rules for computing and valuing Brick and Brick Work, Stone Work, Painting, Plastering, with a Vocabulary of technical terms. Price, $1.50, postage free. Published by Henry Carey Baird & Co., 810 Walnut street, Philadelphia, Pa.

FROM OUR MAILS.

Hamilton, Canada.

Trade is getting dull. We have set the ball in motion to have a Building Trades League in this city. New members are joining us at every meeting.

Baltimore, Md.

Trade is just fair, not so brisk as it was, with the prospect [illegible] for the Winter. Some of the bosses are beginning to talk of cutting down, as the days are getting short, but we intend to resist it and expect to resist it successfully. Our Building League is progressing, and we expect good things from it early in the Spring. Union No. 29 has come to an agreement with the Ship Joiners' Union (which has always been very exclusive), and hereafter they will recognize each other's cards, and recognize none of either craft without their cards, which will work to the benefit of both Unions.

San Rafael, Cal.

Work fair; all union men employed; cost of living high; wages same as last month. Lots of men coming in from the country looking for work for the Winter. But if they don't belong to our Carpenters' Union, there is no show for them, and they have to soon go back to where they came from. Union No. 35 resolved that none of its members be allowed to work on a job where there is a sub-contract, nor shall they work for a sub-contractor, nor take sub-contracts in violation of our rules. [illegible]

St. Louis, Mo.

[illegible]

Victoria, British Columbia.

[illegible]

Cincinnati, Ohio.

[illegible]

Boston, Mass.

[illegible]

Indianapolis, Ind.

[illegible]

[illegible]

J. R. WHITESIDE.

Germantown, Pa.

[illegible]

Brownsville, Mo.

[illegible]

Cheyenne, Wyoming Terr.

[illegible]

J. R. G.

Rushville, Ind.

[illegible]

[illegible]

Stair Builders of Cincinnati.

[illegible]

LOUIS BRAND.

Halifax, Nova Scotia.

[illegible]

Chicago Reports.

[illegible]

Toronto, Canada.

[illegible]

[illegible]

Philadelphia, Pa.

[illegible]

Washington, D. C.

[illegible]

Providence, R.I.

[illegible]

Alameda, Cal.

[illegible]

JOHN J. BOYLE.

Oakland, Cal.

[illegible]

YOU MEN OF CHIPS AND SHAVINGS!

You men of chips and shavings!
You men of saws and planes!
Arise, and in your manhood break
Your fetters and your chains.
Too long our craft has been oppressed,
And we must break the ban,
So come and help us in the fight
And be a "Union Man."

The money king has ruled us
With an iron-scepterd sway
He is striving to control us
In each and every way.
But we're risen to defeat him,
So come and join our clan,
And profit by our victory
By being a "Union man."

The man who has the money
Has set a price on you,
And bound you as a fettered slave,
And there's but one thing to do;
Your own strength is only weakness.
Deny it, if you can;
But you'll find that you are powerful,
If you are a "Union Man."

When we are all united,
Labor hours will not be long,
We shall have an hour for study
And an hour to right each wrong.
No longer shall starvation
Haunt you so grim and wan,
For you can get good wages,
If you're a "Union Man."

So come and join the Union,
'Tis the best thing you can do,
And leave your scab companions,
The act you'll never rue.
Not long the day, till you'll rejoice
You did these verses scan,
And took the kind advice intended
To make you a "Union Man."

J. C. ORROD.

EVANSVILLE, Indiana.

A CONTEMPTIBLE PRACTICE.

Cincinnati Union No. 2 of the Brotherhood of Carpenters and Joiners of North America, desires to warn all Union carpenters of the way J. C. & F. G. Huntington, builders, do business. Through the Summer months they employ first-class workmen to do their heavy out-door work on buildings; but in Winter, when the weather is inclement, and indoor work is therefore at a premium, they sub-contract the finishing work to "scabs," thus working a great wrong to the men who have done the heavy work. Union men should see to it that such firms are spotted. When the building season opens next Spring, and first-class carpenters are in demand, these builders should be compelled to get along with their cheap, incompetent "scabs."—*Cincinnati Unionist.*

COMPLIMENTARY TO OUR NEW OFFICERS.

The Chicago *Truth* in speaking of our newly elected general officers says: A new and additional honor has been bestowed upon our city by the recent election of J. P. McGinley as the general president of the Brotherhood of Carpenters and Joiners. No more worthy selection could have been made and we predict that that large organization will be greatly pleased with its action in that respect during the term of his office, and the usefulness of the brotherhood to its members greatly enhanced by him. T. F. Blair, also of this city and a great worker, was elected first vice-president. The other general officers are well known and earnest men and will fill their places to the entire satisfaction of the brotherhood.

—The Union of Boss Carpenters in New York has informed the members of the Journeymen Carpenters' Union that it has passed a resolution to employ henceforth only union members, provided that union members henceforth apply for employment only to members of the union of bosses. The journeymen will agree to that proposition.

—There is no better wood in the world for shingles, tanks, [illegible] doors, blinds, sash, etc., than cypress. It is also excellent for [illegible] ties, telegraph poles, fence [illegible]. Roofs of cypress shingles have [illegible] to remain tight and good for [illegible] is very slow and difficult to [illegible] soft and easy to work as [illegible] *Worker.*

[illegible] toil. But [illegible] in New York is very [illegible] organized, we [illegible] per day. Through the [illegible], and it is only for [illegible] League the carpenters in some places that [illegible] very weak has [illegible] of recruits. On [illegible] the trade was [illegible]

VIEWS OF THOMAS BURTT ON THE LABOR QUESTION.

Thomas Burtt is a member of the British Parliament, twenty years ago he was handling a pick in a coal mine in the North of England. He is one of the foremost champions of the laboring classes in his native land, and was recently on a visit to this country studying the labor conditions of America, especially in the coal and iron industries. He is president of the Miners National Union of England. In a speech delivered in Pittsburgh, Pa., on Oct. 10th, he said:

A revolution, bloodless but radical in its results, had been accomplished in the labor circles of England, and especially in the Northern counties. Forty years ago boys of seven years worked in the mines, from sixteen to eighteen hours each day; then it was enacted that no boy under ten years should be allowed to work and his labor per day was cut down to twelve hours, now, by legislative enactment—and in England the laws enacted are strictly carried out—the laborer in the mines must be over thirteen years of age and he must not be kept in the pit, until he is sixteen years old, over ten hours in each twenty-four. Forty years ago it was a common thing to see woman at work in the mines; now no women can be employed under ground. And the moral status of the laborer has greatly been improved. Years ago the man of wealth had the laborer under complete subjection; now, the laborer, if he has any grievance, boldly faces his employer and, with head erect, demands redress; the laborer is conscious that he is just as much of a man as his master. There are no victims now-a-days; you never hear that a man has been dismissed for advocating the rights of his fellow-laborers. This great change in condition and sentiment had to be fought for inch by inch and it required the united efforts of the miners themselves; it was by wise combination alone that the laborers improved their condition.

In past years those labor movements were fitful and of little service; now the labor organizations are permanent institutions, and their good services are steadily increasing. Most of them have accumulated large funds. They find this large fund a power, and it enables them to secure remedial measures without the necessity of resorting to strikes. They had learned from sad experience the necessity of concentrating their funds; experience had taught them that they could not make a successful strike without the sinews of war. There is not a labor union in England that has been successful with capital unless it had accumulated a round sum in the general treasury. As a rule, the funds are placed in the hands of reliable and responsible trustees.

The trade unions in England make very few changes in their responsible offices. In no case is any officer dismissed unless he has in some way misconducted himself in office. No incapable, no false man, however, is kept long in office. When an officer's popularity is lost he loses his usefulness. Only men of convictions are placed in high places; men who will even face their fellow laborers and stand and fall by the force of their convictions. The trades unionists have confidence in each other. Reasonableness is another prominent trait. A desire on the part of the workmen to be fair and modest in their demands has done much to consolidate their unions, to make them invincible and thus to greatly improve the condition of the laboring classes.

The trouble is that neither labor nor capital will look into the future to see what the ultimate interests may be; unfortunately both sides only consider their present interests. How can an identity of interests be secured? Only by co-operation. He was confident that in the near future the relationship of labor and capital would be one of hearty, earnest, healthy co-operation.

Laborers must trust one another; they must be fair and just, and above all, they must be intelligent. Turn the labor question as you may and it inevitably resolves itself into a mental and educational problem. The laborer must have character and he must seek education. Every workman should have better wages, short hours of labor and a good house to live in; but above all, he should have solid manhood and genuine honesty. With a good education and organization the workingman is the peer of the foremost in the land.

—Work is slacking off in Trenton, N. J., but organization is growing.

A VOICE FROM CLEVELAND.

Carpenters of Cleveland are the poorest paid mechanics in the city. And what is the cause of it? Nothing but so large a number of their trade keeping out of the union. Unorganized labor can never increase wages a single cent. Carpenters require more outlay for tools than almost any other trade, and should in justice receive even higher wages than almost any other trade, and should in justice receive even higher wages than bricklayers and stone masons. Yet they receive from $1 to $1.50 per day less. That men who are obliged to lie idle several months in each year should only receive $2.50 per day is outrageous. There is one remedy, and one only, and that is organization. The bosses will give no more than they are obliged to. Organize, agitate, educate!—*Cleveland Labor Star.*

THE EFFECT OF ORGANIZATION.

In speaking on this point, *The Craftsman*, published in Washington, D. C., takes the Washington carpenters as an example, and says: Right here at home, only a year ago the wages paid to carpenters were hardly two dollars a day, and apparently the supply of men willing to labor for that small sum was equal to the demand. No more was offered, and, not being in a condition to insist on more, the men took what they could get. A change, however, came o'er the spirit of the dreams of those, who thought they could procure all the skilled labor they might require at about half its value. Stimulated by the action of other classes of mechanics, the Carpenters' Union became a well organized body, a fair scale of wages was formulated, and notice given to the employers in time to base their bids on the new schedule. The result is briefly and satisfactorily told in the simple statement that wages paid to carpenters are fully 30 per cent higher than a few years ago, and the bosses, to all appearances, are making just as fair a profit from their operations as before.

SWISS CARVERS.

The first attempt to introduce wood-carving into Berne was made half a century ago by Christian Fischer, of Brienz, who may be called the father of the art; for, after acquiring it himself, he taught it to others and founded a school. Besides being an artist in wood, Fischer taught music, made musical boxes, and practiced the healing art, but, like many other clever fellows, he died in poverty. Sometime after Fischer began wood-carving at Brienz, a certain Peter Baumann began at Grindelwald, the making of the miniature Swiss chalets which are now so popular. He afterwards removed to Meyringen, where he taught his art to his three sons, one of whom, Andreas, proved to be a genius of the first order, and was equally distinguished for originality of design and skill in execution. He was the first to practice carving in relief. His roses are still regarded as master-pieces and serve as models for young sculptors. The success of the Baumanns encouraged others to follow their example, and wood-carving soon became a winter occupation in nearly every cottage of the valley of the Hasli. But the sale of carvings and chalets being restricted to foreign tourist in the summer season, principally through the intermediary of hotel porters, the trade for a long while was limited and unremunerative. But it struggled on, and in the course of time attracted the attention of local capitalists, who started workshops, opened depots for the sale of their products, and began an export trade which, with some fluctuations, goes on steadily increasing. The business of wood-carving now finds employment for several thousand individuals. In one establishment alone—that of the Brothers Worth—three or four hundred sculptors of both sexes are regularly occupied. Each has his or her specialty, the choice of which is left to individual taste. Some have an aptitude for, and excel in, the modeling of groups of animals; others, again, prefer to carve ornamental caskets and build miniature chalets. The women have great delicacy of touch, and their work in certain branches is preferred to that of men. One thing leads to another, and the abundance of certain sorts of wood in the district suggested the idea of adding to wood-carving the production of what may be called fancy furniture—carved chairs and tables, napkin-rings, and such articles. A factory has also been started at Interlaken, and is now in successful operation for making habitable chalets on a large scale. You have only to select your design, give the order, and all the parts of a chalet are sent to any destination, so arranged and marked that an intelligent joiner can put them together, and you have a handsome and picturesque house which you may live in as long as you like and even carry about on your travels.

Der Carpenter.

New York, November 1883.

Schutz- und Trutz-Bündnisse.

Arbeiter-Organisationen bedeuten Schutz- und Trutzbündnisse, sie sind ein Mittel gegen lange Arbeitsstunden und niedrige Löhne; sie sind eine Waffe gegen die Uebergriffe pläneschmiedender Monopolisten; sie dienen zur gegenseitigen Aufklärung der Mitglieder. Als Individuen sind die Arbeiter eine ganze Reihe von Nullen, vor denen die betreffende Zahl fehlt, um sie zu achtunggebietenden Millionen umzuwandeln; vereinigt, ist die Umwandlung da. Die Kasse des einzelnen Arbeiters ist nur zu schnell leer, wenn nicht täglich oder wöchentlich hinzugethan wird; vereinigt können die gesteuerten Beiträge über alle Schwierigkeiten der Einzelnen siegen. Jeder Arbeiter sollte einer Arbeiter-Organisation angehören. Schaut um Euch! Welche Arbeit ist die am meisten anerkannte? Die der organisirten Arbeiter. Welche Arbeit wird am besten bezahlt? Die der organisirten Arbeiter. Welche Arbeiter haben die kürzesten Arbeitsstunden und werden am besten behandelt? Die organisirten Arbeiter. Arbeiter-Vereine haben ihre Versammlungen, wo gegenseitiger Austausch von Ideen, Ansichten und Erfahrungen die Mitglieder aufklärt, und sie zur Erkenntniß ihres eignen Werthes bringt. Verschiedene Köpfe haben verschiedene Sinne, und Austausch derselben dient dazu, den Gesichtskreis der einzelnen zu erweitern und ihren eigentlichen Werth kennen zu lernen; es ermuthigt den Einzelnen, die Sklavenketten abzuschütteln und zu fordern: „So viel will ich für meine Arbeit; wollt ihr mir das nicht geben, so arbeitet selber und seht wie lange euch's behagt!" Arbeiter, es ist eure Pflicht, gegen euch selbst und eure Familien, daß ihr euch Arbeiter-Organisationen anschließt. Organisirt euch, daß ihr im Stande seid, die Anmaßungen eurer Unterdrücker zurückzuweisen und mit Herz und Hand für euer gutes Recht einzustehen; einzeln seid ihr auf Gnade oder Ungnade eurem Arbeitgeber [illegible] Denjenigen, den ihr durch euren Fleiß zum Herrscher gemacht habt [illegible] unterthan. Leser, gehörst du einer Gewerkschafts-Organisation an? Wenn nicht, versäume keine Gelegenheit.

Die Zeit naht mit Riesenschritten, wo organisirtes Monopol und vereinigtes Kapital den Arbeiter zwingen wird, energischen Widerstand gegen Uebergriffe zu leisten oder sich zur Leibeigenschaft degradiren zu lassen.

Der mächtige Einfluß einer starken Organisation.

In dem Bericht des Präsidenten der „International Cigar Makers Union" steht Folgendes: Die Int. Union bestand 1877 aus 17 Lokal-Unionen, jetzt existiren deren 185; die Mitgliederzahl war in dem genannten Jahre 1016, gegenwärtig sind es ca. 11,000. Ueber Strikes sagt der Bericht [illegible]: „Wir begünstigen dieselben nicht. Sie sollten nicht angewandt werden, bevor alle friedlichen Mittel versucht und erschöpft sind. Einen Ausstand zu beginnen, ohne kalte und ruhige Ueberlegung, wobei die obwaltenden Verhältnisse gehörig erwogen werden müssen, ist weder heroisch noch der Nachahmung werth. Der Zweck jeder gut organisirten Gewerkschaft ist, häufige Konflikte zu vermeiden zu suchen und Lohnerhöhungen zu erlangen, wenn immer die Geschäftslage günstig ist, ohne zum Ausstand schreiten zu müssen."

Während der verflossenen zwei Jahre bewilligte die Int. Union 191 Ausstände, größtentheils hervorgerufen durch die Verminderung der Revenue Taxe, wobei $77,[illegible].47 von der Int. Union verausgabt wurden. Außerdem wurden noch mindestens [illegible] freiwillige Beiträge für diese Ausstände gegeben. Für folgende Zwecke wurden diese Strikes begonnen: 97 für Lohnerhöhung, 52 gegen Reduktionen und 45 wegen verschiedenen anderen Ursachen. Von diesen waren 135 erfolgreich, 47 gingen verloren und 12 blieben unentschieden. Nach den monatlichen Berichten der letzten vier Jahre wurde eine sorgfältige Schätzung der erzielten Lohnerhöhungen vorgenommen und der Int. Präsident berichtet, daß dieselben jetzt ca. $150,000 per Monat, oder $1,800,000 per Jahr betragen. Die vereitelten Lohnreduktionen bewiesen daß die Mitglieder der Int. Union jetzt ca. $500,000 per Jahr mehr erhalten, als wenn die Versuche erfolgreich gewesen wären. Das demonstrirt den mächtigen Einfluß einer gut organisirten Gewerkschaft auf den Arbeitsmarkt.

Aufruf an die deutschen Carpenter.

Dieser Aufruf ist von unserer Milwaukeeer Union ausgegeben, aber er paßt eben so gut für andere Städte.

Kameraden!

Schon mehrere Male wurde es versucht, die hiesigen Carpenter in einer großen Union zu vereinigen, welches aber leider an der Theilnahmlosigkeit der Mehrheit unserer Kameraden scheiterte. Die hiesige noch bestehende Union hat daher beschlossen, an der Südseite und Nordseite je eine deutsche Union zu gründen, in denen alle Verhandlungen in deutscher Sprache geführt werden sollen. Es ist nicht zu läugnen, daß die Schwierigkeit der Sprache ein großes Hinderniß der Vereinigung entgegen setzen, was wir auf diese Weise zu überwinden hoffen.

Wenn diesen Sommer die Carpenter Milwaukee's vereinigt gewesen wären, so hätten sie eben so gut drei Dollars den Tag verdienen können, wie es unsere Kameraden in Chicago, St. Louis und anderen Orten erhalten. Allein das Nichtzusammenhalten ist der theuerste Fehler, welchen die Arbeiter nur zu oft begehen. Aber was dieses Jahr versäumt worden ist, darf nicht für nächstes Jahr verbummelt werden. Deshalb laßt uns zusammentreten und uns zu einem festen Bunde vereinigen. In kurzer Zeit wird ein Jeder ausfinden, daß dies der praktische Weg ist, wodurch wir unsere Stellung etwas verbessern können.

Wir sollten aber nicht blos die Lohnerhöhung im Auge haben, sondern auch für eine gute Gewerks-Krankenkasse Sorge tragen, damit im Falle der Noth wir uns einander beistehen. Unsere Kameraden in New York, Chicago, San Francisco ꝛc. sind uns in dieser Hinsicht weit voraus. Vor 5 Jahren war der Lohn in New York bis auf $1.50 und $1.75 gefallen; dann traten die deutschen Zimmerleute zusammen und gründeten eine Union und richteten eine Kranken- und Sterbekasse, sowie auch eine Unterstützung für Arbeitslosigkeit ein. Ist ein Mitglied der Union außer Arbeit, so erhält es aus der Kasse $5 per Woche. Der Lohn ist seit der Zeit auf $3 bis $3.50 gestiegen und die Krankenunterstützung ist $5 per Woche. Dies Alles ist durch einen Beitrag von 35 Cents per Woche erreicht worden. Hätten unsere Kameraden sich nicht vereinigt, so wäre ihr Lohn auf unter $2 zu stehen geblieben und sie hätten weder Kranken- noch Sterbegeld, noch würden sie, wenn außer Arbeit, $5 per Woche erhalten. Also ohne Union verdienten sie $8 bis $12 die Woche, ohne jede Unterstützung in der Noth; — mit der Union verdienen sie von $18 bis $21 per Woche und erhalten $5 per Woche in jedem Nothfalle, und das Alles durch eine Ausgabe von 35 Cents per Woche. Es sind also immer noch [illegible] Dollars und [illegible] Cents Ueberschuß per Woche.

Ihr seht also, daß es keine bessere Sparkasse für uns gibt, als eine gute Union. Natürlich kann Niemand erwarten, daß eine solche Union in einem Monat fertig ist. Die Erfahrung lehrt uns, daß die Arbeiter immer Geld für irgend einen Schwindel haben, der ihnen von den Kapitalisten aufgetischt wird, aber sehr selten die Lust und Ausdauer haben, [illegible] den Weg zu ihrem eignen Besten zu [illegible], und die Carpenter sind eben durchschnittlich wie alle anderen Arbeiter, sie kümmern sich blutwenig um das, was ihnen nöthig ist.

Kameraden, legt diesen Schlendrian bei Seite und tretet Mann für Mann zu einer Union zusammen, und laßt es uns ebenso machen, wie unsere Kameraden in New York. Noch ist Arbeit genug vorhanden, um unsern Vorsatz, den Lohn auf drei Dollars per Tag zu erhöhen, durchführen zu können. Freilich können dies keine 20 oder 30 Mann durchsetzen, sondern es kann nur durch die vereinigte Kraft aller Kameraden geschehen. Wenn erst die Krisis da ist, dann ist an keine Besserung mehr zu denken. Vereinigen wir uns aber noch vor dem kommenden Krach, dann sind wir im Stande, den Lohn aufrecht zu erhalten, wie es die Bricklayer, die Heizer und Lokomotivführer während der letzten großen Panik gethan.

So z. B. war der Lohn der Bricklayer in Cincinnati während der ganzen schlechten Zeit nie unter $4 per Tag, weil sie alle zur Union gehörten. Der Lohn der Bricklayer in Pittsburg und Allegheny City dagegen, wo keine Union war, betrug nur $2 bis $2.25. Hieraus geht klar hervor, daß auch wir Carpenter in Milwaukee einen besseren Verdienst erringen können, wenn wir Mann für Mann zusammenstehen.

Mancher wird sagen, die Bosse bezahlen das nicht. Das ist allerdings wahr, so lange wir es nicht fordern. Von selbst werden sie nicht kommen und zu uns sagen, ich gebe Ihnen 50 Cents mehr per Tag, obgleich das sehr in ihrem Interesse ist.

Allerdings glauben die meisten Bosse kurzsichtiger Weise, daß sie bei niedrigen Löhnen mehr Profit haben als bei hohen. Der harte Concurrenzkampf untereinander bringt ihnen diese Meinung bei. Ein Jeder sucht durch niedrige Contrakte mehr Arbeit zu erhalten, und versucht dann, seinen Profit von den Löhnen seiner Arbeiter abzuziehen. Geben die Arbeiter nach, so versucht ein anderer Boß dasselbe Manöver und in kurzer Zeit sind die Löhne überall gefallen. Die Bosse vergessen aber, daß sie dadurch ihr eigenes Geschäft ruiniren, indem durch niedrige Löhne die Kaufkraft der Arbeiterklasse verringert wird, was bald eine Stockung aller Geschäfte nach sich zieht. Hat die Majorität des Volkes — und das ist die Arbeiterklasse — kein Geld, so kann nichts consumiren, und bald häufen sich die Waaren in allen Fabriken an, Handel und Wandel stockt, und die Bosse selbst verlieren am meisten, indem dann sehr wenig gebaut wird und viele bankerott machen müssen.

Hohe Löhne bedingen einen guten Geschäftsgang, niedrige Löhne einen schlechten.

Wenn wir Carpenter aber zusammentreten und den Bossen kund thun, nächstes Jahr verlangen wir $3 per Tag, so können sie ihre Contrakte danach einrichten. Die Bosse haben diese Lohnzulage nicht aus ihrer Tasche zu zahlen, sondern wir ringen es den Groß-Kapitalisten ab. Und das ist eine Wohlthat für das ganze Geschäftsleben, indem dann mehr Geld in Cirkulation kommt. Jedermann, der nur das A B C der National-Oekonomie kennt, wird diese Wahrheit anerkennen.

Das Comite ist der Ansicht, daß die meisten Bosse dieser Stadt sich gar nicht weigern würden, einen Lohnsatz von $3 per Tag anzuerkennen, sobald sie wissen, daß wir nicht billiger arbeiten und daß jeder Boß dies zahlen muß. Dann ist der Konkurrenzkampf unter den Bossen derselbe geblieben, wie er jetzt ist, und keiner kann den andern mit den Löhnen unterbieten.

Dieses durchzusetzen, ist unsere Aufgabe, und wir fordern jeden Carpenter auf, sich der neuen Union anzuschließen und dabei zu bleiben, dann, aber auch nur dann werden wir unser Vorhaben durchsetzen können.

Unsere Versammlungen finden statt jeden zweiten und vierten Mittwoch jedes Monats in der Casino Halle, Ecke der 7. und State Straße, Westseite, Abends 8 Uhr, statt.

Die deutsche Abtheilung auf der Südseite versammelt sich jeden ersten und dritten Samstag im Monat, Abends 8 Uhr, in Mechanics Halle, Ecke Grove und Park Straße.

Mit kameradschaftlichem Gruß

Das Comite.

Spähne aller Art.

Die Nationale Association der Fensterglasarbeiter in Pittsburg hat infolge der in letzter Zeit im Gewerke stattgefundenen Strikes und Mißhelligkeiten mit den Bosses beschlossen, selbst Unternehmer zu werden. Die Association zählt 1700 Mitglieder und glauben dieselben unter sich $1,000,000 Anlage-Kapital aufbringen zu können, um die Fabrikation, deren Arbeitskräfte ziemlich beschränkt sind hier im Lande, selbst in die Hand zu nehmen.

— Die International Brotherhood of Locomotive Engineers hielt ihre 2[illegible]. Jahressitzung vom 27. Okt. ab in Buffalo. Es waren 3[illegible] Delegaten anwesend. Die Verhandlungen waren meistens geheim. Diese Gesellschaft ist eine der ältesten und bestorganisirten des Landes.

— Mr. Thomas Burt, einer der Vertreter der englischen Trades Unions im Parlament und seit 30 Jahren ein Trades Unionist, sagte kürzlich in Pittsburg, die Centralisation der Fonds sei das beste Schutzmittel gegen Strikes und habe in England mehr gethan, dieselben zu verhindern, als alle andern Mittel zusammen genommen.

— Ein internationaler Kongreß englischer und französischer Gewerkschaften fand Ende vorigen Monats in Paris statt, um die internationalen Beziehungen der Gewerkschaften zu diskutiren.

Der nächste finanzielle Krach wird schwer auf Diejenigen fallen, welche nicht zu einer gut organisirten Arbeiter-Vereinigung gehören. Ihr Schicksal wird in der That ein trauriges sein.

— Beinahe alle Kohlenländereien in Colorado und Missouri sind schon jetzt durch die großen Eisenbahn-Corporationen oder europäische Kapitalisten monopolisirt. Und schlimmer wird's immer.

— Warum sollen die Arbeiter die Welt mit Ueberfluß beladen, und selbst in Noth und äußerstem Elend leben? Es muß ein grenzenloses Unrecht herrschen, wo Diejenigen, welche Alles schaffen, nichts haben.

— Hand in Hand mit der fortschreitenden Civilisation gehen Bettler und Millionäre. Um 1[illegible] Clara Millionen Dollars zu führen, ist es nöthig, daß eine Million Menschen zu Bettlern wird.

Allerlei.

— Unionleute sollten einander stets zu Beschäftigung verhelfen. Sobald Ihr wißt, wo ein Job offen ist, lauft nicht hinter Non-Unionleuten her, noch sagt ihnen, wo der Job ist. Sehl Euch um und sorgt dafür, daß ein Union-Mann die Stelle kriegt. Haltet fest zusammen und seid einander treu. Die Scabs mögen für sich selbst sorgen!

Die Kesselschmiede und Schiffsbauer-Gesellschaft von Großbritanien hat 28,243 Mitglieder und ein Einkommen von $85,[illegible] pro Jahr.

— Die Brüderschaft der Lokomotive Engineure hat während der letzten 15 Jahre im Ganzen $1,[illegible] an Unterstützungsgeldern, d. h. $[illegible] im Durchschnitt für jeden Fall ausgezahlt und dafür zahlte jedes Mitglied jährlich $[illegible] pro Jahr ein. Die Bruderschaft bezahlt Versicherungen für den Verlust einer Hand, eines Armes, irgend eines anderen Gliedes oder eines Auges, gerade so viel, als wenn ein Mitglied stirbt.

— Die Carpenters in Baltimore haben ein System, welches ihre Mitglieder zwingt, erst ihre Beiträge zu zahlen, bevor sie einen Job kriegen können und der Scab, welcher keine „klare" Karte zeigen kann, hat niemals Aussicht auf Arbeit.

— Jeder Unionmann sollte den Versammlungen seiner Union beiwohnen; viele Unions sind kaput gegangen, weil ihre Mitglieder von den Versammlungen wegblieben, oder sonst nachlässig wurden. Wenn die Leute erst eingesehen haben, daß das Bestehen ihrer Union vom Besuch der Versammlungen abhängt, dann kann es ihnen nicht mehr mißlingen, ihre Organisation zu einer unbezwinglichen Macht zu erheben. Seid auf Eure Interessen so versessen wie die Bosse auf die ihrigen.

— Einer der häufigsten Irrthümer ist es, sich einzubilden, daß eine Union mit kleinen Beiträgen erfolgreich wirken kann. Das einzig Richtige ist, die Beiträge so hoch zu machen, daß man einen Fond ansammeln kann, mit dem jeder Kampf, und sei es der schwerste, durchgefochten werden kann.

— Horace Mann, Amerika's großer Patron der Erziehung, sagte: „Trotzdem durch die Ingenuosität des amerikanischen Erfindungsgeistes die Arbeitsprodukte verdoppelt und vervierfacht werden, ist doch nicht ein einziger Schritt gethan worden, um eine gerechte Vertheilung dieses Produkts zu erzielen.

— Die Gewerkschaften müssen auf ihr Banner schreiben: Nieder mit der Lohnarbeit! Nieder mit dem heutigen System und deren Träger, damit jedem Arbeiter der volle Ertrag seiner Arbeit werde:

Vereint sind wir alles,
Vereinzelt sind wir Sclaven.

Das beste Mittel.

Den gesellschaftlichen Frieden haben die Trades Unions freilich nicht herzustellen vermocht; es fehlt auch gegenwärtig nicht an Streitigkeiten zwischen Arbeitern und Arbeitgebern, und die Lohnkämpfe haben nicht aufgehört. Aber sie sind wenigstens auf eine verhältnißmäßig geringe Zahl reduzirt worden. Dank der Organisation der Arbeiter, welche ihre eigene Kraft, sowie die der Gegner genau kennen, sich also nicht in Illusionen wiegen, werden die meisten Differenzen gütlich geschlichtet, so daß man sagen kann, jeder Strike, der zum Ausbruch kommt, repräsentirt [illegible], die nicht zum Ausbruch gekommen sind. Die Entwickelung der Industrie und die Zahl der Arbeiter in Betracht gezogen, ist England dasjenige Industrieland, in welchem die Strikes am seltensten sind. Und heute, wo die Arbeiterzahl die fünffache ist, giebt es dort lange nicht so viele Strikes, als zu Anfang dieses Jahrhunderts. Den Einigungsämtern und Schiedsgerichten, sei es nach Vorschrift des liberalen Fabrikanten Mundella oder nach der des Friedensrichters Kettle, ist freilich dieses Ergebniß nicht zuzuschreiben, wie Herr Brentano es meint, sondern vor Allem der Tüchtigkeit der Organisation, welche die Gegner von leichtfertigem Angriff und die Mitglieder von gefährlicher Selbstüberschätzung abhält. Die Arbeitgeber haben dies auch [illegible] eingesehen, und in manchen Gewerben ist es zur Vereinbarung bestimmter Lohnnormen gekommen, [illegible] nannter sliding scales [illegible]

[illegible]

[illegible] Wahrheit sind die [illegible] das beste Mittel gegen [illegible], [illegible] Organisationslosigkeit [illegible] Mutter von Strikes [illegible]

Chicagoer Brief.

Redaktion des „Carpenter".

Auf Ihr zweimaliges Ersuchen, Berichte Branch 7, Union 21, für unsere Zeitung zu senden, bin ich beauftragt worden, dieses zu übernehmen und werde ich von jetzt ab jeden Monat einen Bericht einsenden.

Zweig 7 hat in dem letzten Halbjahr die Werbetrommel tüchtig gerührt und hat es verstanden, durch öffentliche Versammlungen, wie durch persönliches Agitiren der Brüder auf den Arbeitsplätzen die Mitgliederzahl bedeutend zu verstärken, so daß sie jetzt 140 Mitglieder zählt. Es giebt hier aber auch noch ein großes Feld zu bearbeiten, da es hier noch viele deutsche Carpenter giebt, die keiner Organisation angehören.

Für Samstag, den 10. Nov., haben wir einen Ball veranstaltet, der in jeder Beziehung, soweit es sich voraussehen läßt, von Erfolg sein wird.

Die hiesige „Trade & Labor Assembly" wird sich an der nächsten Herbstwahl betheiligen, indem 2 Delegaten auf dem demokratischen resp. republikanischen Ticket als Countybeamte laufen werden und auf die Stimmen der Gewerkschaftsmitglieder rechnen. Zweig 7 hat dagegen Stellung genommen und erklärt, daß sie dagegen protestirt und denen ihre Unterstützung versagt, da erstens die Konstitution verbietet, innerhalb der Gewerkschaften Politik zu betreiben, sie sich nie dazu hergeben wird, für die alten Ausbeutungsparteien (Demokraten und Republikaner), die nur die Vertreter und politischen Handlanger des Kapitals und Monopols, unserer Feinde, sind, ihre Stimmen herzugeben. Doch würden wir es immerhin als einen Fortschritt in der Gewerkschaftsbewegung begrüßen, wenn die Gewerkschaften selbstständige Arbeiterpolitik treiben würden.

Arbeiter! Wann werdet Ihr endlich Eure Feinde erkennen?

Chas. Giedelberg.

Chicago, 1. Nov. 1883.

Wie kann das arbeitende Volk seine Freiheit erringen?

Ist der Reichthum ein Produkt der beständigen Beraubung des arbeitenden Volkes? Doch wie kann die Arbeit so kolossal betrogen werden? warum kann das arbeitende Volk im Rahmen der heutigen Gesellschaft sich nicht der Folge dieser Beraubung erwehren?

Das arbeitende Volk ist nicht im Besitze der Arbeitsmittel (Maschinen, Grund und Boden, Verkehrswege, Kapitalien ꝛc.), es steht im Abhängigkeitsverhältniß zu den Besitzern dieser Arbeitsmittel, muß diesen seine Arbeitskraft nach dem Gesetze von Angebot und Nachfrage verkaufen und ist darum auch den Schwankungen überwiesen, welche in Folge der planlosen Produktionsweise entstehen. Weil bei der heutigen Entwicklung der technischen Hülfsmittel menschliche Arbeitskraft im Ueberfluß vorhanden ist, also eine Reservearmee von Arbeitern stets bereit ist, die Plätze der Beschäftigten einzunehmen, so wird der Arbeitslohn auf die denkbar niedrigste Stufe gedrückt und das um so mehr, je weniger die Arbeiter organisirt sind. Die beste Organisation aber vermag an diesem Abhängigkeitsverhältniß wenig zu ändern, wenn die Ursache der Abhängigkeit, der Privatbesitz an Arbeitsmitteln, nicht beseitigt ist. So lange dieser besteht, werden die Arbeitenden eben immer Vasallen des Geldsacks sein.

Die Lohnarbeit, wie die andern Abhängigkeitsverhältnisse des gesammten arbeitenden Volkes vom Kapital, durch welche es Einzelnen möglich wird, sich auf Kosten der Massen immerzu zu bereichern, sind innerhalb dem Rahmen der heutigen Gesellschaft nicht zu beseitigen. Lohnarbeit und Privateigenthum an Arbeitsmitteln bilden die Grundlage der heutigen Gesellschaft, der Staat hat die Kapitalherrschaft sanktionirt.

Soll das Volk die ökonomische Freiheit erobern, soll der Arbeitsertrag des Volkes dem Volke und nicht einzelnen Bevorzugten zufließen, soll die Existenz der Arbeitswilligen eine gesicherte und nicht wie heute stets bedrohte sein, dann muß die Grundlage der Gesellschaft eine andere werden: An Stelle des Privatbesitzes muß der Gemeinbesitz an Arbeitsmitteln treten, und an Stelle der Lohnarbeit die staatlich geregelte genossenschaftliche Arbeit.

Das sind die Grundlagen der neuen, besseren Gesellschaft, des sozialen Volksstaates, den wir an die Stelle des heutigen Klassenstaates setzen wollen.

(Arbeiter-Stimme.)

[illegible]rung.

[illegible] Union von Cincinnati [illegible] Mitglieder der der [illegible] und J. G. Huntington, [illegible] des Sommers Unionl[illegible] auftellt, und im [illegible] Contrakte [illegible]

THE CARPENTER

A MONTHLY JOURNAL FOR CARPENTERS AND JOINERS.

VOLUME III. NEW YORK, DECEMBER, 1883. NUMBER 12.

THE FRENCH DELEGATES.

During the past month we have had the pleasure of a visit of 14 delegates from the Trades Unions of Paris to the Boston Exhibition. They represent 82 trades unions or "syndical chambers" of Paris, and arrived in New York on Nov. 30, and returned on Dec. 19—after 19 days stay in America, during which time they visited Boston, Lynn, Quincy, Lowell, Providence, Fall River, New Haven, Hartford, Philadelphia, Jersey City, and several other places. Their mission was to investigate the industries of our country, the social condition of our people and to establish friendly relations with the workingmen of the United States. Everywhere they went they were met by public receptions and the utmost hospitality was extended to them, except in a few instances where some manufacturers denied them admission to their factories. In New York a banquet was given them by the Central Labor Union on the night of their arrival, and on the 17th inst. an immense demonstration of workingmen was held in their honor at Cooper Institute. This is the second delegation of workingmen that has visited America, the first coming here to the Centennial Exhibition. These industrial missions are indications of a growing sentiment of fraternity among the workingmen of all nations.

CAPITAL AND LABOR.

We hear and see so much nonsense said and written on the labor and capital question, and much of it growing out of a confusion of terms that I will beg a small space in your paper for explanation. A great portion of this comes from using the terms capital and labor, for capitalists and laborers. The monopolists started this, for it is their desire to confuse the minds of the people to keep them from understanding, but why it should be kept up by intelligent persons who claim to be reformers I cannot understand. Now we hear them discussing the rights of labor and capital. As rights belong to persons exclusively I cannot see how capital which is but a thing, can have rights. If they mean the rights of laborers and capitalists, let them say so; but then the rights adhere in them, because they are persons and not because they chance to hold capital. If we admit otherwise we open the door to class legislation. It is when men undertake to separate them and bestow all the capital upon one class, and throw all the labor upon another, that the conflict begins, and that conflict is irrepressible. There can be but two ends to it; Either the laborers must own the capital with which they work, or the capitalists will own the laborers. The people can pay their money and take their choice, but it is useless to try to patch up a compromise, for no compromise can stand. Labor and capital are inseparable, and those who control the one will possess the other in the end, and no power can prevent it.—H. G. THURMAN, Senator of Ohio.

—A French labor paper, *L'Ouvrier*, will soon appear in Montreal. This is very important, as it will eventually lead to the organisation of the French Canadians.

— This month we publish a very interesting letter in German from the Carpenters' National Union of Germany, in which
gard
thems
hours

STRAY CHIPS.

—Dennis Kearney, the sand-lot hoodlum, is in the employ of the San Francisco *Call* and *Bulletin*, the boycotted papers of that city.

—The Wharf Builders of San Francisco have followed the example of the Carpenters of that city, and adopted the nine-hour rule with success.

—In the next convention of the International Typographical Union the adoption of a mortality fund will have an important place in the discussions.

—An item in the Detroit *Spectator* reads as follows: The same series of labor lectures being published in THE CARPENTER have been commenced in the *Journal of United Labor*, central organ of the K. of L.

—Some of the trades Unions at Barcelona, Spain, have opened houses of refuge for poor foreign workmen who come there to compete. In this way they win them over to unionism.

—Denver, Col., has a live Trades Assembly and it has made a movement to build a Workingmen's Hall in that city. The indications are that the project will be carried out.

—The fight against Stilson Hutchins, of "rat" newspaper fame, still continues with the odds in favor of organized labor, while Hutchins becomes more desperate every day and threatens all manner of legal and illegal violence.

—On December 9, the question of abolishing the prison contract system in Texas was submitted to the people of that State, and by a majority of 84,976 they declared that prison contract labor must go. A similar agitation is now going on in Kentucky.

—The average pay of those employed by the Pullman Palace Car Co., of Detroit, Mich., is $1.96 per day. This includes the wages of managers and foremen, some of whom get $5 to $6 a day. A few receive as low as 60 cents a day. Over 800 workmen are employed and labor organization is forbidden among them.

—For tyranny unexampled the course of the oil cloth firms of Philadelphia and the contracting tailor bosses of New York are notable instances. Both demand that their employes shall sign away their right to membership in any labor organization. The oil cloth printers have submitted to the yoke of slavery, the tailors of New York refuse to do so.

—The Commissioner of Labor Statistics for the State of Missouri, Henry Newman, has been indicted for corruption in office, having sold a notaryship. This is the political bummer against whose appointment as Labor Commissioner the organized workmen of the whole State protested. We wonder what Governor Crittenden thinks of his protege?

BOYCOTT CLARK'S THREAD.

"Clark's O. N. T. Sewing Cotton" should be boycotted everywhere. The working people use it very largely and our wives and families everywhere should drop it entirely. The reason for this is that the Clark Estate is erecting a row of buildings in 73d St., this city, and refuses to pay union wages or hire union men. They have called out the police force and de-

IMPORTING FOREIGN LABOR UNDER CONTRACT.

A circular demanding the suppression of the unjust system of importing foreign labor to America under the contract system, and which will be presented before the next meeting of Congress, has been distributed among the labor organizations of this country to be signed by men and women who toil for a living, but are often compelled to suffer, because this foreign element come here from abroad and work for a mere pittance. The petition gives opinions of the American Consuls in all foreign countries relative to the degrading manner in which these Old World people live, and in the way in which American agents for a certain sum induce men to come to America, "the land of the free and the home of the brave." Such glowing stories are told them that they pack up and come without ceremony. It is desired and intended, if possible, to make this importation of foreign labor a criminal offense, and everything possible will be done to prevent its continuance.—*Labor Tribune.*

COURAGEOUS STRUGGLE OF THE GLASS WORKERS.

Since June 30, two-thirds of the Window Glass Workers' Association, in all 1,700 members, have been standing out against a reduction in wages of from 10 to 30 per cent. This comes now directly after the fight of last year when $73,000 was spent by the union in maintaining its scale of wages which, of course, makes the fight at present all the more severe. By years of patient endeavor the men succeeded in reducing the hours of labor to eight and a half per day, but the employers now demand that the workmen perform extra work which will increase the hours of work to more than nine per day.

To give an idea of the means employed by the National Association of Window Glass Manufacturers to effect a reduction of the wages of the workmen of America, we quote from the minutes of their last annual meeting held at Saratoga, July 11, 1883: "Resolved, That the treasurer be authorised to pay a sum not exceeding $30 per man for each blower or gatherer brought over from Europe after September 1, 1883, provided the same is employed by some member of this association.

In spite of this the workmen feel confident of success, and with the pecuniary assistance of their co-workers will doubtless bring the Manufacturers' Association to terms.

SERIOUS TIMES IN TROY.

There are indications of a bloody struggle in Troy, N. Y. The ninety scab molders in Schleicher's foundry, after six months' scabbing, have become disgusted and joined the union in a body. Those men took the places of the strikers early last Summer and then, according to reports of the press, a reign of terror ensued. Shooting, clubbing, rioting, etc., in which one man was killed and several permanently disabled, was the order of the day. On account of low wages and bad treatment the scabs at last left the foundry and joined the union. The owners of the works say they will keep up the fight and import non-union men to supply their needs.

TRADE JOTTINGS.

—The Amalgamated Carpenters now number 22,369 members with 389 branches, all over the globe.

—Carpenters in Australia work only eight hours per day and have a half-holiday on Saturdays.

—International Convention of Bricklayers and Masons will be held in Cincinnati, O., January 14, next.

—Reduction of wages and discharge of men seem to be the rule at present very largely in the iron industries.

—During the strike of the carpenters in Berlin, last May, 10,777 marks or $3,696 were collected in support of the men.

—The wood carvers of Boston have obtained the nine-hour system without any trouble in all the leading shops of that city.

—The International Convention of the Lake Seamen's Union opened at Detroit, Mich., on December 10, and was largely attended.

—Cabinet makers in Louisville, Ky., are becoming Vanderbilts on $8 per week and, of course, they are so contented they don't want to organize.

—A largely attended meeting of the carpenters of Covington, Ky., was held on the 16th inst., and a union under our jurisdiction is the result.

—In Cincinnati the Trades Assembly is engaged in a very interesting discussion with the clergy in reference to laws for the advancement of the working classes.

—A strong disposition prevails among the building trades of this city to make a general nine-hour movement next Spring and the prospects are it will be successful.

—All the carpenters employed by Williams & Parkhurst and Cooke & Berryman, of Orange, N. J., have struck because the employers will not pay for a full day's work when only nine and a half hours can be made.

—In the Hawaiian Islands there has just been formed a large and radical labor organization under the presidency of Sigismund Danielewicz, who was formerly one of the leaders in the labor movement on the Pacific coast.

—There were 71 applications for the job of putting in one load of coal at a hotel in this city last week. This fact is commended to the attention of the fellows who say that any man who wants wo[rk] can get it.—*Irish World.*

—New Orleans freight handlers wo[n] their strike and now the railroads must deal with the union to get men. Unlike their New York friends, the New Orleans men were well organized and had plenty of money.

—The quarrel between the Internat[ional] and Progressive Cigar Makers ought [to be] settled on some fair and just b[asis] ... welfare of the trade cannot ... tention; the bosses gloat ... good union men deplore ...

—Reports from Englan[d] ... show that carpenter work ...

... edition.

FEDERATION OF TRADES.

To Labor Societies and Friends of Organized Labor.

The Federation of Organized Trades and Labor Unions of the United States and Canada asks your co-operation with it for the purpose of securing the accomplishment of the following results during the coming year:—

I.—The better organization of labor, especially among the working women and factory operatives of the country. Financial aid for this work is needed. Let all who can contribute money do so, and the sum, however small, will be gratefully received and rigidly applied for this work.

II.—The collecting of data about labor troubles,—their cause, duration, effect, etc. A slight amount of personal effort in forwarding accounts of the strikes and lockouts of which you have knowledge will assist the Legislative Committee in obtaining information of much value.

III.—The creation of labor literature. The Federation offers a prize of $50 for the best Essay on Trade Unions and Strikes, said essay to make not more than twenty-four nor less than eight pages of the size of our Annual Report. By bringing this offer to the attention of your friends you will enable us to secure a wider range of talent from which to select. Manuscript should be forwarded to the Secretary as soon as completed.

IV.—The Federation urgently requests all labor organizations to consider the question of universal federation, and respectfully asks that the result of such deliberation—scheme of organization, platform, etc.—be sent to the Legislative Committee, in order that they may lay before the next Labor Congress some practical plan for the unification of labor.

V.—We ask that copies of all labor bills submitted to the various Legislatures and to Congress be forwarded to us, and the Legislative Committee will assist to the best of their ability in furthering the same.

VI.—The obtaining of names to a monster petition for the enforcement of the National Eight-Hour Law, and the immediate forwarding of such names to the Secretary of the Federation.

The Fourth Annual Session of the Federation will be held in Chicago, Ill., commencing on the first Tuesday in October, 1884. All labor organizations are cordially invited to send delegates. The following is the basis of representation:—

From National or International Unions, for 1,000 members or less, one delegate; for 4,000, two delegates; for 8,000, three delegates; for 16,000, four delegates; for 32,000, five delegates; and so on. From State or Provincial Federations of Trades Unions, two delegates. From local Trade Assemblies or Councils, District Assemblies of the Knights of Labor, or local Trades Unions, one delegate. But no local Trades Union shall be entitled to representation which has not been organized six months prior to the session of this body.

The revenue of this Federation shall be derived from each National or International Trade or Labor Union, and each Trades Assembly or Council, or District Assembly of the Knights of Labor affiliated with this Federation, and shall be assessed upon the following basis: For 1,000 members or less, $10 per annum; 1,000 to 4,000, $20; 4,000 to 8,000, $25; 8,000 to 12,000, $30; 12,000 to 20,000, $40; over 20,000, $50. Local Trades Unions may be entitled to representation upon payment of $10 per annum. State or Provincial Federations of Trades Unions shall pay $10 per annum for each delegate sent by them to the sessions of this Federation.

The Reports of the Third Annual Congress may be had on application to the General Secretary. Single copies 10 cents, or twenty copies for one dollar.

FRANK K. FOSTER,
Secretary.

QUANTITY VS. QUALITY.

When Oscar Wilde was in this country it was reported in the papers that "he wondered how it was that mechanics did not show a greater taste in the development of the artistic." It may have been said at the time by the majority of employes, in answer to his remarks, that quantity and not quality was the end in view by the majority of employers. Of course, there are some employers and architects who aim at quality, but at the same time there must be a sufficient quantity necessary to qualify a workman's standing as first-class.

It is not quality alone that was the aim of our old masters, but speed is necessary for this new age and country.

Now is this really as it should be? Do employers and architects and those who have the building up of this young country desire quantity before quality? I have worked at the bench in this country since 1856, and my experience has been that quantity takes precedence over quality. And employers, with rare exceptions, want all that you can give them in the form of quantity. If you can give in addition to quantity the appearance of quality, so much the better is your standing as a workman. Here, again, is a wrong when the economic view of the question is considered; to give with quantity the additional quality is a tax wrongly wrung from one's physical energies. For this is what is termed "high pressure" working. And one who has a practical knowledge of over twenty years' experience knows that it is a cause of undue waste to the system. It is the case sometimes that the workman combines strength with quality and quantity, and is thus enabled to work on this high pressure system longer than the ordinary workman. But it is an undue waste to the system nevertheless. Is this undue waste to the physical and brain energies a thing to be encouraged? No true man will say it should be encouraged. Why then is it? It is said alas! too frequently that machinery is the cause of this high pressure working. And that if the workman, particularly in some branches, wants to hold his own, he must work with all his brain power and physical strength to compete with it, and no truthful workman will deny it. Why it should be so is beyond my comprehension, when we have been told so often that machinery was introduced to ease off the heavier burdens in the various trades. I am cognizant of the fact that machinery does take off some of the heavier work in my trade, but the fact is there nevertheless that our trade has to work harder to-day than in my younger days. I cannot account for it in any other way than that speed or high pressure working is the cause of the mischief. It is quantity to-day, but it was quality in my younger days. In my younger days it was, do your work well, if you didn't you were discharged; but to-day it is "rush your work through, if you don't I don't want you," or "I can't pay you the full wages."

The plea is often put in that this young country is too poor for quality of workmanship. "It wants all the work possible for its money." Selfishness was born from the beginning in us. Selfishness often gives rise to the plea of self-preservation. But selfishness, in the main, has not shown itself to be a thing always desirable and encouraged. Rather the other way. It encourages a false economy. Its aim is to live at another's expense, and the weaker in all cases are the sufferers by it, and who the weaker are there is not a single employe but that can tell you.

W. H. STEVENS.

TORONTO, Canada.

WHEN THE END WILL COME.

Strikes are expensive, wasteful, disorganizing. But the intervention of force, invariably on the side of the employers, is

EMBRACING OUR GENERAL PRESIDENT.

BRANCH 4 held a regular weekly meeting at their Hall, 106 E. Randolph street, on October 24. Brother Francis in the chair. After the usual routine business Bro. W. T. Henderson called attention to the fact that our new General President, J. P. McGinley was present in the hall, and after a few remarks on the valuable services rendered to the Brotherhood and Union No. 21, by Bro. McGinley in the past, he predicted that the Brotherhood would increase and be prosperous during President McGinley's term, and concluded by moving: "That all the members of Branch 4 who were present should embrace our new President." The motion was seconded by Bro. John Cornwell and was carried unanimously.

Bro. McGinley replied by thanking the brothers for their good wishes and hoped they would say when his term of office was ended "Well done, thou good and faithful servant!" He thought there was some radical changes needed in the Brotherhood to make it a grand success. He was in favor of equalization of funds and universal dues, if we only pay 5 cents a month, let us all pay alike. He thought, however that we could all pay 60 cents per month and have a tool insurance benefit, also a sick benefit (same as now exists in Union No. 21), and apply it to the whole of the Brotherhood. He thought the death and accident benefit required to be revised. He was in favor of having a General President to act as salaried organizer for the Brotherhood, and said if all the brothers in the different Locals will go to work and get advertisements for our journal, THE CARPENTER, it can be made self-supporting, and the money thus saved go toward paying the new officer. He was also in favor of having the headquarters for five years in one city and providing for a Board of Trustees of say five members to be elected from the Local in the city where the headquarters are established, and all money, etc., to be voted by that body. A General Council to be selected from all the Locals, said Council to have the power to rescind any act or resolution of the Board of Trustees. He thought the plan of electing the officers of the Brotherhood by "popular vote" had been a grand success, and was of the opinion that all proposed changes in the Brotherhood should be voted upon by popular vote, but he thought it was a mistake to vote for eight vice presidents at large. Chicago had two vice presidents and she only needed one; he thought the Brotherhood ought to be divided into districts for the purpose of electing vice presidents. Bro. McGinley then thanked the brothers for their good wishes and took his seat amidst long applause. After Bro. McGinley's speech all the brothers present "embraced" him, according to the resolution.

CHICAGO, Ill.

—Work has closed for the Winter at Rushville, Ind., and not much prospect for Spring.

—In Indianapolis wages are 20 to 25 cents per hour; a few men out of work. Men working on short time.

RESOLUTIONS ADOPTED BY BALTIMORE UNION No. 29.

At a regular meeting of Union No. 29, Brotherhood of Carpenters and Joiners, held Dec. 10th, 1883, the following preamble and resolutions were unanimously adopted. Whereas, the members of this union accepted an invitation from Union No. 1 of Washington, D. C., to visit them and believing that fraternal greetings should be of more frequent occurrence,

Resolved, that this union return to our brothers of Washington Union No. 1 our thanks for their hearty reception and banquet, given to the members of this union, on their visit to Washington.

Resolved, that we shall ever cherish in our memory the action of our brothers, who though bound together by the ties of our noble Brotherhood were strangers, but who proved by their action, that the living stream of good fellowship in our noble organization had but to be touched by such worthy fellow craftsmen as our brothers of Union No. 1, to produce plenty of goodly cheer for the inner man.

Resolved, that we hope if ever any question comes before us as a Brotherhood, no matter whether disagreeable to us as a union or individually, we shall ever remain in the ranks keeping a steady hold of the great principles underlying our organization, and though differing in some points, all should labor, for a common object, "THE BETTERING OF OUR CONDITION," through a noble band of brothers, the Brotherhood of Carpenters and Joiners of America.

Resolved, that should it be our good fortune to have the pleasure of a visit from our brothers of Union No. 1, we shall endeavor to repay the debt.

Resolved, that a copy of the above preamble and resolutions be published in THE CARPENTER and LABOR FREE PRESS, and a copy be sent also to Union No. 1 of Washington, D. C.

By order of Union No. 29.

J. W. PUGSLEY, }
J. S. BYE, } Committee.
J. J. BENTLEY. }

CHICAGO REPORTS.

At the Executive Council the following reports were presented:

BRANCH 11 made the motion that whenever strangers visited the Executive Council, that on entering the the conductor should conduct them into the middle of the Hall and introduce the President and Secretary; also when any officer of the E. C. visited any Branch other than his own, the Branch conductor should go through the same ceremony. The object of this, as will be seen, was to show courtesy to strangers visiting our Union and also to the President and Officers of the E. C. Branch 11 had a fine social entertainment on November 26th. The hall was crowded to its utmost.

BRANCH 7 made a motion to introduce a Tool Benefit in the Brotherhood. It was unanimously agreed on all sides that such a benefit would be a means of great strength to the Brotherhood, but some of the brothers thought the benefit ought to be introduced into Union No. 21, locally at first, and then try and make the benefit universal throughout the Brotherhood. It was pointed out by some members that just as soon as the benefits in our Brotherhood were valued by members who did not take an active part in the management of the union, just so soon would we be able to retain members, as at present many members who joined the Union paid their entrance fee and one month's dues in advance and never came near the union after, and this tool benefit would strike home to every carpenter.

After some discussion a committee was appointed to draft a scheme to introduce a tool benefit into Union No. 21. The committee appointed were Bros. Boyer, [illegible] and [illegible].

BRANCH 4 offered a resolution that a committee be appointed to wait upon the Chicago branch of the Amalgamated Society of Carpenters and Joiners at their next meeting to invite them to appoint delegates to attend the meeting of our E. C. The committee appointed were Bros. [illegible] and Boyer with the President Blair.

After the meeting the Committee had an interview with Mr. Ralph Inglelow, Secretary of the Chicago branch of the Amalgamated, who stated that the matter had been brought up in their branch some time ago, and that all the brothers of his society were heartily in favor of such a scheme, the Chicago branch of the Amalgamated now contains 110 members in good standing, which would make quite an acquisition to the force in Union No. 21.

Toronto, Canada.

The Canadian Trades Congress will be held December 26-28, in this city, and the indications are it will be well attended by Delegates from all parts of the Dominion.

The Plasterers' strike will be long remembered here as a rather novel affair in trade conflicts. The bosses instituted action for $1,000 damages and sued out an injunction against the union for interfering with the men employed by them. And in this all the [illegible]

Alameda, Cal.

At our meeting Nov. 15, we had a very full attendance to receive our brothers of San Francisco Union No. 22, who had paid us a fraternal visit and thereby revived the lagging energy of some of our members. These fraternal visits should be encouraged in every possible way, especially visits of large unions to small unions as opposition falls heaviest on the latter, and a fraternal visit strengthens and revives the weaker union.

Special-Advertisements

THE CARPENTER.
PUBLISHED MONTHLY
BY THE
Brotherhood of Carpenters and Joiners,
OF AMERICA.
Office: 184 William St., New York.
TERMS.—Fifty cents a year, in advance, post-paid.
Send all moneys and correspondence for this Journal to
P. J. McGUIRE, Secretary,
184 William St., New York

NEW YORK, NOVEMBER, 1883.

— A Merry Christmas and a Happy New Year to all our readors and to all members of our Brotherhood! Let each one of us make the coming year more productive of actual good than even this year has been, let us hope our success in organizing the trade will be even greater, and that we may each one of us point with pride to the work we have done in the glorious cause of Labor's Emancipation.

WAR UPON LABOR.

Everywhere the hands of the capitalists are raised against trades and labor unions. They demand that workingmen shall sign contracts not to belong to any such organizations. Among the oil cloth printers in Philadelphia, among the silk weavers, the tailors and the cigar-box makers of New York, among the shoemakers of St. Louis, among many other trades and in many other localities, the edicts of the bosses have gone forth in opposition to the right of the workers to form associations for their own protection and security. This is one of the plainest signs that the capitalists fear trades unions, because through them the workers will soon be educated into the fulness of their manhood and will not be the slaves of others. The capitalists by making war upon trades unions are only bringing destruction upon their own heads. They are simply inciting the basest passions of a disorganized mob, instead of dealing with bodies of organized men, trained and disciplined, and fully responsible for their acts. Has it come to this that the capitalists alone can have the right to organize, and when workingmen attempt it, they shall be locked out and driven into starvation?

HARD TIMES COMING.

Some asinine creature in Milwaukee, who calls himself the editor of the *Evening Wisconsin*, has the effrontery to pen the following article in regard to the prospects of a panic:

> There are indications from all sections of the country that there must soon be a readjustment of the rate of wages in order to prevent the discharge of tens of thousands of workmen on the eve of Winter when the wants of the household are the greatest and the most pressing. The demand for all kinds of manufactures has become so slack, and the prices offered are so low that operations cannot be continued except at a ruinous loss unless labor consents to a reduction in wages. The steel rail mills of Cleveland will shut down on the first of December, as will also other mills in that hive of industry. And so it will all over the country.

So then this fledging of a political economist has no better remedy for an impending panic than reduce the wages of the workingmen. That, he holds, will prevent the discharge of tens of thousands of workmen. Such shallow reasoning is not uncommon to the press generally. During the last panic the same arguments were used and with disastrous results. Just think, because the demand for goods slackens there must be a reduction in wages, or else business will stop! Is that the best remedy that our business men and editorial flunkies can discover? To our mind every reduction in wages simply cripples the purchasing power of the workers, and to that extent curtails the demand for goods, and this adds to the intensity of the panic.

Instead of reducing wages, why not reduce the hours of labor to equal the demand for goods? That would be the better way. But to do so, of course, is not the desire of the bosses, as long as Labor is not organized well enough to compel them. The only way to prepare for the hard times approaching is for every workman to become a member of his trade union or to join some labor organization.

POINTS TO STUDY.

Do ye want to understand the principle underlying the nine-hour movement? If you do read this. If not, then let it alone and grunt and toil 10 hours a day. But if you want to know how to uplift yourselves how to get more manhood, more liberty, and more rest, then listen to what we have to say and don't throw this down to read some article in a sporting paper, or some novel, or some sensational suicide in the daily press.

If ten men go to a shop where only nine were wanted (wages $3 per day), one is refused. When men are out of work, they are often willing to work cheaper. The man out of work accordingly visits the shops and offers to work for less than $3 per day, and each one of the nine, fearing he may be discharged to make place for the cheap, idle man, drops his price to keep his place, say to $2.50. This is a plain illustration of the principle that competition regulates wages by reducing them below the level they would be if there were no competition. Each of the nine men lose 50 cents a day by the competition of one, and still that man is idle.

The nine men working each ten hours a day would make ninety hours a day in all. Suppose now the nine men agree to work only nine hours a day which would be a loss of one hour from each of the nine men, or a total of nine hours loss. What would the employer do, if he could not induce the men to keep on at ten hours or get other ten-hour men to take their places. He would then hire the one idle man.

But, you say, these nine men would get only nine hours' pay, or $2.25 a day instead of $2.50, thereby losing 25 cents a day, simply to oblige an employer to employ one extra man. This, you say, would be a loss of $1.50 per week to each man under the nine-hour system, and that, you say, is the squre reason why you don't believe in it.

Stop, not too fast. Here comes in a principle you don't know much about evidently, or you would not say so.

Granted the men are reduced to $2.25 per day. What then? The ten men are at work, the one idle man whose competition obliged the others to take $2.50 a day, is at work. He is not outside to beat down competition. There is no competition except among the ten, and they stick together. What is the result? There being no outsiders to bid for work and underbid the rest, their request for more wages is conceded, and wages go back to $3 by a law as universal and unerring as the law of gravitation.

Therefore, reduction in the hours of labor does not in the long run reduce wages. And our first move should be to establish nine hours as a day's work all over the land.

AN ORGANIZER IN THE FIELD.

Bro. R. Stephens, Oakland, Cal., fourth Vice President, writes that at an early day he will start out on a trip in the interest of the Brotherhood. He will visit various cities in California, and organize carpenters Unions. He will proceed to Santa Clara, Los Angeles, Stockton and Sacramento; after remaining in the latter place a few weeks he will stop off at each of the above places on his way home and give them further instructions. In this trip Bro. Stephens should have the financial assistance of every one of our California unions, especially San Francisco and Oakland.

—Persons wishing competent carpenters can procure the same by applying to John McCartney, 221 South Desplaines street, Chicago, Ill.

AN ADDRESS FROM OUR GENERAL PRESIDENT.

TO THE OFFICERS AND MEMBERS OF THE BROTHERHOOD:

Brothers:—In accordance with the usual custom it becomes my pleasing duty to not only thank you for the honor you have conferred upon me by placing me in the position I now occupy. But also to ask you all as Unions and individuals to give your newly elected general officers, not only your hearty confidence, but also your cooperation. And if you do so I assure you that at the end of our terms of office, you will feel as I do now that your confidence will not be misplaced.

I wish to call your attention to the fact that some very important changes are necessary in our constitution. One of the most important of which is, that portion governing the election of general officers on page 5 of our constitution. All general officers, in my opinion, should be elected by a general vote and the nominations should be made at the regular convention and submitted to the unions, unless said convention should be deemed unnecessary, and in that case the system adopted this year will give general satisfaction.

Another very important change is necessary in the number and mode of electing Vice-Presidents of the Brotherhood, we should have but two Vice-Presidents, who with the G. P. should constitute the Executive Board, and in place of the other six, we should have district organizers. The United States and Canada should be divided into districts, and these organizers should be elected by and from the unions, located within the boundaries of each of the respective districts and not by a general vote of the whole Brotherhood.

I am also in favor of changes in that portion of our general laws relative to the Endowment Fund, by which it can be made more secure, and the payments more prompt. I would also recommend the adoption of a system of universal dues, initiations, benefits, etc. In the case of new unions, a union should be six months in good standing in the Brotherhood, before it should be required to comply with said system.

I would also respectfully ask all members of the Brotherhood to cease to criticise our present system so severely, but put your shoulders to the wheel, and let us move our young organization forward, until we have complete control of our craft. You may rest assured that your General President will do his whole duty and he in return asks you to do yours. The only drawback we will have for the present, will be the lack of funds with which to perfect the organization of new unions but that difficulty. We hope to be able to overcome this in the near future.

In conclusion I respectfully ask you to kindly criticise my actions during my term of office, and overlook my mistakes.

Hoping our concerted actions may be productive of the greatest possible results, I have the honor to be fraternally yours,

JOHN P. McGINLEY, Gen'l Pres.

Chicago, Nov. 15th, 1883.

THE POWER OF AN IDEA.

A profound sensation has recently been created in Oxford, and indeed throughout England, by a lecture delivered by William Morris, the poet, in that conservative University town, in response to an invitation from a society of undergraduates. A sufficiently commonplace occurrence, one would think at first blush, but not a little startling when one learns that the lecture consisted of an indictment of our present industrial system, and a championship of modern socialism from the standpoint of art. Professor Ruskin gave his presence in sanction of the lecturer, and social and literary circles are stirred to their depths. At this rate the universities of England may become, before long, like those of England, "hotbeds of Nihilism." Who knows? Mr. Morris, we believe, has already been followed by Mr. Hyndman of the Democratic Federation, and a lecture is announced for February by Ruskin himself on the significant subject: "The Storm-Cloud of the Nineteenth Century." From Mr. Morris' lecture we quote the following: "One man has an idea, and you say he is mad. Two men have the idea, and they are fools. One thousand have it, and you hear of a new religion. Ten thousand, and society trembles. One hundred thousand, and there is war. A million, and there is peace on earth."—*Liberty.*

BROTHERHOOD NOTES.

—New By-Laws, embracing a sick benefit have been adopted by Oakland Union No. 36.

—Constant accessions of new members is the report from San Francisco Union No. 22.

—Union No. 2, of Cincinnati, is having a boom of new members; initiated a whole raft full lately.

—Charleston Union No. 52 has initiated 113 members, and they are greatly pleased with our ritual.

—Washington Union No. 1 has accepted the endowment plan and is in splendid working order.

—Trenton, N. J.; work is fair, all union men at work, men at work 9 hours per day and getting 9 hours' pay.

— A Carpenters' Union has been formed this month in Utica, N. Y. It promises to be a thrifty organization.

—Bro. Philip H. Fagan, President of Hartford Union No. 43, is President of the newly formed Trades Assembly of that city.

—Bro. R. Stevens, of Oakland, Cal., our fourth Vice President, will soon start out to organize the interior towns of California, at the expense of the California unions.

—Bro. J. T. Bentley, of Baltimore Union No. 29, started out the other day and got several subscribers for our journal and promises to get more. Other brothers might follow his example.

—Union No. 2, of Cincinnati, is picking up wonderfully; many new members. The Fin. Secretary of this Union, Bro. G. Brethauer, and the Cor. Secretary, Chas. Rumpler, as well as all the officers, are good, active men.

—Bro. G. Edmonston, Washington, D. C., has been appointed Carpenter for the House of Representatives. W. Dove, a politician, and not even a carpenter, was a candidate. Our Brotherhood demanded a union man for the place and got him.

—Philadelphia Union No. 8 has established a Labor Bureau at D. R. Macomlvin, 1727½ Lombard street, Philadelphia, Pa. Members in good standing, wanting employment, will report there, also those knowing where employment can be procured.

—A new charter has been granted to the carpenters of St. Louis, Mo., and a strong organization is springing up. The charters of Unions No. 5, No. 12 and No. 14 are revoked. Only one union will be recognized hereafter in St. Louis, and that union will be known as Union No. 5, and is so chartered.

—Fraternal visits of one local union to another should be encouraged. They lead to a better understanding between the unions, and cement the bonds of solidarity all the stronger. The visit of our Baltimore Union to Washington had that effect. So had the visits of San Francisco Union No. 22 to Alameda, Oakland and San Rafael.

—In another column we publish a list of the Corresponding Secretaries of Carpenters' Local Unions. This will be an aid to our travelling brothers, so that when they come to any of the cities on the list, they will know where to inquire for the meeting place of the union, etc. Any errors in this list will be corrected upon due notice.

—Union No. 29, Baltimore, Md., has adopted the following resolution in regard to the first meeting in every month: "That after initiation there will be no business transacted, but the remainder of the evening shall be devoted to a free discussion of such subjects as may be most beneficial to Labor." The report says that this step has had a good effect in bringing members to the Union.

—Portland Union No. 50 has $2.50 initiation fee and 50 cents a month dues, and it fines any member 25 cents who does not attend the meetings at least once a month. It pays $10 per week accident benefit until $50 are paid, in case injuries are received at work. From May 1, 1884, nine hours shall constitute a day's work, from 7 A. M. to 12 M.—1 to 5 P. M., and union men not work with non-union men who refuse to comply.

a hard struggle last May. To obviate this [illegible] journeymen held an immense meeting lately [and] resolved to stand firmly by their scale of [prices].—Active agitation is going on among the [b]inders, turners and cabinet makers of Ber[lin to] strengthen their unions.—In Munich, Dres[den, H]anover and other cities the trades union [move]ment is assuming gigantic proportions, in [which] the shoemakers propose to move for a [reduc]tion of the hours of labor from 15-16 per day [to] eleven.—The carpenters have formed [unions] in Breslau, Brandenburg, Rathenow, Me[iningen] and Frankfort, and joined the National Car[pente]rs' Union of Germany. In Frankfort and [vicinit]y the wages are 22 pfennige an hour.

[EQUA]LIZE THE HOURS OF LABOR IN SUMMER AND WINTER.

[I no]tice several places complain of the reduction [of wages] on account of the short days. And this is [not con]fined to carpenters alone; all the building [trades] in nearly every instance make the same [compla]int. I know of a Boss Painter in this city [that cu]t his employes twice this fall, two weeks in [succes]sion, on account of short time. In some [places] Carpenters, Bricklayers, Plasterers, and [Painte]rs are getting a full days pay for the short [days]. But in many cases the wages in Winter are [paid b]y the hour. Now my remedy is: Let the [journeym]en say to their employers when they com[mence] the cutting down, that we journeymen will [work] the same number of hours next Spring and [Summ]er, let it be 8 or 9 hours—no matter what [the sca]le. For if a man can live through Winter [on 8 h]ours or 8½ hours pay, in the season when [everyt]hing he uses is much dearer, then I am sure [he can] do the same in Summer and even live better.

[WAS]HINGTON, D. C. J. G. B.

FROM OUR MAILS.

Toledo, Ohio.

[Busi]ness is slacking off here; wages $2.00 to $2.50 [per da]y. From the 1st of December our monthly [dues h]ave been 50 cents per month and the initia[tion fe]e $2.00. The weekly sick benefit of $4.00 will [comm]ence six months afterwards.

Cleveland, Ohio.

[On] Saturday, December 1, Carpenters' Union [No. 11] got a judgment in the Common Pleas Court [of thi]s County for $184.70 against Patrick Doyle [who a]t one time was treasurer of our union, and [who so]me time ago claimed to have been knocked [down] and robbed of the money. The first hearing [was ha]d before a Justice of the Peace, and judg[ment] was obtained against the defendant, where[upon] he took an appeal to the Common Pleas. And [that] Court has decided against him. John F. [illegible] and Mr. Phibbs were our attorneys, and [they d]eserve great credit for the manner in which [they co]nducted the case. Trade is getting pretty [dull h]ere, although most all union men are em[ploye]d. Wages $2.25 and $2.50. A dull Winter is [expect]ed. The union is doing well, but we cannot [expect] much growth until next Spring.

Boston, Mass.

[Matters] are moving slowly at present; times are [very] slack; quite a number of carpenters walking [idle]. But the best of it is they are non-union [men], and I hope that it will be always so while [they k]eep out of the union. The Central Trades [and L]abor Union entertained the workingmen's [delega]tes from Paris on December 3, at the Parker [House]. Over 150 persons sat down to supper at [that fi]rst-class hotel. Carriages were furnished to [escor]t the delegates around to the principal [work]shops, and all the bills were paid for by the [Gove]rnment of Boston. Our committee, F. K. [illegible], John Cluskey, and Geo. E. McNeill waited on [the M]ayor and explained that the French dele[gates] were here and expected to be entertained [by th]e workingmen of Boston, whereupon the [Mayor] agreed that the city should foot the bill. [This i]s the first time in the history of this city that [the Go]vernment has been so ready to recognize [the wo]rkingmen.

Victoria, British Columbia.

[Trad]e is good, although we are on short time, [averag]e wages $3 per day. There is a great deal [of lost] time in winter on account of wet weather. [Our un]ion still keeps growing, constant initiations [and a]pplications. All work has been stopped for [the wh]ile on the Canadian Pacific R. R. in British [Colum]bia, and the men are all flocking down here [lookin]g work, but they find out by inquiry that [the va]cancies are filled by union men when they [arrive], retreat Eastward and leave us uninjured [by the]ir visit. We would not advise any one to [come] here at present for they will find it up hill [work t]o get employment.

[At ou]r last meeting I was ordered to contradict [the st]atement that Bro. H. Whitten of San Fran[cisco] had organized our union. The way in which [it was o]rganized was: Several of the chips of this city [met to] discuss the advisability of forming a union. [Those p]resent were: J. Murchison, late of Hamilton [Union] No. 18; S. Anderson; A. Noble; D. G. Mc[Donal]d; and Joshua Holland. We then called a [mass] meeting of the trade. D. G. McDonald was [voted] in the chair. He addressed the meeting on [the b]enefits of unionism and the necessity of or[ganizatio]n, and spoke of the Brotherhood. 17 men [came] forward and signed the roll. That was the [start]. Although disheartened at the small num[ber, w]e persevered until now we number 75 per [cent. o]f the carpenters of this city in our ranks.

Denver, Col.

[A few] of the carpenters and joiners of Denver [met o]n December 6, and passed a resolution in [favor] of organizing a union. It was a stormy night [and on]ly a few were present. Our idea is now that [as soo]n as we can get a respectable number together [and co]llect the money, we will send for a charter [an]d to proceed to organize. An organization [is badl]y needed in Denver. No established wages, [and n]o difference made between good workmen [and p]oor ones. Wages all the way from $2.25 to [$4 per] day, so the average is a paltry $2.75. Be[cause s]ome of the contractors and bosses here cut the wages some time ago to $4.00 per day; pay all men or nearly all the same. That was their first move; the next was to cut down time to nine hours and only pay for the hours at the rate of $2.50 per day. Work is not very plenty here now; weather cold, living higher than in Summer. If the bosses would pay full pay for nine hours it would be better and more like business. It is just what they should do. For now a man has to work hard and fast to keep warm and can do about as much work in 9 hours now as in 10 in extreme hot weather. In Winter here coal, provisions and everything a workingman has to buy goes up, and his work becomes scarcer, and his wages go down, so it is a hard struggle to live at all.

Baltimore, Md.

FRATERNAL VISIT OF UNION NO. 29 OF BALTIMORE TO WASHINGTON UNION NO. 1.

At 6.25 P. M. on Thursday, Nov. 15th 1883, a delegation from Union No. 29 left Camden station of this city for the purpose of paying a fraternal visit to Union No. 1 of Washington. The delegation was composed of J. W. Pugsley, J. J. Bentley, John Rye, Felix Gruber, G. H. Striewig, J. H. Craddick, Thos. Keenan, John Bond, W. H. McKenney, W. H. Beam and Robert McKinley. Arriving in Washington at 7.35, the delegation was met by a Reception Committee from Union No. 1, when there was a general hand shaking and greetings were exchanged. The Reception Committee then escorted the visiting brethren to Abner's hall, where a general reception took place. The address of welcome was made by President George Suter of Union No. 1, who was followed by G. Elmendorf of the same union. Response was made by President J. W. Pugsley of Union No. 29, in a very appropriate manner. He thanked the members of Union No. 1 for the kind reception, and also discussed the principles and workings of the Brotherhood of Carpenters, paying particular attention to the 8 hour system, also the contract convict labor system. J. J. Bentley of Union No. 29 was next called to the stand, throwing every other question aside he paid particular attention to the endowment feature of the Brotherhood, explaining the plan thoroughly, and proved that the action of the General Convention in 1882 was perfect in every detail, except in case of an epidemic, or some accident when a large number of members might lose their lives. The address was received with great enthusiasm by all present.

J. H. Craddick, Vice-President of Union No. 29, was next called on.

After short addresses made by members of Union No. 1, Felix Gruber of Union No. 29 made quite an extended address regarding the principles of the Brotherhood. When the President arose to announce the adjournment, Mr. Bentley stepped forward and in the name and in behalf of the delegation from Union No. 29, presented the President of Union No. 1, Bro. George Suter, with a handsome gold badge—the emblem of the Brotherhood—stating that it was typical of the principles of the Brotherhood, and that he hoped it would be received not for its mere intrinsic value, but as a testimonial of the friendship and good feeling displayed by the visiting brethren, hoping he would hold it as a memento of the occasion. The presentation was responded to in a very appropriate manner by the President, who stated he would hold it in kind remembrance of the first fraternal visit of Union No. 29 to Union No. 1. This little episode was quite a surprise to all present.

After this the banquet hall was visited and full justice done to the choice viands provided. Supper being over the pleasures of the evening commenced in good shape. Ex-President Elmendorf presided and stated that the different members would be called on for toasts, to spin a yarn or recite a poem, commencing with the recitation of a poem and a toast to Union No. 29, which was responded to by J. W. Pugsley, who after a neat address gave a toast to the President and members of Union No. 1, which was responded to by Pres. Suter to the Order at large. J. J. Bentley gave the following toast: "The Bald Eagle, the glorious emblem of American liberty, may she ever flap her wings with prosperity around the members of Union No. 1." After short speeches by Felix Gruber, Ward, Bond, Crandall, Galloway and W. E. Ringwalt of the *Washington Critic*, the visitors left for Baltimore at 11.30 P. M. with a high appreciation of the manner in which they were entertained, which was fully expressed by the cheering that greeted each other as the train departed from the depot.

Cincinnati, Ohio.

The complimentary entertainment given by Union No. 2, on December 2, at Workman's Hall, was a splendid affair in every way. The programme opened with an overture and then a song by the Cincinnati Glee Club; an address by Otto Brethauer in the interest of unionism and organization among carpenters. Among the many arguments he used, he demonstrated that Union No. 2 had brought the wages up to the present standard. He narrated the history of the union and its strikes, and said the second strike was not a complete failure, because after that it taught the bosses a good lesson, and if it were not for that strike carpenters would have less wages to-day in Cincinnati. Piece work was denounced by the speaker as demoralizing, and if it were generally introduced, two-thirds of all the carpenters employed now could do all the work and the others would be thrown idle, which would result in reducing wages. And by joining the union this might be stopped. Those who stay back are keeping others from joining, and the ones who always have excuses about "Carpenters won't stick together," are the ones who don't want to stick themselves. Throw these petty excuses to the winds and come forward and act like men. Bro. Brethauer then appealed to the ladies and urged them to appeal to their husbands and brothers to attend the meetings and join the union, and in an effective manner he presented the reasons why women should be interested in trades unionism. Brethauer's remarks were loudly applauded.

The hall was overcrowded, every seat was taken before 8 o'clock and the stairways and galleries were packed. These entertainments prove more successful than mass meetings in drawing in non-union men.

Master Alex Rampler recited a poem dedicated to the journeymen carpenters. After several songs and a comic sketch, a brilliant tableau, entitled "The Combined Building Trades," was displayed. The balance of the programme consisted of an address by Henry Behrens who appealed to non-union men to come into the fold of union. Then songs and an operatic sketch, which called great mirth, followed; the whole concluding with a soiree.

On December 15, 1883, the grand ball of the combined Trades Unions of this city will take place.

Portland, Oregon.

Our union is prospering beyond our most sanguine expectations; we have now over 70 members and are initiating at the rate of 40 per month. We appointed a committee at the last meeting to secure a larger hall and intend to give a grand ball soon. The union is just beginning to be known. Some carpenters do not know of it yet, though it has been advertised in the different papers. We expect to have 200 members this winter; our initiation fee is $1.00, and 50 cents monthly dues until the end of this quarter when the initiation will undoubtedly be raised to $2.50. Portland has a population of 35,000 and is rapidly increasing; of that number there is at least 300 carpenters so we have the material here for a large union. We dont take any but first class mechanics; all our men are employed, but others are idle; work is getting slack.

Troy, N. Y.

The Carpenters Union of this city is in a first class condition; our organization is increasing very rapidly and we have now the leading and best carpenters and joiners in the city. One of our members died a few weeks ago, we had a short notice. However a special meeting was called and we drafted a set of resolutions of respect, and sent a delegation of 75 members, headed by Doring's Troy City Band, to attend the funeral wearing the usual badge of mourning. Our charter is draped in mourning for 30 days. I have distributed copies of THE CARPENTER among our members and they speak in the highest praise of it. I will send you subscribers to commence with the new year. This winter we will have a mass meeting at the City Hall. Several of our members speak very highly of the Brotherhood. The Barbers of Troy have formed a strong union.

Washington, D. C.

On last Thursday night a new era was inaugurated in the history of our Brotherhood, which was a practical illustration of the spirit of unity that pervades our craft.

Local Union No. 29 of Baltimore paid us a fraternal visit and created an impression that will not soon be forgotten. Local Union No. 1 received the visiting brothers at the depot and escorted them to Abner's spacious hall, where addresses of welcome were delivered, and responded to. After a few moments spent in greetings, Pres. Pugsley of Union No. 29 in a neat little speech presented Pres. Geo. Suter of Union No. 1 with a beautiful gold pin emblematic of our order. This act of brotherly consideration took our President so by surprise that he stood like a bashful maiden, embarrassed for the want of fitting words to express his feelings of grateful acknowledgment. President Suter is not a speech maker but an active sensible worker, who commands the respect of all for his sincerity. At the banquet table speeches were made by nearly all the visiting brothers, and several of Union No. 1, as well as Mr. Ringwalt of the *Evening Critic*, who presented the claims of the "pencil pushers" to recognition of their product, as a part of the industries of our land. In a short but impressive speech, Pres. Pugsley in responding to the address of welcome made a very forcible speech on the objects of organization. Bro. Beatty of Union No. 29 followed and spoke of the benefits of the endowments. Bro. Chas. Galloway of Local Union No. 1 made the speech of the occasion. He said, that while workmen were ready to complain of the abuses of power, very few gave much thought to a permanent remedy. He thought the non-enforcement of the 8 hour law was enough to teach the working classes that they had been giving their political support to a class of men, who cared but little for their welfare, and while he had his party bias he was ready to abandon it for the good of his class. He thought the labor element as an independent factor in politics could make itself felt more effectually than in strikes, or disjointed movements of a mighty rabble with no systematic course of action.

San Rafael, Cal.

Union No. 35 has expelled A. Geraper for violating our rules in working piece work, and we also got the sub-contractor on that job discharged. Wages $3.50; union men all employed.

St. Louis, Mo.

Building is very nearly at a standstill, everything dull; plenty of men idle. Strangers are taking what little work there is at low wages, offering themselves at $1.50—$2 per day. Union No. 5 is making glorious headway.

Utica, N. Y.

Wages vary from $2.50 to $2.75, and from that down to $1.25. Heretofore the bosses have made a practice of cutting down wages about December 1, but this Fall they have feared to do it on account of our union being organized.

Philadelphia, Pa.

Seeing so much spicy news in the trade columns of our journal last month, it makes me believe that the old ship is not so rotten as I have heard some fellows say. But there are croakers everywhere. And to tell the truth, it is enough to make Philadelphia carpenters ashamed that they have not been better represented in the paper than they were. We have never been able to find out whether it has been the fault of our C. S. or the laziness of some of our members that we had no news before now. We are confident now of plenty of news from all quarters, as Bro. Chas. Wells has been deputized by Union No. 8 to correspond with all local unions. It is to be hoped they will reply. Bro. Wells has been working on the energy of our worthy C. S. for some time to get him to correspond with the various unions, but the C. S. not receiving any answers, his veracity was questioned. Hence Bro. Wells has kicked and [illegible] saddled the labor of one month's [illegible] on him as a punishment for [illegible] is believed that a little [illegible] between the unions [illegible] and beneficially well [illegible] on the dep[illegible] member [illegible] will [illegible]

per Jahr

$2.00 per J[ahr]

Die Expedition.

THE LABOR QUESTION.

HOW SOCIETY IS CONSTITUTED.

LECTURE XII.

In treating the labor question we have to deal with that complex body known as society, and we have seen that society can only exist by industry, which manifests itself through certain elements, which are five—Land, Labor, Capital, Exchange, Insurance.

The question naturally arises, of what is this complex thing, which we call society, composed?

We shall find, upon investigation, that this thing, or collective body or being, which we call society, is, itself, composed of two separate factors, viz., *man* and the planet which he inhabits, or, in other words, man and his environment.

Therefore, we find that it is necessary to go back, and, as it were, get behind what we have previously said in relation to the elements which enter into the activities of society, and find out of what factors that society is, itself, constituted.

Now it is evident that without those two factors, man and the planet, society would have no being. Given the planet only, without man, there would be no society; given man only without the planet, evidently man could not exist.

If we can imagine a man in full possession of his faculties suddenly placed upon the planet, the first question he would probably ask himself would be—*Where am I?*

With the knowledge we at present possess, which is very limited compared with our possible knowledge in the future, the reply would be: You are placed upon a planet, the surface of which is described and explained by geography; it is made up of materials, the knowledge and arrangement of which deal with the composition of that planet, and comprise the sciences of geology, mineralogy and chemistry.

Its inhabitants are the subject of natural history, both animal and vegetable. The structure of these things and their explanation, is the province of biology, and its subdivisions, anatomy, physiology and psychology. In relation to the highest type of them, *man*, there is the record of history.

The laws of the motion of the atmosphere which surrounds the planet, comprise the sciences of pneumatics, optics and acoustics.

The science of hydraulics, mechanics and hydrostatics, explain the motion of the earth and the waters.

The planet is, permeated by forces of incessant and tremendous power, which may, perhaps, be but one force in various forms, as the "correlation of forces" would seem to demonstrate, but which are at present known and investigated under the names of magnetism, galvanism, heat, light and electricity, but each is, at present, the subject of a distinct branch of science. And, finally, the science of astronomy deals with the knowledge that this planet is one of many planets floating in space, and as being part of a system of planets, that system but part of another system, and so onward beyond the power of the human mind to conceive.

This shows how comprehensive the question, and how comparatively great the amount of knowledge necessary to reply intelligently and fully to the question, *Where am I?*

With the comparatively limited knowledge which we at present possess, the answer to the question, *What am I?*—which is, probably, the second question which this man, in full possession of his faculties, would put, if suddenly placed in our midst, would relate exclusively to man, not to the male or female, the white, the black or the red, not to the Aryan, Semetic, Turanian, African or Australian, the Asiatic or European, the savage or the civilized, the slave or the freeman, but to *man*, contemplated as a being of peculiar form, possessing physical, mental and moral attributes and forces, endowed with intelligence, subjected to certain laws which specially govern his organic structure, and to certain other laws which specially govern his physical or mental structure, and as knowledge increases it may be found that there are laws which govern the moral domain of his nature.

As viewed externally, anatomy and physiology would reply to the question, What [illegible] that thus: You are a com[illegible] provision and [illegible] structure, adapted by [illegible] adaptation to the con[illegible] and b[illegible] in which you are [illegible] their b[illegible] a me[illegible]

and whose actions are directed by self-contained intelligence.

The human structure is a machine of infinite complication in detail, but extremely simple in design. This structure is evidently formed to exist upon a planet composed of matter having a specific degree of substance, and of what is known as solidity. Every part of the body is framed to act upon the matter which surrounds it; therefore the man and the environment are incessantly acting and reacting—the one upon the other.

The body is simply the instrument with which man communicates with the external world; the limbs are the means of locomotion; the head is the centre where the mental faculties generate that volition which directs their movements.

The trunk is the laboratory, where the machinery of the body prepares for use the material for growth and repair, and where what is exhausted and useless is extracted and carried off.

And above and superior to all these, man has feelings, sympathies and emotions of a most complex and extraordinary nature, which cannot be located, but which are the source of his highest and purest happiness, the consensus of which are expressed under the head of moral sentiments.

If this man, suddenly appearing in the full possession of his faculties, should further follow the bent of his curiosity and ask, *Why am I?* he would be referred to political science and sociology for an answer, as those sciences should teach what his duties are, what are his relations to beings similarly constructed, that is, to other members of society as well as to himself.

So much for the scientific, or, as it may be considered by some, the theoretical view of the case, let us now turn to the practical. We men of the labor movement desire to secure the means of existence to every member of society who is desirous and willing to work for a living and to make life harmonious, which can never be done until poverty is eliminated from society.

The word "poverty," of course, conveys different meanings of different minds; we simply mean here, and for the moment, physical poverty—the want of food, clothing and shelter—of good, wholesome and varied quality in sufficiency, and even abundance, to maintain a healthy physical, mental and moral condition in man.

If we take the definition of William Cobbet we may, perhaps, be able to agree with it, as far as it goes. "Poverty is, except where there is an actual want of food and raiment, a thing much more imaginary than real; the shame of poverty, the shame of being thought poor, is a great and fatal weakness, though arising in this country from the fashion of the times themse ves."

Cobbet was an Englishman, and wrote at a time when education was not considered necessary for the "common people" by the "Lords" of creation, the aristocracy; and while we may agree with Cobbet we must extend the signification of poverty until it covers the absence of intellectual education and moral training.

To eliminate poverty we must control the elements of industry. To do this we must employ the means. What are the means to employ?

The problem is, to give to labor all that labor creates, and to all the other elements that which equity and the strictest justice should determine to be their share of the wealth produced by their joint action; in a word, the equitable distribution of wealth.

(To be continued.)

FOREIGN SURPLUS LABOR.

Mr. Robert Howard, of the Cotton Spinners' Union at Fall River, Mass., proposes a remedy for the competition of English operatives. He says:

"A great portion of the surplus labor, not only of Oldham, but of other towns in England, finds its way to this city, coming in direct competition with labor here, crowding our factories and tending in no small measure to increase the burdens of our operatives. On this account we intend to submit a scheme, on a co-operative basis, by which land can be purchased at low rates in the Southern States and colonized by the unemployed operatives from this city, whom we can send there from time to time, when the condition of the labor market warrants such action.

— Union No 53 has been organized this month in Benecia, Cal., by Bro. Stephens, of Oakland, Cal. The new union starts out with a large roll of members.

SOME CHANGES OF IMPORTANCE PROPOSED BY A CHICAGO MEMBER.

I take issue with J. T. B., as to the Endowment Fund. I hold that benefits when thoroughly established and well understood by our members, will be the means of *retaining* nearly all our members. We admit plenty of new members in the course of the year in our various Locals, but the number of suspended members for non-payment of arrears by far outnumbers the new ones. Indeed, in our local union many new members only pay their initiation fee and the first month's dues in advance, and that is the last seen of them. Now, why is this? My answer is, for the want of a universal system of dues and benefits.

What is it that makes the Amalgamated Society of Carpenters a power? Because they have a good system, which is universal, and benefits which are of practical value to the members in this world. To be sure it is very good to provide for one's family after we leave this world. But tell me how far will the balance of $250 go for a family after all the expenses of burial have been paid. After death it will at best only afford temporary relief, to say nothing of the cumbersome way of collecting our endowment benefit according to our present constitution.

What is required, is that the benefits should be paid promptly, to be a source of strength to the Brotherhood, and that can not be done, unless our Constitution is so changed, as to enable a local union to pay the benefit as soon as it is due, which cannot be done unless the members of every Local pay alike the same dues, and there is an equalization of the funds of the various Locals once a year.

The trouble of our Endowment is that it concentrates all the resources of our Brotherhood on one benefit which is no benefit to a man while he lives. Of all my experience in both benevolent and trade societies I do not know of one that pays more death benefit than will pay the expenses of a decent burial. I know of some that have a kind of insurance fund where members can insure their lives for a thousand dollars if they wish, but we cannot establish those things yet in our Brotherhood. Nor do I think it would be advisable to do so, even were we in shape to do it. What I want to see is benefits that would help to *retain* members in our Brotherhood, and if we do that I am quite sure that our Brotherhood will be a power in the land.

Now, our Union, like Union No. 20, has complied with the endowment law to the letter, we have laid aside the required 10 cents per member since September, 1882, and we have done more than paid our share of each assessment promptly. We have had 10 deaths in the B. in as many months, and at our present strength we collect only enough to pay one death benefit per month, if all the unions comply with the endowment law. Even at that we collect only enough to pay benefits that have accrued, and leave nothing in the fund to meet future calls.

Now I am in favor of reversing the existing order of things. I think, if we make the death benefit $100, and the accident benefit $250, we will be doing about what is right. Then we will be able at the same rate as we now pay, to create a Fund to meet future calls and pay benefits promptly. If a member wishes to provide for his family after death, he can take out a life insurance policy in any life insurance society.

Why not establish a Tool Benefit in our Brotherhood? Such a benefit would be of practical use to every carpenter, and would be valued by every carpenter, single or married. Ten cents per member per month on 1000 carpenters would be $100 per month, and 1000 carpenters, if they are careful about their tools, are not going to lose half that much per month. You can establish a universal sick benefit of $5 per week. Some of our Locals have such a benefit now. These benefits would be of practical value to a member in this life, and such benefits would be a source of great strength to our Brotherhood, but by centring all our resources upon one benefit which we cannot maintain, which is of no value to a man in this life and which takes months after his death before his family receives it, will not increase the strength of our Brotherhood.

With $3 initiation fee and 60 cents per month dues, universal all over the Brotherhood, giving new Locals the privilege of charging only $1 initiation for the first year of existence we can pay $5 per week sick benefit, $100 death benefit, $250 accident benefit, and a tool benefit of not less than 50 cents, or more than $30 on one claim.

Adopt these ideas, Brothers, and make our Brotherhood strong and powerful!

L. J. B.

UNION 21, CHICAGO, ILL.

Der Carpenter.

New York, Dezember 1883.

Das Wirken der Trades Unions.

Wird dem Arbeiter, der Mitglied einer „Gesellschaft" ist, ein zu niedriger Lohn angeboten oder zu lange Arbeitszeit zugemuthet, so steht er nicht hülflos da, wie der einzelne Arbeiter, der keine Wahl hat, als sich zu fügen oder zu verhungern: er wendet sich an seine Trades Union, und diese erhält ihn nicht nur, sondern ergreift sofort die nöthigen Maßregeln, um den Arbeitgeber, der die Löhne zu drücken sucht, entweder durch Verhandlungen auf andere Wege zu bringen, oder durch eine Arbeitseinstellung zu Paaren zu treiben. Für jedes Mitglied einer Gewerkschaft gilt im Inlande das berühmte Civis Romanus sum! (ich bin ein römischer Bürger) — das stolze Wort, welches nach Lord Palmerston jeder Engländer im Auslande von sich sagen kann. „Ich bin Mitglied einer Gewerksgenossenschaft und die ganze Macht meiner Gewerksgenossenschaft steht hinter mir!"

Die Trades Unions — und das bildet ihre ungeheure Macht — sind zu klug, ihre Kräfte zu zersplittern, sie concentriren dieselben auf einen Punkt, der aber der entscheidendste ist; sie richten alle ihre Anstrengungen ausschließlich darauf, die Klassenlage der Arbeiter zu verbessern. Von der richtigen Ueberzeugung ausgehend, daß die wirthschaftliche Lage und die sociale Stellung des Arbeiters eine Machtfrage ist, richten sie ihr Augenmerk zunächst darauf, den Arbeiter mächtig zu machen. Zu einer ehrfurchtgebietenden Machtstellung gehört aber zweierlei: Organisation und Geld. Wie die Trades Unions ihre Organisation nach und nach verbessert haben, wurde schon früher mitgetheilt. Aus rein lokalen Vereinen [illegible] Gesellschaften entwickelten sie sich allmälig zu stramm gefestigten, über ganze Gewerbe oder doch größere Theile von ganzen Gewerben sich erstreckenden Arbeiterheeren, bei welchen mehr und mehr das Gefühl der allgemeinen Zusammengehörigkeit hervortritt. Man kann wohl sagen, daß die Organisation der englischen Gewerksgenossenschaften eine mustergültige ist. Die Organisation ist der Hebel. Damit aber der Hebel funktioniren kann, bedarf es einer festen materiellen Grundlage, und das ist eine gefüllte Kasse. Was nützt die beste Armee ohne Geld? Die Kasse in einen solchen Zustand zu setzen, daß sie allen Eventualitäten, auch den äußersten, einem Strike oder Lockout, gewachsen sei — das ist nun das erste Ziel der Trades Unions. Und sie haben es erreicht. Die Kassenverhältnisse der englischen Gewerksgenossenschaften sind geradezu bewundernswerth. Aber die Strike-Kasse, wenn auch ursprünglich die Hauptsache und sogar der Kern, um die sich alles andere krystallisirt hat, ist nicht die einzige Kasse. Besser ausgedrückt: das Striken und überhaupt der Klassenkampf ist nicht das einzige Objekt der Kasse. Die Kasse der Trades Unions ist in allen Fällen auch Unterstützungskasse für Arbeitslosigkeit, Krankenkasse, Begräbnißkasse und in vielen Fällen bei den bestorganisirten Gesellschaften auch Unfalls- und Altersversorgungskasse. Eine Trennung dieser verschiedenen Funktionen findet nicht statt, was den außerordentlichen Vortheil hat, daß die Gewerksgenossenschaften, wie dies Gierke von den Gilden des Mittelalters sagt hat, „den ganzen Menschen ergriffen haben".

(Neue Tischler-Zeitung.)

— In Canada besteht ein Conspirationsgesetz. Die Trades Assembly in Toronto beabsichtigt nun zu versuchen, ob dies nicht zu Gunsten der Arbeiter angewandt werden kann. Torontoer „Master-Bosses" haben sich verbunden, um alle Arbeiter auszuschließen, welche Union-Mitglieder sind, und es wird behauptet, daß sie sich dadurch gegen dies Gesetz vergangen haben. Da wird's wohl ebenso wie auswärts auch auf die Richter ankommen.

Ein brauchbares Buch.

Unter dem Titel: „Handbuch der parlamentarischen Praxis" hat Herr Geo. G. Block in New York ein Buch in Taschenformat herausgegeben, welches sämmtliche parlamentarische Regeln in leicht [illegible] Form enthält und ein unentbehrliches Buch für Jeden ist, der Vereinen oder Logen angehört. Der Preis ist nur 25 Cents und das Buch kann durch jede deutsche Buchhandlung im Lande bezogen werden.

Eine sociale Rundschau.

Die Krisis rückt näher. Herunterdrücken der Löhne ist das Mittel der Kapitalisten und ihrer Lügenpresse. Die Arbeiter in Milwaukee schlafen. Die Mich. Walsh Affaire erledigt.

Milwaukee, 20. November 1883.

Bald ist das Jahr 1883 dahin und es geziemt sich wohl, eine Umschau zu halten, wie unsere Union steht und wie die Lage der ganzen Arbeiterklasse ist. Nur durch ein richtiges Erkennen der Dinge sind wir im Stande, ein treffendes Urtheil zu fällen und werden in den Stand gesetzt, Fehler, welche begangen sind, für die Zukunft zu vermeiden.

Das Baugeschäft florirt in diesem Jahre nicht so gut als im letzten. Die Löhne sind, im Ganzen genommen, eher gefallen als gestiegen, und nur an Orten, wo gute Unions sind, haben sie sich gehalten. Nur an der pacifischen Küste sind sie durch die Anstrengung unserer dortigen Mitglieder in die Höhe gegangen. In den Prairiestaaten und Minengegenden, als Texas, Kansas, Colorado, Montana, Nevada und Utah war das Baugeschäft bedeutend schwächer wie im Vorjahre, weil die mit einander konkurrirenden Eisenbahnen ihre durchgehenden Linien größtentheils vollendet haben und nur noch kurze Zweigbahnen im Bau sind. Hierdurch ist eine bedeutende Flauheit in der Eisenindustrie eingetreten, was eine Lähmung aller anderen Geschäfte und namentlich im Bau nach sich zieht.

Durch die große Krisis von 1873 bis 1878 sind die Großfabrikanten etwas vorsichtiger geworden und die großen Eisen- und Stahlfabriken haben beschlossen, die Arbeit zeitweise ganz einzustellen. Andere Fabrikanten folgen ihrem Beispiele, z. B. die Nägelfabrikanten, die Glashüttenbesitzer &c., so daß nach Weihnachten eine sehr flaue Zeit auch in unserm Geschäfte eintreten muß.

Die Zeitungen der Kapitalistenklasse und besonders die hiesigen republikanischen englischen Blätter, werden nicht müde, ein Universalmittel gegen die Krisis auszuschreien, nämlich Herabsetzen der Arbeitslöhne! Trotzdem, daß dieses ein sicheres Zeichen der schlechten Zeiten ist, lassen die hiesigen Arbeiter sich nicht aus ihrem Schlendrian bringen. Selbst die Unions sind mäuschenstill und beweisen dadurch, daß sie ihre Pflicht noch nicht erkannt haben, oder wenigstens nicht thun. Ich lasse eine Uebersetzung eines Artikels folgen, der vor einigen Tagen hier im „Evening Wisconsin" erschien und so recht die Anschauung der Kapitalisten repräsentirt. Derselbe lautet:

„Der Arbeitsmarkt.

Es sind Anzeichen in allen Theilen des Landes vorhanden, daß bald eine Regulirung der Arbeitslöhne stattfinden muß, um die Entlassung von 10 Tausend von Arbeitern im Angesicht des Winters, wenn die Bedürfnisse im Haushalte die größten sind, zu verhindern. Die Nachfrage nach allen Arten der industriellen Waaren ist so schwach geworden, und die Preise, welche geboten worden sind, so niedrig, daß eine weitere Fabrikation dieser Waaren nicht fortgesetzt werden kann, ausgenommen mit einem bedeutenden Verlust, wenn die Arbeiter nicht in eine Reduzirung der Löhne willigen. Die Stahlschienen-Fabriken in Cleveland, Ohio, werden am ersten December geschlossen, welchen andere Fabriken in diesem Industriezweige folgen werden.

Die Lage ist so ernst, daß die Fabrikanten die Arbeiter nicht fragen, kleine Löhne anzunehmen, sondern sie sagen, sie können unter den obwaltenden Umständen nicht arbeiten lassen. Jedermann will die Waaren billig einkaufen und Fabrikwaaren erst recht billig. Wir mögen sagen, Niemand mehr als der Arbeiter. Doch wenn er billig zu kaufen gedenkt, muß er billig arbeiten. Dies ist die ganze Sachlage in einer Nußschale und ist die wirkliche Situation in England, Belgien, Frankreich und Deutschland.

Nun, kann das Volk der Vereinigten Staaten billig kaufen und zu gleicher Zeit seine Arbeit für einen hohen Preis verkaufen? Das, erklären politische Oekonomisten, ist wirklich eine Unmöglichkeit!"

Hier ist das Rezept, der Löhne auf die Stufe der europäischen herabzudrücken, klar und deutlich ausgesprochen, und die hiesigen Eisenbahn-Compagnien haben es sofort gethan. Vier Fünftel aller Zimmerleute, welche sie beschäftigen, erhielten letzten Sommer $1.75 per Tag, jetzt ist fast allen Arbeitern noch 12½ Cts. abgezogen worden, so daß dieselben bei neunstündiger Arbeitszeit nur $1.46½ erhalten. Die gewöhnlichen Handarbeiter verdienen ungefähr einen Dollar per Tag. Nehmen wir die hiesigen Preise für Miethe und Lebensmittel in Betracht, so ist dies schon unter die Lebensverhältnisse vieler europäischer Arbeiter gesunken und es liegt kein Grund vor, die Konkurrenz des Auslandes zu befürchten.

Die Kapitalistenpresse lügt, wenn sie behauptet, daß niedrige Löhne das Mittel sind, um die Arbeiter vor Entlassung zu schützen.

Im Gegentheil, niedrige Löhne verschlechtern es und werfen immer mehr Arbeiter außer Beschäftigung, aber es gibt den reichen und mächtigen Compagnien einen größeren Kapitalprofit, es gibt den Aktionären höhere Dividenden und darum allein ist es diesen Ausbeutern zu thun. Die Arbeiter müssen bis auf die Knochen geschunden werden, damit jene Faulenzer die Millionen einsacken können, und deshalb ist das Geschrei für niedrige Löhne erhoben.

Trotz diesen Zuständen verhalten sich die hiesigen Arbeiter sehr still und die einzige Antwort, wenn man sie zum Widerstande auffordert, ist: „Ja, was soll man machen, es ist Winter!"

Zu den Trades Unions hat die Masse der Arbeiter hier wenig Vertrauen, erstens weil der große Strike der Cigarrenmacher Union gegen die Firma Fischermann & Co. verloren ging, und zweitens weil die hiesige Trades Assembly voriges Frühjahr in die Politik eingriff und sich der demokratischen Partei anschloß. Ein hier sehr bekannter Unionmann Namens Michael Walsh wurde auf diese Weise in die Legislatur gewählt und hat sich seit der Zeit bemüht, die Legislatur des Staates zu bewegen, ein statistisches Arbeitsbureau für den Staat Wisconsin einzurichten, was denn auch schließlich gelungen ist.

Die republikanischen Politiker hetzten nun ihre Anhänger in den Unions auf und Streit und Zank waren seit langer Zeit an der Tagesordnung, was fast alle Unions sehr geschwächt und einige der Auflösung nahe gebracht hat.

Dies liefert auf's Neue den Beweis, daß die amerikanischen Arbeiter unfähig sind, ihre Klassenlage zu verbessern, weil sie dieselbe nicht erkennen und es noch eine Weile nehmen wird, bevor sie von ihren kapitalistischen Anschauungen kurirt sind.

Um nun diese Streitigkeiten endlich zu beseitigen, wählten die verschiedenen Unions einen Delegaten, um die Sache zu prüfen. Indem man aber dem Herrn M. Walsh nichts anderes vorwarf, als mit den Demokraten gegangen zu sein, was ja alle Anderen auch gethan hätten und er also nicht besser und nicht schlechter war, als die für ihn gestimmt, so hielt das Untersuchungs-Comite die Anklage nicht für genügend, um ihn deshalb zu verdammen. Hiermit werden hoffentlich die unerquicklichen Debatten über diese Affaire ein Ende haben und die verschiedenen Unions können nun daran gehen, ihre Reihen zu stärken.

Die hiesige Plasterers Union hat ihren Bossen die Erklärung zugeschickt, daß sie vom 1. April an anstatt 30 Cts. per Stunde 35 Cts. verlangen.

Unsere Anstrengung, die Masse der hiesigen deutschen Zimmerleute zu vereinigen, war bisher von geringem Erfolg und wird auch nicht vor dem Frühling möglich sein.

Unser Organ wird hier sehr gerne gesehen und freut sich ein Jeder, einmal zu erfahren, wie es anderwärts aussieht. G. L.

Die Nothwendigkeit genügender Beiträge und Agitation.

Der folgende lehrreiche Artikel ist dem Bericht des englischen Gewerkschafts-Congresses entnommen:

Alles, was wir den Arbeitern rathen können, ist die Nothwendigkeit für eine verbesserte Organisation. Eine starke Organisation mit großen Fonds ist unbedingt nöthig für einen erfolgreichen Mitbewerb mit dem Kapital in der Arbeiterpolitik. Der Werthmesser einer starken Union liegt nicht so sehr in der Durchführung erfolgreicher Strikes, als vielmehr in der Zahl derjenigen Streitfälle, welche durch die moralische Macht einer Union verhindert werden. Das sind die großen Siege, weil sie blutlos sind und keinen Groll und keine Leiden hinterlassen. Solche Verbindungen zu schaffen, ist gewöhnlich das Werk von mehr als einer Generation. Aber jede solche Organisation muß einen Anfang haben, die Mitglieder müssen gewonnen werden, die Fonds wollen Zeit haben, sich anzusammeln. Die Jugend einer Union sollte deshalb vor Conflikten ebenso beschützt werden, wie wir die jugendlichen Arbeiter vor der Arbeit schützen, welche nur für Erwachsene geeignet ist. Genügende Beiträge für die wirksame Durchführung der erforderlichen Funktionen sind absolut nothwendig. Billige Beiträge sind oft sehr gefährlich am Tage des Kampfes als ein zerbrochenes Rohr.

Zum Schluß wird auf die geringe Agitation hingewiesen, welche die Unions den jungen Leuten und den weiblichen Arbeitern, sowie denjenigen Geschäftsbranchen angedeihen lassen, welche als „verlorene Posten" in dem großen politischen Körper zu betrachten seien. Namentlich in den großen Städten sollte durch Agitation diese verstreuten Gewerke in die Bewegung zu ziehen versucht werden.

Die Pinkerton'sche Rowdybande.

welche von den Kohlenbossen in Bradford, Pa., gegen die strikenden Arbeiter daselbst angeworben ist und über hundert Mann stark, mit Winchester-Gewehren und Revolvern bewaffnet ist, hat erklärt, daß sie die Scabs zur Arbeit bringen werde und wenn sie auch erst alle 600 Strikers todtschießen müßte! Die Pinkerton'sche Rowdybande steht, indem sie im Dienste der Ausbeuter steht, über dem Gesetz. Ueberhaupt ist dies ja die Organisation des Meineids, die jeden Menschen in diesem Lande für gute Bezahlung durch massenhafte Meineide des Mordes bezüchtigen und an den Galgen bringen kann und die genau ebenso gut für gute Bezahlung Jeden, selbst den bei der That ergriffenen Räuber und Mörder, freischwören kann.

Dieses organisirte und privilegirte Verbrechergesindel hat nun selbstverständlich noch eine Anzahl anderer Strolche als Specialpolizisten einzeschworen und diese Mörderbande tritt den Strikern bewaffnet entgegen. Sich in das Sklavenjoch fügen oder todtgeschossen zu werden, zwischen diesen beiden Uebeln haben die Striker nun zu wählen. Das ist die „Freiheit" der Besitzlosen in diesem Lande! Wie lange wird dies Schandsystem noch anhalten, bis der Mann der Arbeit, müde seiner Last, sich erhebt und fürchterliche Musterung unter seinen Feinden und Abrechnung mit den Ausbeutern hält? (Der Hammer.)

Bericht von Union No. 21, Chicago, Branch 7.

Zweig 7 fährt fort, eine rege Agitation zu unterhalten, wenn auch der Erfolg kein derartiger war, wie in anderen Monaten.

Die regelmäßigen Versammlungen sind stets gut besucht und zeigt sich bei allen Mitgliedern ein lebhaftes Interesse sowohl für Vereinsangelegenheiten, wie für Diskussionen über allgemeine Arbeiterfragen. Auf Sonntag, den 16. December haben wieder eine allgemeine Agitationsversammlung einberufen.

In einer der letzten Versammlungen war ein Comite der Cigarrenmacher Progressive Union erschienen, welches um Unterstützung bat in dem Kampfe, den die Internationale Cigarrenmacher Union gegen sie begonnen. Nachdem das Comite angehört war, sprachen sich alle Mitglieder zu Gunsten desselben aus und wurde eine dem entsprechende Resolution einstimmig angenommen.

Die Anregung im „Carpenter" betreffs der Werkzeug-Versicherung ist nicht ohne Wirkung geblieben. Zweig 7, von der Nützlichkeit derselben für die Carpenter überzeugt, hat die Angelegenheit im Exekutivrath zur Sprache gebracht und hoffentlich wird es von Erfolg sein. Ueber den Verlauf das nächste Mal.

Im Auftrage der Zimmerleute- und Bauschreiner Gewerkschaft, Lokal Union 21, Branch 7, Chicago, ersuche ich Sie um Aufnahme von Folgendem im „Carpenter":

In der Versammlung am 13 November 1883 von Union 21, Zweig 7, der Brüderschaft der Zimmerleute und Bauschreiner von Amerika wurde folgende Resolution angenommen:

In Anbetracht des Strikes der Inter. Cigarrenmacher-Union No 14 gegen die Cigarrenmacher Progressiv Union No 15, erklären wir, daß wir das Vorgehen der Intern. Cigarrenmacher-Union verdammen, weil wir niemals mit einer Arbeiter Organisation sympathisiren können, welche eine weiter fortgeschrittene Organisation bekämpft; wir versprechen daher der Cigarrenmacher-Progressiv Union den kräftigsten Beistand mit Rath und That in diesem Kampfe und werden nur noch Progressiv Union-Label-Cigarren rauchen — rothe Labels.

Beschlossen, diese Erklärung in allen Arbeiterblättern zu veröffentlichen. I. A.:

Charles Eickelberg, Sekr.

— Die organisirten Holzbildhauer in Boston haben in vielen Shops die neunstündige Arbeitszeit eingeführt und zwar ohne dafür striken zu müssen.

— Eine Anzahl Delegaten französischer Gewerkschaften sind vorige Woche hier eingetroffen und wurden von den hiesigen Arbeiterorganisationen und französischen Gesellschaften auf's Herzlichste empfangen und bewillkommnet. Zweck ihrer Reise ist der Besuch der internationalen Industrie-Ausstellung in Boston, um die Erzeugnisse anderer Länder kennen zu lernen. Die Delegaten wurde in Folge eines Beschlusses des Gemeinderaths von Paris hierher gesandt, welcher auch die Geldmittel theilweise dazu bewilligt hat. Dieselben haben außerdem noch verschiedene Städte des Landes besucht, um die Arbeiterverhältnisse des Landes kennen zu lernen und wenn möglich dauernde Verbindungen zwischen den Arbeitern beider Länder herzustellen.

Agitation gegen die Importation Europäischer Paupers.

Das Exekutiv-Comite der Knights of Labor hat einen Aufruf an alle amerikanischen Arbeiter erlassen, um sie zu ersuchen, ein Dokument zu unterzeichnen, das dem Congreß vorgelegt werden soll, um ihn zu veranlassen, gegen die Importation von Paupers aus Europa Schritte zu thun. In dem Aufruf werden die Aussagen amerikanischer Consuln in Europa angeführt, welche erklären, daß Agenten hiesiger Fabrikanten in Europa umherreisen, um den dortigen Arbeitern glänzende Versprechungen zu machen und sie dann hierher in die Lohnsklaverei zu verlocken. Die Listen, auf welchen die Unterschriften der Arbeiter gesammelt werden sollen, tragen die folgende Aufforderung an den Congreß:

An die Repräsentanten des Volkes im Congreß:

Wir fordern Euch auf, im Namen der intelligenten Lohnarbeiter der Ver. Staaten, Gesetze zu erlassen, welche die Importation fremder Arbeiter, die sich in anderen Ländern verdingen, nach den Ver. Staaten zu kommen, auf immer verhindern soll. Wir lenken Eure Aufmerksamkeit auf die Thatsache, daß dieses System der Importation um sich greift und den Bestand der amerikanischen Institutionen bedroht; daß es ein tödtlicher Schlag gegen die Seele des kommerziellen Lebens der Nation ist, indem es durch ein unredliches Mittel versucht, die Lebenshaltung der hiesigen Arbeiter auf das Hungerniveau von Europa herabzudrücken. Das Uebel ist bereits derart gewachsen, daß unsere Consuln im Auslande bereits auf seine Folgen hingewiesen und darüber spezielle Berichte erstattet. Wir heißen mit Freuden alle diejenigen an unseren Gestaden willkommen, welche die Ketten ihrer Unterdrücker abgeworfen haben, um unter uns zu weilen; aber wir protestiren allen Ernstes gegen das Landen von Sklaven, für deren Leiber in manchen Fällen Staatsgeld bis zum Betrage von $30 bezahlt worden ist und die ihre Arbeit abgeschworen haben, bevor ihr Geburtsland ihren Blicken entschwand. Deshalb fordern wir Euch im Namen der Arbeiter Amerikas auf, Gesetze zu erlassen, welche es zu einem Kriminalverbrechen machen sollen, Leute nach unserem Land zu bringen, deren Freiheit verkauft ist, wie dies nur zu leicht geschehen kann, wenn Agenten unter dem schlecht gezahlten Volke Europas herumreisen, welches in überfüllten Industrie-Centren der alten Welt wohnenden Arbeitermassen ausbeuten, welche erregt und fast zu jedem Preise zur Auswanderung bewogen werden können.

Die Listen sind zu haben bei John G. McClelland, No. 374 Washington Str., Hoboken, N. J.

Aus Deutschland.

Berlin, am 15. November 1883.

Geehrte Kameraden Nord Amerikas!

Hiermit erlaube ich mir, den gegenwärtigen Stand der Bewegung der deutschen Zimmerleute zu unterbreiten. Von dem Grundsatze der Aufstellung der Forderung eines neunstündigen Normal-Arbeitstages für die Zimmerleute mußte Abstand genommen werden, denn erstens steckt noch ein bedeutender Theil Indifferentismus und Egoismus in den Köpfen der deutschen Zimmerleute, zweitens konnten wir d. J. nicht das genügende Kapital zur Durchsetzung einer solchen bedeutenden und eingreifenden Forderung aufbringen, um diesen Kampf aufzunehmen.

Wir haben jedoch 6 Wochen gestrickt und einen Lohnsatz von 40 Pfg. per Stunde gleich 4 Mark per Tag bei zehnstündiger Normal-Arbeitszeit erreicht.

Nun haben wir eine Organisation über Deutschland für alle Zimmerleute in's Leben gerufen, „Verband deutscher Zimmerleute".

Hierzu bitte ich die verschiedenen Zeitungsberichte (beiliegend) zu beachten, vielleicht ist es uns dann möglich, nach einer regulären Organisation in einigen Jahren den neunstündigen Normal-Arbeitstag zu fordern und auch durchzusetzen — dieses ist meine persönliche Bestrebung — und bitte ich alle Kameraden, Zimmerleute, Carpenters um Beistand im solidarischen Interesse.

Geehrte Kameraden, Brüder, ich bitte sehr, es vielleicht möglich zu machen, daß eine große Versammlung (Carpenters' Meeting) in verschiedenen größeren Städten Amerikas aus Anlaß der Errichtung eines Verbandes deutscher Zimmerleute auf solidarischer Grundlage, eine Glückwunsch-Adresse beschließen und dieselbe ihren deutschen Brüdern übersenden möge. Dieses soll den Zweck haben, den Geist des deutschen Michels unter den deutschen Kameraden zu beleben und anzufeuern zu reger Thatkraft. Gewähret mir diese Bitte im Interesse Eurer Brüder, die noch so sehr der Aufmunterung aus dem lethargischen Schlummer bedürfen.

Bitte meinen Brief nicht mit meiner Unterschrift, sondern als Bericht einfach abdrucken zu wollen, denn nach dem preußischen Vereinsgesetz vom 11. März 1850 ist eine jede solche Korrespondenz strafbar. Es kann also Geeignetes nach Belieben gedruckt werden, aber ohne meinen Namen.

Die Zimmerleute in K... [illegible] ... sen Sommer (Juli, ... weiß ich nicht. Die ... und ... Verdienste ... per Jahr ... $2.00 per ... Killian ... Germany.

Die Expedition.

BLACK LIST.

ANDREW MOE has been expelled from Branch 8, Union No. 21, on several charges.

THOS. PORTLEY was suspended from Branch 8, Union No. 21, Chicago, Ill., for non-payment of dues, fines and assessment, and also for drawing a loan of $10 from our branch, which he failed to return. He has also abandoned his wife, and it is understood he has gone to California. He is stoutly built, about 40 years old, blue eyes, large nose, bald-headed, black moustache, small face, speaks English with a slight Norwegian accent.

G. E. GRIMES, late Treasurer of Philad. Union No. 8, has been expelled for defrauding the Union out of $562.15. The money was obtained in the following manner: 1—Grimes had $79.25 in hand for which no orders were drawn; 2—an order of $100 was drawn in favor of the striking Telegraphers, which he did not pay; 3—he represented to the Auditing Committee that he paid an order of $25.90 for June capital tax; 4—he had not paid three other orders amounting to $105, and had in his possession $60 more belonging to the Excursion Committee. He was in the hands of the Auditing Committee at the time he left but they appointed one of their number as a detective, who traced him to Kansas City. A government detective was then sent and he brought Grimes back; Geo. E. Grimes is now serving a term of 9 months in the State Prison for these embezzlements. It cost the Union $700 to punish him (including his peculations). But we are not broken up, and it goes to show that Union No. 8 will not be trifled with by rogues and swindlers.

W. F. EHRHARDT, Rec. Sec'y Union No. 8.

CORRESPONDENCE.

New Orleans, La.

Weather fine and cool, plenty of work, city quite clear of sickness. Several jobs in the market; wages average $2.50 per day.

The carpenters of this city propose forming a Building Trades League. All union men are employed.

St. Catherines, Canada

Trade dull, all union men employed, but the prospects for Winter are not extra bright. Wages firm, work from 9 to 9½ hours.

Hamilton, Canada.

We are glad to see that other unions are bracing themselves to the work of the Brotherhood. Union No. 18 is moving along safely and has some influence in this city. Trade, however, is very dull, and the cost of living very high. A strike of the iron molders against 20 per cent. reduction is expected.

Indianapolis, Ind.

Trade slack; plenty of carpenters out of work. Wages tending lower. Unionism growing stronger every day, but when some men were offered a chance to organize they held back. No doubt they thought they were doing too well, but now when work is getting scarce they begin to howl and want to join our union. Before workingmen can ever hope to assume their rightful place, they will have to display more independence and manhood, and not cringe and crawl at sight of a boss, they will have to join with each other in unions and protect their own common interests.

Hartford, Conn.

Our journal last month has pleased us all. It is full of sound advice, that ought to be carried out just as it is laid down. It is the workmen's own fault if they are debased and defrauded. If they would only wake up to their duties and stand together like men—and they can readily do it if they want to—then they could benefit themselves and all dependent upon them. Trade is fair in this city, a few men idle, work on short time—only 9 hours a day. We are adding members at every meeting and purpose doing so right along. We will have a family sociable on Jan. 15 in Allyn Hall.

Seattle, Washington Territory.

Carpenters Union 15 of this city is progressing finely and our membership will soon comprise the majority of good workmen here. Times are likely to be dull here this winter as the largest new buildings will shut down soon until spring. Most of the union men are at work, while non-union men are nearly all out of work. I fear short hours will soon reduce the wages to $2.50 and $3.00 while at present they are from $3.00 to $3.75 for first class men. Our journal, *The Carpenter*, is the thing all the local unions need, and if all goes well it will be a power before many years.

St. Louis, Mo.

Union No. 5 is growing with a vigor that promises well. From December 2, the initiation fee will be $2.00, and for the present our dues will be 35 cents per month, but it will not be long until we will raise them. We are getting new members at every meeting. On Nov. 25, we elected new officers with the following result: President, Aug. Oberbeck; Vice-President, Robert Becker; Rec. Sec'y, Aug. Daniel; Fin. Sec'y, P. H. Blattner; Treasurer, Aug. Stade; Sergeant-at-Arms, John Reincke. All the members entertain the right kind of spirit and energy to make a strong union.

St. Catherines, Canada.

We are "holding the fort" and occasionally getting recruits; initiated five last meeting, and have made arrangements to form a sick benefit. Our dues to 25 cents per month. ... very firm and dues are fairly ... speaking we are in a ... party in our delegate to ... and appliances, in Toronto, Dec. 26 ...

www.ingramcontent.com/pod-product-compliance
Lightning Source LLC
Chambersburg PA
CBHW022009050726
47499CB00008BA/2758
* 9 7 8 3 3 3 7 3 8 3 4 3 5 *